THE NECROMANCER

VALANCOURT CLASSICS

THE

NECROMANCER

A ROMANCE

BY

GEORGE W. M. REYNOLDS

Edited with a biographical sketch by
Dick Collins

𝕶𝖆𝖓𝖘𝖆𝖘 𝕮𝖎𝖙𝖞:
VALANCOURT BOOKS
2007

The Necromancer by George W. M. Reynolds
Originally serialised in *Reynolds's Miscellany*, 1851-1852
First published in book form in 1857
First Valancourt Books edition, December 2007

Biographical sketch, afterword, and notes © 2007 by Dick Collins
This edition © 2007 by Valancourt Books

Library of Congress Cataloguing-in-Publication Data

Reynolds, George W. M. (George William MacArthur), 1814-1879.
The necromancer / by George W. M. Reynolds ; edited with a
biographical sketch by Dick Collins. – 1st Valancourt Books ed.
p. cm. – (Valancourt classics)
ISBN 1-934555-32-0 (alk. paper)
1. Henry VIII, King of England, 1491-1547–Fiction. 2. Great Britain–
History–Henry VIII, 1509-1547–Fiction. I. Collins, Dick. II. Title.
PR5221.R35N4 2007
823'.8–dc22

2007045573

Design and typography by James D. Jenkins
Published by Valancourt Books
Kansas City, Missouri
http://www.valancourtbooks.com

CONTENTS

GEORGE WILLIAM MCARTHUR REYNOLDS:[*]

A BIOGRAPHICAL SKETCH

The Necromancer was published in *Reynolds's Miscellany* in weekly parts, beginning on 27 December 1851, and ending on 31 July 1852. The best way to read it is the way Reynolds expected his first readers to: start at the Prologue, and read each chapter one after the other, until you reach the end. The worst way would be to read an introduction or summary first. It is a book of thrills and surprises, of shocks and revelations: if you already know what you are going to find, you won't find it. Worse still, from an introduction, you'll only find what the guide thinks is there. So discussion of the text is relegated to an Afterword, and you are on your honour not to read it first.

On the other hand few writers put so much of themselves, so many of their own convictions and prejudices, in their books as G.W.M. Reynolds, and a knowledge of his life and ideas will be indispensable in following the story. His readers knew he was a Chartist, a Republican, a Tee-Totaller, a Feminist, a Philo-Semite and pro-Arab, because he told them so, relentlessly, in every work he wrote. His personal obsessions—notably with strong, often violent and murderous women—spill out perhaps despite himself. The facts of his life are thus of the first importance. But the accounts we have are very brief and partial, and frankly contain many errors and false assumptions.[1] What follows is therefore an attempt to write, not a full biography of Reynolds, but at least a more complete and accurate sketch of his life.

Family Myths

Reynolds's father came from Eastry, Kent, at the very south-eastern tip of England, and looking straight over to France. Eastry is about three miles south of Sandwich, and about four miles southeast of Ash-next-Sandwich, on the Roman road from Woodnesburgh to Dover. Still beautiful, it is deep in the rural heart of Kent, as well as in the most strongly maritime area of England. The village has a long and rather romantic history. Egbert, one

---

[*] Most commentators give Reynolds's name as "George William MacArthur Reynolds"; however, numerous official documents, such as his marriage certificate and death certificate, use the spelling "McArthur."

of the ancient Kings of Kent, had a palace there in 664 A.D. The princes
Æthelbert and Æthelred, his two young cousins, were murdered there,
and buried in the King's Hall, on the site of the present Eastry Court.
In 1164 Thomas Becket, archbishop of Canterbury, hid out for a week in
Eastry from Henry II and his men. From there, he fled to France via Sandwich. Tradition has it that there is a secret passage leading from Eastry
Court to the Parish Church of St. Mary the Virgin—but the place seems
to demand the story. There are certainly romantic caves just to the north
of the village, which may have been used for ancient worship, and which
were believed to go as far as Canterbury to the west, and Sandwich to the
east. More recent legends include that of Thomas Russell who, despite
his very English name, was said to have been Prince of North Bohemia,
and to have had no penis. In modern times the village is very proud of the
ghost of a rather comfortable-looking clergyman, photographed sitting in
a pew in the church, though how seriously they take it is another matter.
All in all, Eastry is a good place to grow up in with an imagination.

    GWMR was born and brought up in the parish of St. Clement, Sand-
wich. One of the Cinque Ports—the five coastal towns on which the Naval
defences of England were founded—it too is a place of history and legend. It was a frequent point of attack from Vikings, and it was here that
Prince Louis of France landed with his troops to fight against King John in
1216. In 1255 the first elephant to be seen in England landed at Sandwich,
a gift from the King of France to John's son, Henry III of England. It was
marched from the port to the Tower, according to the tale killing a bull
that attacked it on the way by throwing the bull over its shoulder. Every-
one knows that the 4th Earl of Sandwich was so busy at the gaming tables
that he refused to leave them even for food, and so tucked a slice of meat
between two slices of bread. More importantly for George Reynolds,
Thomas Paine, the great English Radical, lived and worked in Sandwich,
where he ran a staymaker's shop in New Street. He married an orphan,
Mary Lambert, who was supported by the parish; she died a few months
later. Paine is credited with inventing the phrase, "The United States of
America;" he was a friend of Benjamin Franklin, and was imprisoned in
France for opposing the death-sentence on Louis XVI. Paine was a big
influence on Reynolds.

    There is a story that his father, George Reynolds, was knighted (Carv-
er 2004). *Burke's Peerage and Landed Gentry* knows nothing of any knighthood; in his marriage licence, marriage certificate, his Will and the certificate of probate he is referred to as "George Reynolds, Esq." Possibly this
tale was spread by GWMR himself; it may also have been invented by a
journalist named John Dix, who found him pompous and self-satisfied.

The story is certainly untrue, and has recently fallen out of fashion, but it still crops up from time to time.

Another story is that in 1830 GWMR inherited a fortune of £12,000. This one is more persistent, and needs to be examined in more detail.

Family Background

George Sayer was born in Woodnesborough—pronounced Winsbrough—in Kent around 1717. On 13 September 1739 he married Mary Shrubsoer, from the same village, and their daughter Mary was baptised in the church of St. Clement, Sandwich, on 19 August 1744. Through Mary the family rose in the world when, on 5 March 1764, she married Robert Monro, a Freeman of Sandwich.

As we said above, Sandwich is one of the Cinque Ports, the five major towns on the Kent and Sussex coast that formed the main defence against the ancient enemy, France. To persuade them to their role, some 900 of the men of Sandwich were called Freemen, and had certain privileges and exemptions. Among the former were the right for five of them to bear the canopy over the monarch's head at a coronation; and while few of them could aspire to such honour, the fact of being part of the group from which they would be chosen conferred great status. It was, of course, a men-only club.

There were (and still are) two ways of becoming a Freeman: by being born into a Freeman family, or by marrying into one. George Sayer earned greater respect for having a Freeman as a son-in-law, but didn't have the status himself. And in any case, the link was soon cut: within six months of marrying, Robert Monro was dead.

With a haste almost indecent for the times, Mary married again on 6 October 1765, in the same church of St. Clement. This time her husband was John Reynolds, a yeoman from Eythorne, Kent, who had come to live in Eastry. In December of that year, John applied for election as a Freeman, and was refused: the Freemen argued that a widow didn't have the right to pass the rights on to a second husband, especially when she herself was not of a Freeman family. John lobbied for support, and at the next election, on 12 December 1766, the refusal was reversed. John had the status he wanted.

John and Mary Reynolds had five children: William and John (dates unknown); George (baptised Eastry 2 February 1769); Mary (baptised Eastry 2 February 1770); and Elizabeth (baptised Eastry 11 July 1771). John's will was signed in 1780, and proved in 1784. Mary and Elizabeth both found good husbands: Elizabeth married Dr. Edward Boys, of Walmer, near

Deal, in 1800, and Mary married Edward George, a farmer from Eastry, on 10 December 1790. Her mother Mary signed as a witness, but, her father being dead, young Mary was "given away" by Benjamin Sayer, a customs man from Deal—we can guess he was an uncle. One wonders if he remembered Tom Paine at all.

George Reynolds entered the Navy, and was commissioned Lieutenant Commander on 21 September 1790. He was obviously a man of some ability, as well as wealth, because on 2 August 1797 he was promoted to Commander, and on 29 April 1802 to full Captain. With his connection to Edward Boys, and his naval rank, it's hardly surprising he met Lieutenant Commander Purser Dowers, Governor of the Royal Naval Hospital in Deal. Dowers had been born in Stepney, near the Tower of London, in 1751: his brother-in-law Thomas Browne-King worked in the Royal Armaments in the Tower. On 21 August 1771 Dowers was commissioned as a Lieutenant Commander, and was never promoted further; but because of his post as Governor in Deal, he was accorded the courtesy title "Captain" Dowers. One of his colleagues at Deal was a Scottish surgeon, living (like Edward Boys) in Walmer, Duncan McArthur.

Dowers married Frances Atherden on 12 September 1781. Their daughter Caroline Frances Dowers was baptised in the church of St. Mary-the-Virgin, the same place they had married, on 8 July 1789. Six days later, the Bastille was stormed in France, and Deal and the other Cinque Ports went on an alert that was to last until 1815. It spelled good times for the town: in 1824, Pigot's Directory of Kent states somewhat rudely: "The town is clean, but owing to the establishment of peace, it presents in many parts, a scene of desertion." The economic boom brought by the war was not quite over on 13 August 1813, when Captain George Reynolds married Caroline Frances Dowers, again in St.-Mary-the-Virgin. He was 44, she twenty years younger.

Their first child was born on 23 July 1814, and baptised in the church of St. Clement, Sandwich, on 26 August. He was named George for his father, William for his uncle, and McArthur for his godfather Duncan McArthur—hereafter, he is GWMR. The parish of St. Clement's comprises only six and a half streets: Upper Strand Street, Fisher Street, Knightrider Street, Church Street St. Clement's, Sandown Road, Millwall Place, The Chain and the eastern half of High Street. The family lived in one of these, though there is no record of exactly where. Their second son, Edward Dowers Reynolds, was baptised at St. Clement's on 2 August 1816. If we apply the roughest rule-of-thumb dating, and assume that there was the same interval between Edward's birth and baptism as there was between his brother George's, he was born around 30 June/1 July 1816. This calculation is more important than it seems.

On 16 October 1822 Captain Reynolds signed his will. In it he describes himself as "George Reynolds of the parish of St. George-the-Martyr in the City of Canterbury Esquire a post-Captain in His Majesty's Royal Navy." How long the family had been in Canterbury we do not know, but Captain Reynolds died there before 28 January 1823, when his will was granted probate.

GWMR's Inheritance

There has been much confusion as to exactly what GWMR inherited from his parents, with estimates and guesses as to what he received, and when he received it, ranging wildly:

—"He inherited a substantial sum on his mother's death in 1830" (Thomas 1994);

—"[A]t twenty-one when his father died [he] inherited £12,000" (James 1973);

—£12,000 from his mother in 1830 (Carver 2004)

—"[O]n his mother's death in 1830 he inherited £12,000" (James 2004)

—"Sir George, however, died before his son had finished his course [at Sandhurst] leaving him a fortune of £120,000, whilst Lady Reynolds only survived her husband a few months." (Summers 1940)

The cause of the confusion is probably GWMR himself. Before the Insolvent Debtors' Court, he declared:

that when he became of age a few years ago, he was left by his father, Capt. John Reynolds, a sum of between 8,000*l.* and 10,000*l.* He was also entitled to share in a small quantity of land in Kent.

In essence this is true, but as expressed it is deceptive (and, given the setting, perhaps deceitful). The answer lies in the dust-dry wills of in the Reynolds family.

Neither John nor Mary Reynolds seem to have left much behind them. In 1810 Edward George, husband of their daughter Mary, died in Eastry. He left everything to Mary, mostly in trust during the term of her life for other members of his family.

Next William Reynolds died, and left everything to his widow, Elizabeth, once more in trust for his own brothers and sister.

In 1820 Mary George died. She and Edward were childless, so she left to each of her surviving siblings, John and George Reynolds and Elizabeth Boys, the sum of £2,000. Once more this was to be held in trust for the terms of their lives and, after their deaths, it was to devolve on their children. In addition, each of the three was to receive a third share of the money that Mary would have received after her sister-in-law Elizabeth's death. A small parcel of land in Eastry, amounting to 2 acres, was also to be shared between them.

When Captain Reynolds came to write his will, therefore, he had received £2,000 from his sister Mary, £3,333.6s.8d from brother William, and a share in a patch of land, again from Mary—all in the last few years of his life. He also expected to get one-third of another £3,333.6s.8d from his sister-in-law Elizabeth, after her death.

The total cash that Captain Reynolds left in his will was £5,800. Of this, all but £466.13s.4d had been left to him in the last couple of years. The income from the land would have been near negligible, and its value barely more. We have a picture, then, of a family living on enough to keep up a shabby-genteel appearance, but far from enough to call them well-off. Probably they relied on Captain Reynolds's half-pay from the Navy, and perhaps this was why they left Sandwich and went to Canterbury.

All the money and real estate were left to Caroline Frances Reynolds, for the term of her life. Her children were to inherit when the younger of the two, Edward, reached the age of twenty-one years—in other words neither would receive anything before 30 June 1837. Provision was made for £1,000 of the money to be used to educate the boys, and as we shall see it almost certainly was used, in its entirety. After payment of debts and "just expenses," each boy would have received from his father £2,400, plus the expectation from their aunt Elizabeth—though there is no record that this was ever paid.

In 1830 Caroline Reynolds died, aged just 40. She left everything in trust with her father for the boys: when each of them reached the age of twenty-one years, they were to receive £400 from her will. Doubtless this was paid out, but Purser Dowers added nothing of his own, omitting all mention of his grandsons from his will. The Dowers family were no richer than the Reynolds: Purser's younger brother George left an unsigned will, in which he said pathetically:

> I am truly sorry I have not the means of leaving to my children any property for themselves but I trust their dear mother will assist them if she has it in power in the best way she can. I desire to be buried at poplar[2] [sic] where my father and Mother lay buried but as there will be very little to spare that the greatest planess [sic] ceremony may be made use of at my funeral

Understandably and rightly, Purser changed his will in favour of his brother's children, though even then he was able to do relatively little for them. We can therefore say with some accuracy exactly what GW-MR's inheritance was: £400 from his mother, on 23 July 1835; £2,400 from his father, on 1 July 1837; roughly an acre of land in Eastry; and, possibly, £1,666.10s from his aunt Elizabeth, at some unstated time. It is a very far cry from £120,000.

Before we leave Reynolds's family, there was one Dowers who went down to fame, if in a distinctly bathetic manner. On 3 July 1689:

> Richard Dowers of Westminster was indicted for robbing Robert Hurlock between Kinsington and London, where he met him holding a pistol to his breast demanding his money, and took from him one watch. value 3 l. and a knife &c. It appeared upon the evidence that the prisoner was a constable belonging to Knightsbridge; and the prosecutor swore, that the prisoner was the person that robbed him. The prisoner denied it, and said, that he did execute his office by way of assisting the prosecutor to find out who robbed him. The prisoner called some witnesses, who gave a good account of the prisoner's behaviour, and it appearing that the prosecutor was mistaken in the person, he was acquitted.

It is something to have a highwayman in the family—even if he turned out not to be one after all.

Education and Infidels

A few weeks after his father's death, young George, then aged eight, started at the Free Grammar School in Ashford. This was a charity school, founded by a local family, the Knatchbulls, and in 1823 was run by the Rev. John Nance, D.D. Nance was born in 1777 in Baxley, just north of Maidstone in Kent, the son of William Baxley; he matriculated at Worcester College, Oxford, 20 June 1794, took his B.A. in 1798 and his M.A. in 1801. In 1803 he graduated Bachelor and Doctor of Divinity. He was appointed Rector of Old Romney, Kent, in 1810, and of All Saints, Hove, Sussex in 1827. He remained there until his death, aged 72, on 21 February 1853. There is no contradiction, at least at that time, in the Rector of Old Romney running a school twenty miles away: many priests were absentees from their parishes, and the work would have been done by a vicar or a curate. Interestingly, the curate of Snargate from 1817 to 1824 was one Richard Harris Barham—better known as Thomas Ingoldsby, the immortal writer of the *Legends*. It would be quite something to connect Reynolds's teacher with one of the glories of English comic literature, and given that Old Romney and Snargate are only three miles apart it is unfeasible that the two men never met; but neither is there any evidence that they did.

What George's status at the Free School was we do not know: presumably he was a paying pupil, and presumably too he boarded at the
school, Ashford being about a dozen miles from Canterbury. Nineteenth
century education has a bad name for brutality, but a Grammar School,
run by a Doctor of Divinity, would at least have provided a sound, and
probably very good, basis in the Liberal Arts: Latin, Greek, History and
Mathematics. Very likely French and Geography were also on the syllabus,
but we should expect the Sciences to be fairly weak. It was as good as you
could hope for.

George stayed there until 12 July 1828, when he was admitted as a
Gentleman Cadet to the Royal Military Academy Sandhurst, Berkshire,
the élite training school for British Army Officers. Since the family was not
rich, he was possibly given a scholarship, which was granted by competi-
tive examination. The fact that his father had been a Captain, R.N., probably helped too. At first he was put in 2 Company, but on 25 December
that same year he was removed to 1 Company. This is slightly odd. The
Companies were simple Divisions, and each had the same status as the
others, so it was neither a promotion nor a demotion, leaving the question of why move him at all. The fact that it was done on Christmas Day
implies some sort of snap decision, and the first thing that springs to mind
is that George was being bullied. Sandhurst had something of a reputation for rowdiness at the time and, as we shall see, Reynolds had a life-long
habit of rubbing people up the wrong way. The records however give no
hint: the *Gentleman Cadet Register* says, in full:

> Name: Geo Wm McA Reynolds
> Father's Occupation: Late Post Captain RN
> Date of Admission to RMC: 12 July 1828
> Age on Admission: 13 Years 7 months
> Height: 5 Feet 1 Inch
> Cadet Company: 2 Company (removed to 1 Company 25 December 1828)
> Date of Leaving RMC: 13 September 1830
> Remarks: Withdrawn by his friends

According to Dr. Anthony Morton, Archivist at Sandhurst:

> The phrase 'withdrawn by his friends' usually meant that the Gentle-
> man Cadet concerned had chosen to leave (or been encouraged to leave)
> either because of poor performance in his studies or because he was
> considered (by himself or others) to be generally unsuitable for a career
> as an officer in the Army. If a Gentleman Cadet was expelled from the
> RMC due to a serious disciplinary offence this would normally be noted
> in the Cadet Register. There is no such note in GC Reynolds's entry.[3]

It is accepted that GWMR was unsuited to military life, and probably the decision to remove him was taken by his grandfather Purser Dowers, shortly after the death of his mother. GWMR came down from Sandhurst on 13 September 1830. This rather scotches another myth, probably put about by Reynolds himself: that he was present in Paris during the Revolution of 1830. He may well have been in Paris sometime that year, but the Sandhurst records show that he was safe at school in Berkshire in July and August, when the brief violence was taking place. Indeed, it is very unlikely that he was allowed to go there at all, until the situation calmed down. His guardians were not the sort to allow it. Duncan McArthur was a former Ship's Doctor, now a surgeon in Walmer Road, Deal, and living in the nearby village of Walmer (one of his neighbours was the Duke of Wellington, at Walmer Castle); Thomas Brown King worked in the Royal Armaments, at the Tower of London. Neither seems obviously the type to allow a sixteen year old boy, who had just failed at military school, to go traipsing off to the Barricades in a foreign (and despised) land. And, of course, the finance for such a trip was lacking, for another seven years. We may add that if Purser Dowers was a typical English sailor of his time, having gone through the Napoleonic Wars at sea, he would not have been a great lover of the French, and no great advocate of his grandson going to live there.

The commonly accepted view is that Reynolds went to France at a very early age, where he met Beau Brummel, and came into contact with French Radical thought. As well as being unlikely, there is no strong evidence for it, and there is no need to posit such a residence before 1835. There was a thriving Radical culture in London, which published the works of Tom Paine, Sade and others who influenced Reynolds. The main centre of publishing was around Wych Street, off the Strand; the Radicals were known as Infidels, from their attacks on Christianity. They were also becoming notorious for bringing out pornography, sometimes with a Radical edge, often smut, pure and simple. The finer attitudes of these people can be exemplified by Richard Carlile (1790-1843). A follower of Paine, he was imprisoned in 1817, and again for six years in 1819. In 1826 he opened a shop in Fleet Street, and became involved with Francis Place, another Radical who placed great emphasis on self-improvement as the way forward for the working classes. They were very advanced for their time, publishing pamphlets in favour of birth control. Despite Place's clean bright reputation, his friend Carlile was rather more earthy: according to Vic Gatrell,

> The infidel bookseller, Richard Carlile, had no doubt (he told Francis Place) that women 'had an almost constant desire for copulation': 'the customs of society alone, I think, deter them from it.' [Gatrell 2006: 304-5]

Gatrell gives a vivid and hilarious picture of life in Carlile's establishment:

> Altogether, then, bookshops had to tread much more cautiously than
> printshops. Here is one measure of this from a few years later. In 1822,
> a Bow Street officer reported that Richard Carlile (or his wife: he was
> in prison) had invented a system in his little bookshop off Fleet Street
> that would thwart *agents provocateurs* by ensuring that the book-sales-
> man's identity was concealed and that sales were wordless. The device
> consisted of two apertures in the back partition [of the shop] one for
> the receipt of money the other for the transmission of the publication
> from behind, over which is a round dial with numbers on it and a move-
> able hand which may be turned so as to point to any number. These
> numbers correspond with others affixed to a list of books stuck up in
> one side of the shop, so that any person by perusing this list may learn
> to what number to affix the hand of the dial. The Carliles might have
> been lampooning the law in the subterfuge. The fact remains that no
> printshop needed to resort to anything like it. It was becoming danger-
> ous to sell obscene prints, but the most scurrilous satires on the regent
> were still sold as openly as ever. [Gatrell: 501-2]

In 1832 Reynolds brought out his first book, *The Errors of the Christian
Religion Exposed, by a Comparison of the Gospels of Matthew and Luke*. It was
published in London by Richard Carlile—or, as Gatrell would say, his wife:
her husband was in prison again. So Reynolds was in London for at least
part of that year, even if he was not based in England full-time. In the
book, he claims to have been a Christian believer until that year, when on
reading Thomas Paine's *The Age of Reason* his eyes were opened. He comes
down in favour of Deism—the belief, popular in the Enlightenment, that
there is a God, but that after creating the world he plays no further part in
human affairs. It is a humanistic view of religion, but still not an atheistic
one. We shall come back to the subject of Reynolds's religion. But we can
note for now that his Deism, his Radicalism, and his later sensuality, all sit
very comfortably with the Infidel Radical community off the Strand. Deism was, moreover, rather more an English thing at the time than a French
one: the prevailing French attitude was an outright anti-clericalism.

To speculate (and nothing more): was Reynolds one of those hidden,
anonymous counter-assistants in Carlile's shop, or one like it? He would
not be the only one to have held such a job, and later become a Chartist
and writer. Thomas Frost was one such. Born (like the great publisher
Edward Lloyd) in Croydon, he passed through various stages of Radicalism, from Marxism to Chartism to Christian Socialism, and ended up a
respectable moral reformer; as did Carlile, who broke off with his sons Al-

fred and Tom Paine Carlile, on account of their Infidel morality. But Frost
began life selling pornography from William Dugdale's shop, and wrote
two (unsuccessful) pornographic novels. GWMR seems to have sprung so
completely from this Infidel soil that it would not be surprising if he had
more links with them than just publishing a book from Carlile's shop.

Duncan McArthur

We can pause for a moment to consider GWMR's godfather, the remarkable Duncan McArthur. He was probably born at Killin, Perthshire,
on 9 January 1772, the son of Duncan McArthur and Janet Anderson. He
studied Medicine in Edinburgh, and was commissioned as a surgeon in
the Royal Navy in 1793. This brought him to Deal, and the Naval Hospital,
whose Governor was Purser Dowers. The two men became friends.

McArthur lived in the Hospital Buildings, off the Strand, Deal, and
practiced as a surgeon in civilian life from Walmer Road, Deal. He never
married, and most of his earnings seem to have gone into buying silver
table-ware. He comes over as an extremely fussy man, perhaps a typical
elderly bachelor: in his will, he identifies certain items in his collection
by where they stand in his house—on the large table in the dining room,
beside his bed, and so on. Clearly, he was a "place for everything" man.
But reading between the lines, his personal life was anything but conventional.

Among his first bequests is one of two silver spoons to his housekeeper, Betsy Marshall, born Chichester, Sussex, 13 December 1780—the
date is important. She had been with him since at least 1818, and later in
the will she receives a rather more generous recompense:

> I give and bequeath the dividends interest and annual produce of one
> thousand pounds three pounds five shillings percent Bank Annuities /
> part of the stock now standing in my name in the books of the Gover-
> nor and Company of the Bank of England unto my said housekeeper
> Betsy Marshall who has served me more than thirty years for and during
> the term of her natural life independent of any and every husband with
> whom she may intermarry

The great majority of his collection goes to his "natural or reputed
son John Francis McArthur of Norwood Argyle New South Wales." He is
careful to mention when an item was a gift from someone: clearly, even
when writing his will, Duncan McArthur cannot resist talking about his
life's passion. There are then several bequests to old friends, mostly naval
men, and the residue of the estate then passes to John Francis. This will

was signed on 26 January 1848. Tucked away in its interminable, tedious legal phraseology is a generous bequest of £100 to Betsy Marshall, his housemaid.

On 5 and 6 April 1850, McArthur added one of six codicils to his will. He requested that his "body linen and cloths" be distributed among his servants, and details further items of his collection to go to various friends. His housemaid Betsy Marshall receives £100. He also makes provision for his burial, writing his own epitaph, so we might guess he was seriously ill at the time. However, he survived to bequeathe another day.

On 14 February 1851 he added a second codicil. Sometime in the last three years he has sent John Francis his legacy, and this must thus be removed from his estate. In addition, he bequeaths a further £100 to his housemaid Betsy Marshall. A third codicil follows on 12 August 1852, in which Betsy is again remembered, and a fourth on 24 March 1853:

> This is a fourth codicil to the last will and testament of me Duncan McArthur of Walmer in the county of Kent Doctor of Medicine which will bears date the twenty sixth day of January one thousand eight hundred and forty eight I bequeath to my present housemaid Betsy Marshall the further sum of fifty pounds to the sums of one hundred pounds one hundred pounds and one hundred and fifty pounds respectively bequeathed to her by my will and first and third codicils and in addition to the other articles bequeathed to her by my said first codicil and I direct that the said several sums and articles so bequeathed to the said Betsy Marshall shall be free of legacy duty which I direct to be paid out of my residuary personal estate ...

On Christmas Eve 1853, Duncan takes time off from the festivities to draw up a fifth codicil, detailing yet more items from his collection off to more friends. Betsy the housekeeper is not mentioned. But on 7 February 1854, there is a very lengthy sixth codicil, which reads in part:

> Whereas by my will and the first third and fourth codicils thereto I have bequeathed to my housemaid Betsy Marshall therein respectively named several legacies or sums amounting in the whole to the sum of four hundred pounds Now I revoke the said several bequests to her ... and instead thereof I bequest to my executors William Walt and George Mercer ... the sum of four hundred pounds And I direct and desire ... in the first place to pay to the said Betsy Marshall the sum of fifty pounds sterling part thereof the same to be for her separate use free from marital control And upon further trust to lay out and invest the sum of three hundred and fifty pounds sterling the residue thereof in their or his names or name in or upon any of the parliamentary stocks or upon government or real securities in the United Kingdom with power to vary

the same from time to time for other investments of the description aforesaid And upon further trust to pay to her the said Betsy Marshall and her assigns during her natural life or to such person or persons as she shall from time to time and not by way of anticipation appoint to receive the same ...

The plain legacy is converted into a trust fund, from which Betsy can draw more or less at will. Provision is also made for any children she might have; and it is at this point the will becomes problematical.

Born in 1780, Betsy Marshall of Chichester was hardly likely to have children in 1854; and indeed Betsy Marshall died in the Spring of 1853, in Walmer. What is going on?

In the 1841 Census, McArthur's household consists of himself and Betsy Marshall, both of whose ages are given as 60—ages in that Census being rounded down to the nearest five years. As well, there are three fifteen year old servants: Hannah Earidge (?), Hannah Decker—and Betsy Marshall. In 1851, Duncan and the older Betsy are still there, and they have been joined by a cook, Elizabeth Wybourne. And the younger Betsy Marshall is also still there, as Duncan's housemaid.

There are two Betsy Marshalls: one the faithful housekeeper, who receives two silver spoons for her years of trouble; and the other a local girl, who receives a trust fund of £400.

Betsy the younger was the daughter of James and Mary Marshall, of Walmer, and was baptised on 11 September 1825. I can find no record of her marrying, or that she had any children, but her remarkable treatment at Duncan McArthur's hands suggests a more intimate relationship than was normal between servant and employer. The fact of having two servants of the same name, who had such astonishingly generous treatment from their employer, suggests a closer relationship still.

Such generosity didn't extend to his godson. GWMR had precisely nineteen guineas from his godfather; but he may have learned something from him that stood him in excellent stead when he came to write—see the Postscript.

Paris and Marriage

By 1835, when he was 20, Reynolds was working at the Librairie des Etrangers, 55 Rue Neuve-Saint-Augustin, Paris. This was a bookshop—not a library, as James says, though it may have operated a circulating library as well. Reynolds went into publishing: in 1835 he brought out his first novel, *The Youthful Imposter*, an apt title since the story was stolen from Edward Bulwer-Lytton. The publisher is given as Librairie des Etrangers. It was republished in 1847 as The Parricide. In a short preface to this second edition he says:

> The Author, when only eighteen years of age, wrote a novel entitled "The Youthful Impostor," which was published in three volumes, in 1835, the Author then being twenty-one.

It is set "about twenty years ago," on "the London side of Bagshot," on the border between Surrey and Berkshire. This is the only surviving fiction he wrote before returning to England, and it is a thoroughly English tale. At the same time, or just after, he was literary editor for the *Paris Literary Gazette*, which was the first magazine to pay William Makepeace Thackeray for his writing. He also published his own translation of Victor Hugo's *Chants du Crépuscule*, under the title *Songs of Twilight*, in 1836.

At the end of June 1835, Reynolds applied at the British Embassy for a licence to marry. In order to do so, certain facts have to be established—for example the age and parentage of both parties. Reynolds was either unable or unwilling to provide these facts, or could not provide documentary proof of them, and so the licence was not granted. Instead, on Sunday 12 July, banns were read in the Anglican church of St. Michael, rue d'Aguesson, and repeated on 19 and 26 July. No one came forward to object to the marriage, possibly because no one in the congregation knew them to object. Thus they passed the test of banns, but no details, beyond names and home parishes, were ever entered in the record.

On Thursday 23 July 1835 GWMR attained the age of 21. He now came into his inheritance of £400 from his mother; but he would still have to wait a further two years before inheriting from his father. On Friday 31 July he was married. The celebrant was Bishop Matthew Henry Thornhill Luscombe, who had been appointed to the post by Prime Minister George Canning in 1825. Up until 1834 weddings had taken place in a room in the Embassy itself, or, for the more traditionally-minded, in a French Protestant church nearby. Bishop Luscombe had the new church of St. Michael built near the Embassy, and it was here that the couple were married.

His bride's name was given in the Register as Susannah Frances Pierson, and she deserves a section all to herself—see below. She was probably only 17 years old. Less than six months later, on 20 January 1836 their first child, George Edward, was baptised in the same church; he was probably born within two months of the marriage.

Whether deliberately or through neglect, George and Susannah obscured the facts of Susannah's early life, and an underage marriage, and a semi-illegitimate child, provide ample reason for two people of their time to do so. Later scholars have assisted the process of confusion:

E.F. Bleiler: By the end of 1837, [GWMR] was ... equipped with a wife, Susannah Frances."
Patrick Kelly [2005]: "probably in 1833, Reynolds married Susanna Frances Pearson."
Trefor Thomas [1996], Steven Carver [2004] "In 1848 he married Susannah Pearson."
Louis James [2004]: "About 1844 he married the writer Susannah Frances Pearson."

There is no record, between 1837 and 1858, of any marriage between anyone named Reynolds and anyone named Pearson, leave alone Pierson, in England and Wales. This rules out the possibility of a second, legitimising marriage, but the entry in the Register of the British Embassy, Paris, is definitive, and there for all to see. Further research—and it is badly needed—should start from there.

We can, however, settle two points suggested by some later writers. If GWMR was married in the British Embassy, he had not become a French citizen. And if he was not a French citizen, he could not have joined the Garde Nationale.

The marriage may have been the cause of a rift between GWMR and his mother's family: it is noticeable that he and Susannah married within days of his being allowed by law to do so without obtaining permission. Whether or not she had her parents' permission is another matter.

According to Bleiler, from January 1836 Reynolds edited the *London and Paris Courier*, an expatriate newspaper. According to Louis James, there is no evidence that the paper ever appeared, and Bleiler himself admits that the files are missing. Probably he put money into the venture, in return for being allowed to edit it. Again according to Bleiler he did very well at it, and soon the *Courier* was challenging the other leading papers on the market. But the money ran out, and Reynolds now quarrelled with his colleagues: he may have been hoping that his grandfather's will would bail him out: it didn't, as we have seen. Bankrupt in France, he paid off his creditors and returned to England in the autumn of 1837. He had probably left the whole of his inheritance behind in Paris.

*   *   *

For someone who spent so long there, Reynolds has left very little trace in the annals of Paris. The British Embassy did not keep files on expatriates unless they had direct dealings with them, and it seems Reynolds did not. He does not appear in the diaries of Lord Granville, the British

Ambassador at the time, nor is he ever mentioned in Galignani's *Messenger*. None of the group of expatriates mentions him, either, except Thackeray—and that mockingly. This is all the more strange since at that time there was a stellar community of English writers and artists in Paris—as well as Thackeray there were Laman Blanchard, Douglas Jerrold, and a host of lesser lights. And then it becomes strange to the point of incredulity. On 20 August 1836, Thackeray married Isabella Shawe. The ceremony took place in the same church of St. Michael, Rue d'Aguesseau, that had seen the nuptials of George and Susannah Reynolds, and it was conducted by the very same Bishop Luscombe. After the ceremony, William and Isabella moved into an apartment at 15 *bis*, Rue Neuve-Saint-Augustin. Neither was it the first time Thackeray had lived in that street; in the Summer of 1830, he had rented rooms at no. 54 right next door to the Librairie des Etrangers that had later been run (according to Summers, owned) by George William McArthur Reynolds. Even if he had not lived there, it is next to impossible to think that literary Englishmen in Paris would not have known, and dropped in on, a bookshop in their area that specialised in English books. Yet, apart from a fleeting mention many years later, none of them seems to have known Reynolds.

In 1852 Thackeray mentioned Reynolds in a lecture, though not by name:

> There was a book which had an immense popularity in England, and I believe has been greatly read here, in which the Mysteries of the Court of London were said to be unveiled by a gentleman who, I suspect, knows about as much about the Court of London as he does of that of Pekin. Years ago I treated myself to sixpenny-worth of this performance at a railway station, and found poor dear George IV., our late most religious and gracious king, occupied in the most flagitious designs against the tradesmen's families in his metropolitan city. A couple of years after, I took sixpenny-worth more of the same delectable history: George IV. was still at work, still ruining the peace of tradesmen's families; he had been at it for two whole years, and a bookseller at the Brighton station told me that this book was by many many times the most popular of all periodical tales then published, because, says he, 'it lashes the aristocracy!' [Thackeray: 280-281]

That is all he has to say, and it doesn't appear to be the work of a man who knew Reynolds well, if at all.

What are we to make of this? There is little or no evidence that GWMR was in Paris before late 1834, at the earliest. This lack of evidence is startling, given the number of people from whom we might expect it, and given the extreme geographical proximity of GWMR to these people—not only the same city, but the same address. One conclusion is that he was not there at all between 1830 and 1834, or, at least, if he was, it was only on short visits: holidays, in a word. So where did the story come from that he was? It is hard not to recall that Thackeray was (genuinely) in Paris in the Summer of 1830; returned a few years later; lost a fortune inherited from his father; lost money on a failed newspaper; contracted a marriage; then returned to London with his tail between his legs. It is remarkably similar to Reynolds's story, and, if that story is full of holes, then those holes may have been put there by GWMR himself, in imitation of Thackeray.

London and Obscurity

In 1838 Susannah and George Reynolds were living in Blackfriars, a poor district just south of London on the Thames. Their daughter Blanche was born there that year.[4] Reynolds was hired as editor of the *Monthly Magazine*, which Bleiler describes as "an unbelievably dull, moribund journal of considerable age." Assisted by Susannah, Reynolds quickly transformed it into one of the most widely-read journals of its day, not least because of his own serials in it. But by December 1838 he had, inevitably, quarrelled with his colleagues, perhaps over those same sensational serials, and he left the editorship. Without George and Susannah Reynolds in the editors' chair, the magazine quickly sank back into mediocrity and died a couple of years later, unregretted.

Having been in Paris, and being fluent in French, Reynolds tried to put his experience to use. In 1839 he published *Reynolds's French Self Instructor*, a language course. *Alfred de Rosann, or, The Adventures of a French Gentleman* came out in 1838, *Robert Macaire in England* in 1840. He also translated Hugo's *Dernier jour d'un condamné*, and Paul de Kock's *Soeur Anne*.

The most interesting of these French-linked books is his *The Modern Literature of France*. On the title-page he styles himself GEORGE W. M. REYNOLDS, MEMBER OF THE FRENCH STATISTICAL AND AGRICULTURAL SOCIETIES, &c., &c. I have no idea what these may have been, but if they are not made up then they may be a weighty clue to what Reynolds was actually doing in France at the time. Let's note, they are hardly what you would make up to bolster your credit as a literary critic. But there are few fields of human activity we would connect less with GWMR than statistics and agriculture, and why he should proclaim himself a member of the French Societies is perplexing, to say the least.

The book is an anthology of extracts, one from each author treated of, and each with a short introduction by Reynolds, so that the actual amount of exposition is small. But it is interesting to see whom he admires, and what he admires in them. As we might expect, he praises Hugo, Dumas and Lamartine; but Eugène Sue is more or less written off as a refined version of Captain Marryat. This is surprising, as Sue's *Mystères de Paris* was the model for Reynolds's greatest work, the *Mysteries of London*. Neither his political nor his social views are mentioned. Where others are admired for their realism, Sue is praised for avoiding it:

> Totally devoid of that intolerable vulgarity that characterises many of the naval novels of English writers, the works of Eugene Sue are as well-fitted for the lady's boudoir as for the officer's ward-room. They are written in a bold and happy style, which never relapses into coarseness; and even his details of the characters and conversations of the rough mariners whom he patronises, are replete with delicacy and simplicity. (79-80)

Reynolds knew more of the realities of sailors' manners than most, and it is hard not to see this as a rejection of his family heritage: sailors who never relapse into coarseness are barely sailors at all. Paradoxically, given Sue's gentility and lady-friendliness, Reynolds makes an interesting comparison:

> *Vigie de Koat Ven* has one parallel work in the French language—a work too licentious to be noticed at length in this book; but a work whose terrible lessons make the hair stand on end, chill the blood in the reader's veins, harrow up his soul, and for hours—perhaps for years after perusal, disgust him with this world and it denizens;—a work that was written by a French nobleman, and that purports to be a history of human nature;—a work, the tendency of which has been vituperated and condemned as pernicious in the extreme;—but a work which, we are fain to confess, tells a tale that is alas! too true. We allude to *Justine, ou Les Malheurs de la Vertu*; and with these two volumes should *Vigie de Koat Ven* be bound and placed upon the shelf of the public circulating library, or the private *bibliothèque*.

Since he is referring to it as a two-volume work, Reynolds presumably means the third edition of 1797. The comparison to Sade seems unfair to Sue, but we take from it the point that was perhaps meant: Reynolds has read a lot more French literature than the Law of England would allow at the time, and wants us all to know it.

One writer for whom Reynolds has nothing but praise is Frédéric Soulié (1800-1847). Now all but forgotten, Soulié was a stalwart of the *roman frénétique*, in which horrors and emotional turmoil are piled onto every page. It is worth quoting at length:

FREDERIC SOULIE

Turn we now to that young and successful writer, who descends into the vault of the dead and snatches the cold corse from the tomb, to introduce it into his tale; who calls in the assistance of plague and fire to add fresh horrors to his romances; and who delights more in the violated sanctuary of Death than in the splendour and gaiety of the drawing-room. Turn we to him who has revived the midnight terrors, the phantoms, the robbers, the murderers, the executioners, and the violaters of virgin innocence, that were wont to dwell in the legends of the olden times, or in the folios of a German library; whose patrons were Maturin, Lewis and Radcliffe; and whose readers were timid school-girls and affrighted nursery maids. Turn we to him who has regenerated that school of horror which had nearly exploded within the last dozen years;—yes, let us turn to him whose favourite subjects are those which we have dreaded to think of at night in the days of our childhood.

The writer of an ordinary novel may possess a weak, pusillanimous and feeble mind, and yet produce an amusing tale. His book may be called a good one; and he himself may pass as a man of talent and capacity. But the author of a romance, in which the feelings are most painfully interested by deeds of blood, vengeance, rape, and horror, must own a powerful mind, a vivid imagination, and a fertile brain; or else his lucubrations will be vain and futile. His murders must not be told with the coolness of a newspaper report: they must seem as if they were written in letters of blood themselves. The very page, which narrates their tale, must be surveyed with awe and a species of pleasing and fascinating abhorrence—if the reader can comprehend the antithesis—which create much more than a common interest in the mind. The romance writer must indulge in nothing puerile: no tame or vapid description will be pardoned in him: his work must be all fire, all vigour, all energy, and capable of producing a species of electric interest throughout.

Such is the system of M. Frederic Soulié, exemplified in his *Deux Cadavres*. This awe-inspiring romance, which seems as if it had been written in a charnel-house, by the light of those flickering candles that in Catholic countries surround the corpse, and by an iron pen dipped in human gore, is the most extraordinary creation of the brain that ever was yet, in the guise of a historical tale, presented to the world. Let the superstitious and the timid beware of it: they would not forget its terrible incidents for many a long night, after they had once perused it. It is a romance which haunts its reader as a man is haunted by a phantom of the victim whom he has slain: it is a book so full of horrors—and all those horrors so natural and so probable—not once exaggerated by the assistance of powers from beyond the tomb—that he, who reads it, lays it aside with the impression that such things might have been, and interrogates himself whether he be just awakened from a nightmare dream, or whether he have witnessed a series of terrible realities.

The scene is laid in England; and the epoch of the tale is the Protectorate of Oliver Cromwell. The work commences with the execution of Charles the First, which is described with painful accuracy. This is the first horror. Then comes the desecration of a grave in Westminster Abbey—the parade of a corpse through the streets of London—the hideous ceremony of presenting a jug of beer to the motionless lips of the dead thing, as the procession moves up the Poultry—the visit of two adventurous men to the Chapel in Windsor Castle at midnight—the exhuming of a coffin—the circumstance of one of those men putting his hand to the dead body which that coffin contained, and finding by the dissevered head that it was the corse of the late King—the journey through dark and dismal roads with that coffin upon a sledge drawn by dogs—rape of a beautiful girl by her lover in an hour of madness—the progress of the plague—murders, duels, riots and deaths—and then the horrid agonies endured by that young girl, who lingered through all the stages of starvation, tied to a tree, till she was wasted away, expired, and was found a fleshless skeleton some time afterwards! This is the brief analysis of *Les Deux Cadavres*: this is the frame-work of the book upon which was built the reputation of M. Frederic Soulié.

The Preface and Introduction are most interesting of all, for their spirited defence of France, and their attack on England. Replying to an article in the *Quarterly Review*, which blamed French morals on their literature, Reynolds says:

> To suppose that the insurrection of 1830,—an insurrection having for its object the working of a great and glorious change in the liberties of a mighty people,—depended on the licentiousness of novels and dramas, is to believe that the heated imaginations of men were fired rather by the contents of a circulating library than by a just sense of wrong and oppression. (iv)

He digresses, a little too lovingly, on the brutality of English murders:

> The abuser of French morals then proceeds to favour us with some extracts from the said *"Gazette des Tribunaux,"* relative to several horrible trials that had lately taken place in France. Amongst the hundreds which occur annually in that as well as in any other country, it is very easy to select half-a-dozen of the most dreadful, "in order to prove that the principles which pervade the novels appear to exhibit themselves elsewhere. In answer to this we declare that the same principles exhibit themselves also in England; particularly when Mrs Brownrigg flogged her appren-

tices to death,⁵ and when Cooke at Leicester murdered Mr. Paas with a log of wood, *and then burnt the body piecemeal on the fire to get rid of all traces that might lead to his discovery.*⁶ The late murder of Mrs. Brown by Greenacre was not attended with any dreadful circumstances, we suppose.⁷ Or may we say nothing to the massacre of Millie in the New-castle Savings' Bank? O! no!—in England murders are always committed *mercifully* and *humanely*, according to the inferences we draw from the *Quarterly Review*; whereas in France they are invariably attended with unusual circumstances of horror. (vi-vii)

Reynolds does not "set out his stall" in *The Modern Literature of France*, but it is a clear statement of his view of writing. As an aid to understanding his later work, it is invaluable.

* * *

During his time at the *Monthly*, Reynolds had begun to publish plagiarisms of Dickens. Everybody was doing it; Reynolds did it well. *Pickwick Abroad; or, The Tour in France* (1837-38) continued Dickens's novel in familiar territory for Reynolds. He also wrote short stories and novels, for example *Grace Darling, or, The Heroine of the Fern Islands* (1839), and *Robert Macaire in England* (1840). On 13 May 1840 he walked past a crowd outside a chapel in Aldersgate Street, London, and stopped to find out what was going on. The Temperance lecturer J. H. Donaldson was in full flow. Reynolds had been drinking that afternoon, though he claims he was not drunk; he heckled Donaldson, and challenged him to a public debate. Donaldson took up the challenge, and several debates ensued, in which Reynolds got the worst of it. He tried to argue for moderation, but was defeated, and on 30 May he signed the Pledge. He suddenly became a leading advocate for Temperance, and started a magazine, *The Tee-Totaller*, in which he printed his own stories, didactic or otherwise. Its first issue was on 27 June 1840. Its last was on 25 September 1841, by which time Reynolds had quarrelled with his colleagues, yet again, and left them.

The period between leaving Paris and signing the Pledge is not well known, aside from his publication history, and the rather tidied-up story of his conversion to Abstinence. The story suggests that he had a problem with alcohol—the sudden, vehement conversion is typical of the recovering addict. From the rift in 1841 until late 1844, even less is known. The argument with his T-T friends may have occurred because of a relapse in his drinking. According to James he was declared bankrupt in England in 1840, which may have been either cause or effect of drinking. Certainly, he and his family were living in poverty: they moved to a house in Suffolk

Place, Bethnal Green, then one of the poorest districts of London—now a fashionable one, and much the poorer for it. There were ten people in the house in all, in five different households, so that the Reynolds family cannot have had more than a single room, in which they would all live together. The ten may have shared a kitchen—it was a common arrangement—and washing facilities were probably at the sink, if there were any at all. Any money he earned was paid to the Official Receiver, through the Bankruptcy Office in Carey Street; his debts were serviced, and he was allowed the rest on which to subsist. It must have been a miserable life, especially for the children.

Around 1844 or 1845, John Dix visited Reynolds at his home, above a greengrocer's shop in King Square, off Goswell Street. There is no record of a grocer's in that square, and this may have been a snobbish dig at GWMR. In fact the street was distinctly up-market from Bethnal Green. At least seven residents were involved in the watch-making or jewellery trade; there were four schools—one for ladies—and a 'professor of music;' there was even a bookseller, Archibald Fullerton & Co., at no. 12, and at the same address was Duncan F. McKay, a publishers' agent. George and Blanche may have attended the National School run by Mr. and Mrs. Bicknell at no. 2, or Jacob Barret's academy at no. 57. "I found him in a back room," says Dix, "wrapped in a dingy dressing-gown, and perched on a stool at a high desk, writing away like a steam-engine." Reynolds was certainly writing prolifically at the time, and it may be that the more salubrious surroundings of King Square were helping him. His second son Frederick was born there in 1844, and their second daughter Theresa Isabella in 1846. And it was probably in King Square that he began his masterpiece, *The Mysteries of London*, that was finally to bring him success.

Reynolds the Chartist

By 1848 Susannah and George were living at 7 Wellington Street, Strand. George's brother Edward lived just across the Strand in Lancaster Place, where he was a journalist. Their third daughter was born in 1848, and named Joanna Frances—Frances, of course, for both her mother and her grandmother. The year of her birth was to be a momentous one for her father.

In 1838, Radical, progressive, and Socialist groups formed a coalition to promote a People's Charter. It was agreed to proceed by constitutional means, and gather a petition demanding implementation of the Six Points of the Charter: universal adult male suffrage; use of the secret ballot; abolition of the property qualification; payment for Members of Parliament; constituencies of equal sizes; and annual Parliaments.

The Charter seems to make very modest demands, and in at least one point the UK has gone beyond what was demanded; but at the time it seemed quite revolutionary. The Chartists, as its supporters were called, joined forces with other left-wing groups, notably Republicans and those agitating for Irish Home Rule.

GWMR had always been on the Radical side of English politics. In recent years the main debate has centred on the sincerity of his beliefs. Let us say straightaway that sincerity can never be proved, just disproved; and GWMR never did anything to show outright that his Radical stance was merely a pose. It is of course a common ploy of the Right-wing to claim that Socialists, Republicans, and the like are chancers, exploiting the workers just as much as the Capitalists—who at least pay their wages, where the demagogue merely fleeces them of their contributions. In the time-worn phrase, they're "only in it for the money." Reynolds made his money from publishing. It can hardly be believed that people bought his magazines and miscellanies because they admired his politics: on the contrary, we might say that Reynolds wrote and published popular, sensational literature to make sure people read his polemic. Thus at the beginning of each issue of *Reynolds's Miscellany* there was an "Address to the Reader:" the stories followed afterwards. Had he adopted a more conventional or even Right-wing stance, sincerely held or not, he might have made a bigger fortune by far.

Most criticism of Reynolds came from the Right of him, if only because—given he was a Radical, a Socialist, a Chartist, a Republican, and an advocate of armed force to achieve his ends—it was hard to be to the Left of him. Even someone as liberal as Dickens was forced into a quintessentially middle-class English, knee-jerk condemnation of him:

> "If 'Mr. G.W. Reynolds' be the Mr. Reynolds who is the author of the *Mysteries of London*, and who took the chair for a mob in Trafalgar Square before they set forth on a window-breaking expedition, I hold his to be a name with which no lady's, and no gentleman's, should be associated." (Quoted in Carver 2004)

We shouldn't be too surprised at such pomposity: Dickens was the author of *Barnaby Rudge* and *A Tale of Two Cities*, both of which show his terror at revolutionary excesses. But as Carver acidly comments:

> Given Dickens's take on the working class movement in *Hard Times*, with trade unionism demonised in favour of a rather insipid appeal to Christian brotherhood, it is obvious why he so disliked the revolutionary rhetoric of the popular author and Chartist Reynolds. Reynolds, in

turn, resented Dickens's image as a man of the people, feeling that his own voice much more accurately reflected the plight of the urban poor. The fact that Reynolds had successfully plagiarised Dickens in the past had not helped matters much either.

The spat between the two writers was rather more than this, and in a way rather less. We shall come back to it in its proper time.

To sum it up, though he sided with the Chartists, Reynolds saw that society's problems went much farther than an unfair franchise; and, having experienced poverty at first hand, he did not believe that those problems could be solved, as Dickens seems sometimes to believe, by the rich having a change of heart. Both seem fair points.

Those whose Socialism was tinged with, or derived from, Christianity did not like him either. The author and Chartist Thomas Frost mentions him only once, as turning up to a meeting in Croydon, in Surrey. But those further down the Victorian social scale had a better opinion of him. Henry Mayhew recalls:

> What they love best to listen to—and, indeed, what they are most eager for—are Reynolds's periodicals, especially the 'Mysteries of the Court.' "They've got tired of Lloyd's blood-stained stories," said one man, who was in the habit of reading to them, "and I'm satisfied that, of all London, Reynolds is the most popular man among them. They stuck to him in Trafalgar-square, and would again. They all say he's 'a trump,' and Feargus O'Connor's another trump with them."

We know that by 1832 Reynolds was reading Tom Paine, and in London and Paris he may have come into contact with Radical thought. The Radicalism in his own writing doesn't really come out until the mid-1840s, when Eugène Sue brought out his *Mystères de Paris* (1842-1843). He now modelled himself on Sue, but, given the run-ins he had had with the *New Monthly* and the *Tee-Totaller*, who had not appreciated his sensational style, he had to keep the tone down. Then in 1845 he met the publisher George Stiff and became the editor of his *London Journal*. It was printed by George Vickers of Holywell Lane, London. He now had the freedom to write as he wished, and the result was an imitation of Sue's *Mystères*, entitled *The Mysteries of London*. Here the Radical tone is strident, and the narrative frequently gives way to long passages of polemic facts, many of which Reynolds made up for the occasion. *The Mysteries* was hugely successful, and Reynolds was finally launched, not only as an author, but as a distinctive and popular political voice.

The year 1848 brought revolution, or the threat of it, to many parts of Europe. It brought Reynolds his finest hour.

Charles Cochrane, the Representative for Paisley on the Chartist Convention, called a meeting in Trafalgar Square for 6 March 1848, to protest against the new Income Tax. The Police ordered him to call it off, which he did, if reluctantly and half-heartedly. In spite of this, an estimated 10,000 people turned up in the Square, which was still under construction; and since Reynolds found himself the only official Chartist present, he promptly climbed up on the builders' scaffolding and began to address the demonstrators.

He spoke briefly against the Income Tax, a little more in favour of the Revolution that was then stirring in France, and then more extensively in favour of the Great Charter. (Was it today that he discovered his "part" in the French Revolution of 1830?) It was all peaceable enough; but then, either because of a fight that broke out with "a well-dressed man," or for no reason at all, the Police charged with their batons, and a general riot ensued. By four o'clock in the afternoon, the Police had cleared the Square of demonstrators. They stayed until about six o'clock, and then started to pack up and go home, confident that it was all over. But as they were moving away the crowd returned in the mood for a fight. They armed themselves with sticks and lumps of stone from the building works in the Square, and fought with the Police all evening. Some of the crowd took their stones and set off down Pall Mall, breaking the windows of gentlemen's clubs as they went. Order was not restored until past midnight.

What had happened to Reynolds in all this? There is some doubt, and some room for doubt. According to the commonest-told story, when the crowd went down the Mall he led them, and addressed them again in front of Buckingham Palace; then, for no easily explained reason, they took him up on their shoulders and carried him home to Wellington Street. Once there, he went out onto his balcony and continued his speeches into the night.

This may have happened; but if it did, it was a smaller section of the crowd that did it. Most of them stayed behind to fight with the Police. Reynolds's name does not appear on the list of those arrested, nor, apart from his speechifying, does he appear to have done anything else. Almost certainly he was not present the next morning, when the crowd returned and began to erect barricades in Trafalgar Square. The fighting now went on for two days, until Wednesday 8 March. There was then a mass movement towards Stepney Green, where another meeting was held; again, Reynolds is not mentioned as having been present.

Despite the fact that the events had little or nothing to do with Chartism, Reynolds had made quite a name for himself in the Movement that day. On 4 April he was asked to represent Derby at the Chartist Convention. Then, on 10 April, came the long-awaited mass meeting on Kennington Common, before presenting the Great Petition to the Government, in which he played a major part—as a speaker.

After the events in Trafalgar Square, the Police banned the meeting the moment they heard about it, but once more the order was ignored. The day began rather farcically. Kennington is in Surrey, south of the Thames; most of the delegates, and most of those wishing to attend, lived north of the river, in London. The Police blockaded the bridges, and much of the morning was spent in a game of cat-and-mouse between Police and demonstrators. In the meantime, the leaders of the Convention had gathered at their Headquarters, the Literary and Scientific Institution on John Street, Fitzroy Square. Feargus O'Connor was due to take the Chair, but when he had not arrived by nine o'clock Reynolds was asked to take his place—though he had to give it back when O'Connor finally turned up. They were told that the meeting had been forbidden, but they decided to carry on with it anyway. A crowd gathered outside the Institute, wearing the red, white, and green colours of the Chartists, and then the leaders set off for Kennington. They had had two coaches made: a squat four-wheeler, to carry the Petition itself, and a larger one to carry themselves; and Reynolds rode with them. Surrounded by supporters, they made their way to Bloomsbury High Street. There, at the offices of the National Land Company they took possession of the Petition itself. With a growing accompaniment of supporters, they went down Holborn to New Bridge Street, and prepared to cross Blackfriars Bridge. There was a great deal of cheering, and even what appears to be a civic reception from a local Alderman: but now a large contingent of Chelsea Pensioners—not old men, as nowadays, but soldiers on the reserve—landed at a nearby wharf. A contingent of the City of London Police guarded the north entrance to the Bridge, and men from L (Lambeth) Division gathered at the south entrance. A troupe of 15 mounted policemen stood by. It was a show of force, rather than force itself: the cavalcade was allowed to cross, though from now on it had a Police escort. By the time they reached Kennington, there were as many as 50,000 people cheering along the Great Petition, and George William McArthur Reynolds, riding proudly behind it.

The Irish Confederalists (Home Rulers) had been on the Common for some time, and the various Trades Union bodies had joined them. There was a wide variety of banners, only some of which touched on the matter of Chartism. The official Chartists joined them, but before they could begin the speeches a Police Inspector came over and asked to speak to Feargus O'Connor. O'Connor and Philip McGrath walked away with him. The rumour quickly struck up that O'Connor was arrested, and the crowd started to murmur. When he strolled back a few minutes later, after a friendly chat with the Inspector, a cry went up as if his return were a great triumph.

O'Connor now proceeded to address the meeting at great length, as was the custom in those times. The *Illustrated London News* reported that:

> During the delivery of Mr. O'Connor's speech, a deputation of the delegates, consisting of Mr. Reynolds, Mr. G. J. Harney, and Mr. West, left the car with a view of addressing the Irish Confederates or democrats, who were drawn up in military array at the south-eastern boundary of the common, headed by a handsome green flag, containing a harp and the words "Irish Confederation." "Let every man have his own country." An audience, which at one time numbered about 5000 persons, assembled here, and were certainly not the least enthusiastic portion of the crowds upon the common. Permission having been obtained for the deputation to speak from the balcony of a window overlooking the common, Mr. Daly said he was glad the Irishmen in the metropolis had taken this first great step of identifying themselves with the body of the English democracy. His friends had advised him not to bring the Irish flag to that meeting, because it had been taken down from the mast at Liverpool, but they were determined to stand by their Chartist friends in the assertion of the great constitutional right now at stake. (Cheers.) The Government must recognise the rights of the working classes in England, as they had been compelled to recognise them in France and elsewhere. He begged they would give a warm reception to their friends who formed the deputation. Mr. Reynolds, Mr. West, the Stockport delegate, and others then spoke at considerable length.

After which they returned to the main meeting. Thomas Clark read out the terms of the Great Petition; a Mr. Kidd proposed that it be presented to Parliament; and George Reynolds seconded the motion. Then, quietly and peaceably, they packed up and went home. The city of London had been in a foment all morning, with some of the choicest residential squares chosen as meeting-places for hordes of rough working men; the Police and even the army had been on high alert for Red Revolution. "At two o'clock," said the *Illustrated London News*,

> not more than 100 persons were to be seen upon the Common. Many of these consisted of its usual occupants—boys playing at trap-ball and other games. [*ILN*, 15 April 1848]

The Great Charter was handed in to the Government—who declared it a fake, and simply ignored it. Although the Chartists claimed 5,000,000 signatures, the Government said there were only 2,000,000, most of which read "Mr. Punch," "Queen Victoria" or "the Duke of Wellington." The Great Chartist Foment ended that day with a few speeches, and boys playing ball.

But Reynolds was on a roll, and typically there now followed a disaster.

The Fight Goes On

In 1846 Reynolds quarrelled with Vickers and Stiff—according to some accounts it was over money—but possibly just because that's what Reynolds did: quarrelled with people. The partnership broke up, and Reynolds took *The Mysteries of London* with him. He soon found another publisher, the young printer John Dicks, and they began a new venture from Reynolds's home: *Reynolds's Miscellany of Romance, General Interest, Science and Art*. It carried a continuation of *The Mysteries*, renamed *Mysteries of the Court of London*. In 1848, they began a new series of the *Miscellany*. This was printed up and sent out to the distributors, including George Vickers, who received a consignment destined for Scotland. The copies arrived in his office on Saturday 24 June 1848: the journal was due to come out on Wednesday 28 June. The intervening Monday, Reynolds received news that Stiff intended to issue his own magazine in competition with the *Miscellany*, and had been looking for a printer to do it. The Wednesday came, and the *Miscellany* came out—and so did *Reynolds's Magazine*, published by George Stiff, and printed by George Vickers of Holywell Lane.

> This spurious work contained a wretched travesty of my tale "The Coral Island," under the title of "Corral Island," Coral being spelt with two r's. It likewise contained a portion of another translation of "The History of the Girondists"—these two features being introduced to mislead the public to follow out the announcement contained in all the advertisements and placards above referred to, and to induce people to take "Reynolds's Magazine" instead of "Reynolds's Miscellany." Even the "Notices to Correspondents" in No. 1 of the new series of "The Miscellany" were travestied or parodied in "The Magazine." Mr. Stiff moreover declared in the presence of witnesses that 'He would spend a thousand pounds to ruin me and the "Miscellany."'

So thundered Reynolds, in a long, impassioned complaint, in the *Miscellany* on 29 July 1848. Of course there was little he could do, and he was in danger of giving people merely a good laugh at his expense: and he made it far worse with a silly, snobbish outburst, that perhaps shows the real Reynolds:

> But upon what pretence did Mr. Stiff issue a work entitled "Reynolds's Magazine"? He has a stoker in his employment of the name of Abraham Reynolds, and *this man, who is perfectly illiterate, and who earns a pound or a guinea a week,* lent his name to the spurious publication! But that name has been withdrawn from the imprint of No. 2 of the said spurious publication; and there is not even now a shadow of a pretence for retaining the name of Reynolds in the title of the work. (Emphasis mine)

Indeed! Whoever heard of a *writer* called Abraham, a stoker? The snobbish, disgraceful point is not that the man is to be despised for being "perfectly illiterate," but for earning only "a pound or a guinea a week." Reynolds may well have been sincere in his Radicalism, but, like Tolstoy, his snobbery never really left him.

Ironically, Reynolds himself might have been glad of that guinea a week: in 1848, for the third time in his life, he declared himself bankrupt. He weathered the storm, perhaps more due to the stolid common-sense of John Dicks than anything else. The family retrenched, moving from Central London to the quieter, cheaper suburb of Islington.

★ ★ ★

In 1849 some Chartists were arrested. Charles Dickens organised a subscription fund to pay bail for one of the young detainees, whose name he does not mention. Reynolds sent some money, and so did various ladies of Dickens's acquaintance: among them Angela Burdett Coutts, Julia Salis Schwabe, and Catherine Ann Cobden. This was where the problem arose.

On 30 August 1849, Dickens wrote to Miss (later Baroness) Burdett Coutts at her home, Holly Lodge, Highgate:

> My Dear Miss Coutts
>   The sense of the question is so clearly stated in your letter received yesterday, that I have no doubt it will be best for Charlie [his son] to go first to Eton, and then (for the professional conclusion of his education) to King's College [London]...
>   In the matter of that unfortunate young chartist, I have done what you kindly empower me to do. I quite agree with you as to the principle of such a subscription, and must add that while I feel for many working men who are Chartists, and mean no ill by it, I have no sympathy for

xxxvi REYNOLDS: A BIOGRAPHICAL SKETCH

the Amateur Members of that body. But I have no doubt that in this instance the money will do good…

  With many thanks for your excellent advice, believe me Dear Miss Coutts

Ever Faithfully Yours

Charles Dickens

(Storey and House, vol. 5, p. 601)

The same day he wrote to his friend William Macready on the same subject:

My Dear Macready

  I have deferred answering your note until I should have heard from Miss Coutts. She doubts (as I must say I do too) the expediency of the *example* of this assistance, however distressing and pitiable the facts of the case. Therefore she cannot appear as a subscriber, or give much. But she begs me to put down "A lady—£2.2.0." I will give you the two guineas when I see you—or I will give them to Mrs Macready if I see her first. Between ourselves, I must observe that I feel strongly for the genuine working men who are Chartists, but have no sympathy whatever with the amateurs. Let me, in confidence, call your attention and that of Mrs Schwabe and Mrs Cobden to the reason of my having separated the statement (in sending it to Miss Coutts) from the list of subscriptions. If 'Mr G.W. Reynolds' be the Mr. Reynolds who is the Author of the Mysteries of London , and took the chair for a mob in Trafalgar Square before they set off on a window-breaking expedition, I hold his to be a name with which no lady's, and no gentleman's, should be associated. And if anything could deprive this unfortunate young man of his liberty ticket, I am pretty confident that it would be a knowledge on the part of the government at home that he had such a champion. It may not be the same person, but the initials are the same…

Ever affectionately

My Dear Macready

Charles Dickens

(Storey and House, vol. 5, p. 603-4)

The root of Dickens's antipathy is in that word *amateur*. Why only *genuine working men* should be Chartists is not explained, neither is why Dickens should be the one to decide who is genuine or not; it might be added, as a note to Dickens, that *genuine working men* do not send their sons to Eton. The opposite of *genuine* is *amateur*, and the genuine chartists "mean no harm by it." In other words, they know their place, and cause no trouble. The amateurs, on the other hand, go off on window-breaking expeditions.

The anxiety comes from Miss Coutts, but Dickens is anxious—more than anxious—on his own part to accommodate her. She was a "millionaire philanthropist" (to use Michael Slater's phrase), one of the family owning Coutts's Bank in the Strand, and had contributed to several good causes Dickens was involved in. She also had a habit of intervening in his private life, as here with the education of his son, and later in the quarrel between Dickens and his wife; and Dickens's attitude towards her is generally rather servile, as the patronised to the patron. If Reynolds's name is to appear on the list of subscribers, then hers must not; and that, says Dickens, is absolutely right. Her less than generous two guineas is not the point: the continuing patronage of Miss Burdett Coutts is what Dickens is trying to save. If Dickens based David Copperfield on himself, he might have found Uriah Heap in the same place.

Having slighted his generosity, Dickens did not leave Reynolds alone. In the first edition of *Household Words*, Dickens continued his attack in a veiled form, speaking of "panders to the basest passions of the lowest natures." It was the aim of *Household Words* to "displace" such abominations. Later, in the edition of April 1851, he was far more explicit. Reynolds was:

a person notorious for his attempts to degrade the working men of England by circulating among them books of a debasing tendency.

On 8 June 1851, Reynolds responded in kind. His leader began:

That lickspittle hanger-on to the skirts of Aristocracy's robes—'Charles Dickens, Esq.'—originally a dinnerless penny-a-liner on the Morning Chronicle [...]

Otherwise, he seems to have ignored him. He could afford to: he was outselling him on all sides.

The exchange seems almost entirely personal. Dickens had sued Edward Lloyd for publishing plagiarisms of his works; he lost, when Lloyd argued, with magnificent cheek, that his thefts were so bad no one would be deceived. A later attempt to control the plagiarists ended badly for Dickens, leaving him feeling as if he had been the criminal, not the victim. He gave up trying, but he didn't give up resenting the thieves. Reynolds was, by general consent, the best of his plagiarists. Subscribing to his enemy's Charity was a generous act, removing his name from the list of givers was a spiteful one, and not for the brightest of motives; suggesting that Reynolds was insincere because of his social origins is a childish point. The chip on Dickens's shoulder never really healed.

★ ★ ★

In 1850 GWMR was elected to the Chartist executive again, and served for two years. He worked with Bronterre O'Brien's National Reform League, a militant Left offshoot of the Chartist movement. He and Dicks, another Chartist sympathiser, started a newspaper, *Reynolds's Political Instructor*, which published articles by O'Brien and other Radicals. Three times Reynolds was proposed as a candidate for Parliament: for Finsbury in 1850, for Bradford the following year, and for Lambeth the year after. His candidacy provoked outrage in some Chartist circles: Thomas Clark published the grandiloquently titled *A letter addressed to G.W.M. Reynolds: reviewing his conduct as a professed Chartist, and also explaining who he is and what he is: together with copious extracts from his most indecent writings: also, a few words of advice to his brother electors of Finsbury*. It was a successful attack; the "copious extracts" can't have hurt its sales.

In 1850, too, Reynolds and Dicks started their own most successful title, *Reynolds's Weekly Newspaper: a Journal of Democratic Progress and General Intelligence*. It was to run for 117 years, and for a while was the most popular working-class print in Britain.

Reynolds's business must have been helped by the departure from the Penny Dreadful scene of his main rival, Edward Lloyd. The Salisbury Square School (named from Lloyd's premises off Fleet Street) had dominated the lower end of the publishing market for more than a decade, but from the early '50s on Lloyd had gone for the life of a respectable newspaper owner. What Reynolds inherited, specifically and among other things, was Lloyd's chief hack-writer, James Malcolm Rymer (1814-1884), author of *Varney the Vampyre*, *Newgate*, and *The String of Pearls*. Rymer came to work for the *Miscellany*, producing notably *Edith the Captive; or, The Robbers of Epping Forest* for John Dicks in 1853. It was classic Lloyd material, from beginning to end, but now it belonged to Reynolds.

★ ★ ★

By the turn of 1850 Reynolds's finances were more settled, and the family could afford a holiday home in Herne Bay, Kent. Perhaps too they felt the air would be better for Susannah, who may have been showing signs of ill-health.

They continued to be based in Islington, and Reynolds not only kept his offices at 7 Wellington Street but opened new ones, at 40 Parker Street, off Drury Lane. In May 1850 another son was born, at Clinsby Villa, Tollington Place, Islington, and in a burst of revolutionary fervour Reynolds named him Kossuth Mazzini—after Lájos Kossuth, the Hungarian free-dom fighter, and the Italian Radical Giuseppe Mazzini. The child must have been so grateful! Strange though it may seem to us these were actu-ally quite popular names at the time: there was even a Thomas Kossuth Reynolds born in Hinckley, Leicestershire, who seems quite unconnected to our man. In later life, Kossuth called himself "George."

In mid-September 1850 the family were in Herne Bay. On or about 15 September George Edward fell ill. He had a persistent fever, already seri-ous enough in those days, but then he developed a red rash over his face and neck, and on Friday 20 September typhoid was diagnosed. On Mon-day 23 September he lost consciousness, and died two hours later.

On Thursday 26 September the Reynolds's neighbour, Celia Ledbet-ter, of Undersdown Row, went to Herne and registered the death with the Registrar, Thomas J. Pope. According to his death certificate, he was 15 years old, and the "Son of George William McArthur Reynolds, Author and Publisher."

George Edward was buried in the churchyard of Christ Church, Herne Bay. The family continued to live in Islington, where a fourth son was born in 1853; he was named for the French Democrat, Ledru Rol-lin.[8] It was here, too, that Reynolds wrote the weekly instalments of *The Necromancer*, starting at the end of 1851. But by now Susannah's health must have been weak, and in 1854 they moved permanently to Herne Bay. They took a lease on Belmore Hall, on the edge of the town, thus for the first time appearing as "gentry" in the local directory. Two daughters were born here: Louise Clarice, in 1854, and Emily, in 1856.

In the Spring of 1858, Blanche Reynolds, now 20, married William Wright Eaden, a thirty-year-old solicitor from Cambridge, then practising in Canterbury. They lived in Canterbury until their first child, Kate, was born, in 1859; but Susannah didn't live to see her first grandchild.

Susannah Frances Pierson; or, The Mysteries of a Wife

On Monday 4 October 1858 Susannah Reynolds collapsed and died at their home in Herne Bay. The doctor certified that the death had been due to "Disease of the Heart," which probably means it had been present for some time. On Wednesday 6 October, Mrs. Esther Goodban, of 11 Abbotts Place, Canterbury, went on the family's behalf to the Registrar, Mr. T. Pope, and gave details of the death. Mrs. Goodban was a dressmaker, but given that her husband had family in Ash-next-Sandwich, near Estry, she was probably a friend of the family. She claimed to have been present at the death, but this is almost always a fiction: the law requires the details to be from someone who witnessed the death for themselves, but in a clear-cut case such as this, no one quibbles.

Susannah Reynolds was buried in the graveyard of Christ Church, Herne Bay, with her son George. Her origins are a mystery. There are precisely 14 references to her in the public records, twelve of them as Mrs Reynolds: the day on which she married GWMR, and where; the dates on which she gave birth to her nine children, and where she was at the time; the details (given by GWMR, not her) in the 1841 and 1851 Censuses; and the date, place and cause of her death;

There is one other, which we shall look at later, but there is no trace of a birth certificate, or certificate of baptism, anywhere in Europe. James tells us she was brought up in France and Belgium. In the 1851 Census, an Alfred Pierson, born in Belgium in 1838, was a pupil at the Roman Catholic College in Stonyhurst, Lancaster; but there is no trace of his parents, and the disparity in ages almost certainly means he was not Susannah's brother. Antoine Joseph Pierson died in Brabant, Belgium, around 1795, and his will was recorded in England; but, again, he doesn't seem to have been a relative. Susannah Frances Pierson springs, a little like Athene, whole from the Register of the British Embassy. From the records we have we can make a few good deductions: but they expand our knowledge really very little, and raise more questions than they answer. According to Diana Neill, of the British Embassy in Paris, the records show some "amazing contradictions." We shall try to resolve them, or at least lay them out for others to do better.

1. Date of Birth

Susannah died on 4 October 1858, aged 40 years. Accepting that this as correct, we can say that she was born between 5 October 1817 and 4 October 1818.

The 1851 Census,[9] taken on 30 March 1851, gives her age last birthday as 32. That gives us a range of between 31 March 1818 and 30 March 1819.

These two statements are consistent, in that they overlap:

5 Oct. 1817—(31 March 1818—4 Oct. 1818)—30 March 1819.

We can take this period of overlap as a "safe zone," that probably contains her true date of birth.

2. Place of Birth

In 1851, her place of birth is given as St. Martin's-in-the-Fields, Middlesex, the district now centred on Trafalgar Square. This is probably her own statement, though the actual informant would have been GWMR, as Head of the Household. In 1841, she is listed as having been born in Middlesex—no other information was sought.

In 1835, she stated to the Registrar at the British Embassy that her *Parish/Residence* was St. James Piccadilly. This parish centres around St. James Square, which is barely a quarter of a mile from Trafalgar Square as the crow flies—assuming a crow could fly straight in London. So there is no real contradiction between the two statements. We must remember that London is divided into a bewildering number of sub-districts, many or most of which have no official existence, and that they overlap at the whim of whoever is describing them at the time. My native Fulham is at least seven different places, and I doubt if any five Fulhamnians would agree on where they began and ended. In Central London, the problem is compounded tenfold. Susannah Pierson was born between Buckingham Palace in the East, and Covent Garden in the West; between Piccadilly in the North, and Trafalgar Square in the South. But there are an awful lot of addresses in that small square of city.

3. Name

No support can be found for any of these assertions, in any other records. The name Susannah Frances Pierson appears in the Register of the British Embassy in Paris, and only there.

Between 1813 and 1837, there is no record of a Susannah (Frances) Pierson being baptised in St. Martin's-in-the-Fields, or anyone with any variant of that name. Of course her parents may have had her christened outside the parish, but there is no record of that name anywhere in England, between the above dates.

Four girls called Pearson were born in St. James, Piccadilly, in 1818 and 1819; two, Hannah and Sarah, were baptised on the same day, 6 September 1818, which happens to be in our "safe zone." Sadly, the parents of both children were William and Isabella Pearson, and they were practicing a not-uncommon delayed baptism: Hannah was born 11 March 1811, and Sarah 6 August 1813. Neither could be SFP in disguise.

Eliza Charlotte Pearson was born on 9 April 1819, and Mary Ann Pearson on 25 November 1817, both in St. James. The surname is wrong, and the dates skew the age for SFP. It is barely possible that one of these was SFP, but there is not a shred of evidence to support such a notion.

Searching for parents is futile when you don't have the child, but one or two names stand out. On 23 October 1823 Samuel Pierson married Ann Maskell, in the church of St. Martin's-in-the-Fields. The date is clearly too late for Susannah to be their daughter—it would mean she was under twelve when she married, and there is no Susannah Maskell. It is just possible that Susannah was Ann's illegitimate daughter, or a daughter by a previous marriage, who later adopted her stepfather's name; but, yet again, this is an pure speculation, without any evidence.[10]

On 20 January 1820 Edward and Susannah Pearson had a daughter, whom they had baptised Susannah in St. Luke's Church, Old Street, Finsbury, on 20 August. It is outside the "safe zone," and again the name is wrong. I suppose there is an outside chance that this was SFP. But why change the spelling of the name? She was educated, so it is not an illiterate mistake. If she wanted to disguise her identity, why not adopt a new name altogether?

In addition, a Susannah Frances Peirson (b. 1796) married James Gabb on 31 October 1817 at St. Mary Magdelene, Bermondsey, London. The Gabbs went to live in Botley, Gloucestershire, where they had two sons, John and Thomas. In 1841, a Susannah Pierson, aged 73, lived in Hitchin in Hertfordshire, and Peter and Frances Pierson (aged 65 and 70 respectively) lived in Tonbridge, in Kent. Edward and Susannah Pierson lived in Herne, Kent; she was too young to be Susannah's mother, though she, and all of these, may be related to her.

4. The Marriage Certificate

The most informative document on Susannah Pierson is the record of her marriage to GWMR. This took place, as we saw, on 31 July 1835, in the church of St. Michael, Rue d'Aguesseau, Paris, the church of the British Embassy in that city. The entire certificate reads as follows:[11]

> Bridegroom's name: George William McArthur Reynolds.
> Age: *not given*.
> Condition: Bachelor.
> Rank/profession: *not given*.
> Parish/residence: St. Clement, Sandwich, Kent.
> Father's name: *not given*.
> Father's profession: *not given*.
>
> Bride's name: Susannah Frances Pierson.
> Age: a minor.
> Condition: Spinster.
> Rank/profession: *not given*.
> Parish/residence: St. James Piccadilly, Middlesex.
> Father's name: *not given*.
> Father's profession: *not given*.

By Banns or Licence: ~~by licence~~.

Witnesses: Edward Dowers Reynolds, James Brooke Irwin, Emelie de Baysen, F. Foucquet.

What immediately strikes us is the amount of information that is *not given*: out of fourteen lines, seven are left blank. Some of these omissions are very surprising. It was usual to give the age as simply *minor* if under twenty-one, and as *full age* if over twenty-one. In the bride's case, it is usual not to give her rank or profession. But given that Susannah *was* a minor, it is most unusual that her father's name is not given and, presumably, not sought or asked for: all the more so because none of the witnesses can be her father, or even a relative. A minor, by definition, does not have the right to marry without her father's permission. Where was he in July 1835?

We know that GWMR's home parish is given correctly, because other records back this up. It refers to his place of baptism, rather than his last residence. As we have seen, there is no record of a Pierson family in the parish of St. James, Piccadilly.

The witnesses are of great interest, and help us fill in a few gaps in the story. The first to sign is, naturally enough, GWMR's brother Edward. It would be interesting to know if he was living in Paris with George, or merely visiting for the wedding. The next is James Brooke Irwin, born in Cumberland in 1811. He married Elizabeth Beavan in the church of St. Andrew, Clifton, Bristol, on 30 June 1843, and died in Stanley Street, Brompton, West London, in 1856. On his return from France he became a clerk at Somerset House, where one of his duties would have been to keep and collate the very records of Births, Marriages, and Deaths we have relied on so heavily here. This means that, in the late 1840s, Reynolds, his brother and Irwin are living and working within a few hundred yards of each other: Reynolds in Wellington Street, Edward in Lancaster Place, and Irwin next door to Edward. If he did not remain a lifelong friend of George Reynolds, he did keep up some sort of contact. In the 1851 Census he is lodging at 3 Mill Street, St. George's Hanover Square. The servant of the household is Edward Tozer—and this gives us a lock on the man who registered the death of GWMR. Through the connection with Irwin we know that he was the Edward Tozer born in Exeter, Devon, in 1826, and that in 1851 he was a hairdresser's assistant. This is interesting, as it is the only indication we have that Reynolds had personal friends—neither of whom have any obvious connections with the world of literature or publishing.

But it tells us nothing about Susannah. The last two witnesses may well have been her friends, rather than George's: they are Emelie de Baysen and F. Foucquet. There is no F. Foucquet, male or female, in any of the records I have been able to check, although there are Fou(c)quets aplenty to be had. As for Emelie de Baysen, the problem is of an entirely different order: there is no record of anyone of that name in France, and neither does the name (de) Baysen appear in any French records. The name Baysen (without the honorific de) is common in the Arab world, and in Denmark and Norway, but nowhere else. Whoever signed the register that day, it probably wasn't "Emelie de Baysen."

The whole marriage smells of elopement, and Paris was the right place for it. The minister who conducted the ceremony was Matthew Henry Thornhill Luscombe (1775-1846). A graduate of St. Catherine's College, Cambridge, he was curate of Clewer, Windsor, then from 1806 to 1819 a master at the East India Company School in Haileybury, Hertfordshire. At the same time, he was curate of St. Andrew's, Haileybury. In 1819 he moved to Caen, and then to Paris. At the time, the Anglican congregations on the Continent had no figure in overall control: in 1824 the Foreign Minister, George Canning, appointed Luscombe Chaplain to the British Embassy in Paris, and general superintendent of the Anglicans on the Continent. In 1825 he was ordained a "missionary" Bishop in the Scottish Episcopal Church. He was not a success. The congregation in Boulogne refused to recognise him, and many others thought he was exceeding his authority. Given his ambiguous status, as an Episcopalian Bishop ordering Anglican congregations, his right to ordain priests was questioned, and in 1840 it was removed from him: casting grave doubts over the legitimacy of those priests he had ordained. He died in Lausanne on 24 August 1846.

Luscombe seems to have been a troublesome priest, an empire builder rather than a peacemaker or an administrator. It was he who built the new church in the rue d'Aguesseau, paying for it in part himself. But the records kept under his administration are not good, and Paris seems to have been a place where people from London went to contract marriages that might have raised an eyebrow or two back home. It is rare to see the name of a father in the marriage registers, and ages are not always given, even to note a minor. Clearly, marrying couples were not pressed for details. This is the case with GWMR and Susannah Pierson.

It isn't hard to see what is going on. If we are correct in the range of dates for her birth, then in July 1835 she was between 16 years 8 months and 17 years and 4 months old. Her first son, George Edward, was baptised on 20 January 1836, in Paris. At his death, on 23 September 1850, his age is given as 15. If this is correct—we must accept it is—then he was born on or before 23 September 1835: in other words, within 54 days of his parents' wedding. Descending into indelicacy, Susannah was a "wide bride." She and George must have known each other since at least January 1835, when Susannah would have been at most 16 years 7 months old, and perhaps not even 16. This extreme irregularity must have prompted some inquiries (is that why Edward came over from England?), which may explain why the words "by licence" have been crossed out in the Register.

5. Other Sources

The only other thing we know for sure about Susannah Reynolds is her publication history, which is brief. Her only novel, *Gretna Green; or, All For Love* came out in 54 weekly parts, between 8 September 1847 and 30 August 1848. It bore the imprint of *Reynolds's Miscellany*, 7 Bridge Street, Covent Garden. It was reissued, and then published in one volume by John Dicks, at GWMR's home address in Wellington Street, in 1849 as *Gretna Green; or, All For Love. A Domestic Tale*. We can mention that this is the tale of an elopement, but not make too much of it. It owes a large debt to Hannah Maria Jones's novel *Gretna Green* (1820).

In 1847, she collaborated with W.E. Hall on *The Household Book of Practical Receipts*. And again, on 25 September 1847, she published a song, *The Belle of the Village*, which Summers says was very popular. The music was supplied by Albert Dawes, organist of Trinity Church, Ryde, Isle of Wight.[12] I have no idea what the connection was with Dawes, but given the setting of much of *The Necromancer* on the Isle of Wight, we wonder whether the Reynolds family spent a holiday there, between 1845, when the church was built, and 1847? Ryde is only four miles from Brading, home of Musidora Sinclair, and the description of the place in Chapter One could have been written by someone with personal knowledge of the place.

On Wednesday 6 September 1848, her *Wealth and Poverty. A Domestic Tale* was published from Wellington Street, and finished on Friday 22 December 1848, having gone through 12 numbers. The whole thing, presumably from remaindered copies, was available from Wellington Street at 1s., but it appears not to have been republished.

6. The Other Susannah Frances Pierson

Let us now pile mystery upon mystery. The public records mention Susannah Frances Pierson only twice by that name. The first is her marriage to GWMR. But there is a second Susannah Frances Pierson; and although the temptation is to write her off as a different person, we cannot altogether do that. The two mentions appear only three years apart, and in the very same MS 10891 of the Guildhall Library in London. On 23 February 1832, a woman of that name married a Thomas Noel, or Thomas Noel, Cleric, in the Chapel of the British Embassy in Paris:

Bridegroom's name: Thomas Noel (Cleric?)
Age: *not given*
Condition: widower
Rank/Profession: *not given*
Parish/residence: St. Marylebone, Middlesex
Father's name: *not given*
Father's profession: *not given*

Bride's name: Susannah Frances Pierson
Age: *not given*
Condition: spinster
Rank/profession: *not given*
Parish/residence: St. Pancras, Middlesex
Father's name: *not given*
Father's profession: *not given*

By banns or licence: licence

Witnesses: Peter Smith, J F Lemaire

Again, half of the fourteen categories are not filled in. There is no more trace of this SFP than of the other. Neither is there a trace, after the wedding, of a Susannah Noel: the only woman bearing that name married John Noel in 1837, and died in 1870 aged 74. She is accounted for; our Susannahs are not.

There was a family of Piersons in St. Pancras: they were Samuel and Miriam Pierson, and their son Richard (b. 15 August 1813). There is no record of a daughter, but it's quite possible they had one: whichever way, they are the nearest thing we have to a reasonable guess at her family.

The witnesses provide a slim but tantalising link. "Peter Smith" is far too common a name to pin him down, and there is no record of such a man in the Embassy Registers. John Francis Lemaire, on the other hand, is present: he married Matilda Macdonogh (MacDonough) at the Embassy Chapel on 12 September 1829. The allegations—the details of bride and groom—have been lost, as indeed they have been for Noel and Pierson. As a witness to the latter wedding, Lemaire's place of origin is not given, so we cannot strictly identify the two men; but there was a James Lemaire, who married Martha Garrud in St. Martin's-in-the-Fields on 18 June 1828.

They may have been related to the John Lemaire who married Ann Burl-inson on 20 December 1794, at St. Dunstan's Stepney. If so, then they are of right age to be brothers, or at least cousins.

The question is, of course: are these two Susannah Frances Piersons one and the same? Given that there are as many or more links to our SFP, it seems highly likely they are, leaving us four options—either Thomas Noel died before 1835; or the marriage was annulled, possibly due to her extreme youth; or there was a divorce, possibly due to her adultery with GWMR; or, finally, Susannah was a bigamist. At this point, with no more facts, we stop.

Last Years and Religion

After Susannah's death GWMR moved back to London, to 41 Woburn Square in Bloomsbury.[13] He had come as far from the poverty of Bethnal Green as it was possible to go, and ended his days in the heart of the wealthiest part of the City of Westminster. Shortly after the move he accused his erstwhile Chartist colleague, Ernest Jones, of financial dishonesty. He and Jones had been at loggerheads for many years, and the insults and accusations had not been from Reynolds's side alone. In 1852, Jones wrote an "Address to the Chartists" which he published in his *Notes to the People*, no. 2. Referring to Reynolds by name, he says:

> When we sit down to the feast of democracy we must not have the table spread with garbage. The man whose taste has led him to dish up Chartism with such trash; and he who is satisfied with it, have alike mistaken their mission, and the nature of the principles they have adopted. (Quoted in Ledger 2002: 45)

Again in 1853:

> [...] when advertising *Woman's Wrongs* in *The People's Paper*, he appealed (doubtless in a sideswipe against Reynolds) "TO THE FRIENDS OF A CHEAP LITERATURE FREE FROM DEMORALISING SENSUALITIES." (Ledger: 63)

Jones won his case against Reynolds in 1859; but the costs of the case were so great that *The People's Paper* was forced to fold. Ledger says this may have been Reynolds's original aim, but this seems doubtful: it was Jones who brought the case, and his motive may have been no higher than to force out a hated rival. It was certainly not a case of despising Reynolds for having made money out of mixing sensationalism and Chartism. Jones himself had done the same, for many years. Like Reynolds, he was heading for respectability, having just resumed his career at the Bar: a taint of dishonesty would have ruined him. And neither was it a working-class Chartist despising the middle-class *parvenu*: Jones came from the same kind of officer class as Reynolds, with the difference that Jones was the godson of the King of Bavaria. We might conclude that both were worse than each other.

* * *

Reynolds's second grandchild, Charles E. Eaden, was born in Canterbury in July 1860, after which Blanche and William moved away to Friern Barnet, to the north of London. He was left a widower at 46, with seven children still at home, the oldest sixteen, the youngest only four. They had a cook in Woburn Square, 43-year old Ann McIvering from Limerick; a housemaid, Annie Smith (31) from Bursey in Hampshire; and a parlour-maid, 23-year old Elizabeth Beckwith, from Plumstead, near Norwich, Norfolk. Now he also brought in a nursemaid, Maria Wood (22) from Clerkenwell, London.

By 1862 Reynolds had ceased to write. Around that time he sold the copyright of all his works to John Dicks, who proceeded to bring out a complete edition—though he omitted the plagiarisms of Dickens. *Reynolds's Miscellany* changed its name to *Bow Bells*, and although Reynolds stayed on as editor, he seems to have been less active even in this.[14]

Reynolds's place as chief writer was taken by James Malcolm Rymer, a veteran Penny Dreadful producer of the old Salisbury Square School. Born on 1 February 1814, he trained as a civil engineer, but turned to editing his own *Queen's Magazine* in 1842. It failed after five issues, and he was taken on by Edward Lloyd, king of the Penny Dreadfuls, in Salisbury Square, off Fleet Street. Rymer produced some of the most famous works in the genre—*Newgate, Varney the Vampyre, The String of Pearls*—and when Lloyd moved away from Dreadfuls he was snapped up by Dicks and Reynolds. He continued to write until the end of the 1860s, by which he had made enough to retire from the trade. With his wife Sarah he moved to Worthing, Sussex, where he ran a hotel on Marine Parade. He too seems to have had Chartist sympathies, or at least connections: Sarah Rebecca Rymer (1824-1909) was the daughter of the Chartist William Carpenter (1797-1874), by his first wife Mary Avey. Carpenter was a left-wing religious author, and an early believer in the British Israelite theory—that is, the idea that the inhabitants of Britain are really the Ten Lost Tribes of Israel. How far Rymer went with his father-in-law's notions is a moot point: for example, Carpenter was an avid Freemason, Rymer was not. (Sarah was even born in Great Queen Street, next to Freemason's Hall.) But it is clear that a career writer, with vaguely liberal views, would be comfortable working with Dicks and Reynolds.

On 21 March 1863, Theresa Reynolds married Archibald Douglas Lamb, in the church of St. Andrew, Wells Street, Marylebone. The Lambs were a very well-to-do middle class family: Samuel Lamb (b. 1812) was a solicitor, originally from Reading, Berkshire; Samuel junior (b. 1837) and Archibald (b. 1843) were articled to solicitors; Victor (b. 1839) was a medical student. The youngest son, Arthur Henry Woodham Lamb (b. 1847), was a law student in the Temple, London. Whether they first met at the wedding or before, Arthur clearly impressed Joanna Reynolds: they were married in the same church on 1 August 1865. In 1865, too, Frederick Reynolds married Kezia Meek, a servant from Cambridge, where he had been studying medicine. Arthur and Joanna moved to Hammersmith, Middlesex, where they had a daughter Edith in 1867; then on to St. Pancras, near her father, where Florence was born in 1868. In 1871 they were lodging at no. 12 Lower Easthorpe Street, St. Pancras, the home of Charles Sheppard, a commercial clerk. Arthur is not at home on the night of the Census, but whether it was just for that night, or more permanently, there is no way of telling. I have found no further trace of Theresa Lamb, and she and Archie may have gone abroad.

One of the few windows into GWMR's world in his later days is the 1871 Census. He is 56, and still describes himself as "Author, Novelist and Journalist." Louisa and Emily are still at home, aged 17 and 15 respectively, and so is Ledru Rollin Reynolds, aged 19, and articled to a Shipping Broker. They are cared for by a staff of four. Their cook is Ellen Quigley, 24, from Woodbridge in Suffolk. The housemaid is Mary Weller, 24, from Battersea, and there is a livery servant, a local boy aged 17, William Wall. The nursemaid is gone, and Louisa now has a lady's maid, 22-year old Jane Overs, from Dereham in Norfolk. For a moment, a slip of the census-taker's pen brings her alive. In London, Dereham is pronounced to rhyme with "fear 'em;" the census-taker has transcribed Jane's Norfolk accent, which rhymes it with "scare 'em:" she is from "Norfolk, *Dareham."*

In 1873 Louisa Reynolds married Adolphus William Bell. In 1875, Ledru Rollin married Marian Rees, and went to live in Kennington, Lambeth, not far from where his mother and father started out, on their return from France—and the scene, of course, of his father's greatest hour. (By 1891 they had four children: Hilda, 12; Vera, 10; Gladys, 5; and Cyril George, 4.) That same year, Emily Reynolds married Clifford Berdoe. This left their father alone in the house.

The story persists that after he retired from writing GWMR was Church Warden for the Church of St. Andrew, Wells Street. Summers wrote:

The famous author and once prominent publicist drew further and further into retirement, and I have been given to understand that latterly he
had a very deep sense and consciousness of religion. (147-148)

Summers is implying that Reynolds's quiet life was a cover for a religious retreat, and, like most of Summers's pronouncements, it can be
politely ignored. There is no evidence at all that Reynolds 'got religion.'
Yet the story grew and took hold, and we must look into it and answer
it. On the surface it is not at all impossible. He was baptised and confirmed into the Church of England; he married Susanna Pierson in an
Anglican chapel, and his first child George Edward was baptised into the
same church, in the same chapel.¹⁵ Being in France, they had the option
of civil marriage; but they did not take it. He was thus a communicating
member of the Church—meaning one that takes communion—or at least
was qualified to be one if he so chose to be; and, at least in his early days,
he did. Throughout his writings, his characters invoke and inveigh against
God and his Providence, and though this is perhaps nothing more than
convention, he never takes the opportunity to deny the existence of God.
Some passages hint at stronger beliefs:

> The infidel may deride as he will,—the scoffer may ridicule the opin-
> ion;—but it is nevertheless a grand and solemn truth, that an act of
> devotion in the hour of danger inspires the soul with confidence and
> with courage,—invoking Providence as it does, to watch over the path
> of peril, and raising up a belief that He will indeed vouchsafe to become
> a guide in the ways of difficulty! (*Faust*, p. 88)

This has the ring of belief. But sceptical opinions alone would not necessarily have stopped him being a church warden. The Church of England
has always avoided clashes of doctrine: that is one of its great strengths,
and also its greatest weakness. It has always comprised an Anglo-Catholic
and an Evangelical wing, and in the middle is a whole spectrum of opinion, tolerated because it is not looked into very assiduously. The Eliza-
bethan and Williamite settlements of Religion stressed Occasional Con-
formity—that is, as long as one conformed outwardly to the rites of the
church, what one believed in one's heart would remain a private matter.
This sane and humane attitude is firmly rooted in English thought, and
survives to this day. A Deist, such as Reynolds proclaimed himself, could
feel quite comfortable as an Anglican: many agnostics have, and not a few
atheists. To be a Churchwarden is not to occupy a religious post, but to
be responsible for the fabric of the church, and the smooth running of its

work, especially charitable works, of which there were many in Marylebone. Reynolds might well have found satisfaction in doing that.

Reynolds's Deism is well-expressed in *The Modern Literature of France.*
Writing of Lamartine, he says:

> [H]e prays to his God in those sweet strains which, if the Almighty re-
> ally listen to the supplications and thanks of men, could not fail to be ac-
> ceptable at the throne of eternal grace [...] Religion made Lamartine a
> poet; but instead of inspiring him with fanatic and gloomy notions, and
> divesting his lips of smiles, and quenching the fire of his eye, it taught
> him to worship his God with gladness as frequently as with plaintive
> measures, and to depict in happy and glowing colours the goodness and
> munificence of the majesty of Heaven [...]
>
> M. de Lamartine worships his Maker through that Maker's works;
> and when he gazes upon the faultless beauty of those Asiatic women,
> whose charms embellish his verse, it is not with the eyes of desire that
> he surveys them; but he dwells on their attractions with the same enthu-
> siasm and the same holy admiration as when occupied in the contem-
> plation of a lovely spot in inanimate nature. The girl, with her naked
> legs encircled by bracelets, and with all the riches of her breast revealed
> to view by the loose vesture which only partially concealed her form,
> was to Lamartine but as another instance and living example of the wis-
> dom and might of his God, who had created that fascinating being also.
> (130-132)

There is however a larger objection to the story. You don't apply for
the job of church warden: you are invited to fill the post. Reynolds's reputation as a sensational novelist, as a Chartist, a Republican, and indeed as a
writer of 'indecent' novels, may well not have made him the first choice of
the Vestry. And there is still more: as well as being a communicating Anglican, a church warden is chosen from amongst those who live in the parish,
or at the very least have a long-standing connection with it. GWMR lived
in Bloomsbury, and the district of St. Giles. St. Andrew's Church, Wells
Street, is in St. Marylebone, a quite distinct borough, and in parochial
terms there is no connection. His daughters may have been married there,
but that was through the Lamb family. GWMR was never a parishioner of
St. John's, and we should take with a large spoonful of salt the idea that he
would have been invited to hold office within it.

If George Reynolds *was* a church warden in that parish, then it was
almost certainly a different George Reynolds; and there was another in
the right place at the right time. A corn-chandler of 398 Edgeware Road,
he was married at St. Andrew's in 1848, and was still at the same address
53 years later. The honour was probably transferred to GWMR because of

his slight connection to St. Andrew's, when his daughters married there; or, more likely, because the second George Reynolds was not only another Kentishman, from Deal, but he was also GWMR's cousin.

Most likely of all, the tale was Summers's vigorous, paranoid imagination. And yet: see below, "A Very Gothic Postscript."

In retirement, Reynolds developed high blood pressure and kidney disease. The two go together, of course, and the death certificate does not state which came first, and so which was the cause and which the effect; but he also grew fat, which with hypertension was probably the aetiology of the renal disease. Under such circumstances, he may also have had a degree of diabetes mellitus. In early 1877 he had a stroke, a cerebrovascular accident that left him paralysed down one side, unable to speak and helpless. He held on like this for another two years. On Thursday 19 June 1879 he collapsed at his home in Woburn Square. S.E. Mullings, a surgeon, was called in, which suggests his relatives thought he had had another stroke. Reynolds died that same day.

There followed something of a flurry. He had clearly made no arrangements for his burial, and something had to be found quickly. Edward Tozer, whose address is given as 41 Woburn Square, was probably a servant at the house. On Saturday morning, 21 June, Mr. Mullings gave Tozer a note certifying the cause, which he took to the Registrar of Births and Deaths for St. George's Bloomsbury, a Mr. Yardley. Tozer agreed with Yardley that he had been present at the death. Yardley entered the information in the Register, and gave Tozer a certified copy of the entry. Reynolds's profession was given as "Newspaper editor." Straightaway, a member of the family—not named beyond "Reynolds"—went to Kensal Green Cemetery, North London, showed the certificate to the officials of the General Cemetery Company, Ltd., and bought Reynolds a place in the Catacombs. The price was fifteen guineas.

In the end, Reynolds did make a return to the Church of England, of a sort. On Monday 23 June his remains were deposited in Catacomb B, Vault 194, Compartment No. 5, beneath the Anglican Chapel, after a service conducted by the cemetery's Church of England chaplain. In the same cemetery lie Richard Harris Barham, William Harrison Ainsworth, Feargus O'Connor, and (nearest to him of all) James Malcolm Rymer.

Originally, he was to have been laid in Vault 198, Compartment 10, but between purchase and burial the location was changed. Perhaps George Reynolds was already quarrelling with his neighbours.

★ ★ ★

A Very Gothic Postscript:
Maundy Thursday, 5 April 2007

Over Easter, 2007, we went to stay with relatives in England, and I took the opportunity to visit Kensal Green Cemetery. I had two purposes in mind: one was to visit Reynolds in the catacombs; the other was to locate the grave of James Malcolm Rymer.

Rymer turned out to be a hard man to find, even using the excellent map provided by the cemetery, and it was more than an hour before I realised the bare patch of grass concealed his tombstone. Then it was another hour's careful, back-stretching dissection before I managed to peel away enough of the grass, using my father-in-law's old trowel, to be able to make out the inscription:

James Malcolm Rymer
born 1 February 1814
died 11 August 1884

Rymer was thus a slightly older contemporary of Reynolds, and had been laid to rest barely two hundred yards from his late friend. With him were his wife Sarah, his son Gerald (1860-1865), and his other son Walter (1840-1926). It was a moving moment: I was greeting the author of *The String of Pearls*, the creator of the immortal Sweeney Todd, for perhaps the first time in eighty years.

You enter Catacomb B of Kensal Green Cemetery through a door in the side, that leads to a shabby, disused chapel. There is a green door, and a flight of stairs past what look like boilers, and at the bottom of the cramped staircase is another door: the space is so narrow you have to get back on the stairs to give it room to open. Beyond this is utter blackness.

My Guide to the Underworld was Peter Hughes, the pleasant, quietly-spoken Chapel Attendant. I followed him into the Catacombs with only the light of his torch to guide me: the place was so cavernous the light didn't seem to touch anything but the floor in front of him. A hundred steps or so into this Hades there was a vent in the ceiling, letting in some weak light. For the first time I could see where I was: in an immensely long tunnel, perhaps twenty feet high, and surrounded on all sides by arches. Each of these arches was divided into ten or twelve squares, most of them plastered over; and with a distinct nervousness I realised that these were the compartments that contained the dead. We were the only living people among 10,000 coffins.

I stayed very close behind Peter.

We found Vault 194 with difficulty—the electric lights were temporarily not working—but at last we were there. Counting from the ground, and from left to right, at about knee-level, we saw the compartment housing Reynolds's mortal remains. It was uncovered, leaving the coffin open to the view. Peter knelt down and polished the name-plate with a cloth. It was worn almost to illegibility, but in the light of his torch we saw it was the right place: the name McArthur was plain. Slowly we made out the simple epitaph:

GEORGE WILLIAM McARTHUR REYNOLDS
DIED 19TH JUNE 1879
AGED 64

The wreaths laid by the mourners were still on top of the coffin, and though blackened now after 128 years, the flowers were still recognisable.

I stood back and looked at the Vault, taking care not to step back too far. An immediate shock: some of his neighbours' compartments had not plaster but wrought-iron cages over them. I asked Peter about what they were:

"That was to stop body-snatchers."

Even fifty years after the Anatomy Act, the shadow of Anthony Tidkins was still strong. The sleepers were secure behind their iron bars, and their families slept soundly at night. I began to wonder if any over-nervous readers of The Mysteries of London had rigged their coffins to fly open at a movement from within, for fear of premature burial, but bravely stopped myself going down that road.

But a second, greater shock was waiting: at the foot of the coffin was a tiny statuette of the Blessed Virgin, bright and shoddy, kneeling in her blue robes.

I cannot explain it. Even if Reynolds were a Church Warden, he was an Anglican Church Warden, and such statuettes are not used in the Church of England. None of his family were Catholic, though I suppose Edward Tozer might have been. At a quick glance, in a very dark place, it appears that the statuette has been placed over accumulated dirt and debris—unlike the blackened wreaths, still present and recognisable, it was not put there at the burial. Two possibilities therefore come to mind—first, that it previously belonged to someone else, dropped to the floor, and was placed in Reynolds's compartment by mistake; or that it was put there deliberately by someone else. Since no one appears to have known where GWMR was buried before I found him, the person that immediately springs to mind is Augustus Montague Summers.

Despite my extreme nervousness at being in a Catacomb, the feeling of being there in the presence of George Reynolds was overpowering. I had finally met the man who had occupied so much of my thoughts and time for so long. Without thinking, when it came time to go, I leant forward and patted the coffin: I was glad I did it. We made our way back up to the air, and the pale sunlight of an English April has never looked so beautiful.

Dick Collins
West Muskerry, Co. Cork

August 31, 2007

NOTES

1   In this respect, I am not the least of sinners. See my introduction to *Wagner the Werewolf* (Ware: Wordsworth, 2006) for a cautionary lesson in checking your sources before you write your introduction.

2   Poplar, Middlesex, now in the East End of London.

3   Personal communication, 18 January 2007.

4   St. Saviours (Southwark) Births March 1838 fol. 4 p. 390.

5   The murder of Mary Clifford by Elizabeth Brownrigg was one of the most famous, and most popular, of all British murders. Brownrigg was hanged at Tyburn on 4 September 1767, for a particularly prolonged and sadistic crime. Scandalously, the girl was at the time under the protection of the Church-wardens of St. Dunstan's, Fleet Street, who appear to have ignored suspicions of the Brownriggs. She is a forerunner of Sweeney Todd, not least because a highly romanticised version of the story was written by Thomas Peckett Prest, and published by Edward Lloyd in 1842.

6   Paas was a bookbinder, James Cook made the brass instruments used in that trade. Cook fell into Paas's debt, and when Paas came to Leicester to collect, Cook murdered him, and burned the body in his fire. The case is full of gory and novelistic touches, and is grist to the *Newgate Calendar's* mill. The account there bears reading. Cook was executed near Aylestone Toll Gate, Leicester, on 10 August.

7   On 28 December 1836 a human trunk and arms were found at Ben Jonson Lock, on the Regent's Canal in Stepney. The head was later found at Camberwell, in Surrey. The remains were those of Mrs. Hannah Brown, who had been about to marry James Greenacre. Greenacre was already cohabiting with a woman, Sarah Gale, with whom he had a child. Part of the material in which Hannah Brown had been wrapped was found at Greenacre's house, off the Edgeware Road in London. Sarah Gale was transported for life, as an accessory after the fact; Greenacre was hanged at Newgate on 2 May 1837.

8   Despite the lines drawn by town planners, most London Boroughs are fairly indistinct in Londoners' minds. Tollington Place is still there, in the north-west of Finsbury Park, somewhere between Islington and Holloway. Kossuth was declared as being born in one area, Ledru in another; but they were probably born in the same place.

9   The 1841 Census is of no help: ages are rounded down to the nearest multiple of five, so that someone of 24 appears as 20.

10 On 22 August 1838 a Charles Pierson married Louisa Amelia Davidson in the Chapel of the British Embassy. He was from Edinburgh, she from Middleby, in Dumfriesshire. We can assume there is no connection.

11 Guildhall Library MS 10891. The document is fragile, and cannot be pho-

tocopied or scanned. Information courtesy of Stephen Freeth, Keeper of Manuscripts, Guildhall Library.

12   Around 1857, Dawes moved to Bermondsey, where he was organist of Christchurch. His collaboration with Susannah appears to have been his only foray into publishing.

13   By coincidence, 41 Woburn Square is only two hundred or so yards from 65 Russell Square, where James Malcolm Rymer lived during the mid-60s.

14   A few years later Rymer, too, left the business, going to manage a hotel in Worthing, Sussex. It suggests writing was always a career for the Dreadful authors, rather than a vocation.

15   Though there is no record of any of the others being christened.

WORKS CITED

Carver, Stephen. "Reynolds, G. W. M." in *The Literary Encyclopedia* (on-line database). Article first published March 5, 2004 (accessed January 12, 2006); available online: http://www.litencyc.com/php/speople.php?rec=true&UID=5614

Frost, Thomas. *Forty Years' Recollections*. London: Sampson Low, Marston, Searle and Rivington, 1880.

Gatrell, Vic. *City of Laughter: Sex and Satire in Eighteenth Century London*. London: Atlantic Books, 2006.

James, Louis. "George William MacArthur Reynolds (1814–1879)" in *Oxford Dictionary of National Biography*, Oxford: Oxford University Press, 2004.

James, Louis. *Fiction for the Working Man*. Harmsworth: Penguin, 1973.

Register of Baptisms, St. Clement's Church, Sandwich

Register of Baptisms, St. Martin's-in-the-Fields, London

Register of Marriages, Chapel of the British Embassy, Paris

Register of Births, Chapel of the British Embassy, Paris

Thomas, Trefor, ed., *The Mysteries of London*. Keele: Keele University Press, 1996.

UK Census 1841, 1851, 1861, 1871, 1891

UK Index of Births, Deaths and Marriages

ACKNOWLEDGEMENTS

Peter Hughes, Kensal Green Cemetery; Joe Hughes, Friends of Kensal Green Cemetery; Dr. Anthony Morton, Deputy Archivist, Royal Military Academy, Sandhurst, Berkshire; Diana Neill, British Embassy, Paris; Dr. Fiona Cox, University College, Cork; Ray Harlow, Curator-Archivist, Guildhall Museum, Sandwich

NOTE ON THE TEXT

The Necromancer was originally serialised in *Reynolds's Miscellany* from 27 December 1851 to 31 July 1852. It first appeared in a one-volume edition in 1857, an illustrated double-column reprint, printed by John Dicks for Reynolds. An undated reprint followed, published at Philadelphia by T. B. Peterson and Brothers, under the title *The Necromancer; or, The Mysteries of the Court of Henry the Eighth*, and in 1884 at New York under the same title. All these editions are quite scarce today.

The present edition follows the text of the 1857 edition. The text presented here is identical to the 1857 text, with the exception of a few minor printer's errors which have been silently corrected. No attempt has been made to modernize spelling or punctuation, and Reynolds's somewhat idiosyncratic use of italics and dashes has been preserved as in the original.

THE NECROMANCER.

PROLOGUE.

OUR narrative opens in the year 1510.

It was night—a cold, clear, beautiful night in the month of March. From the deep blue heaven the moon, ravishingly bright as an orb of silver, looked down on the sleeping earth and the tranquil sea—while countless stars, spangling the celestial canopy, seemed angel-eyes sending forth looks of hope for the desolate, love for the forlorn, and consolation for the sorrowful.

The pure effulgence brought forth all the prominent features of the land into strong relief, and overlaid the sea with a sheet of living lustre. On lofty eminences did old frowning castles look grey; and on slopes, or in valleys, the dingy brick buildings of town and villages seemed white in the argentine flood.

On the land the busy hum of mankind was hushed in sleep; and on the ocean there was a mystic silence broken only by the mellow lisp of the gentle ripples dissolving upon the shore.

Through a range of lofty windows the cold white beams of moon and stars penetrated into a vast Gothic hall; and as those rays rested upon the shafts of many pillars, they seemed like long straight transparent lines of ice reaching slantwise across the spacious apartment. That hall was hung with suits of armour, implements of war, and weapons of the chase; and above them were suspended the banners of battle—the decaying trophies of deeds whose heroes slept in the deep vaults beneath, and whose arms were rusting within that ancient hall!

The moon shone with so full a power through the windows as to make every object distinct and clear as if it were daylight, save in the corners and behind the pillars, whither those ice-like shafts of light could not penetrate. It was a grand, a solemn, and a strange thing to contemplate the interior of this great hall, with its range of high narrow arched windows—its double row of pillars supporting a vaulted ceiling and producing a cathedral effect—the pavement of block and white marble in diamond-like arrangement—and the warlike embellishments of mouldering banners and rusting armour that covered the walls. In such a place and in the deep midnight hour, silence itself seemed more solemn, more awful, than elsewhere—a silence on which neither voice nor foot could scarcely dare intrude!

And yet both voices and footsteps *were* now wakening the echoes that long, long had slumbered undisturbed within that Gothic hall. Yes, but gently, very gently were, the voices speaking and the feet treading: for it was impossible that those who were now advancing there, could do otherwise than feel the solemnity of the scene, the silence, and the hour.

Who were they that whispered in subdued, hushed voices, and advanced with slow and even hesitating steps? One was a man who appeared to be some four-and-twenty years of age, and the elegance of whose apparel matched well with the high order of his masculine beauty. His hair was dark as jet, clustering in rich natural curls about a head of the most perfect classic shape—while the light of no ordinary intellect and the power of no common mind flashed in the remarkable brilliancy of his fine dark eyes. His apparel consisted of a purple velvet doublet—black silk hose fitting tight upon the limbs—cavalier boots of Spanish leather but of buskin-shape—a short cloak, of the same material as the doublet, worn over the left shoulder—and a dark velvet cap with a long drooping sable plume. Such was the attire that set off the tall, slender, but well-knit and graceful person of this individual to the fullest advantage.

His companion was a young girl of about eighteen, and of the most exquisite beauty. Myriads of dark brown ringlets fell in a hyperion-like shower upon shoulders the admirable slope of which enhanced the beauty of a figure cast in a faultless mould and endowed with every grace. Her eyes, at once lustrous and languishing, were of that deep blue which was as clear and transparent as the heaven whence the moonlight now poured; while between the parting of the well-cut rosy lips shone teeth white as pearls. She too was apparelled with mingled elegance and richness; and indeed, as this noble-looking, interesting pair advanced slowly through the moonlit hall,—she hanging upon his arm and gazing up into his fine countenance with all a young maiden's clinging tenderness and intense devotion—it was fair to argue that they were of rank and birth, as it was also natural to conclude that they were lovers. For upon the lady's hand no marriage ring appeared amidst the jewels which gemmed her taper fingers: and there was too unmistakable an air of candour and innocence about her to warrant the belief for a single moment that she was bound to her companion by any dishonourable tie. No—notwithstanding the immensity of her love, 'twas of virgin chastity, and no sentiment of a gross contexture marred the immaculate purity of her soul.

Through the hall did the young cavalier and his beauteous companion proceed, their footsteps raising the dust collected upon the pavement and which settled upon the polished boots of the former and the ermine-bordered velvet robe of the latter. The cold atmosphere of the place seemed to be put in motion by the visitors who were now passing through it; for the flags suspended to the walls slowly trembled and waved above the rusting armour, and then drooped into perfect stillness again.

"Do you feel cold, dearest?" asked the cavalier, in that manly melody of voice which was so sweet to her ears and so ravishing to her senses.

"I think not of the coldness, nor the solemnity, nor the chill silence of the place, so long as I am with you," was the answer which she gave in soft fluid accents, as she still gazed up into his countenance with an expression of love so intense that it proved the immensity of the power which that man exercised over her trustful, devoted heart.

"This is the home of my ancestors, beloved Clara," he continued, in that same deep melody of voice, and with a look as if the whole fire of an illimitable love shone out of his magnificent eyes. "Their ashes repose in the vaults beneath where we are treading: their armour hangs upon these walls! And you are not afraid, my Clara, to venture hither with me at this solemn hour—in this stealthy manner—unattended and alone—as if we ourselves were spirits of the departed, instead of——"

"Oh! speak not thus," interrupted the beauteous Clara with a chiding gesture: and now a gleam of anxiety—almost of sudden terror—glittered in her loving deep blue eyes.

"Well, well, I will not repeat so strange a comparison," her lover hastened to reply: and as he strained her closer to him and pressed his lips to her pure polished forehead, the caressing tenderness of his manner was far more potent than even his words to sooth her.

"Oh! my worshipped idol, what happiness exists in your love!" she murmured in a low and scarcely audible voice, as one who gives utterance to the dearest secret of her heart: and in that moment it was evident she forgot alike the place and the hour in the all-absorbing nature of her feelings.

This manifestation of her soul's illimitable tenderness seemed suddenly to touch a strange chord in her lover's heart; and an expression very much like that of a mortal agony swept over his features. And at this very moment was it that Clara raised her eyes and caught that anguished soul-tortured look just as it was vanishing from the countenance it for the swift brief instant convulsed so fearfully. The effect upon her was rapid as the blasting lightning upon the tree which it strikes with its zig-zag tongue of fire. A maddening misgiving fastened upon her soul: she shivered with a violent tremor in the very agony of her apprehension, and would have dropped down abruptly on the dust-covered pavement had not her lover at the moment encircled her beautiful shape with his arms.

"Clara—dearest Clara," he said, with a strange and even wild agitation; "what has alarmed you thus?"

"I know not—I dare not—no, no, I cannot tell you," she gasped forth in faltering accents; and at the same time she endeavoured to overcome her feelings and fling off as it were that vague indefinite sensation of uneasiness which had seized upon her heart: but she could not—it appeared as if a blight had fallen with cruel suddenness upon that heart's happiness!

"Oh! do not, do not give way thus to idle and unfounded terrors," said her companion, straining her so forcibly, so fervently to his breast that it seemed as if he almost sought to subdue her form's quivering by the very violence of his embrace, because mistrusting the power of his words' tenderness to lull it.

"Oh! pardon me, pardon me this weakness!" said Clara, still in a murmuring faltering tone: and as she gazed up with those large blue eyes, in whose liquid beauty the deep blue of heaven had seemed to settle, she met the strange wild look which her lover was at the instant fixing upon her, and which again sent a thrill of icy anguish through her frame—for she had never seen him look thus upon her before.

"An unknown and mysterious apprehension has seized upon you, my Clara," he said, once more adopting the caressing manner and soothing voice of the most affectionate tenderness. "That foolish comparison on my part demolished as it were all your fortitude in a moment. But surely, surely that sublime faith—that trusting devotion—that illimitable confidence which you have hitherto placed in me, cannot have received so severe a shock—much less have been annihilated altogether?"

"No, no," she hastened to observe, as if terrified at the bare suspicion which his word conveyed: and now again was her voice full of the purest and most exquisite tenderness as the rich bright glow of mingled confidence and joy mantled upon her soft damask cheek up to her stainless brow.

"Come then—come, dearest Clara," he said, "let us proceed:"—and as she again took his arm, her agitation having considerably subsided, he led her onward through the hall.

Still it was not altogether with the same assurance and utter absence of alarm as at first that she suffered him thus to conduct her onward. At first suspicion and misgiving were undreamt of: now they were floating dimly and vaguely in her mind; and the composure she had assumed was the result of an effort—not the spontaneity of nature. Her companion, who watched every varying expression of her countenance,—and whose looks, when seemingly fraught with the deepest tenderness, were also penetrated with uneasiness and uncertainty—now endeavoured to hurry her pace somewhat through the hall, on reaching the extremity of which an immense staircase made of solid oak, and with a massive balustrade as if the whole belonged to a giant's dwelling, appeared before them.

At the foot of this broad and vast ascent of steps, stood two suits of complete armour, with the visors down and a sword grasped in the right gauntlet of each—so that as the moonlight shone through a tall window of painted glass upon the first landing, the prismatic beams fell with a strange effect upon those two figures and made them seem like living sentinels guarding the staircase. A few words tenderly whispered in Clara's ear had prepared her for this spectacle: nevertheless she recoiled and shuddered for a moment and clung more closely to her lover, as he led her between the statue-like and rustling panoplies.

They ascended the stairs, Clara's lover continuing to breathe the tenderest and most encouraging words in her ears—while she, feeling that her strength of mind was not altogether equal to the task she had this night consented to undertake, clung as it were all the more lovingly and trustfully to him from whose lips those reassuring syllables were alike so welcome and so necessary.

The tall narrow window of painted glass was so much darkened with the collected dust, that all the upper portion of the staircase was involved in obscurity; and the higher they ascended, the deeper the gloom grew in perspective. Clara felt all her remaining courage proportionately ebbing away; and a thousand wild ideas began to flash through her brain. She even for a moment felt a cruel doubt arise as to the feasibility, or indeed truth, of the tale which her lover had told her in order to induce her to accompany him this night to the deserted halls of his ancestors. But instantaneously stifling the suspicion in the bottom of her soul, as most injurious to one who had ever been all fondness and manly affection towards her since the first day she knew him, Clara clung to his arm with a pressure the very feeling of which mutely but eloquently made him aware that her unyielding faith, her blind confidence, and her unasking devotion were given up to him!

On reaching the second landing, which was involved in complete darkness, they paused for a moment while the cavalier opened a door; and then the moonbeams again flashed suddenly through an array of windows, thus lighting a long narrow gallery crowded with large pictures. Upon these the slant rays fell: but so blackened were they with collected dust, or so marred was the canvass by the ravages of time and the canker-worm of decay, that it was impossible to obtain more than a feeble idea of what their subjects were. Nevertheless Clara was enabled to perceive that those which were at all discernible were the portraits of men in armour and ladies in old-fashioned dresses; and when her lover whispered to her that these were the portraits of his ancestors, male and female, Clara could not repress a shudder as she fancied that the dark shapes were about to come slowly forth from the frames and beckon both him and her amongst them!

Her companion, feeling that she trembled with a sudden recoil, hastened to breathe fresh words of encouragement in her ears, as he led her on into a suite of rooms communicating with arched Gothic doorways, and having rows of windows elaborately sculptured. In these apartments the furniture all appeared to be blackened with dust, and the feet left prints upon the floor in the same way as upon the hard snow in the middle of winter.

At the end of this suite of rooms, which were of grand and noble dimensions, the lovers entered a narrow passage where utter darkness prevailed. But in a few moments they stopped short: a sharp click was then heard as of some bolt giving way by means of a secret spring that was touched; and then a low narrow door immediately flew open.

Again did the pure moonlight appear to dispel the vague terrors of darkness; and Clara's lover led her forward once more, closing the door behind them. It shut with the same sharp clicking noise that had marked its opening: and as Clara mechanically looked back she could observe neither latch nor key-hole. Then, her glances being rapidly swept around, she perceived that she was in a room of moderate dimensions, but perfectly square, and with the windows so high up that it was impossible to look out even though mounted on a chair for the purpose. There were two windows on each of the four sides of the room; and it was consequently evident that the apartment itself was in some detached tower wherewith the narrow passage thus threaded alone communicated. For there was no other door in the room, and therefore no visible means of egress besides that one.

We have not however altogether finished our description of this apartment, which indeed was of peculiar aspect. The walls around, up as high as the window-ledges, were covered with carved oak panels—or what in later times would have been called wainscoting. But on that side of the room which immediately faced the door there were six small squares painted black, marked with a bold red outline, and the whole filling up the place of one of the oaken panels. They were numbered; and their arrangement was in this wise:—

I	II
III	IV
V	VI

On each of the first four black squares there was a name with a date, as follows:—

1. BIANCA LANDINI	1390
2. MARGARET DUNHAVEN	1407
3. ARLINE DE ST. LOUIS	1463
4. DOLOROSA CORTEZ	1500

These inscriptions evidently were not painted; and it was difficult to discern their exact nature. But they appeared to be formed of letters and numerals of glass, set into fitting places cut completely through the black squares in order to receive them, and shining as if with the glare of a powerful lamp burning behind. Such at least was the appearance which the inscriptions had,—looking like letters of flame—not lambent and oscillating, but burning steadily and uniformly like fixed fire.

It must be observed that the two last black panels had not inscriptions upon them—merely the figures V and VI respectively, but which seemed to denote that they were not destined to remain for ever different from the rest, but that they would some day or another have inscriptions also. The furniture in this room consisted of a table and chairs of massive oak, so as to match the wainscot of the walls. A velvet carpet covered the floor; and so far from the apartment bearing any appearance of the ravages of time, it formed a remarkable exception in this respect, from the other portions of the edifice through which Clara had been led. Not a particle of dust was to be seen upon any of the furniture: the velvet floor-cloth looked as if it had only been recently brushed; and the entire aspect of the room denoted care and attention.

Clara had experienced a sudden thrill of alarm on beholding that door with the invisible bolt, close so abruptly in the manner already described; and a sense of captivity instantaneously fastened upon her mind. Thence sprang a wilder feeling of terror than she had as yet experienced; and this was heightened on beholding those names shining upon the wall and looking as if they had been traced with a pen of fire. Full of misgivings and suspicions, which she could neither control nor conceal, Clara flung her looks upon her lover; and a still more violent tremor seized upon her as she felt his large black eyes flashing into her very heart with a lightning power!

But the next moment his looks changed—so suddenly indeed as to leave a doubt whether his glance had really flashed with the expression she had just imagined: and becoming all love, all softness, all tenderness again, he gazed upon her with that deep impassioned fondness, that adoring earnestness, which had ever as yet characterized his love and called forth a kindred worship from her own soul.

"Dearest, dearest Clara," he said; "why for a moment does the shade of doubt cross your angelic features? why does the tremor of suspicion pass over your frame? Have you no longer any trust in me? do you imagine that I am capable of breathing a single syllable to shock the purity of your soul, or mar the innocence of that love which flows like an ethereal essence from your virgin heart?"

"I know—I know—that not for worlds would you harm a hair of my head," said Clara, as she suffered him to lead her to a seat. "But those names—apparently written in fire—and the effect of which is so ominous, so terrible——"

"Calm and tranquillize yourself, dearest, dearest Clara," her lover hastened to observe, as placing himself in another chair by her side, he pressed her hand between both his own and gazed upon her with all that deep, unalloyed, and impassioned tenderness which found so genuine a reflection in her looks and in her heart. "The meaning of those names I will explain presently, and you will then chide yourself for this momentary alarm."

"But why are they thus traced in characters of fire?" asked Clara, with another sidelong glance of apprehension flung towards those ominous panels.

"It is in appearance only—a strange whim of one of my ancestors—the condition, indeed, upon which I hold the estates—the tenure of my titles and fortunes."

"Ah! pardon me, then, this painful curiosity which has made me perhaps unkind and mistrustful!—pardon me, pardon me, I say!"—and the beauteous Clara, fearing in her heart's natural generosity and frankness, that she had wounded her lover's feelings, suddenly slipped from her chair and fell upon her knees at his feet.

"Oh! then you do love me—love me passionately, adoringly?" he cried, in a voice of such strange exultation and even intoxicated wildness of triumph, and *again* would his manner have struck her as singular to a degree, had not her own feelings been at the moment so profoundly absorbed in regret and self-reproach at having mistrusted him. "Yes—you love me—you love me," he cried, "my own worshipped Clara!"—and he raised her, or rather snatched her up from her suppliant posture, strained her to his breast, and then deposited her with a sudden and delicate gentleness in the chair.

"Then you forgive me?" she said, her cheeks suffused with the blushes which the ardour of his caresses had conjured up.

"Oh! forgive you—what have I to forgive?" he exclaimed: "and how could you possibly offend me? No, no: not for an instant could I experience resentment against *you!* Besides, it is so natural for you to pass through the ordeal of many strange and varied feelings under such circumstances as the present! To issue forth by stealth from your father's house at such an hour—to ride with me for such a distance and at such a pace——"

"Heavens, what a pace!" echoed Clara, her look suddenly expressing the astonishment which accompanied the circumstances brought back to her mind.

"Aye," said her lover, "mine are no ordinary steeds:"—and she fancied for a moment that his eyes had a wicked and sneering glance; but if it were so it was transitory as a passing shadow—and with a deepening tenderness of look and manner he said, "Yes, dearest, you have indeed had enough to agitate and bewilder you this night. But you know how necessary it was to pass through this strange ordeal: you are aware that my ancestor, the founder of my family, decreed that every one inheriting his name should receive in this room the solemn pledge and plight of love from the lips of her whom he proposed to lead unto the altar."

"How strange the whim!" observed Clara, shuddering with a vague presentiment of evil as she spoke; but the next instant her hand was pressed to her lover's lips—and as she gazed upon the proud and indeed glorious beauty of his countenance, her heart grew warm and gushing again with the tenderest emotions of love and hope, and confidence.

"Yes—it is indeed a strange whim, my beloved Clara," he replied; "but not the less needful to be fulfilled by every descendant of the half-crazed ancestor of mine! Loving each other as we do—with the holiest bond of affection so indissolubly uniting our hearts—and with your sire's permission that our nuptials shall take place ten days hence—it was scarcely indelicate for me to implore and beseech that you would steal forth to-night, journey with me hither to my own ancestral hall, and accompany me alone to this apartment where our solemn vows must be exchanged. For in the immensity of the love which binds us to each other, consists not only in the security which *you* must experience in my company, but also the pride which *I* feel in being your protector and the guardian of your honour. But not long need we tarry here. Let our vows be spoken—our troth be plighted—and then we will away back to London again!"

"But this ancient castle of yours, my beloved one," said Clara, suddenly inspired by a strange and mystic sentiment of curiosity,—"where is it situated? how far from London? Surely we must have come many, many miles in that hour's ride—and methought that we dashed through a river—but it was so momentary that I immediately afterwards fancied I must have been deceived——Besides, the skirt of my robe was dry as I dismounted, and the steed too dripped not."

"No—it was but fancy on your part, dearest Clara," returned her lover. "As for the castle, it is not so very far from the metropolis——But when we are united and I can call thee by the endeared and endearing name of *wife*, we will come hither in the broad daylight and explore the ruined home of mine ancestors."

"Oh! yes," exclaimed Clara, joyfully;—"when it is daylight I shall be so fond of examining all those warlike weapons and suits of armour in the great hall below—the portraits too in the gallery which we threaded—and all the curiosities of the ancient fortalice——But surely the moon is now waning?" she suddenly exclaimed, as it struck her that the argentine flood which had hitherto rendered the interior of the apartment as distinct as in the daylight had grown somewhat obscured.

"Yes—it is time we should be gone, dear Clara," responded her lover. "Come, let us plight those solemn vows for the record of which we have come hither—and first—Oh! first, dearest Clara—worshipped angel of beauty—first let me declare unto thee, by that Power to which I am devoted, and with as much solemn sincerity as there is truth and justice in that Power—that I am thine—wholly and solely thine, in love, and tenderness, and devotion!"

While thus speaking, he sank at her feet and bent his head over the hand which he held in his grasp and which he pressed with a sort of wild ardour to his lips, as if in the delirium of ecstatic passion, when he had thus recorded his solemn oath.

"O my beloved one," exclaimed the fond, confiding beauteous girl, as her head swam with a sort of pleasurable dizziness—and the very air, instead of being cold in the moonlight, seemed to burn with the impassioned and glowing language that her companion's lips had sent forth: "O my beloved one! accept the unspeakable thanks of an affectionate and loving heart for that vow of thine! And this vow I re-echo and give back again—I call heaven to witness that naught can ever mar—no, nor ever exceed this love of mine! And I am thine—wholly and solely thine—in all tenderness and devotion!"

"Oh! now it is for me to proclaim my thanks," cried her lover, gazing up into her countenance with looks that poured a flood of inconceivable rapture into her heart. But tell me once more that you are mine!"

"Yes—thine, thine for ever!" she murmured, the warm blood mantling with heightened hue upon her cheeks.

"Mine!" exclaimed her lover, with an exaltation as if his voice were the pæan of victory. "Mine, you say?—mine for ever—body and soul?"

"Yes," returned Clara, in the heartfelt fullness of her love: "thine for ever—body and soul!"

Scarcely had the fond and truthful girl given utterance to this fearful vow, when her lover sprang from his knees and started up to his feet with the wildest abruptness.

With a faint shriek, and with a marble whiteness suddenly chasing away the bloom from her cheeks, she glanced up at his countenance. But heavens! what a change had all in a moment been worked there!—for triumph and despair, joy and agony, were ineffably mingled in those features which seemed of a fearful beauty now, like the face of a fallen angel!

But in that self-same moment—quick as the eye can wink—a blackness fell down upon the scene, like a heavy pall covering every window with its dread cere-cloth. And then, from the midst of that pitchy blackness, came cry after cry—and shriek after shriek resounded wild and piercing, from the extremest agony of a female heart, and thrilling through that room as if they would rend and crack the very walls!

For nearly a minute did that Egyptian darkness and those appalling shrieks endure: then, in a moment the pitchy cloud vanished—and all was still!

Again was the apartment flooded with the silver light, brilliant and cold: and the lover stood *alone* there, in the midst of that effulgence. But his wild glowing eyes—his lips blanched and quivering—the panting breath—and the dark unearthly thoughts that sat like a Cain-brand upon his brow—*these* were a sufficient indication of the strong agony that convulsed the soul within!

But on what object did his eyes glare in such fierce intenseness, through which a frenzied exultation also penetrated? Upon the fifth black square upon the wall: for on it the following inscription was now traced in letters of living fire, like the rest:—

CLARA MANNERS   1510.

So that the inscriptions upon the five squares might now be recorded thus:—

1. BIANCA LANDINI   1390.
2. MARGARET DUNHAVEN   1407.
3. ARLINE DE ST. LOUIS   1403.
4. DOLOROSA CORTEZ   1500.
5. CLARA MANNERS   1510.

And now, then, there was but *one* black square left without its tracery of fiery name and date!

But not alone that fifth black square was the fearful man now watching. Beneath the panel in which those six squares were set, did a small trap door—not half-a-dozen inches broad or high—suddenly open; and the arm of a skeleton was thrust forth. Between the fleshless fore-finger and thumb something glittering was held; and the cavalier seized it eagerly. It was a ring of plain gold enamelled in black, and with a name round it. This the fearful man hastily attached to a chain which he wore concealed in his breast, and on which there were already *four* rings—the one he had just received making the *fifth*.

The skeleton arm was withdrawn as abruptly as it was thrust forth; the little trap-door was closed again—and the cavalier slowly quitted the apartment where these scenes of a wild and terrible mystery had taken place.

But who is this man that his destiny seems linked with such transcending horrors?—what meant those fiery inscriptions upon the wall, and those rings which he wore secured beneath the folds of his doublet?

CHAPTER I.

MUSIDORA.

FEW of our readers will require to be told that the Isle of Wight is situated on the southern coast of England, separated only from the mainland of Hampshire by a narrow channel called the Solent Sea. The average width of this channel is between three and four miles, so that the isle and the mainland are in sight of each other. Between the two is the famous anchorage for shipping known as Spithead: but in the time of which we are writing—namely, the reign of Henry VIII—it was a rare occurrence to behold any war-ships moored there.

For the most part the Isle of Wight presents a wall of precipitous cliffs or steep slopes to the sea on every side; and in some places the natural ramparts of the lozenge-shaped isle rise to an elevation of five or six hundred feet. There is much grandeur in those eminences overlooking the sea; while all the interior of the insular tract is characterized by the most beautiful scenery; and the mildness of the climate causes myrtles, laurels, geraniums, and various kinds of delicate evergreens to flourish throughout the winter.

Brading Castle is situated on the north-eastern point of the island— the town from which it takes its name being at no great distance from another equally well known—we mean St. Helens. At high water the haven is a beautiful lake covering an extent of a thousand acres; but at low water it presents to the view naught but a surface of sand traversed by the river Yar. Still at the present day the lands about the haven are well wooded; but at the period of which we are writing all that part of the island had the appearance of a forest, the little towns of Brading and St. Helens being embowered as it were by giant oaks which spread their verdure down to the very edge of the haven.

On the rising coast that ascends from Brading Haven, stood a large house—or indeed mansion—consisting of dingy red brick supported and as it were interwoven by a massive timber frame-work. It was an ancient building, with many straggling offices and outhouses in the rear, and standing on an eminence where the trees had been cleared away to afford room for a shrubbery and lawn in front, an orchard on one side, an immense kitchen-garden on the other, and a large field behind. It commanded a splendid view of the sea, overlooking the entire range of forest that stretched upon all the proclivities around.

This house was the property and residence of an old knight named Sir Lewis Sinclair. He was a widower, devotedly attached to hunting, good living, and the bottle, to all of which perhaps he accorded a greater share of his love than to his beautiful daughter Musidora. She was an only child; her mother had died in her infancy;—and when she grew up the chief care of the household devolved upon herself.

Sir Lewis Sinclair had reached the good ripe age of sixty-two at the time when we thus introduce him to our readers, and which was in the year 1516. He belonged to an ancient and honourable family, some of whose more distant members were ennobled; although the scions of this particular branch from which he himself sprung, had never risen beyond the plain rank of commoner, until Sir Lewis by siding with the cause of Henry VII against Richard III, at the battle of Bosworth Field, received the distinction of Knight-Banneret, of which he was not a little proud. Edmund Dudley, one of the principal and most infamous Ministers of Henry VII, was a relation of Sir Lewis Sinclair's, and had procured for the knight a sinecure post as Ranger of the Forests in the Isle of Wight: but when Henry VIII[1] came to the throne, he not only put Dudley to death, but to the best of his power cancelled every appointment which that individual had made. Thus, when advanced in years, Sir Lewis Sinclair lost the Rangership of the forests, and in losing that was deprived of the principal source of revenue remaining to him. For what with having equipped a troop at his own expense to fight against Richard III and what with a life of unbridled extravagance, profusion, and improvidence, he had so hampered his hereditary possession that when the income of the Rangership suddenly ceased, he found that it was absolutely necessary to curtail his expenses. He had therefore then dismissed the greater number of his retainers; so that for five or six years previous to the date at which this chapter opens, himself, Musidora, two female and two male dependants had been the only occupants of the spacious mansion.

And now let us endeavour to describe the old knight's daughter—if language can indeed be made to assume any form that shall do justice to the superb beauty of Musidora Sinclair.

At the time when we thus present her to our readers she was in her twenty-first year. Without being too tall for grace and elegance, she was nevertheless of a noble stature; and without losing its fine feminine qualities, her beauty was of a most commanding and exalted order. Though pale as an image of statuary marble, it was no dead inanimate pallor that thus formed her complexion: nor was there aught of sickliness or ill-health in her appearance. Her's was the grandeur of a proud classic beauty uniting all the fullness and polish of the chiselled alabaster with the softness of nature. No mark of time—no ravage of care—no trace of disease, marred the unsullied purity of the high expansive brow: and though no roseate tint was ever seen to settle—scarcely even to wander—upon the marble fairness of the cheeks, yet were they of a wholesome living white, firm as flesh should be, and of damask softness. Her features had the exquisite regularity of the Grecian profile—the lofty forehead, the nose perfectly straight, the short-arched upper lip with its slightly haughty wreathing, and the small delicately-rounded chin. Her countenance was an oval, and with its superb features possessed all the glorious dignity of the proud Norman type, just sufficiently attempered with a smile—but coldly brilliant—to prove that there was no undue pride nor overbearing arrogance in Musidora's nature.

Her raven hair, parted exactly in the middle of her head, was thus divided as it were by a delicate line of ivory whiteness into two masses which lay smooth and glossy as velvet above the temples, and then gradually broke, not exactly into tresses, but into accumulated clusters of the thickest and most luxuriant redundancy. Thus did it flow—that dark, dark hair—like a sable cloud upon the superb shoulders, enhancing the marble fairness of the countenance, and making the ivory neck stand out as it were in dazzling relief against that ebon background. Thus, too, did the polish, the animation, and the stainless transparency of Musidora's complexion strike the beholder all the more brilliantly in contrast with the cloud-like darkness of her hair. And yet this hair, so magnificent in its luxuriance and so silken in its softness, was not of a dull dead blackness: but it shone with the purply metallic lustre which glows upon the raven's wing or which forms the rich gloss of velvet.

Her brows were nobly arched and distinctly though not severely pencilled: but these ebon lines, with the eyes of glorious eastern darkness so thickly fringed with long lashes slightly curling, suited well that Grecian countenance so proudly beautiful. And what eyes were they through which Musidora's soul looked forth,—that soul which it seemed impossible to read in the unfathomable depths of those large lustrous orbs! There was a kind of weird mystery in their glance—not a restless flashing—no, but rather a steadiness of gaze—a look which stole strangely upon the heart of the beholder at the time and haunted him long, long afterwards.

We have said that Musidora's lips were formed to suit her Grecian profile: we should add that in their hue, with the rich blood crimsoning them, they were of a vivid scarlet; and in their dewy moisture they seemed like wet coral. When closed, they bespoke a certain energy of character: but when those bright lips parted, they revealed a set of teeth so brilliant that the purity of ivory was outshone and the delicate transparency of pearl could best be likened to their exquisite enamel. As the predominant expression of Musidora's countenance was the half-unconscious dignity of stillness, bordering upon the settled placidity of a queenly coldness,— so did a certain majesty of air blend with the grace of her attitudes and the elegance of all her movements: Each gesture had its own peculiar charm; and though never impulsive and quick, but always slow even to an appearance of measured deliberation, yet was there no striving after effect—no studied calculation on her part, either to appear singular or to please in her own particular manner. With that imperial air of her's was mingled a sufficiency of softness and gentleness to render her agreeable and even amiable: so that her's was not a beauty which chilled the heart with its frozen grandeur—for if coldly proud, it was also proudly radiant. The Olympian loveliness of Juno, the cold chastity of Diana, the high intelligence of Minerva, and the gracefulness of Venus,—all seemed to be combined in the aspect of Musidora. And indeed no form of a rarer symmetry did Grecian chisel ever shape in marble: never did sculptured effigy of beauty breathe with an ideal dignity and grace more exquisite than the combined reality which characterized Musidora's person. Her classic shape blended in admirable unison the lithe symmetry of maiden youthfulness with the mature developments of perfect womanhood: the fine slope of the shoulders, the noble contours of the bust, the rounded fulness of the arms, the sylphid slenderness of the waist, and the faultless modelling of the feet and ankles—these details of beauty, aided by a statuesque elegance of gait, constituted the perfection of Musidora's form.

But what was the disposition—what were the mental and moral attributes of this splendid creature? It was impossible to contemplate her countenance without reading the noblest traits of intellect and of mind in every feature. Could that high and polished forehead be the seat of aught save the diadem of genius?—could those well-cut lips fail to express the power of self-control and inward discipline through the medium of a strong, indomitable will?—was not all the noble pride of woman's self-reliance displayed in the thin arched nostrils? And yet all unfeminine expression of the countenance was absorbed in the silver radiance of that beauty which shone upon every lineament. But if her intellect were thus powerful and her character thus energetic, what can we say of the feelings of her heart? Ah! now we are at fault. We have already hinted that her soul was unfathomable: for her eyes betrayed not the inward emotions as woman's eyes are wont to do—nor did she ever seem to feel that quickening of the pulse nor to experience that flush upon the cheeks which in *her* sex bespeak the vibration of the heart's chords to every varying passion and sentiment. Whatever thoughts, or secrets, or emotions harboured in her bosom, no visible trace thereof was ever revealed by her countenance. The mountains of Iceland may be volcanoes internally; but their outward surface is ice—yet not dull, dead, and inanimate, but with the sunlight shining upon its whiteness and illumining its very coldness. Was it so with Musidora?—did the queenly, chill quiescence of her manner conceal the tumult of fervid feelings within?—or was it that the youthful freshness of her heart had faded altogether ere Time had swept over it his frozen wings?

We cannot say: we must repeat what we have already hinted, that her soul was unfathomable. And yet it had not always been so. In her childhood she was a merry, joyous, laughing thing—never with any particular ruddiness of countenance, but still with a roseate bloom upon her cheeks: and when she merged into the period of girlhood, she was still ever smiling, gay, and happy—and still was there a delicate tinge of the carnation visible beneath the transparent purity of her complexion. In her infancy was it that she had lost her mother, whom therefore she never knew, and whose departure from this world could not have left any melancholy shadow suddenly to rise up and darken Musidora's soul, or to remain in abeyance for years and then fall as it were with the virulence of a blight upon her heart. How was it, then, that at the age of seventeen, her manner underwent so abrupt an alteration that it seemed as if her very nature had been changed? And mark! this alteration was not worked gradually as if by the insidiously stealing inroad of a cankering care: but it was accomplished all in a moment—in a single day! She had retired to her chamber at night with sunny smiles upon her lip, roseate hues upon her cheeks, and brightness dancing in her glorious eyes; and when she descended to the breakfast-table in the morning, her cheeks were marble, her look was cold as ice, and her very nature seemed to have turned from the warmth of glowing youthfulness into the freezing insensibility of a glacier. Her father questioned her: but she seemed astonished at the idea that any change had taken place in her demeanour at all: and as Sir Lewis Sinclair was not a man to trouble himself much on such points, he took no farther notice of the matter,—soon getting accustomed to his daughter's altered nature, and apparently ceasing to remember that she had ever been otherwise.

It was at the age of seventeen, we stated, when this remarkable change took place in Musidora. She was now nearly one-and-twenty. Three years and a half had therefore elapsed since the spell—for such indeed it seemed—had fallen upon her. During this interval no alteration, either for better or worse, had occurred; so that if she recovered none of the sunny joyousness of her girlhood, she gave no farther indication of any concealed unhappiness. Generous-hearted and charitable—full of benevolence in respect to the poor—kind, tolerant, and forbearing towards the household menials—dutiful and attentive to her father—bearing herself with a dignified and lady-like courtesy towards his male friends, and with an easy hospitable politeness towards female visitors,—Musidora was not only admired and esteemed, but also loved by all who knew her. Many of her own sex proffered their tenderest friendship and sought her confidence: but while she received all these advances with gratitude, she declined them in a manner that could not possibly give any offence. Indeed, the dignified urbanity of her manner, though so graceful in its courtesy, had just enough of a polished reserve to render familiarity impossible on her part, and even to arrest the growth of intimacy. There seemed to be a line up to which persons might advance in their acquaintance and intercourse with Musidora, but beyond which it was impossible to proceed, and the attempt to overstep which would have amounted to rudeness.

Musidora was therefore a beautiful mystery—the lovely incarnation of an enigma. As a matter of course, conjecture had been rife amongst all who knew her relative to the change that had so suddenly come over her when at the age of seventeen, and which had now lasted for three years and a half. Some fancied that it must have been a disappointed love: but others declared that this was impossible, inasmuch as she had never been known to love at all. Though many a highborn, wealthy, and handsome cavalier had sued for Musidora's hand, even from the time she was in the girlhood of fifteen, yet all had been refused; and if she had really fixed her affections on any one of them, there could have been no hindrance to the match—no stern decree of separation to blight her passion and wither her hopes. Indeed, it was positively declared that Musidora had never known the melting influence of the tender feeling—that her soul was inaccessible to the sun-light of love—and that her heart was a sepulchre of ice whence none had ever rolled the stone to enter and sit in it an angel.

Some conjectured that an evil enchantment had thrown a spell upon her: but others ridiculed such an idea, so motiveless and aimless. Some imagined that a sudden discovery of her father's embarrassed finances had produced upon her an effect from which she had not recovered: but others insisted that her sire's true position had been previously well known to her, inasmuch as the loss of the Rangership and the consequent reduction of his establishment had taken place a couple of years before that wondrous change in Musidora's nature. Besides, it was urged that she was a damsel of too high an order of intellect and too strong a mind, to be thus influenced by even the falling fortunes of her family.

Then what was the origin of the almost magical alteration alluded to? Ah! none could tell: it defied all conjecture. And yet, where speculation was most rife amongst gossips and scandal-mongers, no word was ever whispered against Musidora's virtue: the breath of calumny never dared attempt to sully the purity of her name. That as a woman she was chaste even to a passionless iciness of heart, was the generally received opinion; and that she could have possibly committed a crime of any other nature, and which might have frozen her innermost feelings with the eternal chill of horror, was not for an instant to be imagined.

Beautiful mystery—splendid enigma! what was the secret of thine heart?—of the many conjectures rife concerning thee which was the true one? We know not. There were a few—but these were a very few indeed—who declared their belief that her bosom cherished no particular secret at all, but that the extraordinary change which had so abruptly turned the warm and gushing springs of her girlish happiness into the brilliant petrifaction of the glacier, was to be ascribed to some mental phenomenon of which she herself was unconscious and which it would perhaps perplex the metaphysician to penetrate or explain. One thing was very certain—that if her heart really did cherish some secret in its unfathomable depths, no visible trace of feeling, passion, sentiment, or suffering, upon her calmly splendid and proudly beautiful countenance, ever betrayed it.

CHAPTER II.

PERCY RIVERS.

It was in the afternoon of a warm and sunny day, at the close of April, 1516, that Musidora was walking alone in the orchard adjoining the house. The trees had put forth the rich emerald garb of Spring—the haven was full with the rippling, glittering water—and the forest-music, made by the voices of myriad birds, filled the cloudless air with a sweet strain of harmony.

Musidora was handsomely but by no means gaily dressed. Her apparel was elegant and tasteful in fashion, and of good material without being rich or costly. The boddice of black velvet was cut square in the neck, the edge having embroidery of lace half an inch wide; and the stomacher was also elaborately embroidered. Demi-sleeves, hanging rather loose, and leaving the arm bare down from the elbow, were slashed, divided, and joined, according to the fashion of the time, and produced a picturesque effect. The skirt of Musidora's dress was of a brown stuff, embroidered all round the hem, which was cut in Vandykes, each having a kind of little tassel at the point; so that as it were from the midst of these the long narrow feet and the well-turned ankles glanced forth as the damsel slowly pursued her walk. She wore no cap, having merely strolled out for an airing within the enclosure of the grounds, and not for the purpose of taking a formal promenade: but a short scarf of figured silk was thrown loosely over her head to protect it from the heat of the sun, and the fringed ends of which fell like lappets upon either shoulder.

To pretend to tell what was occupying Musidora's thoughts at that moment were impossible: for though now completely alone, and free to give way to any reflections which might rise uppermost in her imagination, yet was her mien as still, as quiescent, and as coldly emotionless as it always was when in the presence of others. But whatever her reverie might be, it was speedily interrupted by the presence of a young horseman who suddenly appeared in the road which, skirting the orchard, led up to the house. As the mounted visitor gracefully raised his cap, Musidora waved her hand with a friendly welcome—a more friendly welcome indeed than any other being of her acquaintance would have received: for this was her cousin Percy Rivers, Secretary to Sir William Woodville, the Captain or Governor of the Isle of Wight.

Riding round to the stables, Percy gave his splendid steed to the keeping of the groom, and then hastened into the orchard to join Musidora. He was a tall handsome young man, of about four-and-twenty—of slender shape but well-knit limbs—and possessing as much strength as gracefulness. His dark brown hair fell in rich wavy curls from beneath a black velvet cap which he wore a little on one side of his well-formed head: and in his fine blue eyes might be read all the generous feelings and chivalrous sentiments of an elevated soul. His doublet, fitting close, displayed the fine symmetry of his shape; the sleeves were slashed with pieces of different colours let in, as were the upper parts of his long trunk-hose. This continuous vestment, uniting breeches and stockings, was worn quite loose over the hips, and then set close to the lower limbs all down, thus delineating their fine Apollo-like modelling. His ruffles and worked collar, as well as a glimpse of the embroidered shirt caught through an opening in front of his doublet, showed that he took some little pains with his toilette; while the rapier by his side indicated that he was of gentle birth.

Such was Percy Rivers—a nephew of Sir Lewis Sinclair, and consequently (as above stated) Musidora's cousin. He was an orphan: but by the excellence of his character and his intellectual accomplishments, he had for some time held the important office of Civil Secretary to Sir William Woodville. This functionary, however, being a very old man and full of infirmities, left the entire administration of the Island's affairs to Percy Rivers, who therefore wielded a large amount of virtual power.

Having spent all their lives in the island, Percy and Musidora had known each other from their earliest infancy; and as they grew up, not only did common rumour declare that they were destined for each other, but common opinion added that their personal attractions and high mental qualities pointed out the fitness of such a union. Such indeed also was Percy's hope: for when he was old enough to experience the sentiment of love—to feel its warmth and to understand its meaning—he perceived that his heart was devoted to his beautiful cousin. But she entertained no such tender feeling towards him. She esteemed him as a friend—liked him as a relative—and was more familiar with him than with any other soul in existence, because they had been playmates in childhood: but as for love— the passion which had quickened in Percy's breast drew no responsive vibration from Musidora's heart! To this sad truth Percy had not been long in opening his eyes; and therefore he had never in words made known his love for her. Friends, neighbours, and acquaintances at last saw that after all there was to be no match in this quarter: and then the sudden change which had come upon the damsel's nature, as before described, made not only *them*, but likewise her cousin Percy *himself*, believe that her heart had turned to ice. The young man had continued to be as constant a visitor as his official duties would permit at Sinclair House; and at least three or four times a week would he mount his horse, when the business of the morning was over, and gallop across from Carisbrook Castle to Brading Haven. For Carisbrook was the residence of the Governor, Sir William Woodville: and the distance between that celebrated fortress and Sinclair House was but ten miles.

Musidora, as already stated, liked her cousin Percy Rivers as well as she seemed capable of liking anybody. But she liked him, not only because they were relatives or because they had known each other so long and had been playmates in earlier years,—but because her cousin was in every way a fine and noble character—frank-hearted, generous, and honourable to a degree—brave, and skilled in all manly exercises—endowed with a rare intelligence—and having neither the frivolities nor the vices which characterized the well-born young men of those times. But more than all this, she liked him because she had read the state of his heart—she knew that he loved her—she compassionated him for that hopeless affection—she admired his delicacy in not having breathed it to her ears—and she was aware that he had never fixed his eyes on any other woman, but remained unmarried through a sort of romantic fidelity to this deep, earnest, but unrequited love of his!

"Good day, my fair cousin," said Percy, as he sped across the orchard to join Musidora. "I do not wonder that you should be enjoying the beauty of the weather, for methinks that never did Nature seem more charming."

"And you, who have a mind to appreciate all its beauties, must enjoy them doubly when escaping from the cabinet of Sir William Woodville:"—and as Musidora thus spoke in a voice which was ineffably musical in its tone, but without much variety of accent, the animation of her countenance brightened into a smile of welcome as she extended her hand to her cousin.

He pressed it quickly as if afraid to trust himself with that beauteous snowy hand in his clasp, but instantaneously offered her his arm, which she took at once; and they crossed the orchard together.

"Musidora," said Percy, now breaking silence with some little embarrassment in his manner and hesitation in his speech, "I am glad I have thus found you alone. I wanted an opportunity to speak confidentially and privately with you."

The damsel raised her eyes with a slow look of mingled astonishment and inquiry to the countenance of her cousin, who thus began to address her with so much unwonted mystery: but she said nothing. It seemed as if she could well wait until he chose to explain himself.

"I know you will forgive me for venturing to broach so delicate, and indeed so disagreeable a topic," he continued, after another pause; and now she gazed at him with a steadier look, as if resolved to penetrate his meaning at once, although she seemed to experience no earthly emotion of either curiosity or suspense—a little astonishment perhaps, but no indication that she cared very much about having it gratified. "It is relative to your father—my revered uncle—that I would speak," added Percy after another pause.

"I am sorry to say," remarked Musidora, her voice now modulated to mournful accents, "that my poor father's health seems to be suffering. Unable to entertain a house full of guests as was once his custom as well as his pride, the sense of loneliness gains day by day upon him; and he has no longer the same inducements to ride forth to the chase or pursue the sports of the field."

"This gradual settling down into more quiet habits," rejoined Percy, "was naturally to be expected from the breaking-up of his large establishment of hunters, hounds, grooms, and falconers; but as this event took place nearly six years ago, the poignancy of the regret attending it must have long since been blunted. I fear me, Musidora, that it is not the remembrance of his studs and his packs that now preys on your father's mind—no, nor even what he considered at the time to be the *shame* and *disgrace* of having to give them all up. But may I proceed in my remarks without the risk of offending you?"

"How can I possibly take offence where none is intended?" asked Musidora, with a sort of chiding look, as much as to reprove him for having even suspected her to be capable of such injustice. "Indeed, I know what you would say, Percy," she continued, in the steady-flowing music of her silver voice. "You no doubt conceive that my father has immediate and present cause for annoyance; and I fear that your surmise is but too correct."

"This is precisely what I desired to know," continued Percy: "for the truth is, my dear cousin—and the sooner I explain myself the more at ease shall I feel—I have this day received the handsome present of five hundred pounds sterling from Sir William Woodville; and if there were possibly a way of inducing my uncle to accept the use of it——"

"Percy, you possess a noble heart," interrupted Musidora, throwing upon him a look of gratitude from her large dark haunting eyes: "but you know full well that my father is in his own way as proud as he is improvident."

"But you, Musidora," urged the young man,—"could *you* not by some means force him to accept this sum which is of no use to me, and which may remove some little difficulty from my uncle's path?"

"I appreciate all the generosity of this proposal on your part," said Musidora; "but I am sure you will pardon me for declining it:"—and while her nostrils dilated and her lip curled with a just perceptible expression of hauteur, it was at the same time counterbalanced by the look of gratitude which she again threw upon Percy from the depths of her fine dark eyes.

For an instant Rivers felt hurt, because he had endeavoured to carry out a generous intent in as delicate a manner as he possibly could. Besides, being so nearly related to the old knight, he could see no harm in a proffer so ingenious and well-meant. But too chivalrous and too magnanimous to experience for many moments this sudden pique, he exclaimed in his usual frank-hearted manner, "I see full well that it is of no use to talk to a lady on matters of business; so I will reserve the point to mention to my uncle at a fitting time and opportunity."

But while he was thus speaking, Sir Lewis Sinclair himself entered the orchard. He was a tall fine-looking old man, who must have been full six feet high ere the weight of years, troubles, and infirmities had bowed his back. But still his stoop was not very great; and by the aid of a stick he walked with great firmness and celerity when his sixty-two winters were taken into consideration. He was particularly neat in his apparel, which was that of the country-squire of those times—consisting of a doublet of grey stuff, slashed with black velvet—buff trunk hose—and high boots, very much resembling the hessians of later times. He wore a cap of very small dimensions, and with a black plume fastened by a mother-of-pearl clasp on the right side. His countenance was composed of the hard and somewhat weather-beaten features of a man who had devoted his life to the sports of the field: but there was wanting in his aspect the bluff genuine frankness which usually characterizes the hardy votary of the chase. For in the twinkle of his small grey eyes there was a certain selfishness which could not fail to strike the near observer. And this indeed was the character of Sir Lewis Sinclair. He thought only *of* himself—he lived only *for* himself; and if he did indeed possess that pride with regard to money-matters to which Musidora had alluded, it arose from no genuine excellence of principle, but from a foolish vanity which strives to conceal the poverty of the purse as if it were a disgrace or indeed a crime.

But on this occasion there was a more than usual cunning sprightliness in the old knight's looks, and a more than his wonted egotistical complacency in his manner, as he approached his daughter and his nephew. Shaking the latter by the hand, and then taking his arm—Musidora still leaning on the other—Sir Lewis observed, "I did not know you were here, Percy. Wanting to speak to 'Dora, I learnt that she was in the orchard and came to join her, little suspecting she had already a companion. But no matter. What I have to say to her may be uttered in your presence, Percy; and so you may both prepare to listen with attention."

Young Rivers gazed with curiosity and interest upon the old gentleman's countenance: but Musidora, without the slightest display of emotion, said calmly, "I can tell by your manner, dear father, that it is something regarding myself: and more than that, I think I can connect it with the letter which arrived yesterday."

"Egad! the girl's a witch," exclaimed Sir Lewis with a chuckle which had something forced and anxious in its mirth. "But you don't mean to say that you have read that letter?" he abruptly asked, no longer able to conceal the sudden apprehension which his daughter's words had excited in his mind.

"Your correspondence is sacred, father," she answered, a sudden light of indignation flashing from her eyes: "and even if I had found your letter lying open in my path, and no human eye upon me to mark my actions, I should not violate its sanctity."

"Well, well, girl, I did not mean to anger you," said the old knight, evidently satisfied by this assurance. "But how on earth came you to conjecture that any idea which I have been revolving in my mind for the last four-and-twenty hours was connected with you?"

"From the simple fact that I beheld you more than usually preoccupied from the moment that letter came," responded Musidora calmly; "while your eyes were frequently thrown upon me, as if I entered deeply into your thoughts. Then too you asked me with a strange significancy this morning how I should like to pay London and its environs a visit?—and when I gave you my response you drew forth your letter and read it all over again."

"See how she puts two and two together, Percy—and how dexterously she arrives at a conclusion," ejaculated Sir Lewis Sinclair. "Well, then she is right too in her inference: it is about herself I wish to speak. The fact is, this letter,"—and as he thus spoke Sir Lewis drew the epistle from the pocket of his trunk-hose, just displayed it, but without opening it, and then returned it to his pocket again,—"is from my noble relative the Earl of Grantham, who has sent me a very pressing invitation for Musidora to pay him and his noble Countess a visit at their villa at Greenwich, which, as you perhaps both well know, is a sweet spot on the banks of the Thames some four or five miles from London."

"And am I to accept this invitation?" asked Musidora, with perhaps the least, least expression of curiosity in the fluid tones of her voice.

"Well, I have been thinking over it until now," responded her father. "I never come to a hasty or rash conclusion: and so I took twenty-four hours to deliberate upon the subject; and my decision is that you will do well, 'Dora, to accept this invitation. It may lead to results which——"

But here Sir Lewis suddenly checked himself, and gave a short cough so as not to appear to have purposely broken in upon his own words.

"Do you mean, uncle," asked Percy, who looked chagrined and annoyed, "that this invitation on the Earl's part is with a view of effecting a complete reconciliation between yourself and him? for if I mistake not, very many years have elapsed since you were on friendly terms with each other."

"Well, I suppose you are right," returned Sir Lewis: "it is but prudent that such reconciliation should take place. However," he added, as if desirous to cut short the conversation, "you will follow my wishes, 'Dora, and accept this invitation?"

"Since it is your pleasure, my dear father," was her reply, "I can have no objection to make:"—but it was impossible to glean from her passionless manner whether she were really pleased or otherwise at the arrangement so abruptly proposed to her and so speedily settled.

Certain however it is that her cousin, the handsome Percy, was very far from relishing the idea. Though hopeless was his love, and though confined as well as it possibly could be within his own breast, yet was it to him a solace and a comfort to be able to enjoy the pleasure of Musidora's society during his leisure hours; and he had taught himself to be contented—nay, even happy, with the privilege of beholding her often—conversing with her—drinking in the placid and even flowing melody of her voice—and accompanying her in her walks. *Now* he was to lose all this, at least for a season; and the thought flung upon his spirits a damp which he could not immediately shake off. But speedily recollecting that it was unworthy of him to exhibit anything savouring of discontent in Musidora's presence, he assumed a forced gaiety as he continued walking up and down the orchard with his splendid cousin leaning upon one arm and his selfish old uncle hanging on the other. At length Musidora remarked that she felt tired and should return into the house. Sir Lewis thereupon bade Percy escort her in-doors, observing "that he no doubt required some refreshment after his ride."

The two cousins accordingly entered the mansion; and Sir Lewis remained alone in the orchard. The truth is that he had thus stayed behind in order to give free vent to the joy experienced at having so easily carried what he had at first expected would prove a very difficult point. This was to persuade his daughter to accept the invitation to pass a few weeks with Lord and Lady Grantham at Greenwich; and if he had kept the letter twenty-four hours ere he broached the subject, but in the meantime had

beaten about the bush by a leading question or two, it was because he had
hesitated to communicate the invitation to Musidora for fear she should
excuse herself. His astonishment was therefore only equalled by his joy,
when he found that she thus yielded so ready an obedience to his wishes.

It was to give free vent to this joy that the old knight remained behind
in the orchard; and getting out of sight of the house, in the shade of a
cluster of trees close by the road which separates the orchard from the
forest, he rubbed his hands, chuckled, laughed, and almost danced with
delight, as he thus yielded to the gilded thoughts that swept through his
imagination. Then, as if to assure himself that there was indeed a chance
of beholding the realization of the ambitious hope which thus inspired
him, he again drew forth Lord Grantham's letter and carefully perused its
contents. These were to the following effect:—

"Grantham Villa, by Greenwich.
"This 27th of April, 1516.

"DEAR AND ESTEEMED COUSIN,

"For some years past an estrangement has existed like a gulf between
your branch of the family and mine; and yet I scarcely know the cause.
And forasmuch as that cause must be so slight, since I have ceased to remember it, let it no longer have existence. Accept then the hand of friendship which by these presents I proffer unto you.

"And now, since I have taken up my pen to write, I will enter upon
certain matters which I herewith submit for your consideration. I am well
aware that the King, in consequence of your relationship to the late Minister Dudley, has deprived you of an honourable post yielding a sufficient
revenue; and I have heard with sorrow that this circumstance has much
impoverished your means and broken your fortunes. Perhaps you are
aware that for the very self-same reason—namely, my kinship with the late
Minister Dudley—King Henry has for some years exiled me from Court:
and shorn me of my pensions, commanding the Countess and myself to
live at this villa of ours under peril of his farther displeasure.

"Now you, my dear cousin, will agree with me that if there be any
means of reconciling the King unto us, and inducing him to take us into
high favour, such means should be adopted. Those means, I think, are
within our reach; or at all events, the experiment may be made without
harm or dishonour.

"Listen. The King has of late frequently visited his Royal Palace at
Greenwich, seeking in disgust to separate himself as much as possible
from his so-called wife, Catherine of Arragon. Now it is notorious that
this marriage of his Highness the King with Catherine of Arragon, is no

marriage at all; and that the King means to divorce her so soon as he shall have found a damsel, beautiful, well mannered, elegant, and accomplished enough to become his wife in Catherine's stead. For on this occasion I am credibly assured that his Grace the King is resolved to choose himself a bride from amongst his female subjects, so that a daughter of England may share with him England's throne!

"Now, my esteemed cousin, knowing that your daughter Musidora is endowed with every charm, elegance, and grace calculated to ensnare the heart and enchant the fancy of our young King—and as it would be most honourable as well as most advantageous to all branches of our family that the Lady Musidora should if possible be elevated to the queenly rank—I pray you, esteemed cousin, if it seem good to you on reading this letter, to permit Musidora to come and pass a few weeks or months, as circumstances may decide, with the Countess and myself. We will be unto her most loving, tender, and affectionate; and while so arranging matters that she shall have every chance of attracting the King's notice, we will watch most scrupulously over her, so that whatever may arise in respect to herself and the King shall only be of the most honourable character. To this the Countess and I solemnly pledge ourselves; and your daughter's own prudence and delicacy will serve as an additional guarantee and safeguard for her virtue.

"Should this proposition meet your approval, it would be as well for all purposes that Musidora should not be previously informed of the part which it is anticipated she may have to play; inasmuch as by shocking her modesty, the result would be to prejudice her against me and the Countess.

"Your very affectionate and faithful cousin,
"GRANTHAM.

"Ride, ride—haste, haste—until these be delivered to the good Sir Lewis Sinclair, Knight-Banneret."

Such was the precious epistle which Sir Lewis Sinclair had received from his noble relative, and which he now perused for the fiftieth time in order to buoy up his spirits with the golden prospect it held forth. Having devoured the letter with as much avidity as if it were only the first time that he read it, he carefully folded it up and consigned it (as he thought) to the pocket in his trunk-hose. But he merely thrust it into one of the slashed plaits, so that on withdrawing his hand it fell out and dropped upon the ground.

Unconscious of the accident which had thus occurred, Sir Lewis Sinclair jauntily retraced his way through the orchard into the house, where he rejoined Musidora and Percy Rivers in a parlour opening upon the lawn in front.

Meantime, scarcely had he thus entered the mansion, when an individual who had been watching all the proceedings in the orchard for the last hour, darted out of his hiding-place in the forest—clambered over the fence—and possessed himself of the letter which the knight had left lying upon the grass. Then, springing lightly back again over the railings, the intruder plunged once more into the depths of the forest.

CHAPTER III.

THE COUSINS.

IN the meantime let us see what had been taking place between Percy Rivers and Musidora during the half-hour that they were alone together in the parlour, until rejoined by Sir Lewis Sinclair.

Immediately upon entering that room, the damsel took up a silver hand-bell which stood upon the table and was about to ring it, when Percy, anticipating her intentions, hastily said, "If, fair cousin, you are about to summon the domestic to serve me up refreshments, I require them not."

We should here observe that the dinner-hour at the period of which we are writing was between twelve and one o'clock, even for the highest grades of society; and therefore that repast had already been partaken of alike by Musidora and her father at Sinclair House, and by Percy Rivers at Carisbrook Castle.

"And yet," said Musidora, in reply to the young gentleman's remark in declining the offered refreshment, "you have had a good ride since the mid-day meal: and it is now verging towards five o'clock," she added, glancing at an old-fashioned but very handsome clepsydra, or water-clock, which stood upon the projecting marble of the huge chimney-piece. "At least you will take a goblet of wine?"

But Percy only shook his head with a gesture bordering on impatience, such as the knight's daughter had never seen him display before. Then he walked towards the open window, and gazed forth upon the magnificent prospect formed by the waving forest that went sloping down the proclivity to the very brink of the haven—the full estuary itself, shining like a lake of quicksilver—the opposite shore, likewise fringed with verdure—and then the open sea, which stretched beyond far as the eye could reach. For two or three minutes did Percy Rivers seem to be absorbed in the contemplation of the beautiful scenery before him; but as Musidora slowly approached that same open window, the first look which she bent upon her cousin showed that he was in reality gazing upon vacancy, and that his thoughts were engrossed by a subject of even a painful character. Nor was she at a loss to divine what this subject was; and therefore, as she continued to gaze in her own peculiar manner upon the young man, the wreathing of her lip changed just perceptibly enough to show that she not merely understood him but likewise pitied him.

"You do not seem pleased with this proposed visit of mine to our noble connexions on the banks of the Thames?" she said, with that serene seriousness which almost invariably characterized the fluid evenness of her silver voice.

Percy started, and turned towards his fair cousin with a look expressive of ineffable feelings: for this was the first time that ever a syllable had fallen from her lips which in any way seemed to allude, or could be even construed into an allusion, to the more than ordinary interest which he cherished in the depths of his soul towards her. For an instant—but only for an instant—a scintillation of hope flashed up in his mind; for it struck him that if she thus noticed that he experienced any special feeling relative to her projected visit, she herself was disposed to pay some deference to that feeling. Besides, how easy is it for the heart, which loves devotedly, to catch at the slightest gleam that suddenly breaks in with the semblance of hope upon its long-endured darkness of despair! And so it was for the moment with Percy Rivers. But when he thus turned abruptly towards his cousin, and beheld her unmoved, icily serene as ever, and with nothing in her deep fathomable eyes to tell even of that sentiment of compassion which she in reality experienced for him, and the evidence of which too had disappeared from her finely arching lip,—that scintillation of hope died as suddenly as it had flashed up, and it was only by a strong effort that Percy was enabled to subdue the feelings which had thus passed through the ordeal of such sudden excitement and equally abrupt revulsion.

"You ask me, Musidora," he said, now casting down his eyes and speaking in a low and somewhat tremulous voice, "whether I am pleased with this proposed visit of yours to Lord and Lady Grantham: and I know you well enough to be aware that in making such an observation, you give me leave to speak my mind—and in speaking my mind, you wish me to do it frankly. Is it not so?"

"Assuredly," was the damsel's response.

"Then listen, Musidora," continued Percy Rivers, speaking now with the manly earnestness and decision of a true, frank-hearted friend. "Lord and Lady Grantham are but remote connexions of our branch of the family; and, there are consequently no near ties of kinship to inspire them with so sudden an affection for you. From some circumstances with which

I am unacquainted, they have long been estranged from your father: and *you* they have never seen at all. Whence, then, can have arisen this desire on their part to have you to visit them?"

"Do you believe it impossible," asked Musidora, "that in their old age they may experience regret for the coldness and slight with which for years past they have treated my father, and that they now seek to afford reparation in as graceful and delicate a manner as they can?"

"Do you yourself really believe in the interpretation which you have thus so charitably given to their conduct?"—and as Percy Rivers put this question, he looked earnestly and even fixedly upon Musidora.

"It was but a speculation on my part," she replied, steadily meeting that gaze, and with an expression of cold, chaste, immaculate candour upon her countenance. "Where any subject is involved in doubt and therefore admits of two interpretations, a good and a bad—I always prefer to adopt the former. But in the present case, what sinister motive can Lord and Lady Grantham possibly have in sending me this invitation?"

"I know not—and yet I can scarcely bring myself to believe that their object is a purely disinterested one:"—and Percy gazed again upon Musidora, as if there were some idea hovering in his mind, but to which he scarcely dared give utterance.

"Speak with candour," she said, perceiving that there was thus something behind. "You know very well that I shall not take offence."

"Lord and Lady Grantham," resumed Percy, still speaking reservedly, though availing himself of his fair cousin's permission to open his mind frankly,—"are old and childless. They have no daughters to prove an attraction to the gay, the youthful, and the high-born; and their gilded saloons are most likely neglected, if not positively deserted, by the brilliant danglers in the train of beauty and fashion. Is it not possible, then, that Lord and Lady Grantham, having heard of your beauty, your intelligence, your accomplishments——Ah! Musidora, you know that I speak not thus to flatter!——having heard, I say, that *you*—their hitherto neglected and ignored relative—are thus richly endowed by nature and by heaven, is it not possible, I ask, that they should seek to have you with them, to make you the object of attraction at their festivals, their banquets, their dances, and their music-parties?"

"If I thought that such was indeed their object," said Musidora, a haughty and indeed half-scornful smile slowly appearing upon her splendid countenance, "I would not leave my father's home to visit these noble relatives of our's. But you had not finished your observations?" she added, her features relapsing into their wonted fathomless expression.

"That your father should wish you to accept this invitation, is natural enough," continued Percy. "He hopes that amongst the brilliant throng of cavaliers, gallants, and nobles, to whom you will be introduced, and who will surround you with their homage, there may perhaps one be found—a fortunate one—" and here the young man's voice trembled—"who may woo and win you."

"Ah!" ejaculated Musidora, suddenly displaying more excitement than her cousin had ever yet observed since the spell-like change came over her three years and a half back—and her eyes flashed forth a strange lightning: but almost instantaneously resuming her most icy manner, she said coldly, "Whatever motives may influence others, I am my own mistress and can act for myself."

"I fear, Musidora," her cousin hastened to observe, "that you fancy I have not altogether dealt candidly with you? Perhaps you suppose that because I, in the selfishness of my own heart,—in the egotism of my own feelings—wish that you should stay, I am capable of having recourse to a base unworthy sophistry in order to disgust you with the very idea of this visit? And now the conversation has taken a turn which compels me to speak upon a subject which I have ever so scrupulously avoided until now—this day—this hour! Yes—it is true—perfectly true," he continued, in a voice of gathering excitement and with looks full of mingled admiration and mournfulness, "that I *do* deplore the thought of your absence: but I am not base enough—no, nor selfish enough, to have recourse to coward subterfuges to induce you to remain at home. Ah! Musidora, whatever sentiment I have felt for you, has been of the purest, holiest nature: and you, who for some years past have read—as I know you *have*—the secret of my heart, can tell me now whether a single deed, or word, or look of mine can be brought in accusation against me? Never, never have I until this moment permitted myself to weary or grieve you with the lament of mine own unavailing affection. Impute not then the slightest shade of lurking selfishness to me: for if you knew as I do what love is—aye, and what the hopelessness of love is—you would understand how the only solace is to be found in the consciousness of its purity and its fidelity!"

"Enough—peace—no more!" said the young damsel, quivering for an instant—but only for a single instant—with the emotion which Percy's words had excited in her soul, whatever that emotion might be; but as this quivering was so transitory as to leave no doubt when it was passed whether it had taken place at all—and as no flush nor glow tinted even for a moment the pure marble of her complexion—he thought that his eyes must have deceived him and that no visible trace of feeling had in reality disturbed the coldly brilliant surface of her beauty.

"Pardon me—I will say no more," he murmured in a low deep voice: then with an impulsive feeling which he could not control, he grasped her hand, exclaiming, "for years I have struggled against this manifestation of weakness into which I have now been betrayed! Tell me—tell me—will you forgive me—can you pardon me?"

"You have not offended me," returned Musidora, now smiling with an encouraging brightness. "But it is for you to pardon me—inasmuch as my words or my manner may have seemed to question ere now the sincerity of your motives in arguing against this promised visit. Percy Rivers," she added, with a slightly deepening earnestness, "if I did not know you to be everything that is honourable, noble-minded, truthful, and frank-hearted, you would not be so frequent a visitor at this house—no, not even on the strength of the kinship existing between us—and much less should we have conversed with such ease, I might almost say familiarity, as we have done today. Therefore, believe me when I assure you that I do *not* suspect the genuine sincerity of your motives in condemning my acceptance of Lord Grantham's invitation. Your conjectures may even be true as to the selfishness which dictated that invitation on the Earl's part, and the hopes which have inspired my father in wishing me to accept it. But you know little of me,"—and once more did a strange light flash in her splendid dark eyes as she spoke,—"if you think that I myself am actuated by the frivolous idea of shining in a patrician circle or the ambitious hope of forming a proud alliance—or rather, I should say, you know me too well to imagine for a single moment that such are my motives in accepting this invitation."

And as Musidora thus spoke, she gradually drew herself up to the full of her noble height, unconsciously enhancing the Juno-like carriage of her splendid head, her arching neck so grandly white, and her bust so superbly modelled—while her lip slowly wreathed with a sovereign hauteur, and her very air was such that it almost seemed as if any one thus gazing upon her queenly form dilating as it were in its goddess-like beauty, must fall down at her feet, crying, "Pardon, pardon!"

Percy Rivers gazed upon her with an admiration which he could not subdue, but which was nevertheless attempted by a respect amounting almost to awe: for he saw indeed full well that she was elevated above the frivolities and vanities of her sex as the Alpine floweret, cradled amidst eternal snows, shines in its cold purity apart from the specimens of floral gaudiness in the vales below. Yes—this much could he understand concerning Musidora—this much did he see: but when she had observed that he knew her too well to mistake her motives, a sigh—a scarcely perceptible and scarcely audible sigh—escaped him; for he could not but think within his own breast that so far from knowing her well, he had not for more than three years past been enabled to comprehend her at all!

The entrance of Sir Lewis Sinclair put an end to the topic of the cousins' discourse, even if it had not reached a crisis that without the old knight's interruption at all would have caused it to be turned at once into another channel. And now Sir Lewis, ordering in wine, began to quaff brimming goblets to sustain the excellent spirits which his adventurous hopes had excited; and while thus indulging in copious libations, he sketched out the plan which he had formed for Musidora's journey to Greenwich. He had calculated that she would not require more than three days to make her preparations, and that therefore on the fourth morning she would be ready to set off, attended by one tire-woman and the groom. He had likewise estimated that she would take three days more to reach the metropolitan suburb of Greenwich—the distance being about seventy five miles, and the journey to be performed on horseback.

To all the arrangements which her father methodically laid down, Musidora gave a dutiful assent in her own quiet emotionless way and the old knight continued to drink goblet after goblet in tolerably quick succession until supper was served up at about eight o'clock. Percy Rivers remained to partake of the meal but when it was over, and he rose to retire, he said in a voice the tremulousness of which he could not subdue as he spoke aside to Musidora, "If you will permit me, I shall call on each of the three days which are to elapse previous to your departure?"

The damsel gave her consent; and Percy mounting his horse, which was in readiness galloped off on his way back to Carisbrook Castle.

It was not till Sir Lewis Sinclair ascended to his own bed-room that he missed Lord Grantham's letter; and as his brain was now somewhat clouded with the effects of the wine he had drunk he could not for the life of him remember where he had last taken out the letter from his pocket. So he went to bed in a painful kind of bewilderment; and when he awoke in the morning after a sound sleep, the first idea which presented itself to his mind was that of the lost letter. While performing his toilet, he recollected how he had drawn forth and perused that letter in the orchard: but the longer he reflected upon this incident the more convinced was he that he had safely consigned the missive to his pocket again. Nevertheless, the moment he was attired in his morning riding-suit, he hastened to the orchard to look for the letter: but it was nowhere to be found. Re-entering the house, he questioned his servants; and they one and all denied having seen it. Indeed, it would not have much mattered if they had, considering their inability to read.

Fearful that after all it might have fallen into Musidora's hands, it was with a certain degree of trepidation and guilty shrinking which he had never experienced before in respect to his daughter, that the old knight entered the parlour where the morning repast was spread. But as Musidora rose from her seat according to custom and advanced to embrace her sire, he felt tolerably assured by the first glance which he threw upon her countenance, that his alarm was unfounded. Not that he, although her father, could pretend to probe the secrets of her heart any more than the rest of the world: but still, when he found that there was not the slightest cloud hanging upon her brow, nor even the faintest expression of chiding or reproach in her look—but that the cold brilliancy of her smile shone upon her countenance with its wonted welcome for *him*—he was justified in the belief that she had not found the letter. Even if she had, he thought within himself, she would not violate its contents but would bring it straight to him.

Making up his mind, therefore, that the letter was lost in one of the thousand ways in which papers do sometimes disappear, without turning up again to the detriment or injury of anybody, Sir Lewis Sinclair soon ceased to trouble himself any more upon the point: but during the three days which elapsed ere his daughter set out upon her journey he gave every proof of having regained much of the good spirits of former times. Indeed, the old gentleman buoyed himself up with the most extravagant hopes; and there were moments when he could scarcely avoid imparting them to Musidora and enjoining her to do her best to bring about their realization.

Percy Rivers passed nearly the whole of each of the three days at Sinclair House: but he maintained so rigidly a guard over his feelings as to prevent the repetition of aught savouring of that weakness which he had displayed in Musidora's presence, as already related.

At length, when the third evening came, he had to say farewell to his beauteous cousin—for it was arranged that she should take her departure at an early hour on the following morning. Full evident was it now that Percy Rivers, despite all his efforts to maintain a becoming fortitude, was shaken to the very depths of his manly nature; and as he gazed upon that splendid being who shone in what might be termed all the glacial glory of her charms, and as he thought within himself that she loved him *not*—that she never could be *his*—but that she might love elsewhere and become *another's*—he felt for a moment as if he could have fallen at her feet and implored her for the love of heaven to have mercy upon him! But she herself, as if reading all that was passing in his mind, gave him her hand with a cordiality more than usually warm;—and at the same time from out the mystic depths of her dark dream-like eyes she threw upon him a look which seemed to remind him of his duty as a man.

"Farewell, dear cousin," he said, feeling grateful—deeply grateful—that she should have thus, though in her own strange manner, reminded him of the due necessity of controlling his emotions. "May all possible happiness attend you!"—then availing himself of the opportunity afforded by her accompanying him into the hall, he said in a rapid but excited whisper, "Musidora, as your cousin, I may say to you what I am about to speak—and that is, if at any time or under any circumstances you require the aid, the defence, or the counsel of a sincere and devoted friend, fail not—Oh! fail not to summon *me!* Were it at the ends of the earth, I should speed as if for life and death, in obedience to your command!"

"I know how well-meant is your proffer," rejoined Musidora; "and my gratitude is proportionate."

They then parted—Percy Rivers flinging himself upon his steed and galloping madly away by the side of the orchard and through the forest, as if anxious to outstrip a presentiment of evil which pertinaciously pursued and taunted him.

Early on the following morning Musidora took leave of her sire. He accompanied her down to the sea-shore near St. Helen's, where she embarked on board the ferry-boat, attended by a tire-woman (or lady's-maid), and by a faithful old groom who had been in the family for many years. The boat—or rather huge clumsy barge—received on board the three horses for the travellers' service, Musidora's wardrobe being contained in a large portmanteau made to strap on to the groom's saddle.

And now, when the moment came for bidding her father farewell, Musidora gave evidence of greater emotion than for a long, long time she had displayed. Those who had believed that her heart was ice in respect to love, had never imagined that it was inaccessibly frozen against filial sympathies: and they were right. For the damsel wept—and assuredly these were no frozen tears that trickled down her marble cheeks: but they were warm from a heart that experienced all affectionate solicitude on behalf of the author of her being. The old knight wept also—but they were tears of joy which he shed in the almost childish delight conjured up in his soul by the brilliant hopes he entertained relative to Musidora's destiny.

The barge was pushed away from the shore—the fresh breeze of morning filled the bellying sail—and Sir Lewis Sinclair remained on the beach, until he could no longer catch the waving of Musidora's handkerchief. He then mounted his horse and galloped up the steep to his now lonely dwelling—while his daughter, seated in the boat, watched the receding shore of the isle of her birth with eyes no longer dimmed with tears. For a calm cold serenity of countenance had full soon succeeded the emotions she betrayed at the instant when imprinting the parting kiss upon her father's cheek.

CHAPTER IV.

GRANTHAM VILLA.

At the period of which we are writing Greenwich was not united to London by the unbroken range of buildings which cover all that portion of
the right bank of the Thames at the present day. Indeed Deptford, now
forming so considerable a portion of that range, was only just beginning
to be called into existence, Henry VIII having at that very time founded
the Dockyard. Such buildings as there were between London and Greenwich were far less of a business-like aspect than those of the existing age;
but many noblemen had beautiful villas along the shore of the noble river,
especially in the neighbourhood of Greenwich itself, where a royal palace
then stood. The site of this regal dwelling, known as "Greenwich House,"
was that where now stands the Hospital of world-wide fame. It was by
no means a large nor imposing edifice; but looking upon the river on one
side, and having the spacious park immediately contiguous in the rear, it
was an agreeable dwelling enough in the summer time. Henry VIII was
frequently there in the early part of his reign; and on those occasions all
the satellites of the Court hastened to take up their abodes in the neighbourhood—so that villas and mansions, either to purchase or hire, in the
Greenwich district, were much in request; and a series of gaieties in the
form of balls, masques, pageants, music-parties, and garden fêtes, were
sustained for the Court's diversion.

The Earl of Grantham's letter to Sir Lewis Sinclair relative to Henry
VIII and Catherine of Arragon, was substantially correct. Catherine, when
espoused by Henry, was the widow of his elder brother; and as he was
young at the time, it was always believed to be a match into which he was
forced by an inhuman policy on the part of his advisers, rather than by his
own inclinations. Certain it is that he was altogether wearied of his alliance—that he had declared it to be null—and that he had more than once
proclaimed his intention of marrying again so soon as he should encounter a lady whose beauty and accomplishments might seem deserving of
his hand.

The house inhabited by the Earl of Grantham had naught resembling
the lightness of architecture and the general cheerfulness of aspect which
the imagination is wont to associate with the term "villa." It was in reality
a large straggling, irregularly built mansion—of stone in some parts, brick-
work in others—and having indeed a sort of castellated appearance. It was
situated about a mile and a half above Greenwich, and therefore so much

nearer to London. Standing back about a hundred yards from the Thames, it had a flower-garden and then a stone terrace reaching completely down to the river's edge; and behind it had spacious gardens, shrubberies, and pleasure-grounds, extending to a distance of nearly half a mile. Though not rich—his resources having been much crippled by the loss of the pensions which he was so anxious to recover, no matter by what means—the Earl of Grantham was well enough off to live comfortably, if not handsomely; and as there were merely himself and the Countess to attend upon, there was no necessity to keep many servants. Seven or eight menials accordingly formed his household; and a gloomy, monotonous, dreary life they led—for as it was well known that his lordship was in complete disgrace with the King, and dared not show himself at Court, few were the acquaintances and fewer still the real friends who ever cheered him or the Countess with their presence. No wonder, then, that the Earl and his lady should have put their heads together and set their wits to work in order to devise some means to regain the royal favour. At length they hit upon the notable project with which the reader is already acquainted; for by some means or another they had heard a most dazzling account of Musidora's remarkable beauty. They had been told of the imperial dignity of her air mingled with feminine gracefulness of manner—of her commanding beauty of person and her high mental accomplishments: and knowing the King's taste well, they had felt persuaded that the charming daughter of Sir Lewis Sinclair was in every way qualified to attract the royal notice and win the royal heart!

A few words more relative to the Earl and Countess—and we will resume the thread of our story. His lordship was a little, thin, miserable-looking man, as far as his physical appearance was concerned; but every line of his wrinkled countenance denoted the craft and astuteness of the politician—while every flexion of the body, every gesture, and every movement indicated the polished courtier. While his eyes evinced the restless cunning of the diplomatist, his language sounded so mellifluous and bland as to appear incapable of veiling deceit: but it did not require any very considerable amount of penetration to read his true character in his looks—namely, that of an ambitious, intriguing, unprincipled time-server. The Countess was a suitable match for such a lord. Thin, hatchet-faced, bustling, and restless—with sharp quick eyes, and a remarkable habit of taking up people's words and finishing their sentences for them—she seemed to possess all the essential aptitudes for intrigue in every one of its phases; while a certain affability of manner—an ingenuous way of conveying compliments without appearing to mean them—and a great facility in discovering a person's weak points and dishing-up her flatteries accordingly,—all these constituted an attractiveness well-calculated to throw people off their guard and induce them to place reliance on her as a very kind-hearted, agreeable, unpretending woman. If we add that the Earl was about sixty years of age, and the Countess four years his junior—and that they both dressed in a style of great elegance, as if indeed they had never lost their position at Court—our sketches of the noble pair will be as complete as it is at present necessary to render them. Indeed, all other traits or peculiarities belonging to the character of either, must be left to develop themselves in their actions and words, which will perhaps constitute the best mirror wherein to regard them.

It was in the evening of the third day of her journey,—and as the white mistiness following the sunset spread its gauzy veil over the fair scenery in the neighbourhood of the river,—that Musidora, attended by the old groom and her young tire-woman, arrived at Grantham Villa. As an especial compliment, the Earl and Countess came forth to welcome her at the front door; and as the former assisted her to alight from her steed, the latter received her in her arms. Then, on being conducted to a spacious saloon where the blaze of chandeliers altogether neutralized the sombre aspect produced by the massive furniture and the tapestry hangings, Musidora at once became the object of much real interest and a vast amount of affected tenderness on the part of the selfish and designing pair. But joyous though rapid were the glances of self-gratulatory intelligence which the Earl and Countess exchanged, as ocular demonstration now proved that the reports which they had heard of Musidora's great beauty were far from exaggerated. For as they contemplated our heroine,—clad as she was in her riding-costume, which, fitting close to her shape, developed the symmetrical grace as well as the fine contours of her form,—with a cloud of raven hair flowing over her shoulders in massive velvetty undulations,—with the serene though glacial dignity upon her brow, and that gleam of a fading smile which imparted its cold animation to the lower half of her countenance,—in a word, as they beheld her in the full glory of her youthful yet commanding beauty, they could not help thinking how utterly impossible it was for rumour to have exaggerated her personal charms in any sense!

An elegant supper was served up; and Musidora found herself the object of the tenderest and most delicate attentions—as they appeared to be—on the part of her noble relatives. Both as a lady endowed with instincts which even excelled the artificialities of the highest breeding, and with that sense of obligation which every guest experiences for the hospitality of the entertainers, Musidora strove to render herself as agreeable as she could; and without unbending from that queenly reserve which was mingled with so much grace—and without as it were manifesting any thaw of that frozen serenity which, though so indicative of a passion-less nature, was at the same time so consonant with the superb brilliancy of her beauty—she soon convinced the Earl and Countess that in man-ner, bearing, and conversation, she was calculated to shine with a dazzling transcendency.

When the hour for retiring arrived, Lady Grantham conducted Musi-dora to the bedchamber which was prepared for her reception. It had been hastily fitted up in the most elegant and cheerful style,—no expense having been spared in thus modernizing its aspect and appointments: for as a matter of calculation the wily Earl and Countess had resolved that nothing should damp the spirits of the young damsel in whom such ex-alted hopes were now centred. Upon an elegant toilet-table appeared two caskets, which Lady Grantham proceeded to open. One contained a mag-nificent set of diamonds—the other a set of pearls of the finest and most brilliant description.

"As your nearest female relative," said the Countess, with winning tone, and kind look, "you will permit me, my dear Musidora, to offer you these trifling tributes of my esteem and affection. Deeply do I deplore the untoward circumstances which have hitherto kept me unacquainted with so charming, beautiful, and intelligent a relation as I now find in you: but it is useless to regret the past. We are at length acquainted with each other; and as I was already prepared to love you well, I now feel that I can experi-ence towards you all the tenderness of a mother. Indeed, it is as a daugh-ter that Lord Grantham and myself wish to regard you: and therefore, whatever we may choose to do for you must not wound your pride—no, nor even make you feel that you are placed under the slightest obligation towards us."

Having thus spoken, and without waiting to afford the young lady any opportunity for a reply, the Countess hastily kissed her cheek and hur-ried from the apartment. There was for a moment a half-scornful, half-disdainful wreathing of Musidora's classic lips as she flung a look upon the caskets, which, lying open upon the toilet-table, displayed their brilliant contents to her view; then, without even experiencing sufficient curios-ity to induce her to inspect those dazzling gems more closely—much less inspired by the least sentiment of vanity to behold the effect which would be produced by placing those pearls upon her brow or those diamonds upon her hair—she carelessly shut the lids of the caskets, and turned away with as much frozen indifference as if their contents were mere worthless dross.

Immediately afterwards, Annette, her young tire-woman, entered to assist in Musidora's night-toilet; and as her mistress was thoughtful and silent, the abigail ventured not to intrude upon her with any remarks of her own. She was soon dismissed for the night; and Musidora then remained alone, to reflect upon the characters of her noble relatives so far as she had as yet been enabled to read them, and also to ponder upon what their real ulterior motives could be in having invited her to stay with them.

CHAPTER V.

THE VENERABLE WANDERER.

THE first dawn of morning was peeping with dim uncertain light from the purple portals of the east—and night, with her black waving pennons, was but slowly passing away in the western horizon—when an old man crept forth from a sort of arbour or summer-house on the extreme boundary of Lord Grantham's pleasure-grounds.

This old man, who was evidently bent down as much by the weight of afflictions as by that of years, had something so venerable and at the same time so woe-begone in his aspect, that an observer would have almost forgotten to notice the mendicant condition of his apparel in the contemplation of his lineaments and looks. All attention would, at least on the first survey, have been absorbed in the mournful—indeed the profoundly melancholy—expression of that countenance which, though covered with wrinkles, had nothing disagreeable nor repulsive in its mien, but on the contrary beamed with a benevolence which implied how undeserved were the sufferings which the poor old man endured. He had a long white beard which gave that venerable look to the features so deeply marked with the lines of despair; and leaning upon a stick to support his tottering limbs as he stole forth from the summer-house, he had the appearance of one of those wandering anchorites or hoary pilgrims who formed a class belonging to an earlier and more Catholic age.

But, as we have hinted, his apparel was in a sad dilapidated condition: indeed they were the veritable rags of beggary which hung upon him—shreds and tatters but ill adapted to protect his form from the cold air which characterizes the nights of spring. Yet in that open summer-house, so slightly built, had the old man spent the past night. A houseless wanderer, there had he crept to shelter himself against the mist, the damp, and the chill,—while he snatched a few hours of troubled repose. At that period the severest penalties were in existence against beggars, mendicants, and vagrants: it was a grievous crime to be houseless; and if frequently convicted of being thus friendless, homeless, and utterly pauperized, death upon the scaffold was the punishment. To the risk of these contingent horrors and barbaric atrocities the old man was not blind; and therefore it was with fear and trembling that he had scaled the low palisade and entered Lord Grantham's grounds to sleep in the arbour, or summer-house alluded to. His fears pursued him in his dreams and caused him to awake at the moment the earliest streak of dawn glimmered in the orient sky. Creeping forth, therefore, in the stealthy manner described, he dragged himself painfully over the railings, and descended into the open field which lay beyond the Earl's pleasure-grounds.

At this moment—just as the old man had scrambled over the palisade—a tall figure, enveloped in a cloak, suddenly appeared round the angle formed by the dark waving evergreens of the shrubbery: and thus did the old man and the cloaked stranger find themselves abruptly and unexpectedly within half a dozen yards of each other.

The stranger was tall, slender, and remarkably handsome; but with a proud haughty countenance, and a sinister expression in the dark eyes and on the curling lip. He was dressed in rich but sombre apparel; and his arms, crossed over his breast, retained the Spanish cloak closely around him.

"Ah! is it *you*?" he ejaculated with a sudden start, as he at once recognised the old man.

"Villain!—my daughter?" exclaimed the latter; for the recognition was mutual and instantaneous. "Give me back my daughter!—where is she?—what has become of her?"—and in a manner half entreating and half-menacing the bereaved father sprang forward and clung to the stranger's cloak.

For a few instants the latter gazed down upon the old man with a wild and inexplicable expression, as if inclined to pity but having another reason to triumph—as if not knowing whether to repel the venerable suppliant with contempt, or sooth him with some specious representation. But altogether there was something inhuman, unnatural, diabolic in the expression of the stranger's countenance. Darkly handsome, with proud haughty outlines, it had now a look so sinister and wicked that it made that stranger seem as if he possessed some mysterious and prescriptive right to trample on all ordinary feelings and spurn all common sympathies.

"My daughter, I say—my daughter! By the great God who hears me now, I adjure you to give me back my daughter!"—and the old man, as he gave utterance to these ejaculations with passionate vehemence, grasped the stranger's cloak with a tenacity which seemed to imply a resolve on his part that they should not separate until he had received satisfaction.

"Your daughter, old man?" at length spoke the stranger, his brows contracting, and his eyes fixing themselves with so sardonic a gaze upon the aged one's countenance, that there was now something more than wicked, but positively infernal, in the dark and terrible beauty of his features: "I know nothing of your daughter! Wherefore should you apply to me? But stay! I see that you are steeped in poverty, and circumstances must have altered with you greatly. Here—take this purse!"

Thus speaking, the stranger suddenly opened his cloak and extended a purse evidently well filled with yellow coin, to the old man.

"Monster—villain!" ejaculated the bereaved father, indignantly pushing back the proffered purse with one hand while he clung to the stranger's mantle with the other. "Having deprived me of my daughter, would you now seek to render me an accomplice in her shame? No, no!—never, never, by means of gold shall you purchase from my lips an assent to my child's disgrace. Give me then my daughter, I say! I will receive her back to my arms polluted though she may be——"

"Dotard!" interrupted the stranger, in his stern deep voice, which sounded as ominous as appeared the light that shone with a sort of mystic unhallowed luridness in his dark, dark eyes: "what know I of your daughter?"—then breaking away from the old man, he tossed the purse upon the ground, and began to move off slowly with scornful unconcern.

"No, no—we do not part thus!" ejaculated the bereaved father. "Ruined—mendicant—houseless—starving beggar that I am, there must nevertheless be law and justice for me!"—and in mingled rage and desperation, which gave vigour to his enfeebled frame and agility to his limbs, he seized upon the departing stranger again.

"Beware how you provoke me!" said the latter in a voice so sombre and with a look so diabolic that the old man felt an unknown terror strike into his heart, as if with the shuddering, withering conviction that he sought to contend against some one possessed of powers of no ordinary description.

A dizziness seized upon his brain—a faintness came over him—and the wretched old man sank back insensible upon the grass that was damp with the glittering dew.

With the first glimmer of that morning's dawn had Musidora opened her eyes in the chamber where she had passed the night; and all sense of fatigue arising from her journey having passed away, she at once rose from her couch. Annetta, who knew her young mistress's habits of rising at the peep of day, was in attendance; and the simple but elegant morning-toilet was soon performed.

Arrayed in a white robe, with the masses of her raven hair rolling in heavy waves upon her shoulders, and even flowing partially down her back, she looked grandly handsome and elegantly graceful, as she issued forth into the gardens to imbibe the freshness of the morning air. Threading the pleasure-grounds, in the silence and dreamy mistiness of that hour when nature begins to awaken to the life of a new-born day, and while industry is likewise arousing itself from slumber, while indolence still remains cradled in oblivion upon downy pillows,—at that hour when the rose begins to expand its modest beauty, and tulips and peonies to display their pompous gaud to the rising sun,—Musidora, even in the matchless perfection of her beauty, seemed to derive additional charms from the scene and the hour. There was something spirit-like in her presence amidst the flowers whilst the dew was still upon them, and with the slant beams of the sun setting forth her form with a dazzling brilliancy in the whiteness of her raiment and the marble fairness of her complexion, and making the raven darkness of her hair shine as with a glory.

Threading her way, we repeat, through the garden, Musidora presently reached the palisade forming the boundary at the end of the pleasure-grounds. But scarcely had she reached that spot, when her eyes, sweeping around to embrace the entire landscape that stretched in its emerald verdancy before her, suddenly settled upon the form of an aged man stretched upon the grass, and either dead or at least deprived of consciousness.

Without an instant's hesitation did Musidora climb over the palisade, by the assistance of a stunted tree—for the fence was scarcely breast high: and the next instant she was bending over the object of her compassionate interest. She at once saw that life was not extinct: she raised him partially up—but his head fell back—and though a low gasping moan indicated returning consciousness, yet was it evident that nature would require some restorative to stimulate its resuscitating energies.

Musidora cast a bewildered look around her. What was she to do? how was she to act? She could not leave the poor old man to lie any longer upon the damp grass: for his clothes—if indeed the rags that wrapped him deserved the denomination—were already saturated; and yet she could do nothing without assistance.

In this moment of uncertainty she heard footsteps approaching; and glancing in the direction whence they came, she beheld a handsomely-dressed man, of medium stature, somewhat stoutly but not ungracefully formed, and whose age might be three or four years under thirty. He had light hair, blue eyes, and but a small quantity of beard and whisker. There was something noble and dignified as well as courteous and high-bred in his appearance; and altogether his air was that of rank and importance.

"Lady," he exclaimed, quickening his pace, "what has occurred? and in what office of angel-ministering are you engaged?"

"From that enclosure," replied Musidora, indicating with a gesture the Earl of Grantham's grounds, "did I behold this poor old man stretched lifeless upon the ground. I fear that he must have been in this deplorable condition some while; for his clothing, already pitiable enough, is saturated with damp, and his limbs seem rigid."

"And you, lady—faithful to woman's angel-mission," said the courtly personage, regarding Musidora with a respectful admiration, but still with an earnestness which she could not help noticing, "have been seeking to recover him? In this good work I must have a hand. What shall we do?"

"Assist the venerable sufferer into the house," rejoined Musidora, glancing towards the villa. "It is the Earl of Grantham's——"

"Yes—I know my Lord of Grantham well," remarked the damsel's new acquaintance. "But see! the old man is recovering——Perhaps he may do so sufficiently to walk between us while we support him into the villa."

While thus speaking, the courtly personage assisted the old man to rise up; and as his senses slowly returned, he seemed bewildered on opening his eyes, to find himself the object of such solicitude on the part of so beauteous a lady and so noble-looking an individual. But they both addressed him in cheering and encouraging terms; and the bereaved father felt the kindness of their language and their manner sink down as an anodyne into his heart. Musidora herself was evidently somewhat prepossessed in favour of her unknown courtly companion: for from the depths of her dark eyes she threw upon him a look which seemed to say that she felt on the old man's behalf the kindness of this benevolent attention— especially as it was shown by one evidently moving in a sphere where contact with rags and beggary was by no means likely to be of common occurrence.

Between them did they support the bereaved father towards the house—leading him along the road skirting the pleasure-grounds, till they reached the front door, where two or three of Lord Grantham's menials at once made their appearance in answer to the ring at the bell. Profound was their astonishment on beholding the scene which thus met their eyes on opening that door: deeply respectful too was the salutation, or rather the low obeisance, which they made to Musidora's courtly companion, whose person was evidently known to them;—and her first suspicion, that he must be an individual of some very high rank, was thus immediately confirmed.

Perceiving that he was interested in the old man thus so strangely but benevolently conducted thither, the domestics at once bustled about to afford the invalid such attentions as he required; and leading the way into the nearest apartment they placed the aged sufferer upon a sort of ottoman or sofa—while one of them hastened to procure wine wherewith to resuscitate his strength.

In the midst of these proceedings the Earl and Countess of Grantham entered the apartment; and while the nobleman at once sank upon his knees in the presence of Musidora's courtly companion, Lady Grantham made a low obeisance indicative of the profoundest reverence.

"My Liege—my Lord—my Sovereign," said the Earl; "welcome to the dwelling of one of your Grace's humblest though most devoted servants!"

Then Musidora knew that it was the King whom accident had thus made her partner in the benevolent work of that memorable morning; and with a graceful dignity did she also express her reverence and her loyalty in a low curtsey.

"Rise, my lord," said Henry VIII, extending his hand to the Earl of Grantham. "Circumstances of an auspicious nature have brought me within your walls; and the same benign influence shall therefore make us friends. The past is forgotten. Rise, my lord, I say: it is your King who commands you!"

But ere the Earl availed himself of this permission, or rather before he obeyed the royal mandate, he took the monarch's hand and respectfully drew it to his lips: then rising from his knees, he hastened to place a chair for the King, remaining standing by his side with that attitude of profound deference which not only as a courtier but also as an astute politician he knew so well how to assume.

"You have to thank that young lady, who is as good as she is beautiful," said Henry, bending his looks upon Musidora, "for the incident which has produced the present reconciliation. But listen," continued the King, in a tone of authority: "it suits my purpose that this reconcilement shall remain secret for the present. Your lordship has potent enemies at Court—enemies to *you*, but friends of *mine*, and whom I choose not to alienate from me by any precipitate deed on my part. It shall be my study to change their feeling towards your lordship, and convert their animosity into a favourable sentiment. Then, this being done, the reconciliation which has ere now taken place in private shall be renewed in public; and again shall your lordship occupy some post of honour about the person of your Sovereign. Relative, then, to my presence here this morning, and every incident concerning it, the strictest secrecy must be maintained: and you will take care, my lord, that your menials babble not elsewhere respecting the occurrence."

"In every respect shall your Highness's commands be attended to," answered the Earl, an enthusiastic joy mingling with the expression of profound deference which he had assumed.

"And you, Countess of Grantham," said the King, turning towards the Earl's wife and proffering her his hand, "shall again shortly mingle amongst the titled dames who throng in the circle of England's Court."

The Countess, also, with joy beaming in her looks, reverently touched the monarch's fingers with her lips, and gave utterance to a few appropriate words of gratitude.

"And now tell me," resumed Henry, once more bending his eyes upon Musidora, who stood surveying the scene with that calmness and serenity of self-possession which seemed to constitute her nature—"tell me who is this angel of beauty and of benevolence whom I found engaged in so noble a work, and in which work I feel so proud to have become a sharer?"

"She of whom your Highness is pleased to speak so graciously," answered the Earl of Grantham, "is the daughter of one who for some years past has pined in wretchedness and affliction beneath the weight of your royal displeasure."

"Then, by my sceptre!" exclaimed the King, speaking with warmth, "that displeasure is at once appeased—nay more, changed into favour and friendship towards the father, whoever he may be, for the daughter's sake. Lady," he continued, now addressing himself direct to our heroine, "what maybe your sire's name?"

"Sir Lewis Sinclair, my liege," answered Musidora,—"a gentleman of an honourable family, and who earned his distinction of Knight-Banneret on the field of Bosworth, when fighting in the cause of your Grace's august father."

"The name is well known to me," said the King; "and if harshness has been done towards your parent, beautiful damsel, the blame must rather be laid to the door of my counsellors, than charged directly against myself. However, full reparation shall be made to Sir Lewis Sinclair for whatsoever he may have suffered. Was he not Ranger of the forest-lands in the Isle of Wight?"

"He was, my liege," responded Musidora, her splendid countenance now expressing a certain degree of interest which enhanced the brilliancy of her smile, though still leaving the alabaster purity of her complexion untinted by aught resembling a roseate flush.

"In all these matters shall amends be made," said the King: but he immediately added as a thought seemed to strike him, "In your correspondence with Sir Lewis Sinclair, young lady—for I can full well understand that your filial affection will prompt you to acquaint him at once with the withdrawal of his Sovereign's displeasure—you will charge him to keep the secret in his own breast until such time as I may give my permission for it to be openly proclaimed."

"Your royal commands shall be my law," said Musidora. "But permit me to add that a daughter's fervid gratitude is proffered to your Highness for all your generous assurances:"—and as Musidora thus spoke, the animation so coldly brilliant, and resembling the unsullied purity of moon-light upon the glacial radiance of her beauty, was enhanced still more.

"I claim no thanks," rejoined the King, taking her hand in his own and pressing it warmly: then turning towards the old man, who was lying a mute but wondering observer of all that had just taken place, the monarch said, "Who are you? and how came you reduced to this lamentable posi-tion?—for there is something in your looks which speaks eloquently and unmistakably of better days."

"Ah! great King," replied the old man, tears trickling down his fur-rowed cheeks, "I have indeed suffered deeply, deeply! But the kindness— the benevolence, which I have now experienced from this angel-lady here, and from your gracious Highness——"

The old man stopped short, ineffable emotions choking further utter-ance; and he would have thrown himself from the sofa at the feet of the King, had not the monarch himself bade him remain where he was, nor strain his exhausted strength by over-exertion.

"His Grace inquires who you are, and how you became thus reduced in the world," said Musidora, addressing the old man in the most soothing tones of her silver voice.

"I once was prosperous and rich," replied the aged sufferer, when his feelings were somewhat composed: "and I was happy too in the possession of a daughter whose beauty was such as only to be outshone by your's, young lady—but whose goodness——alas! that I, her loving father, should have to say so—was not equal to her beauty! She yielded to the honied words of a villain, and abandoned me in my old age. Affliction came not alone—for O! misfortune is wonderfully prolific: and no sooner had this first calamity stricken me, when a thousand others entered my house like a desolating army, sweeping away wealth, possessions—all—all—even to the very bed from under me! Oh! sad, sad indeed is my fate! But heaven be thanked, it is not I who have brought dishonour on a once respected name:—and sadder, sadder still, I fear me, is the fate of my lost daughter— the beguiled and guilty Clara Manners!" With a movement resembling a sudden start—but so quick and transitory as to be scarcely perceptible, even if it occurred at all—did Musidora fling a strange inexplicable look from the lustrous depths of her unfathomable eyes upon the countenance of the old man: and then, taking his hand, she said in a more subdued tone than was her wont, "You shall not speak of your sufferings now. Another time—when your strength is restored—you shall unburden your heart to the ears of friendly sympathizers."

"Yes—another time," said the King, who was earnestly watching Musidora's countenance while she spoke; as if he had perceived or fancied he had perceived that sudden but evanescent display of emotion on her part. "I must bid you all farewell now: but this evening, at nine o'clock, I shall come, unattended and alone—in the strictest privacy—to hear more of this poor old man's history and see what can be done to serve him."

Having thus spoken, the King took a hurried leave of the Granthams and Musidora, and quitted the house.

Our heroine remained standing near the sofa on which the aged sufferer lay—gazing upon him with a look as much expressive of mournful compassion as any look of her's could ever express aught bordering upon a definite sentiment: while the Earl and Countess, the moment the King's back was turned, exchanged glances of joyous triumph and satisfaction.

CHAPTER VI.

THE SUPPER.

PUNCTUAL to the appointment which he himself had made for nine o'clock in the evening, King Henry VIII arrived, unattended and alone, at Grantham Villa. He was enveloped in a cloak, and evidently was studious to shroud his visit with as much secrecy as possible.

Great preparations had nevertheless been made for his reception. The principal saloon was a blaze of light; and the supper-table was resplendent with plate, glass, and porcelain. The Earl and Countess of Grantham were apparelled in the most elegant manner; and if there were any drawback to their joy and exultation at the royal visit, it was in the circumstance that Musidora had not decorated herself either with the diamonds or pearls that had been presented to her on the previous evening. Any sentiment however of annoyance which the noble couple experienced on this account, was rather one of mortification to perceive that their splendid gifts should have been thus slighted, than of disappointment at the effect of Musidora's charms on the present occasion. Indeed, as they gazed upon her while, with a serene but cold dignity, she saluted the monarch on his entrance, the Earl and Countess could not help feeling that her's was indeed a loveliness which needed no brilliancy of ornament to enhance it.

She wore a dress of white brocaded satin, the body of which fitted close to her well developed shape, while the ample skirt seemed to flow around her from the waist downwards in heavy waves of silver. The raven masses of her hair hung in cloud-like redundancy upon the beautifully sloping shoulders, and down the back even to the slender waist. In brilliant contrast with that thick natural veil thus floating behind her, shone the dazzling purity of her complexion, with no insipid whiteness, but in all the polish and animation of glowing life itself. Yes—glowing, but not with a blush—no, nor even with roseate tint,—but glowing as that marble statue might have been supposed to glow, when warming with Pygmalion's ardent gaze, it gradually expanded into being.

For all ornament, a single white rose—placed upon the shining masses of Musidora's hair—indeed appeared the most appropriate, and of the only kind that was at all necessary. For the natural gloss which rested like a glory upon that dark hair outshone the effect which even a queenly crown might have produced: nor could the richest gems have shed around her a brighter halo than that with which she was invested by the lustre of her own transcending beauty.

The King had seen her in the morning in the simple robe of white which she had worn: he beheld her now clad in white again—but of a rich and costly material. And yet, if in the morning her toilet was altogether plain and simple, it was now characterized by a not less tasteful blending of chaste elegance and virginal splendour. That he was struck by the brilliancy of her appearance, which dazzled with a beauty of whose power she herself seemed altogether unconscious, was evident from the gaze of respectful admiration that he fixed upon her. It was the homage which an impassioned nature seemed irresistibly led to pay to such transcending charms, and which though manifested with mingled earnestness and enthusiasm, was still so attempered by delicate courtesy and profound respect, that it was impossible for any woman to take offence at such a tribute offered to her beauty.

The Earl and Countess exchanged vivid glances, significant with satisfaction, at the effect which Musidora's appearance produced upon the susceptible heart of the King; and they no longer regretted that she had passed over the diamonds and the pearls in the details of her evening toilet. On the contrary, they now felt convinced that her's was a style of beauty of so superior an order and also invested with a charm so peculiarly its own, as to be entirely independent of all the appliances to which even the most lovely women are accustomed to resort in order to assist the effect of nature with that of art.

The table was laid for four: and soon after the King's arrival the repast was served up. Handing Musidora to a seat at the board, the monarch as a matter of course placed himself next her, and at once made her the object of the most marked, continuous, yet delicate attentions. These she accepted with the mingled dignity and grace which were alike the characteristics of her beauty and her manners. She did not however seem flattered by his attentions; nor from the mien and bearing could it be discovered that she even noticed that they were in any way more pointed or more significant than those which every lady expects, and is indeed accustomed to receive, from any well-bred gentleman whom chance may render her companion at table. Her noble relatives began to be at a loss to comprehend her. That the King was already smitten with her beauty, they were well convinced. Indeed, this much they had seen in the morning; and the admiration which now shone forth in every look which he flung upon Musidora confirmed that opinion beyond the possibility of mistake. But was she unconscious of this impression which she had made upon him?—or if not unconscious, was she indifferent to the effect thus produced by the power of her charms?—or again, if not indifferent, was it that she was playing a part with admirable tact and the most exquisite finesse? Such were the questions which both the Earl and Countess asked themselves as they sat at table, but to which they could not find any positive solution. Musidora's manner was unexceptionably ladylike, calmly dignified, and courteously graceful: but neither by look or word had she as yet shown either that she felt flattered by Henry's attentions, or that the complimentary language which he addressed to her afforded her the slightest pleasure. She smiled—she conversed with gaiety—she sustained her part in the conversation, and did all that a well-bred lady ought to have done to make the time pass agreeably for the royal guest of her relatives: but over all she did, or said, or looked, there was still that cold but brilliant polish as if everything connected with her shone but in the grand brightness of a glacier!

"And so," observed the King, when the more substantial portion of the repast was removed, and a choice dessert accompanied with a variety of exquisite wines was placed upon the table, "and so, fair lady, you have been but a few hours as it were in this neighbourhood—or I might say, within the atmosphere of the Court?"

"As I informed your Grace ere now," answered Musidora, "I arrived here only last evening."

"But once arrived, it is your intent," he continued, "to remain for some time in a neighbourhood which, appearing to me so much brighter by your presence, would become proportionately darkened by your absence?"

"Your Grace is pleased thus to address me in the complimentary language of the day," answered Musidora, as if now for the first time noticing his flatteries.

"No—by, heaven!" exclaimed Henry, "I was perfectly serious in what I said:"—and somewhat warmed by the wine which he drunk, he was emboldened to fix upon Musidora a meaning look but in which however there was nothing disrespectful.

"Your Highness," she observed, "has the peculiar privilege, by virtue of your sovereign rank, of giving utterance to whatsoever may suit your royal whim and pleasure at the moment:"—and if it were not precisely in a tone of rebuke that Musidora thus spoke, it was nevertheless with a maiden dignity which had all the effect of a remonstrance when coming from one whose appearance was so queen-like and whose nature seemed to be so incomparably above the reach of all commonplace flatteries.

"Whatever my privileges as a Sovereign may be," rejoined Henry, with a slight bow, as if to show that he understood the rebuke but nevertheless would not take offence at it, "I invariably lay them aside when in the presence of those rare specimens of the fair sex whom nature evidently intended to be the queens of the earth: for who indeed can be the world's virtual rulers save those who govern proud man by the magic influence they exercise over his heart?"

"Your Grace acts only in accordance with the true principle of chivalry," said Musidora, not for a moment appearing to take the King's compliment exclusively unto herself, "in setting an example of courtly attention and magnanimous deference, so far as prudence may warrant, to the sympathies of the weaker sex."

There was a slight pause, of which the Earl of Grantham now availed himself to offer a remark in answer to a question which the King had ere now put to Musidora.

"Your Grace," said the nobleman, in his bland courtier-like tones, "addressed my fair young relative a short while back concerning the probable length of her sojourn beneath my roof. I can take it upon myself to respond on her account, that she is not shackled by any paternal injunction on that head; and it will most assuredly be the constant study of the Countess and myself to——"

"To make the time pass as agreeably to her as possible," added her ladyship, finishing her husband's sentence for him.

"So that she may prolong the visit which has commenced in such an auspicious manner for us," continued the Earl: "I mean *auspicious*, my liege, inasmuch as it has been the means of restoring us to the light of our Sovereign's royal favour."

"And as Musidora is now visiting the neighbourhood of the metropolis for the first time," observed the Countess, again taking up the thread of her husband's remarks, "she is anxious to inspect all that is worth seeing in your Highness's fair capital. Moreover she shall have an opportunity of beholding such gaieties and pastimes as are in vogue amongst the aristocracy and fashion; and as all this cannot be accomplished in a few days—scarcely in a few weeks—it is more than probable that our sweet young relative's visit will extend to some months."

"So much depends," observed Musidora, in a gently corrective tone, "upon the way in which my beloved father supports my absence—also upon the tidings I receive concerning his health: for were I to hear any unfavourable account, I should at once speed back with the least possible delay to my native home."

"I thank you most sincerely for this speech, fair damsel," said the King: "because you have now made me comprehend upon what conditions your visit to your noble relatives here may be prolonged. To-morrow, my lord," he added, turning towards the Earl of Grantham, "you and I will have some private discourse together respecting the best mode of ensuring Sir Lewis Sinclair's comfort, prosperity, and happiness. As for the worthy knight's health," continued the monarch, now again reverting his looks upon Musidora, "if you think that it is at all precarious, or that it would be benefited by the constant attention of some eminent physician, I will in the course of the coming week send a most skilful doctor to take up his abode at Sinclair House—so that not merely may his professional knowledge be rendered available for the knight's behoof, but his companionship also prove agreeable."

"Your Grace," said Musidora, in a voice that was somewhat tinged with seriousness, while at the same time she bent upon him an earnest searching look from the depths of her superb dark eyes,—"has already conferred so many favours upon me during the few hours that I have had the honour of becoming known to your Highness—I mean since first we met this morning—that I am utterly unable to find adequate terms wherein to express my gratitude. Your Highness has restored unto your royal favour not only my relatives here, but likewise my father, who is absent: you have also promised, sire, to do many things for them all—and within the last few minutes your Grace has furthermore manifested a generous spirit towards my father. Pardon me, great King, if I must observe that I fear to accept, even on my sire's account, too much at your hands—because of the utter impossibility of ever repaying the smallest part of this immense obligation. Indeed, your Highness *must* know that I have naught but words wherewith to express my thanks."

As Musidora thus spoke—the silver fluency of her voice being slightly marked by solemnity of tone and accompanied with a perceptible seriousness of look—the King gazed upon her with an air of the deepest interest, mingled with the most respectful admiration. The Earl and Countess felt annoyed; for they feared that Musidora, by this address, would throw a damp upon the ardour of the monarch, and make him look upon her either as a cold passionless prude, or else as a wily tactician somewhat overacting her part. Yet, as she proceeded in her speech, and the old courtier and his wife beheld nature's own diadem of candour seated upon her brow, and the most genuine sincerity characterizing—or at least appearing to characterize—her looks, her words, her mien—in fine, breathing as it were through her entire being—they scarcely knew what to think: and when she had ceased speaking their eyes settled with misgiving and suspense upon the King, to see how he would take the damsel's proceeding. For in terms as plain as so delicately-worded a speech could possibly be, it seemed as if Musidora meant him to understand that if he had any ulterior object in heaping favours upon the heads of her relatives that object would *not* be gained.

"I have listened to you fair lady," said the King, assuming a manner as gaily courteous as it seemed frank and open-hearted, "with the utmost attention—not so much because I recognized any need on your part to deliver yourself of that speech, but because I could sit in silence for ever to drink in the music of your voice and listen to that language which sounds like the silver flow of a stream chastely pellucid and coldly crystal! As for obligation, Musidora," added the King, with a gracious smile, "who ever heard of a Sovereign conferring marks of his pleasure upon his subjects and expecting aught in return saving their allegiance and good faith? But observe!—this last allusion of mine is meant for your father and your noble relatives here. I spoke not of you, fair damsel, as my subject—because I have already this evening told you that it is chivalrous and proper for man to acknowledge woman's empire—and faithful to my own precept, I profess my allegiance to *you!*"

"Your Grace is in every way determined that I shall remain indebted to your courteous gallantry as well as your royal favour:"—and again did Musidora's smile and manner seem to indicate that she only regarded the monarch's words as the passing compliment of the moment, to which neither her dignity nor her modesty—no, nor yet her intelligence, would for an instant permit her to attach any other meaning.

"Since you are determined," resumed the King, with a gay laugh, "to regard everything I propose in the light of a favour, perhaps I ought not to make the suggestion which I am about to offer. And yet on the other hand, it were most discourteous not to do so. Indeed, I was about to observe, beautiful Musidora, that since your sojourn with your noble relatives will allow of ample time for you to visit all places that are worth seeing within a reasonable circuit, I may perhaps be allowed to furnish you with the proper passports to obtain admission to my royal palaces of the Tower, St. James, and Windsor. The Earl and Countess will escort you thither; and in each and all will a lady of your good taste and fine intelligence behold much to excite admiration and interest."

"Again do I thank your Grace for this proffered kindness," said Musidora, "and which I gratefully accept. But pardon me if I remind your Highness that you this morning testified some degree of interest on behalf of that poor old man——"

"Aye!" ejaculated the King, with a slight appearance of impatience in his manner—as if he would have much rather continued discoursing with Musidora than have allowed aught to interrupt the present scene: but instantaneously subduing any such feeling of vexation, if such it were that he indeed felt, he said, "And how fares the old man?"

"Seeing how profoundly he had won your Grace's sympathy," the Earl of Grantham now hastened to observe, with his courtier-like blandness of tone and manner, "I ordered that he should be treated with all possible attention. Accordingly he has been comfortably lodged—suitable raiment has been provided for his use—and I believe that he is now in a more tranquil, if not a happier frame of mind, than he has been for a long time past. Because it is evident that he has suffered much——"

"Well," interrupted the King, turning somewhat abruptly towards Musidora,—"and has he yet told you the tale of his sufferings?"

"Ere taking your departure this morning, sire," returned Musidora, "you intimated your royal pleasure to hear this evening that tale from the lips of the poor old man. Whatever curiosity, then, I have experienced on the subject, I have controlled until now—not choosing to torture the venerable sufferer too much, nor allow his heart's wounds to be opened too often, by a needless repetition of his history. Now therefore, if your Grace be agreeable, the old man can be introduced; and we will hear the narrative of his misfortunes?"

"Be it so," said the King.

Thereupon the Earl of Grantham rang a silver hand-bell which stood close by him: and on a lacquey answering the summons, he desired that old Master Manners—for so was the bereaved father called—might be introduced to the saloon. This command was speedily obeyed: and in a few minutes the venerable man, leaning upon his stick, made his appearance. On perceiving the King he sank down upon his knees and poured forth his gratitude for the generous kindness shown him in the morning: but Henry hastily compelled him to rise and bade him sit down, while Musidora handed him a cup of wine.

Tears trickled down the furrowed cheeks of old Manners as he found himself the object of so many and such delicate attentions: but having quaffed the generous wine, he felt cheered; and in compliance with the request now made him, he proceeded to unfold the narrative of his afflictions in the following terms.

CHAPTER VII.

THE HISTORY OF CLARA MANNERS.

"UNTIL within the last few years there was not in all London a mercantile warehouse enjoying a higher repute than that which was known by the sign of the *Golden Fleece* suspended over the door. My father, who was for many, many years Alderman of the ward of Cheap, and who was thrice Lord Mayor of London, founded that establishment; and when he died he left it to me, his only son. I was so wedded to habits of business that I thought but little of the serene comforts and tranquil pleasures of domestic life; and it was not indeed till verging towards the age of forty that I began seriously to think of marriage. Then, scarcely had I formed the wish to find a suitable companion to become the sharer of my fortune and the partaker of my prosperity, when accident threw me in the way of the beautiful widow of a brave officer who had fallen when gloriously fighting the battles of his country. She was poor, but amiable and virtuous as she was beautiful. After a short courtship we were married: and a proud as well as a happy day was it for me when I bore my bride home. Our happiness continued without alloy, while my commercial prosperity increased. I had ships of my own trading in the Levant; and my warehouse was stored with all the choicest produce of the East. Nobles and titled dames were wont to visit my establishment to inspect the brilliant assortment of precious stones, shawls, silks, brocades, and costly stuffs which were amongst the numerous imports that formed the basis of my transactions. Some of those ladies had been previously acquainted with my wife, and their friendship was not discontinued because she had married a trader—for they all knew that I was one of those rich merchants whose spirit of enterprise conferred immense benefits upon the country. We were therefore caressed and courted by many of the nobility; and we not only visited at their mansions, but also received them at our own house in return.

"Three years after our marriage, our happiness was augmented by the birth of a daughter, on whom the name of Clara was bestowed. In this being was centred all the fondest parental love, alike on my part and on that of my wife. Clara grew up beautiful and affectionate: we had no other children,—and I need scarcely say how indescribably dear she was to us. My wife, who was a clever and elegant as well as beautiful woman, took a delight in training the mind of her daughter; and thus at the age of fifteen, when her education was finished, Clara was as intelligent, accomplished, and well-bred as any damsel belonging to even the highest grades of soci-

ety. Thus was it that from her mother she not only inherited all the beauties of person and acquired all the graces of mind, but likewise derived the
elegancies of manner; and any stranger who had seen my beloved Clara,
would have fancied that she was the daughter of some titled personage
instead of a City merchant.

"But it was at this very period of which I am speaking, and when just
about to enter as it were upon life, that Clara lost that excellent and affectionate mother who had reared her so carefully and so tenderly. Yes—my
wife was snatched away from me by an epidemic malady; and so great was
my grief that had it not been necessary to live for the sake of my child, I do
not think that I could have borne up against the loss. Clara felt the shock as
acutely as myself: for though so young, yet she had alike intelligence and
feeling enough to be aware that she had lost her dearest and best friend.
Yes—for no matter how earnest and how deep may be a father's love for
his daughter—no matter how proudly he may regard her, how fondly he
may cherish her—it is after all the mother who is the best calculated to
guide her on as she enters upon the great pathways of life, and point out a
myriad dangers which the more hasty and superficial glance of the father
cannot descry, or with which his different experience renders him altogether unacquainted.

"We mingled our tears together; and as time passed on, the keen
sense of our affliction was mitigated and its poignancy mellowed down,
as is ever the case even where the lost one is most deeply valued. Two
years elapsed; and at the end of that interval I considered it expedient to
introduce my daughter into society. She at once became the admiration of
all who formed her acquaintance; and in a very short space she had several
suitors for her hand. But eighteen months and upwards passed away, without any indication being afforded that her affections were engaged. We
visited not only the circles of our civic friends, but likewise the mansions
of the nobility; and although Clara had several eligible proposals made to
her by suitors in both spheres, yet did her heart remain untouched, and
she assured me that she had determined never to bestow her hand where
her affections were not also engaged. I applauded her resolve—admired
her prudence—and was indeed so well convinced that any attachment she
might sooner or later form, would be in every way worthy of her good
sense, her virtue, and her position, that I bade her consider her matrimonial destiny to be entirely in her own hands; as any choice she might make
would be certain to meet my approval.

"Shortly after this conversation, and when Clara was within a few
months of nineteen, we received an invitation to an autumnal festival giv-
en in the spacious pleasure-grounds of Lady Wilbraham, who had been

intimate with my wife. Never shall I forget the evening! Not that I thought at the time it was destined to become so memorable as to have even its slightest incidents impressed upon my brain as if seared there with red-hot iron: but the circumstances to which it led has thus caused all its minutest details to be so indelibly written on my mind. I recollect, then, that as the sun was setting behind the trees, at the close of a splendid September day, I entered the immense garden where the festival was to take place, with Clara leaning on my arm. A brilliant company had already arrived; and those walks, avenues, arbours, and recesses were gloriously lighted with rows of lamps hanging in festoons; and being of different colours, they resembled wreaths of flowers shining with a living light. Scarcely had we arrived when, as usual, I noticed that Clara at once became the object of general admiration; and I experienced all the father's pride at the homage which was thus paid to my beautiful daughter. Presently, however, there was a moment when we were left alone together. I remember well how it occurred: it was because some masque or pageant was suddenly introduced upon a stage, and all the guests at once sped in that direction. Clara and I remained near a fountain formed by the water playing through the mouths of wild animals beautifully sculptured. By the aid of the myriad lamps suspended in all directions, the scene was as light as day. On a sort of trellis-work over the basin some beautiful roses were twining; and Clara, as she surveyed the fount, directed my attention to the charming flowers. That very moment a figure swept by us—stepped into the basin—then climbed up on the marble effigies with as much graceful ease as lightness—gathered the most delicious flower;—and leaping back again, presented it to Clara.

"All this was the work of a few moments, and indeed took place with a startling rapidity that produced an amazement from which my daughter had not recovered when the stranger with the rose in one hand and his plumed cap in the other, was gracefully saluting her. A glance was sufficient to show that he was a tall, slender, symmetrically-made cavalier—elegantly dressed—and perhaps of the most perfect masculine beauty that ever distinguished the human countenance. He was dark; and his hair was black as night. His eyes shone like lustrous jet—and his look though slightly tinged with hauteur, seemed full of a chivalrous generosity. Indeed he appeared just the cavalier who was likely to perform a deed of such gallant courtesy as the one which he had that moment accomplished, for be it observed that he had plunged knee-deep in the water in order to reach the overhanging flower. Clara expressed her thanks in a becoming manner as she accepted the rose; and our new acquaintance walked by her side as we slowly proceeded through the garden.

"In the course of conversation he gave us to understand that he was Lord Danvers, the only surviving scion of a family which had once been the most considerable in the country, and was descended from one of the Norman Barons who had accompanied William the Conqueror on his invasion. It appeared that he had been much abroad: he had travelled in many foreign lands—and his mind being stored with all he had seen or heard, his conversation was not merely agreeable and instructive, but also of the most fascinating description. Indeed such was the impression which he made alike upon Clara and myself, that hours slipped by as we walked in the brilliantly lighted avenues listening to the discourse of Lionel Danvers. Yes—*hours* thus passed: for it was scarcely nine o'clock on that memorable evening when the incident at the fountain made us acquainted; and when midnight was proclaimed by the cry of the watchman in the road adjoining the gardens, Clara and I were still walking with Danvers—still drinking in his lively descriptions, pathetic tales, or brilliant anecdotes connected with his foreign travel. Those three hours had glided away as if they had scarcely been more than a few minutes. Sometimes sitting in the arbours—sometimes walking to and fro—had we thus traversed a space of three hours with an inconceivable rapidity.

"The splendid saloons of the hostess were thrown open for supper; and thither did we repair. Danvers now offered my daughter his arm; and I, as a matter of course, surrendered her to his temporary care, withdrawing to another part of the room according to the prescribed custom which forbids a father to monopolize his daughter when in society. Infinitely pleased with my new acquaintance, I accosted Lady Wilbraham, to ascertain from her something more concerning him.—'Is he not a splendid young man?' she immediately exclaimed; and being an elderly lady she might be allowed to pass her opinion upon him. 'I do not know,' she continued, 'that ever I beheld an Englishman of such perfect masculine beauty before. He has the true Norman type of features, with the Saxon slenderness and symmetry. The elegance of his manner is that of a Spanish cavalier, like whom indeed he wears that short cloak of his so gracefully over his left shoulder. Indeed, there is not a single gallant here to-night who wears his apparel with an equal gracefulness and ease. Then, would you not think that all the impassioned soul of the Italian glowed in those fine dark eyes of his? And again, are not Grecian thoughts seated upon his noble brow—thoughts fervid with classic fire, and irresistibly reminding one of poetry, and sculpture, and all the arts belonging to that world-renowned clime?'

"I observed in answer to this eulogy, that I really did not think it was too highly drawn; and I declared how fascinated both myself and Clara had been with his conversation for the last three hours. Thereupon my noble hostess, drawing me still farther apart from the gay company, said in a more subdued voice and also with a sudden mysteriousness of manner, 'He belongs to a strange family; or rather, as I believe, he is the last scion of his race.'—I here observed that Lord Danvers had just now told me as much.—'I thought so,' continued Lady Wilbraham. 'From all I have learnt, it is more than a century and a half since the family ceased to reside habitually in this country. The Lord Danvers of that day (his Christian name, I have heard, was Walter) went abroad and seldom, if ever, came back again. His descendants have followed his example, living almost entirely upon the Continent—I do not exactly know where—but sometimes, though seldom, revisiting England. This present Lord Danvers,' and she glanced towards the handsome young nobleman who was now seated next to Clara at the supper-table, 'seems to be true to the family type, fulfilling the traditions of his ancestors and living habitually abroad.'

" 'But the family estates, castles, and mansions?' said I: 'for I suppose that these Danvers must have possessed, even if they do not still hold, lands and dwellings in this country?'—'Yes,' continued Lady Wilbraham, in farther explanation, 'I believe that Lord Danvers has no less than three mansions in different parts of the kingdom, with estates belonging to each. Indeed, so far as I have ever heard anything concerning this family, I believe that since Lord Walter Danvers removed altogether from England, a hundred and fifty or sixty years ago, the holders of the title have only returned into this country at different times for the mere purpose of visiting their estates and receiving the revenues from the agent in Lombard Street, to whom all moneys are paid by the stewards managing the property.'—I then asked where these castles and estates were situated: for I know not how it was, but I already felt a deep interest in Lionel Danvers, and perhaps was struck with a presentiment that the acquaintance just formed between him and my daughter would ripen into a more tender feeling.—'I do not exactly know where his estates are situated,' returned Lady Wilbraham. 'But stop! now that I bethink me, I recollect he has a castle situated in the Isle of Wight—at that point where certain pieces of isolated rock stand out into the sea and are known by the name of the Needles. But where his other ancestral mansions are, I cannot recollect at this moment—even indeed if I ever knew. However, that he is immensely rich, I am certain—and so generous too! When I first became acquainted with him—that was about three or four years ago, when he was quite a youth, and he had just come over to this country, as he told me, to take possession of his estates in consequence of his father's death—he insisted upon making me the almoner of his charity to the poor of this neighbourhood; and I forget how much gold he placed in my hands—but a very large sum.'—'And how came your ladyship to be acquainted with him?' I asked, impelled I know not by what irresistible sentiment of curiosity to put these questions.—'I was acquainted with his father,' was the response; 'and therefore, of course, when the son presented himself at my house, I gave him a cordial welcome. Indeed, who could do otherwise towards a young nobleman, so elegant and so accomplished? Ah! Master Manners,' she added, 'it will be a happy day for you should he become captivated by your Clara and propose to make her Lady Danvers!'—'And yet your lady-ship says that there is something mysterious connected with his family?' I observed: 'and for my part, I detest everything savouring of mystery.'

"To this observation Lady Wilbraham replied in the following man-ner:—'I did not tell you that there was anything mysterious connected with him; or at all events I did not mean you to receive that impression. What I *did* intend you to understand, was that some century and a half, or perhaps two centuries ago, there was some mysterious occurrence, I know not what, that induced Lord Walter Danvers, this young man's far back ancestor, to leave England and remove to the Continent, where he fixed his abode. All his successors have followed his example in abjuring his country—and I suppose the present Lord Danvers yonder will do the same. But habit runs in families; and it is natural we should prefer the clime wherein we are brought up. So it has doubtless been with all the de-scendants of Lord Walter Danvers: and we may thence conclude that Lord Lionel, now seated by your daughter's side, has inherited the traditionary taste of his family.'

"Having thus spoken, Lady Wilbraham quitted me to attend to some of her guests in another part of the room; and I joined a group of noble-men and gentlemen with whom I was acquainted. Presently I felt a gentle tap on the shoulder, and turning round beheld my daughter Clara leaning on Lord Danvers' arm. She had come to remind me that it was growing very late: and I accordingly intimated my readiness to conduct her home. Lord Danvers insisted upon accompanying us; and the horses being or-dered, we took leave of our kind hostess, mounted our steeds, and rode away. His lordship saw us safe to our own door, and requested permission to call upon some future occasion. This was of course granted; and he took his departure.

"I need not dwell at any length upon this part of my narrative. You are all prepared to hear that Lionel Danvers became the lover of my daughter; and to him were her most enthusiastic affections given. She loved him as perhaps never woman loved before—and methought that he idolized her in return. Nor can I wonder for a moment that Clara should thus have loved him: for it is impossible to conceive a being of the male sex more fitted by nature to win and secure the ardent attachment of a young, beautiful, confiding, and unsuspicious girl. I have already spoken of his great personal beauty; and in that respect I must repeat that he was the most faultless—I will even say the most *perfect* specimen of the male creation. Had a sculptor taken him as a model, the statue chiselled therefrom would have represented the finest Apollo that human genius ever conceived as the personification of a god-like beauty. And yet there were times when it struck me for a moment—but only for a moment on each occasion—that a strange and mystic light flashed from his eyes, and that his lips curled with an expression which did me harm to observe, yet leaving me unable to define what the exact impression was that it left upon my mind. Besides, those instants when it thus struck me that I beheld the wild gleaming of the eye and the sinister curling of the lip were so transitory, so evanescent—and his countenance so immediately recovered its wonted expression of frank urbanity and generous open-heartedness again—that I felt as it were bewildered, and thought it must have been mere fancy on my part. Then I would go back to my counting-house and plunge deep into business, in order to escape from the impression so disagreeably made upon me. But it would sometimes haunt me for hours; and I would see those eyes before me flashing dread lightnings, and that lip wreathing with the mocking scorn of a fiend—so that to such a morbid state did my fancy grow that I would conjure up the handsome countenance of the young nobleman, dwell upon it in my solitude, and thus contemplate it till my disordered brain gave it the aspect of that fearful beauty which we may suppose to be characteristic of a fallen angel.

"Oh! how I used to reason with myself against these dreadful visions: but I could not always master them. Though strong was my mind, and I may say sterling my common sense—though business-habits too had made me essentially a practical man and not a dreamer, a reasoner and not a visionary—yet did I find that the impression thus made upon me by Danvers' look and smile, grew more powerful than myself. It haunted me like a remorse—it followed me like a presentiment of evil. As time wore on, and I beheld my daughter becoming, if possible, each day more and more infatuated with Danvers, I grew alarmed, and resolved to make farther inquiries concerning him. I called upon several persons of rank whom he had named as his acquaintances; and everything I heard from their lips was satisfactory beyond a possibility of doubt. He was represented as immensely rich—as a young nobleman of unimpeachable honour—and in every way calculated to constitute a most eligible, indeed desirable alliance for my daughter, then felt angry—nay more, deeply indignant with myself for having yielded, as I thought, to such ridiculous misgivings. But

I was rejoiced to reflect that even when most cruelly taunted thereby, I had always studiously and successfully concealed the circumstance from my daughter. Moreover, when, in brighter moods and in hours of re-established confidence, I surveyed that noble-looking elegant young man, endowed with every superb quality alike of person and of mind—when I examined the expression of his countenance with the most earnest attention and beheld nothing but lofty frankness and an elevated chivalry breathing forth from every lineament—I not merely cursed what I deemed my folly in giving way to monomaniac notions, but even felt that I was mean and despicable to a degree to offer that splendid young noble even the tacit insult of groundless suspicion!

"Thus was it that perhaps for days I would surmount my misgivings and behold the progress of my daughter's love with unfeigned joy. But all in a moment—it might be at the very instant that my spirits were most elevated, my contentment most complete, my satisfaction most decisive—the wild unearthly light would flash forth from Danvers' eyes, and that mocking wicked smile of utter sardonism would curl his haughty lip! Then as I gazed again, it was all gone—the eyes shining with a natural lustre, the lip wearing a smile of honest frankness and devoted love, as he turned his looks upon Clara. I would pass my hands before my face as if to dispel a mist gathering there—or I would sweep that hand rapidly athwart my eyes to banish the film which I fancied must have made me see as if through a glass darkly: then would I gaze upon Danvers, saying to myself, 'No, it is impossible! That countenance, so noble in its perfect beauty, could not serve as a means to express a diabolic mockery, or reflect in its frank and candid lineaments the malice-mirth of a fiend!'

"Still, however, in these suspicious moods, did I seek additional evidence to satisfy myself that Danvers was all he represented himself to be. I even visited the clerks at the House of Lords, to inquire whether there were such a peerage, and if so, who was its present possessor. Again I found that all was correct. There was not only such a peerage; but it was now held by Lionel Danvers, who had within the last two or three years produced the necessary certificates not only of his father's death, but also to prove his own identity as the legitimate claimant of the said peerage. I then asked for a personal description of this Lionel Danvers, and found that it was the same as that of my daughter's suitor. Again did I return home bewildered—indeed almost dismayed—by the unaccountable presentiment which filled my mind. But another interval of confidence and satisfaction ensued, till in some flitting, transitory moment the sinister phenomenon occurred again—the unearthly flashing of the eye and the diabolic curling of the lip! My suspicions all blazing up again, like combustibles exploding furiously in my mind, I sought an opportunity to question him relative to his castles and estates. This I did in the most delicate manner possible, and not as if I had really any doubts or misgivings hovering in my mind. Nor did he appear to think that I touched upon the subject from any other motive than a passing curiosity; and with all that frankness of manner which was wont to characterize him, he said, 'I possess a mansion with a considerable estate attached thereto, in the county of Essex, at no great distance from the ancient town of Chelmsford. I have another mansion—or I might almost denominate it a castle—with a much larger estate than the Essex domain, in Cumberland. But the ancestral castle—the feudal dwelling-place of mine ancestors—is that which towers aloft upon the rocky eminences forming the south-western point of the Isle of Wight. This ancient fortalice has long, long been untenanted, and is gradually yielding to the ravages of time: for however great might have been its advantages as a place of residence for powerful feudal chiefs in the troublous ages which have passed, it is by no means suited for a family-dwelling at this period of refinement and civilization. But my mansions in Essex and in Cumberland are occupied by domestics who maintain those establishments in fitting order and in constant readiness to receive their owner or his friends. As for the revenues arising from my estates,' added Lord Danvers, in a careless manner, 'the venerable Master Landini, the eminent goldsmith of Lombard Street,[2] could give you a pretty favourable account on *that* head.'

"There the conversation ended; and when I was again alone I bitterly, bitterly reproached myself for having even ventured to question the young nobleman relative to his estates. For all suspicion was again banished from my mind; and when I contrasted the noble frankness with which he had at once given me the explanations I sought, with the doubting humour which had made me thus seek them, I could not help thinking that there was something mean, contemptible, and paltry in my conduct. I even feared he might fancy that I was naught but an abject, selfish money-maker, having no ideas more lofty than those connected with lucre; and, in a word, that I had been questioning him for the sake of discovering the amount of riches which he possessed and of which my daughter was to become the sharer. I therefore did indeed feel more little, more abject, in my own estimation than I can well describe; and I vowed that never, never again would I permit suspicions so injurious to an honourable man to obtain an entry into my mind.

"But it was easy to make such resolves, and far more difficult to adhere to them: for who can undertake to exercise a despotic sway over his volition? Two or three weeks passed; and again, on some particular occasion, was my heart smitten as with an avenging blight on beholding that lurid lightning flashing from Danvers' large black eyes, and a smile which seemed worthy of Lucifer wavering upon his lip. O God! how indescribably wicked was his look for that moment—but only for a moment!—and then it was frank, generous, and serene as ever. I turned away—for there was a dizziness in my brain, and I feared lest my countenance should serve as an index to the dread emotions that were now re-awakened in my breast. I went forth into the streets to seek the fresh air; and whom should I run against in this mood but Master Landini, the eminent goldsmith of Lombard Street? We were known to each other, having occasionally had some business transactions; and we accordingly stopped and spoke. He at once began to speak of Lord Danvers, saying that he understood his lordship was engaged to my daughter, and congratulating me on the brilliant alliance which she would thus form.—'You are fully able to judge,' said he, 'of the moral and intellectual qualifications of him whom you have accepted as your son-in-law; and I believe there is not a lady in the land who would not admit that his lordship is the handsomest and most fascinating cavalier that ever shone in the brilliant circles of nobility and fashion. As for his wealth,' added Master Landini, 'I can answer for him on *that* head. The revenues arising from his English estates are immense; and I know that he has possessions in France, in Spain, and in Italy.'—'Yes,' I observed, 'I have understood that Lord Danvers is immensely rich.'—'From my experience in those matters,' continued Landini, 'I have no hesitation in declaring that Lionel Danvers is the richest nobleman in Europe: My father was agent and banker to his lordship's grandfather, as I myself have been agent and banker to his lordship's father, and am now continued in the same capacity towards his lordship himself. For more than a century, then, has that agency been enjoyed by the firm of Landini; and you will therefore readily believe, Master Manners, that I can speak with confidence when giving you this information relative to the immense prosperity and indeed increasing wealth of the noble house of Danvers. Once more then do I congratulate you on the splendid alliance which your daughter is about to form.'

"I thanked the eminent goldsmith for his kindness, and we parted. Slowly did I return to my counting-house, pondering upon all I had heard. Master Landini, though naturalized in England, and indeed an Englishman by education and habit, was sprung from an Italian family who had acquired considerable repute and great riches as merchants at Genoa. It was his father who had first come over to settle in England, and had opened the banking establishment in Lombard Street. The present proprietor of that establishment, and with whom I had just been conversing, was a man well stricken in years—known to be enormously rich—of unimpeachable integrity—and universally respected, although supposed to be somewhat miserly in his habits. At all events, he was a man on whose slightest word implicit reliance was to be placed: and therefore it was impossible, after all he had just told me, to entertain the faintest doubt as to the brilliant position of Lord Danvers. Again therefore was I indignant—even enraged—at what I was constrained to look upon as my intense folly in conjuring up phantoms to haunt me and actually allowing my thoughts to weave themselves into scourges wherewith to lash myself!

"Several months had by this time passed away since the memorable evening which first introduced Lord Danvers to Clara and me. He had been a daily visitor at my house: in due course he had proposed for Clara's hand, and was accepted. I have already said she loved him passionately—devotedly—fondly. Her whole soul was wrapped up in him: he was all in all to her—and so intricately had love thus interwoven the threads of her destiny with his own, that her very existence might now be said to depend upon his look, his word, his smile. And he in return had all the appearance of experiencing a kindred attachment. Indeed, that he loved her is beyond all doubt; and I must confess that when I call to mind all the many proofs he gave of that earnest love—the delicacy of the attentions which he paid to Clara—and the honourable manner in which he conducted his suit, I am bewildered and astounded when I think of the catastrophe.

And to *this* am I now bringing my narrative. It was in the month of September, 1509, that Lionel Danvers first became acquainted with Clara and me: it was in the month of March, 1510, that I was besought to allow the day to be fixed for the nuptials. I did so—and scarcely had the assent gone from my lips when I felt as if a secret voice whispered a solemn warning in my soul bidding me beware. But, good heavens! of what was I to beware? in what direction did this mystic warning point? Again was I confused—bewildered—almost maddened. There was a presentiment in my mind that bade me break off this contemplated match at once—some secret influence appeared to urge me to separate Clara for ever from her lover. But why?—was he not in every way eligible?—had I not satisfied myself with even more than strict paternal solicitude, on every point regarding his social position—his property—even to his identity with the veritable Lionel Danvers, the rightful possessor of the peerage and estates belonging to that family? What more could I do? indeed what more could I want? Did it not seem as if I should experience a deep gratitude to heaven for having prepared so brilliant a destiny for my beloved daughter, rather than thus allow my morbid mind and diseased fancy to suggest misgivings and suspicions which, so far from having any foundation, I actually could not define to myself? It was thus I reasoned: and yet I was neither perfectly consoled nor altogether reassured.

"The bridal day was now approaching; and great preparations had been made for the ceremony. A select number of friends was invited to be present at the nuptials, after the celebration of which it was arranged that the young couple were to repair to the estate in Essex where the honeymoon was to be passed. But as all these details were discussed in my presence, and as every additional step was taken which seemed to ratify as it were the progress of my daughter's destiny, I grew more and more uneasy in my mind. Nevertheless, by dint of a powerful effort—or rather of a continuous series of efforts that were as painful as they were powerful—I veiled all that was passing within me. To show misgiving, and to suffer my presentient suspicions to appear, would be alike to insult the noble Danvers and to throw a damp upon my daughter's happiness. Such were my reflections—and I felt that in the absence of anything like a reason for my misgivings, I had no right to offer an outrage to the feelings of the former, or do aught to mar the happiness of the latter. Besides, had I not promised to allow Clara to be the arbitress of her own matrimonial destiny?—had I not professed my complete reliance upon her prudence?—how, then, could I now interfere to break off this match without appearing in the light of a capricious tyrant? And lastly, was it not evident that Clara herself was disturbed by none of those misgivings which haunted me? She never caught that flitting sardonism of expression on her lover's countenance which had struck me so forcibly and which haunted me so cruelly? Then was it not imagination—pure imagination—on my part? Heavens! how arduously I strove to think so!

"It now wanted but ten days to that fixed for the bridal; and I took an opportunity when alone with Clara to ask her if she were perfectly happy at the change in which she was about to embark. I conjured her to examine deep into her soul, and satisfy herself that she was consulting her best sense of felicity in bestowing her hand upon Lord Danvers. This discourse I held to her in a manner which suffered her not to perceive that I myself entertained the slightest presentiment of evil—much less of regret—in connexion with the subject; and throwing herself into my arms, she thanked me for all the fond paternal affection I had lavished upon her from her infancy upward, as well as for this last proof of a father's solicitude on my part. But she assured me, with even an exultant joy and an enthusiasm alike of language and of looks, that her happiness was all concentrated in her love for Danvers; and that confident as she was in the strength and sincerity of her own love for him, so sure was she of his fervid and genuine love for her! What more could I say? I saw her radiant—I saw her enthusiastic, in the confidence of a love that was reciprocated; and I felt my own spirits rise—my suspicions grow dim—and the presentiment of approaching evil losing its power. Indeed, I was almost satisfied that I *had* been the dupe of a fancy at times fevered by an over-anxiety on account of one so inestimably dear to me. This, in a word, now seemed to be the explanation of all those vague misgivings and evil forebodings which had arisen in my mind.

"It was in the afternoon part of the day that this conversation between me and Clara took place; and soon afterwards Danvers called as usual. He remained to a later hour than was his wont; and I subsequently remembered well that on taking leave of Clara at about ten o'clock that evening, he flung upon her a look of mysterious significancy. I did not, however, appear to notice it, being well aware that lovers have their own little secrets into which even parents may not penetrate; and moreover I was in a happier mood than I of late had known, and was not at that time labouring under the influence of presentient misgivings. Indeed, the conversation with Clara that day had restored me to serenity and inspired me with confidence. Embracing my daughter, I ascended my bed-chamber and slept profoundly. But on descending at the usual hour in the morning, I found that Clara had disappeared. Heavens! what a blow was this for me! All my former suspicions seemed justified in a moment. But I scarcely had time for thought: indeed thought itself was too agonizing to be endured. What had become of my daughter? Her bed had not been slept in during the night. It was therefore to be inferred that she had stolen forth soon after the household had retired in the evening. I flew to Lord Danvers' lodgings: he likewise had been absent all night. Wild with despair, I despatched mounted messengers in all directions to search for the fugitives: but everything proved of no avail. A terrible illness seized upon me; and for weeks I raved in the fever of delirium. When I returned to consciousness and was enabled to leave my couch, I found that misfortune had not come alone, but that a perfect hailstorm of calamities had vented its rage upon my fated head. Two of my most richly-freighted ships had been wrecked on the Goodwin Sands; and a third had been captured by Algerine pirates in the Mediterranean. But what to me was now the loss of wealth, since she to whom alone I should have bequeathed it was gone? No tidings had been heard of my daughter! When able to drag myself over the threshold of my house, I called upon Landini, who had already heard of the circumstance and offered me his sincerest sympathies. But while so addressing me, he shook his head in a mysterious manner, murmuring, 'It is sad—most sad—that Lionel Danvers should thus emulate the dark treachery of his grandsire!'

"I did not ask the meaning of those words. I was too much absorbed in my own grief at the time to entertain thought or care for the concerns of others. But subsequently I remembered that remark which fell from Landini's lips; and calling on him again, I reminded him of it, and sought an explanation. But he avoided the subject; and I therefore know not the particular circumstances to which he may have alluded.

"With regard to my own unhappy history, a few more words will suffice to complete it. I have already stated that a storm of calamities assailed me: I may now add that the violence of the tempest was overpowering. Ruin entered my house with the remorseless fury of a ravaging army; and my possessions were swept away, leaving me as poor as I had once been rich—as wretched as I had once been prosperous. The friends who were wont to gather around me and partake of my hospitality, were now no longer to be seen: their backs were turned upon me—and if I sought them at their own houses, they found a myriad pretexts to avoid an interview with the bankrupt merchant. Master Landini proffered me assistance, and afforded it with readiness; though reputed to be avaricious and money-loving, he opened his purse-strings to me. Lady Wilbraham also at whose house I first met Danvers, gave me her sincerest sympathy, and forced a sum of gold upon me. She died recently; and in her I lost a kind and generous friend. Six years have now elapsed since the unfortunate Clara's disappearance, and not once have I heard of her. Not the slightest clue have I obtained to discover her fate: I know not even whether she be alive or dead. Neither have I been able to glean any tidings of Lionel Danvers, who during this interval has appeared not again in London. Nor has even his agent Landini received any tidings from him—or if he has, he reveals them not.

"I have wandered everywhere in search of my lost daughter. I have visited Danvers' Castle in the Isle of Wight—I have journeyed into Essex many times—many times also have I travelled into Cumberland to visit the treacherous lord's estates and prosecute my inquiries there—but all in vain! Rapidly sinking lower and lower in the slough of misery, and not daring to intrude again upon the generosity of Landini, I have for some time past been enduring the cruellest privations and have at length fallen into the completest destitution.

"Last evening my wandering footsteps brought me into this neighbourhood. I passed the night in the summer-house at the bottom of these grounds. Creeping stealthily forth at an early hour this morning, whom should I suddenly encounter but Lionel Danvers? I demanded of him my daughter! I scarcely know now what I said, but I believe that I alike entreated and menaced. He regarded me no longer with a fleeting and dubious sardonism: it was with a look of such unmistakable wickedness and so full of a diabolic expression, that it sent a train of dreadful unutterable thoughts through my mind! Indeed, it struck me that he must be something less or something more than man, though wearing the most perfect of human shapes: for at that moment, when he stood with all the tremendous power of his awful looks fixed upon me, it seemed as if he were a being having the privilege to trample upon every holy tie and to laugh in scorn at the laws of God and the statutes of man. I remember too that he tossed me his purse: but not for worlds would I have accepted aught at his hands, although on the brink of starvation at the time. My brain was on fire—my heart was rent with lancinating tortures—and I recollect that I clung to him in desperation. But there was a power in his looks which overwhelmed me: my senses fled—and when I awoke to consciousness again, it was to find myself the object of the most generous solicitude on the part of those to whom I now renew the fervid expression of my gratitude."

And as the old man gave utterance to these last words, he bent his tearful eyes upon Musidora and the King.

CHAPTER VIII.

THE ROYAL PROMISES.

FRAUGHT with romantic wildness, pathos, and interest, as was the narrative of the ruined merchant, yet were it difficult to gather from the countenances of the listeners the feelings it excited in their breasts.

The Earl and Countess of Grantham had at the outset assumed each a look as if they were prepared to pay the profoundest attention to the old man's story. This, however, they did not from any curiosity to hear it, nor from any real sentiment of sympathy towards himself; but because they fancied that the King experienced considerable interest in him, and with true parasitical prudence the wily old couple gave themselves the air of being swayed by the same feelings that influenced Royalty. But as in the course of the narrative they observed that his Majesty grew abstracted, and even at times had a preoccupied air, as if his thoughts were travelling quite in another direction,—the Earl and his wife conceived that the great length of the tale proved tiresome to the King; and they therefore thought it right to yawn and even manifest impatience. At times they remarked that the King, throwing himself back in his seat and folding his arms, appeared to be listening with real and earnest attention; but the penetration of the astute old couple enabled them to observe that the monarch was in reality surveying Musidora with scrutinizing looks, which were not altogether those of admiration, but had in them a searching keenness that strove to dive into the innermost recesses of her soul.

But impossible indeed was it for human regards to plunge into those unfathomable depths. For there sat Musidora—her eyes fixed upon the old man's countenance and evidently listening with the profoundest attention to every syllable of his strange and wildly romantic narrative; but of the extent to which her feelings might be moved or the mystic chords which vibrated in her heart be touched, it were impossible to say. True was it that the half-vanishing gleam of a smile which was wont to sit upon her countenance, had now disappeared altogether; and a solemn seriousness of look uniting with a perfect stillness of attitude, gave her the air of a splendid statue chiselled from Parian marble. It might be—and indeed it seemed—that she was so profoundly absorbed in the deep mystic interest of the ruined merchant's history, that she had no thought for anything beside while he continued speaking. At all events, certain it was that she did not once notice those earnest scrutinizing looks which the King fixed upon her—much less the occasional remarks of impatience made by her noble relatives.

As for old Manners himself,—fancying that Musidora was the most profoundly interested—or, at any rate, perceiving that she was the most attentive of his listeners—he addressed himself almost exclusively to her; and though no changing colour upon the cheeks, no movement of the lips, much less any ejaculation from the tongue, afforded an index of the degree of interest she might really feel in his narrative, yet as he beheld her large dark lustrous eyes fixed steadfastly upon him the whole time, it was natural for him to suppose that the recital of his misfortunes and his wrongs enthralled, not merely the deepest attention but likewise the most generous sympathies of that young damsel who had already shown herself so kind-hearted towards him.

But for more than a minute after the old man had brought his narrative to a close—and during the brief interval of profound silence which followed the last words to which he had given utterance—Musidora still remained motionless and statue-like in her chair—still kept her countenance turned towards the bereaved father—still also retained her looks fixed upon his venerable features. It seemed as if the impression made by his tale continued to enthral every sense and hold captive every faculty—as the soul remains for a brief space under the empire of a religious awe inspired by a solemn strain of music, even after the grand swell of the cathedral organ has died away.

"Fair lady, what think you of the old man's tale?" asked the King, leaning forward from his chair and gently touching Musidora's arm. She gave a slight and barely perceptible start, while for a moment—and only a single moment—a strange light flashed from her eyes and as weird-like an expression swept over her features. But the next instant she turned upon the King that countenance from which all traces of unusual emotion had vanished as quickly as they had sprang up, even if they were at all anything more than the effect of so abruptly changing her position and bringing her features as it were into a new light.

"There can be;" she said, with the wonted fluid evenness of her silvery voice, "but one opinion as to the painful narrative we have just heard. It strikes deep at every sympathy finding a habitation in the human heart; and I for one," she added, rising from her seat, "proffer the venerable sufferer my sincerest condolence."

Thus speaking, she approached the ruined merchant who likewise rose as she thus accosted him: but beckoning with her snowy hand for him to retain his place, she said in a voice that was now unmistakably tremulous and full of emotion, "Poor bereaved old man! may God Almighty give you strength to support your heavy afflictions! But as for your wrongs, it is not for short-sighted humanity to grasp heaven's lightnings and invoke its thunder to deal vengeance upon the head of him who has so deeply, deeply injured you!"

"Ah! dearest lady," said the old man, taking her proffered hand and respectfully raising it to his lips: "your words are full of solace—but, alas! as a moral lesson, they are ineffective. Your sympathy pours like a balm upon the still bleeding wounds of my lacerated heart: but you bid me lay aside all thought of vengeance—and *that* is impossible! O lady! young, beautiful, and good as you are, you never can have known—and God send you never may know—an anguish half so poignant as that which I have felt for six years past and which tortures me now! It is only a parent who can appreciate all this agony of agonies that teems within me and craves the volcanic vent of deadly vengeance. Great King!" continued the old man, now painfully excited; and springing past Musidora, he threw himself at Henry's feet—"I beseech your Grace to see that justice is done me. The villain who has deprived me of my daughter is a subject of your Highness: he has castles, and estates, and great wealth in this kingdom, over which God has set you to reign. Perhaps the threat of confiscation, if promulgated by your Grace's royal authority, would induce the proud Lord Danvers to do justice to a poor old man? Oh! intercede on my behalf, excellent young lady!" added the ruined merchant, turning his head partly round so as to look appealingly up into Musidora's countenance: "intercede, I beseech you, that the cruel, pitiless Danvers——"

But he suddenly stopped short: for that countenance—always of marble fairness—was now, if possible, more deadly pale still—indeed pale even unto ghastliness; while so strange and ineffable a look was now plainly visible upon her exquisitely chiselled features, on which it lingered for a few moments, that there was this time no doubt as to the possibil- ity of Musidora being sometimes moved by what was passing within her bosom.

"Yes, I will join my intercession with your's," she said, hastily recov- ering herself, but with a strong perceptible effort and even with a slight shudder passing through her frame: "I do unite my prayers with yours—if the intercession will do any good at all," she added in a voice of ice and with a manner that suddenly became cold and emotionless as the look of a marble statue.

At the same instant she tranquilly resumed her seat, while the old man continued to gaze upon her in mingled doubt, sorrow, and amaze- ment, as if he feared that he had given her some offence but he knew not how he could possibly have done so. A pause of nearly a minute now ensued in the conversation.

"About the purse which Lord Danvers flung to you this morning?" at length said the Earl of Grantham, perceiving that there was some little awkward constraint or embarrassment at this juncture on the part of his guests; and though he could not exactly understand how it had arisen, he nevertheless thought that the best plan was to set the discourse flowing again by suggesting some topic.

"I took it not. No—not for worlds would I receive it!" exclaimed old Manners. "Where it was thrown on the grass, there did it lie."

"I marked it not when I beheld you stretched senseless in the field," said Musidora, addressing the observation to the old man and speaking in her usual tone and with her wonted manner, while the coldly brilliant smile of affability came back to her countenance.

"Doubtless some passer-by has picked it up," said the King, "and as a matter of course self-appropriated the treasure. And now, with regard to the request you have made me, worthy Master Manners, and in which en- treaty the lovely Musidora has united her own prayer,—I can only say that anything which as a King I may reasonably and properly do, shall be done. But though experiencing all possible sympathy with your misfortune, I dare not go to the extremes which you have suggested. What? threaten to confiscate a powerful noble's castles and estates, because, forsooth, he has broken his word in respect to marriage with a young damsel—and even of that we have no sufficient evidence."

"Evidence?—too much, great King!" cried Manners, clasping his hands despairingly. "If Lord Danvers had intended to prove faithful to his promise and make my Clara his honourable wife, of what need to bear her away for the purpose?—and if he *did* espouse her, wherefore keep her thus secluded from all intercourse with her only surviving parent? No, my liege—Danvers was forsworn—was perjured—and Clara was beguiled—betrayed! No marriage has hallowed the love—the fatal love—which she entertained for him!"

"Look you, old man," said the King; "I am inclined to believe that what your own fears suggest must have been the case; and deeply sympathizing with you, as I have ere now said, I will cause secret but searching inquiries to be made respecting your lost daughter, and also concerning the whereabouts of this Lord Danvers. If these researches prove successful, I will order Danvers to appear before me; and privately and secretly will I counsel him to do you complete justice by espousing your daughter, if she be alive—or at all events, of giving you some account concerning her. This will I do, Master Manners; and in the meantime you must observe strict secrecy relative to your success in enlisting your Sovereign's sympathy in your favour. I know not this Danvers—I have never seen him: but he appears to be a strange personage, from all you have been saying; and should he learn that inquiries are set afoot regarding him, he might speed away from England at once and return to his Continental home, wherever it may be. As for your present condition, poor old man! it shall be your Sovereign's care to provide you against want in your old age. Here, take this purse—return to London to-morrow—and name some place where any person whom I may send to make known my farther plans for your welfare, can be sure to meet with you."

"Kind, generous, noble-hearted prince!" exclaimed the old man, once more throwing himself upon his knees at the monarch's feet, and reverently kissing the hand which was extending to him a well-filled purse. "Thanks to your royal bounty, I shall at least be secured against poverty for the remainder of my days! This purse is heavy—the gold it contains will suffice for all my wants during the brief space I may yet linger in this world of sorrow——"

"Nay, but I am resolved to do more for you, old man," exclaimed the King; "and tomorrow I will appoint some trusty person to meet you in London for the purpose of carrying out my designs. Name some place of appointment for five of the clock to-morrow afternoon. Or I will settle this point for thee! Be the meeting-place the Temple Gardens—and I shall so well describe your person to the individual I may send, that there shall be no error on his part as to the facility of recognising you."

The ruined merchant, with tears trickling down his furrowed cheeks, reiterated his thanks to the monarch for these instances of kindness; and slowly rising from his knees, he turned towards Musidora, saying, "With

the earliest beams of the morning sun shall I be on my road back to London. Perhaps, beautiful damsel, I may never see you again: but morning
and evening will a prayer go up from the depths of my heart to the throne
of the Eternal, imploring that heaven's choicest blessings may descend
upon the head of the young maiden who took compassion upon the poor
helpless old man!"

Musidora extended her hand to him, and he pressed it to his lips. He
then turned towards the Earl and Countess of Grantham, to whom he
poured forth his gratitude for the generous hospitality he had received
beneath their roof; and having observed "that with their permission he
would trespass upon their goodness for an asylum till the morrow," the
poor old man passed out of the room.

It being now close upon midnight, Henry rose to depart. The Earl
of Grantham offered to accompany his Grace to Greenwich House, as
the way was lonely and the distance was a mile and a half. But the King,
significantly tapping the handle of his rapier, declared that he experienced
no fear so long as he had the companionship of his faithful Sheffield blade,
while at the same time he courteously acknowledged the Earl's proposal.

"Beautiful Musidora," continued the monarch as he turned towards
our heroine; and taking her hand, he held it between both his own,—
"write to your father to-morrow—say what you will to make him happy—but enjoin him to observe strict secrecy for the present relative to
his restoration to the royal favour. All that concerns the poor ruined merchant, too, shall be my care: because," he added with a significant look and
a tender tone, "I see that you experience a deep sympathy in his behalf.
But may I, if the pressing affairs of public business permit, renew my visit
to Grantham Villa to-morrow evening, with the certainty that the lovely
Musidora will join her noble relatives in giving me a cordial welcome?"

"After all the benefits so generously volunteered by your Highness,"
began Musidora, "it would be ungrateful in me——"

"Ah! do not address me as your Sovereign," interrupted the King,
pressing the hand which he still retained in his own, but which was now
instantaneously withdrawn the moment that pressure was felt—while the
damsel's lip suddenly gave a haughty curl and her eye flashed the quick
transitory look of woman's stately pride; so that Henry, with deprecating glances and increasing tenderness of tone, hastened to observe, "Ah!
take no offence from word, or deed, or look of mine—because he who
courts your smiles is not the one willingly to provoke your displeasure.
And henceforth," he added, "speak to me—regard me—think of me, *not*
as your Sovereign——but as your friend!"

Having given utterance to these last words in a somewhat excited—or

we might almost say impassioned tone, the King hurriedly bade farewell
to the Earl and Countess of Grantham, and took his departure.

CHAPTER IX.

THE TWO HORSEMEN.

WE have already intimated that the bank of the Thames between Greenwich and London was dotted with noblemen's villas, the grounds attached
to which extended several hundred yards—in some instances even to a distance of about half-a-mile. At the back of all these villas, and skirting the
end of the grounds, ran a winding road that led into Greenwich. On one
side were the railings, hedges, or boundary-walls belonging to the villa-
gardens; and on the opposite side of the road was a long line of trees, the
overhanging branches of which formed a grateful shade for the lounger
in the midst of a summer-day's heat, but rendered the pathway gloomy
enough by night.

It was close upon midnight when two horsemen turned out of the
Blackheath Road into this bye-path which we have just been describing. In
the clear and beautiful moonlight it might have been observed that there
was something suspicious not only in the movements, but also in the demeanour and dress of these men. One was between forty and fifty years
of age—tall, but awkwardly built—and had a partial stoop which gave him
a most uncouth appearance on horseback. His countenance bore all the
unmistakable marks of inveterate dissipation, which were equally discernible in his toilet—for his garments were covered with stains of wine or
grease, proving him to be a frequenter of low taverns and eating-houses.
He had a heavy broadsword by his side, pistols in his holsters, and a dagger
in his belt: moreover, by a string fastened to one of the buttons of his doublet hung a black silk mask, which he could put on at a moment's warning,
and which was so elastic with whalebone that it would keep fast upon the
countenance when once assumed.

The companion of this individual was much younger—indeed, not
above five-and-twenty. He was tolerably good-looking, but was also of
very dissipated appearance. There was however nothing so ignoble in his
looks—nothing so thoroughly vile and degraded in his general aspect, as
in that of his companion: but his face had a wild kind of expression of
mingled recklessness and care—a look of sorrow and regret drowned in
the full tide of vice. His raiment had seen as much service as that of his
comrade, and likewise bore evidences of an acquaintance with the tavern
and the low eating-house. Armed also was he to the teeth, in the same

manner as his friend: nor was the black mask wanting to complete the similitude of this portion of the portraiture.

Both were mounted on tolerably good steeds, which were not how-ever their own, but had been let to them for a special purpose and on a special consideration, the nature of which will very soon transpire.

"No luck as yet, friend Welford," said the younger individual, in a tone of petulance and disappointment, after a ten minutes interval of si-lence, during which they had ridden some way down the bye-road at the back of the villa-gardens.

"You are too impatient, my dear St. Louis," was the response given by the senior. "This is your characteristic in everything—always precipi-tate and premature, whether in throwing a die before you have secured it in your finger in such a way as to make it come up what number you choose—or in calling for your tavern bill before you have convinced your-self that the coast is clear enough for you to slip off while the waiter has gone to fetch it."

"Well, well, you are perhaps more truthful than complimentary in your allusions," replied St. Louis. "But I fancy that I never should have been reduced to such straits as to want to secure a die, conceal a trump card in my sleeve, or bilk the waiter of a slap-bang shop at all, unless I had been so kindly and generously helped by you to run through the hand-some fortune which I had left me by my uncle."

"I never in my life knew such unpardonable ingratitude," exclaimed Welford, with a sort of ironical amazement. "Did I not attach myself most lovingly unto you at the moment your worthy uncle died, leaving you without a relation or friend in the whole world to take care of you—and leaving you likewise that fortune to which you have alluded, and which did require such special taking care of? Why, young sir, may I never handle pestle and mortar again, if you were not the most inexperienced, foolish, unlearned, and insipid young gentleman, when first I knew you four years ago, that ever found himself his own master when he ought still to have been in swaddling clothes!"

"And I, thinking you were a respectable apothecary and leech," re-torted St. Louis, "was fool enough to put implicit confidence in you. You came to feel my pulse when I was ill, and you staid to thrust your hand into my purse long after I was well."

"You ungrateful young rapscallion," exclaimed Welford, in a sort of good-humoured bantering, or rather ironical jocularity of tone; "you are indebted to me for all the really valuable and practical part of the educa-tion you possess! From a monk you learnt Latin; and being descended from French parents, there is no very great credit to you in being able to speak the French tongue. Well then, Latin and French—with just enough geography to make you know that Europe is in the world and England is in Europe—combined with a sufficiency of arithmetic to add up your housekeeper's bills and see that they were right,—and this was the sum of all your qualifications when first I fell in with you. How on earth could you expect to get through the world with such a handful of knowledge as that? And mark, I pray you, in comparison, the pleasing nature, infinite variety, and truly practical value of the education you received from me. Why, no young nobleman with a tutor ever went through a more complete finish! Did I not introduce you to the finest set of daredevils in all London, who taught you to drink like a fish, quarrel like a bully, and swear like a trooper? Did I not initiate you in all the sublime mysteries of the cock-pit, the tennis-court, and the gaming-table? Did I not show you the true exemplary manner of thrashing a watchman within an inch of his life, and shifting shop-signs in such an improved style as to throw all London into confusion,—so that the man who went to bed a barber rose up in the morning to find himself a grocer—at least so far as the substitution of gilt sugar-loaves for the parti-coloured pole was concerned? Did I not, in a word, lead you into the very best society——"

"Blacklegs, sharpers, bullies, and counterfeits," interjected St. Louis, in a tone of mingled recklessness and sorrow.

"Well, and where could you look for better society?" continued his elderly companion: "or with whom could you have more agreeably spent your money? But when that money was all spent——and, egad! I never yet heard that gold was intended for any other purpose——who was it that still kept you by the hand and showed you how to live handsomely upon nothing? Who taught you how to chaunt a horse, secure a die, always cut a trump card, and chouse at tennis? Who initiated you into the mysteries of bilking taverns, getting into debt, feeing bailiffs and the City Marshal's men, and doing everything *against* the law in defiance of the law? If you ask who in fact was the learned professor that finished your education, every echo must answer that it was the erudite and accomplished Benjamin Welford, Licentiate in Medicine, Apothecary, and Dispenser of Drugs—in other words, your humble servant."

"Yes, I have indeed to thank you for completing my education," observed St. Louis, with accents of mingled bitterness and devil-me-care recklessness. "You found me inexperienced enough, heaven knows! and receiving me into your school, you have rendered me so proficient that I am prepared to take the highest degrees as swindler, blackleg, cheat, and scoundrel. But now—as if it were necessary to cap them all—you are about to make me a highwayman!"

"Egad! it is not I exactly, but necessity," exclaimed Benjamin Welford. "Things are so very slack now in those spheres where we have recently been accustomed to shine—and moreover, to speak candidly, we are better known than trusted at cock-pit and tennis-court. As for taverns and ordinaries, I verily believe there is not one in the good city of London which hath escaped our presence. Even the lowest ale-houses have received our favours and do not seem anxious for a renewal of them. Accordingly, it was my advice that we should take to the road, as other high-spirited gentlemen have done before. Indeed, inasmuch as my doctor's shop is so infested by duns that it was impossible to hold out there any longer, necessity ordained that I should go upon the highway. Consequently, as the pupil accompanies the master and the lieutenant goes with the captain, so are you side by side with me this night."

"And if our ramblings prove ineffectual," observed St. Louis, "how are we to manage? You know that in leaving that casket as a pledge with the horse-dealer, it was my last earthly possession, so to speak, from which I thus parted. You know also the value I attach thereto, and the thought of which alone seems like some better influence penetrating through the dense mist of vices, rascalities, debaucheries, and scoundrelisms whereby I am enveloped."

"Oh! perdition upon your sentimentalism," interrupted Welford impatiently. "The casket is pretty enough as a trinket, and the legend attached to it is romantic enough as a story. But as for any real value belonging to it, beyond that of some four pounds sterling or so, which is about the price of these two hacks——"

"Now, mark me, friend Welford!" interrupted St. Louis, speaking in a resolute tone and with peremptory manner: "that casket I will have back again either by fair or foul means. If we find gold in a traveller's pocket, well and good: we shall take home the horses—pay for the hire thereof—and get back the casket. But if on the other hand luck should *not* befriend us, and we are compelled to return into London with naught in our pockets, I give you due warning that I will blow out the old horse-dealer's brains with one of his own pistols which he has lent us, unless he gives up my casket."

"One would take you for some superstitious maudlin fool," observed Welford contemptuously, "unless they happened to know that you were in reality a dicer, gamester, chaunter, tavern-bilker, and blackleg—soon, I hope, to be a practised highway-robber also."

"Aye—and the sooner the better too," rejoined St. Louis emphatically: "or else there will be murder done in the morning at Deadman's Place, when I go to demand back my casket! You may think what you like of me and my love for that trinket. Indeed, I do not mind confessing that I *do* feel a certain superstitious awe connected therewith. A mission was entrusted to me by my late uncle—a task was enjoined me as the condition on which he left me his fortune: and even amidst the most uproarious scenes of debauchery, has a still small voice appeared to whisper in my ear like conscience speaking from the depth of my soul, reminding me of that mission and that task! Yes—and even when reeling beneath the maddening influence of fiery alcohol—or when stupefied with the vapours of a debauch that was over—though all other ideas were either in whirling confusion or in cloudy indistinctness, yet has that *one* recollection been ever definite, palpable, bright, and steady in my brain, like a fixed star always shining in the midst of a heaven where at one time the moonbeams play fitfully and vibratingly, and at another the clouds form an opaque veil. Now, then, my friend—for so I call you rather from habit than from taste—you understand me in my superstitious affection and solemn reverence for that casket and its contents?"

"A portrait and a few scarcely legible pages of writing!" ejaculated Welford contemptuously.

"Aye, to be sure!" rejoined St. Louis, with a sort of fierce earnestness: "and why should these *not* be the objects of such a feeling on my part? I tell you, sir," he continued in an excited tone, "that the mission connected with those articles should have been regarded as of a sanctity sufficient to keep me virtuous, and ought now at all events to be potent enough to recall me from this desperate and depraved career in which I have embarked. That casket haunts me as it were like a remorse—though I myself am innocent of anything connected with its sad legend!"

"St. Louis," observed Welford, "I am ashamed to hear you talk thus. You are in a strange mood to-night! For a long, long time you have not thus given way to your silly feelings; and it is particularly inopportune, now that perchance all your presence of mind may be needed and your courage put to the test at any moment. It is truly astonishing how an old casket, containing the portrait of a girl who certainly is pretty enough, and a few papers recording the most trashy old woman's gossip that ever I read, should have turned your brain thus."

"Silence—no more of this!" ejaculated St. Louis with unmistakable ferocity. "If you desire that we should remain friends—such friends as circumstances have made us—you will do well to avoid *that* topic—unless indeed you can approach it without the use of a bantering tone and ironical manner."

"Well, we will be friends again, then," said Welford, now adopting a conciliatory policy: for it did not suit his purpose to quarrel with the young man, whom however he could not help teasing and worrying at times—partly to gratify a disposition naturally bad, and partly as one of the means by which he maintained his influence over him.

And lest this last observation may appear paradoxical, let it be remarked that to enact the bully occasionally was to assert a power which remained dominant so long as it was not absolutely disputed; and if it were not disputed, it was not that St. Louis was a coward, but because his ruined fortunes and frequent violation of the laws had placed him in a complete state of dependence on his more experienced, more cool-headed, and also more unprincipled preceptor in vice.

While the preceding conversation was taking place, the two horsemen had advanced a considerable distance along the lane; and during the interval of silence which followed Welford's last remark, they stopped to allow their horses to drink at a pond by the side of the road. For this purpose they dismounted, holding the bridles while the animals walked a little way into the water. There was a gap in the line of trees at this point; and the moon shone down upon that part of the road without obstruction—for it was a night of unrivalled splendour, and, except in the shade, almost as bright as day.

While the horses were drinking, the sounds of advancing footsteps suddenly reached the ears of the two men; and they nudged each other with a significant intimation that the moment was probably at hand when they were to make their first experience in the capacity of highwaymen. Almost immediately, from the deep shade thrown by the trees a little farther on, did the tall figure of a man on foot emerge into the sphere of silver moonlight; and the two desperadoes at once saw by the plume that waved from his cap and the rapier by his side, as well as by his lofty bearing, that he was a personage of rank and consequence.

"Good night, sir traveller," exclaimed Welford, who had already slipped one of his pistols from the holster, while St. Louis had done precisely the same thing and at the same moment.

"Good night to you," answered the stranger, in a tone the hauteur of which had something sullen in it, while the manner in which he pursued his way without doing more than just deigning to cast a single glance upon the dismounted horsemen, showed that he did not choose to tarry for any farther converse.

Until this moment Welford and St. Louis had averted their countenances in such a manner that the stranger could not possibly obtain a full view of them even if he had cared to regard them. But now, quick as thought, did they slip on their black masks; and precipitating themselves upon him, seized hold of his arms—each presenting a heavy pistol, at the same moment, and demanding the instantaneous surrender of his purse.

"Ah, villains!" he said in an under-tone, and with a marvellous degree of coolness: then disengaging himself from their grasp with a sudden
jerk,—which must indeed have been singularly managed to shake off those
two strong men and make them even reel for a moment backward,—he
drew his rapier from its sheath.

"Take this then!" said Welford doggedly; and he fired his pistol point-
blank at the stranger, whom the bullet however did not touch.

"Then this will do it!" exclaimed St. Louis: and the words were accompanied by a flash and a report.

"Fools that ye are!" said the stranger, still remaining unscathed by the
second shot, though also fired within a couple of yards of his head. "Miserable wretches!" and he spoke in a tone of the coldest and most ineffable
contempt, as without the least excitement he easily parried by means of
his light rapier the furious blows which the two men at once levelled at
him with their heavy broadswords.

"Get another barker," cried Welford; "or both! I'll keep him employed:"—and he re-redoubled the fury of his attack upon the stranger.

But the next moment—just as St. Louis had turned away to reach
the other pistols from the holsters—the stranger, with perhaps a slight
display of some additional effort, made the blade of his rapier twine as
it were snake-like about Welford's broadsword, which was in an instant
torn from his grasp and sent whirling over the fence against which the
stranger stood. The discomfited desperado sprang backward with the instinctive impulse to save the life that was now placed all in a moment at
the stranger's mercy: but this individual did not seem to think it worth
while to follow up his advantage—although had he chosen, he might at
once have pierced Welford through and through.

But the few instants' suspension of hostilities which thus ensued was
promptly broken by St. Louis, who now returned to the attack, discharg-
ing first one pistol at the stranger and then the other with scarcely a moment's interval; and still that personage stood unhurt before them, a smile
of the most withering contempt, or rather of blighting scorn, upon his
darkly handsome countenance,—while his tall, well-knit, and admirably
shaped form, instead of being drawn up to the full of its commanding
height, had assumed an attitude of listless ease and indolent indifference,
as if he cared not whether the attack were renewed or not, and at all events
did not choose to follow up his own advantages against men whom he appeared to consider too despicable for chastisement.

"By heavens, that look—that terrible smile of diabolic scorn!" exclaimed St. Louis, now staggering backward, and dropping the two pistols
from his hands as well as the broadsword, which he had retained naked
under his arm while holding the other weapons in his grasp.

"Ah! who are you?" cried the stranger, now suddenly appearing to be interested and even excited at the few words that had just been uttered—he who had hitherto remained so indifferent to the attack alike of pistol and of sword!

"Nay, tell me first who *you* are?" cried St. Louis, seeming to be maddened with some thought that had sprung up in his mind. "But I know who you are—I can guess full well! You are a descendant of a fearful race—and there is now an hereditary hatred on the part of my family against your's! It is a death-struggle, then, between us!"

Having given utterance to these words with the wildest excitement of manner and a frenzied vehemence of tone, St. Louis snatched up his broadsword, which lay shining at his feet like the fragment of a spent lightning-shaft in the silver moonlight: and apparently armed with the courage of a maddening fury, he sprang upon the stranger. Their weapons clashed—but only *once!* For, quick as the eye could wink, the broadsword was whirled from the young man's grasp and sent whistling through the air; and at the same instant that it fell with a splashing noise into the pond, did the stranger grasp St. Louis' arm—force him down upon his knees—and tear the black mask from his face: then, seizing the young man's head with his two hands, he made him upturn his countenance so that the moonlight should fall full upon it.

"Ah! you are a St. Louis," said the stranger, in one swift brief moment making the recognition.

"And you are a Danvers!" returned the young man, as he slowly rose from his knees and gazed with a mingling of mysterious awe and profound hate upon the proudly handsome countenance of the nobleman.

CHAPTER X.

THE PROPOSALS.

At the point where we broke off the preceding chapter, the scene in the bye-road had all in a moment become one of those spectacles, so full of dramatic effect, wherein a strange solemnity is mingled with a wild romance. The two most prominent figures of the group at that instant were Lord Danvers and St. Louis—while Welford, having retreated a few paces back towards the spot where the horses were standing on the verge of the pond, was gazing through his mask with blended interest and amazement upon the countenance of the nobleman. For Welford was acquainted with all the reasons which St. Louis had for proclaiming himself an hereditary hater of the Danvers family; and there seemed to be a kind of superstitious singularity in the coincidence of Lord Danvers' sudden appearance at the very time when the conversation had been turning on the cause of that traditionary hatred. No less was Welford struck with an unknown terror at the seemingly preternatural escape of Danvers from the pistol-bullets, as well as the ease wherewith he repelled the attacks made upon him and worsted his assailants. Indeed, it appeared as if he bore a charmed life; and the reckless, hardened spirit of the finished ruffian was smitten with a species of superstitious awe.

A similar kind of feeling was it that had seized upon St. Louis, when having slowly risen from his knees again after his recognition by Danvers, he stood gazing in mingled consternation and irresolution upon that haughty noble's countenance.

"Is it thus," asked Danvers, at length breaking the solemn silence, and now speaking with an expression of blighting scorn upon his darkly handsome countenance,—"is it thus a wretched outlaw who lies in wait to plunder the passer-by, dares to assume the dignified position of an avowed foe to the scion of a proud and mighty race?"

"I know not by what means your lordship has escaped death on this occasion," replied St. Louis: "but if at any future time we should meet on equal terms, rest assured I shall not hesitate to renew the conflict!"

"Equal terms!" echoed Lionel Danvers with that sardonic wreathing of the lips which gave him the wicked look of a fallen angel; "do you mean that you are to be armed with loaded pistols and heavy broadsword, while I am but to wield a poor thin rapier? But enough of this exchange of angry words and looks! Wherefore seek to make an enemy of one whom you doubtless never saw before, but who nevertheless would rather befriend than injure *you?*"

"If I never saw you before, my lord," replied St. Louis, still in bitter accents, "you will perhaps confess that I have good reason to be acquainted with the name you bear?"

"I am no stranger to the incident unto which you allude," replied Danvers: "but I am not responsible for a father's transgression."

"How knew you, my lord," demanded the young man, suddenly struck by the strangeness of the incident to which he was about to allude,—"how knew you that my name was St. Louis?—how, by the examination of my features, did you trace the resemblance to that family to which I belong?"

"Is it so many years, then," asked Danvers, with a peculiar smile, "since your uncle died? Methinks that 'tis but three summers since the old man was seated in front of his dwelling, beneath the rose-covered portico, enjoying the warmth of the sunshine?"

"Ah! then your lordship saw him at that time?" observed St. Louis.

"Yes—and even in his old age," returned Danvers, "did he retain that well-preserved facial outline which, once seen, is not easily forgotten. You have a proof indeed that it was not forgotten by *me*, since I have just recognised its living counterpart in your profile. But tell me in return, how came *you* at once to recognise *me*—since, as I believe, you never beheld me before?"

"No, my lord—it is the first time you and I have ever met," answered St. Louis,—"at least to my knowledge. But I have *heard* and likewise *read* so perfect a description of your father, that I could not fail to recognise in you, my lord, a descendant of the haughty house of Danvers. Indeed, were I not aware that your lordship's father is no more—and even if he were alive, the snows of many, many winters would be upon his brow—I should fancy that I beheld him now before me. For he who ruined the fond confiding Arline fifty-three long years ago, and whose portraiture is so well preserved not only in written description but also by the oral traditions which have reached my ears,—must at that time have been in appearance such as your lordship is now. Yes—the stature—the shape—the style of countenance—the eyes—the hair,—but chief of all that strange, wild, scornful look which was upon your lordship's features at the moment I recognised you ere now,—these are all the same! And in sooth, it was that look which served as it were in a moment as a spark to light up a whole train of smouldering memories—memories of what I had read and what I had heard concerning your sire!"

"Enough of this long parley—at least upon the present topic," said Danvers, curtly. "Your appearance does not proclaim easiness of circumstances; and your manner of introduction to me this night necessarily leads me to infer that distress has made you alike desperate and unscrupulous as to the means of replenishing your purse. Is it not so?"

"Your lordship has but asserted what it were useless on my part to contradict," replied St. Louis, "because all appearances are against me."

"What if I were to offer to serve you?" said Danvers, fixing his dark eyes keenly upon the young man, as if to ascertain how the proposition would be met.

"I thought my case ere now," answered St. Louis, "so very desperate, that had Satan himself tendered me his assistance I should have accepted it without being over nice as to the terms. But a St. Louis to receive assistance from a Danvers!—no, no—it may not be!"—and he shook his head gloomily.

"Do not be a fool, friend and companion of mine!" now interjected Welford, stepping forward and thus officiously thrusting his counsel upon

St. Louis. "If his lordship shows such good feeling towards you under all circumstances, it would be the height of churlishness as well as madness on your part to reject his good offices. What? we have assailed his lordship with murderous weapons—and verily it was not our fault if they took not fatal effect:—then you plainly and flatly informed his lordship that you entertain a family hatred for him, and that you mean to seek another opportunity to take his life! But all these grave causes of offence does this generous noble forget and forgive;—and doubtless with the anxiety to make such atonement as he may unto you for the wrong inflicted by his father on your ancestress, he proffers you his friendship. This, to my thinking, is carrying out the good Christian maxim of doing good for evil."

"Cease, reprobate!" exclaimed St. Louis, now turning with savage suddenness upon his comrade. "Though heaven knows that I of late years have had little enough to do with religion in any shape, yet does it make my blood run cold to hear a wretch like you bringing his tongue to the quoting of Scripture."

"And yet altogether, Master St. Louis," said Lord Danvers, "your friend there has given you very excellent advice, and has put the matter in its most tangible form. You have proclaimed to me your hatred—and I in return offer you my friendship. If your deceased uncle instilled malignant feelings into your soul, it is for you to exhibit the moral courage and the magnanimity sufficient to subdue them. Even if you had no personal interest to serve, such a hatred as this which you have professed against me were vile, unnatural and dastard to a degree: but since your own welfare has positively become interested in the matter, by the proposal I have made, you will not exhibit your good sense as a man of the world by refusing it."

"And recollect," Welford hastened to whisper in his friend's ear, "that we have not the smallest coin bearing King Harry's face."

St. Louis still shook his head ominously.

"And you must have the wherewith," added Welford, still in a low but persuasive whisper, "to redeem your casket from the old horse-dealer in Deadman's Place."

St. Louis was now evidently moved. All the difficulties, embarrassments, and even horrors, of his desperate condition rose up vividly in his mind. He had already entered upon a career which might speedily terminate at the gallows; and he shuddered at the thought. There—before him—stood a nobleman, immensely rich, and who with every appearance of a generosity as singular as it was magnanimous, had proffered his friendship. Should he accept it? Yes: but the oath he had sworn to his deceased uncle, vowing an implacable hatred to the house of Danvers?

Well, but had he not done his best to take the life of him whom chance had thus thrown in his way?—and was he not defeated in a manner but too well calculated to prove how incomparably superior Danvers was a swordsman?—and did it not even seem as if heaven itself had interposed to shield the nobleman's life against the pistol-balls?

"What is it that your lordship proposes to do for me?" asked St. Louis, his tone and manner alike showing how his resolution now wavered.

"Were you to accept my proffers with becoming cordiality," replied Danvers, seeming to unbend strangely from his wonted hauteur, "I should perhaps be found capable of doing much for you—far more than you can possibly imagine."

"It will be rank staring madness for you to hold out against such generosity," whispered the doctor, still more earnestly than before. "Only conceive the advantages of plenty of money—good clothes——"

"Well, my lord," St. Louis abruptly exclaimed, his countenance all in a moment brightening up with the resolve to which he had come,—"here is an end of hatred; and from henceforth shall I tutor my feelings to enter upon the career of friendship. Pardon me, my lord, if I have been somewhat laggard and hesitating in accepting this proposal."

"Enough of apologies," exclaimed Danvers, a peculiar smile, like that of a sardonic triumph, for a moment—a single moment, appearing upon his strikingly handsome countenance, and then the next instant leaving it full of a warm, generous, and frank-hearted expression again. "Rest assured, St. Louis," he hastened to observe, as he saw that the young man's features darkened slightly again, "that I am not merely anxious and willing, but also able to serve you. Tell me, however, do you write a good, clear clerkly hand?"

"Without vanity, my lord, I can declare myself a good penman," answered St. Louis, the momentary cloud passing away from his features even as quickly as the peculiar smile on Danvers' lip which had conjured it up.

"Good! you are an able penman, then?" exclaimed the nobleman. "And now say—is your name offensively known in high quarters?—that is, have you by any indiscretion rendered yourself the subject of outlawry or proclamation?"

"No, my lord," replied St. Louis. "In the City of London my name smells not over sweet amongst tradesmen and tavern-keepers——"

"But it has never been positively stigmatized in a court of justice?" asked Danvers.

"Never, my lord," was the response. "But wherefore these questions?"

"Because there is a post of honour now vacant at the Court," answered the nobleman, "and which post is in the gift of a worthy friend of mine——"

"A post at Court!" exclaimed Welford, in such a sudden paroxysm of joy that he tore off his mask and tossed it up in the air. "Only conceive, my worthy friend, a post at Court! It will be the making of you! Down upon your knees and breathe forth your gratitude to his lordship! But pray, when you are a great man, don't forget your excellent tutor, guide, and comrade, Dr. Benjamin Welford, Licentiate in Medicine, Apothecary, and Dispenser of Drugs."

"Ah! is that your style and title?" asked Danvers, now fixing his keen dark eyes with a sort of suddenly inspired interest upon St. Louis's worthless comrade.

"Yes—at your lordship's service," replied Welford: "and if having done your best for St. Louis here, your lordship would only extend your generosity towards me——"

"Judging by your years, Master Welford," interrupted the nobleman, "it is most likely *you* who have corrupted this unfortunate young man. But as he is to be unfortunate no longer, it shall be my care to remove you from too close a neighbourhood unto him. Therefore if you really wish me to serve you also, make speedy preparations to repair to some distant part of the kingdom, where I will ensure you a maintenance."

"Is your lordship serious?" exclaimed Welford, his ignoble countenance beaming with a sort of lurid satisfaction. "For I do not think that your lordship would jest with a poor reduced gentleman like me?"

"I never jest," answered Danvers, in a severe tone, and with a haughty look. "Where do you live, sir?"

"I have a tenement—such as it is—in the Old Bailey, my lord," replied Welford: "but I dare not return thither just at present, inasmuch as the calls of tradesmen and tavern-keepers are so numerous that they disturb my slumbers."

"Enough! we will see to all that," said Lionel Danvers: then turning towards St. Louis, he asked, "Are you contented with these arrangements which I am shadowing forth?—will you accept a post of honour, emolument, and trust about the person of the King?—and are you willing that I should do something for your friend here, in order that ye may henceforth be separated?"

"Ah! my lord," returned St. Louis, "how can I ever sufficiently express my gratitude for all these demonstrations of kindness? I am ready to curse my own folly in having ere now hesitated for a moment to accept your lordship's friendship——"

"And of all that we will think no more," interrupted Danvers. "Here—
take this purse," he continued, producing one that was heavily filled:
"you can give a portion of the gold to your companion, so that he may
hesitate not to return home to his residence in the Old Bailey. But you,
St. Louis, will to-morrow purchase suitable raiment—apparel yourself
handsomely—and go boldly to yon palace where the King now holds his
Court——"

"To Greenwich House, my lord?" asked St. Louis, his heart fluttering
with such joyous feelings that he had not experienced for many and many
a day.

"Yes—to Greenwich House," replied Danvers: "and you will present
yourself to Sir Edward Poynings, the Comptroller of the Royal Establishment. Tell the worthy knight you are he whom Lord Danvers recommends
for the post of Private Secretary to his Highness the King. This post is at
the moment vacant: and you shall obtain it."

"Oh, my lord!" cried St. Louis, now bursting into tears, "if any one
had told me an hour back that it was possible for my life to experience
such a change, I should have thought that the assertion was a mere mockery. Indeed, all that is now occurring seems so marvellous—so full of romance—that I can scarcely believe my own senses. It must be a dream—a
brilliant dream—from which there will be the awakening of a bitter disappointment!"

"It is true—all true," said Danvers. "For my part, I am incapable of
deceiving you," he added in a tone of easy assurance.

"And the gold is in your hands," whispered Welford. "It is no dream
that I am to have a share."

"My lord, I have not words to thank you," murmured St. Louis, his
voice tremulous with emotions. "From this hour do I enter upon a new
existence! You have saved me from perdition:"—and taking the hand of
Lionel Danvers, he pressed it to his lips, moistening it with his tears.

"Of your past life you need say to Sir Edward Poynings nothing de-
preciatory," remarked the nobleman. "I shall see him early in the morning,
and will speak sufficiently in your behalf, so that without compromising
my own truthfulness, I may dispose him favourably towards you. The
way will therefore be prepared: and again I tell you that the vacant post
shall be yours. As for you, Master Welford," continued Danvers, turning
towards the apothecary, "you may expect a visit from me to-morrow at
about mid-day, when I shall develop the plan which I may have devised on
your account. At all events, hold yourself in readiness to quit London at
the shortest notice: for I repeat it is my intention to despatch you to some
distance. And now good night."

Having thus spoken, Lord Danvers turned quickly away; and a bend in the lane speedily concealed him from the view of the two individuals who stood gazing after him as if still in a state of uncertainty whether they were not the sport of an hallucination as pleasing as it was visionary.

CHAPTER XI.

DEADMAN'S PLACE.

LONDON, at the time of which we are writing, was but a small town in comparison with the London of the present day. A reference to the maps of that period will show that Cornhill was an open space; the districts of Whitechapel and Houndsditch, now so densely populated, were chiefly gardens and grounds shaded by immense trees; and the laundresses of the City used to dry their linen in Moorfields. Finsbury consisted of pasture-lands where cattle grazed; and where Finsbury Square is now laid out, there were three windmills. Goswell Street[3] was a bye-lane, so lonely that it was unsafe for travellers to journey there after nightfall; and Islington Church stood at a distance, with a few houses about it, the whole group forming a picturesque little village. St. Giles's—a name with which is associated every idea of squalor, demoralization, and misery—was a hamlet as detached as Islington: the Strand was an avenue of palatial mansions with splendid gardens; and St. Martin's Lane was a shady walk lined with trees.

On the Surrey side of the River Thames, the Borough of Southwark consisted of but a dozen streets—St. Olave's (now called Tooley Street) being the principal. Rotherhithe and Bermondsey were detached villages: Walworth was also an isolated hamlet; and the chronicles of that day speak pompously of the "independent and important market-town of Lambeth, the residence of the Primate." Bankside was a noted place for infamous houses and the lowest dens of corruption, as well as for bear-gardens and amphitheatres for bull-baiting. Despite however the ill-repute of that neighbourhood, it was the site of an episcopal palace, the Bishop of Winchester having his dwelling there.

This rapid glance at the metropolis in the time of Henry VIII will be sufficient to show those who are familiar with it now-a-days, how very different it was from its present magnitude. The discrepancy was quite as great in reference to its general aspect. With the exception of a very few good thoroughfares—such as the Strand, Aldersgate, Cheapside, Holborn, &c., the streets were for the most part as bad as the wretched bye-lanes, vile alleys, and low courts belonging to the poorest neighbourhood of

the present day. Unpaved, the streets were full of holes, and littered with
rubbish, rendering locomotion alike difficult and disagreeable even in the
broad day light, but making it actually perilous in the night-time when
these wretched thoroughfares were involved in total darkness. Narrow and
crooked, with great overhanging gables, they were gloomy enough when
the sun shone bright in the heavens: but when plunged into obscurity, they
constituted a maze of dangers which it was a perfect venture to encounter.
The dwellings themselves were, generally speaking, of a proportionately
wretched description, consisting chiefly of plaster and timber, thatched on
the roof, and having each storey overhanging that immediately beneath
it—so that if two opposite houses were six yards apart from threshold to
threshold, there would be scarcely two yards interval between attic and
attic. Be it observed that while in many parts of the country—especially
in the Isle of Wight—substantial brick buildings had for some time been
in vogue, yet in the metropolis nine out of every ten houses consisted of
the trumpery and combustible materials above named; so that it can be
no wonder if London were so often ravaged by conflagrations, consum-
ing thousands of houses ere their rage was spent. Nor, on looking at the
wretchedness of the streets—their narrowness—the density with which
the population was packed—the accumulations of filth and garbage of all
kinds—the deficiency of water—and the absence of anything like proper
ventilation,—can we be astonished if pestilence should have been as frequent and as insatiate a visitor as conflagration.

Fixing the special attention of the reader for the present on the
Borough of Southwark, we must observe that it had been from a very
early period a refuge for all kinds of depraved, infamous, and dangerous
characters. It was this circumstance, which indeed constituted a growing
evil, that induced Edward III to place Southwark under the jurisdiction
of the corporation of London: but while in that and succeeding reigns
some feeble efforts were made to purge the Borough of the shoals of bad
characters swarming there, one particular spot remained invested with
all the privileges of a "sanctuary."[4] This was known as Deadman's Place,
and lay between St. Olave's Street and the river, just where Mill Lane is at
the present day. Picture to yourself a little nest of the narrowest streets,
the closest courts, and alleys so confined that scarcely two people could
walk abreast, and where hands might be shaken easily from opposite windows—abounding in the most offensive odours, or rather having an atmosphere appearing to hang like a black plague-mist over the spot,—and
the reader may form an idea of what that sanctuary was which bore the
dreadful name of Deadman's Place.

How it had become a Sanctuary no one could exactly tell: for there was assuredly no written charter extant, guaranteeing it such privileges. But certain was it that never did the constables or any law-authorities venture to make an irruption into Deadman's Place in pursuit of an offender, cases of high treason being alone excepted. If even a murderer were chased by the officials of the law, the moment he stepped across the boundary of St. Olave's Street into Deadman's Place, he was safe: the constables would stop short as if a wall of adamant had suddenly sprung up between them and the object of their pursuit! It may therefore be easily imagined that the Sanctuary was ever crowded with the very worst characters, and that in its confined state it could not always find room for the numbers seeking refuge there. Thus, often were the redundant refugees compelled to pass the night in the open air,—that night which under such circumstances they rendered terrible by their uproarious shouts, bacchanalian songs, and uncouth noises.

To continue our tale. It was about two o'clock in the morning, as Welford and St. Louis rode along St. Olave's Street and turned into Deadman's Place. Here they were compelled by the narrowness of the thoroughfare to proceed one in advance of the other; and in a few minutes they stopped at the dark-mouthed entrance to a stable-yard attached to a house which stood completely upon the bank of the river. On Welford making a certain signal, a light presently appeared; and from a building at the end of the yard an ill-looking fellow came forth with a lantern to receive the horses, from which the two riders now dismounted.

"Well, what luck?" he asked, in a growling tone, as if he had just been disturbed from his slumbers in the hay-loft.

"Oh! tolerably good," exclaimed Welford. "At all events you need not put so sullen a face on it; for we shall perhaps find an odd coin for you. Where is the old man?"

"In-doors: and I don't think he is gone to bed yet—for there has been a terrible fight in the Sanctuary, and he as ward's-man was called out to exercise his authority."

"Well, but all is quiet now?" observed Welford.

"O yes," answered the man: "it was only one of those drunken riots that are frequent enough here. But do you want to see the old man at this hour? It's past two, and I should think you would both be glad to take a little rest?"

"What say you, friend of mine?" asked Welford, turning to St. Louis: "shall we stretch ourselves in the hay-loft for three or four hours—or go over to the Old Bailey, and then come back again at breakfast-time?"

"No—I will see the old man at once," replied St. Louis, sternly. "Come, let us seek him!"

Welford accordingly led the way down the stable-yard, in the same direction whither the man had already conducted the horses. He knocked with his fist at a little low door in the side-wall, which was opened in a few minutes by an old man, upwards of sixty, and whose aspect was of a very vile and sinister nature. He had but a few garments, negligently huddled on, and which showed that he was preparing for rest when thus disturbed by his two visitors. At first he was evidently inclined to demand savagely why he was thus intruded on: but so soon as he distinguished the countenance of Welford and St. Louis, by the light which he carried in his hand, he assumed a more amiable aspect.

"Ah! is it you come back?" he said. "Walk in, walk in."

"Old Dunhaven," observed Welford, with a coarse laugh, "only bids us thus courteously to enter, because he smells the gold in our pockets."

"Ah, gold?" ejaculated the horse-dealer, greedily. "Well, I am glad to hear that you have experienced such good luck."

"Good luck indeed!" ejaculated Welford, as he followed Dunhaven into a little close dirty room, of which two or three clumsy stools, an equally uncouth table, and a hard pallet stretched upon a long chest, or trunk, in one corner constituted the furniture. The ceiling was so low that a tall man would have touched it with his head; and the atmosphere was perfectly stifling. This was the old horse-dealer's own chamber. He was unmarried and childless, and had neither kith nor kin to bear him company: so he dwelt all alone in this room, the remainder of his house being occupied by lodgers—these consisting, as a matter of course, of some of the desperate characters taking refuge in the Sanctuary.

We may here seize the opportunity to observe that Dunhaven, being the oldest inhabitant in Deadman's Place, and also reputed to be the wealthiest (his ostensible trade being that of horse-dealer) was invested with the authority of "ward's-man," or governor as it were of this colony of society's most desperate outcasts. Not that his authority was either conferred or recognised by the law: it was merely accorded to him by the suffrages of the householders in the Sanctuary; and he exercised it in pursuance of a code of laws which might be termed the Constitution of the Sanctuary's government. In exercising this authority and carrying out these laws, he was sure to be efficiently backed by the other householders, all of whom recognised the necessity of having something like a penal code amongst them. The punishments which this code inflicted, were necessarily of a limited character,—consisting of fines in money or liquor—a good ducking in the Thames, which flowed handy—or expulsion from the Sanctuary,—this last being only inflicted for the most serious offences. But it can be easily understood how a sentence of expulsion might in reality become one of *death*: for to expel a criminal was as a matter of course to throw him into the hands of justice outside the circle of the Sanctuary; and through those hands he was pretty sure to pass to the scaffold.

We may now pursue the thread of our narrative without the necessity of farther interruptions. On introducing Welford and St. Louis into his own room, Dunhaven placed the light upon the table; and producing a bottle of spirits, he offered his two visitors a dram. This Welford accepted; but St. Louis declined—a circumstance which made the old horse-dealer regard him with an earnest attention mingled with amazement.

"Ah! you may well look at our young friend in that manner," said Welford. "A complete change seems to have come over him within the last two hours—in fact, since a little adventure——"

"Silence!" ejaculated St. Louis, turning sharply round upon his companion. "You surely are not going to let your tongue babble in the usual style about *this* occurrence, at all events?"

"Well, well—it shall be a secret then," said the doctor somewhat sullenly.

"Ah! where are your swords?" suddenly exclaimed Dunhaven, "You have the sheaths hanging to your sides; but the weapons are gone. What can this mean? Surely, surely, if you murdered some traveller for his purse, you have not been foolish enough to leave those weapons behind you? For there is no knowing how they may be recognised and lead to your capture—that is to say, unless you mean to remain in the Sanctuary all the rest of your lives?"

"Make yourself perfectly easy on this score," interrupted St. Louis, almost sternly. "No murder has been done—nor indeed robbery, for that matter."

"No—Danvers was generous enough with his gold," exclaimed Welford, with a coarse chuckle, and he bestowed a sly vulgar wink upon his companion.

"Danvers!" echoed the old horse-dealer, with sudden start.

"Silence, fool," interjected St. Louis, turning sharp round upon the doctor, and seizing him fiercely by the doublet. "You have already remarked that a change has recently come over me—and you spoke truly: for it is such a change as releases me from the thraldom in which you have so long kept me. Therefore understand me well—if you dare venture to breathe another word concerning all that has taken place to-night, I will make you bitterly repent it."

"Come, hands off, St. Louis!" said Welford suddenly. "I did not mean to blab—but merely let slip the name by accident."

"And that name?" cried old Dunhaven, with intense eagerness: "was it not Danvers?"

"No matter," answered St. Louis shortly.

"Yes, yes—but it does matter," said the horse-dealer, evidently labouring under considerable excitement. "It is not a common name; and of the noble race that bore it for centuries, not a soul remains alive."

"You are wrong, old man," exclaimed Welford, forgetting St. Louis's last injunction and menace, "for it was Lord Danvers whom we saw to-night."

"No, no—impossible, impossible!" cried Dunhaven, trembling all over with the excitement of strange terror mingled with amazed incredulity.

"But why do you speak thus positively?" asked St. Louis, struck by the peculiarity of the old man's tone and look.

"Because," he answered, fixing his small grey eyes with an ominous significancy upon the young man, "Lionel Danvers, the last of his race, ceased to exist two years ago!"

"Describe him—describe him!" exclaimed St. Louis.

"When last I saw him," returned Dunhaven—"that was two years ago—he seemed about eight-and-twenty years of age—tall, slender, of wondrous personal beauty—hair dark as jet—eyes flashing strange wild fires—and a look at times of such ineffable scorn as if a diabolic malice curled his lips."

"By heaven, 'tis the same!" cried St. Louis, now no longer thinking it necessary to guard the secret—or rather, perhaps, not pausing to think upon the point at all.

"Yes—the very same that we saw to-night!" added Welford. "But assuredly it was no ghost—for he wielded his rapier in a most swordsman-like manner——"

"What is this I hear?" cried Dunhaven, his aged form quivering perceptibly from head to foot, and his whole countenance convulsed with horror. "You say that you have this night encountered such a man as he whom I have described, and bearing the name of Danvers?"

"Aye, verily it is so," Welford hastened to respond: "and by the token that he sent my broadsword over into an enclosed ground, and dashed the one wielded by St. Louis to the bottom of a pond."

"Tell me—tell me," interrupted the old man, his nervous agitation increasing,—and he caught hold of St. Louis' arm as he spoke,—"tell me, my young friend—for *you* are not accustomed to speak at random—besides, you have a solemn demeanour at this hour and will adhere to the truth—tell me, I say, is all this substantially correct?"

"Accurate to the very letter, as you are a living man!" returned St. Louis, almost confounded with what was now taking place. "But it is for you to explain yourself. What mean you," he demanded impatiently, "by the averment that Lord Danvers is no more—that he ceased to exist two years back?—since in living flesh and blood we have encountered him within the last few hours!"

Dunhaven did not immediately answer the question: but stepping back, he raised his hand to his brow as if to steady his thoughts and commune with himself. Both Welford and St. Louis gazed with earnest curiosity upon him, both alike wondering whether he were in his right senses, and if so, under what strange mistake he could be labouring to declare that an individual whom they had encountered so very recently, had ceased for two years past to be in the land of the living.

"You, St. Louis," said Dunhaven, slowly arousing himself from his reverie, and fixing a look of deep meaning upon the young man's countenance—"you are interested in the fate of the family of Danvers!"

"How know you this, old man?" demanded St. Louis, quickly. "I suppose your chattering tongue again," he added, turning sharply round upon Welford, "has revealed those family secrets which in a friendly mood of confidence I entrusted to you?"

"No, no—I declare that I never thought it of sufficient importance to trouble my head about it," exclaimed Welford.

"Ah! then, I comprehend it!" ejaculated St. Louis: and reverting his looks menacingly upon Dunhaven, he said, "You have violated the sanctity of that casket which I deposited in your hands?—you have read the paper which it contains?"

"There is no denying it," answered the horse dealer. "But do not strike!" he exclaimed as St. Louis raised his hand to inflict a blow: "touch me not—and I will tell you a strange and wondrous secret!"

"Well, for thy secret then?" demanded St. Louis restraining his anger, "But why did you open my casket?—how dared you break the wax fastening the paper that contained it?"

"One word of explanation," answered Dunhaven, eager to exculpate himself through fear of harsh treatment: for there was something terribly wrathful and determined in St. Louis' looks. "I trusted you and your companion here with horses and pistols for your night's enterprise; and you left me in pledge a casket of sandal-wood inlaid with gold. When you were gone I rather repented of the arrangement,—fearing that, after all, the settings of the casket might be only of polished brass. This suspicion seemed to be confirmed by the fact that you had insisted on having it enveloped in paper and sealed in your presence. I felt assured I was duped, and that I should never see horses nor pistols again."

"Well, well," interrupted St. Louis impatiently, "to make a long story short, you tore open the envelope and examined the casket?"

"I did so, and satisfied myself that it was good jeweller's gold, such as would be bought in Lombard Street. But in so examining the casket, the lid flew open——"

"Yes—you must have touched the secret spring," remarked St. Louis, somewhat mollified by the old man's explanation, which certainly absolved him from any deliberate treachery respecting the casket. "Well, you found the papers?"

"And I read them," replied Dunhaven. "Ah! you know not what fearful sensation of interest was excited within me when I beheld the portrait of a lovely female set in the lid of the casket, with that inscription beneath— '*Arline de St. Louis, Victim of Lord Humphrey Danvers, in the year 1463.*'"

"But why, why," demanded St. Louis, now greatly agitated, "should you have experienced such a feeling? Did you know the unfortunate Arline? No—for you must have been but a mere boy at the time."

"I knew her not—I never heard of her before," replied Dunhaven: then in a solemn tone he added, "But I am smitten with a feeling of the deepest interest, because I know of *another* sad and mournful history, in which a lovely damsel was the heroine and a scion of the house of Danvers the hero!"

"Indeed! a case resembling this of Arline?" asked St. Louis, eagerly.

"Yes—the exact parallel," returned Dunhaven. "In a word, it was an ancestress of mine—the lovely Margaret—the fairest maid of Cumberland—and it was in the year 1407.——Oh! the date has been religiously preserved——that she became the victim of Lord Ranulph Danvers!"

"Then perhaps *you* also, worthy Dunhaven," interposed Welford, with a coarse attempt to give the conversation a jocular turn, "have cherished an hereditary hatred against the house of Danvers!"

"Aye—a mortal hatred!" answered the old man, evidently feeling deeply the words that he uttered. "Would you like a proof of this hatred of mine?" he abruptly demanded with a diabolic look. "Well, you shall have it! It will reveal the secret to which I ere now alluded; and it will also explain wherefore I so positively announced that Lord Lionel Danvers, the last of his race, ceased to exist two years ago. Follow me."

Thus speaking, the old man took up the candle from the table, and opening the door, led the way along a narrow passage, Welford and St. Louis following close behind. In a few moments he paused at a door which he unfastened with some difficulty; for the bolts which closed it were fixed with rust in their sockets. At length however it yielded; and Dunhaven passed on into a small room without any window, totally denuded of furniture, and the walls of which were green and mildewed with the damp. Both Welford and St. Louis cast their eyes around; and beholding nothing in this room, they simultaneously fixed their looks inquiringly upon the old man.

"Do you feel nothing?" he asked, with a look maliciously significant.

"The boards quivering under my feet!" cried St. Louis, at the moment experiencing what he thus described: and instantaneously suspecting some treachery, he bounded back to the threshold, where indeed Welford had halted at the first.

"Fear nothing," said Dunhaven, placing himself close against the wall, so as to leave the middle of the room quite clear. "Now observe!"—and as he thus spoke, he pressed his hand against an iron knob in the wall where he thus leant.

The effect was instantaneous. The whole flooring in the middle of the room seemed to give way quickly as the eye can wink,—half of it disappearing downward and half of it tilting upward. In a word, it was a trap-door about a yard and a-half square, fixed upon an axle, so that by touching a spring the bolts which held it tight in its place were drawn back, and by the semi-revolution of the axle, the trap suddenly took a vertical instead of a horizontal position—thus forming a chasm the mouth of which the axle intersected.

St. Louis could not repress a quick start, while Welford gave vent to an ejaculation of alarm at this sudden opening of the floor: but immediately perceiving what it was, they turned their looks upon old Dunhaven for farther explanations.

"Hush!" he said, raising his finger to command silence: and they listened accordingly.

The dull eddying sounds of flowing water met their ears; and knowing how closely the house was situated upon the bank of the Thames—recollecting moreover that it had an overhanging out-building—they instantaneously understood that it must be the river itself which was rolling beneath. St. Louis shuddered; and Welford, bold though he were in all desperate ventures, drew still farther back even from the threshold.

"And now what would you have us to gather from this revelation of the murderous mystery of your house?" asked St. Louis, more than half suspecting what the reply would be.

"Upwards of two years ago," responded Dunhaven, in a deep voice and with sombre look,—"in the middle of a dark night—when neither moon nor star shone upon the face of heaven, but the wild March winds were raving and moaning and sighing as if bearing on their wings the cries of murder sent up from dead men's graves—on that night, I say, Lionel Danvers, lured hither no matter how, was precipitated down the abyss, which suddenly opened beneath his feet, and plunged into the tide beneath! The river was swollen at the time—the current rushed onward with a strength bidding defiance to the power and the skill of the strongest swimmer. Think you, then, it was without good ground and sufficient cause I ere now affirmed that Lord Danvers had ceased to exist?"

St. Louis advanced towards the edge of the chasm—took the candle from Dunhaven's hand—and held it over the opening, while he endeavoured to plunge his looks into the gulf. But it was an inky darkness that prevailed within—a darkness which no eyes might penetrate. Shaking his head dubiously, St. Louis handed back the candle to the old man: then, as the marvellous manner in which Danvers had ere now escaped unhurt from the four pistol-shots flashed to his mind, he said, "Of a surety that man must bear a charmed life!"

"Yes—if it indeed be he whom, as you declare, you have seen this night," responded Dunhaven.

While thus speaking, he touched the spring, and the revolving trap-door at once resumed its place, a sharp metallic sound indicating that the bolts which retained it in a fixed position level with the floor, had shot back into their sockets. Then, with a species of superstitious awe hanging like an oppressive cloud upon their minds, did both St. Louis and Welford accompany the old horse-dealer back to his own room, on reaching which he was beginning to renew the conversation on the same topic, when all in a moment a loud knocking was heard at the door leading into the stable-yard. With a low-muttered imprecation, Dunhaven hastened to answer the summons; and the moment he opened the outer door, a female voice exclaimed, "For heaven's sake, come directly, good Master Dunhaven, to the *Gallows Tavern*: for some new comers are brawling and fighting at a terrific rate, and blood will be shed ere long."

"Well, well—go back to your master, young-woman," replied Dunhaven, "and tell him that I will be over there in a minute or two."

"Yes—pray do: for your authority alone will restore order."

"I come in a minute," answered Dunhaven: and he then shut the door impatiently.

"More work for you to-night," observed Welford. "But I wonder you are not afraid of thrusting yourself into those commotions? A man of your years, and somewhat ricketty on your legs——"

"Ah, well! I am compelled to put up with it," returned Dunhaven, with a sigh. "If it were not that my little authority here makes my person as it were sacred, I should not be able to live in this dreadful place a single night in safety."

"Then why continue here at all?" demanded Welford. "What a thrice-soddened old fool you must be!"

"Mind your own business," interrupted Dunhaven sternly; then approaching his bed, he drew the pallet off the trunk whereupon it was stretched, and opening the immense box, which was filled with a most miscellaneous assortment of articles—such as plate, fire-arms, swords, daggers, and garments—he drew forth an object enveloped in a piece of paper.

St. Louis, on receiving it from his hands, hastily satisfied himself that it was his much-prized casket; and he proceeded to secure it about his person. He then produced the purse which he had received from Danvers, and whence he took two pieces of gold. These he presented to the old horse-dealer, who clutched the coin with a glittering eagerness in the eyes and an avidity of look that showed how deeply was the love of lucre implanted in his tainted soul. "Now let us depart," exclaimed St. Louis.

"Yes—and leave the ward's-man here to go and attend to his duties at the *Gallows*," observed Welford—immediately adding with a coarse laugh, "Perchance he will someday swing to one."

"No—rest assured *that* will be *your* fate!" retorted the old man, in a tone of fierce resentment: then as Welford with a continuation of his rough laugh opened the outer door, Dunhaven caught St. Louis by the arm and whispered hastily, "You and I must meet again! We have much to talk about. Will you come to-morrow by yourself?"

"No—not to-morrow: but as soon as convenient," answered St. Louis. "But rest assured that I *will* come!"

He then quitted the house; and rejoining Welford who was waiting outside the door, they hastened away from the Sanctuary of Deadman's Place.

CHAPTER XII.

THE COMPTROLLER OF THE ROYAL HOUSEHOLD.

It was about eleven o'clock on the following morning that St. Louis, handsomely dressed, landed from a boat at Greenwich and bent his steps towards the side-entrance of the palace.

A considerable change had taken place in his appearance, not merely on account of the improved character of his wardrobe, but also in his looks. Hope now beamed in his eyes—the flush of confidence was upon his countenance—and a certain polished air of gentility had succeeded that wild recklessness which was wont to mark his demeanour.

Ascending the steps of the side-door, St. Louis entered a marble hall, where several of the Court lacqueys and menials were lounging. Accost-

ing one of them, St. Louis inquired whether he could obtain an interview
with Sir Edward Poynings, the Comptroller of the Royal Household; and
a response was at once given in the affirmative. St. Louis was thereupon
conducted up a staircase to a handsome apartment, where a fine, tall,
good-looking man, splendidly dressed, and whose age might have been
about forty, was seated at a table covered with bills, receipts, and account-
books. This was Sir Edward Poynings; and upon St. Louis being introduced into his presence, he at once received him with a most encouraging
courtesy and bade him be seated.

"My name is Gerald St. Louis," said the young man; "and I venture to
intrude myself upon your notice, having heard that his Highness our most
gracious King is in need of a confidential secretary."

"You are he whom Lord Danvers has already spoken of to me?" observed Sir Edward Poynings, inquiringly.

"I have the honour to be acquainted with that nobleman," answered
St. Louis; "and it was at his suggestion that I have become emboldened to
solicit the vacant situation."

"Lord Danvers is an intimate friend of mine," observed the Comptroller; "and on all occasions should I prove most anxious to oblige him.
He has been with me this morning, and has specially recommended you
to my notice as a young man every way adapted to fill this important and
trustworthy post about the person of his Highness. By your name I conceive you to be of French extraction?"

"My parents, may it please you, sir, were French," responded St. Louis: "but I may truthfully style myself an Englishman, inasmuch as I was
born in the suburbs of London, and my Christian name, as you perceive,
is English."

"But you doubtless speak the French language?" asked Sir Edward.

"As well as the English tongue," answered St. Louis.

"That qualification is an indispensable one for an aspirant to the post
of Royal Secretary," observed the Comptroller; "inasmuch as the greater
portion of our State papers and diplomatic communications, as well as
the correspondence which the King maintains with foreign potentates,
are couched in the Gallic tongue. And now relative to your penmanship,
Lord Danvers assured me that you could write a fluent, plain, and clerkly
hand?"

"Permit me, sir, to give you a specimen," St. Louis exclaimed; and
drawing his chair close to the table, he wrote a few lines upon a piece of
paper.

"This is most scholarly and excellent," remarked Sir Edward, as he
examined the specimen of the candidate's penmanship. "I have received at

least a hundred applications for this vacant post, which I may affirm to be within my gift, inasmuch as his Highness, who deigns to place great confidence in me, his humble servant, has commanded that I should find him a fit and proper person to serve as his private secretary with as short a delay as possible. Out of the host of applications whereof I have just spoken, I have so far entertained ten or a dozen that I have kept them specially in view, so that their relative merits being compared, the best qualified of the number might be finally selected. But your personal qualifications, Master St. Louis, rise superior to those of all the others—especially when so well backed with the favour and countenance of the noble Lord Danvers. Will you, however, be grateful and recognisant if I induct you into this important situation?"—and as Sir Edward Poynings put the question his countenance assumed a certain mysterious significancy which at once struck St. Louis.

"I will testify my gratitude to the utmost of my power," he answered. "Indeed, you have but to indicate the manner whereby I may demonstrate my feelings of thankfulness, and the test will show that I am sincere."

"I have no doubt of it," rejoined Sir Edward emphatically. "You are all well aware," he continued in a lower and more confidential tone, and still with a certain significance in his looks, "that those who are attached to Courts, while performing their public duties, are also justified in forwarding their private interests? I presume you are not merely acquainted with this fact, but are prepared to act accordingly."

St. Louis was for a moment embarrassed how to reply. He fancied that Sir Edward Poynings was merely putting the question to him in order to try his trustworthiness and integrity: yet when he looked into the Comptroller's countenance he beheld that peculiar significancy of look which seemed to corroborate the idea that there was really something behind. He accordingly observed in a guarded manner, "It is you, sir, who are placing me in this honourable position about the person of the King: and recognizing you as my patron, I shall ever obey whatever commands you may issue, or follow whatever advice you may choose to give me."

"Answered with true courtier-like diplomacy!" exclaimed Sir Edward, laughing; then, as his countenance instantaneously grew serious again, he observed, "Master St. Louis, you and I must understand each other before I confirm you in your appointment and present you to the King. You speak fairly enough now, and your promises look sincere: but thus is it always with a candidate for office. What guarantee have I that when once installed about the person of the King, you will not toss all idea of gratitude to the winds, and so far from following my advice, run exactly counter to my wishes?"

"What guarantee can I give you, sir," asked St. Louis, "as a proof of my good faith?"

"What guarantee?" repeated the Comptroller in a musing tone. "I know not exactly. And yet it is necessary that I should have some security of the sort; because from the moment your appointment receives the royal sanction you become independent of me, holding your post at the pleasure of the King and of none other. You may become a favourite with his Highness: it is possible—it is even likely—considering the trustworthy and confidential office that you will fill. Your opinion may have weight with his Highness: you may be enabled to exercise some degree of influence in many respects. Now let us understand each other at once, St. Louis," added Sir Edward Poynings, fixing his eyes full upon the countenance of the young man. "The power which I have shadowed out is what I will not see entrusted to any one!"

St. Louis now comprehended altogether the meaning of Sir Edward Poynings. He saw that this personage was resolved to fill up the vacant post with some creature of his own—or, at all events, with an individual who would hold himself entirely at his disposal. But the fortunes of St. Louis were otherwise too desperate not to render him willing to make any sacrifice rather than allow the present opportunity of re-establishing them to slip through his fingers. Of little consequence was it to him how completely he might become bound hand and foot to Sir Edward Poynings, so long as he obtained a post of honour and emolument about the person of the King. Nevertheless, while thus making up his mind to accept any terms and subscribe to any conditions in order to secure the place, St. Louis could not help feeling galled by the reflection that Lord Danvers had most probably been all along aware that some such peculiar terms and conditions would be insisted upon, and that he had therefore recommended him (St. Louis) rather as a tool to serve Sir Edward's purposes than from the purely generous motive which had at first appeared to influence him. Veiling however the disagreeable feeling which these reflections excited, and resolving to play his cards with courtier-like diplomacy which Sir Edward Poynings had already jocularly commended, St. Louis proceeded to observe "that he had no personal interests of a selfish character to minister unto; that he was anxious to push his way in the world; and that he placed himself wholly and entirely at the disposal of Sir Edward Poynings."

"But you must do more than *that*," said the Comptroller, bending upon him an earnest look: "you must not merely place yourself at my disposal, but also in my power!"

"I am prepared to do so," responded St. Louis. "Have I not already said that whatever proof of my sincerity you demand shall be cheerfully accorded?"

"You speak like a man—aye, and like a man of the world too," observed Sir Edward. "Methinks that you will push your way well at Court, and in time be enabled to command the adhesion, the services, and the fidelities of others as I am now securing your's unto myself. But to the point. You must place yourself, I say, in my power—you must be as it were, at my mercy; and your office, your honour—nay, your very life, must be in my hands!"

"My life?" exclaimed St. Louis, startled by the terrific import of the conditions thus chalked out, and which so far transcended any thing he had preconceived.

"Yes—your life!" repeated Sir Edward Poynings, looking him resolutely and even sternly in the face. "If I ask too much, that is an end of our conference, and no harm done."

"Well then," cried St. Louis, "since it is but a guarantee and a test of sincerity you require, and as I never mean by any infidelity or ingratitude on my part to make the forfeit, I may as well place my life, honour, and everything in your hands. But how is this to be done?"

"It is easily arranged," rejoined Sir Edward. "Commit some act which at once places you in my power. For instance, take a slip paper—write an acknowledgement for certain moneys—sign the name of Lionel Danvers thereto——"

"What! forge the name of Lord Danvers?" ejaculated St. Louis, irresistibly struck by the idea that all this must be a preconcerted conspiracy to ruin him, and that Danvers himself was a party to it.

"And why not?" demanded Sir Edward coldly. "Think you that I wish to ensnare you for any other purpose than that which I have named? It is preposterous! What interest can I have in accomplishing your ruin? But it seems as if we did not yet quite understand each other—or rather that *you* have not altogether understood *me*. I will therefore speak more plainly than I have been doing, and there shall be no possibility of mistaking my language. What, then, are the facts? Here is a particular situation, of emolument and honour, which is virtually in my gift. But inasmuch as it suits me to place a sworn adherent and friend of my own in that office, I choose to take adequate guarantees that trust shall not be abused, and that he in whom I hope to find a staunch ally may not become converted by selfish considerations into a rival or an enemy."

While Sir Edward Poynings was thus candidly, frankly, and explicitly detailing his views and motives, Gerald St. Louis had leisure to recover from the alarm into which the proposed forgery had plunged him; and a moment's reflection convinced him that the exact truth was as the Comp-troller now explained it. For if Lord Danvers wished to destroy him, could he not have taken his life on the preceding night—could he not have thrust him through and through with his rapier?—would he have given him a purse of gold instead of taking measures to hand him over to the grasp of justice? Such were the questions which St. Louis hastily revolved in his mind; and the result of his deliberation was to abandon himself entirely to this new current of events on which his destiny seemed to have cast him.

"You will admit, sir," he observed when the Comptroller had done speaking, "that to propose a forgery to an honest and well intentioned man such as I,"—and he blushed not as he thus vaunted an integrity from which he had been so long estranged,—"it is but well calculated to startle and dismay. But considering it more calmly, I can now only regard the sug-gestion as a legitimate guarantee which you have a right, under circum-stances, to demand. Therefore I have no longer any hesitation in acceding to your conditions."

Thereupon Gerald took up the pen once more, and drew out a docu-ment to the following effect:—

"This 9th day of May, 1516.
"By these presents, I acknowledge myself bound to pay unto Master Gerald St. Louis the sum of one hundred pounds sterling, on his demand or to his order.
"As witness my hand,
"DANVERS.

"To be paid at the Counting house of Master Landini, Goldsmith, Lombard Street."

"In some such form as this, I presume?" said Gerald St. Louis, inter-rogatively, when he had drawn up the note of hand.

"Nothing can be more clerkly in penmanship or more business-like in draft," exclaimed Sir Edward. "Now endorse it, as an acknowledgement that you have received the amount specified."

"There!" said the young man, as he signed his name at the back of the forged bill: but it was not altogether without a secret misgiving that he did so.

However this sentiment of mingling doubt and apprehension speed-ily vanished, when Sir Edward Poynings, having locked up the forged bill in an iron casket which stood upon the table, said, "Now come with me, and I will introduce you to the King, so that your appointment may be ratified at once."

The animation of joy lighted up St. Louis' countenance, which had grown serious and moody-looking during the latter portion of the above colloquy; and with a fluttering heart he followed Sir Edward Poynings from the room. They descended the staircase; and the moment they reached the marble hall below, all the lacqueys and menials lounging idly there, at once formed themselves into two lines leading up to a pair of folding doors at the extremity of that hall. Then these two ranks of Court dependants made a low obeisance as the Comptroller passed between them, closely followed by Gerald St. Louis. The folding-doors flew open; and Sir Edward Poynings led on into a spacious apartment where a guard of Buffetiers, or Royal Yeomen, was stationed. Several officers command- ing this corps, and clad in their magnificent uniforms, were playing with dice at a table in a bay-window looking towards the Park: but the moment the Comptroller made his appearance they rose out of respect, while the guard saluted with their halberds.

Passing onward, Sir Edward Poynings led Gerald St. Louis through another apartment, where a number of splendidly-dressed pages and eq- uerries were lounging about. Thence they traversed two more rooms, also crowded with Court officials: and at length they paused in an ante-cham- ber, where two or three Lords-in-waiting were seated. Having ascertained that the King was in the Council-room, Sir Edward Poynings passed on once more, St. Louis closely following; and now, as a pair of gilded fold- ing-doors fell back, the young man was conducted into the presence of the King.

His Majesty was seated in a large arm-chair, raised upon a dais ap- proached by three or four steps; and at a table in front were placed several of the great Officers of State. There was Warham, Archbishop of Can- terbury and Lord High Chancellor of the Kingdom, dressed his pontifical robes, with the mitre upon his head and the crosier in his hand. Next to him sat Lord Herbert, the Chamberlain—an old man with a venerable countenance and having the unmistakable evidences of wisdom in every line that marked his brow. On his right hand was the Earl of Shrewsbury, Lord High Steward; and next to him was Sir Thomas Lovel, Constable of the Tower. Opposite were placed Sir Henry Marney, Sir Thomas Darcy, Henry Wyatt, and Doctor Ruthal. There were the Earl of Surrey, Lord High Treasurer; and the Bishop of Winchester, Lord Privy Seal. These were the members of the Council of State, with whom the King was in deliberation at the moment when Sir Edward Poynings, who was himself a member also, introduced Gerald St. Louis.

The young man experienced a sensation of awe on finding himself in the presence of the King and this august conclave: but he made low and most respectful salutation, and then remained standing near the door, while the Comptroller of the Household accosted his Highness and said a few words in a subdued tone. Henry VIII now beckoned St. Louis to approach, and proceeded to question him relative to his abilities and qualifications. The young man answered in a way which proved altogether satisfactory; and the appointment was at once ratified.

CHAPTER XIII.

THE GOLDSMITH OF LOMBARD STREET.

It has already been stated that Master Landini was one of the richest goldsmith-bankers of Lombard Street; and we may now observe that the largest as well as the handsomest house in that street belonged to him. He was an old man—had long been a widower—and having no children of his own, had adopted a nephew of the same name, and whom he had destined to be the inheritor of his colossal wealth. This nephew, whose Christian name was Marco—abbreviated into the English *Mark*—was a man of about six-and-thirty—as devoted to business as his uncle, and, as his friends were wont to say of him, too completely wedded to the delights of money-making to think of wedding a bride.

In a large but ill-lighted counting-house, on the ground-floor, the nephew of Mark Landini and two clerks might be seen seated at desks, poring over correspondence from almost all the civilized parts of the world as well as from the principal trading towns in England. There was no display of jewellery in the windows: on the contrary, a range of massive iron bars not only protected but likewise darkened each casement. But on a counter inside, were displayed the most costly as well as the most beautiful specimens of jewellery; and on another part of the same counter there was number of wooden bowls containing an infinite variety of coins belonging to the mintage of almost every European country—for the business of money-changing was in those times connected with that of bullion-dealing and banking. At the end of the counting-house a door opened into a private office where Master Landini himself might likewise have been seen profoundly engrossed in the perusal of a mass of correspondence.

It was about two o'clock, on the same day of which we have been writing in the last chapter, when Lord Danvers entered the banking-house. Mark Landini, thrusting his pen behind his ear, hastened round from his desk to receive the nobleman, to whom he made a profound salutation; and officiously opening the door leading into the inner office, he said, "Uncle, our kind patron the Lord Lionel Danvers."

The nobleman passed into the office, where the elder Landini rose from his chair to welcome him—while Mark, shutting the door, went back to his desk in the counting-house.

"You have received your correspondence from abroad?" said Lord Danvers interrogatively, as he carelessly took a seat.

"I have, my lord: a courier arrived this morning. I have letters from my correspondents in Paris, Madrid, Genoa, and Venice."

"And they contain reports relative to my stewards and intendants?" asked Danvers.

"All, my lord," returned Landini; "and every one most favourable as usual. According to your lordship's order, remittances have been made of the various sums in my continental agents' hands, belonging to your lordship. I have not yet added up the amount of the bills of exchange," he continued, pointing to a pile of such commercial papers; "but the sum total of these several remittances must be enormous. What your lordship will do with the money I am at a loss to conceive: but perhaps your lordship will allow me to think of some means of disposing of it to the best advantage. For, assuredly, your lordship has already more estates in different parts of the world than any other nobleman that ever lived."

"Possibly," remarked Danvers, with an air of the most perfect indifference. "I dare say you can recommend some eligible employment for the money; and you must see about it. Has any one called to ask concerning me this morning?"

"Yes, my lord," answered Landini, in a hesitating manner, as if not exactly liking to give an affirmative response, and yet fearing to return a negative. "There has been a person——But it's of no great consequence——I gave him an answer——"

"Well, but who was he?" asked Danvers.

"An old man, my lord——I fear me he is half-crazed: he tells some strange wild tale——"

"I presume you mean an individual by the name of Manners," said the nobleman; "the same who has called here on previous occasions, as you told me yesterday?"

"Well, I think it is the same, my lord," answered Landini, evidently fearful of saying anything that might give the least offence to his immensely rich client.

"And so he has called again this morning?" said Danvers, half carelessly and half with a faint show of interest. "I thought that he would: I saw him the night before last. Did he tell you that he had seen me?"

"He did, my lord," answered Landini. "I offered him money: but he declared that heaven had sent him a friend."

"Did he mention whom?"

"He did not, my lord."

"But I suppose he gave you some particulars of our interview?" said Danvers inquiringly.

"Yes—he said something, my lord," returned the old goldsmith; "but being very, very busy at the time, I did not pay much attention."

"Well, no matter," remarked Danvers carelessly. "The fact is, worthy Master Landini, that old man believes I spirited away his daughter. It was nothing of the kind. For certain reasons she and I separated with the mutual agreement that we were never to meet again; and she—worthless creature that she was!—fled the same night with a rival. That is the whole history of the matter:"—and as Lord Danvers gave utterance to these last words, a strange and almost fearful expression swept, or indeed flashed over his countenance, disappearing with lightning suddenness, and leaving it the next moment with that careless indifferent look which it had worn just before.

"Shall I add up these amounts, my lord?" asked old Landini, in a confused muttering tone: for he had caught that strange and mystic look which passed, fleet as a whirlwind over a lake, athwart the features of the nobleman: but not choosing to appear to have observed it, he affected to be very busy with the papers that lay before him.

"No, no—not now," replied Danvers. "I do not care to trouble myself about money-matters at this moment. By the bye, my good friend Sir Edward Poynings is anxious to purchase an estate in Kent: the sum is considerable—at least for him—but I have agreed to lend it to him. He will most probably call on you this afternoon with the draft I have given him for the amount."

"Prompt attention shall be paid thereto, my lord," answered Landini. "Has your lordship any farther commands?"

"While I think of it," resumed Danvers, "I must observe that some one has been defrauding Sir Edward with a forged draft purporting to be signed by me and to be drawn upon you——"

"A forgery, my lord!" ejaculated Landini. "We must set the officers of justice to work——"

"No such thing," interrupted Danvers. "I know something of the culprit and do not wish to persecute him. Besides, it is only for a poor paltry hundred pounds——"

"Ah, my lord! how generous, how noble-hearted you are!" exclaimed the old banker, who knew how to play the sycophant almost as well as a courtier.

"No, no," returned Danvers; "there is little generosity in suffering a poor wretch like this to escape the scaffold. Indeed, I should not have mentioned it at all, only Sir Edward Poynings insists upon presenting the document here for form's sake, so that you may at once brand it as a forgery."

"And impound it, my lord?" asked Landini.

"No—give it back to Sir Edward Poynings," replied Danvers; "and let him do with it as he thinks fit."

"Ah! I understand," ejaculated the ancient goldsmith. "You and Sir Edward have arranged it all between you! You mean to take the bill to the culprit, display it to his eyes with the word *forgery* written on it in red ink, and then tear it up before his face in the hope that it will serve as a salutary warning for the future. Is it not so, my lord?"

"It may be just as you say, worthy Landini," responded Danvers, smiling. "However, you will do as I have enjoined you in this matter; and see that the thing is not talked about."

"Not a syllable of the transaction shall transpire from this establishment," said Landini.

"Good," observed Danvers: then rising from his seat, he said, "and you are sure that old Manners did not tell you anything else of any consequence? He did not hint who his generous friend might be?"

"He did not, my lord. He said it was a solemn secret. He asked if your lordship had been hither; and I of course said that you had—that you had returned within the last few days from the Continent——"

"And I presume he was most anxious to ascertain where I was to be found and all about me?" said Danvers.

"Precisely so, my lord, I answered that you were staying with some friend in the neighbourhood of London; but that I neither knew with whom nor where—as your lordship had come over quite in a private manner, with no retinue, but merely on a business visit."

"And what said he then?" asked Danvers.

"But little more, my lord: for as I have ere now observed, I was so busy at the moment that even if I had experienced the liveliest interest in the visit and its object, I could have spared no time for discourse. The arrival of my courier from abroad poured as it were a flood of business within these walls——"

"And therefore I will not occupy your attention farther," said Lord Danvers, smiling.

The old banker, confounding himself in bowings and scrapings, assured his lordship that however occupied he might be in respect to others, he always had ample time to discourse with *him*.

"Pray therefore, my lord," he continued, "do not hurry away thus. Permit me to have refreshments served up. I have wine which might tempt the palate of an anchorite——You shake your head, my lord, in refusal?

Well, but another time you must honour my humble dwelling with your presence, so that I may entertain your lordship in a fitting manner. I can never forget that my family owes all its prosperity to your's——"

Suddenly did the brow of Danvers darken: and again did that weird-like mystery of expression sweep over his countenance, as if he experienced a pang of agony as excruciating as it was evanescent.

"Thanks for all your hospitable proposals, my good friend," he said, that singularly agonizing look having passed away as completely as if it had never appeared upon his features at all. "I can remain with you no longer now—I have an appointment elsewhere."

With these words Danvers shook the old banker by the hand, and passed out of the establishment, Mark the nephew speeding to escort him to the threshold of the street-door.

So soon as the nobleman had taken his departure, Mark Landini proceeded into the private office; and closing the door, said to his uncle, "What brought Danvers hither this afternoon?"

"Ostensibly to inquire if we had received our foreign letters," returned the old banker, "but in reality to ascertain whether poor Manners had been to see us—and if so, what he said."

"But you did not suffer Danvers to perceive that you showed any sympathy with him?" said Mark, in a tone of anxious interrogatory.

"Nephew, have I reached this age without knowing how to command my looks, veil my feelings, and measure my words to suit all men and all occasions?"—and there was an accent of grave rebuke in the venerable goldsmith's tone and manner as he thus spoke.

"Pardon me, my dear and respected uncle," said Mark. "Lionel Danvers is so shrewd and keen-sighted—so observant and penetrating, even at the very moment when he seems most careless and indifferent——"

"That has been the character of his ancestors for generations back," interrupted the elder Landini. "No, it is not probable that I should suffer my real feelings to transpire in his presence. Little, little does he imagine how deep—how insatiate—how implacable is the hatred which I bear towards him——"

"And I also, uncle!" added Mark, his plain but by no means ill-looking countenance expressing a deep concentration of feeling as he thus spoke. "But think you that the day of vengeance is drawing near?"

"Let us hope so," answered his uncle. "A vengeance which has been dissimulated in our family for a hundred and twenty-six years, without having lost any of its original intenseness, but has been preserved in all its pristine power until the present moment,—such a vengeance, nephew, is sure to accomplish its aim at last! Indeed, is not the first step already taken towards the working out of this hereditary revenge of our's?"

"Yes—it is true that you have so well managed, uncle, as to induce Lord Danvers to begin to concentrate all his revenues in your hands. But let us suppose that this scheme proves fully successful, and that the bulk of his immense wealth becomes invested with us—even then I do not see how you will strike the grand blow which shall accomplish his ruin."

"My dear nephew," answered the elder Landini, "I thought that I had already explained myself sufficiently on this head. At all events, if I have not done so, it is high time that such explanations were now given. For if the opportunity should not fully serve while I am yet alive, to denude Lionel Danvers of his colossal wealth—strip him of his vast estates—and send him an outcast, a wanderer, and a beggar upon the face of the earth—then must all this be consummated by *you!* As a lineal descendant of the race of Landini—as the only surviving son of my younger brother, long since dead—*you* are the inheritor of my wealth, as you are likewise the inheritor of that mission of vengeance which by my father was entrusted to me?"

"Aye—and I shall prove no traitor to the solemn bequeathment," answered the nephew. "Though born in England, and with my Christian name anglicised, yet do I feel Italian blood burning in my veins, and my heart throbs with all the fervid emotion which prompts an Italian vengeance! Implacable then as thou art, uncle, in this cherished vengeance against the accursed house of Danvers——"

At this moment the door of the private office was suddenly opened; and to the dismay of the uncle and nephew, the object of their discourse re-appeared before them. But well, and indeed exquisitely practised in the art of dissimulation towards him, they both instantaneously recovered their presence of mind; and when they observed, each with a quick glance, that the countenance of Lionel was perfectly unruffled, they felt convinced that his ear had not caught a single syllable of the words which were being uttered at the moment he opened the door.

"Pardon this interruption, my good friends," said Danvers, in that frank style of off-hand but high-bred courtesy which he was wont to adopt towards those whom he honoured with his intimacy: "but I had forgotten one object of my visit just now."

The manner of the uncle and nephew had again become so profoundly respectful, and their looks so replete with an almost reverential courtesy, that it scarcely seemed possible they could be the same men who a few moments back had been discussing plans of fearfullest vengeance and direst hate against the object of their present attention. So however it was; and while Mark officiously placed a chair for Lord Danvers, the elder Landini stood obsequiously waiting his commands.

"No—I will not sit down—I am not going to wait a minute," observed

Danvers. "What I came back for may be promptly settled. Give me the finest and costliest set of diamonds you have in your collection."

A great variety of the most brilliant gems was now exhibited to Lionel Danvers: but without lingering many moments over the inspection, he chose a set valued at a price which was equivalent to a monarch's ransom; and thrusting the flat case which contained them into the breast of his doublet, he once more took his departure.

But as he walked leisurely forth from the goldsmith's establishment, had any one been attentively observing his features at the moment, it might have been seen that a proud expression of scornful defiance swept over his darkly handsome countenance, and for an instant gave to his beauty the aspect of Lucifer in his fall.

CHAPTER XIV.

THE TEMPLE GARDENS.

THE Temple, at the time of which we are writing, was occupied by law-students and gentlemen of the legal profession, as at the present day; and the gardens, stretching down to the margin of the Thames, were a favourite lounge for the citizens of London and their wives on a fine summer's evening.

It was not much later than half-past four o'clock when old Master Manners entered those gardens, and proceeded to place himself on a bench commanding a prospect of the river. Clad in the comfortable clothing which he had received at Grantham Villa—with his mind tranquillized as to his own lot in the world—and entertaining some considerable hope from the promised intervention of the King to find Danvers and induce him to espouse Clara, if she were still alive—the old man presented a much improved appearance in contrast with his condition when we first introduced him to the reader. But though there was upon his features an expression of serenity to which they had been long estranged, yet it cannot of course be said that he was altogether happy. No—far from that! Happy he never could be again—unless indeed his beloved daughter should be restored, pure and immaculate, or an honourably wedded wife, to his arms. But dared he hope in such a blissful consummation? No: if she were alive he felt persuaded that she was beguiled and betrayed—the mistress and not the wife of Danvers! Therefore, even if by the royal intervention that nobleman should be led to do her a tardy justice, it would be the best reparation that could be made, but incompetent to efface the memory of past degradation and shame.

The reader will remember that Master Manners had received the King's order to be in the Temple Gardens at five o'clock: but it was quite natural that the old man, in his over-anxiety to be punctual, should have repaired thither half-an-hour before the time. Seating himself therefore on the bench, as above described, he gave way to his reflections, with his eyes fixed on the broad river which stretched before him, and on whose surface numerous pleasure-boats and ferry-barges were floating.

He had been seated thus for a few minutes, when he was suddenly aroused from his reverie by hearing himself addressed by name: and turning his head, he beheld a person of tall ungainly form, stooping considerably in his gait, but handsomely dressed in a suit of dark cloth and velvet. This individual's countenance was not of a prepossessing description: otherwise there would have been little to cavil at in his general aspect; and indeed, notwithstanding the drawback of his ignoble and sinister mien, he might readily be taken for a respectable member of the medical profession, the distinctive garb of which he wore. Old Manners had some indistinct recollection of this person, but could not tax his memory so far as to recall to mind who he was or where they had previously met.

"Yes—it must be you yourself, Master Manners!" exclaimed the medical gentleman fixing his eyes upon the venerable countenance which was now upturned towards his own. "Some years have elapsed since last I saw you—indeed not since your misfortunes, which I can assure you I heard with very great regret. However, all men must have their due share of adversity in this world; and I have had mine as well as the rest. But really you seem as if you did not recognise me?"

"Your features are not unknown," said Manners; "and yet I cannot recollect who you are."

"What! is your memory so treacherous," exclaimed the medical gentleman, "that you have forgotten the learned Licentiate, Apothecary, and Dispenser of Drugs, who attended your head clerk in his illness, and who was once called in to prescribe for yourself, when your own medical attendant had gone upon a journey?"

"Ah! I do now remember you," responded old Manners, his countenance assuming a grave look and his bearing becoming reserved and distant: for at the same moment that the apothecary of the Old Bailey was thus brought back to his recollection, was he likewise reminded that the said apothecary had been ordered to discontinue visiting at his house on account of certain evil reports which had been whispered concerning him.

"You did not treat me very handsomely at the time," continued Dr. Benjamin Welford; "but I am not a man to cherish rancour. I therefore pitied your misfortunes when I heard of them:"—then placing himself by the old man's side upon the bench, Welford took a flask from the pocket of his trunk-hose, and pulling out the cork, handed it to the ruined merchant, saying, "Here—drink a stoup of this prime sack: it will warm your very heart's core."

"I thank you, but I am not athirst," responded Manners coldly: and he edged off from the close proximity of the doctor.

"Oh, well! if you object to a dram, I will e'en drink two—one for yourself and one for me:"—and with these words, Welford poured the best portion of the contents of his flask, which held a good pint, down his throat. "Ah! it is indeed cheering," he continued, smacking his lips. "But really I am well pleased, Master Manners, to behold you in such good form: inasmuch as from all I had heard, I imagined you to have been very much reduced. As for myself, I have just kicked the shop in the Old Bailey to the dogs. I go to it no more. I am now a gentleman at large, and am tomorrow morning going to set out on my travels. In fact, I have got a good situation, cut and dried, and ready prepared for me. But it was with the greatest trouble I induced my generous patron to let me tarry in London until the first glimpse of dawn tomorrow. However, I pleaded hard that I had divers indispensable duties to perform, and one or two friends to take leave of—so that I carried my point. And now, what do you think I am going to do, and why I came to the Temple Gardens at this hour?"

"It is impossible that I can conjecture," said Manners, with a cold reserve, but still not choosing to risk giving the doctor offence by at once breaking off the conversation.

"Why; the fact is, worthy Master Manners," continued Benjamin Welford, "I have become quite a steady character. Indeed, I should not have even produced this flask, had you been a perfect stranger: but knowing that you are somewhat acquainted with my antecedents, it is of course no use to go into extremes and play the hypocrite in your presence. But so far as my general conduct is concerned, I am resolved to turn over a new leaf,—beginning as it were a fresh chapter with some very excellent motto at the head. So I mean to *look* the doctor as well as practice the profession of one. I am going to be steady and sedate—*respectable*, in a word. You see I have got the necessary garb to fulfil this part," he continued, glancing down complacently at his black apparel: "and I am determined that my deportment, my language, and my behaviour shall all be in due accordance. Do you approve of my resolution?"

"I cannot do otherwise than applaud the resolve of any person to reform his character and conduct," answered the old man, but still with a look that implied his doubt as to the sincerity of the vaunted self amelioration.

"But I have not yet told you wherefore I have sought these gardens at the present hour," resumed Welford. "Know then that I leave London, as I ere now stated, at peep of dawn to-morrow morning. I am pledged and bound to be off—otherwise I forfeit the good opinion of the excellent patron whom chance has thrown in my way. But this evening am I resolved to have a quiet and comfortable carouse, with just one boon companion, at the best tavern in Fleet Street. Now, as circumstances have separated me from a most excellent young gentleman with whom I have for some time past been on terms of intimacy, I positively and truly at the moment have no familiar acquaintance whom I can make the companion of my festivity. As for carousing alone, such a proceeding were not to be thought of. No, no: it is not so much for the eating and drinking, as for the sake of agreeable discourse—to which however the aforesaid eating and drinking are potent auxiliaries. Well, then, it is absolutely necessary that I should find a suitable comrade for my projected farewell supper in Fleet Street: and where could I stand a better chance of either renewing some old friendship or forming a fresh one, than at these gardens which in the evening are so favourite a resort? Such are my motives for coming hither; and forasmuch as accident has thrown me in your way, it is you, worthy Master Manners, who will be my supper-companion this night."

CHAPTER XV.

THE INTERVIEW.

VERY different was the demeanour of Lionel Danvers on this occasion from what it was when he encountered the ruined merchant outside the grounds of Grantham Villa; and the old man was at once struck by the change. For there was something regretful and conciliatory in Danvers' aspect—nothing abject or servile however, nothing grovelling nor abased: for alike in his attitude and his look was all that dignified grace which at a moment could so readily elevate itself into a haughty courtesy. But it seemed as if the proud and imperious disposition, yielding to a consciousness of wrong and swayed by those generous feelings which were not altogether foreign to it, was now prepared to make reparation or atonement.

"My lord, dare I hope for aught that will soothe me in my affliction?" asked Manners, in accents tremulous with suspense: for Danvers gazed upon him without speaking.

"Let us sit down and discourse tranquilly," said the nobleman. "There are many persons walking about in these grounds, and it were neither prudent nor agreeable to attract their notice by any outward display of extraordinary feeling."

Thus speaking, Lionel placed himself upon the bench, where Manners also resumed his seat; and as the old man surveyed that elegant and symmetrical form—that countenance which, with its duskiness of complexion, was of such perfect masculine beauty—those lips, surmounted with the slight moustache, and which now, slightly parted, bespoke mournful meditativeness—those eyes whose gaze, half-veiled beneath the long lashes, beamed not at present with lightning-fires but appeared to express the remorsefulness of a proud soul,—the bereaved father felt that he could even forgive this nobleman for the past, provided he undertook to make all possible reparation.

"You doubtless know by whose command I come hither?" said Danvers, again breaking silence, after a few moments' pause.

"Yes: his gracious Highness the King must have sent you hither," exclaimed Manners. "But one word, my lord—I beseech you, one word! Is Clara alive?"

"She is," responded Danvers, quickly averting his head as he spoke: but almost instantaneously turning his looks back again upon the old man, he said, "I am prepared to give you a strange surprise."

"A surprise, my lord!" exclaimed Manners, with mingled joy and misgiving: for while he inwardly thanked heaven for the assurance that Clara was alive, still was he troubled by the tone in which that assurance was given and the suddenly averted look that accompanied it.

"Yes—a surprise of a nature alike startling and pleasurable," continued Danvers, "Indeed, I feel but too profoundly that my conduct has been ungenerous—unkind—unwarrantable: and yielding to the persuasion of the King, whom I saw this morning, I am here now to give you the assurance that all mystery shall cease—all uncertainty be cleared up."

"Then Clara is alive?" exclaimed Manners, his joy now triumphing completely over his misgivings. "She is alive—Clara is alive—my beloved daughter is alive! Oh! what deep, deep gratitude do I feel to heaven, that it has granted me this moment of recompense for the days, and weeks, and months, and years of wretchedness, suspense, and horrible uncertainty which I have endured!"—and as the old man thus spoke, the tears trickled down his cheeks and rolled upon his beard.

"Tranquillize yourself—master your emotions," said Danvers, "or we shall be observed!"

"True, my lord," returned Manners: "I forgot at the moment that we were in a public place. Indeed, I remembered nothing save the *one* blissful thought that was uppermost in my mind—the thought that my Clara is alive! But where is she, my lord? does she love her old father as was her wont? is she acquainted with the misfortunes that have overwhelmed me? is she aware that I have wandered as a houseless beggar upon the face of the earth? Tell me everything, my lord, I beseech you! But first of all, is my Clara near? is she in London? If so, take me to her—let me embrace her—let me pardon her if she be guilty!——But that surprise, my lord, which you promised?"—and having thus given vent to his feelings and anxieties in quick and broken sentences, the old man began to sob like a child.

"Your daughter is not guilty: she is my wife," answered Danvers—and again was his head suddenly averted as he spoke: but on the vanishing profile did Manners, as he raised his tearful eyes, catch that wicked look of awful mystery in the wreathing lips and flashing eyes of Lionel Danvers.

A horrible feeling seized upon the old man: it appeared as if a voice from another world had whispered in his ear that he was deceived;—and from having experienced a brief interval of thrilling hope, he was now suddenly plunged into a maze of the most poignant and agonizing uncertainties.

"Good heaven, my lord! if you were deceiving me?" he cried, snatching the hand of Danvers so as to make him turn round again.

"Deceive you?" ejaculated Lionel, his countenance all in a moment assuming a look of haughty indignation, as he *did* turn and bend his inscrutable eyes upon the old man. "Ever these doubts—these misgivings!—But if they are to continue, the sooner our interview ends the better:"—and he rose from the bench.

"No, no—depart not thus, my lord—I implore, I beseech you!" exclaimed Manners, in bewilderment and confusion—neither reassured in his previous hopes nor knowing how to regard his misgivings—not daring to relapse into confidence and staggered as to his unbelief. "Pardon me if I have wronged you, my lord: but consider how much reason I have to doubt! Think of all that has occurred to make me distrustful—remember everything I have gone through——"

"Well, well," said Danvers, half impatiently and half soothingly, as he sat down again; "I do make all possible allowances for you. But listen, and endeavour to interrupt me not. I have already assured you that your daughter is alive; and now I emphatically add that she is my wife—that she has all along been my wife! But it was the pride of a scion of the mighty house of Danvers which made me ashamed of acknowledging the low plebeian family to which she belonged. Nor was this all! Think you that I was unaware of all the keen pryings, the impertinent scrutinies, and the incessant peerings which you carried on with, regard to me? What! I, the descendant of one of the proudest families in Christendom, and whose hand would have been accepted without question or reference by peeresses or princesses, to find myself the object of all your mean, base, low-minded inquiries?—it was more than I could endure! Therefore was it that I made up my mind how to act. I said to Clara, '*If you love me, abandon home, father, everything, and come with me; but if you value home, and father more than this love of mine, then farewell for ever!*'—Was it doubtful which course a fond devoted maiden could adopt? She fled with me to the Continent—we were wedded—and she is now dwelling in splendour, surrounded by domestics, courted and admired by all who know her!"

"Where, my lord—where?" demanded the old man, now elate with confidence once more.

"At my castle in the Isle of Wight," returned Danvers.

"What, my lord—the Isle of Wight?" exclaimed Manners, his wild hopes all dashed down again in a moment. "I have been thither—the castle is deserted——you yourself told me when first I knew you that it was untenanted——"

"But it is occupied *now*—and Clara is *there*," observed Danvers, speaking with the haughty air of one who with difficulty condescends to explain away a doubt accusatory of himself. "Within the last few weeks have I made that castle my home again—and money, lavishly expended, soon rendered the long-deserted fortalice as sumptuous as a royal dwelling."

"Oh! again and again," cried Manners, "do I implore your lordship's pardon for these doubts—these misgivings—these suspicions on my part! But since Clara is really at your castle in the Isle of Wight, let me hasten thither," continued the old man in a tone of fervid entreaty,—"let me hasten thither, I say, and behold my Clara once again! If you, my lord, deem that the alliance is a stigma and a stain—and even if *she* should hesitate to acknowledge her poor, bankrupt, lately mendicant sire, in the presence of the brilliant circle which, as you say, surrounds her—Oh! then will I consent to see her from a distance! I will not accost her—I will even stifle her loved name when rising to my lips——nay, more, I will mingle with the menial herd, if your lordship wills it, and become your own and my daughter's servitor, provided I may but see her!"—and as he thus spoke, again did the tears pour down his cheeks.

Fortunately the place where the old man and Lionel Danvers were seated was at some little distance from the spot principally chosen by the loungers: otherwise his emotions and the impassioned vehemence of his utterance would have attracted attention. As it was, the nobleman was compelled once more to enjoin him to be tranquil.

"Calm yourself," he said; "calm yourself! You have asked me to yield my permission that you shall see your daughter, and I will take you to her."

"O joy, joy!" ejaculated the old man, utterly unmindly of the injunction to be calm: "all this is happiness so unexpected, so undreamt of, that I know not what to say or what to think! It appears to me like a vision, presently to melt away and leave naught but disappointment behind. Ah! my lord, how bitterly do I deplore that conduct on my part which gave you offence and has aided to produce so much misery! But peradventure your lordship set down my motives as mercenary? perchance you believed that I sought to pry into your affairs to ascertain the amount of your wealth? I take heaven to witness it was not so! O my lord, I dare not explain to you what those motives really were. It was a cause which may have been imaginary—visionary—delusive: but it was a superstition stronger than myself. It was a belief that hung like an iron chain around me—it was an influence that sat upon me like a spell. Ah! and that same cause it was which ere now again, but a few minutes back, made me provoke your wrath by that sudden appearance of misgiving on my part——O God! and I behold it *now!*" he cried in a sudden paroxysm of mental anguish, as he caught that same look flitting in its fearful sardonism and diabolic mystery over the countenance of the listening Danvers.

"What madness is this?" exclaimed the nobleman, seizing the old man's wrist and wrenching it forcibly for an instant: while the look—that fearful look of infernal wickedness—swept again over his countenance.

"God forgive me if I wrong you," murmured the old man in accents so deep, so piteous, that it seemed like the voice of a crushed and ruined spirit; "but you have a look at times, my lord, as if Lucifer himself were gazing out of your eyes and reflecting his scorn upon your lips!"

"Ah! because a sudden pang convulses me," exclaimed Danvers,—"a pang arising from some internal malady—am I to be judged thus uncharitably by you? Does not all your conduct warrant me in separating myself entirely from you—in bearing away your daughter—and in adopting all the measures which I have used to keep *her* on whom the proud name of Danvers is bestowed, afar from these base and grovelling influences which pertain unto her sire?"

Once more did old Manners experience a sudden and powerful revulsion of feeling; and it was accompanied with a shock that agitated him from head to foot. What if that explanation were indeed true, that it was the pang from a hidden malady, which from time to time swept athwart Danvers' countenance? And after all, what explanation could possibly be more natural? How was it to be doubted? did it not seem the simplest but at the same time the most rational solution of a mystery which had haunted the old man for years past? And if this were indeed the truth, was it wonderful that Danvers should have felt aggrieved, hurt, and insulted at all the inquiries, suspicions, and misgivings of which he had been the object when paying his suit to Clara? was it wonderful that *he*—a great, wealthy, and proud nobleman—should have borne away his bride in the manner he did, leaving her father in disgust, and compelling her to choose between that father and himself?

Such were the reflections which swept rapid as a whirlwind through the old man's brain; and he felt an ineffable humiliation—a profound mortification—as he was thus led to regard Danvers as the injured person and himself the injurer—Danvers the provoked and himself the provocator.

"My lord," he said, in a tone of deep contrition, "I begin to think that, after all, much of the wretchedness and sorrow which I have endured has been of my own making. But will you pardon a poor ruined old man, who whatever his foibles, his weaknesses, and his faults may have been, has bitterly paid the penalty?"

"This is the hour, then, for mutual forgiveness," said Lord Danvers: and taking the bereaved father's hand, he wrung it with all the apparent cordiality of those times when he visited at the merchant's house as the suitor of his daughter. "Nevertheless," he continued, "I most candidly inform you that had it not been for the intervention of his Highness the King, I do not think these explanations would ever have taken place. His Grace is well disposed towards you, and purposed to have sent some trusty emissary to provide you with a considerable sum of gold to commence a mercantile career again. But I assured the generous monarch that, yielding to his wishes, I would make your future welfare the object of my attention. Henceforth shall you abide with your daughter."

The old man was about to fling himself upon his knees at the feet of Danvers; but his lordship, catching him by the arm, bade him beware how he attracted the notice of the loungers who had within the last half-hour grown tolerably numerous. Clara's father accordingly retained his place upon the bench; but fixing his tearful eyes upon the nobleman, he poured forth his gratitude in the most earnest and the most fervid manner. Danvers himself seemed to be affected—at least the old man thought so, for the proud lord averted his countenance and held his handkerchief to his face for several moments.

"Have you any preparations to make ere you leave London?" asked Danvers at length; "for we will begin our journey in a few hours."

"To-night, my lord? Oh! the earlier the better!" exclaimed the old man, scarcely able to restrain his enthusiasm.

"Yes—to-night at ten o'clock." rejoined Danvers. "I shall not be able to leave before."

"Your lordship will find me ready, and indeed anxious to commence the journey," said Manners. "I will go forthwith, on leaving your lordship, and purchase a steed. I have gold, thanks to the bounty of the King——"

"No, it is not necessary for you to trouble yourself on that head," interrupted Danvers: "I myself will provide the horses. You must meet me punctually at ten o'clock, under the walls of the Convent Garden."

"The wall that overlooks the Strand, my lord?" said Manners.

"Yes: be punctual to the hour, and you will find me at the place of appointment. The steed shall be in readiness, so that there will be naught to do save to mount and gallop away."

"O, my lord! you are placing me under an obligation which I can never repay—you are filling me with a happiness which I never thought would be mine in this life again!"

It was thus, in deep tremulous accents, that the old man spoke; and Lionel Danvers, again pressing his hand, rose abruptly and sped away. For some minutes did Manners remain seated upon that bench, gating after the retreating nobleman as his form, so full of youthful vigour and characterized by so much symmetrical grace, as well as being so lofty and dignified, stood out as it were conspicuously from the now thickening crowd of loungers amongst whom he passed. At length the dark mantle so gracefully worn over the left shoulder, and the sable plume floating over the cap that rested upon the raven masses of hair clustering about the classic head, disappeared from the old man's view; and then reverting his eyes towards the Thames, he fell into a long reverie.

Now did he examine every minute detail and every particular of the interview which had just taken place. But why, as he thus pondered on all the circumstances that had occurred and the syllables that had been uttered, did a grave seriousness come gradually over his countenance? It was because his convictions were not established so completely, so irrefragibly, in favour of Danvers and all that he had said, as to preclude the access of a faint foreboding into his mind. He knew not why his thoughts should thus as it were be sobering down into sadness again; and he tried to persuade himself that it was only the reaction naturally following upon so much enthusiasm as he had been experiencing. But no! ardently and energetically as he strove to feel convinced—profoundly and earnestly as he strained every nerve to fortify his soul against farther doubts and misgiving—*still* did a presentiment, faint as a fleecy vapour in the distant horizon steal over his mind, and a suspicion indefinite as the ringing of far-off bells in the ears arise in his imagination.

CHAPTER XVI.

THE JOURNEY.

It was not therefore with complete assurance and unalloyed confidence that Master Manners found himself wending his way along the Strand a little before ten o'clock. Very different was that thoroughfare from what it is in the present day. *Then* no crowds thronged on either side—no double line of vehicles occupied the road-way: the roar, and din, and bustle, and agitation of wheels, and horses, and men, which *now* characterize the place, gave not in those days even a sign that they were ever destined to be.

The night was dark and cloudy—the Strand was involved in an obscurity relieved only by the faint beams of light struggling from the casements of the mansions on either side of the road: for a road rather than a street it assuredly was. Few and far between were the passengers walking in either direction; and if here and there a female form were visible, it was hurrying along as though in terror of foot-pads or insolent gallants.

But the old man was too deeply absorbed in his own reflections to observe any external objects with more than a cursory attention. As a matter of course he was thinking of Danvers, and likewise of his beloved Clara. Indeed, to think of one was to think of the other: it was impossible to keep them separate in his mind, or conjure up the image of the former without beholding the latter also. Ah! if it were indeed true that he was about to enter upon a journey which was to take him to his daughter—how happy he would be! But if Danvers were to deceive him? Yet what possible interest could he have? Why make matters worse than they were by additional wrong? No, no—it could not be: Danvers dared not to superadd such flagrant injury to a monstrous outrage!

Thus did the old man endeavour to buoy up his hopes: and yet he could not altogether divest himself of the dim foreboding nor stifle the faint suspicion that vibrated troublously amidst the gush of his hopes, like the venomous water-snake in the midst of the crystal stream that flows in its pebbly bed.

"O Lionel Danvers!" thought Manners to himself, "how is it that there seems to be within thee a hidden spirit of evil from which I have found myself shrinking instinctively? It is like a spectre looming through the twilight, and appearing to blacken where it stands, but which vanishes in a moment, leaving the awe-stricken beholder in doubt and perplexity whether it were ever there at all. Oh! what is this mystery that hangs around thee, Lionel Danvers? Is it indeed naught but fevered fancy on my part? Was the explanation which thou gavest of the sudden pang springing up at times from an inward malady, the true one? God grant that it was! But why did not thy words impress a lasting conviction upon my soul?—why was the effect fleeting and transitory? Why indeed these ever-recurring doubts concerning thy truthfulness? Why these dark imaginings relative to the influence thou hast upon all these latter circumstances of my life? Is it that even when thou didst speak with the most assurance, and even with a wrathful resentment of suspicion, I nevertheless could detect a consciousness of deceit within thee which thou didst vainly endeavour to conceal? I know not whether it were so. Perhaps even now I am doing thee flagrant injustice again, by suffering the faintest whisper injurious to thy integrity and truthfulness to arise in the depths of my soul. God grant that it may be!"

Thus musing, Master Manners proceeded along the Strand, until he reached the place of appointment. This was the wall that then enclosed the Convent Garden of Westminster, the site of which is the market known as *Covent Garden* at the present day.

In that spot it was almost pitch dark: for there was no mansion near at hand to send forth beams of straggling light from the windows. The clouds had spread a funeral pall over the sky—neither moon nor stars were visible—and everything portended a storm. Such a night was by no means calculated to dispel whatever amount of gloomy feeling still marred the trustfulness and confidence of the old man, but rather appeared of a nature to strengthen his forebodings.

On reaching the wall, Master Manners began to skirt it slowly; and in a few minutes he suddenly came upon some objects which were visible, as being darker than the darkness. These were two horses, on one of which a rider was seated, the other being as yet riderless.

"My lord," said Manners, "is that you?"

"Yes—it is I," responded Lionel. "Mount and let us away. These are steeds of a mettle rarely equalled!"

The old man fancied that this observation was made in a sort of mocking tone: but ashamed of himself for allowing every look, action, gesture and word of Lord Danvers constantly to assume an unnatural aspect in his imagination, he endeavoured to speak cheerfully as he said, "It is the fashion for great noblemen of the present day to have high-spirited steeds."

"Aye—but few so fleet of limb as these," replied Danvers, assisting the old man to mount the horse that was intended for him. "And now let us away!"

At this instant the moon broke feebly and faintly from behind a cloud; and her dim watery rays fell upon Danvers' countenance. The old man instinctively threw a swift searching glance on the nobleman, half in terror lest he should behold that expression on those features that ever sent a cold chill to his heart's core. And sure enough it was so! There was the fire flashing from the deep dark eyes, and seeming to shed an unearthly glow upon that countenance which at the instant was invested with all the terrible beauty of the ruined angel. A cry rose up to the old man's lips; but he stifled it as it were ere it found vent;—and the next instant he was speeding along by the side of Danvers towards Charing Cross.

The road lay in the direction which is now called Piccadilly: and skirting Hyde Park—then a private pleasure-ground—it was lined with a continuous row of trees on either side. Wilder grew the night, though a few faint beams still managed to struggle from behind a break in the dense clouds; and presently the moon itself came out, chill and wan like the eye-ball of a dead man through a jagged rent in a sable cere-cloth. Instead of diffusing a sweet silver lustre, it only seemed to illume the black air with a feeble ghastliness, like the effect of a lantern in an immense cavern. It was such a night as one would deem fitted for any purposes of ill—a night which, without storm or tempest, seemed full of a silent awe that enwrapped as it were the soul. The dark shapes of the towering trees might themselves be taken for ominous portents; and in the utter darkness that prevailed on either side of the road where the moonbeams could not penetrate, black sinister forms appeared to be gliding. The old man knew that all these effects were but the fevered imaginings of his own brain: but vainly did he endeavour to struggle against the superstitious dread in which they enthralled him.

"Let us speed onward," said Danvers: and putting spurs to his horse he dashed along.

His aged companion was too much under the influence of consternation to do aught to impel his own courser forward: nevertheless the animal bounded on, keeping abreast with the steed which Lionel Danvers bestrode. They were horses of colossal size and as black as night. Wondrous was the speed which they now put forth; and every minute they appeared to be going quicker and quicker, until they reached a degree of swiftness that seemed like that of a hurricane. The trees flew past as if they themselves were rushing in the contrary direction; and as Danvers looked round towards the old man, it struck the latter that the noble's dark eyes were now flashing continuous fires, and that the awful expression of satanic scorn and withering contempt instead of flitting over his features, was stationary there. Horrible ideas flowed through the ruined merchant's brain, like a trail of scorching flame. He felt as if he were in the power of some unearthly being who was whirling him on at a maddening rate that might have outstripped the whirlwind!

Away, away!—along the road they rush, the horses' hoofs beating with thundering din upon the hard ground—while trees, and sign-posts, and all objects that could serve to mark distances flitted past like a moving panorama speeding one way as the horsemen were dashing on in another. Through a village were they borne: another moment and it was out of sight! Now they suddenly emerged upon the wide open heath of Bagshot; and in a few minutes Danvers abruptly reined in his steed—the one which the old man bestrode sympathetically relaxing its pace also. Then they stopped; and a creaking sound smote hideously upon the ears.

"Behold where the murderer swings!" cried Danvers: and through the darkness he pointed with outstretched arm.

Manners mechanically glanced in the direction thus indicated, and beheld a gibbet by the road-side, to each arm of which a malefactor hung in chains; and as the bodies swayed gently to and fro, the rusty iron groaned as if the sounds came up from the hollow throats of the dead. The hideous spectacle, darkly defined in the obscurity which the wan moon feebly illumined, caused the flesh to creep upon the old man's bones and the blood to stagnate icily in his veins: but the next moment the steeds dashed on again, with wildering, whirling, maddening pace; and a tremendous weight of awful consternation sat upon the old man, as a foul night-hag sits upon the breast of a sleeper in a fearful dream.

Away, away! over the wild heath the horsemen sped; and as Danvers' short Spanish mantle of sable velvet flew out straight from his shoulders, it seemed as if huge bat-like wings were thus spread open, giving a horrible completeness to the idea that his shape was that of a fallen angel. The old man gazed upon him as if his very eyes would burst from their sockets—gazed indeed with looks so full of wild terror and awful dread that had it been some hideous spectral form seated on the coal-black steed, it could not have inspired a more stupendous horror. And Danvers bent upon him a countenance which had a look glowing with a wild and singular exultation that mingled with a terrific scorn and blighting irony. Yet all the remarkable beauty of the features struck the eye forcibly still—a beauty which in its masculine perfection resembled that of an archangel, but at the same time appeared to he naught save a mask beneath which all the passions of hell were raging, gnawing, agitating, struggling, corroding,—aye, and devouring too the heart of that man who was thus clothed in so tremendous a mystery!

The ruined merchant endeavoured to cry aloud: but the faculty of speech failed him. Then he turned away his head in order to shut out the spectacle from his view and by a desperate effort regain something like composure. But a wild and unearthly laugh rang in his ears; and he knew that it came from the lips of his companion. Irresistibly his eyes were reverted upon that individual, whose tall, elegant, and graceful form, seated upon the coal-black steed, with the mantle streaming from his back and the sable plume stretched out straight as a pine-bough from his cap, seemed awful as that of Lucifer. And, O horror! was it imagination or a dread reality?—but now living lightnings seemed to flash from his eyes, play around his lofty forehead, and illumine the wild beauty of his countenance with their baleful fires! At the same time the wind swept over the heath; and with such suddenness came on the tempest, that in less than a minute it blew a hurricane. Now a wood of fir-trees was reached; and as the sable chargers skirted it in their maddening career, the wind whistled, and shrieked, and roared, and moaned by turns amidst the trees, so that it appeared as if the voices of ruined spirits falling in headlong flight were sending forth the tones of agony that mingled with the malice-mirth of fiends!

Heavens! how haggard, wild, and horror-stricken the old man looked: desperation sat on his features—the most appalling terror was in his fixed and staring eyes. It seemed as if demons had him in their grasp and vultures had fastened on his brain. His imagination, wrought up to a frenzied pitch, appeared to torture itself by enhancing the horrors of everything that was already so transcendingly horrible. The notes of the wind, as it swept through the forest of firs, now seemed to him to be giving utterance to articulate sounds—cries of murder blending with the shrieks of tortured maidens—the wild wail of young children uniting with the yells of strong and powerful men in mortal agonies! "O God, I can endure this no longer!" exclaimed Manners, suddenly recovering the faculty of speech with a great effort, and thus giving vent to the horror that filled his soul.

"Away, away!" cried Danvers: and as the two black coursers redoubled their speed, the wild winds echoed the cry of "Away, away!" and in the far-off depths of the forest of firs did raving echoes prolong the words, "Away, away!"

We said that the horses redoubled their speed—and it was so. If they had travelled hitherto with the celerity of the hurricane, they now rivalled the vivid swiftness of the lightning. Their long black manes streamed out and shone with a bright gloss like meteors: their eyes lashed fire—and the breath through their nostrils instead of being of fleecy transparency, was like a glowing vapour. Seen from a distance, it must have appeared as if meteor-lights were being borne along with a celerity at which electric fires alone can travel: and notwithstanding this fearful velocity wherewith he was wafted onward, the old man experienced not the least difficulty in retaining his seat, but on the contrary appeared to be kept in the saddle by some spell which was stronger than himself.

He shut his eyes in order to concentrate all his ideas internally, and thus shield his imagination as it were against the influence of external objects. He asked himself whether all these things were a reality or a delusion?—whether, in a word, he was merely performing a very rapid journey with Lord Danvers, and that his own fevered fancy had invested it with such an assemblage of wild and mystic terrors? For upwards of a minute did he thus reason with his eyes shut close; and in the depths of his soul did he murmur, "Yes, it must be all the work of imagination!"

But when he felt the night-air keen and piercing as if blowing upon him from Spitzbergen's ice, and recollected that it was a night in the genial month of May, he was struck with the conviction that the atmosphere only seemed thus penetratingly cold, because he was being whirled with such headlong rapidity through it. For indeed it was like speeding full in the teeth of a strong gushing wind; and therefore the old man knew that the pace must be terrific. Ah! how then could it all be a delusion? Feeling as if suddenly goaded well-nigh to insanity, he opened his eyes and threw a quick shuddering look upon his companion. Danvers appeared at the moment to have some intuitive knowledge that the old man thus regarded him with a glance of agonizing inquiry; and he turned upon him all the terrific lightnings of his looks. Yes—there indeed was still that awful beauty of the noble's countenance: there too were the fires flashing from his eyes and playing like blasting lightnings about his brow;—and his very lips, wreathing in satanic scorn and withering irony, seemed to breathe fire also!

Away, away!—on thundered the steeds—a town is reached—it is a large one—and yet it is traversed and passed quick as if it were but a single house that had appeared on either side of the road. On, on—and in a few minutes they reach the bank of a broad river on whose bosom the wan moon plays. The steeds dash in!—a moment and they are upon the opposite bank! It was as if a mere puddle had been plashed by their tramping feet for an instant. Then away, away again! and the steeds snort flames from their nostrils, and toss their heads as if to shake off meteoric fire-sparks from their manes—while lightnings flash from their eyes, and they have the appearance of maddened animals rushing along in the wildest affright. Another town is reached: some grand funeral ceremony is taking place in the churchyard; and torches waving to and fro, fling a lurid light with a magical effect upon the white grave-stones and the grey walls of the sacred edifice. Danvers reins in his steed for a moment, and pointing to the churchyard, exclaims in a wild and mocking tone, "They are busy with the dead this night!" Then away, away dash the two coal-black chargers again—the town is passed—and along the lonely road they thunder on once more. The winds continue to rave through the trees; and spirit-voices appear to shriek, and scream, and moan, and howl, above—below—behind—before—on every side!

Presently the way lies through a part of the country singularly wild and fitted for such a dread nocturnal journey. The road passes round a tremendous hollow, into the black depths of which the eye cannot plunge; while on the other side of the beaten pathway rugged heights tower upward.

"It is the Devil's Hole!" exclaimed Danvers, pointing into the abyss: and then he gave so wild and terrific a laugh that it woke a thousand echoes far wilder and more terrific still; and ere they had died in the distance he shouted "Away, away!"—the hills and hollows again reverberating the sound, as if the whole neighbourhood were peopled with fiends whose voices kept passing on the words "Away, away!"

The old man felt as if his senses were now leaving him; and he had no longer the power to reflect and think upon what was passing. But still, of all that was taking place he remained painfully sensible: only he had no longer sufficient control over his ideas as to deliberate within himself whether these transcending horrors and stupendous mysteries were stern realities or the mere phantasmagoria of a fevered fancy. The wild winds raved—the air was keen as if formed of myriads of ice-shafts all shooting in one direction while he was rushing on against the piercing shower—the eyes of the horses continued to flash forth living flames—and when he looked upon Danvers, he still beheld the awful expression of scorn and malignant triumph upon his countenance, illumined by the fires which shot from the eyes and played like forked tongues of lambent flame around his brows.

Away, away!—more maddening, frenzied, and furious becomes the pace at which the coal-black steeds dash along, bearing with them the unearthly halo of the fires which they *look* and *breathe!* It is as a trail of meteor-like flames sweeping onward over the surface of the earth. The old man loses all power of reckoning, or even guessing at the lapse of time. At last another mass of water is suddenly reached: but it seems not like a river—for he cannot see the opposite bank or shore. Not another moment has he to reflect upon this. The steeds dash on—the spray is thrown up thickly around him—and immediately afterwards the horses' hoofs tramp upon the rattling beach of some shore on which they have just landed. Here there is a sudden halt: and the old man flings a fevered anxious glance around. Where is he? whither has Danvers brought him? has the sea been passed? They stand upon a beach at the foot of high and escarped cliffs, which gleam white as snow in the wan moonlight. On the summit may be seen a pile of castellated buildings—ramparts, turrets, and towers, looking like a black cloud of fantastic shape that had settled down there from the dark vaults of heaven. Below—at a little distance from the beach which the ebb had now left bare—two or three shafts of rock are seen shooting abruptly out of the water. The old man gazes for a few moments in the wildest amaze; and then he gives utterance to a loud and terrible cry—for he recognises the spot—he knows the scene—he has beheld it before!

Yes—for in his search after his lost daughter Clara, had he visited the Isle of Wight, at the south-western point of which stood Danvers Castle, frowning from its rocky eminence above the sea, and overlooking the spot where the Needles uprear their heads like the last vestiges of some temple built by gigantic hands, and which the ocean has overwhelmed.

No wonder, then, that on recognising the spot to which he had been brought a terrific cry escaped the old man's lips! For the moon was still high in the heavens—the night was not waning yet—no glimmer of dawn appeared in the east—and therefore was the astounding, wildering, whelming fact apparent, that in three or four short hours a journey of eighty miles had been accomplished! Aye—and the sea had been traversed, too, by the coal-black steeds, which now stood snorting, and champing, and pawing the beach, as if anxious to start on their preternatural journey anew!

Oh! as these convictions flashed, soul-harrowing and brain-scorching, to the old man's mind, he felt that he was in the power of one who was indeed above all earthly laws—an exception to the very human race itself! But his daughter——Ah! horrifying thought! what could her doom be, in the hands of such a being?

"Be you a fiend in mortal shape," cried the old man, now driven to the frenzy of utter despair, "I will resist until the last!"—and in his maddened wildness, he rushed upon Danvers, heaven only knows with what aim or with what hope.

"Fool—dotard!" muttered Lionel Danvers in a tone of withering scorn: and all the terrors of his countenance—the lightning of the eyes and the satanic sardonism of the wreathing lips—were turned full upon the old man.

"O God, that look!" he exclaimed, stopping suddenly short in dread consternation: then turning half round, he reeled—staggered back a pace or two—and fell heavily—deprived of consciousness.

When he recovered his senses again, he was in a dungeon.

CHAPTER XVII.

THE LADY AND HER TIRE-MAID.

A MONTH elapsed; and during this interval the King was a constant visitor at Grantham Villa. Scarcely an evening passed without his Majesty's presence at the Earl's abode. Sometimes he would sup there: at others he would merely walk for an hour or two in the garden and shrubbery in company with Musidora and her two noble relatives;—but on all occasions his attentions to our heroine plainly indicated that she was the object of attraction for him. Indeed, those attentions became more and more tender in their nature and more pointed in their significancy. Though always characterized by an ardent admiration, they were nevertheless blended with the utmost respect, and so far from having anything of a libertine aspect, were those of a suitor wooing a damsel to be his bride. Never once, either in word or look, did the monarch transgress the bounds of the strictest delicacy. Not that Musidora would for a single instant have tolerated such transgression: but there was nevertheless, all circumstances considered, a merit in this forbearance on Henry's part. For inasmuch as a King in those times assumed to himself a sort of prescriptive right to exercise the fullest control over the hearts of his female subjects, as he held the lives, liberties, and fortunes of *all* at his own disposal,—the respectful conduct which his Highness observed towards Musidora would have been regarded by any other lady as a homage of the most flattering description. It was at once the most exalted compliment which the Royalty of that age, especially when personified in such a monarch as Henry VIII, could possibly offer to the beauty, the virtue, and the other merits of an English damsel. But Musidora, while receiving these delicate and respectful attentions from the King, appeared to regard them only in the light of ordinary courtesies, and did not seem to attach any more significant meaning to them.

But we shall gather a better idea of the occurrences of the month which had elapsed since Musidora's arrival at Grantham Villa, if we peep into her own chamber, and listen to the conversation which was taking place one evening between herself and Annetta. The King was expected to supper at nine: it was now eight o'clock, and our heroine was commencing her toilet a little earlier than usual.

Seated near the window, which was open, and through the lattice-work of which shone the prismatic lustre of the descending sun, Musidora gazed down into the beautiful garden below—while Annetta was arranging the long shining masses of the lady's raven hair. It was a delicious evening in the month of June: the air that was wafted into the chamber, was filled with the fragrance of the sweetest flowers, yet not to a degree to produce a sickly sensation, nor to mar the freshness of the gentle breeze. And Musidora appeared to woo that breeze as it came through the lattice-blind. Not that there was the flash of excited thoughts upon her cheeks: no, pale as the purest Parian marble were they—and the serenity of her alabaster forehead forbade the supposition that her brain throbbed behind those brows. And yet did she court the breeze as if there were some in-ward excitement which its freshness soothed. Yet who that gazed upon Musidora's countenance, with its ice-like placidity, and beheld her in all the glacier-brilliancy of her beauty, could for a moment imagine that it was possible for her heart to be swayed or her soul to be excited by the feelings with which other hearts are touched and other souls are moved?

"His Highness comes *again* to-night?" said Annetta inquiringly, as she combed out the long tresses of her lady's hair.

"Yes," replied Musidora; "the King comes again to-night:"—and her voice usually characterized by a fluid evenness which would have been monotonous were it not for its ineffable melody, gave a just perceptible accentuation to the word *again*.

"And are you not pleased, dear lady?" asked Annetta, who was a shrewd and intelligent, but frank-hearted and well-meaning, as well as very pretty and interesting girl of about eighteen. "I am sure that if I had the good fortune to be regarded as a fit companion for the King, I should be ready to go out of my senses with sheer delight."

"Then in order to retain your senses, Annetta," said Musidora, "it will be as well for you to avoid the chance of ever falling in with Royalty."

"It is not likely that I shall have such a chance at all," rejoined Annetta. "But you, mistress, who are so very fortunate in this respect, do not seem near so happy as, frankly speaking, you really ought to be."

"And why do you think that I ought to be so supremely happy?" asked Musidora, in a tone of placid indifference, as she threw herself farther back in her chair, over the crimson velvet of which the raven masses of her hair flowed like a dark cloud: but as Annetta did not answer the ques-tion, Musidora glanced slowly round; and as she caught a glimpse of her young dependant's countenance, she observed, "You wish to say some-thing, minion, to which you hesitate to give utterance?"

"May I then speak freely?" asked Annetta, encouraged by Musidora's words and manner: for the term *minion* was in those times one of endear-ing familiarity addressed by ladies to their favourite abigails.

"Assuredly! say what you will," returned Musidora. "You have been with me nearly three years—have you not, Annetta?—and during that interval I have received every proof of your natural goodness of heart, as well as of your candour and prudence. I therefore suffer you to speak more familiarly to me than any one else. And now say what you wish."

"I was about to observe, dear lady," continued Annetta, "that his gracious Highness must be deeply and sincerely in love with you to come so often to the villa. Of course it is not through friendship for Lord and Lady Grantham that his Grace comes; because I have learnt from the servants of the household that the King never came hither at all till you were an inmate of the house; but on the contrary, I understand the Earl and Countess were in deep disgrace. It is therefore evident enough that the King is in love with you, dear lady; and as his present marriage is said to be no marriage at all, and his present wife no wife at all, it follows that he is at perfect liberty to contract another marriage and choose another wife. Oh! my dear mistress," exclaimed Annetta, enthusiastically, "proud I shall be to see you Queen of England!"

"Annetta, I have suffered you to go on talking thus," said Musidora, calmly, "because I in the first instance gave you full and free permission to speak your thoughts. But I did not anticipate that you were about to indulge in such wild dreams on my behalf. Do the servants of the household permit themselves the liberty of talking in a similar manner?"

"There is no doubt that they whisper amongst themselves," replied Annetta, "and that they sometimes exchange looks which mean quite as much as words can say. But they are very cautious alike in speech and looks with regard to this matter: for there is scarcely a day that passes without the Earl and Countess renewing the injunction to keep his Grace's frequent visits a profound secret, and never to allude to them outside the walls of the villa, under pain not only of instant dismissal but also of the King's sorest displeasure."

"And what do the domestics think of this incessantly-renewed injunction," asked Musidora, "accompanied as it is with threats and warnings?"

"They say little on the point, but yield implicit obedience, so far as I can learn," replied Annetta. "The servants, both male and female, are, as you must have observed, all elderly people, and have been in Lord Grantham's service for some years; and therefore they are not likely to risk their own situations, much less dare the royal vengeance, by carrying tittle-tattle outside the walls of the villa. Besides, there is the old housekeeper, Dame Bertha, who keeps a lynx-eye upon them all; and she takes care that none of them ever set foot over the threshold without her permission."

"But what opinion do the domestics seem to have formed relative to the injunction which the Earl and Countess have given them?" asked Musidora, though in a cold indifferent manner, as if rather for the sake of saying something than because she felt the slightest interest in the topic.

"I have heard Dame Bertha herself say," answered Annetta, "that his Highness is not so completely his own master but that he to some extent follows the advice of his councillors—the Lord Chancellor Warham, the Earl of Surrey, Sir Edward Poynings, and others—and that they are all bitterly opposed to Lord Grantham. Therefore his Grace does not choose all in a moment to inform his courtiers that he has forgiven Lord Grantham;—and so for the present he visits here *incognito*. Thus says Dame Bertha."

"And is that all she says?" asked Musidora: for it was easy to perceive by Annetta's tone and the way in which she suddenly stopped short, that she had really more to tell.

"That is all Dame Bertha says," replied the girl: "but the servants generally fancy that this is *not* the only reason why his Grace comes hither under such circumstances of strict secrecy."

"Proceed, Annetta," said Musidora, as her dependant again stopped short: but still the lady spoke in her wonted manner of calm indifference and passionless quiescence.

"Well, dear mistress, since you permit me to speak," continued Annetta, "it must frankly be told that the prevailing impression in the servants' hall is that King Henry comes here so often and in such rigid *incognito*, because he is wooing you as his bride, but does not choose to let the circumstance become public until he has sent to Rome to obtain from the Pope a bull divorcing him from the present Queen."

"Now, supposing that all these conjectures be well founded," said Musidora, "should you not think me very wrong, Annetta, to become the cause of severing the King from Queen Catherine, whether she be or be not an estimable woman?"

"If, dear lady, by intrigue or treachery," replied Annetta, after a few moments' consideration, "you had succeeded in alienating King Henry's heart from Queen Catherine, I should certainly think the deed most ungenerous for any woman to perform, and most unworthy of the character of Musidora Sinclair. But inasmuch as it appears from all I can have learnt, that his Highness had resolved, *before* he ever saw or even heard of you, to divorce Queen Catherine and to proclaim the nullity of a marriage which he believes to have no legal tie, I cannot for a single moment see that you are to blame if his Grace has chosen to fall in love with you."

Annetta ceased speaking, and Musidora made no reply nor comment for nearly a minute. The young damsel, while arranging the superb tresses that flowed over the crimson back of the chair, passed round from behind the seat so as to catch a glimpse of her mistress's countenance, and ascertain, if possible, whether she could read therein the effect which her

words had produced. But no!—there was that ice-like brilliancy of the lady's beauty, with the fading gleam of a smile upon the lower part of the
face; and there also was the superb lustre of the fine dark eyes: but the
expression of all the features was as inscrutable as ever—so that as Annetta
passed behind the chair again, she wondered how it possibly could be that
never, never could she glean from Musidora's looks the slightest, faintest
clue to what was passing in her soul.

"You have spoken like a very sensible and intelligent girl, as you are,"
said Musidora, at length breaking silence again; "but recollect that I only
supposed your conjectures to be true for an instant, in order to give you
an opportunity of expressing your opinion on a certain point. Let me now
assure you, my dear Annetta, that whatever brilliant hopes you in your
kindness may have conceived on my behalf, have never once as yet been
fostered by my ambition. The King has proffered me many civilities, but
has never hitherto breathed a word which might be construed into a direct
proposal."

"But he means it—he means it, dear lady!" exclaimed Annetta: "and
I shall yet have the honour—Oh! the supreme, the matchless honour of
dressing the hair of the Queen of England! How grandly would a diadem
rest upon this head!"—and as she spoke with a heartfelt enthusiasm, she
with her two pretty white hands smoothed down the redundant masses of
her mistress's hair. "Yes—and it *will* be so too," she continued, rather in a
musing strain to herself, though speaking aloud, than actually addressing
Musidora: "every sign, every token proves that the King loves you. Has he
not sent a learned physician to the Isle of Wight, to take up his abode at
Sinclair House?—not merely that your father's health may be duly cared
for and cherished, but also that the worthy knight may have the society
of a gay and intellectual companion to make him miss his daughter's absence all the less. And in the letter which you received the other day from
Sir Lewis, and of which you so kindly read a portion to me, did not your
father declare that he had never been happier in his life than with this individual whom the King had sent to him, and who served the purpose of
comrade, physician, and friend? Yes—those were Sir Lewis's very words:
and surely it was most considerate and most kind on the part of the King
to send so agreeable a person to keep Sir Lewis company? But that is not
all," continued Annetta, in her almost unconscious musings. "Has not
his Highness provided you with written orders and passports, bearing his
own gracious sign-manual, to enable you to visit the Tower, St. James's
Palace, and other places under the royal authority and which he thought
you would like to inspect? Did you not likewise receive an order to visit
Windsor Castle?—and was not that a pleasant day which we spent on the

jaunt thither? It must be quite a change for the Earl and Countess thus to go about with you, mistress, after being so long confined, as one may say, to this particular spot. They have to thank you for getting out of disgrace with the King, and into favour again. But as I was saying, dear mistress, all those civilities and favours which the King has shown you, speak eloquent enough of his intentions——Ah! I quite forgot the magnificent set of diamonds which his Highness gave you——"

"And which I accepted at the time with so much reluctance," added Musidora, "and have so completely forgotten ever since."

"You are incomprehensible in all but the kindness of your disposition," remarked Annetta, encouraged, by the turn the conversation had taken, to a somewhat greater familiarity than she was wont to venture upon with her young mistress: but at the same time she meant no harm. "I do not pretend to know anything about the value of precious stones; but the most ignorant could tell that these are beyond all price. I thought the set beautiful enough which the Countess presented to you the day of your arrival, and wondered more than once why you wore them not. But bright as I deemed *them*, they appear absolutely pale and dim in comparison with those resplendent gems which his Highness gave you. Ah! dear lady, if you would only permit me to decorate you with them this evening, how ravishingly beautiful would you look! Beautiful you always are—beautiful you ever must be: but still this loveliness of your's may be set off, if not enhanced, and displayed in the light of flashing gems as a contrast to the simplicity which mingles with the glory wherewith it is wont to shine."

"Annetta—my dear Annetta!" exclaimed Musidora, smiling with a sudden gaiety, which nevertheless was but the heightening of the cold brilliancy over her alabaster features—while the pearls shone between the parting coral of her lips: "you have been studying in the school of flattery. Do you know that if I were more girlish than I am, you would render me quite vain?"

"O dear lady! you *must* know—you cannot help knowing," cried Annetta, now passing from behind the chair and gazing upon her young mistress with a sincere enthusiasm, "that you are splendidly beautiful. Yes—though of the same sex, yet do I feel a pleasure in contemplating such transcending loveliness as your's. Aye, and it is an honour likewise to be permitted to serve as the handmaiden of one so superbly handsome."

For an instant—but only for a single instant—an expression of proud triumph shone upon Musidora's countenance: but the next moment it settled like a spirit of mockery in the depths of her dark haunting eyes, as if even the consciousness of her own miraculous beauty was not able to excite more than the slightest and most transient emotion.

"It does not even appear to give you pleasure, dear lady," said Annetta, with a look of affectionate regretfulness, "to know that you are beautiful. Either you will not allow the thought to harbour in your bosom, because you deem it a weakness—or else it is absorbed by *other* thoughts, which make you indifferent to the possession of such rare loveliness."

"Annetta, you have never spoken to me in such a strain before," said Musidora, bending her dark eyes for an instant in an inquiring manner upon her abigail's countenance.

"Because you never permitted the conversation to take such a turn before," answered Annetta.

"Then you are discoursing on things concerning which you have often wished to speak on former occasions?"

"Yes, dear lady, such is the truth: I will not deny it."

"And these things on which you desire to speak?" said Musidora, her dark eyes resting more searchingly and penetratingly upon Annetta.

"Did I not just now take the liberty of observing that you are incomprehensible? O lady, to be beautiful as you are, and yet to remain emotionless when told that you are beautiful—in one short month to have brought the King of England to your feet, and yet to remain as indifferent to the consummation of so proud a triumph as if it were some poor knight or humble gentleman instead of a mighty monarch whom you had thus inspired with such a passion—to possess the richest diamonds that ever were yielded up by oriental mine, and yet leave them neglected and forgotten in the casket, preferring to place a simple white rose or a camellia upon your hair, or else to leave it entirely unadorned, as if its own dark glory were a brighter halo than diamonds could shed upon it,—Oh! there is something strange—I might almost say *unnatural*, in all this!"

Annetta stopped short: for her mistress's eyes appeared all in a moment to glow with a wild and unearthly lustre; and on her countenance there suddenly sprang up an expression so strange, so full of ineffable emotions—anger, dismay, affright, and entreaty, all combined—that no wonder was it the young damsel ceased abruptly and even started back at thus beholding on the part of her mistress a display of feeling such as the girl had never seen before. But with phantom-like swiftness, and indeed with the suddenness of a passing shade flitting away, did that wild expression vanish from Musidora's countenance and her eyes shone with their natural lustre once more.

"Did I say anything to offend you, dearest lady?" asked Annetta, with timid manner and deprecating look.

"No. What made you think so?" asked Musidora, with the air of one who fancied that not the slightest ground had been afforded for such an idea.

"Methought you looked as if suddenly angered," returned the abigail: "yes—and not only angered, but also grieved."

"If you had done wrong wilfully, I should have chided you," said Musidora, in her usual tone and without the least excitement. "But tell me all you wish to say: I shall not be angry with you. Speak, Annetta. You know that I am not often swayed by mere curiosity: but it suits my humour at the present moment to hear you explain your thoughts concerning me. You said that I am incomprehensible? Is it because my mind possesses a placidity not easily ruffled, and because it is not so readily moved by the vanities and the follies of the world as the generality of our sex?"

"I know not exactly how to answer," replied Annetta, somewhat perplexed and bewildered by these questions. "And yet it does seem strange that one who is herself so lovely and so loveable, should notwithstanding possess a heart so little accessible to love——"

"Love!" repeated Musidora: and then again did that same ineffable expression sweep over her countenance.

"There! are you not angry with me?" cried Annetta, gazing half in affright upon her young mistress.

"Angry?—no!" exclaimed Musidora: and she smiled with such transcending sweetness that the impression produced by the *other* look was effaced all in a moment. "Go on Annetta: let me hear what you have to say, since it is evident you have thoughts unto which you are desirous to give expression."

"Dearest lady," resumed the young tirewoman, "I cannot help thinking that you are a being infinitely superior to myself. I fancy that were I possessed of your superb beauty, I should not prove indifferent to compliments: did I possess such gems as those which have been gifts to you, I should long for every fitting occasion to deck myself therewith: but oh! were I fortunate enough to win a monarch's love, my heart would not remain like a fragment of an unsunned glacier!"

"Do you not see, my dear Annetta," asked Musidora, rising from her seat and tapping her abigail with caressing good-humour upon the cheek, "that if I were all you suppose I ought to be I should seem the most monstrous embodiment of every sentiment of vanity, conceit, pride, and vain-glory that ever combined to render a human being odious and insufferable? Better, better far," she added with some little degree of emotion, "that my heart should remain (if your description be correct) the fragment of an unsunned glacier!—better also that my smiles should be like snow-wreaths, and my tears, if ever I weep, like drops distilled from icicles!"

There was a strange energy in these last words which fell from Musidora's lips—not strange for any other human being, because such words had something too much of bitterness in them not to be spoken with energy; but strange for her who so seldom—so very seldom—displayed aught resembling emotion at all! Yet strange as this manifestation of feeling was on Musidora's part, stranger still—aye, and also far more unnatural—was the sudden coldness which supervened—the iciness of manner and of look which succeeded that swift brief moment of excitement—while the petrifying brilliancy of the smile settled again upon her countenance, and she became the unfathomable, inscrutable being she of late years had seemed to be!

"However," she said, as if by way of winding up the observations she had just made, or of putting a finish upon the topic of conversation, "since you wish to have the pleasure of bedecking me with the gems which his Highness the King has given me—and inasmuch as the circumstance of never having yet worn them may indeed appear somewhat neglectful and might be construed into a prideful eccentricity on my part, of which feelings I am utterly incapable—you shall have your own way this evening."

"What! and you will wear the diamonds?" exclaimed Annetta, joyfully, as if she had achieved a brilliant triumph in persuading her young mistress thus to adorn herself.

"Yes—I will wear the gems this evening," responded Musidora;—and the delighted abigail proceeded to open the wardrobe in which the jewels were kept.

CHAPTER XVIII.

THE KING'S STRATAGEM.

IT was close upon nine o'clock, when the door of the saloon where the Earl and Countess of Grantham were seated, was thrown open and a domestic announced the King. The nobleman and his wife rose and advanced with true parasite servility to greet the monarch, who on his part treated them with most condescending courtesy. But at the same time his eyes glanced rapidly around; and the Earl, anticipating his meaning, observed with a low bow, "Sire, the fair Musidora will doubtless make her appearance in a few minutes."

"Ah! your lordship divined then full easily for whom my eyes sought?" exclaimed the King. "But tell me, what think you is the impression I have made upon her, if any at all? Do not flatter me—do not at once begin with the wonted courtesy-like assurances that wherever I bend my looks, *there* must I find yielding hearts. No, my lord: it is not always so!—the knee sometimes bends in the cringing servility which sordid interest prompts or selfishness suggests; and yet the heart may rebel! Now, it is a week since I privately and confidentially whispered in the ears of yourself and her ladyship the Countess that your fair young relative has won my heart——"

"Which secret, gracious liege," observed Lord Grantham, "the Countess and I have, according to your royal commands, retained solemnly and sacredly in our own breasts."

"Aye, that much I expected at your hands," rejoined the monarch. "But for what purpose did I thus soon make you my confidants? Was it not that you might observe Musidora well—gather up all her words—endeavour to penetrate the meaning of her looks—watch whether you could ever surprise a sigh escaping her bosom—and take opportunities when alone with her, to turn the conversation upon me, so as to ascertain what her opinion is of her King? Have you done all this?—for during the past week I have not had an opportunity of speaking to you alone?"

"We have watched—we have observed—and we have discoursed, in the manner which your Highness pointed out," returned Lord Grantham.

"Yes—and I have sought opportunities of being alone with Musidora," interposed the Countess, taking up as usual the unfinished thread of her husband's remark. "I have spoken to her about your Highness in various terms—sometimes extolling the generosity of your character, at others lauding your proficiency in martial sports and chivalrous tilt; now alluding to your Grace as a polished gentleman and accomplished gallant, and then praising your domestic virtues and describing how admirably your Highness's qualifications are adapted, all monarch though you are, to ensure the happiness of a loving and tender wife."

"Well, and what does the fair Musidora say to all this?" asked the King. "Come, tell me the precise truth. I do not wish you to deceive me in a single point. On the contrary, I should be mortally offended with you, were I to discover that you misled me."

"I will candidly tell your Highness the truth," answered the Countess of Grantham. "Musidora exhibits no particular inclination at any time to make your Grace the topic of discourse; but she never absolutely avoids that topic when I suggest it. She does not appear moved by the eulogies which I pass upon you; whereas she herself occasionally suggests faults which she believes you to possess."

"Ah! you have been indiscreet in plastering me too thickly over with those eulogies," exclaimed the King, in a tone of vexation. "Instead of laying a delicate gloss over your picture, you have doubtless put on so thick a daub of varnish as to make all the rich colouring appear through a suspicious medium."

"No, my liege—I flatter myself," responded the Countess, "that in this respect I have acted ingeniously enough. For when Musidora has hinted at any of your faults, I have spoken with great apparent freedom on the subject—with much greater freedom, indeed, than is consonant with the respect I owe and the veneration I feel towards your Grace——"

"Tush! spare the compliments," cried the King. "We have not perhaps many minutes to converse ere Musidora will make her appearance: and in the interval I wish to glean what I can relative to the impression, if any, which my assiduities, my bounties, and my qualifications may have made upon her. As for my sovereign rank, I believe it is well-nigh valueless in her estimation——"

"No, my liege: Musidora has her ambition, I am convinced of it!" exclaimed the Countess of Grantham. "The very style in which she discusses what she is pleased to term your Highness's *faults*, has once or twice caused her to let slip a word or two——"

"Well, and that word or two?" asked the King. "And about the faults too? Tell me what are my faults in her estimation, that I may know how to amend them."

"Musidora thinks, from all she has heard, that your Highness attends too much to pleasure and too little to the interests of your people—that there is a vast amount of misery and poverty into which your Highness never condescends to look; and she has once or twice observed that if she had the power, she would accomplish such and such reforms and effect such and such beneficial changes."

"Ah! then her's is the ambition to do good?" and a look very much resembling scornful disgust appeared upon the monarch's countenance. "However," he immediately added, "if such be her desire, we will see if it cannot be gratified. But candidly speaking, Lord Grantham, do you not find your young relative a beautiful and charming enigma? Such indeed she appears to me. She resembles the water-lily upon the crystal brook when the moon illumines the scene and bathes the flower with its silver flood."

"The comparison is most admirable, my liege," responded the Earl of Grantham. "It is on account of her very purity that she is so slowly accessible to love."

"Yes, her virtue is of the iciest quality," added the Countess. "And yet she is not passionless! It is impossible with her radiant beauty, and with that voluptuous grandeur of form, together with the deep fire that burns in her splendid eyes,—impossible, I say, that she can be passionless!"

"But surely your Grace can form some idea of the impression which your brilliant qualities as a man and as a Sovereign," said the Earl of Grantham, "have made upon Musidora."

"Flattery again? sheer flattery on your part!" exclaimed the King, with an impatient movement of haughty disgust. "Will you forget the habits of a courtier for a few minutes, and speak as an adviser, a friend, and a confidant if you can?"

"It is difficult, sire, to throw off habits of deference and respect," rejoined the Earl of Grantham. "But to speak in the plainest and simplest language, may I be permitted to ask how Musidora comports herself towards your Highness at such times when you happen to he alone with her? For instance, occasionally when we have walked in the gardens of an evening, the Countess and I have purposely lingered behind to afford your Grace an opportunity of saying sweet things to Musidora——"

"Aye," interrupted King Henry, "and on those occasions to which you refer, has Musidora penetrated the stratagem, and either loitered or actually stopped short in the shady avenue until ye two have overtaken us again. In a word, she has ever avoided being left alone with me in the pleasure-grounds."

"Ah!—that very rigidity of virtue whereof I ere now spoke!" exclaimed the Countess. "It is the purity of admirable principles most highly wrought—the innocence and bashful reserve of girlhood embellishing the charms of splendid womanhood!"

"Well," said the King, "I must devise some means to ascertain how I really stand in Musidora's heart. Therefore if you hear me telling any strange tale this evening, calculated to pique her curiosity, jealousy, or any other sentiment on which I may choose to play, do you appear to enter into the spirit thereof. It will be hard indeed if I do not think of some method of probing the mysteries of the maiden's soul. Perhaps I may even thaw that iciness of look which she wears—call up a blush to the cheeks which are as stainless as marble—and convert into the ruddy glow of the tropics that smile which is as brilliant but as cold as the sun shining on the frozen regions of eternal winter."

"Whatever stratagem your Highness may have recourse to, we shall comprehend it," said the Earl of Grantham.

"Yes," added the Countess; "and I shall be glad for your Grace to devise a means to compel Musidora to give some sign or evidence relative to what she really thinks of your Highness. But," added the titled dame hesitatingly, "if I might be permitted to suggest the easiest, the simplest, and the shortest method——"

"What?" demanded the King, turning with something like choleric abruptness upon the Countess.

"I would advise that your Grace should at once announce your royal pleasure to Musidora," responded her ladyship, timidly and hesitatingly: "for it is impossible to conceive that a young lady—so highly honoured, so transcendingly flattered—should hesitate to fall on her knees and pour forth her gratitude to the great King who purposes to make her the partner of his throne."

"Nonsense, madam!" exclaimed Henry VIII. "I anticipated that such was the idea which had entered your head. But you do not know your young relative Musidora so well as I, if you imagine that she is to be dazzled all in a moment by a brilliant offer. Why, she has scarcely seemed pleased at the civilities I have shown her! She has accepted them in the light of common-place courtesies—save and except the diamonds; and those she positively refused at first to receive at all, until I commanded her as her Sovereign to take them. Even then I beheld, in the quick flashing of her eyes and the sudden wreathing of her beauteous lips, the impatience of a proud spirit rebelling against that despotic mandate of mine. Aye, for she did regard it as despotic, though it was a mandate which forced upon her a gift worth well-nigh a monarch's ransom. Yes, she accepted those jewels because I commanded her—and because almost at the same time I told her how I sent off a learned physician to take care of her sire's health. But has she worn those diamonds once?—has she condescended to appear in them on a single occasion? No. Think you then that she has not a proud, a haughty, a peculiar—aye, and an indomitable spirit? How know you what iron energies may exist in the inscrutable depths of her soul? Believe me, Musidora is not to be driven: but she may be led! It is possible at least—and we will try. But were I to *command* her to accompany me to the altar, she would bend upon me her large dark eyes, and her splendid countenance would beam with scornful defiance. You surely then, madam," added the King, fixing his looks upon the Countess of Grantham, "cannot wish to expose *me*, your Sovereign—the King of England—to the ignominy of being refused by one who, after all, is but an obscure girl? Aye, obscure—but heavens! how wonderfully beautiful! what a marvel of loveliness! The earth never possessed her equal. Talk of Oriental odalisques, of whom my Ambassadors to the Ottoman Porte have spoken in such rapturous terms! they are naught in comparison with Musidora Sinclair. I am convinced that all the boasted brilliancy of the brightest Sultanas' charms would pale into dimness and sicken into misty gloom, before the transcending splendour of Musidora's loveliness."

The Earl and Countess of Grantham exchanged quick looks of significancy as they listened to this excited rhapsody on the part of the King: for they saw that he was so enamoured of Musidora—so utterly captivated with the magic glory of her beauty—that he would raise heaven and earth to win her heart and make her his own.

Scarcely had King Henry concluded his fervid speech, when the door opened and the object of his eulogy made her appearance. But it would be impossible to describe the dazzling brilliancy—the almost overwhelming splendour of her presence, as she thus burst as it were upon the eyes of her relatives and the King. The diamonds in which she had suffered the admiring Annetta to bedeck her, were indeed of the rarest and costliest description: and well did they become her! Shining with the concentrated light of all the stars of the firmament, upon the raven darkness of her hair—around the polished column of her neck—upon the dazzling whiteness of her bosom—and circling the plump symmetry of the snowy arms, those gems did indeed, as Annetta had presaged, set off Musidora's charms to a new and indescribable advantage. Yet brilliant though the shafts of vivid lustre were which the gems shot forth, yet not more lustrous than the light which shone in the large dark eyes—those eyes that seemed of jet filled with electric fire!

An expression of satisfaction burst from the lips of the King as he thus beheld Musidora decorated for the first time with the diamonds which were his gift; while the Earl and Countess exchanged meaning looks once more, not only to imply that they saw how the King evidently felt the compliment, tardily though it was paid, but also to express their hope that their beauteous young relative had at length determined upon riveting the chains which her charms had thrown around Henry's heart.

After some little discourse, they all four repaired to the supper-room, and sat down to table. As usual, the King was assiduous in his attentions to Musidora; and according to her wont, she received them with that dignified courtesy and polished ease of manner which left it to be supposed that she took them as the ordinary demonstrations of politeness, and nothing more.

During a pause in the conversation, Musidora, suddenly recollecting the adventure which first introduced her to the King, said, "I have been somewhat remiss in one respect; and that is in not making very recent inquiries relative to the poor old man in whom your Highness so deeply and so generously interested yourself."

"I have heard naught of him since last I gave you tidings on the subject," responded the King.

"That was ten days ago," observed Musidora; "and he had arrived in Edinburgh on the special mission upon which your Highness had despatched him."

"Doubtless more will be heard from him shortly," rejoined the monarch. "There are various points in which the commerce between the two countries may be improved; and as Manners is eminently proficient in all subjects of that kind, I thought it best to despatch him to the Scottish capital as a special Commissioner to treat with the Regency of that kingdom. He set off, as I informed you at the time, within a very few days after we saw him here; and, as I have likewise informed you, I learnt ten days back that he had arrived safely and was entering with spirit upon the object of his mission."

"Was it not a long journey for so aged a man to undertake?" asked Musidora, her memory dwelling compassionately upon the ruined merchant's infirmities and sorrows.

"As I have already informed you, it was his own wish to remove from London for the present. After mature reflection he made that statement to the trusty person whom I sent, according to appointment, to meet him in the Temple Gardens; and in consequence of what the old man then said to my messenger, did I subsequently act. Rest assured, Musidora, that Master Manners has every reason to bless the hour when you testified so much sympathy in his behalf."

"Your Highness has done more—far more—than I could have foreseen or than he could possibly have expected," observed Musidora.

"Dear young lady," said the King, "there are no doubt many, many sad cases of distress and woe within my realms; and my heart often bleeds when imagination depicts those unseen sorrows to which I would so cheerfully stretch forth a ministering hand if I did but know where such sorrows hide themselves. Indeed, to discover the seclusions, the lurking-holes, and the dens where poverty requires assistance, vice needs reform, and disease languishes for the physician's help, a Queen should take the task in hand. The affairs of State are already heavy enough for me. Scandalous tongues and evil-disposed persons have dared to represent that I expend in pleasure much of that time which should be devoted to my subjects. But this is not the case. Throughout whole days do I sit in deliberation with my Council—or in the inspection of State documents—and in the consideration of plans to benefit my people."

Musidora listened to the King with an interest which she made no attempt to conceal; and as he paused, she said, "It is with unfeigned delight that I hear your Grace thus speak. Heaven will prosper all the endeavours you may make for the amelioration of your subjects."

"Had I been blessed," continued Henry, in a grave tone and assuming a serious look, "with a Queen who would second those endeavours to which you have just alluded, fair Musidora, I should have been happy indeed. But it is otherwise. My marriage being illegal, and the Queen herself knowing that a divorce has been applied for, is too much occupied with her own sorrows to devote any attention to those of my subjects. Therefore, when I resolved to procure the annulment of this most unlawful and most unfortunate union into which I was half beguiled and half forced at the time, I determined that the wife whom I should choose to share my throne must be a woman of a disposition, a character, and a soul that would qualify her to become the veritable mother of my people. I said to myself," continued Henry, now appearing to address himself to the Earl of Grantham, and not to Musidora, "that if amongst the daughters of England I could find one who combined personal beauty with mental accomplishments—a stainless character with a benevolent heart—and a mind that so far from yielding itself up to the seductiveness of the pleasures and delights which belong to a Court, would become devoted to the task of ameliorating the condition of her people,—I vowed, I say, that the damsel, wherever I could find her, and whoever she might be, should receive the offer of my hand!"

"It was a resolve worthy of a great and generous-hearted monarch," said the Earl of Grantham.

"And one," added the Countess, "which history will not forget to record in its brightest page."

"Well," continued Henry, "I have sought after a lady possessing all the requisites which I have specified—I have caused secret inquiries to made in various parts of England, even the most distant, to ascertain if such a young damsel could be found. I myself thought for a moment,"—and here he glanced round at Musidora, with a half-significant and half-reproachful look—"that I had discovered the fitting object of my researches: and I strove to win her heart. I wooed her as significantly and as tenderly as became a prince who could not descend altogether from the summit of his pedestal. But I failed with the voice of affection to awaken a responsive echo in her heart. She would not comprehend me—or she could not. If the former, she was wilfully blind: if the latter she is to be deplored—but I dared not, considering my own rank and dignity, be more explicit. This day I have received a communication from a trusty emissary, whom I sent to a distant county, and who in his despatch informs me that he has heard of a maiden who fully merits the high distinction I proposed to confer on the most worthy. This damsel," continued Henry, still addressing himself to the Earl of Grantham, "is as perfect as a matchless beauty, a cultivated mind, a charitable disposition, and an affectionate heart can possibly render her. To-morrow, therefore, do I propose to journey *incognito* to the dwelling of this damsel's father—remain there for a few days—assure myself that she is in reality all that has been represented—and then act accordingly. Do you approve of this intention, my lord?"

"Most decidedly," answered the Earl of Grantham, remembering the cue he had received from the King previous to Musidora's appearance.

"And I echo the approval," cried Lady Grantham.

"But you, fair Musidora, what say you upon the subject?"—and as the King put this question, he turned slowly round and fixed his eyes upon our heroine.

"Since your Grace has done me the honour to consult me," responded Musidora, with nothing in her tone or her look to indicate the stir of any unusual emotion in her bosom, "I will frankly declare my opinion to be that every part of your Highness's plan relative to the choice of a future Queen is admirable and most praiseworthy, but that the courtship your Grace proposes to make is too short."

"What mean you, Musidora?" asked the King, as if really puzzled to comprehend her words.

"Simple enough though my answer was," she said, in the same placid and passionless manner as before,—so superb and so dignified too in the alpine splendour of her beauty,—"I will nevertheless endeavour to make myself more explicit."

"Proceed," said the King. "I am most anxious to hear you."

"What I meant your Highness to understand," continued Musidora, "is that no woman would be really and truly worthy of your Grace, who suffered herself to be wooed by a short courtship; nor could there be any true delicacy and real feminine dignity in the heart of her who would advance half-way to meet the overtures of a suitor, even though that suitor were the Sovereign himself."

"Ah! it is admirably spoken," exclaimed the King, with a quick glance of intelligence and satisfaction towards Lord and Lady Grantham: then rising from his seat, he advanced to the window, which, stretching down to the floor, looked upon a lawn at the back of the villa;—and perceiving that it was brilliant moonlight without, he drew back the curtain and opened the casement. For a few instants he stood upon the threshold gazing forth upon the scene of garden and shrubbery, with the field and the shady lane beyond, all of which were bathed in the silver flood of argentine splendour:—then turning somewhat abruptly away, he accosted Musidora, extending his hand and saying, "Come! the evening is delicious—let us walk for a while in the garden."

Our heroine rose from her seat—paused for an instant—and the glance which she flung rapidly upon the Earl and Countess, showed that she hesitated whether to desire them to accompany her, or not; but making up her mind the next moment, she gave her hand to King Henry and suffered him to lead her forth from the apartment.

CHAPTER XIX.

THE MOON-LIGHT WALK.

MUSIDORA's diamonds glistened brightly in the silver flood of lustre that poured down from heaven upon the garden-scene of dewy verdure and slumbering flowers: and the marble fairness of her splendid countenance, her grandly-arching neck, and her sloping shoulders, appeared in dazzling contrast with the dark but glossy cloud of her flowing hair. Her hand was still retained in the King's as he led her down the gravel-walk that intersected the sloping lawn: but it trembled not;—it lay there, in his clasp, passive and almost listless, as if no emotion swelled in the heart of her to whom it belonged. And upon her countenance was that same serene seriousness, gently softened by the gleam of a half-vanishing smile upon her scarlet lips: but though her features were thus statuesque and grave almost to a solemn fixedness, yet did that faintly beaming smile, together with the glorious lustre that shone in her superb dark eyes, relieve her countenance of all monotony, and even lead the beholder to suspect that it was *possible* for this ice-like being to become all that could be desired of feminine and tender feelings.

The King gazed upon her with a look of unmistakable admiration, and in which there was perhaps fondness also: but for the first minute or two that they were thus alone together in the garden he spoke not a word. It was nearly as light as day; and they could see each other quite plainly. Musidora flung from the depths of her large inscrutable eyes a quick glance upon the monarch's countenance, as if to penetrate his thoughts with that lightning-look: but it lingered not to mingle with his own—and as he gently pressed her hand, it gave no silently responsive token of tender feeling. In short, not the slightest encouragement of any kind did the King receive from this splendid but mysterious being. Yet surely it was an hour, it was an occasion, and it was altogether under the influence of circumstances, which might have induced her to unbend from her chill reserve and suffer the ice of her heart to melt somewhat?—for this was a moonlight scene, so congenial to the tender passion,—and moreover, it was the mightiest King of Christendom that walked by the side of Musidora now!

"And so, fair one," began the monarch, still retaining in his own that hand which was not withdrawn: but in thus suffering it to remain in his clasp, there was nothing significant—for in those times a lady, when walking with a cavalier, was as often accustomed to hold the hand as to hang upon the arm:—"and so, fair one, you approve of my resolve to raise the most deserving of England's daughters to the seat beside me on my throne? But you disapprove of the brief courtship of three or four weeks?"

"The opinion which I ventured to give your Highness upon that point ere now," answered Musidora, "was one which I can conscientiously reiterate."

"And if I decide upon espousing this damsel of whom I have spoken," continued Henry, "will you be present at the bridal?"

"I should be bound to obey your Highness's commands," responded Musidora, still speaking in the same even and emotionless tone as was her wont.

"I can assure you, from all that I have heard, she is eminently beautiful," resumed the monarch; "and her qualities, though somewhat peculiar, are excellent. I already love her! Love is ever the more profound when it is tinged with romance: and there is something especially romantic in choosing a wife in such a manner as this. Do you not think that she will be flattered by the choice that I thus make?"

"She must undoubtedly feel herself honoured by so marked and distinguishing a proof of her Sovereign's favour," replied Musidora. "But if she be a woman of really fine character, elevated thoughts, and noble disposition, she will feel a laudable gratification of pride rather in the fact that so lofty a tribute is paid to her virtues, than in the mere abstract circumstance of being raised to a throne."

"You mean that she must feel herself to be a woman of no common order thus to have won the good opinion and gained the favour of the King? Is it not so, Musidora?" he asked, gazing upon her.

"Yes," was her tranquil reply: "the Sovereign is the fountain of all honour; and it is therefore natural that his good opinion should be appreciated far more highly than that of a humbler individual. Therefore the woman who is fortunate enough to win this good opinion has reason to be proud: she is even justified in being proud;—and she were something less or something more than woman, did she remain unmoved by such a magnificent tribute paid to her merits. Nevertheless——But perhaps I shall offend by the remark to which I would give utterance?"

"No—you cannot offend me," exclaimed the King. "I value your opinion so highly that I purposely asked you to walk forth with me from the supper-room that I might receive it unreservedly from your lips. I know you to be a lady not merely of very superior intellect, but also of fine taste and exquisite delicacy in all your sentiments. Moreover, a sort of friendship, I flatter myself, has sprung up between you and me; and we are now conversing in this spirit. You must forget that I am the King, while offering me your opinion. Suppose, for instance, that you fancy yourself my sister—then all restraint and all embarrassment can be laid aside, and you may speak to me in the fullest confidence and with the utmost assurance. Do you consent to talk with me on such terms?"

"I do," answered Musidora.

"Now then, proceed with the remark which you were about to make," said the King.

"I had been observing, as your Highness will remember," continued Musidora, "that the lady who becomes the object of so special a mark of royal favour as that which you purpose to bestow upon the country damsel of whom your Grace has spoken, cannot fail to appreciate such a tribute to her merits. But it is at such a time and under such circumstances, that she ought to show the true greatness of her character: for she must remember that, as a woman, she has a duty to perform towards herself and her sex. If she suffer herself to be dazzled by the brilliancy of the offer, and thus accept it readily, your Highness may rest assured that there is some weak point in her character. True, it would be a woman's weakness, and assuredly a pardonable one: but still it would be not the less a weakness."

"Then what would you have her do?" asked the King.

"I would have her frankly and candidly tell your Majesty," rejoined Musidora, "that while she feels flattered by the honour you confer upon her, she nevertheless cannot give an immediate answer—that she requires some little time to study your disposition, and assure herself that her own will appropriately mate with it—that although it is her King who seeks her hand, yet that it is but a man after all who woos her heart—and that it is therefore imperiously necessary she should have some leisure to search into her own soul, and analyse her own feelings, in order to come to a right conclusion whether it will be for the advantage of her monarch that she should accompany him to the altar."

"You reason like a discreet and prudent woman, fair Musidora," said the King—and he pressed her soft hand tenderly: but still did she walk on in serene and placid dignity by his side, without appearing to notice the circumstance. "To sum up all your arguments in a few words, you think that there ought to be a proper period of courtship; and that a King has no exclusive patent or special prerogative to claim exemption from such tardy process of love-making."

"Your Grace has rightly interpreted my meaning," rejoined Musidora.

"In that respect, then, will I follow your advice," continued Henry: "for I am not one of those who seek a friend's counsel without the intention of adopting it. But to another point:—and again do I wish you to speak freely and candidly. You are aware, my dear Musidora,—for in these affectionate terms do I address you by right of the tacit friendship which has sprung up between us,—you are aware, I say, that I am for the moment trammelled by my unfortunate marriage with Queen Catherine: but I have applied to his Holiness the Pope for annulment and divorce. Now, that this dispensation or decree will arrive in England in a few days, I have secret but positive information. Nevertheless, the Queen has a somewhat powerful party in the country; and were the Pope's decree made public all in a moment and the Queen divorced on a sudden, there would be a civil war. The nation would be plunged into the miseries of intestine strife, and my very throne would be endangered. Are not these deplorable catastrophes to be avoided?"

"Most assuredly," was our heroine's reply.

"But the perils of which we are speaking are only to be averted by a temporising policy," proceeded the King, "and this may involve a period of several months. Do you understand me well? From the very moment that the Pope's decree reaches my hand, my marriage with Queen Catherine is dissolved. Shall I be justified in contracting *another*, privately and secretly, but with all the fitting rites and sacred ceremonies so as to render it legal in the eyes of the church and of heaven?"

"If such a marriage will also be legal whenever it may be proclaimed in the eyes of men," was the answer that Musidora gave, in a more deliberate tone and with deeper solemnity of manner than she had before spoken. "Because," she continued, but still speaking with measured accents, as if she well weighed every word ere she gave it utterance, "many marriages take place privately in the world, from a variety of circumstances: but if the circumstances be imperious and the marriages themselves are solemnised in good faith and with priestly sanction, it would be the veriest affectation of heartless stoicism or refined prudery to object to them."

"I thank you for this clear and lucid enunciation of opinion," said the King: and he gazed long and intently upon Musidora's countenance: but not the slightest evidence of emotion ruffled its serenity; and still did her hand remain passive as that of a statue—but with the living warmth which the marble hath not—in his own. "To be more explicit still," he continued, after a long pause, "let us suppose that I avow my intentions to this damsel of whom we have all along been speaking, and that I grant her full power and license to fix the duration of courtship: suppose also that at the end of this courtship my own love is confirmed and her good opinion of me is strengthened to the requisite degree to warrant her in entrusting her happiness to my keeping. Then let us suppose that reasons of policy render it necessary that a *private marriage* should take place, but with the solemn understanding that such marriage is to be proclaimed so soon as the way can be properly prepared for its enunciation. In this case would you advise the damsel to consent to such private marriage?"

"Yes—under such circumstances I would," answered Musidora.

Again did the King fix his eyes earnestly upon our heroine; and still did her countenance preserve all its wonted serenity, though perhaps there was a stranger and even wilder light than usual shining in her glorious eyes. But this might be fancy on the monarch's part: for no other evidence of feeling or emotion did she betray. Her hand, warm with healthful animation, lay listlessly in his own; and the grand outline of her bust moved not with a quicker undulation than was the natural accompaniment of her regular breathing. No—nor did even the faintest semblance of a roseate tint appear upon the pure living white of her cheeks. Her step too was as firm and as even in its graceful dignity and its elegant lightness as ever; and thus was she to all outward appearances as passionless and emotionless as it seemed her fixed nature to be.

"If you were the bosom-friend of this damsel of whom we are speaking," continued Henry, in a slower and deeper tone,—"or to make the question more pointed still, if you were the damsel herself, would you act in the manner we have been describing?"

"It would be either a wretched display of sophistry or else of base duplicity on my part," returned Musidora, "were I to express an opinion to your Highness which I would not give to another; or if I were to approve of a course for that other to pursue, when I myself should shrink from adopting it."

"Then, Musidora," exclaimed the King, "tell me—have you not understood me all along?"

"Certainly," she replied, answering mechanically, as if without effort and without emotion. "You sought my advice as a friend, and I have given it in that spirit."

"And have you not a deeper interest in the topic?"

"No."

"And your heart whispers nothing?"

"No."

"But you have foreseen what was to follow from my words?"

"No."

"No—no—always no!" ejaculated the King in an excited tone. "Your chill replies fall like ice-flakes upon my heart. Ah! but they shall melt there—and *your* heart shall warm also yet! Cruel, cruel Musidora—as lovely as you are cruel—as adorable as you are incomprehensible! You know—Ah! you *must* know full well what I mean!" cried Henry, now

pressing her hand between both his own, and fixing upon her looks as tender and as significant as they were earnest. "Wherefore do you tantalize
me thus? Wherefore continue thus cold—thus freezing? Tell me—is your
heart indeed of ice? have all the feelings of a woman frozen into adamantine sternness within you?"

Musidora spoke not immediately: but now her hand *did* tremble, and
perceptibly too, in the monarch's grasp;—and not merely the semblance
of a roseate tint, but the crimson hue itself mantled upon her pure cheeks,
like the flush of morning on the virginal whiteness of the lily;—and
stranger and wilder flashed the light from her dark haunting eyes—and
the superb outline of her bust swelled and sank with quick and visible
undulations.

"Oh! then you *do* possess the feelings of a woman! The proud soul of
ice can melt—the haughty marble statue can unbend from its pedestal!"—
and as the King thus spoke, he pressed her hand with renewed rapture;
and inclining his head to a level with her eyes, he gazed deep down into
the profundities of those magnificent orbs. "Musidora," he continued, in
a low deep tone of impassioned feeling, "you know that I love you! You
must have seen it! Even if your own heart beat with no responsive chord,
nevertheless you would have been blind not to perceive all the many evidences of that devotion which my soul has offered up at the shrine of
your beauty and your worth! Tell me—tell me, lovely enigma—beautiful
embodiment of the most enchanting mystery—tell me, sweet dissembler,
that you have understood me all along!"

The flush had passed away from Musidora's cheeks—her bosom's
swell was regular once more—proudly she stood and proudly too she
looked, as she withdrew her hand and gave the cold reply, "Your Highness
must not accuse me of dissembling."

"Ah! you are angry with me, then? you are offended?" he cried, looking as if he thought he had gone too far or had spoken too fast. "Incomprehensible being that you are, why this frigid reserve? You know that I love
you—at least, if you knew it not before, you know it now—for I declare
it! The whole tale of the damsel in a distant county was a fiction invented
to serve as a preface for this avowal, and as the means indeed of conveying it. All King as I am, I felt that I could not speak to you, Musidora, as I
should have spoken to any other woman on the face of the earth. There
sits not a queen upon the throne, before whom the heart of man must
humble itself so utterly as mine is humbled in the presence of your lofty
loveliness and proud yet graceful dignity! If, then, in a moment of natural
enthusiasm I forgot the amount of homage which is your due—if, hurried away by the wild and impassioned hopes of a lover, I addressed you

in terms which have given offence, I crave your pardon—I beseech your forgiveness. But at the same time I implore your love; and in bestowing that love upon me, it is for *you* to fix all the conditions of my courtship in pursuance of the opinions you have expressed and the rules of propriety you have laid down."

"Great King," answered Musidora, her voice now perceptibly tremulous, and a beauteous smile of mingled gratification and affability—we cannot exactly say *tenderness*—expanding upon her splendid features,—"I seek no self-humiliation on your part: I demand it not—I deserve it not. I am but a humble mortal—a poor weak woman——"

"Oh! now you are melting—you are yielding—you are about to give me hope and encouragement!" exclaimed the King—and he pressed her hand in rapture to his lips; then sinking upon one knee—there, in the gravel-walk of that garden, and in the pellucid flood of argentine moonlight—the monarch knelt at Musidora's feet, saying, "Tell me that I am not indifferent to you. Say that if I woo honourably and tenderly, you are to be won?"

"Rise, sire—rise," said Musidora, her lips now quivering with emotion, her voice trembling, and the roseate hue again mantling upon the alabaster of her countenance. "I feel honoured—flattered—by your Grace's kindness——But rise—for it is not fit that my Sovereign should kneel to me."

"I obey you, beautiful Musidora," said the King, as he rose from his suppliant posture:—and again did he snatch her hand and press it to his lips: but as she gently though firmly withdrew it, he exclaimed, "Oh! you doubtless imagine that it is impossible for me to love tenderly and sincerely after so brief an acquaintance? But from the very first instant that we met, was I stricken with an eternal sentiment, and your image was indelibly impressed upon my heart. A month has elapsed since then. A month!—Oh! it is a short period in the life of man; but it is full of experiences for one who loves—because every day, every hour, every minute, aye, every flitting second is characterized by a worship that perishes not, but the incense of which grows stronger as it fills the soul. Already then do I love you adoringly and devotedly; and it seems to me as I if had known you for years!"

Musidora listened with visible interest though with disappearing emotions: yet even when the flush had again vanished from her cheeks, and her lips had grown still once more, did she continue to gaze with earnestness upon the monarch's countenance as if to read to what extent his heart echoed the impassioned accents of his tongue.

"Do you doubt me—do you disbelieve me?" he inquired, with a slight tinge of proud annoyance.

"No, sire," she answered: "I do not doubt you—I do not disbelieve you. Why should I? There is sincerity in your words, in your manner, and in your looks. Besides," she added, suddenly drawing herself up to the full of her stately height, "if you know me at all, you must know me too well to have any object in deceiving me."

"No—not for worlds!" exclaimed the King: and again he took her hand, which she unhesitatingly abandoned to him. "Now relieve me, my beloved Musidora, from suspense: tell me how long my courtship is to last. But, Oh! in pronouncing this sentence, be merciful!—doom me not to a delay that will prove intolerable!"—and as he thus spoke he passed his arm around her waist.

But instantaneously disengaging herself, and once more standing and looking proudly before him, she said in a lofty tone and with a magnificent expression of woman's virtuous pride upon her countenance, "If you love me with a hasty burning passion only—if your feelings be made up of frenzy and impetuosity—let there be at once an end of everything between us! Musidora Sinclair will not become the object of a sensual fantasy as transient as it is gross: she was not formed to be the toy of so grovelling a sentiment. But if your Highness seeks in me a true friend—a companion to journey with you along the vista of existence,—if you feel that there is refinement, and tenderness, and delicacy in your affection, and that as years pass on you will cherish me with becoming fondness, even when my beauty shall have faded, my hair shall be streaked with silver, the fire of my eyes shall be dimmed, and time shall have planted wrinkles on my brow,—if such a love as this your Grace can offer me, then will I accept it. I shall esteem it an honour—I shall ever strive to deserve it; and in me will you find a true, a faithful, and an attached wife, until the hand of death shall separate us!"

Every individual existence has had its proud moment at least once during its passage along life's highway from the cradle to the grave; and the career of such a being as Musidora was infallibly destined to be marked by many such moments as that. But this was perhaps her proudest moment: this was the era in her life when she assuredly shone to the grandest advantage and stood upon the loftiest pedestal. Undazzled by the presence of a King—retaining the full possession of all her strength of mind, and supreme command over every feeling that was now so well calculated to sway her heart,—proving indeed that her's was no common nature, and that if her soul were indeed cradled amongst the eternal snows of an alpine height, she at least appreciated all the grandeur of that sublime elevation,—Musidora Sinclair shone forth in all the glorious pride of woman now. Repulsing that tender and indeed pardonable familiarity on the part of the man who had just declared *his love*—and that man too a King,—disengaging her waist from the contact of his arm, and without a single instant's loss of self-possession,—she at once made him to know not only by that movement, but also by the eloquent language in which she addressed him, that if he regarded her with a mere brute passion and as an object to gratify a gross longing, she would scorn his advances, repudiate what he termed *his love*, and renounce even the brilliant prospect of sitting upon a throne. And in perfect keeping, too, with her high moral courage and the immaculate purity of her conduct, was her appearance then. Whatever opinion the King might have formed of her,—however unfathomable her character might have been to him,—yet did all the haughty truthfulness of her spirit shine through her now. It was read in the animation of her looks—it flashed in the fires of her splendid dark eyes—it played upon the wreathing coral of her classic lips—it sat upon her high and polished brow—it swelled in the glowing expansion of her bosom—it gave an added loftiness to her tall and stately form.

"Believe me—O believe me, my beauteous Musidora," exclaimed the King, surveying her with love and admiration, but not for a moment taken aback by her manner or her words—for it seemed as if he understood her enough not to be astonished at this display of haughty virtue on her part,—"believe me, I conjure you, when I declare that the love I bear you is that with which you desire to be regarded. *I* also might answer you with pride and in deprecating language; for I might ask if either by word or deed I have given you reason to suspect me of ungenerous thought or dishonourable intent—whether from the first day we met until the present time, my conduct has not been a series of delicate attentions, such as a true cavalier may offer to a charming and virtuous damsel? I might even go farther and ask whether all I have said this evening has been calculated to inspire confidence or to awaken mistrust. No—Musidora: in offering you the homage of my heart, it is the purest and sincerest ever presented at the shrine of a beauteous and deserving woman. I love you now—I shall love you ever—and will cherish you to the end! Have I not promised to subscribe to any conditions you may impose? But if I besought you to limit the period of courtship to as short a space as is consistent with your sense of propriety, I merely displayed a natural anxiety to become the possessor, as soon as may be, of a treasure which I long to make mine. Am I to be blamed for this?—is there aught unreasonable in such a request?—or does it not prove alike the depth and the sincerity of my love?"

"I thank your Highness for these assurances," said Musidora; "and I am satisfied with them. Perhaps you will not think the worse of me for having required them?"

"No—nothing can injure you in my estimation," said the King. "Say then, you accept my love."

"I accept it," she answered: and of her own accord she tendered him her hand.

"And do you love me in return?" he asked, pressing it to his lips.

"Your attentions are agreeable to me," she replied.

"Ah! you do not then love me yet?" he said in a tone of gentle reproach. "But think you that you will be enabled to love me."

"I will endeavour to do so," she rejoined: and a strange light flashed as it were from her eyes, playing over her countenance.

"You will endeavour to do so?" said the King, repeating her words, but not noticing that look: perhaps he thought that it was but the moonbeams reflected brilliantly in the diamonds that adorned her raven hair. "And is it to tutor your heart to love me that you require the delay of a courtship?"

"And also that I may know and understand you well," rejoined Musidora, gazing upon him with the most truthful sincerity; and there was nothing proud nor haughty now in her bearing—but a womanly gentleness mingling with the most graceful dignity.

"How long is the delay to be?" asked the King: and he evidently awaited the answer with suspense.

"Two months from the present date," she replied, after a few moments' deliberation.

"Two months!" he ejaculated. "It is an age!"—and he looked disappointed.

"Take back your avowal of love then," said Musidora, all her coldness instantly returning.

"Oh! again do I ask you to pardon me," exclaimed the King. "Heavens! are we thus to continue alternating between angering and forgiving?"

"It is indeed an evil augury for our courtship," observed the lady in a freezing tone.

"Musidora, you will drive me mad!" cried the monarch. "If any one had told me five weeks ago that I, the King of England, should thus become utterly captive to a woman, I should have rejected the idea with scornful incredulity. But it is so!—and yet how readily—Oh! how cheerfully do I wear the chains which love has fastened upon my limbs! Musidora, I will be all submission to you: I will not anger you again, but will study to win your esteem and your confidence; so that you may give me your love. You shall behold no more impetuosity on my part. Since you are to be my Queen, we are equal: the natural imperiousness of my sovereign rank shall not display itself in my bearing towards you. Musidora, I love you—I love you: and from this minute forth shall I study to prove how fond and how devoted is this love of mine!"

"Now your Grace speaks to me in a manner which penetrates to my heart," said Musidora: and for the first time she returned the pressure of the King's hand.

"You permit me to love you, then—and you allow me to hope that at the end of two months from the present date you will be mine?"

Thus speaking, he again gently encircled her waist with his arm: and this time she did not resist. Emboldened by that yielding manner on her part, he imprinted a kiss upon her cheek; and she did not chide him—she did not disengage herself from the half embrace in which he held her. And he saw a vivid blush mantle upon her countenance—that countenance which in its marble fairness had until this evening appeared virgin of all blushes! The smile too that ever seemed half fading and vanishing from her lips, expanded into one of unmistakable sweetness; and at that moment Musidora looked not as if she were ice to the very heart's core.

"Now," she said, at length disengaging herself gently from the King's arm, "let us re-enter the house. But one word!" she exclaimed as a sudden thought struck her. "Your Grace will yourself communicate to the Earl and Countess the proposal with which I am honoured—and you will permit me to write and acquaint my father with the honour which the King has conferred upon his daughter by offering her his hand?"

"Yes—without hesitation do I accede to your request," replied Henry. "But for the reasons already explained, and which I need not recapitulate, we must enjoin the Earl and Countess of Grantham to observe the strictest secrecy for the present——the same also with your father."

Musidora answered in the affirmative; and taking the King's arm, she accompanied him back into the supper-room. But there she only remained for two or three minutes: she was anxious to be alone to give free vent to her thoughts after the momentous occurrence that had taken place. She accordingly bade the King and her noble relatives good night, and ascended to her own chamber, where, at once dispensing with the attendance of her maid, she sat down and fell into a long reverie. Indeed, an hour elapsed ere Musidora made the slightest preparation for retiring to rest.

CHAPTER XX.

THE COUSINS AGAIN.

ABOUT a fortnight after the King's avowal of love, Musidora was walking alone in the garden one forenoon, when a domestic came to announce that a gentleman had just called to see her. She repaired to the apartment where the visitor was waiting; and she found that it was Percy Rivers. She at once welcomed him with her wonted affability of manner; and his bearing towards her was equally friendly and cordial. They sat down together and began to converse.

"I am delighted to see you again, fair cousin," said Rivers. "Although but little more than six weeks have elapsed since you left the Isle of Wight, I can assure you that it has appeared to me a perfect age. I miss the pleasant conversations we used to have together and the rambles in the garden."

"But doubtless you still visit Sinclair House as usual?" asked Musidora. "And tell me," she continued, without waiting for a reply, "how is my dear father? The last letter I received, which was two or three days ago, represents him as in excellent health and spirits."

"Yes—the tidings have not deceived you," said Rivers; "and I can fully corroborate them. You are of course aware that he has found a companion in a certain Dr. Bertram——"

"I was aware of it," observed Musidora: and she threw a rapid but searching glance upon her cousin to ascertain whether he had heard anything relative to what had taken place in respect to herself and the King: for in her letters to her father, while strictly enjoining him to keep all those matters a profound secret, she had made no exception in favour of Percy: yet still she did not know whether, in some good-natured mood of confidence or in some unguarded moment, Sir Lewis might not have whispered the matter in the ears of the young man.

"Do you know anything of this Dr. Bertram?" he asked: and she felt convinced by his look, his words, and his manner, that he had been kept utterly in the dark as to her acquaintance with the King and her engagement to become his royal bride.

"No—nothing," answered Musidora, in reply to Percy's question. "I never saw him in my life."

"Then you do not even know how your father scraped acquaintance with him, or what brought them together?"—then as Musidora did not answer, he took her silence for a negative; and without at all suspecting that any secret lay behind this guarded silence, he went on to observe, "One morning—it was perhaps about a week after you left—on riding over to Sinclair House to see my uncle, I found him walking up and down the orchard with this individual, whom he introduced to me as Dr. Bertram. It appeared that the Doctor had only arrived the night before, but was already on the closest terms of intimacy with Sir Lewis. Indeed, so amazingly fond of my uncle does the Doctor seem, that he is constantly with him; and never once have I been enabled to say a word to Sir Lewis alone, since Bertram's arrival at Sinclair House."

"Then the physician takes great care of my dear father?" said Musidora, well pleased at the impression which her cousin's words thus conveyed.

"Oh, excellent care!" answered Percy, but somewhat dryly. "Do you know what I suspect?"

"Tell me your thoughts," said Musidora, calm and unmoved as was her wont.

"It is my idea that our relatives here, Lord and Lady Grantham, sent this Dr. Bertram to be a companion to Sir Lewis, so that he may not miss your absence; and if my conjecture be right," added Percy, "the inference is that, the Earl and Countess intend to keep you a long time, if not altogether, with them."

"Have you yet seen his Lordship and the Countess?" asked Musidora.

"No," returned Percy. "I have only just arrived, and inquired at once for you. I thought I would see you first, and ascertain from your lips whether it would prove agreeable for Lord and Lady Grantham to receive me at all. Because, you must remember, Musidora, that although after the lapse of so many years they at length awoke as it were to the consciousness of your existence, they have never made the slightest advance towards me."

"But I have spoken to them concerning you in such terms as you deserved," remarked Musidora; "and I have no doubt they will give you a cordial welcome. Shall I go myself to seek them in the apartment where they may be, and tell them that you are here? It will be perhaps better than to transmit a message by a servant."

"Presently, my fair cousin," rejoined Percy. "I would rather, if you be agreeable, remain to converse a little with you first. Will you not give me credit for some anxiety to learn whether you are happy in your new abode, and whether you find these noble relatives of our's kind, amiable, and good towards you?"

"Yes—after their own fashion they are kind and indulgent," said Musidora. "They belong to the true courtier-school——"

"And therefore have not much sincerity and heartiness in their conduct," interrupted Percy. "But—but," he went on to say, in a somewhat faltering and hesitating manner, "was I wrong in the opinion that I formed of their motives for inviting you to stay with them? You recollect my belief was that in the selfishness of neglected old age they sought to make you the star of attraction to fill their saloons with brilliant guests."

"In all that, Percy," replied Musidora, "you were mistaken. Nothing could be more quiet, so far as numbers of guests are concerned, than the life we lead here. Indeed the villa is almost as tranquil in that respect as Sinclair House."

"Ah! then," exclaimed Rivers, a slight glow of satisfaction appearing upon his handsome features, as if he took Musidora's words to be a proof that she had encountered no courtly cavalier or noble gallant who had in any way made an impression upon her; and though the young man had long bade adieu to the idea that his fair cousin would .ever become his bride, still perhaps at this moment he felt the fluttering of a feebly awakening hope in his heart:—"Ah! then, you have seen little or nothing of the gaieties of the Court and Aristocracy? I presume that the Earl is still in disgrace with the King——"

"Do let me proceed to inform his lordship and the Countess that you are here," said Musidora: and perhaps at that moment there was the faintest agitation in her manner—but so faint indeed, and so evanescent, that though it escaped not the eyes of her cousin and even troubled him for a single instant—he knew not why—yet the next moment he felt convinced it must have been pure fancy on his part.

She had risen from her chair as she spoke, and was moving towards the door when Rivers hastened to stop her; and in a quick voice he said, "Do grant me a few minutes. You have scarcely replied to any question I put to you. Indeed, I am almost in doubt whether you are pleased at my visit."

"You must not speak thus, Percy," replied Musidora. "You ought to know that I am glad to see you: it is unkind to give utterance to such a reproach."

"Pardon me then, my dear cousin," said Rivers, taking her hand and pressing it cordially: then instantaneously loosening it again, he observed, "I asked you whether you were happy here: and I expect you to tell me whether you prefer the banks of the Thames, or whether you long to get back again to the old house overlooking Brading Haven, with the shady walks of the forest close by."

"Home will be sweeter to me after an absence," replied Musidora. "For a change, I am well pleased with my present abode; and since I know that my dear father is happy and has an agreeable companion who also watches closely over his health, I am spared all anxiety on his account. I have already assured you that Lord and Lady Grantham are as kind and indulgent as it is their nature to be: and therefore I am happy. And now tell me," she added, "when you arrived in these parts, and what has brought you hither: for I do indeed perceive that we have left many things unspoken of, on which we might converse ere I inform the Earl and Countess of your presence."

"Ah! I am glad that you have said that!" exclaimed Rivers, a beam of joy again lighting up his handsome countenance: "for it looks like former times. I was afraid just now that I was intruding: for though your manner is kind and amiable towards me as it always was, yet methought I perceived in it a certain constraint, as if I had come inopportunely."

"No—I was alone in the garden when the domestic announced your arrival," said Musidora; "and again I beseech you not to do me such an injustice as to suppose that I would receive you with intentional coolness. But you have not told me upon what errand you have quitted the Isle of Wight:"—and thus speaking, she returned to her seat.

"My patron and friend Sir William Woodville is dead," replied Rivers, his countenance suddenly becoming serious. "The excellent old man expired in my arms; and so soon as the funeral rites were performed, I hurried off, as in duty bound, to make known the event to Lord Chancellor Warham, Archbishop of Canterbury."

"Sir William Woodville dead!" exclaimed Musidora. "You have lost a kind friend in him, Percy. But have you yet been to the Lord Chancellor?"

"I am now on my way to his residence, which I understand to be for the present near the Royal House at Greenwich. But on my road thither I could not resist the opportunity of pausing to assure myself of your health and happiness. My horse is at the garden-gate: and therefore it is but a flying visit that I pay you."

"But I shall see you again ere you leave for the Isle of Wight?" said Musidora. "I will take upon myself to say that the Earl and Countess will give you a most cordial reception."

"My stay, and indeed all my future movements, must depend entirely upon my interview with Lord Warham," returned Rivers: "for by the death of my patron I have of course lost my official situation."

"And what are your prospects, my dear cousin?" asked Musidora, with evident interest in his welfare.

"I can scarcely hope to be appointed successor to Sir William Woodville in the government of the Isle of Wight. I shall be considered too young: and besides, I lack powerful recommendations. Without great interest to support my appeal, it were useless to make it: and I have no influential friends to assist me. Doubtless my name stands well in the estimation of the Archbishop Chancellor: but mere character is but a poor recommendation at Court. However, I shall supplicate at the Chancellor's hands for some kind of employment, which I have no doubt of obtaining. Were Lord Grantham reinstated in the royal favour, and suppose he had the inclination to assist me——"

"Stop one moment," exclaimed Musidora: "this must be seen to! I will return in a few minutes."

Thus speaking, and with more haste than it was by any means her wont to display, she quitted the room, and proceeded to the apartment where the Earl and Countess were seated together, discussing all the brilliant prospects which they considered themselves justified in entertaining on their own account when Musidora should become Queen of England.

"My lord," she said, advancing towards her noble relative, "my cousin Percy Rivers, of whom I have frequently spoken to you, has just arrived on a hurried visit. You are aware that he occupied the post of Civil Secretary to Sir William Woodville, Captain-Governor of the Isle of Wight. Sir William is dead; and Percy requires interest to support him in an endeavour to obtain the appointment. What is to be done?"

"You have not told him, Musidora, of your engagement to the King?" said the Earl, looking frightened.

"Because," immediately added the Countess, "you know how strict his Grace's injunctions have been on that head, and what mischief might be occasioned by disobeying them."

"I have told him nothing," answered Musidora, in her cold tranquil manner. "Surely I should be the last to betray his Highness's secrets."

"Then what do you wish us to do?" asked the Earl. "You know that although in reality restored to his Grace's favour, yet that to suit his own purposes *this* is likewise one of the secrets to be religiously kept for the present: and therefore I dare not proceed to the palace and ask an audience of his Highness."

"And his Grace will not be here this evening," observed Musidora: "not until tomorrow night—and in the meantime the appointment may be given away to some one else. Immediate measures must be taken. Would it be indiscreet if a letter were written to his Majesty?"

"I do not think it would be indiscreet for you to write it, Musidora," said the Earl.

"No—certainly not," promptly added the Countess: "and it can at once be despatched to the Royal House."

"But of course you will not tell Rivers what is being done," said the Earl. "Would it not be better for me to see him?"

"I wish your lordship to give him a welcome reception," said Musidora.

"Ah! but I cannot ask him to take up his quarters here—nor even encourage his visits," cried the nobleman.

"No, not by any means," added the Countess: "his Highness might be angry."

"If the King," said Musidora, in a cold slow tone, but with eyes that flashed fire, "were capable of such miserable, mean, and grovelling jealousy, I would at once proclaim an end to everything between us."

"Hush, my dear girl!" said the Earl, in a sort of consternation at this display of spirit on his young relative's part: then instantly recovering himself he observed, "You misunderstood my meaning."

"Yes—and mine also," the Countess hastened to superadd. "What we intended to say was that it would be indiscreet to encourage Master Percy Rivers too much at the villa, because his presence here would necessarily prevent his Highness from paying his accustomed visits; and *that*, you know, would be a severe punishment for him, seeing how fondly he loves you and what pleasure he takes in your company."

"Let us proceed to the other apartment," said Musidora, her coral lips perceptibly wreathing with a scornful smile at these shallow excuses whereby the Earl and Countess endeavoured to explain away their previous remark.

They all three repaired to the room, where Percy Rivers was waiting;—and most cordial, in outward appearance, was the greeting which the old courtier and his wily Countess gave the young man, who stood in about the same degree of distant relationship to them as did Musidora.

"My dear young friend," said the Earl, speedily coming to the main point, "our sweet relative, Musidora, has explained to me your exact position; and though I myself have no direct influence at Court at the present moment, yet will I exert myself without delay amongst others who are in favour there. Rest assured all I can do in your behalf shall cheerfully be done; and I have very little hesitation in promising you that the appointment is your's. Go then—see the Lord Archbishop Chancellor—and prefer your claim. But say naught relative to any interest that will be made in your behalf. Leave that to work as I shall see fit and prudent. The Chancellor is certain to give you no definite reply at once; and therefore you must call again upon me in two or three days, when I shall be enabled to communicate the result of the endeavours I am about to make on your account."

Percy Rivers was of too independent a disposition to suffer it to appear that he comprehended the meaning of his lordship's invitation for him to call again *in two or three days*; though he fully understood the hint that his presence was not desired at the villa pending the promised exertions in his favour. He noticed, however, the sudden look of indignation which Musidora's eyes shot forth: but she also deemed it prudent to offer no verbal interference. The young man almost immediately took his leave, after making suitable acknowledgments to the Earl for his volunteered endeavour to promote his interest; and it was perhaps with more than usual kindness—as if to atone for her relatives' inhospitable conduct—that Musidora shook hands with him at parting.

Immediately after he had mounted his horse and galloped away, our heroine sat down and penned a note to the King, frankly stating all the circumstances of Percy Rivers' case and soliciting the royal favour in the young man's behalf, provided that it should seem good to his Highness to confer the appointment upon him.

CHAPTER XXI.

THE RESULT OF MUSIDORA'S LETTER.

WHEN Percy Rivers had taken his leave, and the letter was despatched by the most discreet of the Earl's men-servants to the Royal House, Musidora was about to retire to her own chamber, when the Countess said, "Stay a few minutes, my dear girl, and converse with the Earl and myself."

"Certainly," was our heroine's response; and she resumed her chair from which she had risen.

"It is most probable," continued Lady Grantham, "that in consequence of your note, dear 'Dora, the King will make it a point of coming this evening, although when taking leave of you last night, he intimated that he should not see you again until to-morrow. But I think, from the tender anxiety which his Highness displays to render himself agreeable to you, that whatever engagement he may have formed for this evening, will be set aside to enable him to pay you a visit."

"It is probable," observed Musidora, in her usual coldly placid manner.

"But do you not hope so, my dear child?" asked the Countess. "I really wish you would endeavour to throw a little more warmth into your manner—at least when in company with the King; or he may perchance imagine that you do not love him."

"I am no hypocrite," replied Musidora, a freezing chill marking her voice.

"But you *do* love him, Musidora?" urged the Countess: "or at all events you begin to feel your heart moved towards him? It is impossible you can remain insensible to his attentions, which are as assiduous as they are delicate? If you have no ambition to become a Queen, you cannot at least be indifferent to the prospect of wedding a cavalier who, setting aside his sovereign rank, is of such goodly presence, such elegant manners, and such courtier-like speech. Besides, my dear 'Dora, I think you ought to feel that his conduct has been most straightforward and honourable, and you cannot possibly have any doubt relative to the sincerity and uprightness of his intentions. Let me recall to your mind a circumstance most highly creditable to his Grace. On returning to the supper-room with him on a certain memorable evening—exactly a fortnight ago," continued her ladyship, with a significant smile, "you almost immediately retired to your own chamber, and he at once availed himself of the opportunity to acquaint the Earl and me with everything that had taken place in the garden."

"Had he not done so," said Musidora, "everything would have been at once at an end between his Highness and me. Living beneath your roof as your relative and guest, and under your care, I cannot be regarded as my own mistress; and therefore it was the King's duty to lose not an instant in acquainting you with the honour he had done me by making an avowal of his attachment and offering me his hand. Indeed, I purposely withdrew to my own chamber on that occasion in order that he might have such an opportunity, if he thought fit to make it available. He did so—and I was well pleased when, on the following morning, I received your congratulations and those of his lordship. Had the King acted otherwise, I should have put no farther faith in his honour, nor his professed intentions of wedding me legally and sacredly."

"Well, my dear 'Dora," resumed the Countess, "I am charmed to find that his Grace's conduct met your approbation: but still I am sorry to reflect upon the remark you ere now made—namely, that you do not as yet love him."

"Would you have me tell an untruth?" asked Musidora proudly.

"No, no," the Earl hastened to observe: "the Countess did not mean *that* for a moment."

"Far from it," cried her ladyship. "But entertaining as I do so deep an interest in you, it is but natural that I should look forward with hope and confidence to a favourable result in respect to this courtship."

"I have not told you that I will not marry the King at the expiration of the prescribed period," said Musidora.

"Ah! then you *will* marry him, my dear child," cried the Countess, scarcely able to restrain the enthusiastic manifestations of her joy, "whether you love him or not?"

"Rest assured," said Musidora, now speaking with the firm tone of a strong-minded woman's decision, "that if I marry his Grace it will be with the intention of proving an attached, faithful, and devoted wife to him—resolved to consider his interests as ever paramount—to assist him to the utmost of my humble ability in the duties of his high station—and to bear myself in a manner that shall best prove the deep gratitude which I experience for the bounties conferred upon myself, and those connected with me. But for all this," added Musidora, in a tone and with a look that seemed for an instant strangely bewildered and mournful, "I may not perhaps love him!"

"Unaccountable being that you are!" cried Lady Grantham. "But no matter for a childish, sickly, and sentimental love, so long as you have made up your mind to accept the monarch's hand."

Musidora rose from her seat, advanced to the window, and stood gazing forth for upwards of a minute. Her back was thus turned towards her noble relatives; and therefore they were unable to perceive whether it was a mere mechanical and listless movement on her part, or whether indeed it was deliberately done for the sake of concealing some emotion suddenly excited. They exchanged rapid and significant glances of mutual inquiry: then they shook their heads at each other, as much as to imply that they could not understand it, and that Musidora was a being who in many traits of her conduct utterly surpassed their power of comprehension. Slowly and calmly did she return to her seat; and both the Earl and Countess thought, that pure and stainless as the alabaster of her countenance ever was, it now seemed paler than before—and that instead of the weird light flashing mystically in her dark eyes, there was now a haunting mournfulness in their unfathomable depths. Fearing however to say or do aught that might offend one whom their entire aim was to conciliate as much as possible, they appeared not to notice that anything peculiar had taken place. "To return then, dear 'Dora," resumed the Countess, "to what I was just now saying,—I think that after the note you have transmitted to his Highness, we may expect him here this evening. At all events arrangements will be made in anticipation of such a visit. And now, to come to the point—what I wished to say to you, Musidora, was that since the evening on which his Grace opened his heart to you and offered his hand, you have not once worn the diamonds which are his gift. And yet I feel convinced that the King never surveyed you with so much admiration as he did that night! Regarding you as his future Queen, it is but natural he should take pride in your beauty and rejoice to behold it set off to the fullest advantage. Besides, if he on his part be ever anxious and willing to demonstrate his love by all possible assiduities and attentions, has he not a right to expect from you some little concessions to his pleasure, even though it be mere whim and fancy on his side?"

"I should most assuredly have worn those diamonds again," said Musidora, "but unfortunately on the first and only occasion that I did wear them, I lost two of the principal gems from their settings."

"Heavens! why did you not tell us that before?" exclaimed the Countess.

"Because I did not discover the loss until this morning," replied Musidora. "I remember putting the jewels somewhat hurriedly away, when retiring to my chamber on the night that I wore them two weeks back, and the casket was not opened again until this morning. Then, as Annetta was searching for something in the casket, she observed that the principal gem was missing from the tiara, and another from one of the bracelets. They must have fallen out when I was walking in the garden with his High-ness."

"And yet I think I should have noticed their absence," said the Coun-tess, "when you returned to the supper-room."

"But you remember that I almost immediately withdrew?" said Musi-dora: "and therefore you had scarcely leisure to observe the loss of the gems. Annetta searched carefully for them, this morning, all over my chamber—but without success. I also went into the garden and looked carefully along the paths where I walked with the King on the evening in question: but I had not much hope of finding the lost diamonds—for it has rained two or three times during the fortnight, and moreover the garden-ers have been at work in the grounds. They may have trodden them into the gravel; or if they have found them and appropriated them to their own purposes, it were useless to make inquiries in a quarter where a negative would be given in order to cover dishonesty."

"And yet you take the circumstance so coldly, Musidora?" said the Countess: "and even now you have only mentioned it incidentally! Per-haps if I had not spoken of the diamonds, you would not have alluded to the circumstance at all?"

"I had certainly forgotten it," observed Musidora: "but as for experi-encing any excitement on account of this loss, it were useless. All the vexa-tion in the world will not restore the missing gems. The only thing to be done is to seek the assistance of some merchant or goldsmith who trades in precious stones."

"Musidora is right," said the Earl of Grantham: "regrets are useless. To-morrow we will repair to London, and endeavour to procure two dia-monds of the proper size and also of suitable brilliancy to match the oth-ers. By the bye, the most eminent dealer is that very Landini, the wealthy goldsmith of Lombard Street, whom the old merchant Master Manners mentioned in the course of the long tale he told us."

At this moment the door opened; and the lacquey who had been des-patched with the note to the palace, made his appearance.

"Have you acquitted yourself of your errand?" asked the Earl.

"I have, my lord," was the reply. "On reaching the Royal House I rep-resented to one of the valets in the great hall that I was charged with a missive of secrecy and importance destined only for the King himself. The menial at once conducted me to the apartment of Master St. Louis——"

"Did you say anything, Musidora!" asked the Earl of Grantham, fan-cying that our heroine had spoken.

"No," was her calm reply. "It was a sudden cough rising up into my throat."

"Proceed then," said Lord Grantham, turning once more to the lac-quey. "You were saying that the royal valet conducted you to the apart-ment of Master St. Louis—who, by the bye, within the last six weeks or so has filled the high and important post of Private Secretary to the King. Well—and what next?"

"I informed Master St. Louis that I was entrusted with a private des-patch for his Highness," continued the lacquey, "and besought him to place it as speedily as possible in the royal hands. Master St. Louis inquired from whom I came: but I most respectfully begged that this question would not be persisted in."

"And was St. Louis offended with your answer?" asked the Earl of Grantham.

"Not at all, my lord," returned the lacquey. "He at once said that if it were a private matter he had no wish to peer into his royal master's se-crets, and assured me that the missive should without delay be delivered to the King. I thanked him, and took my departure."

"You have behaved discreetly," said the Earl.

The lacquey then retired: and almost immediately afterwards Musi-dora went up to her own chamber.

As the Earl and Countess of Grantham had anticipated, the King made his appearance in the evening, a little before nine o'clock; and at once accosting Musidora, he took her hand, saying with the utmost kind-ness of manner and with love beaming in his looks, "I am glad that you have asked me a favour—still more delighted that I am enabled to grant it. Where is this cousin of your's?"

"He is not staying here, may it please your Highness," the Earl of Grantham hastened to observe. "Although connected with us in some dis-tant degree of relationship, we nevertheless did not deem it exactly pru-dent for him to lodge beneath our roof——"

"And why not?" asked the King, with an appearance of such noble frankness, alike of look and manner, that Musidora threw upon him a glance of mingled gratitude and admiration—which he instantaneously perceiving, hastened to observe, "If he be the meritorious, well-conduct-ed, and high-minded young man described in my dear 'Dora's note, you Lord Grantham, should have shown him all becoming hospitalities. I am not jealous," he added, with a smile, as he pressed our heroine's hand tenderly; "I have too much vanity on my own account, and too sublime a confidence in her to whom my heart is devoted, to entertain a sentiment alike humiliating and derogatory to us both."

"I thank your Grace for this observation so well worthy of a true cav-alier and chivalrous King," said Musidora: and her dark eyes dwelt with a look of deeper admiration and also with a more eloquent gratitude upon the royal countenance than ever they had displayed before.

"Your Highness altogether mistakes me," said the Earl of Grantham, adopting his blandest tones of cavalier-like servility: for he saw that in his somewhat unguarded zeal to please the King he had unfortunately produced the contrary effect.

"Deign to hear the explanation, sire," exclaimed the Countess, hastening to put in a word on her husband's behalf. "What the Earl meant was that in consequence of the strict commands issued by your Highness that your royal visits to the Villa, and their objects most especially, should be shrouded in all possible secrecy, it would have been inconvenient to harbour Master Percy Rivers within these walls: for either your Grace must have suffered him to learn the secret, or must else have abstained from honouring this humble dwelling with your august presence so long as Master Rivers remained our guest."

"I receive the explanation in the good spirit which dictates it," said the King, now suffering himself to be mollified. "But at the same time," he added, reverting his gaze upon Musidora's splendid countenance, and now addressing himself to her, "I should be truly grieved, my sweet friend, if you were in any way vexed at this treatment which your cousin may have experienced, and which may appear unaccountably inhospitable to him. Rather would I have punished myself by remaining absent from you for a few days, than that you should feel any annoyance on his account."

"I can make no other return for your Grace's goodness," said Musidora, "than to declare that I feel and appreciate all that is kind, and generous, and noble in your conduct and words."

"Since I have pleased you, sweet friend," rejoined the King, raising her snowy hand to his lips, "I am truly happy. But where lodges the object of our discourse? or when and where are you likely to see him again?"

"He will call at Grantham Villa in two or three days," answered Musidora. "But your Highness must permit me to apologise and beseech your excuse if there were aught of indiscretion or freedom in the appeal that I ventured to make on his behalf."

"Ah! Musidora, do you demand forgiveness of me—you who cannot possibly have offended?"—and as the King thus spoke he pressed the lady's hand, which he still retained, most tenderly between both his own. "Did I not ere now assure you that I was charmed to be at length asked a favour by you? Soon, my dear 'Dora, you yourself shall be in a position to bestow places and honours, pensions and titles. For the present you have only to ask in order to have your wish. Here are two parchments, each bearing my sign-manual; and they are each stamped with my royal seal. One," continued Henry, as he drew forth the documents from the breast of his doublet, "contains the nomination of Percy Rivers to the post of Governor of the Isle of Wight, with the same emoluments, privileges, and powers, as were enjoyed by the late Sir William Woodville. And this other parchment contains a decree restoring your revered and respected father, Sir Lewis Sinclair, to the Ranger of the forests and woodlands of the said Isle of Wight. Here also is my sign-manual—and here likewise my sovereign seal."

"My liege," said Musidora—and now her voice was perceptibly tremulous and her looks indicated an emotion that was beyond all doubt,—"how can I find words to thank you for these proofs of generosity and goodness——"

"And of love!" added the King, approaching his lips to Musidora's ear—and he felt her hand, which he still retained, tremble in his own. "But of course, my charmer," he continued, "Master Percy Rivers will be suffered to understand that these bequests have been obtained solely and entirely through the private and secret interest which the Earl of Grantham has made with high officials at the Royal Court. My lord," he added, turning towards the Earl, "it will be for you to make this statement to Master Rivers—as I am well aware that my beloved 'Dora can but indifferently tutor her sweet lips to frame an apology or excuse that has the slightest tinge of falsehood."

The Earl bowed, as if he felt that a high compliment was thus paid to himself, although indeed it was but his power of duplicity which evoked the royal flattery in so equivocal a manner. Immediately afterwards a page announced that supper was served up; and to the room where the repast was in readiness, did the King conduct Musidora—preceded, according to the etiquette of the time, by the Earl and Countess. It is not, however, necessary to dwell at any greater length upon the incidents of this particular evening: suffice it to say that ere the King took his departure he found an opportunity of whispering these words in Lord Grantham's ear:—

"I was not really offended with you for having avoided to receive Percy Rivers as your guest. On the contrary, I am well pleased with your prudence. Musidora must be kept as secluded as possible, so that the presence of no friends or acquaintance may in any way interfere with my courtship. Not that I am jealous of this Percy Rivers. From certain sources I am aware that though he loves Musidora madly and devotedly, and that for some time all who knew them in the Isle of Wight fancied it was to be a match, yet that she never entertained any other sentiment save friendship for him. Again I declare I am not angry with your lordship for having treated him somewhat inhospitably. But I saw that it was a fine opportunity to play off a stroke of dramatic noble-mindedness in Musidora's presence; and you must have observed with what telling effect it succeeded. She already admires my character and feels profoundly grateful for my bounties. Admiration and gratitude, when combining in a woman's heart, are so near akin to love, that if they never do ripen into the more tender sentiment, they are still sufficiently powerful in themselves to ensure the suitor's success. Therefore, my lord, it is beyond all doubt that your incomprehensible young relative will bestow her hand on me. To you I do not speak about reward and recompense at present. You shall see that I know how to be grateful. But ere I depart, one word more in your ear! Percy Rivers must lose not a minute, upon receiving those documents, in speeding back to the Isle of Wight, where he can of course present the one containing Sir Lewis Sinclair's appointment, personally to the worthy knight. And now farewell till the day after to-morrow, when I shall return at the same hour as usual."

CHAPTER XXII.

THE DIAMONDS.

IT was a little past noon, on the following day, that a handsome barge with six rowers, and containing the Earl and Countess of Grantham and Musidora on the cushioned seats in the stern, came along the City Stairs at London Bridge. The Earl assisted his wife and beauteous relative to land; and having ascended the steps, they proceeded to Lombard Street. There they entered the establishment of Master Landini, the richest goldsmith-banker of that already immensely wealthy street; and Mark Landini, the old man's nephew, at once came forward to learn their business.

Perceiving that they were personages of distinction, he at once proposed to conduct them to the private office; and they were accordingly shown into the inner room, where Master Landini himself was seated. Musidora immediately fixed her eyes with a more than ordinary interest upon the old man: that is to say, an interest which was *perceptible*—and any emotion or feeling which her usually unfathomable countenance suffered to appear, may be accurately described as of no ordinary character.

The Earl of Grantham announced his name, as Mark officiously placed seats for the accommodation of the visitors; and old Landini, with his wonted urbanity, bowed low alike to the nobleman and the ladies.

"I have called upon you, Master Landini," said the Earl, now opening the business, "for the purpose of ascertaining if in your valuable collection of precious stones you possess any that will match with a set of gems of the rarest brilliancy and of which two have been unfortunately lost. This is the more annoying, because the set was a present, under particular circumstances, to my relative Mistress* Musidora Sinclair:"—and he glanced at our heroine to intimate to the banker and the nephew that it was to this young lady he alluded.

"I may say, my lord, without vanity," replied the old banker, "that there can scarcely be any diamonds for which my collection will not furnish a suitable match; and rare indeed must they be if they even come up in the fineness of their water to some which I possess. Mark, fetch in some caskets."

"Or wait one moment," exclaimed the Earl. "You had better see these diamonds of which I have spoken:"—then producing the jewel-case containing the set which Musidora had received from the King, he opened it, at once displaying its brilliant contents.

"Ah!" ejaculated Landini: and a quiet glance of intelligence passed between him and his nephew.

"I comprehend!" cried the Earl of Grantham, who, as well as the two ladies, had observed that rapid exchange of looks: "these diamonds were purchased at your establishment? You recognize them? Is it not so?"

As he thus spoke, the nobleman and his Countess became confused and troubled: for it instantaneously struck them that if the King had really bought the diamonds here, and that the Landinis knew to whom they were selling them at the time, they could not fail now to see at once that it was from the royal hands Musidora had received the gift. The young lady herself was likewise evidently annoyed, and for the very same reason: but *her* feeling on the subject was but just perceptible beneath the icy brilliancy of her looks.

"Yes—I think that the diamonds were bought here—but I do not recollect exactly when or by whom," said the elder Landini, now off-hand and business-like: then turning to his nephew, he continued, "Do you not think they were bought here, Mark—or possibly at our wealthy neighbour's opposite—eh?"

"They were bought of us," replied the younger Landini. "I recollect perfectly well a strange gentleman coming for them. He paid liberally and took them away with him without a word."

"Yes—I do now remember the transaction." observed the uncle: then again addressing himself to the nobleman, he said with a tone and manner of the blandest courtesy, "We cannot always remember our customers, my lord—it is quite impossible."

---

* The diminutive *Miss* was not used in the times of which we are writing. Spinster-ladies were denominated *Mistress*, the introduction of the Christian name showing that they were spinsters.

"Oh! certainly," rejoined the Earl: and he darted a quick glance upon the Countess and Musidora, as much as to imply that their previous apprehensions were unfounded and that the secret was safe relative to the diamonds being the gift of the King.

"They are very splendid," continued the elder Landini: "but we shall be enabled full easily to match them in respect to these missing ones. I see that the tiara has lost its finest gem, and this bracelet the centre stone of its star. Now, Mark, fetch the caskets numbered 7, 8, and 9."

The nephew disappeared for a few minutes; and when he returned he carried in his hand the jewel-boxes he had been to fetch. His uncle examined the contents with the rapid but keen glance of one fully experienced in the nature of precious stones; and in a very few minutes he selected two which he pronounced to be of an equally fine water and of the exact size as those that were lost. The Earl and Countess examined them narrowly, to satisfy themselves that such were the facts; and they had not the slightest objection to raise. Musidora, with her wonted indifference, paid but little attention to the proceeding—satisfied no doubt that the set of diamonds would be made up again in a proper manner.

"And now, when will the work be done?" asked the nobleman.

"In three hours, if urgent," replied the elder Landini: "but if your lordship be anxious to return to Greenwich, my nephew shall bring the diamonds to Grantham Villa in the evening?"

"That would be dangerous," exclaimed the Earl: "there are robbers both on the Thames and in the high road—and it were folly for a man to travel at dusk with such valuables about his person."

"It would be our risk, my lord," said the banker with a polite smile: "if the diamonds were lost we should have to make them good. But if your lordship has another visit to pay in London, and could pass the time for three hours, I can guarantee that the new diamonds shall be securely fixed in these settings. Or if your lordship would honour my humble habitation by waiting a while, I shall feel proud to harbour such guests:"—and again the old man made a courteous salutation. The Earl exchanged a look with the Countess, who gave a slight nod, as much as to imply that it would be far better to accept the banker's invitation. Lord Grantham accordingly conveyed this decision to Master Landini.

"I am highly flattered, my lord," said the banker. "Now, Mark, hasten you up to the workshop, and let the men set about this at once; while I escort his lordship and the ladies to our best apartment."

The nephew accordingly issued forth from the private room; and turning into a little narrow passage in one corner of the front office he hurried up a dark break-neck staircase to the workshop on the highest storey of the house—while his uncle, opening an inner door from his own private office, courteously conducted the Earl, the Countess, and Musidora up the principal staircase into a handsomely furnished apartment on the first floor. Having officiously placed chairs for his guests' accommodation, he begged to be excused remaining with them, "on account of extreme pressure of business," and then withdrew. But ere he returned to his office and his papers, he summoned his housekeeper—a matronly-looking woman, with a great bunch of keys suspended to her side—and bade her hasten to convey up-stairs the best refreshments in the shape of wine, viands, fruits, and cakes that the cellar, larder, and buffet would afford. Then he retraced his way to his great arm-chair behind his desk, and continued the perusal of the pile of letters that lay before him.

"I was marvellously afraid for the moment," said the Earl of Grantham, so soon as the door of the drawing-room had closed behind the old banker, "that we had betrayed the grand secret by coming to this establishment. But it is evident enough, from what both uncle and nephew said, that they do not know who was their customer when these diamonds were par-chased."

"And yet," observed the Countess, "there was something strange in their manner which I do not altogether like."

"Oh! I understand that full well," said the Earl, with a very knowing look. "Why, my dear, it is as transparent as possible! The fact is that these two mean money-making citizens were uncommonly annoyed at so unguardedly betraying the circumstance of the diamonds having been originally purchased at their establishment; because they were afraid that I should turn upon them and insist that as the diamonds were lost through some fault or flaw in the setting, it was their duty to make them good again without charge or expense to me! I do really believe that the old curmudgeon purposely threw out hints, as broad as he dared, to induce his nephew to venture the bold declaration that the diamonds were not bought at this establishment at all: but either Master Mark Landini did not exactly understand the old man's meaning, or else had not impudence enough to proclaim so brazen a falsehood."

"Ah! you have indeed hit upon the truth," said the Countess. "I think that there is a great deal of hypocrisy concealed beneath that excessive politeness of the old banker, and that colder but still very servile and cringing courtesy of the nephew."

At this moment the door opened; and the portly housekeeper entered, followed by a younger servant-woman, both bearing trays covered with refreshments, which they spread upon the table. They then retired; and the Earl, approaching the table, filled a glass with some foreign wine, which he tasted and then drank off, the satisfaction of his looks proving that it was excellent. The Countess was easily persuaded to taste the same nectar; and finding it extremely palatable, she sat down to form a farther acquaintance with the refreshments thus served up. The Earl likewise took a seat at the table, remarking that the breeze on the Thames had given him a little appetite.

"Will you not join us, dear 'Dora?" asked the Countess.

"No—I need not any refreshment," was her answer.

"But what are you doing there, my dear child?" inquired her lady-ship.

"There are three or four curious old manuscript volumes," replied Musidora; "and with your permission I intend to amuse myself awhile in examining them: for it appears that we are to pass three hours here."

Opening from the spacious drawing-room was a little inner chamber without a door—or rather a sort of recess—where, upon a curious piece of foreign furniture resembling in shape a modern chiffonier, lay the volumes to which our heroine alluded. Her eye had caught sight of them; and while her two noble relatives had begun to taste the refreshments for which the river breeze had given them an appetite, Musidora had commenced turning over the leaves of one of the books. It was in manuscript, but written in a very plain and legible hand; and as Musidora at no time admired the conversation of the Earl and Countess—their topics being either of the most frivolous or worldly-minded character—she was not sorry at thus discovering the means of whiling away the three hours that had to be passed beneath Landini's roof.

She found that the volume which thus engaged her attention, was composed of a series of biographies connected with the Landini family. It was a very common custom, in the age of which we are writing, for eminent Italian families to keep written records of the principal transactions of their various scions; and this habit was particularly adopted by the wealthy mercantile firms of the Italian Republics in the fourteenth and fifteenth centuries. We may likewise add that inasmuch as the volume was thus left lying in the room—or at least in a recess adjoining that room—and therefore accessible to any one who might be shown thither, there was no indiscretion in the circumstance of Musidora examining its contents.

But so soon as she discovered what the nature of those contents actually was, and how they treated of the deeds of note and the personages of importance connected with the great commercial family of Landini, how deep and absorbing became the interest with which she slowly and carefully turned over the pages! Was she seeking some particular chapter for perusal? or was she merely looking, as persons when taking up a strange book often do, for some part that might seem to possess greater attractions than the rest? We know not. But now she no longer continues to turn over the leaves without stopping to read them thoroughly: she appears to have lighted upon some passage that rivets her attention; and with the air of one profoundly wrapped up in the subject of an engrossing study, she begins to read carefully on without skipping a line—aye, and without missing a single word!

But what is it that she thus reads? The particular episode in which her attention is thus absorbed, will be found in the following chapter.

CHAPTER XXIII.

THE HISTORY OF BIANCA LANDINI.

"IT was a dark night, in the beginning of January of the year 1390; and the wind swept down from the lofty Apennines upon the city of Genoa. Like a bodiless fiend, wingless and footless, but with a howling and roaring voice, the tempest sent forth its wild and terrific dirge from the mountain clouds; and its breath was laden with a storm of pelting sleet such as was seldom known to visit that southern clime on the Mediterranean shore. The sea, in wild magnificence of sound, mingled its mighty voice with that of the wind, and in its convulsive play seem to wrestle even with the power of its Creator. It was indeed a night of fearful storm; and as the inhabitants of Genoa, in their mansions or their huts, huddled more closely round the fire, many of them thought or said amongst themselves, 'It seems as if nature itself were determined that the Doge's decree shall be thoroughly respected this night!'

"To what did the allusion refer? It appears that early in the forenoon of this day of which we are writing, his Highness the Doge of Genoa, Angelo Visconti,—as if to strike fresh terror into the hearts of the Genoese, and consummate the execrable tyrannies which had already marked his ducal reign of three years,—had promulgated a decree to the effect that no one was to appear abroad in the streets, under any pretext whatsoever, after eight o'clock in the evening. Exception was alone made in favour of the sbirri—those detestable police-agents who were all creatures of his own special choosing, and who were charged to watch that this new decree was executed to the very letter. But why had the Duke Angelo Visconti promulgated such an ordinance? We must explain. Having been elected Doge of Genoa, on account of his great valour in battle against the Pisans and the Venetians, he refused to surrender the seals of office, according to custom, at the expiration of a year; and in defiance of all the constitutional rights of the Genoese Republic, had proclaimed himself Doge for life. Having amassed immense treasures when in command of the Genoese armies, in the wars that created his renown, he had no difficulty in bribing a venal soldiery and in winning over the Admiral of the fleets to his cause. His usurpation was thus established by means of corruption, and consolidated by force. The democracy of Genoa, which for centuries past had so nobly resisted the arrogance of the aristocracy, were paralysed, and indeed rendered powerless, by the tyranny of Angelo Visconti; and not the slightest attempt was even made to resist the domination of the usurper. Latterly awakening, however, from the stupor of apathy, the patriots of Genoa conspired in secret: but the Duke's spies introduced themselves amongst those brave men and betrayed them to the tyrant. A special tribunal, armed with extraordinary powers and clothed with all imaginable terrors, was instituted for the trial of those who were termed 'rebels;' and having undergone the tortures of the rack and other fearful instruments for mutilating and dislocating their limbs, they were put to frightful deaths. Some were roasted upon gridirons—others were hacked to pieces with knives and scissors: some were thrown into caldrons of boiling oil—and others again were delivered over to the wild beasts in the ducal menagerie. Nevertheless, discontent still brooded in secret; and if fresh conspiracies did not really exist, at all events they were dreaded. Then came a proclamation to prevent persons from harbouring in their houses more than a certain number of guests. But still the tyrant's fears were not silenced; and his last resource was to prevent all meetings whatsoever, even those of a family nature or of the most innocent kind, by the decree above alluded to, forbidding all persons, no matter of what rank or on what pretext, from quitting their homes after a stated hour in the evening.

"The first night on which this decree came into operation, was marked by the tempest, as described at the opening of this chapter. It was therefore a night on which no one would have thought of leaving his dwelling, unless impelled by some urgent necessity; and hence the observation so prevalent throughout Genoa, that nature itself seemed determined to aid, at least for this once, the effectual carrying out of the ducal decree.

"In a magnificently furnished apartment belonging to one of the finest mansions of Genoa, a man of handsome person, and whose age was about forty, was pacing to and fro with uneasy looks and agitated steps. This was Nino Landini, one of the wealthiest merchants not merely of Genoa, but in all Europe. The light of a splendid lamp suspended to the ceiling, as it fell upon his countenance every time he passed beneath it

in his troubled walk, showed that his fine features were convulsed with
workings of mingled affliction and rage; and the frequency with which he
clenched his hands and set his teeth together, afforded farther indication
of the strong excitement under which he was labouring. Sometimes he
paused near a door communicating with an inner apartment, but which
was shut close; and as he thus gazed upon it his passion subsided into the
agony of suspense. Then, as no one came forth with the tidings which he
was evidently awaiting, he would turn away again and resume his troubled walk, muttering to himself, 'If it should be necessary after all, what
is to be done? Duty and love prompt me on the one hand how to act: but
that dreadful decree stares me in the face on the other hand. Oh, the execrable tyrant! Pitiless as he is and daring too in his despotism, is there no
vengeance as remorseless and as bold to overwhelm him? But my mind
is made up! I need be I will go forth, at any risk and at all peril. Peril! it is
great!—there is death in the undertaking! The Doge hates me, because I
have refused to become the partisan of his cause and the creature of his
will. Were I not so highly placed amongst the merchants of Genoa, and
that he hesitates to outrage so powerful a class by venting his spite on me,
he would have crushed me long ago. As it is, he would gladly seize upon
the first pretext to immolate me to his rancour. But, Ah! there is a chance!
If I be compelled to go forth, gold will perhaps bribe the sbirri, should I
meet them? Yes—that is indeed the only chance of escaping the danger.
But they are venal, and would even sell their souls to the Evil One for
gold!'

"The musings of Nino Landini were suddenly interrupted by the
opening of that door on which he had so frequently paused to gaze in
breathless suspense; and a beautiful creature came forth. This was a
young lady of about twenty, in all the pride of that matchless loveliness
which characterizes the daughters of the sunny south. Tall and splendidly formed, she had all the voluptuousness of a Hebe, mingled with the
graces of a Sylph. Her large dark eyes, full of fire, now shone with the
restlessness of agitation; and through the clear olive of her complexion
the rich carnation mantled, from the same cause, with heightened glow.
A profusion of the darkest and glossiest hair was fastened with a golden
arrow at the back of her nobly-shaped head; and from the Grecian knot in
which it was thus tied, hung down two long tresses, reaching below her
slender waist. Altogether she was one of the brightest embodiments of
female charms that ever broke upon the view of man.

"This splendid creature was Bianca Landini, the merchant's sister.
Of a very large family of children which their parents possessed, the eld-
est and the youngest had alone survived. These were Nino and Bianca.

A pestilence which some years past ravaged Genoa, had swept away all the brothers and sisters of intermediate ages; and these two had alone survived of that once numerous and happy family. The natural bonds of affection would in any case have rendered them deeply attached to each other; but the circumstance which had thus left them the only survivors of their parents' large progeny, was full well calculated to rivet those bonds and cement the affection subsisting between them. Bianca, though so beautiful and likewise so wealthy, was still unmarried—not for want of many offers, but because her disposition was too noble and her mind too pure to allow her to wed where she could not bestow her heart; and hitherto that heart had remained virgin of love's impressions. Her brother too had long remained single. Indeed, but little more than a year had elapsed since he espoused the charming daughter of a merchant nearly as rich and as eminent as himself; and on this very night of which we are speaking was the beloved Genevra seized with those symptoms which appeared to be the warnings heralding the birth of a child.

"The moment Bianca emerged from the inner apartment, her brother Nino hastened to accost her; and he at once saw by the expression of her countenance that it was as had been suspected. The aid of the medical man was therefore necessary; and indeed, from a few hurried words which Bianca spoke, in a voice filled with the golden harmony of her own glorious clime, the need was urgent and imperious.—'Then I will go forth,' said Nino.—Bianca clasped her hands despairingly; and yet under the circumstances she dared not bid him stay. At the same time she dreaded, with the profoundest terror, to see him go forth in contravention of that decree whose penalty was death! He comprehended full well all that was passing in her mind, and hastened to observe, 'Fear not, sweet sister: it is most probable that on such a night as this the sbirri will not watch; but if I should chance to meet them I will lavish gold to purchase their secrecy.'—Bianca shook her head despondingly: she could not help it—it was an improvised movement, spasmodically arising as it were from the tension of her feelings. Her brother strove to reassure her.—'My dear Nino,' she said, a thought suddenly striking her; and she gazed up appealingly into his countenance; 'your life is far more precious than mine: you are a husband, and you are about to become a father. Let me go. If gold will really succeed in bribing the sbirri, what matters it whether it be lavished by your hand or mine?'—'Bianca,' answered Nino Landini, profoundly affected, 'of all the proofs of sisterly love that you have ever given me, this is the deepest and the most touching. But not for worlds would I allow your life to be thus perilled! Even if you returned safe, I should loathe and detest myself as a coward for having permitted you to incur such danger:

but if any evil did ensue, the thought of my dastard conduct would drive me mad.'—Bianca still urged her project; but Nino would not listen to it.—'Then have you not,' she asked, 'in your numerous household of well fed and well paid menials, a single one who will dare this venture for the sake of a kind master?'—'No, not one whom I could venture to trust,' hastily responded Landini. 'Besides, we have lately received new servants beneath our roof; and I have positive information that one is a spy: but which of them it is I know not. I could not lay my finger upon the trai- tor. No; I must go forth myself. The private door will give me safe egress, unobserved by a single soul within the dwelling: the doctor dwells not far off; and in a quarter of an hour I hope to be safe back again.'—Bianca said no more: she dared not, for Genevra's sake, utter a remonstrance against her brother's intention; and she dared not, for his sake, encourage him to go forth. She was almost bewildered with despair; and there was a strong presentiment of evil in her mind. He muffled himself up in his mantle; and as he once more turned to his sister to embrace her ere hurry- ing forth, he said in a low quick voice, 'Genevra knows naught of this atro- cious decree of Angelo Visconti's?'—'No: according to your instructions, my dear brother,' she answered, 'I have carefully kept from her this fresh proof of the tyrant's despotism. Feeling so deeply as she does on behalf of the crushed liberties of our once free and proud Genoa, it would have grieved her sorely.'—Nino Landini now embraced his sister tenderly, and descending a private staircase, issued forth from his mansion by a door of which he alone possessed the key.

"It can hardly be necessary to state that during the day, and indeed up to a late hour of the evening, no suspicion had been entertained that Ge- nevra's time was so near: otherwise, as a matter of course, common pru- dence would have suggested the propriety of sending for the medical at- tendant previous to the hour set forth in the Doge's arbitrary decree. The symptoms of approaching maternity had seized with suddenness upon Signora Landini; and thus was it that her affectionate husband was now compelled to dare so tremendous a peril on her behalf. But as he hurried along the dark and deserted street, holding his cloak tightly around his per- son to prevent it from being torn away by the wind which came sweeping along with fearful violence as he faced it, the thought suddenly struck him for the first time, that the doctor himself might refuse to violate a decree which, in its diabolic tyranny, had made no exception even for such a case as this. For an instant Nino Landini was staggered with the thought: but a few moments' reflection made him reason thus within himself:—'Dr. Forli is a humane as well as brave man; he is moreover my devoted friend, and he will not refuse to run this risk on any account. Besides, even if we were both arrested, surely the Doge never would dare to push his tyranny to such a frightful extreme as to punish a medical man of eminence for obeying the solemn and sacred duties of his profession? If anything would goad the Genoese to desperation and make them fly to arms, it would be such a satanic tyranny as that.'—Reassured by these reflections, Nino Landini pursued his way, having however literally to struggle against the fury of the tempest, and pained by the beating of the sleet upon his countenance, which his plumed cap scarcely protected.

"In little more than five minutes he reached Dr. Forli's house; and was at once admitted by the worthy physician himself, who had been somewhat astonished at hearing a summons at his gate under existing circumstances. But upon recognising Landini he at once suspected the object of his coming; and his looks grew troubled.—'Will you not venture?' asked Nino in acute suspense.—'Yes,' replied the physician boldly; 'but if you saw me tremble, it was on your account. It is to be hoped that my profession would serve as a guarantee for my security, and that even such a tyrant as Angelo Visconti would not dare to wreak his vengeance upon me. But you, my dear friend, are different; and the Doge hates you. Let me then repair to your house, and you remain here till morning.'—Nino Landini objected to this arrangement, alleging his deep anxiety to be near his wife on such an occasion. But the doctor at once adopted a decisive bearing towards the merchant, though with a most friendly intention.—'I will only go to your house,' he said, 'on condition that you remain here in mine until the morning. Better to endure some anxiety than run the fearful risk of giving the tyrant a hold upon you: better to remain away from your dwelling for a few hours, than incur the peril of being snatched from it for ever.'—The doctor was firm in his friendly advice; and Nino Landini was compelled to submit. He accordingly remained where he was; while Forli, hastily wrapping himself in a thick cloak, and drawing his cap over his countenance to protect it from the nipping chill of the tempest, sallied forth, promising however to return so soon as he had any intelligence to report relative to the expected little one.

"Not a quarter of an hour had elapsed after the doctor's departure, when a loud and imperious knocking was heard at the gate; and the merchant's heart was seized with a sudden misgiving. What if the sbirri had traced him? For a moment he thought of concealing himself—then of flying: but the next instant he discarded both ideas, angry with himself for having even entertained them. The gate was opened by Dr. Forli's domestics; and the house was immediately invaded by the sbirri. They burst into the room where Nino Landini was, and at once made him their prisoner. Behind them, in the shade of the doorway, appeared a countenance which shrank back the moment its eyes were met by his own: but it did not thus disappear before he recognised Thomaso, one of his own servants. The truth flashed to him: this man was the spy, of whose presence in his household he had a short time back received a hint from a friendly quarter! And it was so. The villain, on hearing that evening that his mistress was taken suddenly ill, at once felt assured that his master would go forth to fetch the physician: he had watched accordingly—his suspicions were confirmed—and hurrying off to the guard-house, he had brought the sbirri to accomplish this arrest.

"Nino Landini bore his calamity with the firmness of a brave man. He asked the officer commanding the force, whether Dr. Forli was likewise arrested? 'No; we do not mean to touch him,' was the response. 'Our orders are to exempt medical men from the operation of the decree; and this much should have been specified when it was promulgated by the heralds this morning. A supplementary ordinance to that effect will be issued to-morrow.'—'But how,' demanded Landini, 'can medical men's services be obtained, unless there is somebody to fetch them?' 'That, signor, you must ask the Judge to-morrow,' was the curt response. 'We are at all events performing our duty now, and know nothing beyond it.'—Landini felt somewhat consoled by the thought that his wife was at least ensured the medical attendance of which she stood in need; and though he remembered his pre-arranged idea of bribing the sbirri, he was nevertheless at the first moment too proud even to seek to purchase his liberty on such conditions. When, however, the officer bade him resume his mantle and come away to the castle-prison, a powerful revulsion of feeling took place all in a moment in the merchant's mind: he thought of his happy home—his beloved wife and his affectionate sister: he thought also that he was full soon to become a father! Then, stifling his pride, he drew the officer apart and offered him a sum one-tenth of which might have been thought tempting enough for that functionary. But the man shook his head; and glancing quickly towards the doorway, said plainly that he dared not accept it. Nino Landini understood what he meant. Thomaso, the Duke's special spy, would betray the circumstance. There consequently seemed no alternative but for the unfortunate merchant to accompany the sbirri to the gaol within the castle walls; and resuming his mantle and cap, he prepared to issue forth with them from the physician's house where the arrest thus took place.

"As the party emerged into the street, the torch, which, according to custom, burnt in an iron ring in what may be termed the hall of the dwelling, flung its strong and lurid light far out of the doorway; and at the instant a tall figure, enveloped in a mantle, and with the sable plumes of his

cap streaming in the wind, passed by. So leisurely was his pace and uncon-
cerned his manner, that it seemed as if he must be utterly ignorant of the
existence of the decree, or else that he most contemptuously disregarded
it. But while some of the sbirri, who were about ten in number, remained
in the gateway to keep charge of Landini, the others moved towards the
daring stranger.—'Back, villains!' he exclaimed, not even attempting to
draw his rapier, but proudly waving them off with his arm which he extended from beneath the folds of his mantle. At the same moment the
light of the torch flashed full upon the stranger's countenance, which was
that of a man of about thirty—perhaps a year or two more—remarkably
handsome, and now displaying the haughtiest scorn as the fine dark eyes
flashed lightnings upon the sbirri. Whether it were that his audacity for
the moment astounded them, or that there was something in his looks
which overawed them, we cannot say; but certain it is that those who had
rushed forward to seize upon him, fell back—and he, turning coolly upon
his heel, was slowly passing on, when the sbirri with one accord feeling
that they were playing a dastard part thus to recoil from the presence of a
single individual, sprang upon him. Nino Landini never afterwards could
exactly tell the precise manner in which the stranger dealt with them: for
what now followed took place as quick as the eye could wink. A single moment—barely a moment—and the five sbirri were hurled away, staggering
back as if a giant-arm had dashed them all off: and the next instant the
stranger was seen standing calm and collected, with his naked rapier now
drawn in his right hand, and his left hand upon the hip—while his cloak
streamed out behind him like huge fluttering wings.

"The officer of the sbirri, who was standing on the threshold by Landini's side, now gave vent to a bitter imprecation against what he naturally
supposed to be the cowardice of the five men who had been thus instantaneously discomfited; and he sprang towards the stranger.—'Back, back,
fool, or you will meet your death,' said the unknown, not labouring under
the least excitement, but speaking with a calm remonstrance, as if wielding a power which he knew to be invincible. The next moment, and the officer fell back in the same dismay which had seized upon his men; and then
Landini, bursting from the palsied grasp of his guards, sprang towards the
stranger, saying, 'Brave unknown, let us resist them together!'—'Ah, you
were their prisoner then, I presume?' said the stranger. 'Well, you shall
not seek for my succour in vain. Keep with me:' then turning the lightnings of his looks once more upon the sbirri, not another man of whom
ventured to approach him, he said, 'Beware how you follow us; for next
time it shall be *death!*'—He then turned away and passed along the street,
accompanied by the amazed and bewildered merchant, who for a few mo-

ments could scarcely believe that what had just passed was otherwise than a dream.

"The sbirri, stricken with an awful consternation, for which they themselves could not account, ventured not to disobey the unknown's last injunctions; and when Landini found that he and his companion were not followed, he experienced a species of awe, as if conscious of the presence of some superior being. But now the stranger laughed—not with a coarse and vulgar triumph, but with the mockery of a haughty scorn—saying, 'Those miscreants are all cowards in their hearts, if one does but know how to deal with them. Had I shed their blood, they would have fought to desperation: but exercising the commanding authority of a superior mind over a common one, I quelled them as you saw.'—Nino Landini, feeling that this was indeed the only means, short of a supernatural power, by which the wonderful event that had just occurred could be possibly accounted for, was satisfied by the explanation; and he proceeded to return his grateful thanks for the succour he had received from the stranger. 'But,' he asked, 'are you aware of the Doge's decree?'—'Assuredly,' was the reply, given in a scornful tone; 'and I laugh at it. If you Genoese are servile enough to submit to such outrageous tyranny, I, as an Englishman, am resolved to assert my right to personal freedom while sojourning in your city.'—'Permit me to warn you,' said Landini, 'that the Doge makes no distinction between natives and strangers in the exercise of his tyranny.'—'But at least,' rejoined the unknown, with cool indifference, and yet with a certain lofty consciousness of power, which was expressed in his tone and manner, 'your Doge will think twice ere he meddles with an English Peer.'—'Then it is to an English Peer that I am indebted?' said Landini, with increased respect towards his companion.—The unknown answered, 'I bear the ancient and honoured name of Danvers. And now tell me whom I have had the pleasure of serving this night?'—'My name is Landini,' replied the merchant.—'Ah, the name is well-known to every one in Genoa,' responded Lord Danvers, 'and it is not strange to my ears.'—Nino Landini again expressed his gratitude to the English nobleman, adding, 'I wish, my lord, that I could invite you to partake of the hospitalities of my dwelling: but I much fear that there is no alternative for me except to fly from Genoa and take refuge at Pisa within as brief a time as possible: for although by your lordship's kindness I am rescued now from the hands of the sbirri, yet will they be sure to return anon in double force to take me.'—'Fear nothing, Signor Landini,' answered Lord Danvers in a tone of confidence. 'Go to your home, attempt not to fly from Genoa, but trust in me.'—'Your lordship amazes me,' exclaimed the merchant: 'but I fear that such good intercessions as you may intend to make on my behalf with the Duke Angelo Visconti, will fail.'—'Again I say fear nothing,' rejoined Lord Danvers, with the emphasis of one who spoke not lightly but knew full well the import of his words. 'You cannot think that I should betray you into a false security. Even if danger were to overtake you for a time, rest assured that I will deliver you. But this is your house,' he said, suddenly pausing in front of the merchant's mansion, which they had now reached.—'Then your lordship knows where I live?' said Landini in some surprise.—'Yes, I have drafts upon you from your Paris agent for a considerable amount; and during the day I took the trouble of ascertaining where you lived. I should have called upon you tomorrow, even had we not met thus to-night. And now farewell. But again I say, yield to no alarm: you have a friend in me.'

"Having thus spoken, Lord Danvers wrung the merchant's hand with a friendly warmth, which seemed all the more cordial inasmuch as it was evident that he was as proud in disposition as he was handsome in person; and as he turned slowly away and disappeared in the surrounding darkness, the merchant re-entered the mansion. Hastening up-stairs to the apartment where we first introduced him to the reader of this narrative, he was clasped in the arms of his delighted sister Bianca, who was rejoiced to find that he had thus returned safe (as she fancied) from molestation. Then in a few hurried but joyous words, she made him aware that he was the father of a son, and that the mother was progressing admirably. The merchant, for the moment forgetting everything that had just taken place, was enraptured with this intelligence. Dr. Forli now made his appearance from the inner apartment, and was amazed on beholding Landini there after he had so strictly enjoined him to remain at his house till the morning. But when the merchant had explained everything that had taken place, he left his sister and the physician to make their comments upon the adventure, while he himself passed into the adjoining room to embrace his beloved Genevra and his new-born babe.

"Resolved to follow the instructions he had received from Lord Danvers, and put the utmost confidence in the assurances of protection which that nobleman had so generously offered, Nino Landini remained tranquilly at his own mansion, and thought no more of flying to the neighbouring Republic of Pisa. On the following morning he went into his counting-house and attended to his business as usual. At about mid-day Lord Danvers made his appearance, and was most cordially received by the grateful merchant, who had now an opportunity of observing his new friend more closely than on the preceding night. It would be difficult to conceive a more perfect masculine beauty than that possessed by Walter Danvers. He was tall—of slender figure—but symmetrical as an Apollo;

and so well knit in all his proportions, that his slightness was not incompatible with strength. His complexion was dark—his hair black and glossy as that of a woman—his eyes were large and strangely brilliant—and his teeth seemed like two rows of ivory beneath the lustrous jet of the moustache which was finely pencilled upon his short and curling upper lip. His costume was of the richest materials and of the most tasteful elegance. Altogether he was a cavalier full well adapted to touch the heart of even the least susceptible of women.

"In the course of conversation with the merchant, Lord Danvers said that being wearied of the constant strifes, contentions, and cabals in which the imbecility of the reigning King of England (Richard II) had plunged his native country, he had resolved to abandon it altogether; that he had realized a considerable portion of his wealth with a view to deposit it in the hands of three or four eminent mercantile firms upon the Continent; and that as accident had thrown him in the way of Nino Landini, he should be most happy if this merchant would become the recipient of a portion of his funds. Landini expressed his gratitude for this proof of confidence, and declared his willingness to accept the trust.—'Our arrangement in this respect,' said Walter Danvers carelessly, 'can be all the more easily effected, inasmuch as I already hold drafts to a considerable amount upon you:' and with the same off-hand easy air of aristocratic indifference, but which nevertheless seemed to be utterly void of affectation, he tossed down a roll of papers upon the desk. With the cool deliberation of business-habits did Nino Landini arrange the papers in an orderly manner, and then scanned them carefully one after the other. An expression of astonishment gradually deepened upon his countenance as he went on; and having thus gone through the documents, he said, 'Your lordship is the bearer of letters of credit upon me for the largest sum which, throughout all my mercantile experience, I was ever called upon to pay to one individual. It is indeed a colossal fortune in itself.'—'You think so, Signor Landini?' said Danvers carelessly. 'I have deposited an equal sum with a mercantile firm in Paris, and nearly as much with another establishment at Madrid.'—Landini, notwithstanding the natural courtesy of his manners, opened his eyes with mingled amazement and incredulity at this announcement: while Lord Danvers went on to say, as he threw down some more documents, 'But here are the receipts of these mercantile firms in Paris and Madrid of which I have spoken; and you can keep them for me for the present.'—Nino Landini made a low bow, and assumed a manner respectfully apologetic for the passing incredulity he had exhibited. Then he began to talk upon the best means of investing the immense funds which Danvers proposed to leave in his hands: but the nobleman cut him short by observing, 'We shall discourse upon these matters another time. I presume you have heard no more of the adventure of last night?'—'Nothing,' replied Landini; 'but the treacherous servant who betrayed me to the sbirri, has not returned to the house; nor should I think he would venture to do so. Yet, being the Doge's spy, he must doubtless have communicated the whole affair to his Highness.'—'I myself called upon the Doge just now,' said Danvers, 'and very candidly explained to him what took place. As frankly did I assure his Highness that I for one, though a stranger in this city, would not submit to the tyrannous decree he had issued.'—'Ah! then your lordship bearded the despot?' exclaimed Landini joyously. 'And what did he say?'—'He evaded the subject; and after some farther discourse,' continued Danvers, 'on indifferent matters, I took my leave. But depend upon it, that so far from offering any additional outrage towards you, he would rather that the incident of last night had never occurred at all.'

"Nino Landini was overjoyed at this intelligence, which seemed to guarantee his safety; and he now invited Lord Walter Danvers into the private apartments of his splendid mansion. There an elegant repast was speedily served up; and the English nobleman was introduced to Bianca. The young lady was already naturally prepossessed in favour of the gallant foreigner who had been the means of rescuing her brother from the sbirri on the preceding night; and she therefore received him with the generous frankness of a grateful heart. Doubtless she was at once struck also by his extraordinary personal beauty; and he on his part could not help gazing upon Bianca with admiration. Indeed, as they sat down to table, and the merchant surveyed his sister seated next to Walter Danvers, the idea gradually stole into his mind that there was a remarkable fitness in the companionship of the two, and that it would be impossible for the world to furnish a handsomer couple. In the course of conversation Lord Walter Danvers suffered it to transpire that he was unmarried, and that as yet he had never been tempted to change his condition; and Bianca's cheeks displayed a slight blush as he thus spoke, for it seemed as if there was a meaning and a purpose in his words which her own heart enabled her to understand. Two or three hours passed in a very agreeable manner; and when Lord Danvers took his leave, it was not without a pressing invitation on behalf of the merchant to call as frequently as he had leisure and inclination.

"Lord Danvers was staying at the principal hostel in Genoa, where, as it appeared, he had not been many days before the incidents we have related thus rendered him intimate at the mansion of the Landinis. He had arrived at Genoa with a numerous suite, all well mounted on splendid chargers; and the evidences of immense wealth he displayed, speedily rendered him a conspicuous personage in the city. The adventure with the sbirri was not one that could be kept secret even by those who were most interested in suppressing it; and thus when it came to be known that the gallant English nobleman had single-handed defied a posse of the police, and even walked off triumphantly with their prisoner before their very eyes, the public admiration for the hero of this exploit amounted to a positive enthusiasm. Every one however was astonished that the Doge should have taken the proceedings so quietly and tamely: but such was the fact, and it led to many and varied conjectures. With these however we need not encumber our narrative. Let us proceed to state that three months passed away—April came with its sunny smiles—and the groves and gardens in the vicinage of Genoa put forth all their verdure. Meanwhile Lord Danvers had been a constant visitor at Signor Landini's house; and by his assiduities, his delicate attentions, and his many noble qualities, had won Bianca's heart. Deeply and enthusiastically did the beauteous damsel love her English suitor; and fervid was the language in which he in due course declared his own passion. There could be no visible objection to such an alliance, in every way so eligible for Bianca: and therefore the assent of her brother Nino and sister-in-law Genevra was at once given when asked. It was decided that the nuptials should take place so soon as Lord Danvers had made up his mind where he thenceforth intended to fix his abode: for, inasmuch as he had conceived a strong aversion for his native country, where his ancestral mansions were situated, he did not choose to bear his bride to either one of his English homes; and therefore must he prepare one somewhere else to receive her. He expressed his desire to settle in France, and intimated his intention of at once repairing thither to purchase a castle and estate which he had learnt were to be sold in Normandy, and which he would lose no time in preparing to receive Bianca when she should become his bride. He declared that his absence would not exceed two months altogether; and on his return the marriage ceremony should be celebrated. Now, though Landini and Genevra, as well as Bianca herself, had hitherto hoped that Lord Danvers would be induced to settle at Genoa—or at least in its neighbourhood—so that the young lady might remain near her brother and sister-in-law, yet it was impossible to dictate to him in this respect; and therefore all his proposed arrangements were assented to. Having taken a tender leave of the charming Bianca and a friendly farewell of Nino and Genevra, Lord Danvers departed with his suite from Genoa.

"When he was gone, an evil presentiment struck to Bianca's heart. It was not on account of her lover that she thus experienced so sad a misgiving: she had all possible confidence in the strength of his affection, his

fidelity, and his honour; but it was on her brother's behalf that she trembled. For now that Lord Danvers had quitted the city, might not the despot Angelo Visconti attempt to wreak his vengeance upon the merchant?
Bianca felt that hitherto her well-beloved Walter had been a safeguard and
a shield for Nino, and that by some means or other, which he had never
exactly explained to her, he had possessed sufficient influence over the
Duke to avert the effects of his rancour from the house of Landini. But
now that he was gone, would the tyrant still remain passive? It is true that
in their parting conversation, Walter, alluding to this matter, had bade her
entertain no fears; and at the moment she was tranquillized by his assurance. But now that he was no longer there, to afford his succour in case
of need, her heart sank within her; and she could not possibly shake off
the gloom of despondency which gathered around her soul. She however veiled her misgivings as well as she was able, so as not to alarm her
brother and Genevra unnecessarily; and when they observed that she was
melancholy, they naturally attributed this mournfulness to the absence of
her lover. Day after day passed without realizing any of the damsel's fears:
her courage and confidence therefore revived; and when seven weeks had
elapsed without the slightest hostile demonstration on the Duke's part
towards her brother, she smiled at the misgivings she had at first entertained. Yes—she smiled *now*, because in another week her Walter was to
return; and then would she become his bride!

"Very nearly five months had thus elapsed since that memorable
night which gave Nino Landini an heir to his name and wealth; and the little Ludovico throve apace. We must also observe that during this interval
the tyrannical conduct of the usurper Angelo Visconti had exhibited no
abatement. All the odious decrees previously enacted continued in force;
and others equally arbitrary had been promulgated. The entire Genoese
Republic was groaning beneath the tyranny of Angelo Visconti: and the
popular spirit appeared to be altogether broken. Suddenly it became ru-
moured that the Doge, who was a widower and childless, had resolved to
take unto himself a second wife, in the hope of obtaining an heir to his
usurped power; for the principle of annual elections for the Chief of the
State had been abolished by him, and he entertained the project of found-
ing a dynasty. Report likewise added that inasmuch as the treasures which
he had amassed in the wars were all expended in consolidating his usurped
authority, he had determined to make his matrimonial views serve also
the purpose of replenishing his empty coffers, and that his confidential
advisers had drawn up a list of all the loveliest and wealthiest damsels in
Genoa.

"This intelligence was whispered through Genoa just at that period when, as above described, it wanted a week to the day fixed for the return of Walter Danvers. In the evening, at about nine o'clock, Landini, Genevra, and Bianca were seated together in one of the splendid apartments of the mansion, and were engaged in earnest discourse. But very far distant from the Doge or his plans was the topic of this conversation. Indeed the merchant, his wife, and sister, were discussing the preparations that were already in progress for the bridal—a letter having been that day received from Lord Danvers, stating that he had purchased the castle and estate in Normandy, and that he should be at Genoa again on the day originally appointed. The reader may therefore easily conceive that the present conversation was of a very interesting character, and that those who were engaged in it had little inclination to trouble themselves with fleeting rumours respecting a tyrant's projects. Presently the door opened, and a domestic entered to announce that a knight, who gave no name, required an immediate audience of the merchant. Landini asked what appearance the visitor had; for the circumstance carried a sudden trouble into his own heart as well as into the hearts of the two ladies. The domestic, in reply to his master's question, observed that the visitor was sheathed in complete armour and wore a helmet with the vizor closed. Scarcely had he thus spoken when the heavy trampling of steel boots was heard in the passage; and the menial, turning round, exclaimed, 'Here is the visitor to speak for himself!'—The intruder, clutching the domestic's arm with his gauntletted hand, thrust him rudely back from the threshold; and passing into the room, closed the door behind him. Nino Landini, Genevra, and Bianca, all three started from their seats on beholding the tall form of the armed warrior thus appear before them; and while the two ladies shrank together, the merchant, though with an increasing uneasiness, assumed a calm demeanour and inquired who the stranger was, and what he wanted?

"But the intrusive knight did not immediately reply. Advancing towards the two ladies, he fixed his looks through the bars of his helmet upon Bianca, and surveyed her with an intentness that was apparent enough, despite the steel veil which covered his features. For she could see his piercing eyes glow as it were through the openings in his vizor; and she shrank back from that gaze so earnest and so fiery. 'By the saints!' exclaimed the intruder, the natural tones of his voice altered so as to be deeply cavern-like and even sepulchral as they issued from the depths of that steel helmet: 'by the saints! report hath not misled me in this instance. Indeed it were impossible for rumour to exaggerate charms so peerless as these. Yes, thou art indeed the loveliest maid of Genoa; and it is sufficient that thou art Landini's sister to be a guarantee for the richness of thy dower.'—Thus speaking, the intruder raised the vizor of his helmet, and revealed the countenance of the Doge Angelo Visconti.

"A half-stifled shriek burst from the lips of Bianca as an awful fear seized upon her heart. Genevra gave vent to a cry of terror; and a similar ejaculation fell from the merchant.—'Do not alarm yourselves,' said the Duke, deliberately seating himself, and imperiously beckoning with his steel-clad arm for the others to follow his example. They obeyed in silence, vainly endeavouring to assume a calmness of demeanour the better to repel the atrocious proposition which their fears too faithfully told them was about to be made.—'Doubtless you have heard,' continued the Doge, his harsh features assuming an expression of condescending familiarity mingled with a patronising imperiousness, 'the rumour which has been spread abroad to-day, trumpet-tongued throughout the city of Genoa? But if you have not, I may as well inform you that it is my intention to raise to a share of my ducal seat the loveliest damsel in the Republic; and as a matter of course her friends, delighted with the honour thus conferred upon her, will bestow the richest dower as a bridal-gift. The loveliest damsel is *here*,' he added, glancing towards the shuddering Bianca; 'and you, Signor Landini, will furnish the dower.'—'My lord,' answered the merchant, feeling his courage rise in proportion to the emergency of the case, 'my sister Bianca is engaged to wed another, to whom her vows are plighted and on whom her affections are likewise bestowed.'—'And that other,' said the Duke sternly, 'is Lord Walter Danvers, the English nobleman who lately sojourned for a few months at Genoa. Now mark you, Signor Landini,' continued the Doge, speaking in a measured voice; 'I was no stranger to the incident which occurred on a certain night in front of Dr. Forli's house: but this Danvers of whom you speak came to me, and by the exercise of some unknown influence, which was powerful enough at the time, actually succeeded in overawing me. I can scarcely account for this weakness on my part: for all the world knows that Angelo Visconti possesses no craven spirit. But that man seemed to have a spell in his looks and to wield a weird-power too well calculated to make even the boldest afraid. I do not mind confessing this much now; because at length I have succeeded in shaking off that mystic influence which by his own unknown subtleties he shed upon me. I come therefore to demand the hand of Bianca in marriage; to demand also that you bestow upon her such dower as becomes the sister of the wealthiest merchant in the world. I give you three clear days to reflect upon the subject. On the fourth morning hence I shall return for your answer. If it be favourable, it were well for ye all: but if unfavourable, then prepare yourself, Nino Landini, to answer before the tribunal of justice for the double charge of having contravened my august decree and having escaped from the authorities of the law on that same night to which I have before alluded.'—Having thus spoken, the Doge Angelo Visconti rose from his seat, drew down the vizor of his helmet once more, and stalked majestically from the room.

CHAPTER XXIV.

CONCLUSION OF THE HISTORY OF BIANCA LANDINI.

"When the Doge Angelo Visconti thus took his departure, he left the wretched Genevra and Bianca overwhelmed with mingled grief and dismay. Bianca, weeping bitterly, threw herself into her brother's arms, exclaiming, 'Oh, now it is I, beloved Nino, who am destined to draw down the direst calamities upon your head!'—but the merchant said all he could to console his afflicted sister and his equally anguished wife, beseeching them both to compose their feelings that they might all three deliberate seriously upon the course to be pursued. That Bianca should sacrifice herself to the ducal tyranny, was not even for an instant thought of: nor did the damsel herself, willing as she would have been to do almost anything to save her brother, suggest such an alternative. She knew his generous heart too well to suppose that he would tolerate the idea for a moment; and the reader may be well assured that she was by no means dazzled by Angelo Visconti's preference. On the contrary, even if her heart were not engaged and her troth plighted to Walter Danvers, she would sooner have wedded the humblest and the meanest inhabitant of Genoa, than become the bride of the proud and unscrupulous usurper. But what was to be done? There was no time to send and inform Danvers of what was taking place; and even if he should return earlier than the day appointed for his coming, how could he avert the menaced catastrophe? Had not the Duke declared that Danvers no longer exercised any influence over him? Again and again did the merchant, Genevra, and Bianca ask each other what was to be done. Should they fly? This was their only alternative: but scarcely had they begun to deliberate upon this step, and arrange a plan for letting Danvers know whither to follow them, when a servant entered the room to announce that half-a-dozen sbirri had just arrived with the intimation that they were to take up their quarters beneath Signor Landini's roof for the next three or four days, and that the merchant himself, as well as his family, must consider themselves prisoners within those walls.

"The domestic withdrew so soon as he had delivered the message of the sbirri; and now the unfortunate victims of Angelo Visconti's detestable tyranny sat gazing upon each other in speechless dismay. Farther deliberation was useless. There was indeed naught to deliberate upon. Every avenue of escape from the dread catastrophe seemed to be shut up. It is scarcely possible to conceive a misery of the soul more truly agonizing than that which the honest, upright merchant and the two amiable and beauteous ladies were now enduring. Till a late hour that night did they remain together, in the vain hope that some happy suggestion would arise for their deliverance. But not a single inspiration of such a cheering nature pierced through the gloom of their souls: they had no longer a hope—no not one!

"When Bianca met her brother and sister-in-law again in the morning, at the meal which passed away untasted, she looked haggard and care-worn. But suddenly the merchant suggested a plan! He would send to the Duke and offer all his wealth—even to the last coin that he possessed—as a propitiation and a compromise. The hearts of the two ladies fluttered anew with hope. A respectful letter was drawn up and forthwith despatched to Angelo Visconti. In a short time the messenger returned, with the intimation that an answer would be sent anon. Oh! then the prayer was not refused abruptly and outright? and this circumstance enhanced the hope already entertained. Hour after hour passed: the sun gained the meridian—and still no response came. How fearful was the suspense which those three victims of tyranny now endured—so fearful as almost to stifle hope altogether! Still the hours dragged their slow length along, and no reply! The sun was sinking into the Mediterranean wave, when a messenger from the palace was announced. He delivered a sealed letter, and immediately departed. Bianca clung in the agony of suspense to her sister-in-law; and the hands of the naturally strong-minded Nino trembled to such a degree that he could scarcely open the missive just received. At length the document was unfolded; and as his eye glanced with lightning speed over its contents, his countenance at once grew pale, and blank, and deathlike with bitterest disappointment. The Doge refused the offer! In terms which were almost insolent, he declared that he wanted a wife as well as a fortune—that this wife must be the most beautiful maid in Genoa—and who so beautiful as Bianca Landini? All was now despair—dumb, blank, awful despair!

"And yet another hope gleamed forth next day. The merchant would offer half his fortune to the sbirri to connive at the escape of himself and those who were dear to him! He descended to the room where the officer of the sbirri was lodged, and propounded his object. It was received with cold contempt; and when the merchant retraced his way to the apartment where his wife and sister were waiting for him, his looks again denoted the futility of his errand. Oh! what was to be done now? It was impossible to yield tamely and without an effort. Despair suggested a dozen schemes—all of which, alas! proved utterly devoid of feasibility the moment they were reasoned upon. Thus the second day passed. The third morning came; and when the three victims of a satanic cruelty met at the breakfast-table, they were horrified at beholding the ravages of care in each other's looks. Genevra pressed her infant with convulsive violence to her bosom; and though she said nothing, yet in the utter woe of her half-stifling sobs, was read the thought that agonized the soul. For as she looked upon the innocent countenance of that sweet child, she thought to herself, 'Just heaven! is it possible that within a few hours, thou, unoffending babe, may'st be deprived of a father?'—And the father also wept as he gazed upon that child: but with a prompt return of manly courage he speedily dried his tears for the sake of those whose grief was already so poign-ant.—'Now, my dear wife, and you also, beloved sister,' he said, 'there is no hope for us but in the mercy of Providence. We have essayed all human means to avert the impending calamity: it is time that we should implore heaven's succour. Rest assured that if it please the Almighty to spare me, He will yet find a means of working out his sublime will. Therefore let us avert our thoughts from all worldly things, and fix our hopes upon that Power which is superior to the dominion of princes and dominant above the will of the proudest tyrants.'—In compliance with this suggestion, the remainder of that day was passed in devotion and pious discourse.

"The fourth morning dawned; it was the memorable one fixed by the Doge Angelo Visconti for the merchant's decision to be given. Nino Landini and his wife, when they met Bianca at the breakfast table, were profoundly afflicted to behold the still greater change which another sleep-less night of torturing thoughts had worked in that charming creature: she was still beautiful—touchingly beautiful: but how sad—Oh! how sad was the look that seemed to have settled indelibly upon her features. Her cheeks were sunken too; and her eyes were dim with weeping. When the three embraced, they mingled their tears together. But again did they have recourse to the consolations of prayer; and scarcely had they concluded their devotions, when the door was thrown open and Angelo Visconti, followed by a party of his body guards, entered the room. He was arrayed in a splendid Court-dress, as if he had come with the certainty of being invited to conduct a bride to the altar: but the instant his looks were swept around upon the countenances of the unfortunate family, he understood the decision that would be given.

" 'Signor Landini,' he exclaimed in a loud imperious tone, 'what says your sister Bianca? and what say you?'—'I say, my lord,' answered the mer-chant, now possessed of all the courage requisite to enable him to face whatever might be in store, 'that my sister Bianca cannot accompany you to the altar. As for my wealth, it is at your service, even to the last ducat: but I cannot permit a beloved sister to make a wreck of her heart's affections, or betray the troth which she has pledged to another.'—'Hah, this insolence!' thundered the Doge. 'Away with him to the tribunal! And see that these women,' he added, with brutal allusion to Genevra and Bianca, 'be still closely guarded here, as I shall bethink me how to deal with them when the arch-traitor Landini has been disposed of by the headsman.' Then followed a wild and terrible scene, the wife and the sister clinging to the merchant on whom the guards rudely seized; he imploring them not to lose confidence in heaven, and they pouring forth the bitterest lamentations; until the merciless soldiers literally wrenched him from their embrace and hurried him away. The Duke departed with his guards and their prisoner: and the almost heart-broken ladies were now left alone together.

"From the mansion to the tribunal of justice—Oh, what a mockery to use the word *justice* in such a sense!—there was no great distance. And now behold the eminent merchant of Genoa standing, with shackles upon his limbs, in the presence of a Judge who was the mere creature and the vile tool of a detestable tyrant! The tribunal was held in a gloomy subterranean, lighted dimly by iron lamps suspended to the low vaulted roof. The torture-room was adjoining; and the door was left wide open on purpose that the hideous instruments of dislocation and mutilation might be seen by the light which also burnt in that horrible place. But Landini maintained a firm and dignified bearing. The bitterness of death was passed at the moment the guards tore him away from the embrace of his agonized wife and sister. He cared not now for torture: had not his soul already endured excruciations more exquisite than any which man's cruelty could inflict upon his body? Nor did he contemplate death with affright: had he not lived too virtuously to tremble at the idea of speedily standing in the presence of his Maker?

"The trial was a mere mockery, and was as brief and hurried as such mockery well might be. Evidence was given to prove that Landini, on a particular night, had violated the ducal decree, and that succoured by an Englishman, not now present, he had escaped from the officers of justice. The merchant frankly and firmly admitted that the allegations were true; although he protested boldly against the infamy of the decree which his duty as a man, as a husband, and as an expectant father, had imperiously compelled him to disobey. But still he admitted the truth of the charges; and consequently there was no need for the horrors of the rack to extort confession. The Judge pronounced sentence of death; and the penalty was ordered to be carried into immediate execution. Indeed, as this result had been foreseen from the first moment of Landini's arrest, the preparations for his doom were made while his trial was progressing; and during the short hour and a half which the mock ordeal occupied, the platform was set up, the block placed upon it, the axe sharpened, and the headsman in readiness, all in the great square opposite to the ducal palace.

"Though public spectacles of this hideous nature had been common enough at Genoa since Angelo Visconti first ascended the ducal throne, yet that morbid curiosity which no frequency of horrors can ever satiate, much less appease altogether, had gathered even in so brief an interval of time a considerable crowd around the paraphernalia of death. It was to be a short shrift for Nino Landini! A priest was summoned to attend upon him; and accompanied by the holy man, the prisoner walked forth with a firm step from the subterranean tribunal. In the street a procession of guards and sbirri was already formed, with the Doge himself at their head. As Landini met the eyes of Angelo Visconti, a demoniac smile of triumph appeared upon the features of that cruel and implacable man: but the merchant fixed upon him a gaze which implied as eloquently as looks could speak, that the day of retribution would assuredly come.— 'Advance!' exclaimed the Duke in a loud tone; and the procession moved on. In a quarter of an hour the great square was reached: but still Landini trembled not on beholding the preparations of death. Yet in his heart there was a poignant anguish, as he reflected that though he was about to die, yet the shedding of his blood might not satisfy the tyrant's rage; but that a defenceless wife, an unprotected sister, and an innocent babe would be left behind him, perchance to become the victims of the ducal fiend's remorseless fury! Oh! now therefore did all the bitterness of death return into Landini's soul again!

On ascending to the platform, the merchant's ear caught subdued murmurs of sympathy from the assembled crowd: but the Doge, who, mounted on horseback, had taken his station close by the scaffold, looked fiercely around; and such was the dread in which all stood of the tyrant, that those murmuring sounds instantaneously ceased and a dead silence prevailed.—'My lord,' exclaimed Landini, in a firm tone, but with respectful demeanour, 'I will meet my death with cheerfulness if from your lips I receive the solemn assurance, in the presence of those now assembled here, that you will not visit upon the friendless females and the innocent babe whom I shall leave behind me, any sin which you imagine that I may have committed against yourself or the law. Nay, I will even breathe a prayer for your welfare in my last moments, if your Highness will condescend to give me the assurance I ask.'—'I will promise nothing,' thundered the tyrant. 'Proceed with the execution of this traitor!'—'Then,' cried the merchant, raising his voice into the swelling enthusiasm of prophesy, 'I invoke upon your head the vengeance of the Eternal if you dare prosecute your odious tyrannies against those whom I leave behind me. People of Genoa! if you have not the spirit to deliver an innocent man from death, at least display sufficient generosity and courage to assure him that when his blood is poured forth ye will become the guardians of his wife, his child, and his sister, who at one fell blow are to be deprived of a husband, a father, and a brother!'—Again did murmurs arise amidst the assembled multitude; and several voices were even hardy enough to give utterance to threats against Angelo Visconti: but the tyrant drew his sword from its sheath, and glancing with the rage of a hyena around, ordered silence to be observed. His bodyguard and the attendant sbirri likewise drew their weapons; so that the unarmed populace, fearful of being mowed down by the monster and his myrmidons, again relapsed into an awe-stricken stillness. Landini fell upon his knees—breathed a short prayer on behalf of Genevra, Bianca, and the infant Ludovico—and then laid his head upon the block. The headsman raised the tremendous axe on high.—ghastly it gleamed in the sun-light: but at the very instant that it was about to descend on the merchant's neck, a sudden noise and confusion on the outskirts of the crowd made the executioner pause: and as the multitude parted in the midst, a small body of horsemen galloped up to the spot.

 " 'Release the prisoner!' cried a loud and commanding voice, which instantaneously fell familiar on the merchant's ears: and starting up from his kneeling position at the block, he beheld Lord Danvers, followed by his retinue of dependants. Shouts of exultation burst forth from several points in the crowd, and in a few moments became general, a myriad voices combining in a chorus of applause on behalf of Danvers and of execration towards the tyrant. As for Angelo Visconti himself, he suddenly grew ghastly pale on meeting the eyes of the English nobleman: but speedily recovering himself, he turned to his guards, exclaiming, 'Arrest this insolent foreigner who dares interfere with the course of justice at Genoa!'—But Danvers spurring his steed close up to the line of guards, bristling though it were with pointed spears and flashing with naked swords, waved his arm with cool disdain, saying, 'No, they dare not lay a finger upon *me!*'—'Cowards! dastards! will ye see me bearded thus?' exclaimed the Duke, literally foaming with rage.—For an instant there seemed to be a movement amongst the guards as if they were about to obey their master's mandate and rush upon the English nobleman: but as Danvers swept his lightning-glances along the serried ranks and threw upon the armed men all the terrors of his scornful looks, they shrank back with dismay—their lances fell suddenly to the ground—and their swords were dropped as if from palsied hands. For an instant the stupor of wonderment held the multitudes motionless and dumb: but in a very brief space the long pent-up excitement of outraged feelings burst forth with the fury and the force of a volcano. The maddened populace tore the Doge from his horse, trod him under their feet, and literally trampled the life out of him. All this was the work of a few seconds; and neither guards nor sbirri attempted to raise a hand or lift one of the dropped weapons in the tyrant's defence. But when the massacre was accomplished, those myrmidons of a dread miscreant's will seemed but too glad to obey the imperious gesture made by Lord Danvers' hand, and save themselves by a precipitate flight from the vengeance of the Genoese populace.

"The chains were knocked off Landini's limbs; and with fervent gratitude did he embrace his deliverer. The multitudes formed a procession to escort him home in triumph; and in this manner, accompanied by Lord Walter Danvers, did the merchant return to that dwelling which three hours back he thought that he had quitted for ever. Oh! what tongue can tell or what pen can record the joy that was experienced by Genevra and Bianca at this most unhoped-for restoration of him whose loss they had been so bitterly, bitterly deploring! But if it were possible that anything could enhance the delight which the charming Bianca felt at her brother's deliverance, it was the circumstance that this rescue had been accomplished by him whom she loved so tenderly and so well. How fond, then, was the embrace in which she clasped her lover! and how affectionate were the caresses which he bestowed upon her in return! So brilliantly did the hues of health come back to her countenance, that the care-worn haggardness of her features was scarcely to be observed: and in a few days all those traces of recent anguish passed away, so that Bianca Landini seemed more beautiful than ever.

"Lord Danvers explained that it was a troubled dream which had induced him to hurry his return to Genoa two or three days before the date previously fixed for his arrival: but what the exact nature of the dream was he did not state. The merchant was however well convinced that the finger of Providence was visible throughout the proceeding; and he was too happy at his restoration to his family to be able to give much time for reflection upon the extraordinary events that had taken place at the scene of his intended execution. But the people of Genoa, who had witnessed the whole occurrence, freely canvassed its details. They asked themselves and each other, who this Lord Danvers was, that he seemed to wield a preterhuman power and paralyze the strength of armed men by his gestures and looks? That was especially a period when the mind of man was

prone to superstitious belief; and many of the Genoese therefore came
to the conclusion that Walter Danvers must be invested with powers not
possessed by ordinary mortals. But others merely beheld in the transaction the influence of a very superior mind wielding its moral power over
the brute instincts of a horde of hireling bravoes; and this was also the
explanation which Danvers himself gave to the Landini and to all those
friends who came to congratulate the merchant upon his rescue. In two or
three days the Genoese people were plunged into the excitement attendant upon the election of a new Doge; and thus the marvellous adventures
that had taken place on the occasion of Landini's deliverance, ceased to
engage public attention.

"The preparations for the bridal were continued in a spirit more blithe
than that with which they were commenced; and Walter Danvers was
now constantly with his Bianca. They rode out together on horseback in
the forenoon—they rambled of an evening upon the sea-shore. The damsel was evidently wrapped up in her lover. She seemed to live and breathe
only for him. And no wonder! Not only was his personal beauty of the
highest order, his manners most fascinating, his intellect most brilliant,
his mind stored with varied information—but he had likewise rendered
such signal services to the Landini family that could not fail to endear him
to the generous-hearted Bianca. And as she had never loved until she first
saw Danvers, she experienced all the bliss which this new sentiment had
excited in her soul; and in proportion as her thoughts were pure, and innocent, and artless, so was her passion illimitable, enthusiastic, and deep.

"It was now the evening preceding the day fixed for the bridal; and
the lovers' walk was prolonged on the sea-shore to a somewhat later hour
than hitherto. When they re-entered the mansion, the merchant and Genevra both observed that there seemed to be something like a trouble in
Bianca's looks and manner—but a trouble, if such it really were, which
she sedulously sought to conceal. Danvers took his leave as usual, and
returned to the hostel where he was staying with his retinue. Bianca then
remained alone with her brother and sister-in-law; and now that species
of uneasiness which they had observed in her air and looks, grew more
apparent.—'I know my beloved sister,' said the merchant, 'what is passing
in your mind. Even across the glorious sunshine of your heart is a cloud
stealing. But, Ah! how slight is that shadow in comparison with the glowing light of happiness through which it is floating. Yes, Bianca, I can read
the thought which troubles you! Although about to become the loved and
honoured bride of him who adores you so enthusiastically, and who is
in every way so well worthy of your heart's best and purest affections,
yet you cannot help regretting that you are about to be borne away from

these walls which from your birth have been your home, and that you are going to the land of the stranger. I also, and Genevra too, feel a similar regret at the prospect of parting with you to-morrow: but this we regard as a selfish feeling on our part, when we take into consideration the certainty of that happiness which you will experience from an alliance so eligible in every sense.'—Bianca endeavoured to murmur some reply: but the words died upon her lips, or rather were lost in sobs; and having tenderly embraced her brother and sister-in-law, she retired somewhat abruptly to her own chamber.

"On the following morning the merchant and Genevra rose at a much earlier hour than usual, in order to see that everything was in readiness for the bridal which was to take place this day, and which was to be celebrated by a grand banquet at noon, whereunto all the friends of the Landini family were invited. But when the breakfast-hour arrived and Bianca did not make her appearance in the apartment where the table was spread, Genevra hastened to the damsel's chamber. It was vacant; and Signora Landini was about to turn away to seek for her sister-in-law in some other room, when she suddenly observed that Bianca's couch had not been slept in all night. Alarmed, she sped back to her husband. Inquiries were now made; but Bianca was nowhere to be found. No one had seen her that morning: nor had any one observed her leave the house on the preceding night. It appeared, however, that on retiring to her chamber she had dispensed with the usual services of her tiring-maid, alleging that she wished to be alone. That was the last trace of Bianca Landini.

"But what had become of her? All was bewilderment and amaze. The merchant hurried to the hostel; but Lord Danvers was not there. He had not been seen since the previous evening; and the servants of his retinue had all taken their departure at a very early hour in the morning. The merchant was staggered, and could scarcely believe the evidence of his senses. That Bianca could have consented to elope as a guilty mistress with one who had been wooing her as an honoured bride, seemed incredible; and that Danvers, even if he were her villanous seducer, could have had any interest in foully murdering her, was equally impossible of belief. The merchant, when enabled somewhat to compose his feelings, made farther inquiries of the keeper of the hostel; when it appeared that about eleven o'clock on the preceding night, Danvers had returned to the establishment and had ordered his grooms to saddle the two splendid coal-black steeds which always served for his own special use; that he mounted one of them and departed, leading the other away by the bridle; that he had thus gone forth alone, having none of his retinue in attendance upon him; and that he had returned no more. It farther appeared that at an early hour in the morning the domestics composing his retinue suddenly ordered all their horses to be saddled; and the principal menial having liberally discharged the account due to the keeper of the hostel, they took their departure.

"These were all the particulars the merchant could glean: this indeed was all that was known at the hostel. He accordingly returned home to communicate the strange details to his wife. That Bianca had fled with Danvers, was beyond all doubt. But for what purpose this flight? There seemed to be not the least necessity for it. It was an enigma defying all conjecture. Nino and Genevra were well nigh heartbroken at the occurrence; and knowing the purity of Bianca's mind so well, they felt convinced that it could have been under the influence of no ordinary infatuation she was thus seduced away from her home. Now however the merchant began to reflect more seriously, and likewise more gloomily, than he had ever done before, upon the conduct of Walter Danvers. The adventure with the sbirri in front of Dr. Forli's house—the influence which the nobleman had managed to exercise over the late Angelo Visconti—and then the circumstances attending Nino Landini's deliverance from death upon the scaffold, all appeared to indicate that Walter Danvers was indeed no common man. But was he a fiend in human shape? The merchant was bewildered. He however felt that he had a duty to perform; and from this he was resolved not to shrink. Bidding his wife farewell, and having affectionately embraced the infant Ludovico, he set out, attended by a small retinue, upon a journey to France. Losing no time by the way, he in a few days reached Normandy; and there he ascertained that everything which Lord Danvers had stated in respect to the purchase of the castle and estate was strictly true. Indeed, the castle was tenanted by the numerous domestics whom Lord Danvers had engaged during his recent sojourn there: but nothing had been seen of him since he had departed thence to return to Genoa. The merchant lost no time in proceeding to England; and on his arrival he visited Lord Danvers' mansion near Chelmsford in Essex: but for the last eight years his lordship had not been there. Thence the merchant proceeded into Cumberland: but the same period of time had elapsed since Lord Walter Danvers was last seen at his castle in that county. With scarcely a hope left, Nino Landini retraced his way southward, and passed over into the Isle of Wight. But there he found that the castle on the point overlooking the Needles, was shut up altogether; and from the inhabitants in the neighbourhood he learnt that it was precisely eight years since young Lord Walter, on coming into possession of the family title and estates, had suddenly broken up his establishment at Danvers Castle and had gone abroad. Having thus fruitlessly prosecuted his inquiries, Nino Landini, with his little retinue, went back to Genoa, which city he reached after

an absence of four months. He was received with open arms by the affectionate Genevra: but they had naught consolatory or hopeful to impart to
each other concerning Bianca. Nothing had been heard of her at Genoa
during the merchant's absence: no letter nor message had been received
from the lost one. Time passed on—weeks swelled into months—months
grew into years; and yet no tidings of Bianca Landini! No, nor was aught
more heard at Genoa of Lord Walter Danvers.

⋆ ⋆ ⋆ ⋆ ⋆

"Twenty years had passed away; and we now behold the eminent
merchant Nino Landini stretched upon the bed of death. By the side of
the couch knelt a handsome youth, wanting but a few months to complete
his twenty-first year; and by the strong likeness which existed between
his features, that were pale with grief, and those of the invalid that were
pale with approaching dissolution, it was easy to distinguish the degree
of relationship in which they stood to each other. At the foot of the bed
was a venerable man, well stricken in years; and a nurse was mixing a
medicament at the side-table. The time was evening; and the light of the
lamp played with sickly effect upon the ghastly countenance of the dying
man. Presently he spoke, saying to the nurse, 'I feel that my last hour is
come; and it is useless to take potion or drug in the hope of wrestling
against the Destroyer. Retire therefore;'—then fixing his eyes upon Dr.
Forli, the venerable man at the foot of the couch, he continued, 'And you
also, my good friend, be kind enough to leave me alone with my son for a
brief space.'—The physician and the nurse accordingly quitted the room,
and the dying merchant then said, 'Remain upon your knees, my dear Ludovico: for it is in that solemn attitude that it becomes thee to hear what I
am about to speak, so that thou may'st give my last instructions thy most
sacred ratification.'

"The youth took his father's hand, pressed it to his lips, and watered
it with his tears. He endeavoured to speak, but could not: sorrow choked
his utterance.—'Tranquillize your feelings, dear boy,' said the merchant;
'for I have grave and serious matters whereof to treat with thee. In the first
place I must speak to you as an honourable man, and faithful to the character of the first merchant in Christendom: but in the second place I shall
speak to you as a man who cherishes a vengeance which for years past
has gnawed his heart with the virulence of an envenomed snake, and has
haunted him like a remorse.'—The merchant stopped for a few minutes to
gather breath, and then proceeded as follows:—'First of all, then, my son,
listen to me while I address you in my capacity of an upright merchant

whose word has ever been stamped with the authority of a bond. I leave you my sole heir. When I am gone to rejoin that beloved wife, your angel-mother, who went before me five years ago to the world beyond the grave, you will take my example as your guide and pursue your mercantile career with the strictest honour and the most scrupulous integrity. At first sight the wealth which you will find at your disposal must appear colossal beyond your wildest imaginings; but when you search amongst my private papers, you will find that only one-half of it is legitimately my own, or can be honourably bequeathed to you. The other half belongs to whomsoever at this moment bears the title of Lord Danvers. Exactly twenty years and six months ago did Lord Walter Danvers deposit an immense sum in my hands. That amount has trebled since then. You will find due specifications relative to this business in my private papers. I know not whether Lord Walter Danvers is still alive, or whether he has even left any heirs. For years past I have heard nothing of the name. But it is most probable that if he himself be not alive, there must be some heir to his wealth. Should this heir ever present himself and demand the restoration of his progenitor's money; or should Lord Walter Danvers himself be living, and come to claim it, you will at once restore the amount, with profit, and interest, and compound interest, according to the specifications in my private papers. Deducting this immense sum from the wealth left at your disposal, you will still be the richest merchant in the world. May you thrive, my beloved son, even as I have thriven.'

"The youth, with tearful eyes and broken voice, faithfully promised to follow his dying parent's injunctions: and Nino Landini then continued as follows:—'I now come to the second portion of my subject. Amongst my secret papers you will discover a history of the loves of Lord Walter Danvers and your long lost aunt Bianca Landini: that is to say, you will find recorded all that was known of those loves down to the moment of her disappearance. These particulars you must cause to be duly recorded amongst the Chronicles of the house of Landini. And now to the point on which I am desirous of fixing your attention. A fearful outrage has been perpetrated by a member of the house of Danvers towards a member of the house of Landini. The former was Lord Walter, of whom I have spoken: the latter was your long lost aunt Bianca. What became of her I have never known. That she was seduced away by Lord Walter is beyond doubt; and we must hence infer that she either perished miserably, with a broken heart through shame and grief; or else that she was foully murdered by her betrayer. Otherwise, had she lived on all these years, there must have been one moment of penitence and contrition, in which her soul would have yearned to communicate with those whom she left behind her in her native land. Whatever be her fate, then, it is clear that a fearful outrage was perpetrated by Walter Danvers against Bianca Landini. This outrage is one demanding a true Italian vengeance. I have had no opportunity of wreaking it. I therefore bequeath it as a heritage unto you; and if you, my son, should likewise fail to wreak it, hand it down as a sacred tradition and an hereditary duty to your children. For never must the race of Landini abandon this vengeance until it be fully gratified and terribly assuaged! No matter that the descendants of Walter Danvers may be held innocent of their progenitor's crime: on them must the penalty fall, if it fail to reach the guilty Lord Walter himself. But to wreak this vengeance effectually, it must not be by means of your weapon, nor of the hired assassin's dagger. There is a vengeance more terrible than that of taking away life. If you take the life of an enemy, you place him beyond the reach of farther pain at once; and this is scarcely a vengeance to be contemplated with satisfaction. But if you get your enemy into your power—involve him in a web of difficulties that shall be inextricable—insidiously draw in the meshes tighter and tighter around him, so that utter ruin at last stares him in the face,—*this* is true vengeance; because he remains alive for you to tell him that you are avenged, and he lives on in wretchedness and misery to feel day after day and hour after hour the effects of your vengeance! Now, my son, do you comprehend me? Will you accept the heritage of this vengeance? and should you yourself fail to wreak it, will you hand it down as a legacy to your posterity?'

" 'I will,' responded Ludovico solemnly.—'You swear?' said his father.—'I swear,' was the answer.—'Then I die content,' rejoined Nino Landini; and he gave up the ghost.

"Ten years had elapsed: it was the middle of the year 1420; and Ludovico Landini, now a little past thirty, was one day seated in his counting-house and with gloomy aspect looking over his books and making calculations. The farther he progressed in this examination the more moody grew his mien; and when at last he added up a long column of figures and compared the total with the sum of another column, his handsome countenance grew pale with despair. At this moment one of his clerks entered to announce a visitor; and Ludovico, settling his features as well as he could into a business-like composure, rose to receive him. This was a tall, handsome man, of slender figure, aristocratic bearing, elegant apparel, and courtly gracefulness of manner. But when Ludovico Landini marked the dusky complexion, the brilliant eyes, and the glossy black hair of his visitor, he was at once struck by the wondrous resemblance which he bore to the portrait of Lord Walter Danvers, as delineated in the written chronicles he had found amongst his father's private papers. Nevertheless, this individual could not possibly be Lord Walter; for he did not seem to be above four-and-thirty years old; whereas if Lord Walter were alive, he must be exactly double that age.

"Ludovico bowed, and requested his visitor to be seated: but that personage, advancing to the desk, with an air of easy courtesy and polished frankness, said, 'You are Signor Ludovico Landini? Permit me to introduce myself as Lord Ranulph Danvers.'—'Ah, Lord Danvers!' repeated the merchant, with the air of one who receives the confirmation of a disagreeable suspicion: but again recovering his self-possession, he said, 'What can I do for your lordship?"—'Perhaps you are aware, signor,' replied the nobleman, 'that about thirty years ago some little trifle was deposited by *my* father in the hands of *your* father?'—'It was so; but not a trifle,' answered Ludovico: then pointing to a piece of paper which lay before him, he added, 'Here is the original amount deposited with my father; and this is its value at the present day. Your lordship will observe that the original sum has very nearly quadrupled, and constitutes an amount larger than the revenues of any two monarchs in Christendom.'—'Indeed,' said Lord Ranulph Danvers, carelessly: 'when will it suit you to pay me this amount?'—'My lord,' answered Ludovico, 'I will deal candidly with you. Your lordship is aware that within the last few years the Genoese Republic has been ravaged by the Pisans, to the great detriment of our native commerce: moreover three rich argosies of mine have been lost at sea; and thirdly, the failure of an eminent mercantile firm at Venice made me a considerable sufferer. Candidly therefore, my lord, I am not in a position to liquidate your claim; no, nor even half of it, nor a quarter of it at the present moment.'—Before Lord Ranulph had time to reply, a clerk entered the office with an abruptness which was however explained by the consternation upon his countenance; and he beckoned Ludovico Landini into the adjoining room. In three or four minutes the merchant returned to Lord Ranulph Danvers: but his countenance was pale as death, and his looks were full of trouble—'Has aught unpleasant occurred?' asked the nobleman.—'My lord,' replied the merchant, 'a large transaction, involving the boldest venture, and by which I hoped to retrieve the losses of the last few years, has utterly failed. The intelligence has this moment arrived. I am now a ruined man; and so far from being enabled to settle any portion of your lordship's claim, I shall be compelled to throw myself upon the mercy of all my creditors. In a word, I am beggared!'—and the representative of the once wealthy house of Landini burst into tears.

" 'As for the sum in which you are indebted to me,' said Lord Ranulph Danvers, as calmly and indeed with as much indifference as if his own loss were of the most paltry description, 'do not let it trouble you.

I shall not ask you for it until fortune smiles upon you again.'—'Oh, my lord,' exclaimed Ludovico, 'this is most generous on your part! Would to heaven that I could hope for similar mercy at the hands of my other creditors, but a gaol stares me in the face.'—'Let us hope not,' observed Lord Ranulph: then after a brief pause, he said, 'I presume that you entertain no goodwill towards any one bearing the name of Danvers?'—Ludovico looked confused, and made no reply. He thought of the legacy of vengeance which had been bequeathed to him, and how circumstances were now laying him under the deepest obligation to the very man who was to be the object of his hate.—'I am no stranger,' continued Danvers, 'to the wrong perpetrated by my father against your aunt Bianca Landini. That was thirty years ago.'—'Ah!' suddenly ejaculated Ludovico, as a thought struck him: 'your lordship must be a trifle over thirty, and was therefore born previously to my aunt's seduction? In that case I presume your father was married at the time when he paid his court to Bianca Landini.'—'Yes, such indeed was the fact,' answered Lord Ranulph; 'and hence his inability to espouse Bianca. Infatuated by her beauty, he was led on to perpetrate that grievous wrong for which I, as his son, am however ready to make atonement.'—'Know you, my lord, the fate of my unfortunate aunt Bianca?" asked Ludovico.—'She died many long years ago,' responded Ranulph: 'my father, when on his death-bed, told me all. But I can remain with you no longer now. On a future occasion we shall converse more on the subject.'—'On a future occasion, my lord,' said the merchant in a tone of deepest despondency, 'you will find me imprisoned in a gaol!'—But Lord Ranulph seemed not to catch this observation; and with a courteous bow he somewhat abruptly took his departure.

"The rumour soon spread abroad that the affairs of Ludovico Landini were in a most disastrous condition; and his creditors came thickly upon him. The law in respect to debt was mercilessly severe at that period: the unfortunate debtor could be thrown into a dungeon amidst rogues and felons, or could even be sent as a slave to toil at the oar on board the galleys of the fleet. The position of the young merchant was therefore unfortunate to a degree: but still he had too much honour to fly from the face of impending danger. He hoped that leniency would be extended towards him in consideration of the integrity of his character, the calamities that had beggared him, and the eminent name which he inherited. But a creditor more spiteful than the rest, caused him to be snatched from his home and plunged into the castle-gaol. Not many hours however had Ludovico thus become the inmate of a prison, when he was informed by the turnkey that a person desired to see him in one of the apartments belonging to the governor of the castle. Thither was Ludovico accordingly conducted; and to his surprise he found that the visitor was Lord Ranulph Danvers.

" 'I scarcely thought that matters would come to *this* when I saw you the other day,' said the nobleman; 'or I should at once have offered to assist you.'—'My lord,' exclaimed the ruined merchant, 'have you not already lost an immense sum by me?'—'Fortune may yet take a turn,' said Lord Danvers. 'What is the amount of your liabilities?'—'Immense, my lord,' was the reply.—'But the amount, I ask?' repeated Danvers.—'Behold,' rejoined Ludovico, presenting a slip of paper to the nobleman.—'Let us go into the governor's own apartment,' said Danvers; and he led the way thither. Then, to the utter amazement alike of the merchant and the governor himself, Danvers wrote orders upon four different mercantile firms of Genoa, the aggregate making the whole amount of Ludovico's liabilities. While the governor's messenger proceeded to satisfy himself that the draughts would be duly honoured, Ranulph Danvers continued to discourse in a frank and easy manner just as if he had merely been transacting some business of very trivial importance instead of an affair involving millions of ducats. The messenger returned in due course; the draughts had all been honoured, and Ludovico Landini was a free man. How could he do otherwise than express his gratitude? But Danvers cut him short by observing, 'Give me no thanks. What I have done for you is merely by way of making atonement for the injury inflicted by my father upon your ancestress. Besides, it is not my intention to leave my work half done. But I should ask whether you intend to resume business again in Genoa?'—'No, my lord,' was the reply. 'Although through your bounty my debts are paid, yet does a stigma rest upon my name; and in consequence of having even for a few days failed to meet my engagements, and being for a few hours the inmate of a prison, I can never hold up my head in Genoa again.'—'That is exactly the answer I expected from you,' said Danvers: 'for I know the pride of you Italian merchants. Will you repair to London, open a mercantile establishment there, and undertake the agency of the revenues derived from my English estates? If you consent, I will furnish you with the necessary capital to commence the world again.'—Ludovico Landini positively refused to incur further obligations to the nobleman: for he could not, as an honourable man, receive favours from an individual belonging to a race against whom he had sworn, by his father's death-bed, to wreak a terrible vengeance. 'But I must insist on your accepting my proposal,' said Lord Danvers, sternly: 'how can you ever repay me all you owe, unless by entering largely into commerce again?'—'Ah, my lord,' exclaimed Ludovico, 'if you put the matter in that light, I am bound to accept your offer. Indeed, your bounty has made me your slave: deal with me as you think fit.'—'Then you shall go to London,' rejoined Lord Ranulph Danvers.

"Accordingly, in a few weeks, Ludovico repaired to England; and on arriving in the metropolis, established himself as a diamond-merchant, goldsmith, and banker, in Lombard Street. His affairs prospered marvellously; every enterprise in which he embarked, proved successful: riches poured in upon him from all quarters; and he renewed his correspondence with those eminent merchants in various parts of Christendom who had been wont to do business with him at Genoa. In the course of fifteen years he was enabled to liquidate the entire amount due to Lord Danvers, whom, we should observe, he saw but twice during this interval, and then only for a few hours on each occasion.

"Four years later (in 1439) Ludovico, being now forty-nine, began to think seriously of matrimony: and he espoused a young lady of his own native land, but whose parents had for some time been settled in England. This lady brought with her a handsome dower; and thus were the riches of Ludovico still farther increased. In due time he was blessed with a son, whom he named Alessandro; and two years afterwards his wife presented him with another boy who was called Cosmo. But in giving birth to the latter, the mother lost her life. Time continued to roll on—years and years passed—old age came upon Ludovico but he looked on his two grown-up sons with pride, as the fitting heritors of his wealth and of that fatal legacy which, in pursuance of his oath, he was bound to bequeath unto them. He himself had found no opportunity of wreaking the family revenge upon Ranulph Danvers whom not even the sense of gratitude could have induced him to spare had the occasion for vengeance presented itself. For paramount above all other considerations—dominant over all other sentiments—must a cherished vengeance be in the Italian breast. When upon his death-bed, at the ripe age of seventy—and therefore in the year 1460—he spoke unto his two sons in the same manner as fifty years back his father had spoken to him. Alessandro and Cosmo, who at this period were respectively but twenty-one and nineteen, received the legacy of vengeance, and swore to fulfil it or else to hand it down to be fulfilled by their posterity.

"Ludovico Landini died; and his sons continued to be the agents of Lord Ranulph Danvers, who however had not visited England for many, many years. In 1462, Lord Humphrey Danvers—an elegant and handsome young man, inheriting all the personal characteristics of his ancestors when at the same age—introduced himself to the brothers Landini, announcing the death of his father Lord Ranulph, and offering to continue them as his agents. The proposal was of course accepted; and the large sums which were at the time in the Landinis' hands, were duly transferred to the name of Humphrey Danvers. Some time afterwards the two brothers fell out and resolved to separate partnership. They divided their wealth equally between them, Alessandro the elder retaining the establishment in Lombard Street, and therewith the agency for the Danvers family. Cosmo married, and in due time had a son, whom he christened Marco. Not being gifted with the intelligence of his brother, he was unfortunate in his speculations—failed—and perished of a broken heart. His wife, who was devotedly attached to him, never recovered the blow, and died shortly after, leaving the orphan Marco dependent upon his uncle Alessandro. Meanwhile Alessandro Landini himself had likewise married but had become a widower and was childless. He therefore adopted his orphan nephew to be the inheritor of his wealth, and if need be, of the legacy of vengeance likewise!

"NOTE TO THE ABOVE HISTORY.

"I, the undersigned Alessandro Landini, having as yet been unable to wreak the hereditary vengeance of my race upon any member of the accursed family of Danvers, and feeling that old age is creeping upon me, have, on this first day of January of the year 1501, revealed to my nephew Marco Landini, who yesterday completed his twenty-first year, the secret of that hereditary vengeance. Therefore if any plot or plan which I may as yet be enabled to devise for executing that vengeance, should remain unfulfilled Marco will at my death accept the heritage of the legacy for himself, and likewise for his heirs, if need be.

"Witness my hand,
"ALESSANDRO LANDINI."

CHAPTER XXV.

ALESSANDRO LANDINI AND MUSIDORA.

WE cannot pretend to fathom the effect which Bianca Landini's history produced upon Musidora: for so seldom was it that her splendid but inscrutable countenance afforded any indication of her inward feelings, and then only when under very extraordinary circumstances of sudden excitement. Certain it was, however, that with a deep and absorbing interest had she perused that chapter in the Landini Chronicles which recorded the untoward loves of the beauteous Bianca. Without once raising her head from the huge volume wherein the chronicles were contained, Musidora read on from the first word till the last; and perhaps a close observer—had any such been nigh—would have fancied that this interest on her part was of a more profound, a more concentrated, and a more engrossing character than even the most ardent admirer of the wild and romantic would have exhibited in the perusal of that history.

While she was engaged in her all-absorbing study, the Earl and Countess of Grantham had been enjoying themselves at the refreshment-table; and when their repast was over, they had drawn their chairs close to each other in order to converse upon their favourite topic. This was Musidora's approaching marriage with the King; for that she would marry him at the expiration of the prescribed period of two months—a fortnight of which had already elapsed—they had not the slightest doubt. Indeed she herself had on the previous day given them to understand that such would be the result of the monarch's courtship; and therefore the Earl and the Countess, looking upon the alliance as a matter that was as good as settled, revolved and discussed with the almost childish delight of anticipation the thousand-and-one-things they would do or have done when their charming relative should be Queen of England. So absorbed did they become in this subject, and so completely were they carried away by its fascinations, that they did not observe the lapse of time; so that while Musidora was reading in the recess and the noble couple were carrying on their whispered discourse at the table, the three hours mentioned by the Landinis as the interval requisite for repairing the set of diamonds, passed away. A beautiful clock upon the mantel-piece made the Earl aware how time had sped; and starting from his seat, he exclaimed, "Come forth from your nook, 'Dora: we shall soon be going."

"My dear child," said the Countess, as our heroine emerged from the recess where she had just finished the narrative of Bianca Landini, "you must have found something very pleasing indeed in that old book thus to have kept you enchained for three mortal hours to your seat. What is it all about, my dear?"

"Some Genoese adventures and historical incidents in the time of the despot Duke Angelo Visconti," was Musidora's reply.

"Will you not change your mind now and take some refreshment?" asked the Countess: then looking fixedly upon her beauteous young relative, she exclaimed, "But I do believe that you are at this moment a little paler than is even your wont. I am sure it is through exhaustion for want of food. See! it is four o'clock. How many hours since you have taken any refreshment!"

"I require none at present," answered Musidora. "I will wait till we return to the villa."

The door now opened; and the two Landinis—uncle and nephew—made their appearance, the latter carrying in his hand the casket of diamonds, which he at once presented to Musidora.

"Be pleased, lady," said Mark, as he thus approached her, "to examine the tiara and the armlet now; and I think you will admit that the gems are admirably matched."

Musidora for courtesy's sake examined the diamonds, and signified her full approval; but as she raised her eyes to Mark's countenance, while speaking, she thought for the moment that the look which she caught him as it were fixing upon her, had something strange in it. He however instantaneously assumed an air of what might be termed the indifference of cold respect; and bowing in acknowledgment of the approbation which she had expressed, he turned away to exhibit the contents of the casket to the Earl and Countess of Grantham.

"The gems are indeed exquisitely matched," said the Earl.

"And the settings are most artistic," added the Countess. "I am so glad to think that we applied to you, Master Landini," she continued, now addressing herself to the uncle; "for I question whether we should have had the loss so easily or so efficiently made good at any other establishment."

Old Alessandro Landini bowed an acknowledgment of this compliment, and immediately said, "I hope that we have not kept your ladyship waiting. It was close upon one o'clock when you were shown up into this room: it is now but a few minutes past four—and thus we have not detained you beyond the three hours originally specified for the requirement of that delicate work:"—and he pointed to the diamonds.

"We not only have to thank you, Master Landini," said the Earl, now taking up the thread of the discourse, "for your exactitude in respect to time, but also for the hospitality you have shown us."

"Yes," added the Countess, "we have done justice to your good fare. That is to say, I and his lordship have partaken with appetite of the repast; but I cannot say the same for our fair relative. Indeed I think, Master Landini, that for her your old musty volumes have greater attractions than your well-spread table."

At these words the two Landinis exchanged a quick look full of consternation; but it flittered away from their countenances as soon as expressed—and Lady Grantham was too superficial an observer to notice it. The Earl at the instant was examining the diamonds in the casket, and wondering how much he would have to pay for the repairs. But Musidora did observe that expression of dismay which for a swift brief moment passed over the features of Alessandro and Marco Landini; and advancing towards them, she said, "It is perfectly true that I took the liberty of turning over a few pages in one of your volumes: but I hope that I have not been guilty of any indiscretion."

"Oh, indiscretion!" exclaimed the Countess, her aristocratic pride shocked to think that her young relative, who was so soon to be Queen of England, should deem it necessary to make such an apology to the plebeian citizens: "I am sure that neither Master Landini nor his worthy nephew can be angry with you for having looked into an old volume. Of course books are written to be read, and when left lying about, may be opened by anybody. Besides, there can be no possible harm in reading about Genoese incidents, the Duke Angelo Visconti, and other Italian matters."

Again did the elder Landini and his nephew exchange that quick and significant glance of consternation which Musidora had already noticed: but again did it pass unperceived by the Earl and Countess of Grantham.

"From what her ladyship has said," Musidora proceeded to remark, still addressing herself to the Landinis, and speaking with greater haste than was her wont, "you perhaps have understood what chapter it was in that volume which I have been reading? But I can assure you——"

"Pray offer no apology," the elder Landini hurriedly exclaimed. "But step with me for a moment into that recess, while I show you one curious anecdote in the book which you may not have seen. I shall not detain you there, young lady, more than two or three minutes: and in the meantime my nephew Mark will explain to his lordship the instructions I have already given him relative to the cost for repairing those diamonds."

"You must not detain her more than a minute," said the Countess of Grantham; "for we are somewhat in a hurry to retrace our way to Greenwich."

"Not more than a minute or two," rejoined Alessandro Landini: and with the courtesy of a well-bred old man, he took Musidora's hand and led her into the recess.

"Now, worthy Master Mark," said the Earl, addressing himself to the nephew, who had thrown a hurried and somewhat singular look after his uncle and Musidora as they passed into the recess,—"what have you to tell me relative to the charge for these diamonds and their setting?"

"My lord," responded Mark, speaking however with a certain abstractedness of manner, which the nobleman set down as diffidence on the part of a citizen in the dazzling light of his own proud aristocracy,—"my uncle desired me to say that considering the diamonds were originally purchased at his establishment, and that therefore he is to some extent responsible for the loss of the two from the tiara and the bracelet, he begs your lordship will not think of offering the slightest remuneration. My uncle is moreover rejoiced that chance should have led your lordship to apply to us for the repairs; inasmuch as it afforded him the opportunity of doing as, under circumstances, he is bound to do—I mean replace them without price or cost to your lordship's self."

"Both you and your uncle are worthy and inestimable men," said the Earl, overjoyed at being spared any outlay on account of the lost diamonds: for his lordship was particularly fond of money, and with all his aristocratic pride, was not above receiving a favour from the plebeian citizen. "This conduct on your part," he added, "is highly creditable to you both."

"And we are bound," said the Countess, who never thought anything which her husband said could be complete unless she appended a few words of her own thereto,—"we are bound to tender our best thanks for the kind hospitality we have received."

At this moment Musidora came forth from the recess, followed by the elder Landini. Mark threw a hasty look upon her, and observed that her large deep eyes shone with a strange unearthly lustre and that a more than ghastly pallor was upon her marble features. But she hastened—with a sort of excitement that was most unusual for her who did everything in so deliberate and leisurely a manner—to snatch up her scarf from the chair upon which she had thrown it when first entering the room; and for an instant she turned her back upon all present as she flung that scarf over her shoulders. Then, on turning round again, everything strange, wild, or unnatural had passed away from her countenance; and she looked the same coldly brilliant being, with the ice-like smile upon the lips, that she was wont to seem.

"Now we are ready for departure," said the Earl of Grantham; and he expressed to the elder Landini the same acknowledgments he had just before vouchsafed to his nephew.

The nobleman and the Countess passed out of the room, accompanied by Musidora, and followed by the two Landinis. They descended the stair-case—threaded the private office—and reached the counting-house, the uncle and nephew attending the nobleman and the two ladies to the very threshold of the street door. Then, as the departing visitors took their leave, Alessandro Landini threw upon Musidora a quick glance of deep meaning, which she returned with a look of equally mysterious significancy ere she turned away to take Lord Grantham's arm.

When the visitors were gone the elder Landini beckoned his nephew to follow him into the private room; and the moment they were alone together he said in a stern voice, "Mark, it is through your carelessness that those volumes were left in the recess of the drawing-room. This is the first time I have ever had to complain of want of precaution or prudence on your part: let it be the last!"

"My dear uncle," replied the nephew, with a tone and manner expressive of deep contrition, "I am indeed blameable in this. You know full well how fond I am of studying the chronicles of our family; and last evening I was reading these volumes after you had retired to rest. By some extraordinary oversight, for which I cannot account, I left them lying in the recess, instead of replacing them in their wonted security. It shall never happen again. But is any mischief done?"

"No—on the contrary, perhaps a warning has been given," responded the elder Landini. "But only reflect, my dear nephew," he continued in a milder tone than at first, "what a terrible inconvenience would have arisen if by any accident Lord Danvers had been shown up into the drawing-room and had found these volumes lying there. He would have seen that chronicle which records—I may say even sustains, keeps alive, and perpetuates, the idea of hereditary vengeance which *our* family cherishes against *his own*."

"I do indeed understand, my dear uncle, all the harm that might have been done by my carelessness," rejoined Mark,—"a carelessness indeed for which, I again assure you, I cannot possibly account. However, you will pardon me?"

"Yes—I forgive you," returned Alessandro Landini. "But now hasten up-stairs and secure those books——"

"Pardon me for delaying to fulfil your commands for one moment," said the nephew: "but might I ask which anecdote it was you wished to show to Musidora Sinclair?"

"What, Mark! is it possible that you did not see through my motive?" exclaimed the uncle. "Whither has fled all your wonted shrewdness and penetration?"

"Ah! I thought at the time," interrupted Mark, "that it was merely an excuse on your part to have an opportunity of exchanging a few words with Musidora!"

"Assuredly," rejoined the uncle. "What think you of her?"

"She is a splendid creature," replied Mark,—"the most beautiful woman I ever beheld in my life! But what means that singular iciness of look—that almost passionless air—that *chilling demeanour*——"

"How can I comprehend it any more than you?" asked the old man. "But hasten you, Mark, and secure those volumes in the iron safe: then come back to me, and I will tell you what passed during the two or three brief minutes that I was with Musidora in the recess."

The nephew accordingly hurried away to execute his uncle's order relative to the volumes: for he was in haste to rejoin the old man and to receive the promised explanations. Not but that he already pretty well divined what it was that his uncle had said to Musidora; but he was anxious to learn what had fallen from *her* lips in reply. For that during the brief colloquy which had taken place between them in the recess, she must have been profoundly moved, he felt assured, from that strange look which she wore for the first moment on issuing forth again.

CHAPTER XXVI.

PERCY'S RETURN TO THE VILLA.

Two days after the one of which we have been writing, and at about noon—which was in those times the approved hour for paying visits—Percy Rivers alighted from his horse at the gate of Grantham villa; and he was immediately conducted into an apartment where the Earl and Countess were seated. They received him with much apparent friendship,—assuring him that Musidora, who was walking in the garden, would be rejoiced to see him; but begging him to sit down for a few minutes ere he proceeded to join her, as they wished to confer with him on some matter of business. The young gentleman accordingly took a seat; and the Earl went on to address him in the following manner:—

"Cousin, when you were here three days back, I promised that whatever little interest I could command should be exercised in your favour. I have fulfilled this promise, and have secretly but earnestly moved several noble friends of mine to represent your case to the King. Nor, while so doing, was I unmindful, of my excellent relative, Musidora's father. For, to tell you the truth, Master Rivers," continued the Earl with a smile, "when a person makes up his mind to ask one favour at Court he may just as well ask two—because whenever the King is in a humour to grant a boon he is profuse in lavishing his benefits."

"Yes—that is exactly the character of his Highness," added Lady Grantham; "and therefore it was sound policy which prompted his lordship to think of Sir Lewis Sinclair while exerting his influence on your behalf."

"The result is," continued the nobleman, taking up the thread of the discourse just where his wife dropped it, "that I have succeeded in both respects. Here is a document conferring upon you, Master Percy Rivers, the style and title of Captain-Governor of the Isle of Wight, with all such powers, emoluments, and immunities as were enjoyed by your predecessor, Sir William Woodville. And here is another parchment, reinstating my worthy relative Sir Lewis Sinclair in the Rangership of the Forests of the Isle of Wight, with all such pensions and authorities as he was wont to enjoy."

While thus speaking, the Earl of Grantham produced the two documents, and spreading them open, displayed the royal sign manual and sovereign seal.

"My lord," exclaimed Percy Rivers, with all the generous enthusiasm of mingled delight and gratitude—not so much on his own account as on that of his uncle Sir Lewis Sinclair—"how can I sufficiently thank you for this kindness—this goodness—this transcending proof of friendship on your part? What can I do to testify all I feel in return for the noble interest you have thus taken in myself and Sir Lewis Sinclair?"

"What can you do?" repeated the Earl, apparently in a musing tone: then seeming suddenly to recollect himself, he exclaimed, "I will tell you what you can do! You must fulfil the condition upon which those appointments have been made:"—and he indicated the parchments.

"What is this condition, my lord?" inquired Percy Rivers.

"That you lose no time in setting off to the Isle of Wight," was the response. "Indeed, I was enjoined by the nobleman through whose most especial interest I procured these benefits, to signify to you that it was the royal pleasure you should take your departure within an hour after the documents were placed in your hands."

"Within an hour, my lord?" exclaimed Rivers, astonished at so peremptory a proceeding.

"Such are the instructions I received," rejoined the Earl. "His Highness the King is naturally anxious that his faithful lieges in the Isle of Wight should not be left in any needless suspense as to who their future governor is to be."

"But the order is not merely peremptory—it is even arbitrary!" cried Rivers, a certain vague and indistinct feeling of uneasiness arising in his mind, as if all was not right and straightforward in the proceeding, but that something hidden lay behind.

"Young man," said the Earl of Grantham, assuming a very serious look, "the King's orders must not be trifled with. And permit me to remind you that it is not altogether a handsome return you make to me in thus hesitating to fulfil the directions whereof I am only the mouthpiece."

"And you should reflect, Master Rivers," the Countess hastened to observe, "that if you prove disobedient to the royal mandates, you will only draw down the King's wrath upon the heads of those who have so kindly interested themselves in your behalf."

"I feel the full force of your ladyship's observation," said Percy Rivers, though with an evident air of perplexity; "and I beseech you, my lord, to acquit me of even the faintest shadow of ingratitude either towards yourself or those friends whose influence you have made available to serve my purposes. I will therefore obey the mandate, which accompanies these appointments, and I crave your forgiveness if my temporary hesitation proved offensive. But pray answer me one thing, my lord. Is it not expected that I should present myself at Court to thank his Highness for these bounties? Or, at all events, must I not convey that gratitude through the Lord High Chancellor?"

"All these ceremonials are needless, young cousin of mine," said the Earl of Grantham. "Have I not demonstrated towards you a friendship deserving your confidence? Why, then, seem to doubt me? What interest can I have in hurrying you away from the metropolis or its neighbourhood in so peremptory a manner? None, I can assure you."

"My lord," answered Rivers, "let us say no more upon the subject. You tell me that I must depart in an hour—and I will obey. Meanwhile, with your permission, I will ask my fair cousin Musidora what messages or letters she may have to send to her father."

"Do so," replied the Earl. "Musidora is in the garden: you can go to her."

Percy Rivers passed through the open casement on to the sloping lawn; and perceiving Musidora at the farther extremity of the spacious garden, he proceeded towards her. But during the three or four minutes that it took him thus to reach her, many uneasy and bewildering reflections swept through his mind. He did not like the apparent mystery which enveloped the granting of these appointments. The boon he had craved for himself seemed to have been bestowed so very, very easily—without delay—without even any interview between himself and the Lord Chancellor: for though he had called two or three times upon that high functionary, he had been unable to obtain an audience. And not only too was this boon so promptly conferred upon himself, but it was accompanied by another that was altogether unasked for and unexpected—namely, the restoration of Sir Lewis Sinclair to the Rangership. Perhaps it would not have struck Percy Rivers that there was any mystery at all attending those appointments and the singular despatch with which they were made, but he would have implicitly set them down to the zealous intervention of the Earl of Grantham acting through the medium of powerful friends at Court, had there not been something so suspicious in the peremptory order which accompanied the granting of these important favours. He could not help thinking that there was an anxiety to get rid of him from the neighbourhood and send him back as speedily as possible to the Isle of Wight. He could not forget the inhospitality of the Earl and Countess of Grantham when he called at the villa three days back: for on that occasion he had seen that he was not wanted. Then too, he bethought himself of that physician who had been sent to take up his abode altogether with Sir Lewis Sinclair;—and weaving all these things together, the uneasiness of suspicion was enhanced in his mind.

"I fear me," he thought in soliloquy, as he traversed the garden, to join Musidora, "that the Earl and the Countess have some sinister design in respect to my fair cousin. They wish to retain her here altogether with them; and they send a person—whom, by the bye, I am very far from liking—to keep her father company and prevent him from feeling lonely during her absence, so that there may be no excuse for his recalling her home. Lastly, it appears as if I am one too many in this neighbourhood, and it is sought to send me back to the Isle of Wight with the least possible delay. What can it all mean? I have too much confidence in the prudence, the virtue, and the pride of my cousin to think that she will suffer herself to be ensnared in any derogatory proceeding: but if I thought that serious dangers really menaced her, I would tear up the parchment containing my appointment—scatter the fragments to the winds—and in defiance of all the royal mandates in the world, remain concealed in this neighbourhood to keep watch over her. But Ah!" he ejaculated within himself, as a thought struck him,—"there is a better way of proceeding than by any rashness of this kind! Yes—I will indeed hasten back to the Isle of Wight; but it shall be to implore and beseech Sir Lewis Sinclair to recall his daughter home without delay!"

Cheered by this resolution—which seemed to the warm-hearted young man, the best, the safest, and the most effectual course to be adopted,—he was enabled to accost Musidora with a smiling countenance; and the moment she beheld him approach, she advanced to meet him with her usual frank cordiality. But it struck him that she did not appear altogether happy. Despite that passionless placidity which sat upon her countenance as well now as it had done for three years past, Percy Rivers fancied there was something that deepened into actual mournfulness in her look when he first met her gaze, and that it was with an effort she put aside as it were the unpleasant thoughts which seemed to be occupying her mind.

"You are come to bid me adieu, Percy?" she said, with that liquid evenness of tone which suited so well her ice-like air and the cold serenity of her manner.

"Ah! then you know," he at once exclaimed, "how peremptory is the order for my departure?"

"I know it," she responded, steadily meeting the gaze which he fixed with earnestness upon her.

"And think you not, my dear cousin," he continued, "that it is somewhat singular as well as harsh to accompany such an immense boon as my appointment in itself is, with a decree which on the other hand half neutralizes the graciousness of the favour itself?"

"I suppose that Lord Grantham has given you some reason for such a proceeding," said Musidora.

"None that is very feasible," rejoined Rivers. "He says that the King hurries my departure because it is desirable that the inhabitants of the Isle of Wight should hear as soon as possible who is to be their new governor. But surely their anxiety on this head cannot be deemed so very great as to compel my departure at a single hour's notice. What say you, my fair cousin?"

"I agree with you, Percy," she replied, "that the mandate does appear somewhat harsh. But surely you will lose all sense of annoyance on that head, in the proud feelings which you must naturally experience at finding yourself in so exalted a position;—for which I pray you to accept my sincerest and most heartfelt congratulations."

"That you are rejoiced on my account, Musidora," answered Rivers, "I am well convinced. Indeed, I have no doubt it was to your prompt and kind intervention the other day that the Earl took up my case with so much apparent zeal and warmth. I need not tell you, my dear cousin, how delighted I shall feel when presenting to your father that royal document which reinstates him in an office the loss of which has so much wounded his pride and impoverished his means."

"Then, have you not another inducement," asked our heroine, "to make you regret all the less this urgency for departure? Knowing your generous heart, I feel assured, Percy, that you long for the moment when you will be enabled to render my dear father so supremely happy?"

"And you, my fair cousin,—shall you not shortly feel desirous of embracing your dear father again? Do you not long to return to Sinclair House?"—and as he thus spoke, the young man again looked earnestly— we might even say penetratingly—upon Musidora's countenance.

"Knowing, Percy, as you do, how fondly devoted I am to my father," she responded, "you must be well aware that nothing would give me greater pleasure than to embrace him at this instant. I therefore think you must have some latent motive for addressing me in so serious a manner. If so, speak frankly: and tell me also why you gaze upon me with this strangeness of look which I cannot understand?"

"Tell me first, Musidora," answered Rivers, with a tremulous voice, "whether you are completely happy?"

"Nay," she exclaimed, with a slight accent of excitement in her voice, "now again you are evidently speaking from some motive that preoccupies you. Do not tell me what it is. I like not," she immediately added, almost coldly, and with the least shade of dignified hauteur in her manner, as she drew her fine form up, "to be questioned in this dark and mysterious strain."

"I know not how to explain myself, my dear cousin," Rivers hastened to observe: for he had in reality no real and tangible ground on which to question her:—the suspicion that had arisen in his mind was only a vague uneasiness, and had assumed no definite shape; and thus was it that he found himself perplexed how to reply—while, at the same time, he would not for worlds say anything to give his fair cousin offence.

"You know not how to explain yourself?" she observed, repeating his words: "and yet you evidently look at me and question me with a motive. Now, Percy Rivers, if you really wish information on any particular point wherein I can enlighten you, speak out frankly at once."

The young gentleman felt confused—almost distressed. What could he say? To declare that he entertained some wild and uncertain suspicion, without being able to define it, would amount almost to an insult. He therefore regretted that he had said as much as had already escaped his lips; and in his perplexity he gazed upon his beauteous cousin, who seemed calm, placid, and inscrutable as ever. If there were indeed any secret unhappiness in her mind, not a trace had it marked upon her magnificent countenance. All the glory of that loveliness was there, fresh and unimpaired, as he had been wont to see it—aye, and adore it! Her glorious eyes had lost not a single beam of their lustre: her head was borne erect as ever;—her form, so grand in its fullness, yet so symmetrical in its grace, showed not a sign of being bowed down with the weight or wasted with the emaciation of care. Was it, then, mere fancy on his part that at the moment when he first encountered her in the garden, there was a shade of sorrow upon her features, clouding the ice-like brilliancy of her smile?

"You ask me whether I am happy," she said. "Have you any reason to suspect that I am otherwise?"—and she fixed upon him the full power of her magnificent looks, as if to read into the depths of his soul.

"No—I have not the slightest reason to believe that you are unhappy," he hastened to reply, "beyond the transitory thought that at the instant we met ere now there was the slightest shade of despondency in your look: but heaven grant that I was deceived—as I now indeed am almost convinced that I was!"

"Almost? and why not *quite* convinced?" she asked, with an expanding smile, which parting the vermilion of her lips, displayed the teeth white as pearls of the East.

"Oh! believe me, Musidora, that I would ten thousand times rather persuade myself that you are happy," cried Percy Rivers, "than torture my heart with groundless imaginings to the contrary!"

"I thank you, my dear cousin," she responded, "for this additional proof of kind feeling on your part:"—then after a brief pause, during which Percy thought that she hesitated whether she should give utterance to what she afterwards went on to say, she added with a slight—but a very slight and barely perceptible tremulousness of tone—"Pray do not breathe aught in my father's ears which may lead him to fancy that I am unhappy. I am well aware that it was only through friendship towards me——"

"Friendship!" murmured Rivers with a sigh: but neither the word nor the long deep respiration were more than just barely audible.

"Through friendship for me," continued Musidora, not seeming to notice the slight zephyr-like interruption, "that you for an instant caught the illusion that I wore an air of sadness. But I had been walking here alone for the last hour, thinking of home; and you are aware, my dear cousin, that the looks may become serious although no positive care weighs upon the heart. Do not therefore, I repeat, on your return to the Isle of Wight, say aught to render my father uneasy respecting me. Will you promise me this? What! you hesitate?" she suddenly exclaimed, perceiving that he looked perplexed and even sorrowful: for be it remembered that Percy had already made up his mind to advise Sir Lewis Sinclair to recall his daughter home, and he feared that any pledge he might now give Musidora in answer to her question would act as a barrier to the carrying out of that resolve.

"I will not tell your father," he at length answered, "that you are unhappy. On the contrary, I will assure him that from your own lips I received the gratifying intelligence of your perfect happiness. May I say that much?"—and again he fixed his eyes upon Musidora.

"You may," she answered;—"always remembering," she added in a sort of qualifying tone, "that I am as happy as can be expected when thus separated from him who is nearest and dearest to me upon earth."

"Then why not return home?" asked Rivers somewhat abruptly.

"Is that a question to be put to one who is paying a visit to relatives that treat her kindly?" asked Musidora, again exhibiting that haughty bridling up which displayed the proud woman's spirit. "If your question meant a remonstrance against my temporary absence from home, would it not imply that no visit is ever to be paid by one relative to another? I might even feel offended by such a question, Percy," she continued; "but I will not take offence where I know that none was meant. I will even add that after the bounties which have been conferred upon yourself and my father, I am compelled by a sense of gratitude to remain where I am—at least for a time."

"Pardon me, my dear cousin, for my injudicious observation," exclaimed Percy. "In fact, I am afraid that I have spoken indiscreetly more than once during our present interview. But you will forgive me all this? And now tell me what messages or letters you have to transmit to Sir Lewis."

"I will give you a letter for my father," returned Musidora.

They then re-entered the villa, where refreshments were served up; and as the young man was about to depart, the Earl and Countess could now induce themselves to give him a somewhat more hospitable entertainment than on the preceding occasion of his visit. He did not however tarry long: for the urgency with which he had been desired to leave was uppermost in his mind.

Having secured the two royal documents about his person, as well as the letter which Musidora gave him for her father, Percy Rivers bade farewell to his cousin, the Earl, and the Countess; and mounting his horse, galloped away towards London, whence that very same afternoon he began his journey back to the Isle of Wight.

CHAPTER XXVII.

DR. BERTRAM.

Turn we now to the Isle of Wight. It was in the evening of the second day after the incidents just related, that Sir Lewis Sinclair and Dr. Bertram were sitting together in a little summer-house commanding a beautiful view of Brading Haven, the sea into which it flowed, and the line of the Hampshire coast that bordered the water in the distance. The weather was serenely beautiful: there was scarcely a breeze to arouse a ripple upon the ocean;—and the birds were pouring forth their gush of melody in the adjacent forest. The table in the summer-house was covered with flasks of wine, drinking-cups, and dishes of fruit; and while the worthy knight and his companion beguiled the time with such discourse as was most to their taste, they did not forget to do ample justice to the dessert—especially the fluid portion of it.

"Yes, my excellent friend," observed Sir Lewis, pursuing the theme of conversation which had already been progressing for an hour past, "you are evidently a man of the world; and I reckon it to be one of the most fortunate days of my life when the King sent you as my companion——"

"Hush, my dear Sir Lewis!" said the doctor: "you know the old proverb that walls have ears; and if that be true, why should not green bushes likewise possess auricular faculties? I am always telling you never to mention the name of a certain personage—I mean his Highness," added Bertram, lowering his voice to a cautious whisper.

"Well, I do forget myself sometimes," remarked Sir Lewis,—"especially at the eighth or ninth cup of wine: but you must admit, my dear friend, that considering all things, I have kept the secrets with marvellous closeness?"

"You have, Sir Lewis," rejoined the doctor: "and pray continue to exercise the same carefulness. It would be a pity indeed to spoil all by any want of caution. Only think, my dear friend," he continued, again speaking in a whisper, "when once a certain lady has acquired rank by marrying a certain person, we shall be as happy as the day is long."

"Ay," responded Sir Lewis; "and we will drink their healths from morning till night."

"That I think we do pretty well already," said Dr. Bertram. "By my faith! you are mighty fond of the wine-stoup, Sir Lewis."

"Egad! and I can return the compliment without the least compromise of my veracity," exclaimed the knight, laughing.

"You see, most worthy friend," answered Bertram, "I was always of a very studious habit, and remarkably steady: therefore, being much addicted to book-learning and to the study of the medical art—in which, forsooth, I excel rarely—I have been obliged to sustain my over-taxed energies with an occasional dose of nature's choicest beverage. And I can assure you that I only drink wine medicinally," added the doctor very gravely.

"What! and ale, hollands, lambswool, wassail, and other good things, also medicinally?" inquired Sir Lewis.

"All medicinally, I can assure you," was the doctor's response, delivered with a solemn shake of the head: "and as your physician, I allow you to partake of these same good things on the same medicinal principle."

"Then are you assuredly the kindest and best physician on the face of the earth," exclaimed Sir Lewis. "But it seems to me," he added in a jocular tone, "that we both take a great deal of this kind of medicine:"—and he raised the brimming goblet which he had just filled.

"When I think you are taking too much, Sir Lewis," replied Bertram, still with an air of gravity, "I shall assuredly exercise the physician's authority and stop you."

"Ah, well! I am not much afraid that the patient and the doctor will fall out," cried Sir Lewis, laughing gleefully. "We seem to be upon an excellent understanding with each other. But tell me—since you have been one of the King's physicians—does his Grace indulge pretty deeply in his potations?"

"Between you and me," answered Bertram, with a knowing wink, "the King likes his glass as well as either of us. He and I have sometimes locked ourselves in his private cabinet and have tossed off glass for glass, till the whole room turned round, and while I saw two Kings he saw two Dr. Bertrams."

"Ha! ha!" laughed Sir Lewis very heartily: then as his mirth subsided, he observed in a grave tone, "But my 'Dora will not much like the King to give way to these drinking bouts."

"Oh!" replied Bertram, "his Grace will abandon all that kind of thing for the young lady's sake. I have not the slightest doubt of that! No one knows King Harry better than I do. In fact," added the doctor in a confidential whisper, "he and I are thick as two——two——"

"Thieves," observed Sir Lewis, by way of helping his friend to a completion of his sentence, and without the slightest attempt at any sinister meaning.

"Nay, nay, that is rather too bad of you, Sir Lewis!" exclaimed Bertram, laughing. "But, as I was saying, the King and I are so very intimate that I can do anything with him. He calls me 'honest Bertram'—thus you perceive," added the doctor pompously, "stamping my high character with his royal approval."

"Well," remarked Sir Lewis, "wherever the Sovereign's seal is set, the article must be genuine; and therefore you, my dear friend, are a genuine good fellow, as you assuredly are a right down worthy boon-companion. But do you, when with the King, recommend him to drink wine on medicinal principles?"

"Certainly I do," responded Bertram. "As I have before told you on divers occasions, I have invented a new system of medicine, the basis of which consists of good living. Don't let me be told that plenty of roast beef, wine, and ale will make invalids! I know better. To the thin and emaciated, I say, 'Eat plentifully, that ye may get fat:' and to the stout and portly I say, 'Eat plentifully, lest ye get thin, and in low condition.' In the same way, to those who are desponding and melancholy I say, 'Drink copiously, in order to raise your spirits;' and to those who are happy and cheerful I say, 'Drink copiously, lest ye experience reaction, and fall into lowness of spirits.' Now I defy any one to prove the fallacy of this system of mine. I maintain that it is consistent with common sense:"—and here Dr. Bertram looked so exceedingly wise that Sir Lewis Sinclair was for a moment confounded by the knock-me-down kind of argument to which he had been listening.

"Yes—I must admit," said the worthy knight, "that your system, doctor, is most reasonable, as it is certainly the most agreeable."

"To be sure!" exclaimed Bertram. "But do you want a proof? your own sensations must have furnished it over and over again. For instance, the other night—be it spoken with due respect—you took so much of the medicine, Sir Lewis, that it overpowered you, and you tumbled under the table——"

"And you, out of kindness, worthy doctor," responded the knight, with a sly look, "lay down beside me, to keep me company, as you assured me the next morning."

"As a matter of course," rejoined Bertram. "Was I not sent hither to minister unto you and make myself agreeable in all things? Therefore, as long as you can sit up at the table, I am bound to sit with you: but if you prefer rolling underneath it, I am equally bound to roll there by your side. But let us continue with the illustration of my medical system. On the morning after that little incident whereof we have been speaking, you awoke with something of a headache——"

"Something of a headache!" ejaculated Sir Lewis: "it was as if ten thousand invisible demon blacksmiths were mistaking my head for an anvil and beating on it with their hammers."

"Just so!" observed the doctor. "And now suppose that I had given you medicine—would it not have reduced your system in a way to render you incapable of bearing up against that pain? And if I had offered you a glass of water, it would have turned your stomach sick. I therefore made you swallow a brimming goblet of good canary wine——"

"Aye—a hair of the tail of the dog that bit me over night," observed Sir Lewis.

"And was not the remedy infallible?" asked the doctor: "and after three or four turns in the orchard, did you not do ample justice to cold sirloin, cakes, and ale, by way of breakfast?"

"In good faith did I," responded the worthy knight: then surveying his companion with great seriousness and admiration, he said, "Ah, doctor! you are a prodigy of learning, and I am well convinced that your system is decidedly the best."

"Whenever I have been consulted by elderly ladies, for instance," continued Bertram, "on the score of spasms in the stomach, cold, rheumatism, or ague, I have invariably prescribed frequent drops of strong waters: and it is astonishing," he added gravely, "what a favourite I became with all the antiquated dames in or about London. But Ah! I hear the sounds of a horse's feet approaching——"

"It is Percy!" ejaculated Sir Lewis, as he beheld his nephew gallop round to the gate of the enclosure.

"Remember," said Bertram, clutching the knight by the arm, and speaking in a serious, almost grave tone,—"remember that you do not commit yourself in any way in the presence of this young man: for if he were ten thousand nephews instead of one, he is not to know what is going on in a certain quarter."

"Trust me, my dear friend," answered Sir Lewis, "I am not such a fool as to spoil everything by any act of indiscretion. Rest assured of that! But now let us go forward and meet him."

The groom belonging to the knight's establishment had already hastened forth from the mansion to receive Percy's horse; and the young gentleman, having dismounted and confided the steed to the domestic, sped toward his uncle and the doctor. To the latter he bowed with marked coldness; for Bertram was very far from being a favourite with Percy Rivers: but there was no love lost, for he in his heart disliked the young man most cordially.

"Well, what news do you bring us, nephew?' inquired Sir Lewis, shaking Percy warmly by the hand.

"Good news, I hope, in some respects," answered Rivers.

"In some respects!" echoed the knight. "Are there, then, any exceptions in the case? But how is Musidora? have you brought a letter from her? and how have you fared in your application to the Chancellor? Has his Right Reverend Lordship given you any hope of future employment? and who is to be the new Governor of the Island?"

"Gently, my dear uncle," responded Rivers, with a half smile at this torrent of questions; "and I will explain everything in due course. First of all, let me assure you that Musidora is well—and, as she declares, happy."

"That's a good beginning," observed the knight. "Come, let us welcome the intelligence with a cup of wine. I have no doubt that you are athirst, nephew?"

"Not at all, my dear uncle," was the response; but as the old man drew him towards the summer-house, he was obliged to accompany him thither, Dr. Bertram taking very good care to be close at the other side of Sir Lewis.

"And now go on with your intelligence," said the knight when he and the doctor had paid their renewed respects to the wine-flask.

"I have already assured you that my fair cousin is well, and, as she says, happy," continued Percy Rivers. "Next, I must deliver you this letter from her."

"I will read it presently," said the knight, as he received the missive and placed it in the breast of his doublet. "What next?"

"The new Governor of the Island is duly appointed," proceeded Percy; "and your old situation of the Rangership, which for the last few years has remained in abeyance, is again filled up."

"Indeed!" ejaculated Sir Lewis. "Who——"

"The Governor, my dear uncle," answered Percy, with a smile, "has the pleasure of addressing the Ranger."

"Eh, what?" cried Sir Lewis, starting up from his seat with an access of almost childish joy.

"Take a cup of wine to drink a welcome to these appointments!" Dr. Bertram hastened to exclaim: for he was fearful that Sir Lewis might let out something to show that this restoration to his former office was not altogether unexpected on his part.

"Dr. Bertram," said Percy Rivers, turning upon the physician a look that was coldly severe, "if you are a medical man who practises his profession honestly, you will not encourage my uncle to address himself too often to these pernicious stimulants."

"Governor Rivers," said Dr. Bertram fiercely, "attend, I pray you, to your own professional duties, and leave me to mine."

"Nay, let there be no angry words," interposed Sir Lewis Sinclair. "Besides, my dear nephew, when we have got more leisure Dr. Bertram shall explain to you his system, according to which I must drink while cheerful, as you see me now, in order to prevent my spirits from experiencing——a——what is it, doctor?——a reaction! Oh, I remember—that's the term!—yes, a reaction."

"What jargon is this that you have been putting into my uncle's head?" demanded Rivers, now fixing a stern look upon the doctor.

"Let me assure you," replied Bertram, nothing discomfited nor abashed, "that this is not the place for you to begin playing off your Governor's airs; nor shall you with impunity level an insult at Dr. Bertram, physician, licentiate, surgeon, apothecary, and divers other qualifications."

Rivers measured for a moment with his eye the tall ungainly form of Dr. Bertram, as if half inclined to knock him down: but the next instant, thinking it beneath him to provoke a quarrel with such a being, he turned his looks contemptuously away; and producing a parchment from his doublet, tendered it to his uncle, saying, with a sudden brightening up of his handsome countenance, "Receive from my hands the sovereign decree which restores you to the Rangership of the forests and woodlands of the Isle of Wight."

Sir Lewis took the parchment and waved it joyously over his head—skipping and dancing with delight at the same time: then exhausted by this display of his exuberant feelings, he sank down upon the seat, saying, "Now, my dear doctor, a little of the medicine."

Bertram accordingly filled a goblet to the rim and handed it to Sir Lewis,—Percy Rivers looking on in silence, but with a countenance that changed rapidly to an expression of compassionating mournfulness: for he not only saw that his uncle was getting more and more in the power of Bertram, but that the latter evidently wielded his influence to encourage him in his wine-bibbing propensities.

"Here," said the doctor, raising his own goblet, which he had likewise taken good care to fill, "is a health to you, Sir Lewis, in your re-appointment to the Rangership: and if I thought that my advances towards a more friendly footing would be well received on your part, Master Rivers, I would equally felicitate you on your good fortune in being raised to the high office which you now occupy."

The young man merely bowed with the most contemptuous coldness, which Bertram did not however choose to observe, but tossed off his wine with the air of one who was as devotedly attached as Sir Lewis himself to the generous fluid.

"But tell us," exclaimed the knight after a pause, "how all this came about?"—for he began to think it probable that his nephew had been let into the secret of Musidora's intended marriage with the King.

"We are indebted, uncle," responded the young Governor, "to the interest which the Earl of Grantham exerted on our behalf by means of some influential friends of his own. I myself did nothing towards the realization of these results, beyond explaining my own position to your daughter; and she it was who, with characteristic generosity and readiness, urged Lord Grantham to use his influence in the matter."

"But did you see the King?" asked the old knight.

"I did not," replied Rivers. "I saw no one at all connected with the Court; and perhaps I should not have returned so speedily, had it not been for a peremptory order to that effect, which was given through Lord Grantham when he placed the documents in my hands the day before yesterday. But will you step aside with me, Sir Lewis, for a few minutes? I wish to hold some private converse with you."

"We are all friends here," Dr. Bertram hastened to observe, as he nudged the old knight.

"Yes, yes," Sir Lewis accordingly exclaimed, in obedience to the private hint thus conveyed by the doctor's elbows. "You can speak out, Percy; I have no secrets from my friend here."

"But my dear uncle," urged the young gentleman, in a tone of remonstrance, "as you are unaware of the subject on which I desire to speak, you cannot possibly undertake to say that it is one which may be discussed in the presence of an individual whom, whatever confidence *you* may choose to place in him, I must decline to regard otherwise than as a stranger."

"Governor Rivers," said Dr. Bertram, in a reproving tone, "it ill becomes you, at your age, to dictate to your uncle."

"No, no, Percy, I must not be dictated to," said the knight. "Remember that the Rangership is independent of the Governor: the authorities are co-equal, yet distinct——"

"Good heavens, my dear uncle!" exclaimed the young man; "I am not addressing you in my official capacity, but as your own nephew; and I think that I have never given you cause to believe that I would bear myself otherwise than respectfully and deferentially towards you. Besides," he added, "if you are so tenacious of your own independence, uncle, and will not suffer dictation, why permit this person"—and he flung a glance of haughty contempt upon the doctor—"to rule you as with a rod of iron?"

"This is downright insolence!" exclaimed Bertram, his sinister-looking countenance becoming purple with indignation.

"My dear uncle," continued Rivers, not deigning to take any farther notice of the doctor, "I conjure you to grant me five minutes' conversation in private."

"But after all that has just taken place," observed Sir Lewis, in obedience to another nudge which he received from the doctor, "it would be a veritable insult to my friend here to yield to your request. Therefore I must again desire you to speak out."

Percy Rivers was both angry and perplexed. He saw with the deepest pain how completely Sir Lewis was under the thumb of Dr. Bertram, and that it would be scarcely possible to carry his point of obtaining an opportunity for a private discourse with his relative. As for uttering in the presence of Bertram what he was desirous of saying to Sir Lewis, he was resolved that he would *not*: for he felt more assured than ever that the doctor was a mere creature of Lord Grantham, to whom everything would be reported by letter. Then also it struck him that even if he did succeed in drawing Sir Lewis apart and privately recommending him to recall Musidora home, the moment he was gone all that he might have said to the knight would be wormed out by Bertram, and thus be equally sure to reach the knowledge of Lord Grantham in due course.

All these reflections occupied but a moment as they traversed the brain of Percy Rivers; and he saw clearly enough that nothing was to be done on the present occasion, but that he must take some little leisure to reflect what course it was best to adopt in order to carry out his design.

"Well, my dear uncle," he accordingly said, "I must take my leave of you now, trusting to a future opportunity to be able to converse with you on family matters."

"But you will remain to supper?" cried Sir Lewis. "See! it is just upon sunset—and hither indeed comes the servant to announce that the repast is served. Besides, we must drink a flask in commemoration of these appointments."

"You will excuse me this evening," said Percy. "I must return to Carisbrook without delay, and indite a proclamation to issue to the inhabitants of the island to-morrow."

"Aye—and by my faith!" cried Sir Lewis, drawing himself up with an air of infinite importance, "I also shall issue my proclamation, warning all knaves and vagabonds to beware how they kill deer or otherwise trespass upon the royal lands whereof the charge is entrusted unto me; and I will make known that they shall be punished according to law and statute."

"Do as you like, uncle," said Rivers, surveying the old man with a melancholy air: for it certainly struck him that the effects of dissipation mingling with sudden joy, were tending to make him somewhat childish: "do as you like, but I scarcely think such a proclamation on your part is necessary."

"Oh! it cannot be dispensed with," exclaimed Sir Lewis pompously. "But if you are determined to leave us so abruptly this evening, my dear nephew, you must promise to come again soon; if not, I shall ride across to Carisbrook and ferret you out. Egad! it will be with a dashing train once more that I shall gallop over the island. I shall have my hunters and my hounds again—my grooms and my pages; and you, doctor," he added, turning towards Bertram, "will always sit on my right hand at the board, and ride in the same place when I make my excursions."

Percy Rivers now took his leave of the old knight, but deigned not to bestow even so much as a look upon the physician, who, the moment the young man had departed, observed to Sir Lewis, "My good friend, that nephew of yours, all Governor though he be, is one of the most unmannerly curs in Christendom. I do not like him; and the less he is encouraged at the house the better."

"Well, well," returned the knight, "we shall see; but I am sorry that such ill-will reigns between you."

He and his boon-companion then entered the mansion, where they sat down to supper; and after the meal they drank success to the Rangership so often that when they awoke in the morning and found themselves in bed, each in his respective chamber, they had not the slightest idea of how they got thither.

CHAPTER XXVIII.

THE LAST DAY OF THE COURTSHIP.

DURING the six weeks which now elapsed from the date of the visit of Musidora and her noble relatives to the Landinis' house in Lombard Street, until the day when her final decision was to be given in respect to the King's suit, there was much in the conduct of the young lady to keep the Earl and Countess in some suspense as to what her ultimate decision might be. For notwithstanding the wonted iciness of her look, the cold placidity of her manner, and the extraordinary control which she evidently possessed over her feelings, there were intervals when she exhibited a certain restlessness and uneasiness that it was impossible for her altogether to conceal.

Sometimes, when the King was at the villa, and they were all seated at the supper-table, she would fix her eyes upon him with so strange, wild, and searching a look that it appeared as if she entertained some vague but torturing suspicion concerning him, and that she endeavoured to satisfy herself by penetrating into the depths of her soul. At other times she would exhibit such a flow of spirits as seemed perfectly incompatible with her frozen nature, and which had an appearance of being artificially forced in the desperate attempt to veil feelings of bitterness that were rankling in her heart. Or again, she would sink into the profoundest despondency, leaning back in her chair, with her arms lying listlessly upon her lap, her white hands lightly clasped, her head bent forward, and the long ebon lashes of her eyes resting upon the marble of her cheeks. Then, if in this mood she were spoken to, she would give no response: it was evident that she heard not the remarks addressed to her, and that her thoughts were far away from the immediate topic of the discourse carried on in her presence. At times she would start from this desponding mood as if suddenly awakening from slumber; and then, after sweeping her quick glance around, as if to ascertain where she was and who were present, she would become collected, calm—or rather coldly passive and inscrutable—as ever!

Sometimes she would endeavour to treat the King with that grateful courtesy and confiding familiarity which a damsel in her position might well be expected to demonstrate towards a Sovereign who was about to make her his wife: but at other times she behaved towards him with a reserve so frigid—a coldness so distant—that both the Earl and Countess trembled lest the King should take offence, abruptly break off everything, and depart from the villa, to return no more! But if ever, mention being

made of her father or Percy Rivers, she was thus reminded of the bounties which King Henry had conferred upon her parent and her cousin, she
would at once assume such a sweetness of manner as, all well-bred lady
though she were, she was not usually wont to display; and even in this was
it evident enough that she was forcing herself to perform a part which a
sense of gratitude alone prompted her to enact.

The King, strange to say, did not appear to notice her changes of
mood. When she was smiling, and courteous, and amiable, then was he
affectionate, winning, and endearing; when she was cold, reserved, and
distant, he continued to discourse gaily with the Earl and Countess;—and
when she sat desponding or wrapped up in reverie, he addressed her not,
but waited until her mood was changed again, and then conversed with
her in as easy and tender a strain as if he had not for an instant noticed
that there had been any passing peculiarity in her conduct. Nor, when
alone with the Earl and Countess, did he ever allude more than in a very
transient and casual manner to these strange humours on her part: at all
events he never expressed chagrin; but the nearer the time approached
for her to give her final decision, the more confident did he appear, when
conversing with her two noble relatives, that this decision would be in his
favour.

The Earl and Countess themselves occasionally questioned Musidora
relative to these phases in her conduct; but she invariably met their queries
with such iciness of manner, such cold brief answers, and such strange,
unfathomable looks, that they knew not what to think. Although, as day
after day passed, the King seemed thus indifferent or else most unaccountably blind to the marked character of her moods, the old courtier and his
intriguing wife certainly fancied that he was putting an extraordinary rein
upon his patience, and that it must reach a point at which he could endure no more; but as each successive occasion proved their misgivings to
be unfounded, they said to each other that never was man so completely
infatuated with a woman as Henry VIII must be with Musidora. For that
he—the proud, haughty, imperious monarch, whose temper was far from
the most amiable—should thus spontaneously lay aside all his lion qualities and become passive, enduring, and tame as a lamb in the presence
of a girl of comparatively obscure birth, was something well calculated
to excite the wonderment of the Earl and Countess of Grantham. Much
did they tremble however at each visit from the royal lover, lest Musidora
should push too far and arouse him all at once from this kind of stupor
of patience and endurance;—and infinite was the relief to their feelings
when, on taking his departure each night, he shook hands with them as
cordially as ever and promised to return on the following evening. Thus

each day brought its misgivings and its apprehensions to the Earl and Countess; and when the ordeal was over, it as regularly left its renewal of confidence behind.

Musidora passed much of her time in her chamber; and each successive day she rambled less and less in the gardens and pleasure-grounds. That her soul was the seat of strange but powerful feelings, was evidently beyond all doubt: for strange and powerful indeed must they have been when thus able to ruffle the surface of that aspect which had remained frozen as it were for more than three long years! Annetta, her maid, could not help observing these evidences of inward agitation on the part of her mistress; and occasionally she hazarded a few words in the hope of being permitted to learn the source of the young lady's grief (if grief it were) or at least to proffer consolation. But though Musidora invariably answered with kindness,—for she liked Annetta, and therefore spoke not in the same brief icy manner as when responding to the questions of her two relatives,—yet did she never encourage the conversation with her maid upon that topic, but at once turned it into some other channel, or else sought an excuse for dismissing her for the time being from her chamber.

But when Musidora was alone, how looked she? what thought she? how passed she her time? did she read? did she work at her embroidery? or did she sit plunged for long hours in deep desponding reverie? We cannot say. As yet it is not permitted even for our hand to raise the veil from the sanctuary of Musidora's heart—no, nor watch her in her solitude. Certain however was it that the glories of her beauty were not dimmed by any shadow that might rest upon her soul: certain was it that if a cloud enveloped her heart, its murkiness marred not the lustre of her splendid eyes—but on the contrary, in the depths of those unfathomable orbs the weird and mystic light was shining there with greater brilliancy if possible than ever!

The reader will naturally ask whether it were that Musidora did not love the King and felt that if she accepted his hand she was sacrificing herself? But this hypothesis could scarcely be the correct one; because from the very first she had given her noble relatives no hope that she should be enabled to tutor herself to love the monarch, while at the same time she had more than hinted at the certainty of her espousing him. Besides, we have seen that she did feel grateful for the bounties he had conferred upon her father and her cousin, as well as for his unchanging tenderness and assiduities towards herself. Therefore, if only with this sentiment of gratitude, and with none of a deeper and more affectionate character, she might have felt herself justified in bestowing her hand upon him: because she assuredly did not hate him, and the alliance was too splendid, too brilliant, and too advantageous in most respects not to tempt any young lady, even though with a mind so strong and with notions so delicate as Musidora's.

Again, the reader may ask whether it were that, through the instigation of Percy Rivers, her father had written to recall her home, or had in any way changed his mind so as to have become opposed to her marriage with the King? But on this point we can speak positively. The young Governor of the Isle of Wight had indeed managed, during a hunting party, to say a few words alone to Sir Lewis Sinclair, earnestly recommending the knight to send for Musidora. But, as he had foreseen, Sir Lewis subsequently communicated to Dr. Bertram everything that had thus passed between himself and his nephew; and the doctor experienced not the slightest difficulty in preventing Sir Lewis from following Percy's advice, because the old man himself was too ambitious to see his daughter a Queen to take any step to thwart the project. Besides, he naturally fancied that Percy Rivers was merely suspicious of some latent evil because he was not initiated in all that was passing; and therefore though he gave his nephew credit for the best possible intentions, he was by no means inclined to follow his counsel. Consequently, Musidora had received no communication from her father to excite her feelings in any way: on the contrary, the answer he had sent to her letter of affection and love which Percy Rivers had delivered to him, was filled with all the congratulations which the mingled selfishness and paternal tenderness of the old man were calculated to suggest.

But we will not tarry longer upon any of the incidents that marked the lapse of that period of courtship which Musidora had stipulated for. Let us suppose the two months ended—the last day arrived. The King was to come in the evening as usual: but on this occasion to receive from Musidora's lips the decision which she had adopted. She descended from her chamber at the usual breakfast-hour in the morning of that day; and the instant she entered the room where the Earl and Countess were already seated, they threw upon her a simultaneous look of the most anxious inquiry. She was calm, serene, and brilliantly smiling, as during the first days of her residence at the villa. She seemed to have resumed all that outward tranquillity which, though so glacial, was nevertheless so animated, and which to the eye of the observer bespoke naught save a corresponding serenity within. She said little during the repast; but what she did say was free from any indication of heartfelt bitterness. Breakfast being over, she accepted with even an amiable cheerfulness a proposition made by the Countess to walk in the garden; and there they rambled for two or three hours without the slightest appearance of ruffle or ripple upon the frozen surface of Musidora's resplendent beauty.

The dinner-hour passed in the same manner; and afterwards she re-tired to her chamber. Then as evening approached, the Earl and Countess felt their anxiety and nervousness painfully increasing as to what might be the issue of the coming crisis. For they could not conceal from themselves that there was something unnatural in Musidora's conduct—to have been for six weeks subject to such strange phases of look, manner, and deport-ment, and now on the last day to be so icily calm, so immoveably tran-quil!

The hour for the King's appearance arrived. He came—and, as usual, was at once shown into the splendid saloon where it was customary to receive him previous to seeking the supper-apartment. Confidence was in his looks, and both the Earl and the Countess caught therefrom a kindred inspiration. Of their own accord, without waiting to be asked, they told him of Musidora's altered aspect and how her demeanour was restored to exactly what it was wont to be during the first few weeks of her sojourn at the villa. Then did a smile of triumph appear upon the countenance of the King; and he said in a voice that was proudly exultant, like that of a General who proclaims his victory over a formidable enemy, "For some weeks past I have experienced but very little doubt as to the result of my courtship. Musidora is mine!" Almost immediately afterwards the young lady herself entered the room. She was arrayed in a dress of dark velvet, which threw out the alabaster purity of her complexion with dazzling effect; and her appearance was rendered the more overpowering by the splendid diamonds—the King's gift—wherewith she had decked herself. Upon the raven glory of her hair did they gleam: around the marble col-umn of her neck, upon the snowy stainlessness of her bosom, and circling the statue-like modelling of her white arms bare to the shoulder, shone the brilliant gems, glittering like icicles upon a being who herself was of icy aspect, so that she appeared the Queen of Winter!

With the serenity of a frozen lake shining in the sunlight of the pure frosty air when the heaven is cloudless all above, Musidora advanced into the room. Nothing was to be gathered from her inscrutable countenance: naught was revealed in the shining depths of her weird-like haunting eyes. At the same time there was nothing to discourage the King, nor to dis-may her noble relatives. The cold brilliancy of the half-vanishing smile was upon her classic lips; and she looked just as she was wont to be until within the last six weeks of the courtship.

"Charming and well-beloved lady," said the King, advancing to meet her with the graceful ease of a royal cavalier, mingled with the respectful and admiring tenderness of a suitor,—"what answer am I to receive from your lips? My happiness hangs upon a single word! Is it *yes*? or is it *no*?"

"Yes!" replied Musidora: but it was in a voice of ice that she spoke; and for an instant—but only for an instant—a shudder swept through her entire frame: then becoming her own cold serene self once more, she extended her alabaster hand to the King.

And cold as alabaster too was it to his touch!

CHAPTER XXIX.

THE CHAPEL.

It was in the first week of August—exactly three months after the date of Musidora's arrival at Grantham Villa—that she thus gave an affirmative answer to the suit of King Henry VIII: and a week later—namely, on the 13th of August, 1516—the scene which we are about to record took place.

Embowered in the midst of a wood, at a distance of three miles from Greenwich, was a small monastery, inhabited only by twelve monks, who led a life of the most ascetic character. Their apparel, as coarse as sack-cloth, was fastened by a rude cord round their waists. They usually went barefooted; but, if going to any distance on their wonted errands of benevolence and piety, they wore sandals composed of flat pieces of wood fastened on by rough leathern thongs. According to the regulations of their establishment, the number of its inmates could never exceed twelve, which number was emblematic of that of the Apostles: and whenever one died, his place was immediately filled up from the order of Mendicant Friars. The little sanctuary was presided over by one of the twelve, who bore the denomination of "Superior;" and his authority was implicitly obeyed by his brethren.

The monastery itself had a castellated appearance, its dark massive walls being perforated with mere loop-holes, to serve as windows, and the huge doors being set in a deep gothic arch. The chapel belonging to the religious establishment, was of similar architecture, and had a large heavy-looking tower frowning above the circumjacent trees. A space to the extent of about two acres was cleared away in the rear of the monastery, to afford room for a cemetery to receive the remains of those who perished within the walls, and also for a garden to yield the fruit and vegetables which constituted, together with coarse barley bread, the principal fare of the holy fathers.

That religious establishment had existed for three centuries,—maintaining with traditionary reverence and exactitude all the pristine simplicity with regard to internal discipline that was originally prescribed by its founder. It therefore enjoyed the veneration and respect of all who dwelt in the surrounding districts; and every Sunday the chapel was crowded with a humble but pious congregation. There was not a peasant's hut nor a rural dwelling within a dozen miles of the Monastery of Twelve—as it was called—that had not been at some time or another indebted to the holy fathers for visits of charity and religious consolation. Many wealthy persons were wont to bestow donations upon the monastery, to be dispensed in alms at the discretion of the inmates; and thus, though they themselves practised the sternest self-denial and clung with devotedness to the principle of poverty—thus emulating in their own lives the example of the Apostles—they nevertheless were enabled to relieve the distresses of many a poor family and bestow pecuniary succour upon many a penniless wayfarer. No wonder was it, therefore, if these good monks enjoyed so excellent a repute and were the objects of so much veneration—a character and a respect which by the purity of their own lives they full well deserved.

It was ten o'clock at night, on the 13th of August, 1516, as above recorded, that the tapers were lighted upon the altar-piece of the chapel, which was spacious and lofty considering the insignificant size of the monastery to which it belonged. Only upon the altar were the candles lighted; and thus but a small portion of the sacred edifice was shown by their feeble, flickering, uncertain gleam. The roof appeared to hang in dense blackness above: the pillars separating the aisles from the nave, shot up likewise into darkness; while the whole of that extremity of the church which was farthest from the altar was involved in the deepest obscurity. There were some large pictures suspended to the walls, the gifts of pious persons at different times: but these looked like mere squares of sable canvass set in huge oaken frames; for it was impossible to discern their subjects in that dim and oscillating light. At the altar one monk alone was kneeling; and this was the Superior—an old man, whose name was Father Paul.

The kneeling priest had on a simple white stole and a plain alb, over his rough sackcloth garments. He was entirely bald on the crown and above the forehead; but from the temples a fringe of thin silvery locks passed round the back of his head, growing longer towards the nape of the neck. His countenance was filled with benevolence and piety; and it was easy to read in his mild blue eyes the unsophisticated sincerity of his soul, as well as the heartfelt depth of the silent devotions in which he was now engaged. As the light from the altar fell upon his up-raised countenance, and brought out his figure with a Rembrandt-like relief from the sphere of obscurity upon the verge of which he touched, and which spread into deepening darkness all behind him, he looked like some venerable patriarch of the ancient time come back again in the spirit to this earth which his example had illuminated in by-gone centuries, and the concerns of which occupied his care even in the unknown world to which he had long since departed. Such, we say, was the impression which his appearance—in his simple apparel, with his venerable looks, and in the uncertain light shed from that altar—might have made upon an observer, had any been nigh: but no patriarchal spirit was it—but the worthy Superior himself, Father Paul, in flesh and blood, who on this night at that hour was praying before the shrine of his adoration.

A solemn silence filled the church—a like stillness prevailed without, around the monastery and in the depths of the circumjacent wood. Not a breeze ruffled the foliage of the trees—not a breath of air whispered through the chapel. The day had been intensely hot—and when the sun went down, he left all his sultriness behind. But dark masses of clouds were piling themselves up against the sky; and everything portended a storm. It was ten o'clock, we say—and Father Paul knelt before the altar in his silent devotions: for he was praying in the heart and not with the lips. Presently his ear caught the sounds of horses' feet approaching the gates of the church; and the old man arose and listened. Certain that he had not mistaken those sounds, and likewise assured by a knocking which he now heard at the door, that those whom he awaited had come, he sped down the nave, or body of the chapel, as fast as his feeble limbs would allow him to proceed; and drawing back the huge bolt which kept the gates fast, unfolded one of the wings of the massive portals. The night was now dark as pitch without, and all that extremity of the church was involved in impervious gloom: but the feeble lights glimmering on the altar at the other extremity, served as a guide to the party now entering. This party consisted of four persons; and, followed by the venerable Superior,—who tarried a moment behind, after he had admitted them, in order to close the door and draw the bolt again,—they proceeded slowly through the obscurity of the place towards the altar.

Upon the arm of King Henry leant Musidora: behind them walked the Earl and Countess of Grantham. There were no bridemaids—no brilliant courtiers—no princely train—no host of friends assembled to felicitate the pair whose hands were now to be united. Yet this was a bridal-party! Were the actors in the scene clad in wedding dresses? No—all four were attired in riding-suits, which gave them the air of being dressed in their plainest garments. The King wore boots reaching nearly up to his knees, and was enveloped in an ample cloak. The Earl of Grantham was dressed in a similar manner: Musidora and the Countess wore riding-habits of dark velvet, and in fashion much resembling those of the present day.

But how looked Musidora? Upon her marble features there was a certain trouble—a perceptible evidence of inward uneasiness—which she nevertheless strove to subdue. Even her very lips were pale—those lips that were wont to be so deliciously red in their dewy freshness! Her large dark eyes, deeper and more unfathomable than the night through which she had just journeyed from the villa to the church, were thrown restlessly all around as she first entered the sacred edifice, and then were fixed upon the altar with its feebly glimmering lights. But her pace was firm and steady—and whatever might have been her inward feelings, it was at all events evident that she was fortified with an unflinching resolve to pass through the present ceremony unto the end.

Upon the countenance of the King there was an expression of joy and triumph, subdued to just that degree which showed that he dared not altogether permit his features to indicate the extent of the emotions that were swelling so exultingly in his breast. For *him* the scene, with its awe-inspiring accompaniments of a dim light within and utter darkness without, had no overpowering effect: the solemnity of the place and the occasion, the hour and the circumstances, which evidently made an impression upon Musidora, was not felt by him. Was his happiness so great that the idea of possessing as a bride this being of wondrous beauty, was all-absorbing—all-engrossing—alike in the heart and the imagination of the monarch?

If Henry experienced no sensation of solemn awe stealing upon him as he entered that dimly-lighted fane and conducted Musidora Sinclair towards the altar, it was by no means likely that the Earl and Countess of Grantham would be more susceptible on that score. Thoroughly selfish and worldly-minded even to heartlessness, their only cause of misgiving or alarm could have been that at the very last moment Musidora might yet recant her promise and refuse to become King Henry's bride. But little of this doubt or apprehension was in their minds: for during the past week—since the day on which she had given her final answer—Musidora had exhibited all her wonted self-possession, all her cold indifference, all her ice-like serenity. Without remonstrance, too, had she listened to the cogent reasons suggested by the King for a private wedding; and without hesitation had she consented to the proposed arrangement that the sacred solemnization should take place at this hour, at that church, and under those circumstances of secrecy and privacy which we have described. Therefore, all these things being considered, there was little scope for apprehension and misgiving on the part of the Earl and Countess of Grantham.

But to continue. The bridal-party paused at the railing which enclosed the altar; and there they waited in silence until Father Paul rejoined them. The venerable Superior was not far behind; and in less than a minute he took his station on one of the steps leading up to the sacred shrine.

"Dread Sovereign and illustrious Prince," said the old man, now breaking the silence which had hitherto prevailed, and speaking in a solemn voice the tones of which sounded strangely deep throughout the sacred edifice,—"all things have been arranged according to the royal mandate which I received from your Highness's lips last night. Of the twelve inmates of the monastery I am alone here;—for in obedience to my Sovereign's will, my brethren are all consigned to their cells and know not what is now passing. Lady," added the Superior, fixing his eyes upon Musidora with a scrutinizing intentness, "is all this with your full and free consent?—for otherwise I would not allow my lips to breathe the bridal prayer nor my tongue to give the marriage blessing—no, not for all the earthly Sovereigns of the universe! Say then, Musidora Sinclair—for such I understand is your name—speak and tell me if all that is doing or to be done, is with your unbiassed, uncoerced assent?"

"It is," was our heroine's response: and passionless as her looks had again become, equally cold was her voice—as if her heart were but the fragment of a glacier and her tongue an ice-shaft.

"And ye, my lord and Countess of Grantham," continued the Superior, now turning his eyes upon those whom he thus addressed, "is it with your full consent and free permission that the damsel here, whom his Highness has described to me as your relative, should contract this solemn alliance? Is it, I ask, in accordance with your unbiassed and unpurchased will?"

"It is," answered the Earl of Grantham.

"It is," echoed the Countess.

"Your Grace," resumed the venerable Superior, now again turning his eyes upon the monarch, "will deign, ere the ceremony commences, to exhibit unto my eyes and give into my hands that decree which bears the signature of his Holiness the Pope, and whereof your Grace spoke to me last night."

"Behold it!" replied the King; and he took from the breast of his doublet a parchment having three leaden seals suspended by ribbons thereto.

Father Paul, upon receiving this document, ascended to the highest step of the altar, so that he might examine it carefully by the light of the tapers. He looked at the seals—he scrutinized the signature—and then in a respectful manner he touched the parchment with his lips, in recognition of the supreme power of the Sovereign Pontiff the Pope of Rome.

"Know ye, all who are now gathered before me," the venerable Superior proceeded to exclaim in a far louder voice than that in which he had before spoken, "that I hold in my hand a Bull bearing the signature of the Holy Father, marked with the Keys of St. Peter, and authenticated by the three leaden seals of Rome! The purport of this high and sacred decree is to absolve Henry Plantagenet,[5] King of England, from all vows which he may have taken and all troths he may have plighted to Catherine of Arragon, either at the altar in the presence of the priest, or elsewhere and under whatsoever circumstances. Farthermore the Sovereign Pontiff doth declare and pronounce such marriage between Henry Plantagenet and Catherine of Arragon to be null and void, each and both to be absolved from the vows plighted and the pledges made aforetime. Finally, this high papal document doth empower and authorise either or both of the said parties, Henry Plantagenet and Catherine of Arragon, to contract other marriage-ties, the same as if none had previously existed;—and that this Bull, bearing the Holy Father's signature, stamped with the Keys of St. Peter, and accompanied by the leaden seals of Rome, is authentic and genuine, I do hereby solemnly avow my belief!"

The Superior ceased—the tones of his voice died away in the aisles— and a solemn silence pervaded the church. He descended the steps of the altar, and displayed the Papal Bull to Musidora, saying, "Daughter, you behold this decree which I have read: satisfy yourself that it is the same which Henry Plantagenet did ere now place in my hands."

"I am satisfied," answered Musidora.

"But you scarcely glance at it, daughter," said the Superior. "Perhaps you have seen it before?"

"I have," returned our heroine: "otherwise, you may rest assured, holy father, that I should not be here upon this occasion and for such a purpose."

"It is well, daughter. Such is the response I was desirous to elicit from your lips:"—then beckoning to the Earl and Countess to step forward, the venerable Superior displayed the Papal Bull to their eyes, and asked them each separately, "Are you satisfied that this is the same identical document which Henry Plantagenet, King of England, did place in my hands as authority for these proceedings?"

"I am satisfied," answered the Earl.

"I am satisfied," added the Countess.

"Now," continued Father Paul, producing a slip of parchment from the folds of his garments, together with an inkhorn and a pen,—"You, my Lord of Grantham, and your ladyship also, will as witnesses append your names to a certificate which I have already prepared, and which is to the effect that ere the commencement of the nuptial ceremony this Papal Bull was duly placed in my hands, read aloud by me in front of the altar, and made plain and apparent to all present, so that none could misapprehend its purport and its meaning."

With these words, Father Paul beckoned the Earl and Countess to approach a little side-table near the altar, and placed conveniently so as to catch the light of the tapers. He then read over the certificate, with the formula of which we shall not trouble our readers, but which was to the effect already explained by the holy father. The Earl and Countess affixed their signatures to the document, which the Superior at once secured about his person—that paper being a guarantee and indemnification for the part which he himself was performing in the present proceedings. The nobleman and his wife returned to their place behind the bridegroom and the bride; and the nuptial ceremony then commenced.

Musidora's countenance had by this time utterly lost that slight expression of uneasiness which it had worn on first entering the chapel; and the colour had come back to her lips, while there even seemed a tinge of the delicate rose-leaf upon her cheeks. But this might have been a deception produced by the flickering gleam of the tapers. Certain it is that she maintained a calmly dignified and devoutly serene look and manner, as Father Paul proceeded with the bridal prayers. At length it was over, that solemn ceremony!—the nuptial blessing was said—the King pressed his lips to Musidora's brow—the Earl and Countess offered their congratulations—and the Superior repeated in his heart that fervid benediction which he had just bestowed with his tongue.

"Holy father," said the King, putting a heavy purse into the monk's hand, "I know that to thee and thy brethren this would be mere dross, were it not that ye may dispense it in charities. For that purpose therefore do I pray thee to accept the gold."

Father Paul received the purse, and blessed the hand which gave it. He then seated himself at the little table and filled up the marriage-certificate, which he had previously prepared. This slip of parchment he handed to Musidora, who read it with attention and carefully placed it in her bosom.

"Now, beloved one," said the King, in a voice of whispering tenderness, as he took his bride's hand, "thou art Queen of England! In as short a time as may be, this marriage and the rank which it confers shall be proclaimed to the world. Let us issue hence, and return at once to Grantham Villa."

But scarcely did the bridal-party turn to quit the altar, when the whole interior of the church was in a moment lighted up by a blaze which threw every feature of the place into fearful distinctness. In the twinkling of an eye that sudden glare was gone—and then a terrific burst of thunder, pealing through the sacred fane, followed the lightning's glow. There was something awful to a degree in this abrupt outburst of the storm, at such a moment and on such an occasion. Musidora's countenance became ghastly: she shuddered from head to foot, and her eyes, settling on her husband's features, surveyed him with a look of wild terror and amaze. Her features were rigid—her lips ashy pale once more. The King himself was evidently confounded for the moment: but instantaneously recovering his presence of mind, he clasped Musidora to his breast—kissed her cold forehead and her death-like cheeks—but spake no word. Perhaps he himself felt at the instant that there was something appallingly ominous in the occurrence, and that it would be a blasphemy to proclaim a confidence which he did not feel—an impiety to impart a reassurance in which he could not partake. Lady Grantham, terribly frightened, clung to her husband who was also startled and overawed; while the reverend Superior, falling upon his knees, began breathing a prayer to heaven.

"Now let us depart ere the storm pours forth all its fury," said the King: and he hurried Musidora along the nave.

But again the obscurity through which they were proceeding was suddenly lighted up by the vivid glare of heaven's storm-fire; and again, as it vanished away, did the thunder roar with deafening, crashing, pealing sound, as if ten thousand chariots of brass were driven madly over the stone-pavement of the sacred edifice.

"Oh, this is terrible, terrible!" murmured Musidora, appalled by the dread omens—for as such did they doubtless strike with the force of hammers upon her heart and brain.

"My love—my dearest—my own sweet bride," whispered the King in a voice that was quivering with heaven only knows what thoughts,—"do not shrink away from me thus!"

"No," Musidora hastened to observe, instantaneously regretting the unpremeditated movement: "my place in the hour of danger is by your side—on your breast!"—and she suffered her husband to fold his arms around her—nay, she even courted that fervid embrace in which he locked her.

Then did a deep silence—a silence profound as that of the tomb—once more prevail in the church; and as they glanced back towards the altar, they perceived that Father Paul was now kneeling with his head bowed down so that his forehead touched, or rather rested upon, the highest step. He was evidently praying devoutly and in silence.

Again did the King lead Musidora on towards the door, the Earl of Grantham and the Countess following close behind. The bolt was drawn back—the portal was opened—and just as they crossed the threshold, another vivid flash of lightning streamed forth, making the whole canopy of heaven appear as if it were on fire. Then, as the celestial flame vanished once more, leaving the deep darkness darker still, the crash of heaven's artillery again rolled forth in fearful reverberations, making the utter blackness of the night terrible indeed.

And again did Musidora cling to her husband—and again did he cover her countenance with impassioned kisses: but she felt that his strong frame was shuddering and quivering in her embrace; and she could not wonder that it did so, for was it possible to remain indifferent to the awful terror of the storm?

No rain was falling; and the air was as hot and sulphurous as if laden with invisible fire. The horses were found to be trembling as if instinct with the same feelings of alarm which agitated their owners. The poor animals were standing as still as statues in the very spot where they had been left, and where their bridles were fastened to a palisade that was just outside the chapel-door. But as if naught were wanting to complete the dread solemnity of the hour and all its circumstances, the united voices of the eleven monks whom the Superior had ordered to their cells, were now rising in lugubrious chant, sending up through the still hot air and the darkness of night a hymn of intercession to the ruler of the storm.

Oh! what a bridal night was this!—with what awful portents did it seem filled! Of a surety our heroine was not all ice; else wherefore should she have shuddered again and again with an icy thrill that vibrated and quivered through her entire form?—and why for an instant did a still deeper feeling than terror—a feeling of a wild and desolating agony—convulse her from head to foot, as she murmured in a sort of frenzied whisper to herself, "My God! what does it all mean? what have I done?"

"Dearest, dearest," said the King, catching her in his arms and pressing her again and again to his breast, "I beseech—I implore you to be calm!"

"Yes, yes—I will—I ought—I must!" she replied in a strange deep voice that had suddenly become as unnaturally calm as her look and manner likewise grew; and whatever painful feelings she now experienced—whatever alarms disquieted her peace, or presentiments of evil horrified her thoughts—they had all in a moment become entombed as it were in an inward darkness—the terrible darkness of the soul!

To be brief, the bridal party remounted their horses, and slowly descended the eminence on which the monastery stood. Their way lay along a narrow path which intersected the wood; but even there the verdant foliage gave no freshness to the hot and heavy air. The heat was stifling to a degree;—and again and again, as they proceeded, did the lightning glare and the thunder send forth its deafening din. Without any accident, however—for they were all good riders and the steeds were manageable—did they succeed in reaching the villa: but scarcely had they entered it, when the rain began to pour down in torrents.

A magnificent repast was spread in the banqueting-room; and the bridal-party,—cheered by the blaze of light and the comfortable aspect which the well-furnished room presented in contrast with the gloom of the night without, and naturally ready also to avail themselves of any encouraging influences which might afford an escape as it were from the ominous impressions so recently made in their minds,—sat down to the board. The rain continued to pour down with a deluging violence; but at each outburst of the thunder it became more and more evident that the storm was passing away. The King, the Earl, and the Countess soon recovered their wonted spirits: but Musidora was not so easily cheered—nor did she regain even as much of that icy animation of look and manner which it was her ordinary wont to display. Still she strove to render herself affable and agreeable to the King—thus proving that inasmuch as she had accepted the position of a wife, she was resolved to the utmost of her power to perform its duties.

Of all the servants beneath the roof of Grantham Villa, two only were entrusted with the secret of this marriage. These were Musidora's own maid Annetta—and Dame Bertha, the housekeeper of the establishment. For obvious reasons it had been requisite that Musidora should take her tirewoman into her confidence; and through prudential motives it had been judged advisable to acquaint the housekeeper with the secret also. Thus, when Musidora quitted the supper-table and repaired to her own chamber, she found the faithful Annetta and the important-looking Dame Bertha in waiting to tend upon her as she sought the nuptial couch.

CHAPTER XXX.

THE VISIT TO DEADMAN'S PLACE.

A FEW days after the incidents just related, a young gentleman, elegantly attired and mounted on a gaily caparisoned steed, rode through the detached villages of Rotherhithe and Bermondsey, and entering St. Olave's Street, turned his horse into the Sanctuary of Deadman's Place. It was about noon, and the sun was shining gloriously: but instead of imparting any cheerfulness to the aspect of this vile neighbourhood, the golden radiance seemed shed in mockery of the wretched habitations constituting

that privileged district. It was evident, however, that the young gentleman had been thither before: for he paused not to survey the features of
the place, but rode on up to the narrow thoroughfare until he reached
the house which stood at the end, and a portion of which so completely
overhung the river as to be supported by piles fixed deep in the mud: for it
was now low water, and the shore consisting of black slime was bare for
a dozen yards out.

Turning into a stable-yard, the young gentleman leaped from his
horse—tossed the bridle to an ill-looking fellow of a groom who immediately came forward to receive it—and then asked, "Is Master Dunhaven
within?"

"I think he is, Sir Cavalier," answered the hostler: then suddenly giving a sort of ironical whistle, he exclaimed, "Well, may I never apply cur-
ry-comb to horse's coat again, if you are not Master St. Louis!"

"And what of that?" inquired the King's Secretary with indignant
hauteur. "Cannot a man's position change through his own merits, and
his ragged doublet be displaced by an embroidered coat, without eliciting
the impudent remarks of such as you? Come, fellow, know your place; or
mayhap I shall teach you:"—and St. Louis placed his hand upon the light
elegant rapier which, as a symbol of gentility, hung by his side.

"My lord—your honour—your worship—or whatever else you may
be," said the hostler, "I meant no offence; and therefore you won't forget
to give me a silver piece presently when you require your steed again? I
am sure, for my part, I am well enough pleased to behold this change in
your circumstances: for I recollect that when you were last here, it was to
borrow a horse and pistols that you might play the highwayman. But now,
if I mistake not, you come to see us upon a horse of your own; and I must
say you look more like a courtier belonging to a palace, than a roystering
ruffler upon the King's highway."

"Here, rascal!" exclaimed St. Louis, who had blushed up to the eyes
at that allusion to the criminal straits to which he was formerly reduced;
"take this gold piece, and see that you drink enough ale or strong waters, according to your taste, to lull into eternal repose that too faithful
memory of your's—I mean so far as it regards me and my antecedents.
You understand?"

"Your worship goes the right way to make one understand," said the
hostler, in huge delight, as he picked up the gold piece which St. Louis had
tossed to him. "From henceforth I have neither eyes, nor ears, nor tongue
for aught that regards you, unless you give me encouragement to look, to
listen, or to speak. Besides," he added, with a knowing grin, "I don't often
stir out of this sanctuary, having done two or three little things in my time

that it might be inconvenient to be questioned about by the King's constables: and therefore, worthy Master St. Louis, you will have little danger of encountering me elsewhere than in Deadman's Place. But I see you are growing impatient. If you step in you will find the old man."

St. Louis accordingly walked down the stable-yard and knocked at a little low door in the side-wall of the house. The summons was immediately answered by Dunhaven himself,—presenting to the young gentleman's view that same vile, sinister, and sordid aspect which once seen could not be well forgotten.

"Ah! is it possible?—worthy Master St. Louis!" exclaimed the old man, instantaneously recognizing his visitor: for his memory was excellent and his perception keen as that of a hawk. "I am right glad to behold you in such good form; and notwithstanding your feathers, your lace, your ruffles, and your ribands, I knew you directly. But walk in, walk in."

St. Louis accordingly followed Dunhaven into the little dirty room which we have before described, and where the old man's bed was stretched upon an enormous trunk, resembling a sea-chest, in one corner.

"Now sit you down," said the owner of the place, pointing to one of the two or three stools that constituted items of the furniture: and placing himself on another, he proceeded to observe, "On that night when you were here last you promised to return shortly."

"But my occupations would not possibly allow me to keep my word until this day," answered the King's Secretary.

"Your occupations, eh? It was three months ago," continued Dunhaven,—"and more than three months too, that you promised to return. Scarce a day has passed but I have thought of you—wondering why you did not keep your word, and wishing I knew where to seek you."

"Ah!—then you really felt anxious to see me?" observed St. Louis inquiringly.

"I did: and perhaps you can guess wherefore?" rejoined Dunhaven, fixing his eyes with a sinister earnestness upon the young man's countenance.

"No, not altogether," was the latter's response; "unless it were that you wished to tell me the history of that ancestress of your's of whom you spoke—the lovely Margaret, I think you said—the fairest maid of Cumberland—and who became the victim of Lord Ranulph Danvers?"

"Your memory serves you aright," answered Dunhaven: "all that you have just repeated, did I say to you the night you were here with Welford. But it is not merely for the sake of telling you the history of my ancestress that I wished we should meet again; it was also to discourse with you at length relative to that man of whom we spoke on the night referred to—a man whom I had thought dead, but of whose existence in the land of the living still, you gave me such positive assurance."

"Lord Danvers you mean?" observed St. Louis: "Lord Lionel Danvers—the same whom you pitched down that trap-door overhanging the river, on a night of darkness, of tempest, and of flood?"

"There your memory serves you well again," responded Dunhaven. "But ere we continue our discourse upon that point," he exclaimed, his small grey eyes wandering with twinkling celerity over every part of St. Louis's person, "tell me—that is to say if the question be not indiscreet—how your fortunes have undergone so striking a change? For that this is no sudden spurt of prosperity which has clothed you in a lace-bedizened doublet, put plumes in your cap, and given you the fine steed which I beheld from my window a few moments back, is pretty evident. You do not wear those gewgaws as if you had purchased them yesterday and stood the chance of being compelled to part with them again to-morrow for the sake of a meal or to satisfy a tavern-score. Ah! Master St. Louis, I have seen too much of the world not to be able to read all these little evidences of men's circumstances with facility enough; and I see that your garments are worn with a confidence as if you had no fear of parting from them. Moreover, there is a comfortable assurance in your manner—the easy gentility of one who feels that he stands secure and safe in a fine position. Pardon me if I say all this: pardon me likewise if I seek the explanation of your prosperity: but I feel interested in you."

"Is it because when I left my casket as a pledge in your hands, you read the papers it contained?" inquired St. Louis, laughing good-naturedly.

"Just so," responded Dunhaven. "Yet not exactly because I read your papers, but because from the circumstances thereby brought to my knowledge, I learnt that there must be one sentiment in your heart which is identical with that which is uppermost in my own—I mean a sentiment of eternal, immitigable hatred against every one belonging to the family of Danvers! Indeed, a relative of Arline de St. Louis cannot fail to have a fellow feeling with a descendant of that family to which Margaret Dunhaven belonged."

"Well, as to the questions you have put to me," replied Gerald St. Louis, evading any comment upon the remarks which the old man had just made, "I will satisfy your curiosity. In a word, I am Private Secretary to his Highness the King."

"Is it possible?" exclaimed the old man, starting up from his seat: then with a mechanical impulse, he made a low bow to the elegant Court-functionary.

"It is quite possible, because it is the truth," returned St. Louis, laughing: "but I did not come hither to astonish you with my good fortune. Therefore resume your seat, and let us continue our discourse."

"A cup of wine, Master St. Louis?" said Dunhaven, now growing excessively pressing with his courtesies: "it shall be of the best, I can assure you."

"I thank you, but must decline. Ever since I was fortunate enough to obtain this place, which is too good to risk its loss through inebriety, I have forsworn liquor, save of an evening."

"Ah! your old friend and boon-companion Welford was the one to drink at all hours and of all sorts!" exclaimed Dunhaven: then as he resumed his seat upon the stool, he asked, "By the bye, what has become of him? Never have I once seen the roystering doctor since the night you were here together."

"He also is in luck's way," returned St. Louis, "and obtained some situation—but of what kind or where I do not know. All correspondence has ceased between us ever since that very night to which you made allusion; and I cannot say that I am grieved thereat—for Benjamin Welford led me into many follies and serious troubles."

"Ah! he was not the wisest of men," observed Dunhaven; "yet a personage of some talent in his way. But may I be permitted to inquire who was the author of this great and sudden good fortune that hath smiled upon ye both?"

"No—that is my secret," returned St. Louis, good-humouredly: for he now recollected that on the night when he was last at Deadman's Place, it had merely been mentioned that he and Welford had received gold from Danvers, but not that his lordship had made any promises beyond that display of his bounty.

"Well, well, I do not wish to be inquisitive," exclaimed Dunhaven.

"Let us revert, then," said the King's Secretary, "to the former topic of our discourse and the object of my visit."

"We will," rejoined the old man, his countenance becoming so grave and solemn that its expression served for a mask, as it were, for the moment,—but not one hypocritically assumed—to veil the wonted sinister aspect of his looks.

"Let me hear, then, the history of Margaret Dunhaven," observed the Secretary; "since you are so well acquainted with that of my unfortunate relative Arline de St. Louis."

"Yes—you shall hear the history of Margaret Dunhaven," replied the old man, in a voice as deep and solemn as his looks. "But first there is a sight for you to see:"—and he rose slowly from his seat.

Gerald St. Louis gazed upon him in surprise, and watched him with an increasing interest, as he drew off the pallet from the immense chest: having done which, the old man proceeded to take out the fire-arms, weapons, garments, silver plate—in fine, the whole miscellaneous assortment of articles which appeared to form the contents of the chest. But those were *not* all the contents. There was a false bottom, made to be lifted out by a ring fixed in the middle. Dunhaven leant down—caught hold of the ring—lifted out the false bottom—and then beckoned St. Louis to approach and look in.

The King's Secretary did so: but he started back with an ejaculation of horror and amazement, on beholding a skeleton stretched out at full length at the bottom of the chest. There it was as if in its coffin—the bleached bones all perfect and connected together—none dismembered, none deficient. The two rows of teeth, which must have been beautiful in the living form, were white and even, but gleaming ghastly in the lipless jaws—while the dread object seemed to look upwards in horrible derision from its eyeless sockets.

Old Dunhaven stood gazing down upon the grim and hideous spectacle for more than a minute; and unutterable things were evidently passing in his mind. Then, slowly replacing the plank which constituted what might be termed the lid of the coffin-part of the chest, he proceeded to pile in upon it all the articles of plate, weapons, and clothes which he had taken forth.

This done, he returned to his seat, and bade St. Louis resume his place also. When the King's Secretary had obeyed the invitation, Dunhaven commenced his narrative in the following manner.

CHAPTER XXXI.

THE HISTORY OF MARGARET DUNHAVEN.

"THE south-western district of Cumberland may be described as a magnificent assemblage of lofty mountains and beautiful lakes, forming the sublimest and at the same time the most charming scenery in all England. Nothing can exceed the diversified and picturesque loveliness of the landscape surrounding the lake of Ennerdale, which is three miles in length, and nearly three in breadth at its widest part. Upon an eminence crowning a gradual slope on one shore of the lake stands the castellated mansion of the Danvers family. It is a vast structure—the solid masses of masonry seeming to be heaped up one above another like the hills and mountains of the adjoining scenery. The castle and grounds occupy an extent of four acres; and the enclosure is surrounded by a battlemented wall, forming a complete square, and having an octagon tower at each angle. High above the other buildings of the castle, the huge Donjon rears its sombre head; and at one angle a tall, narrow circular tower shoots up like a shaft of masonry, and is surrounded at the top by an embattled overhanging gallery, where in times of trouble or of feudal strife the sentinels were wont to pace day and night. From that elevated point they could look down, with the view of a bird, upon the buildings, grounds, and walls of the castle—the slopes on every side—the lake occupying the valley with its silver sheen—and the whole circumjacent country far and wide. The grand front of the castle, looking towards the lake, is comparatively of modern architecture, viewed in contrast with the heavy structures and majestic towers forming the other lines of the square array of buildings that enclose the court-yard wherein the Donjon is situated. Outside these lines of building, to the foot of the exterior walls, the well-cultivated gardens, the lawns surrounded by noble trees looking as if they were the growth of ages, and the pleasant walks embowered with lofty acacias, occupy the enclosure.

"On the opposite shore of the lake, and at a distance of three miles in a straight line from the castellated mansion just described, stood a somewhat humbler abode,—humbler only however in comparison with that spacious feudal fortress: for Dunhaven Hall, to which I thus allude, was alike a spacious edifice and a comfortable home. It had a garden reaching down to the very shore of Ennerdale lake, from the brink of which the Hall itself was situated about three hundred yards;—and in the rear of the edifice were shrubberies, pleasure-grounds, and orchards. The year 1407 is the period of which I am about to speak in my narrative; and Dunhaven Hall was then the property of a worthy knight who had inherited the estate from his ancestors. The family of Dunhaven was an old one, and in earlier times had been very powerful and very wealthy. Far as the eye could reach on that side of Ennerdale lake, did the hills, the valleys, the woods, and the pasture-lands all once belong to the knights of Dunhaven. Their retainers and vassals were numerous and bold,—renowned in border-warfare when the Scots made incursions into Cumberland,—and formidable likewise to the feudal chiefs of the surrounding district. A mortal enmity had long existed between the Knights of Dunhaven and the Lords of Danvers. This inveterate hatred frequently exploded in hostile aggressions; and on more occasions than one during the progress of two or three centuries, was Dunhaven Hall sacked, pillaged, and burnt by the Danvers and their vassals. The Hall was however speedily built up again; and inasmuch as Danvers Castle was too strong and too impregnable to admit of a like retaliation, the Knights of Dunhaven were wont to avenge themselves

by destroying the huts and habitations of the Danvers' vassals, and taking possession of their flocks and herds. Thus, for a long, long time, the
feudal warfare was waged upon tolerably equal terms between the two
families of Danvers and Dunhaven: but at last the former began to reap
advantages over the latter on each successive outbreak of hostilities. The
Knights of Dunhaven, too, being traditionally lavish and extravagant in
their expenditure, fell into pecuniary difficulties—mortgaged their broad
lands to usurers—and by degrees had to surrender up parcel after parcel
of their territorial possessions to the money-lenders of Carlisle. There was
nothing nobly forbearing in the conduct of the Lords of Danvers towards
the Knights of Dunhaven: for in proportion as the latter grew weak and
impoverished, did the former become more encroaching and predatory. It
was now the Dunhavens' turn to have their flocks and herds swept away;
and thus, though the hatred between the two families increased in rancour, yet year after year beheld the Dunhavens becoming more and more
exposed to the vengeance of the Danvers.

"Great therefore was the relief experienced by the falling and half-ru-
ined Dunhavens when in the year 1389, or 1390—I forget which—Lord Walter Danvers, who had but very recently succeeded to the title and estates,
quitted his native land, for some reasons not very generally known, but
supposed to be through disgust at the troubles into which King Richard
II, who reigned at the time, had plunged the country. To a very considerable extent he broke up the warlike establishment which his ancestors had
ever maintained at their castle in Cumberland; and in this circumstance Sir
Poniers Dunhaven, the then possessor of the Hall and of the little estate to
which the once extensive territory of his forefathers had dwindled down,
beheld a guarantee for peace and tranquillity. But with this sense of security the family hatred experienced by Sir Poniers Dunhaven against his
more powerful rival, was by no means mitigated: on the contrary it was
perhaps rather increased by a sense of his own utter impotence to wreak
it upon the vast territorial possessions and the numerous vassals that Lord
Walter Danvers had thus left.

"I have already said it was in the year 1407 to which I specially seek to
direct your attention. Picture to yourself a fine, tall, middle-aged man, with
a charming girl of seventeen leaning on his arm, walking by the shore of
the lake in the cool of a September evening in the year just named. These
individuals were Sir Poniers Dunhaven and his beautiful daughter Margaret. The martial air of the knight—his powerful well-knit form—the
blended hauteur and sternness of his looks—and the pride exhibited in
his gait, were the true characteristics of the race to which he belonged,
and afforded no mean indication of his qualities and his attributes, alike

physical and moral. His arm had been tried in battle; and where danger was most imminent in the ranks of death, there was he ever found. He was proud too of the name he bore—a name known for centuries on the banks of the Ennerdale, and indeed throughout the county of Cumberland: but with the laurels of bravery upon his brow, and with the pride of an ancient name throbbing in his heart, he was nevertheless a disappointed man. Yes—he was disappointed; because his courage in fighting the battles of several Sovereigns had earned him no rewards; and because the comparative poverty to which he was reduced, and the narrow limits to which his estates had dwindled down, permitted him not to sustain the honour of his rank and name with what he fancied to be a becoming dignity.

"Margaret Dunhaven was the fairest maid in Cumberland. A profusion of soft and golden tresses were parted above a brow of alabaster purity, and fell in sunny luxuriance upon her ivory shoulders. Her complexion was dazzlingly transparent, with the roseate bloom of health upon her cheeks, and so pure a lily fairness upon the brow, the shoulders, and the neck, that each delicately pencilled violet vein might be clearly traced. Her figure was tall, slight, and exquisitely modelled—with just sufficient fulness of contours to mark how the beauty of womanhood was unfolding into richer proportions without destroying the charm of girlish elegance and grace. Light and playful as the fawn, she could be the dignified damsel and enact the part of the chieftain's daughter when occasion required. Innocence and candour were in all her looks, and sat upon her sweet and tranquil brow; truth and artlessness like guardian angels seemed to hover around her. Her beauty was peculiar—sunny and seraphic, yet glowing and dazzling. Her eyes were large and of the deepest blue, fringed with long lashes, and surmounted with brows which were of delicately pencilled brown, but deep enough to form a contrast with the golden glory of her hair. Each varying expression which swept across her speaking features, though full of animation, served but as an index to the artless purity of her thoughts and to the generous feelings of her nature. It was impossible to view that bright, that nymph-like beauty, without feeling interested in her welfare, and without a sentiment of regret that such an exquisite being could belong to a world the sweetest ornaments of which are frequently doomed to the saddest destinies.

"From all that I have been saying relative to Margaret Dunhaven, it has doubtless become apparent that hers was not a nature to imbibe as a prejudice that feeling of rancorous hatred which her father experienced for the very name of Danvers. As a matter of course she regretted—and deeply regretted—the long series of feuds which had raged between her own ancestors and their rivals on the opposite bank of Ennerdale water: but if she felt no vindictive hatred against that family, she nevertheless would not have been very ready to welcome any member of it as a friend. Her spirits were too buoyant, her disposition too ingenuously gay, and her instincts at once too pure and noble to permit her to dwell with anything of a brooding hate in respect to whomsoever might bear the name of Danvers; and her good sense taught her that in the origin of this traditionary strife between the two families, her own ancestors had been as much to blame as the founders of the rival race.

"Margaret was an only child, and she had lost her mother when at a tender age: but an old aunt had supplied with much affectionate care that mother's place, and the good dame had preferred leaving her niece's instincts to their natural course in respect to the family feud, rather than warp the ingenuousness of her young mind by inculcating sentiments of rancorous malignity and bitter hatred. That aunt had died when Margaret was fifteen, and therefore tolerably well able to think for herself: but the kind old relative had lived long enough to screen her niece as it were from the influence of those traditionary prejudices which corroded the heart of her father.

"Such was Margaret Dunhaven, the flower of Cumberland—the fairest damsel of the north. To return to that September evening on which we found her walking with her sire upon the borders of Lake Ennerdale, it must be observed that while she herself seemed more serious than usual, Sir Poniers wore a look more amiable than was his wont. Not that he was ever harsh or unkind to his daughter: no—he loved her too well for that: she was his joy and his darling—and she was also his hope; because in her he beheld the only possible means of amending the broken fortunes of his race. He therefore cherished her with feelings that were a strange admixture of fondness and selfishness—fondness for the innocent, charming, affectionate, and dutiful girl whose gentle ministrations and artless gaiety cheered his gloomy hours; and selfishness in the thought and intention of bestowing the hand of his beautiful Margaret upon a rich and powerful chief whose wealth might enable Sir Poniers to purchase back the broad lands which usury had wrested from his forefathers. Upon this topic to a certain extent, was the conversation turning, as the Knight and his daughter rambled along the shore of Lake Ennerdale; and hence was it that while a cloud gradually darkened upon Margaret's features, her father assumed a look more tender and more conciliatory than was his wont.

" 'Lord Glenmorris has many noble and excellent qualities, my dear child,' said the Knight, continuing the topic of the discourse which he had already commenced as delicately as his somewhat coarse nature, and habitual bluntness of speech would allow. 'He is thirty years of age, exceedingly handsome, has distinguished himself in the border forays and feuds against the Scotch, and possesses so many broad acres that when he stands on the summit of his castle-tower the whole district which he surveys, far as his eye can reach, is his own. What thinks, then, my gentle Margaret of becoming the Lady of Glenmorris?'—The young damsel threw a quick inquiring look up at her father's countenance, as if to assure herself that she had comprehended his meaning aright, and that her previous fears and suspicions relative to the aim of his discourse were now really confirmed by the explicit crisis to which he had brought it.—'My dear daughter,' continued Sir Poniers Dunhaven, 'you have now reached an age when it is right that I should become thoughtful for your welfare. Amongst the chiefs of the surrounding district, several have cast their eyes lovingly upon you; and several have dropped a hint in my ears that it would be a proud day for them to make Margaret Dunhaven their bride. But of all who have thus looked or spoken, none seems more eligible than Lord Glenmorris. To be candid with you, Margaret, I have given this nobleman an encouraging answer: I have promised to speak with you on the subject; and he waits but for the word from my lips to throw himself at your feet and demand your permission to pay you his honourable suit.'—'But my dear father,' returned Margaret, whose maiden modesty was both shocked and alarmed at what she could not help regarding as very precipitate, if not positively indelicate, in this proceeding on the part of her father, 'I am so little acquainted with the Lord of Glenmorris!'—'And yet he has of late visited Dunhaven Hall frequently enough,' rejoined her father.—'True,' answered Margaret; 'but on those occasions I have been little in his company, retiring from the board when the repast was over and leaving you and his lordship to enjoy your flagon together.'—'It is not necessary you should be well acquainted with him, Margaret,' resumed the Knight, 'in order to be convinced of the excellence of his character or the generosity of his heart, much less the valour of his arm or the wealth in his coffers. It is sufficient that I give you suitable assurances on all these points. As for his personal appearance, you have at least seen him often enough to be well aware of his good looks; and that his manners are sufficiently courteous, you have likewise had ample opportunity of judging. What more then can you require?'—'My dear father,' returned Margaret, 'I have always understood, and my good aunt, who is now, alas! no more, frequently informed me, that you espoused my mother because you were deeply attached to each other, and that your love was a sentiment of spontaneous growth. Therefore does it seem to me unmaidenly and improper that I should allow myself to think of marriage where my heart entertains no feeling of

affection.'—'Ah!' ejaculated Sir Poniers, somewhat angrily, 'then I see that
your head is filled with love-sick sentimentalism! Tell me, child,' he added,
bending a stern look upon his daughter, 'do you love any other? has any
one of the chiefs who occasionally visit Dunhaven Hall, whispered sweet
words in your ear and engaged your heart?'—There was a blush upon the
maiden's cheek as she lifted her countenance towards her father's: but it
was not the tell-tale blush of love—it was the glow of mingled shame and
grief at being thus rudely addressed and searchingly questioned by him
whom she had never in her life deceived. But if there were that mantling
hue upon her cheeks, there was candour upon her brow, and the proud
consciousness of innocence in her eyes, as she said in a firm voice, 'No,
father; I have never listened to such language as that of which you speak;
nor do I experience the least liking for any one of your visitors more than
for another.'

"Sir Poniers Dunhaven was annoyed with himself that he had thus
wounded the tender sensibilities of his charming daughter; and at once
assuming a kinder look and milder tone, he said, 'I am glad to receive this
assurance from your lips. I did not think you would deceive me; but for
a moment your observations somewhat startled me and made me afraid.
However, since you tell me that your heart is altogether disengaged, I tell
you in return that the image of Lord Glenmorris is well worthy of filling it; and as an obedient daughter I trust that you will permit him to
pay you his courtship.'—Margaret gave no answer: but her heart swelled
with rebellious feelings against this mandate on the part of her sire. It was
the first time in her life she had ever felt her thoughts rise in insurrection
against his commands: but with all her innocence, her purity, and her artlessness, the young girl had a proper spirit; and this spirit revolted against
the idea that her hand was to be disposed of with or without her own
concurrence.

" 'For more reasons than one,' continued Sir Poniers after a brief
pause, 'it is necessary that I should think of settling you in life. My own
means are gradually becoming more and more impoverished; and the little estate to which the territory of Dunhaven has dwindled down, pro-
duces so beggarly a revenue as to fill me with cares for the future. Ah!' exclaimed the Knight, as he stopped short, and looking across the lake fixed
his eyes upon the castellated mansion on the summit of the hill on the
opposite shore; 'would that I had the power to wreak upon my haughty
rival the vengeance which my soul cherishes!'—'But my dear father,' observed Margaret, by no means displeased to turn the conversation from its
former topic, 'Lord Walter Danvers, the present owner of that castle, has
never done you any harm.'—'Harm!' echoed the Knight, his whole coun-

tenance becoming distorted with rage: 'is he not the representative of a race which has been the mortal enemy of my ancestors? O Margaret, let me not be compelled to think that you are a degenerate scion of the Dunhaven family, and that you have no rancour in your heart against every one bearing the hated name of Danvers!'—'My dear father," replied the young girl timidly and hesitatingly, 'I never saw Lord Walter Danvers in my life. It was when I was an infant in the cradle that he broke up his establishment at yonder castle and quitted England altogether. How, then, would you have me hate an individual whom I have never seen, and who, in his own person, has never done harm to you? Besides,' she added suddenly, as a thought struck her, 'was there not a rumour current a few weeks ago that Lord Walter has died abroad and that he has been succeeded by his son Lord Ranulph, a very young man?'—'Yes, there was such a rumour rife,' answered Sir Poniers gloomily: 'but whether it be true or no, I care not. No matter what the Christian name of the owner of yon castle may be, whether Walter or Ranulph, he is not the less my foe, nor am I the less inveterate against him.'—'Suppose, my dear father,' Margaret ventured to remonstrate, 'that Lord Ranulph Danvers (presuming it to be true that he is now the possessor of the family castles and estates in England and the Isle of Wight) should be more friendly inclined towards you than his ancestors have been to your's, would you still hate him?'—'I would, I would,' exclaimed the Knight with a fierce bitterness in his tone. 'Enough however upon this subject! It is for you to bethink yourself of that *other* topic on which we have been speaking: for to-morrow I shall ride across to Glenmorris Castle and assure his lordship that he will not be rejected when he comes to pay his courtship to my daughter.'—Margaret's bosom heaved with a low sigh as she thus beheld in her father's words an additional proof of his intention to make her wed Lord Glenmorris whatever her own inclination might be: but she offered not another word of remonstrance. Though her spirit had rebelled for a moment, and she had perhaps spoken to her father with a bolder frankness than she ever dared exhibit before, she nevertheless stood too much in awe of him and was likewise habitually too obedient to carry her opposition any farther. But he, thinking perhaps that she would say more upon the subject, and anxious to escape from the necessity of a prolonged argument, abruptly observed, 'I shall now re-enter the house; but you need not come in immediately, unless it be your pleasure. I know that you are fond of an evening walk on the bank of the Ennerdale; and you may prolong it a little on this occasion if you choose.'—With these words he hastened away; and as it was close by the wall of the garden where the concluding part of the colloquy had taken place, he quickly disappeared through the little low door opening into the enclosure.

"Margaret turned and slowly retraced her way along the border of the lake. There was a mournfulness in her thoughts such as she had not known for a long time: no, not since the influence of her aunt's death had shed its cloud upon her mind. It was not that the maiden loved another, for her heart was as yet virgin of the sentiment of love: nor was it that she positively disliked Glenmorris, because she had really no feeling of either aversion or liking at all in the matter. But the purity of her mind had been shocked, the delicacy of her feelings had been hurt, by the bare idea that her hand was to be disposed of in so arbitrary a manner, and that she was to be sacrificed to motives of self-interest. For inexperienced though she were in the ways of the world—unsuspicious and unsophisticated as by nature and circumstances she was—she nevertheless could not help understanding that through this contemplated marriage her father hoped to redeem his broken fortunes. In her love and her tenderness for him she would gladly lay down her life on his behalf: but her soul revolted against the thought of being made the object of a mercenary bargain and thus sacrificed to a cold worldly selfishness.

"Revolving all these things in her mind, Margaret continued her way along the shore of the lake. The sun was disappearing behind the hill-tops in the west: the mists, in fleecy lightness, were gathering over the lake and the surrounding scenery. From behind the mountains the rays of the sinking sun shot upward and away to the right and left, spreading out fan-like in their lambent glory, until gradually becoming fainter and fainter, they gave place to long streaks of orange, and purple, crimson and gold, which blended their gorgeous hues in lines of richness along the horizon. Still the young damsel walked on,—beholding not the beauty of the sunset, nor warned by the gathering mists that it was time to retrace her steps. Indeed so profoundly was she absorbed in her reflections that she did not notice—well as she knew the spot—the presence of a little river which branched off from the lake and might be crossed by a bridge a few yards higher up. But coming upon it suddenly, in the profound distraction of her thoughts, she slipped down the bank, and the next moment was immersed in the water. A rending shriek, ringing from her lips, swept over the lake; for she was out of her depth and unable to regain the land. But, ah! that piercing cry for help is suddenly answered! A young man, elegantly dressed, and who, unnoticed by her, had been observing her with attention for the last few minutes, now suddenly sprang forward—plunged into the lake—caught her as she was sinking a second time—and in a few moments laid her safely upon the bank. But he did not altogether disengage her from his clasp. Kneeling by her side, he sustained her in his arms—bent over her—whispered cheering words in her ears—and wrung out the water from the long heavy tresses of her golden hair. Her senses were so bewildered, her thoughts so confused, that for upwards of a minute she scarcely knew where she was—what had happened—or whether it were all a dream: but the words which were breathed in her ear gradually became comprehensible in their cheering effect; and rising to her feet, the maiden began to falter forth a few syllables expressive of gratitude. The young stranger besought her not to tarry there, but urged her to allow him to conduct her homeward; and compelling her to take his arm, he hurried her along the border of the lake towards Dunhaven Hall. But few words were spoken between them: for dripping wet as they both were, small was the opportunity for the stranger to improve his acquaintance with the damsel whose beauty had evidently produced no trifling effect upon him; and she on her part was still too much bewildered and confused by what had occurred, as well as by the awkwardness of her position in company with the unknown, to say anything beyond a repetition of her thanks. The low door in the garden-wall was reached in ten minutes; and then, as the stranger spoke a few words of farewell, Margaret, suddenly awakening to a sense of the courtesy requisite for the occasion, invited him to enter that he might receive her father's acknowledgments and procure a change of raiment. But a singular smile flitted across the wondrously handsome countenance of the youthful stranger as he declined the invitation,—but declined it in such a manner as not to offend the hospitable feelings of Margaret Dunhaven. He then sped away, and was soon concealed from her view by the increasing obscurity of the hour. For, to tell the truth, dripping wet though she were, the damsel remained standing at the gate for several moments, gazing after him, transfixed in surprise that he should have hastened away so abruptly, and also annoyed to think that he would not even enter to change his dripping garments.

"On reaching the house, Margaret sped up to her own chamber, and putting off her wet clothing, apparelled herself in other raiment. She then descended to the room where her father awaited her for the evening meal, and at once explained to him what had occurred.—'You silly girl,' he cried, 'I should be angry with you for your carelessness in meeting with such an accident, were it not that I am too rejoiced to have you restored safe and sound. But it is singular that this gallant unknown would not enter the house. If he be, as we must suppose, the guest of some neighbouring chief, he must at all events have a considerable distance to run ere he regains his place of abode: or it may be that he is a tourist on a visit to the Lakes, and lodging at some adjacent cottage. Doubtless he will call to-morrow to make courteous inquiries concerning you; and then we shall learn who he is.'—Sir Poniers said no more upon the subject, but addressed himself to the cold viands upon the board, not forgetting to pay his respects frequently enough to the goblet which he filled from a flagon placed near him.

"That night Margaret Dunhaven slept but little: for the image of the handsome, elegant, and noble-looking youth who had rescued her from a watery grave was uppermost in her mind. On the following day Sir Poniers Dunhaven mounted his horse to ride over to Glenmorris Castle, which was about six miles distant. His daughter, who knew full well whither he was gone, and felt more unhappy than even she had done the evening before at the thought of being forced into a union with Lord Glenmorris, went forth alone to take her usual walk on the bank of the lake. Her young female dependant Alice offered to accompany her: but Margaret wished to be left to the solitude of her own reflections; and she accordingly dispensed with the attendance of her abigail. Insensibly her steps led her towards the scene of the last evening's accident: but this time, though still giving way to her thoughts, she was more careful as she approached the river. It was not however until she reached its bank that she noticed there was some one seated on a high stone at the foot of the bridge at a little distance. That individual immediately arose, doffed his plumed cap gracefully, and advanced towards her: then did an involuntary blush mantle upon the maiden's cheek as she immediately recognised the hero of the previous evening's adventure. He took her hand, and kept it in his own a little longer than was warranted by the slightness of their acquaintance: but then *this* the maiden might have thought pardonable considering the circumstance under which that acquaintance had commenced. For such a circumstance might be looked upon as at once establishing a sort of friendship instead of a mere acquaintanceship, the stranger having saved her life. Be it as it may, Margaret did not immediately withdraw her hand from the youth's clasp; and doubtless it trembled in his own, for she felt her heart fluttering with sensations such as she had never experienced before.

"They crossed the bridge—they walked together along the border of the lake—and they conversed upon the beauty of the scenery, the accident of the previous evening, and the loveliness of the present morning, with the sky of unclouded azure and the sun making the lake glow like a molten mass of silver. Gradually the youth turned the conversation upon other topics, and spoke of foreign climes which he had visited. He depicted his travels in France, in Spain, in Germany, in Italy, and in Greece, with an eloquence that enchanted the young maiden. His melodious voice, manly however in its harmony, poured forth a flow of beautiful language that delighted the ear with its masculine music and sank down into the heart with its fervour. She gazed upon him with a rapture of which she herself was almost unconscious; and she beheld his splendid countenance beaming with intellect, while every additional word he uttered was a fresh draught that her young heart drank in from the ineffable fountain of love. And was it surprising that she should thus in every way have been fascinated by her companion? To say that he was handsome, were to say nothing: he was perfectly god-like in his beauty. Tall of stature, his slender figure was marked by an aristocratic bearing attempered by courtly elegance and grace: his locks were long and of raven glossiness: his eyes, dark as jet, nevertheless burnt with living fire; his mouth, cut with classic perfection, was surmounted by a very slight moustache, though his chin was beardless; and when he smiled, his teeth were white, even, and faultless like those of the loveliest woman.

"After rambling for nearly three hours on the shores of the lake, but at such a distance from the Hall as not to be seen from its windows, Margaret suddenly observed that the sun was high and recollected that her father would speedily be returning for the midday meal. With a heightened colour upon her cheeks and somewhat downcast looks, she informed her companion in faltering tones that she must retrace her way; and he accompanied her as far as the bridge over the rivulet: but there he paused to say farewell. She gazed upon him with unfeigned surprise; and then exclaimed in the artlessness of her thoughts, 'But you must come and be introduced to my father! He expects that you will call to-day: he is anxious to express his acknowledgments for the immense service you rendered me last evening.'—'Lady, I cannot have the honour of seeing Sir Poniers Dunhaven to-day,' replied the unknown with a serious look and impressive manner.—'But you really must come, if only for a moment,' rejoined the ingenuous Margaret: 'it ought not to be that I have an acquaintance who is unknown to my father. Come then, I ask it as a favour to myself:' and again the sweet damsel blushed at the vehemence of her own words.—'Dear lady,' replied the stranger, taking her hand and pressing it in his own, 'if you really conceive yourself under the slightest obligation to me for the service, as you are pleased to term it, which I was enabled to render you last evening, I beseech and implore that you will not urge me to accompany you now. Besides,' he added, his voice sinking to a low and plaintively earnest tone, 'if you desire ever to see me more, you will not even mention to your father that you have met me again to-day. But if you will condescend to be here to-morrow, I will explain to you the meaning of my words.'—Having thus spoken, and allowing the amazed damsel no time to reply, he pressed her hand to his lips, and sped away.

"She stood for some time with her eyes fixed upon his retreating form—that form so full of youthful elegance and manly grace: and as he reached the angle of a grove at a short distance, he turned, doffed his plumed cap, and then disappeared from her view. Slowly and pensively did Margaret Dunhaven retrace her way to the Hall. A suspicion of the real truth relative to the young stranger was expanding in her mind, acquiring greater consistency the longer she reflected upon his conduct in not accompanying her home and the words he had used at parting. But what course was she to pursue? To behave with duplicity towards her sire, was an alternative which shocked her pure soul: but to resign the chance of ever beholding her youthful deliverer again, was bitterness to the heart that already in a few short hours had begun to experience the bliss of love, though she as yet did not comprehend what her feelings were. With a sense of duty warring against the influence of a nascent passion, Margaret Dunhaven pursued her way homeward, and re-entered the Hall without having resolved upon any settled course to adopt. She learnt that her father had just returned—that he was accompanied by Lord Glenmorris—and that he was inquiring after her. Accordingly, so soon as she had put off her walking-raiment and assumed another toilet for the dinner-table (this repast being in those times taken at noon) she repaired to the apartment where Sir Poniers and Lord Glenmorris were awaiting her. A variety of conflicting feelings sent the blood mantling up to Margaret's cheeks, so that Lord Glenmorris fancied she looked more lovely than ever in this sweet confusion, the cause of which he utterly mistook. Being rich and handsome, nobly-born and valorous—endowed indeed with all the qualities that were well calculated to win the female heart—the nobleman, with a very pardonable vanity, beheld in the damsel's emotions everything that was flattering to himself; and he interpreted them as being favourable to his own suit. He accordingly advanced to meet her, and taking her hand gallantly raised it to his lips, saying in a low tone and with meaning look, 'Fair lady, this is the happiest day of my life!'—Margaret was so bewildered with the thoughts which crowded in upon her brain, that she could not utter a word of reply, but her father, fearing that she might say something that would damp the young nobleman's ardour, stepped forward, and smoothing down her golden hair with the caressing appearance of paternal fondness, observed, 'Margaret, like a good and obedient child, entrusts to her parent the duty of providing for her happiness: and as you behold her, my lord, a docile daughter, so will you find her a loving and affectionate wife.'—Again did Lord Glenmorris bend down to kiss Margaret's hand: but had his eyes remained fixed upon her countenance at the moment, he would have seen a strange sickly look waver upon her features, and the mantling blood suddenly disappear, leaving her cheeks for the instant as pale as marble. Her father *did* notice this evidence of emotion on her part; but bending upon her a look unusually severe, he turned away.

"They sat down to table; and in the course of the repast Sir Poniers Dunhaven recited to Lord Glenmorris the accident which had occurred to his daughter on the previous evening. Then turning towards her, he said, 'By the bye, has the chivalrous young gentleman who rescued you made his appearance this forenoon at the Hall? or have you seen him again?'— The truth trembled for an instant upon Margaret's tongue—but only for an instant: the next moment she looked her father full in the face, and answered, 'No.'

"How was it that Margaret Dunhaven—the pure, the innocent, the ingenuous, artless girl—thus boldly gave utterance to an untruth? how was it also, that while thus sending forth a falsehood from her tongue, her countenance still wore that angelic look of candour and sincerity which had ever been wont to characterize it? It was because her father himself had within the hour that was passing taught her a lesson of dissimulation. He had audaciously given Lord Glenmorris to understand that his suit was welcome to the damsel; and having proclaimed this falsehood, Sir Poniers had bent upon his daughter that look of stern severity which bade her beware how she contradicted him. Think you, then, that Margaret, ingenuous though she ever was wont to be, failed to profit by the teachings of her sire, in a matter which now so intimately regarded her own happiness? No: she *did* profit by that example! She had this day received her first lesson in duplicity and dissimulation: in a single hour she had grown years older in worldly-minded experience;—a moment of a father's tyranny, falsehood, and severity had taught her what a whole lifetime of happiness, truthfulness, and parental love would have failed to impart.

"I need scarcely tell you, then, that on the following morning, soon after nine o'clock, Margaret Dunhaven wended her way alone along the bank of the lake; and on reaching the bridge over the little river she found the fascinating young stranger—scarcely however a stranger to her now—anxiously awaiting her arrival. Joy beamed upon his splendid countenance, glowing through the olive duskiness of his complexion, as he advanced to meet her; and snatching her fair hand in his own, he pressed it to his lips. Again and again he kissed it—and it was not withdrawn.—'Margaret, dearest Margaret,' he said, with that low deep music of a manly voice which, when quivering with enthusiasm, no young maiden can listen to with impunity, 'you are come, and I am not disappointed! I knew you would come; not because I for a moment fancied that you were inspired by a mere sentiment of curiosity to know who I am; for that doubtless you have already conjectured; but because it was your destiny to come and meet me here again, inasmuch as we were made for each other! Yes, my lovely, my adored Margaret, though I have known you but for a few hours, I love you as if I had lived whole centuries and your image had been cherished in my heart throughout that immense period of time. I love you, Oh! you cannot conceive how I love you; and perhaps this love of mine is all the more adoring, all the more nearly approaching a worship, because the life which animates you now was saved by me! Yes, dearest, I love you thus madly, thus devotedly, and I claim your love also thus earnestly, thus enthusiastically, because Death had you in his embrace and I snatched you from him! I vanquished the destroyer who had you in his grasp: I bore you from destruction in that deep water, to this bank of flowers where I now kneel to demand and implore your love!'—and the young man knelt at her feet; and again and again did he press her hand to his lips; and the damsel felt the wildest but tenderest flutterings in her young bosom. Her heart throbbed with pulses never stirred before: she now comprehended why it was that the image of her adoring suitor had filled her mind throughout the past night; and when he again besought her, in a fresh torrent of rich, glowing, and impassioned language, to declare that she would love him, she murmured, 'Yes.'—He sprang to his feet, he caught her in his arms, he strained her to his breast, and upon her virgin lips did he imprint the warmest kisses.

"Then they wandered again together along the margin of the lake; and on this occasion the youthful lover spoke not of the beauty of the scenery, nor of the sunlit glory of the day, nor of the things he had seen in foreign climes: but he spoke of love—of love alone—that passion whose feeling was so new to her heart, and whose language was so novel to her ears, but which was so ineffably sweet to both: and though for hours the discourse lasted, yet the topic had no sameness, no weariness, no monotony for the young damsel. She listened with subdued rapture—she felt as if new worlds of elysian bliss had suddenly opened their golden portals to her view, and admitted her into their realms of delight and joy. Again was she warned by the vertical beams of the noonday sun that it was time to return—again did her lover accompany her as far as the bridge—and again did they pause there to exchange their farewells. Yes, and not only to exchange farewells, but likewise to arrange an appointment for the morrow: then as they were about to part, Margaret suddenly recollected that she had an inquiry to make in order to confirm her conjecture relative to her lover.

"With a blush upon her cheeks and with downcast looks—for she felt that in the bliss of the last three hours she had forgotten to put the question she was about to ask—she murmuringly said, 'You have not told me your name?'—He caught her by the hand and held her tightly, as if to imply that whatever were the effect of the answer he was about to give she should not flee away from him: then he said, 'Bitter as was the hatred of my ancestors for your's, so fond and devoted is my love for you. I am Ranulph Danvers!'—'I guessed it, I knew it,' returned Margaret. 'Oh, what would my father say, or what would he do, if he beheld me thus with one bearing the name of Danvers?'—'He would slay us both, dearest Margaret,' replied Lord Ranulph; 'and therefore must the secret of our love be inviolably kept.'—'Yes, it must be so,' rejoined the maiden: and with another fond embrace the lovers separated.

CHAPTER XXXII

CONCLUSION OF THE HISTORY OF MARGARET DUNHAVEN.

"Every day, for six weeks, did Margaret Dunhaven and Lord Ranulph Danvers meet at the stone bridge and pass hours in each other's society. The maiden informed her lover of the courtship which Lord Glenmorris was paying her, and of the dissimulation she was compelled to practise at home in order to avert her father's suspicion that *another* image than that of *his* candidate for her hand occupied her heart. Lord Ranulph spoke—but spoke delicately—of the necessity of a secret marriage, and solicited Margaret to make up her mind to fly with him. But deeply, tenderly, devotedly as the young maiden loved him, she could not so soon come to the resolve of abandoning her home, deserting her father, and rushing precipitately upon this new career which her lover developed to her contemplation. Nevertheless, she promised that if Sir Poniers Dunhaven should persist in his attempt to sacrifice her to Lord Glenmorris, and if circumstances should take such a course as to leave her no hope that there could ever be a reconciliation between her sire and the present bearer of the name of Danvers,—then would she, as her only alternative, fly away with him and become his bride. It will therefore be perceived that though Margaret's love amounted to a positive infatuation, yet that the natural rectitude of her character still asserted its authority to a degree sufficient to make her reflect ere she took any rash or precipitate step. Lord Ranulph, with every appearance of an affection as generous as it was enthusiastic—as elevated in sentiment as it was profound in devotion—yielded to the young damsel's delicate scruples, and never urged his point to an extent that might shock her sensibilities or make her suspect the ethereal character of his love. This very forbearance on his part endeared him all the more fully to the confiding Margaret, and she felt assured that he possessed the noblest of natures.

"Meanwhile Lord Glenmorris had been a constant visitor at Dunhaven Hall: but in his presence Margaret was ever silent and reserved, submitting to his courtesies, receiving but never encouraging his attentions, and, covering her own preoccupation of heart and abstraction of thought with the veil of concealment, which was however too cold and too devoid of studied affectation or artifice to be a downright hypocrisy. Lord Glenmorris attributed her conduct to maiden bashfulness; while her father troubled himself very little about it, since she ventured no overt remonstrance against the contemplated match. Perhaps he thought she was passively resigned: at all events he purposely avoided finding himself alone with her, lest any disagreeable scene might take place. That she loved another he did not for an instant suspect: nor did he even know that Lord Ranulph Danvers was in the neighbourhood at all; for the young nobleman contrived to keep this circumstance a profound secret.

"There was one, however, beneath the roof of Dunhaven Hall who failed not to notice the singularity of the young lady's proceedings; and this was the female dependant, Alice. The abigail had been in the habit of walking out with her young mistress: but for the last six weeks Margaret had altogether dispensed with her company. Moreover, Alice observed a considerable change in Margaret's manner; and being sharp-witted and shrewd, she was not long in arriving at two conclusions. The first was that her young mistress did not love Lord Glenmorris; and the second was that she loved some one else. Alice, being a faithful dependant, was somewhat piqued at Margaret's reserve, or rather studied silence towards her; and with true feminine curiosity, she resolved to watch the young lady's movements. This she did through no malicious intent, nor with any ulterior view of betraying whatever she might discover: it was merely to gratify that sentiment which the whole sex in general, and Alice in particular, cherished in the heart—the legacy of their first mother Eve! Accordingly, one morning when Margaret Dunhaven went forth to take her usual walk on the bank of Ennerdale Water, Alice followed at a distance; and by taking a circuitous route, amidst the groves upon the hill-slopes and behind the fragments of rock which lay scattered about in various parts, she managed, without being seen herself, to keep her mistress in view. Her suspicions were speedily confirmed by beholding Margaret Dunhaven encounter an elegant young gallant by the stone bridge; and the affectionate embrace in which she saw them clasped, showed full well that they were not merely friends but tender lovers. Alice could not however, without revealing herself, approach near enough to obtain a full view of her young mistress's admirer; and contented with what she had already discovered, she retraced her way, unperceived by the fond couple, to Dunhaven Hall.

"In the evening, when Alice was assisting her young lady to disapparel herself ere retiring for the night, she dropped a significant hint which at once startled Margaret Dunhaven. That hint made her aware that her secret was known to Alice; and suddenly bursting into tears, she threw her arms round the young abigail's neck, murmuring, 'My dear Alice; I have been wrong not to make you my confidante! Oh, I have wanted to do so on many and many an occasion; but I was afraid. Yet it would have been a relief indeed to me to impart a secret which seems too much for my own bosom to contain. It was not that I feared you would betray me; but it was because I trembled lest you should be both frightened and shocked at the mere mention of the name of him whom I love. But tell me, how did you discover my secret? is it known to any other beneath this roof?'—Alice, who was really most devotedly attached to her young mistress, hastened to relieve her apprehensions on this score, by explaining how she had obtained an insight into what was going on—not admitting however that she had purposely watched the young lady, but alleging that having occasion to pass near the bridge on an errand to a neighbouring farm, she noticed Margaret and her lover. The young lady then revealed to the ears of Alice the name of that lover; and the abigail was astounded on thus learning that a daughter of Dunhaven had bestowed her heart upon one who bore the name of Danvers. Margaret, with that tender longing which young ladies in her circumstances ever experience to pour forth their thoughts, emotions, and feelings into the bosom of a confidante, proceeded to enter into the minutest details with regard to everything that had taken place between herself and Lord Ranulph Danvers; Alice, who was young, high-spirited, and kind-hearted, was not only flattered at being thus admitted to Margaret's fullest confidence, put also sympathized with her young mistress; and so far from counselling her to accept Lord Glenmorris, she advised her to consult her own happiness by marrying Lord Ranulph Danvers.—'Your father, dear lady,' she said, 'only seeks to bestow your hand upon Lord Glenmorris, in order that from the treasures of your intended husband he may purchase back the lost estates of his ancestors: but if report speaks truly, for every piece of gold that Lord Glenmorris can produce, Lord Danvers possesses ten; and surely, therefore, if Lord Danvers can so far forget the traditionary feudal hatred as to espouse Dunhaven's daughter, he will not scruple to place a portion of his treasures at the service of Dunhaven himself?'—'Alas, but would my father accept of such succour?' said Margaret mournfully, 'little more than six weeks have elapsed since, in my hearing, he proclaimed the inveteracy and the immortality of his hatred for every one belonging to the house of Danvers! What can I do? what course would you counsel me to adopt? Shall I throw myself at my father's feet, confess everything, and beseech him to abjure his hatred of Ranulph Danvers for my sake?'—'I know not how to advise you, dear lady,' returned Alice; 'but I should tremble to see you dare your father's wrath by confessing this love of your's. What says Lord Ranulph himself!'—'He asks me to fly with him that I may become his bride,' responded the blushing Margaret: then perceiving that Alice offered no comment, she said, 'You are silent: what think you?'—'I think, lady, that if I were in your place I should yield to the prayer of Lord Ranulph Danvers:' and this answer was delivered by Alice in a firm and decisive tone.

"On the following morning, when Margaret Dunhaven descended to the room where the early meal was served up, her father, who was already there, said, 'My dear child, Lord Glenmorris your suitor is anxious that the bridal should take place with as little delay as possible; and I have therefore fixed this day week for the solemn ceremony. The holy rites will be celebrated in the chapel of Glenmorris Castle; and therefore at an early hour in the morning of Wednesday next, will the bridegroom come with a glittering train of nobles, knights, and fair ladies, to escort you thither. I give you this timely notice in order that you may make fitting preparations in respect to raiment. In the course of this day a large mail-trunk will arrive from Carlisle, containing everything requisite for the seemly apparelment of Dunhaven's daughter.'—Margaret made no reply; and as she had been very taciturn and reserved of late, her father was not troubled by her silence, which he still regarded as indicative of a positive resignation.— 'Lord Glenmorris,' he continued after a brief pause, 'has behaved to me in a manner which should command your esteem, my dear Margaret, even if you cannot bestow upon him your love; and I am about to give you these particulars in order to convince you how worthy a son-in-law I shall find in that nobleman. In the first place, negotiations are already opened with a scrivener at Carlisle for the repurchase of those immense tracts which in times past belonged to the members of our family, but which have been alienated from them. The present owner is willing to dispose of these lands, and in a very short time they will revert to my possession. But this is not all. Glenmorris has formed a solemn league and bond of friendship with me; and within one week from your bridal-day will he place at my disposal all his armed retainers, for a purpose which you can well guess.'—'And that purpose?' said the young maiden, an ice-chill striking to her very heart's core.—'Yon castle,' returned Sir Poniers, pointing towards a castellated mansion on the opposite shore of the lake, 'has been left comparatively undefended by its owner. The report which we some weeks since received respecting Lord Walter's death, is now confirmed; and it is said that Lord Ranulph intends to follow his father's example and remain abroad. Those who are left in charge of the castle, and all the vassals upon the Danvers estate, believe me to be too poor, too friendless, and too much broken down in circumstances every way, to be enabled to make the slightest attempt at a renewal of the ancient feuds. They are therefore lulled into security: but this security is false! Glenmorris will furnish me with a gallant band; and taking advantage of some dark night, when the moon appears not and the stars are hidden, will I storm yon castle and carry the vengeance of fire and sword over the whole domain of Danvers.'—'But my dear father,' said Margaret, shocked at this terrible revelation, 'will it not be an unworthy thing for a valorous chief to do this deed in suddenness and darkness?'—'Daughter,' responded the Knight sternly, 'you know not what you say. Often and often in times past have the Danvers harried the lands of Dunhaven by night; aye, and burnt our mansion to the ground. Think you, then, that I will hesitate to deal forth a terrific retribution, now that opportunity will so shortly serve?'—'But those poor vassals, with their innocent wives and children, have done you no harm,' remonstrated Margaret, an expression of exquisite pain and anguish upon her lovely countenance.—'And the poor vassals of Dunhaven, with their innocent wives and children, who never did the Lords of Danvers any harm?" exclaimed her father in bitter scorn.—'But surely, surely, my dear parent,' cried the young damsel, the tears streaming down her cheeks, 'there must be a time for all those horrors to cease?'—'Yes, they shall cease only when the castellated mansion of the proud Danvers is levelled with the dust and their lands are made a desert!' Having thus spoken with a savage energy, Sir Poniers Dunhaven rose from his seat and abruptly quitted the room.

"With a heavy heart did Margaret ascend to her chamber to put on her walking apparel, preparatory to going forth to meet her lover; and to Alice she told all that had just taken place between herself and her father. Scarcely was she ready to descend from her chamber again, when a horseman galloped up to the entrance of Dunhaven Hall. This was Roger Dunhaven, one of the Knight's nephews and the heir to the title. He was a young man of three-and-twenty, of noble form, handsome but stern countenance, and already celebrated not merely in tilt and tournament, but also as a warrior in the ranks of battle. His father, the younger brother of Sir Poniers, had been dead some years: and Roger as well as his younger brother Euric, had attached himself to the household of a powerful Baron dwelling in a midland county. Sir Poniers had sent Roger and Euric a message to the effect that Margaret was about to become the bride of Lord

Glenmorris; and Roger Dunhaven had accordingly arrived as a visitor at the Hall to be present at the wedding and its attendant festivities,—his brother Euric being unable to accompany him.

"Sir Poniers hastened forth to greet his elder nephew, whom he loved well, not only on account of his warlike renown but likewise because he was an individual after his own heart—fond of carousing at the board, and inheriting with due implacability the traditionary hatred of the Dunhavens for the family of Danvers. Tossing the reins of his steed to the groom who was in attendance, Roger entered the hall with his uncle; and a message was immediately sent up to summon Margaret from her chamber. She accordingly descended in obedience to her father's mandate; and her cousin congratulated her in somewhat rough and uncouth terms, not only upon her approaching marriage with Lord Glenmorris, but also upon the wondrous beauty of her person.—'It is four or five years since I saw you last, fair cousin,' said Roger, 'and in the interval you have shot up from a saucy frolicsome light-headed girl to a splendid womanhood. Why, how old are you? Not much above seventeen; and yet you are as tall as a dart. Higher than my shoulder, I declare!' and then Roger Dunhaven laughed loudly. He sat down to table, ate voraciously, and drank in proportion. Poor Margaret was compelled to remain in the room, although disgusted with her cousin, and longing to speed away and keep the usual appointment with her lover. But this appointment was not to be kept on the present occasion: for when Roger had finished his meal, he said, 'Now, fair cousin, you and I will go and take a long walk together, either upon the shore of the lake or else amongst the hills, whichever you choose.'—Margaret began to murmur an excuse to the effect that she did not feel well, and moreover that she had occupations at home. But Roger insisted—Sir Poniers gave an authoritative look—and the unhappy Margaret was compelled to sally forth with her coarse-minded rough-mannered cousin. She purposely took him amongst the hills, in order to avoid the chance of meeting Ranulph on the borders of the lake; and when they returned to the Hall the dinner was served up. Immediately afterwards the mail-trunk arrived from Carlisle; and Sir Poniers insisted that Margaret should inspect all its contents at once. In short, the day passed without her being able to steal forth from the mansion and meet her lover.

"On the following day the rains poured down in torrents, and there was no possibility of Margaret's stirring out. The bad weather continued for the three days next ensuing: and the young damsel dared not excite suspicion by venturing forth in the deluging rain. Five whole days had now passed, and Margaret had not seen Ranulph Danvers: yet never had she so much wanted to behold him—never had her heart so yearned towards him! She was profoundly unhappy. Her father was sternly bent upon her marriage with Lord Glenmorris; her cousin Roger was constantly obtruding himself with his coarse but not ill-meant familiarity upon her presence: and in addition to these sources of annoyance, she was forced, in order to avert suspicion from the secret of her love, to superintend the making up of the wedding-raiment. The five days which thus elapsed since last she met Lord Ranulph, were the most miserable the poor girl had ever known; and each evening, when alone with Alice, did she give vent to her grief in bitter, burning tears. The sixth day came: it was Monday morning—and the weather had once more changed. It was beautiful, but very cold: for the end of October had now arrived. Margaret was resolved at any risk to meet her lover this day: therefore as soon as breakfast was over, she retreated to her own room, hastily donned her walking-apparel, issued stealthily forth from the Hall by a back door, and sped towards the stone bridge. Lord Ranulph was there. Even before her eyes caught sight of his elegant form, her heart told her that he was sure to be at the usual place of appointment. More tender if possible than ever was the embrace in which they were now locked: more affectionate were the syllables to which they gave utterance! All that had occurred since they had last met was speedily explained by the damsel; nor did she even hesitate to reveal to her lover the hostile intentions which her father contemplated, and which he purposed to carry out with the assistance of Lord Glenmorris's armed vassals.

" 'Now, dearest Margaret,' said Ranulph, straining her to his breast, 'you will no longer hesitate when I implore you to fly?'—The young maiden said nothing; but the look which she gave and the tenderness with which she clung to her handsome admirer, afforded him an answer as intelligible as words themselves could have been.—'The day after tomorrow, you say, dearest Margaret,' resumed Ranulph Danvers, 'will Glenmorris, with a lordly and a brilliant retinue, come to bear you away to his castle, where all the preparations are made upon a splendid scale for the nuptials? But when he, and his lords, and his knights, and his dames arrive at Dunhaven Hall, it must be only to experience the bitterest disappointment, and to learn that the sweet bird has flown. Shall it not be so, Margaret?'—'It shall,' she replied in a faint tone: for she doubtless felt that the alternative she had to adopt was a desperate one.—'To-day and to-morrow,' resumed Lord Ranulph Danvers, 'must I occupy myself in certain preparations, which, after all you have told me relative to your father's hostile intent, are requisite to place my castle and domain in a condition of defence. But these arrangements will be conducted with such secrecy and precaution that my presence in this part of the country shall still continue unsuspected in those quarters it is desirable for it to remain unknown.

And believe me, my sweet Margaret, when I solemnly assure you that whatever vengeance your sire may endeavour to wreak upon my fortalice or domain, shall provoke no active hostility on the part of my vassals. If attacked, they shall merely display an imposing force, in the presence of which the invaders will quail. But when once you are far away and Glenmorris has lost you as his bride, he will not be so zealous in taking up the feudal quarrels of Sir Poniers Dunhaven: and thus there is in reality no fear of a revival of hostilities.'—Margaret was reassured and cheered by the language of her lover; and she resolved to confide in all things to his prudence and his affection.—'We will not remain long together now,' he said, 'lest that rude cousin of your's should chance to behold us in his rambles; and though my good sword would teach him courteous manners, yet it were well to risk nothing that might threaten to mar our projects. Beloved Margaret, to-morrow night at eleven o'clock I shall be here, at this very spot, with two fleet horses; and the minutes will be anxiously counted until you make your appearance.'—'But Alice, is she not to accompany me?' asked the young damsel: 'you know that I have told her everything: I explained this much to you just now.'—'Margaret,' replied Lord Ranulph, 'if you entertain the slightest doubt relative to my honour, you then can have no confidence in my love. It will multiply the chances of discovery if Alice accompanies you in your flight. One person may steal forth from a house, where two would be observed. Besides, I have a pair of steeds of wondrous swiftness, and which will outstrip any others in my castle-stables. Were Alice to go with us, the steed provided for her use, would prove a laggard in comparison with the two that must bear my beloved Margaret and myself.'—But still the damsel hesitated: her instinctive delicacy made her feel that it were more consistent with propriety for her to be accompanied by her maid. Lord Ranulph Danvers, however, advanced fresh arguments against the necessity of such a step, assuring Margaret Dunhaven that ere the sun should rise upon the night of their intended elopement the priest's blessing would give her the sacred name of wife. The young damsel glanced across the lake towards her lover's castellated mansion, and asked, with blushing cheeks, 'Wherefore not solemnize the nuptials there?'—'Because, dearest Margaret,' he at once answered, 'if it were known that it was I who had borne you away, and that you were an inmate of yonder towers, then indeed would Glenmorris and your father come with all the armed strength they could muster to wrest you from my embrace: and *then* indeed would the deadly feud revive, and heaven alone could tell whose blood might flow! But I have *another* castle which can be reached in a few hours; and thither shall I bear you.'—The result of the discourse was that Margaret assented to everything her lover proposed;

and they parted with the renewed understanding that on the night of the next day they were to meet at the bridge at eleven o'clock.

"The young damsel sped back to the Hall, where she was well pleased to find that her absence had not been particularly noticed by her father or her cousin. Repairing to her own chamber, she confided to Alice all that had just taken place between herself and Lord Ranulph Danvers, not even omitting a single word that he had uttered, or a single argument that he had used in order to induce her to fall into his arrangements. Alice listened in silence: and her looks gradually became gloomy.—'You had expected to accompany me in my flight?' said Margaret; 'and I could have wished it also; but rest assured, dear girl, that I shall lose no time after my union with Ranulph in sending for you. The same messenger who will bear to my father a letter explaining all that I have done, will be charged to escort you to my dwelling-place.'—Alice was cheered by this assurance; but as a thought struck her, she observed, 'It is singular that I never learnt till now that the Danvers family had *another* castle so near to that of Ennerdale as to be reached in a few short hours. We have heard that they have a castle in Essex, and a castle in the Isle of Wight: but besides the three thus known of, I have heard of no other.'—'It is not, my dear Alice, because we have never heard of a fourth castle,' answered the confiding Margaret, 'that there should not be one in existence. Oh, do not for an instant even seem to think that Lord Ranulph could deceive me!'—'Heaven forbid, dear lady!' rejoined Alice: 'it was only a passing reflection, without real importance, to which I gave expression. So far from counselling you against the course which you have chosen to adopt, I have advised it before, and I advise it again.'—At this moment the dinner-bell rang, and Margaret was compelled to descend to the room where the repast was served up.

"The better to ward off all possibility of suspicion, she worked for the remainder of that day and throughout all the next at the wedding-raiment—that raiment which in her heart she had vowed never to wear! Her father seemed well pleased that she should thus devote herself to the task; and as her cousin was out pursuing the pleasures of the chase amidst the adjacent mountains, during the whole of that memorable Tuesday, she had not to endure the annoyance of his company. He did not return till supper-time; and soon afterwards Margaret, according to her wont, retired to her chamber.

"It was now past ten o'clock; and Sir Poniers Dunhaven sat drinking deep draughts of wine with his nephew Roger. They discussed the plan of the attack which was contemplated to be made the first fitting opportunity upon the castellated mansion on the other shore of Lake Ennerdale, and they likewise talked gleefully of the negotiations then in progress, and which in a few days were to restore the Dunhaven estate to its ancient boundaries. But principally they dwelt upon the proposed incursion on the domains of their rival and the beleaguerment of his castle. This subject they discussed with a ferocious joy: but presently they began to differ in opinion as to the best method of assailing the fortalice, so as to carry it by storm at a single blow. Sir Poniers, dipping his finger into the goblet, traced various lines upon the table to describe the exact position of the castle on the opposite bank; on the other hand, Roger declared that he was well enough acquainted with every feature of it; and while the Knight advocated an onslaught upon one point, the nephew as vehemently insisted that the attack should be made upon another. The discussion grew warm; and without exactly quarrelling, they disputed in a loud tone and strong language. At length Sir Poniers, starting up, exclaimed, 'Let us go at once and examine well those points of the fortress concerning which we are at variance. The moon is shining brightly and we shall be enabled to pursue our investigation with ease.'—'Agreed!' ejaculated Roger; and they sallied forth together.

"Hastening down the garden, they passed out of the side door in the wall, and sped along the border of the lake so as to make its circuit and gain the opposite side. They had proceeded some little distance and were approaching the stone bridge, when they observed a female form hurrying along in the same direction; and as she threw an affrighted glance behind, on hearing the steps of those whom she took to be pursuers, the powerful moonlight revealed to their eyes the countenance of Margaret. They were so astonished for a few moments as to be transfixed to the spot—both stopping suddenly short as the same idea struck them. They thought they beheld a spirit in Margaret's shape! Thanks to that superstitious belief on their part, and which so abruptly struck them motionless, the young damsel, flying as if wings were fastened to her feet, gained the bridge: and shrieking forth, 'My father and cousin!' sank senseless into the arms of her lover, who was already there.

"Sir Poniers Dunhaven and his nephew Roger were near enough to behold what thus took place, and even to catch the words which Margaret had uttered; and drawing their swords, they sprang forward to cut down the individual in whose embrace she had thus fainted. At the same instant also they perceived two colossal coal-black steeds fastened by the bridles to the other end of the bridge; and thus there could be no doubt as to the motive which had brought Margaret thither. But her lover, still retaining her clasped in his left arm, waved his naked rapier with his right, saying in a cold and even indifferent voice, 'Back, back; ye cannot war against me!'—'Ah!' exclaimed Sir Poniers, as both he and his nephew Roger *did* fall back, repelled as it were by an irresistible power; 'it is Danvers, the hated Danvers! That look, that scornful smile, those eyes, I know them well! they are the characteristics of his detested race!'—'Then let him perish!' thundered Roger: and with upraised claymore he bounded forward to cut Lord Ranulph down. Not a pace did the young nobleman retreat; but still holding the unconscious maiden with his left arm thrown around her form, with his rapier he thrust aside the heavy weapon of the furious Roger, and then the next instant sent his lithe thin blade through his conquered assailant's heart. With a low moan Roger fell back, stone dead; and the next instant Lord Ranulph Danvers crossed the bridge, sprang upon the back of one of the steeds, still retaining Margaret in his arms—and away sped the mettled courser with its burden, and the other horse galloping by the side.

"There is in this portion of the narrative a mystery which cannot be altogether unravelled. Sir Poniers Dunhaven beheld his nephew slain and his daughter carried off before his eyes; and yet he made not the slightest attempt to wreak his vengeance upon Lord Ranulph—no, nor even to snatch Margaret from the young noble's arms. Sir Poniers himself could never afterwards explain how it was that the valour of his arm was paralysed at such a moment, and that he was reduced to powerlessness not only in the presence of his hated enemy, but even under circumstances which, apart from his hereditary enmity, were of themselves sufficient to goad him to desperation. Paralysed and powerless, however, he *did* find himself at that moment: a spell had suddenly fallen upon him, holding him fast with its supernal influence, and depriving him of even the will to act or speak. It was not until the sounds of the retreating steeds had ceased to reach his ear that the spell was lifted from him, and he was master of his own actions once again. Then he rushed madly in the direction taken by the fugitives; but after running a long distance, he sank down exhausted and shed tears of rage at the futility of his chase. Returning to the bridge, he beheld his nephew still lying motionless there, and found that the vital spark had indeed fled for ever. Then he hurried in frenzy back to the hall, and speeding up to his daughter's chamber, found Alice there. The young girl, deeply anxious on account of her mistress, had not as yet retired to rest. She had heard the Knight and his nephew go forth a very few minutes after Margaret herself had stealthily issued from the mansion; and naturally supposing that a pursuit was taking place, she set up to learn the result. Now, on beholding Sir Poniers rush in with wild looks, distorted features, and foam upon the lips, Alice threw herself upon her knees and implored his mercy. She thought that he had come to kill her as the confidante of his daughter's flight. Her terrified looks, her suppliant attitude, and the words which she uttered, at once betrayed her knowledge of Margaret's escape; and the infuriate Sir Poniers vowed that he would slay her unless she told all she knew. She accordingly revealed everything; and her confession, which was subsequently taken down in writing at full length, and in all its details, served as the basis of this narrative. Indeed, from no other source could the various circumstances connected with the loves of Lord Ranulph Danvers and Margaret Dunhaven become known. For never from that day forth was Margaret seen or heard of more!

"The corpse of Roger Dunhaven was fetched from the bridge and borne to the Hall. Then, as it lay stretched upon the couch where it was deposited, Sir Poniers Dunhaven, standing by the side of that bed, and in the presence of all his dependants, took a terrible and fearful oath, to the effect that ere *the bones of his murdered nephew received the rites of Christian sepulture, his death would be fearfully avenged!* Messengers were at once despatched to the Knight's only surviving nephew Euric, to acquaint him with all that had taken place, and request him to repair without delay to Dunhaven Hall. Sir Poniers then lost no time in speeding to Glenmorris Castle, the noble owner of which was almost wild with rage on learning that the beauteous damsel, whom he so much coveted as his bride, had fled with a rival. As it was known that Lord Ranulph had really no castle within a few hours ride of Lake Ennerdale, it was supposed, notwithstanding the statements made by Alice when repeating all she had heard from her young mistress, that Danvers had borne Margaret to his castellated mansion on the adjacent eminence; and a general gathering of all the feudal retainers of Lord Glenmorris at once took place. Five hundred stalwart men were thus assembled; and in the afternoon of the day which followed the night of Margaret's flight, this force, with Lord Glenmorris and Sir Poniers Dunhaven at its head, marched to the assault of Lord Ranulph's castle. The sun was setting behind the western hills as the serried armament, having rounded the extremity of the lake, ascended the eminence towards the castle: but on arriving beneath its walls, the troops of Glenmorris were received with such a shower of arrows and such a hailstorm of ponderous missiles, as to show full well that the garrison was by no means weak nor unprepared, and that the fortalice was admirably defended. The besiegers, thus baffled, fled in confusion—their chieftain Lord Glenmorris was slain by an arrow—and Sir Poniers Dunhaven received a mortal wound from the bolt of an arblast. The inmates of the castle, contented with having thus put the enemy to flight, sallied not forth to follow up the victory; and thus Sir Poniers Dunhaven's immediate followers were enabled to bear their wounded chief unmolested to the Hall.

"The Knight lived for two days,—indeed until his nephew Euric arrived at the mansion. Then Sir Poniers, making the young man kneel down by the side of his couch, addressed him as follows:—'Euric, I have sworn the most sacred and solemn of oaths that the bones of your murdered brother shall never receive Christian sepulture until his death is avenged! It is for you to ratify this oath as your own, so that my soul may not be troubled with the foul sin of perjury in another world.'—The young Euric swore to fulfil his uncle's commands, and Sir Poniers breathed his last. A cunning leech, well skilled in anatomical pursuits, was sent for from Carlisle; and beneath his scalpel and dissecting-knife, Roger Dunhaven's flesh separated from the bones. The skeleton was bleached, and treated in some peculiar manner so as to preserve it; it was then deposited in a chest, and became an heir-loom in the family of Dunhaven,—the Knight's vow prohibiting the interment of those bones until such day that the fullest vengeance should have been wreaked upon some scion of the house of Danvers!

"The body of Sir Poniers Dunhaven and the flesh stripped from Roger's bones were duly buried. As for the young damsel Alice—well-nigh heartbroken at all that had occurred, she retired to a convent, where she languished a few years and then sank into an early grave. But during the remainder of her short life she heard nothing more of Margaret Dunhaven. Euric inherited the little estate, together with the pecuniary difficulties of his deceased uncle; and in the course of a few years he was compelled to surrender up the last remnants of his ancestral patrimony to the hands of usurers. From that period the name of Dunhaven ceased to be known in Cumberland. It was not however extinguished altogether: but its subsequent possessors inherited naught save the family vengeance, the skeleton of Roger, and the obligations imposed by Sir Ponier's vow."

CHAPTER XXXIII.

THE TRAP-DOOR.

Such was the history which old Dunhaven related to Gerald St. Louis, on the occasion of the latter's revisit to Deadman's Place. The King's Private Secretary had listened with an augmenting interest as the old man proceeded; nor did he once interrupt the recital, with either question or comment, until it was brought to an end. Even then, at the conclusion of the history, he did not immediately speak, but remained absorbed in deep thought for several minutes. During this interval of silence, old Dunhaven sat with his elbow upon his knee and his hand supporting his head,—profoundly buried in the many memories connected with his ancestry, which had just been so vividly wakened up in his mind.

"And you still cherish the family vengeance against the house of Danvers?" observed St. Louis, at length breaking silence, and fixing his eyes with a sort of melancholy expression upon the old man.

"Yes—it has descended to me together with my name," was the response; "and though you behold me here—a denizen of this district of squalor and crime, and therefore in one sense unworthy to bear the whilome proud and haughty name of Dunhaven—yet in another sense am I a true scion of that race, inasmuch as I remain faithful to the only heritage which has descended to me from my ancestors—namely, the oath of vengeance!"

"But if it wound not your feelings by asking such a question," observed St. Louis, "how came a man inheriting such a name and so true a spirit, to be a denizen of this sanctuary of crime?"

"Ah!" ejaculated Dunhaven, flinging a quick and meaning glance upon the King's Private Secretary, "is there naught in your own career which might serve as a clue to the unravelment of that enigma?—have *your* experiences failed to teach you how a dashing gallant, who has ruffled it boldly and joyously for a time, becomes reduced to all sorts of shifts when his pockets are empty and his friends fall off? Suppose, Master St. Louis, that when you were down in the world some months ago—at that time, I mean, when you came to borrow horses and weapons of me,—suppose, I say, that no good fortune had turned up to pitchfork you into the royal service, is it by any means improbable that you would have been led to deeds compelling you to make Deadman's Place your home for the remainder of your days?"

"Enough! I did not mean to offend you," exclaimed Gerald St. Louis, liking as little as might be that allusion to his *one* night's experience as a highwayman: "neither will I ask you farther relative to your own circumstances. At all events you are not poor now; and though compelled to live in this sanctuary, are still in possession of much worldly substance?"

"Aye—and men repute me a miser," rejoined Dunhaven. "Perhaps I am—perhaps I am: and if so, it may be that gold is the only source of joy left to me upon this earth. When I first came to this sanctuary, hunted hither by the blood-hounds of the law, I was in poverty and rags—of fortunes so desperate and with feelings so despondent that I cared not what became of me: for the wife of my bosom, whom I had loved fondly, and to shield whom against want I had plunged into crime, deserted me in my utmost need and fled with some lordly seducer. Long years have elapsed since then; and, as you may suppose, there have been times when I have stealthily gone forth from the sanctuary and visited the somewhat more agreeable parts of this capital. Otherwise, when first hunted hither by the officers of justice, I should not have been able to fetch to my new abode, when once settled down in it, those ghastly relics of my ancestor:"—and thus speaking, the old man flung a look towards the huge chest that contained the skeleton. "Now," he continued, "I am the last of my race; and if our family vengeance be not wreaked by my hand upon Lionel Danvers, there is none to inherit the name of Dunhaven and menace him hereafter. There was a time—somewhat more than two years back—when I *did* fancy that by my means this hereditary vengeance was inflicted——"

"But when you had thrown Lionel Danvers down your singularly-contrived trap-door," interrupted St. Louis, "wherefore did you not give Christian burial to the bones of your ancestor Roger Dunhaven?"

"More reasons than one occurred," replied the old man, "to make me hesitate ere adopting any measure to give those bones the rites of Christian sepulture. I have ere now hinted that in this sanctuary I am reputed to be a miser; and it is known—or at least suspected—that I have some hoard of wealth: for during a long series of years have I carried on a variety of transactions in this place,—transactions by which some little wealth has doubtless accrued to me, but not to the extent which my neighbours suppose. However, of late years it has been difficult for me to leave the sanctuary, even for a few hours, no matter how stealthily——"

"But methought," interrupted St. Louis, "that such a good understanding prevailed amongst ye dwellers in Deadman's Place, that ye seldom if ever preyed on each other,—your own penal code sufficing to maintain the most rigid discipline?"

"Aye, true!" replied Dunhaven: "but it is not to the fear of being robbed that I made allusion. Can you not understand that if it were known I stole out of the sanctuary, information might be given to the King's officers, so that my arrest being effected, the informant would receive half the amount of all my property? For whatsoever were found in my house would devolve to the Crown on my conviction for felony. Thus, you see, I was compelled to wait for a fitting opportunity to carry forth those bones and give them Christian burial in some churchyard; and such opportunity did not present itself. Moreover, although in my own mind I felt full well assured that Lionel Danvers must have perished on that night of storm when I flung him down the trap-door, yet still at times there was a slight misgiving which suggested the possibility of his escape; and if he had so escaped, to give the bones the rite of burial would have been to falsify the oath sworn by Sir Poniers long years ago,—that oath which became a heritage together with the pledge of vengeance itself! And fortunate was it that these various reasons should have delayed the interment of Roger Dunhaven's bones: for you may imagine my surprise—indeed you beheld it—when you and Welford came hither with the information some few months back that you had met Lord Lionel Danvers!"

"And now, Master Dunhaven," observed St. Louis, "you have not told me how you managed to inveigle Lord Lionel hither on that night of tempest and storm when you made him issue from your dwelling again, not through the doorway by which I presume he entered it, but by that strange revolving trap of yours overhanging the Thames. And were I to give additional rein to my curiosity, I might perhaps venture to ask for what purpose such a trap-door was ever contrived at all?"

"I am disposed, Master Secretary, to give you my fullest confidence," replied Dunhaven, "and will answer both your questions. But the latter one first. And therefore, as to the trap-door, let me at once inform you it existed when I took the house some years ago. That such a contrivance should be found in a place tenanted by desperadoes of all kinds, cannot be very wonderful; and at the time it was made, the penal code of the sanctuary may not have been quite so stringent as it at present is. Suppose some wealthy individual—may be a lord belonging to the Court—was compelled to seek refuge for a season in the sanctuary: then suppose this house tenanted by murderous ruffians, and that the refugee in question either took up his abode here, or was inveigled hither by some means or other:—in such a case, to strip him of all he possessed, even perhaps of his very raiment—make away with him, and thrust him down the trap-door,—such, in a few words, might be supposed as the summing up of the whole tragedy. But as I am a living man, for no evil purpose has that trap-door been used since the house fell into my hands—save and except in the case of Lionel Danvers: and if you are as faithful to the hereditary vengeance of the family of St. Louis as I am to that of the race of Dunhaven, you will agree that it was no evil at all in seeking to give Lionel Danvers his doom by means of that trap-door!"

"Well, but relative to the inveigling him hither?" cried Gerald St. Louis, evading any comment upon that remark in which the old man had just coupled the two family names together.

"Ah! that was your first question," returned Dunhaven, "and now I proceed to answer it:"—then with a deepening solemnity of tone and manner, he said, "I must begin by informing you that it is about six years ago that I first beheld Lionel Danvers. It was evening, and I had been to call upon Master Landini, the banker in Lombard Street, to ascertain whether the young lord, who had then recently succeeded to the family title and estate, was likely to visit England. Master Landini, as you are doubtless aware, is the banker and agent for the Danvers family. I received an unsatisfactory reply; but as I was turning away from the door of the bank an individual came forth; and in the stream of the lamplight gushing forth from within, I caught a glimpse of him ere he hurried away and disappeared in the surrounding darkness. But that glimpse—Oh! it was sufficient to tell me who the individual was: for *one* style of beauty characterizes the scions of the Danvers family—that strange, wondrous, and almost preterhuman beauty which is as hereditary with them as the family hatred is with us. Tall and slender—with hair dark as the raven's wing—eyes of an uncommon lustre—the proud lip curling haughtily—and with a look of the loftiest superiority,—such were the traits which marked the individual whom I then knew to be Lionel Danvers. But, as I have stated, he at once disappeared from my view, and it were vain to follow him in the darkness of the hour and the mazes of the streets. A short time afterwards I beheld him again. It was night, as on the former occasion; and he was issuing forth from the house of a merchant named Manners. Then also did he at once speed away, neither appearing to behold me nor affording me the slightest opportunity of addressing him. But, oh! in the transitory glimpse which I caught of him on that second occasion, how full of a Satanic mockery and devilish triumph was the smile that curled his haughty lips! A few days afterwards I learnt that he had eloped with the merchant's daughter, and that she had disappeared altogether—even as my ancestress Margaret had done with Lord Ranulph!"

"And as my ancestress Arline did with Lord Humphrey!" added St. Louis, in a deep tone and with a gloomy look.

There was then a brief pause; at the expiration of which old Dunhaven resumed his narrative in the following manner:—

"Four years elapsed, and I neither heard nor saw anything more of Lionel Danvers. One evening, in the month of March, 1514, I paid a visit to Lombard Street, and renewed my periodical inquiry at Master Landini's. I should observe that I never told the banker who I was, nor wherefore I was solicitous relative to the movements of Lord Danvers; and I am certain that Master Landini on his side had no means of ascertaining who I was. Therefore what I am about to state becomes all the more extraordinary and unaccountable, as you will soon perceive. On the occasion referred to, I received as usual a vague and unsatisfactory answer from Master Landini, our interview not lasting above a minute. It was about nine o'clock; and I proceeded to spend an hour or two at that tavern in the Old Bailey which Master Benjamin Welford was wont to frequent, and where indeed I originally formed his acquaintance. Having passed some two or three hours at the tavern, I began to retrace my way homeward; but scarcely had I reached the middle of London Bridge, when the violence of the wind came with so sudden a gust as well-nigh to wrest my mantle from around me. Indeed, the fastenings were riven by the fury of the gale; and I was compelled to take refuge for a few moments in the deep-arched doorway of one of the houses on the bridge, for the purpose of re-adjusting my garment. It was a night of pitchy darkness; there was neither moon nor star upon the vault of heaven; and the winds were raging, and roaring, and rushing with maniac fury over the inky waters of the Thames. It was a night indeed to make a man afraid if he had aught upon his conscience; and that my conscience was very clear, I do not pretend to say. Were it so, I should never have been an inmate of Deadman's Place. At that moment, as I stood in the deep darkness of the doorway, fastening my mantle around me as well as I could, all the evil I had ever done in my life seemed to rise up suddenly in my mind,—incident after incident and detail upon detail crowding thickly and arraying themselves like a troop of grim spectres in my imagination; so that my brain seemed thronged with all the horrors of the prison-house and the churchyard. I felt that the loneliness of the hour and the place was awful to a degree; and I said aloud, 'Would that I had a companion to cheer me for the rest of my walk;'—although indeed it was a bare ten minutes' run from that spot on London Bridge to this house in Deadman's Place. But scarcely had I given utterance to those words, spoken in a sort of involuntary soliloquy, when I was startled, or rather filled with consternation, on hearing a voice, speaking close by me, exclaim, 'I will be your companion!'—For a few moments I was so completely transfixed with terror that I could neither move nor speak; but at length with a desperate effort I thrust forth my hand, and it encountered a velvet cloak.—'What?' cried the same voice that had before spoken, and now its tones were filled with a strange mocking irony, 'do you doubt whether I am a being of flesh and blood? Here, satisfy yourself at once!'— and now my hand was grasped by one that was soft and warm, feeling like that of a young man who earned not his living by hard toil.—'Who are you?' I demanded, taking courage. 'One who, doubtless like yourself, took shelter for a minute or two against that gust which, more pitiless than previous ones, swept across the bridge with such terrific violence.'—While the individual was yet speaking, methought I could perceive the flashing of his eyes, as if they were of superhuman brightness; and I again felt somewhat afraid, not knowing what snare the Evil One might be laying for me.—'You expressed a wish for a companion,' he continued, 'and I offer myself to you as such. Besides, if I mistake not, you will be rather well pleased to have thus encountered me.'—There seemed a strange lurking irony in his accents; but his voice was of perfect masculine melody, flute-like and deep without being either feminine or sonorous.—'Yes, a companion,' I said hesitatingly, 'but not without knowing who he is. Besides, you would please me by explaining what you meant by the remark that I should rejoice at this encounter.'—'When a person,' he responded, 'has been inquiring for another, it is that he wishes to see him. Now then do you comprehend me?'—A suspicion of the truth instantaneously flashed to my mind, and with a thrill of exultation vibrating through my heart, I exclaimed, 'Is it possible, Lord Danvers!'—'The same,' he rejoined; 'and now come on.'—So we continued our way across the bridge together.

"Then he must have known you before?" exclaimed St. Louis. "But even if he *had* known you before, how could he recognise you in the deep darkness of that place and hour?"

"These things have much puzzled me since," answered Dunhaven: "but I did not pause to think of them at the time, all my ideas and all my feelings being so suddenly engrossed in the one grand thought that at length the hereditary object of an hereditary vengeance was by my side— perhaps in my power! How he knew me I cannot conjecture; or if knowing me, how he recognised me then, I am equally at a loss to conceive."

"Proceed, proceed!" exclaimed St. Louis, much excited by the narrative. "This grows marvellously interesting."

"Well," continued Dunhaven, "we walked on in silence. Indeed not a word was spoken till we reached the entrance of Deadman's Place: and then, fearing that he might hesitate to accompany me any farther, I said, 'My lord, my humble habitation is in this quarter: deign to proceed with me thither and accept a cup of wine after this chilling walk.'—'Go on, Master Dunhaven,' was Danvers' reply: 'I will follow you.'—Then nothing more was said until we reached this house; and I introduced his lordship into the very room where you and I, Master St. Louis, are now seated. But it was not until I had lighted a lamp that I for the third time beheld the countenance of this young man on whom I had resolved to wreak a terrible though tardy vengeance. I say *tardy*, because, though during the many years of my life I had never forgotten the heritage of vengeance, yet it was not until very lately, and when I began to find myself tottering towards the grave with no heir to leave behind me, that I had begun seriously to think of fulfilling the duty which my ancestors had bequeathed to me——"

"Spare so many comments, worthy Master Dunhaven," interrupted St. Louis, "and come to the point at once. You had inveigled Lord Lionel to this house—to this very room;—you had lighted your lamp—and you then beheld each other. How looked he when, as the lamp flamed up, you cast your eyes upon his countenance?"

"Ah! that look—never shall I forget it!" exclaimed Dunhaven. "For an instant it sent a shudder quivering through my entire form; and had not my hereditary hate risen superior to my first feeling of terror, I should have sunk down at his feet, with the thought that he had detected my purpose in bringing him thither, and that his vengeance was about to fall upon me instead of *mine* on him,—so that I should have cried, 'Pardon, pardon!'—But I speedily recovered my firmness——"

"And his look?" again demanded St. Louis.

"It was fraught," replied Dunhaven, "with all those terrors which sacred legends attribute to the fallen angels—a look so full of mingled mockery, wickedness, and haughty scorn," he continued, "that it seemed as if he were a man who felt himself privileged to trample upon all things human!"

"The same, the same," muttered St. Louis to himself, "as when we met that night in the lane near Greenwich."

"What say you, Master Secretary?" inquired Dunhaven, thinking that the young man had made some remark the purport of which he had not caught.

"Nothing. Proceed!" returned Gerald. "What followed when you and your enemy were alone in this room together?"

"There was at first a long silence," resumed Dunhaven,—"but a silence intruded upon however by the wild winds that were wailing, and howling, and shrieking, and crying without: and to my ears those blasts seemed laden with the voices of agonizing victims in the last moments of murder, of drowning, and of violent death. But still I was nerved with a courage that surprised myself.—'Hark!' suddenly exclaimed Lord Danvers, raising his finger with a warning gesture; 'what sound was that? Heard you not a noise as of bones rattling in their coffin?'—Then indeed for a moment did a mortal terror come over me; for as the nobleman spoke, my ear had too plainly caught the awful sound to which he alluded. Yes, Gerald St. Louis," continued Dunhaven in a firm voice, and with the air of a man who speaks of things too solemn to be made a jest, "as true as you are there—as surely as you hear me speak at this moment—aye, and as certain," he added more solemnly still, "as there is a God above us, did I hear the skeleton of Roger Dunhaven moving in that chest!"

"Heavens! is it possible?" faltered St. Louis, his countenance turning ghastly pale and a visible tremor agitating his entire form: then, all in a moment becoming ashamed of his fears, he cried, "Pshaw! it must have been only fancy on your part. On my soul, Master Dunhaven, were it not broad daylight, and with the sun powerful enough to send its beams even through that narrow dingy lattice of your's, I should have grown quite pusillanimous at your tale."

"Whether it were fancy on my part," replied Dunhaven, his tone and look again expressing the deepest solemnity, "you shall judge for yourself presently. Meanwhile let me make an end of my narrative. As I have already declared, a mortal terror came over me when those awful sounds of rattling bones reached my ear; and then ineffable grew the wickedness of Lord Lionel Danvers' countenance. But the expression that it wore was not one which marred its wondrously handsome modelling, but gave to all its lineaments the terrific beauty of Lucifer in his fall.—'What?' he said in a contemptuous voice, 'are you frightened at such sounds as those?' then immediately resuming his natural look, and speaking in a cold careless tone, he added, 'But you have inquired concerning me this evening: for what purpose do you seek me?'—'How knew you, my lord,' I asked, 'that I was the individual who had thus inquired concerning you? how came you to recognise me on the bridge in the depth of a darkness which methought no human eyes could penetrate?'—'Let us not waste time with trivial questions and answers,' was the nobleman's reply: 'but tell me wherefore you seek me and what you want?'—'My lord,' I immediately rejoined, 'be pleased to follow me, and I will explain myself more fully.'— 'Oh, if we cannot converse here, I have no objection to go elsewhere,' he observed with a calm indifference: 'so lead on, Master Dunhaven.'—I took up the lamp and conducted Lord Danvers along the narrow passage into the room containing the trap-door; and hurrying on somewhat in advance, I reached that part of the wall where the iron knob connected with the spring is fixed. A glance thrown over my shoulder, showed that Danvers was following me—most probably thinking that I was about to lead into some room farther on still. Oh! never shall I forget the sensation which I at that instant experienced: my veins all in a moment seemed to run with liquid fire—the wildest joy was flaming in my soul! Danvers, apparently unsuspicious, and with that dignified ease of bearing which gives him a look at once so lordly and so graceful, was advancing. He was now upon the middle of the trap-door—I touched the knob—the effect was instantaneous—the floor gave way beneath his feet—and down he fell. If his lips gave utterance to a cry or word, it was drowned in the rush of the rapid waters eddying beneath: and the next moment the trap-door closed again. Then I exclaimed in the fulness of my exultant joy, 'Margaret my ancestress, thou art avenged! Sir Poniers, thy vow shall he fulfilled! Roger Dunhaven, thy bones may at length receive Christian burial!'—Having thus spoken in a loud voice, and with a sensation as if my veins were still running liquid fire, I quitted that chamber and returned hither—to *this* room—where, a few minutes before, Danvers was seated with me, but where I was now alone. "No, not altogether alone," added Dunhaven in a deepening voice: "for I am never alone so long as I hold companionship with the grim tenant of yon box!"—and he pointed towards the chest.

There was another pause, during which Gerald St. Louis gazed earnestly and inquiringly upon the old man's countenance, the expression of which indicated that he had something more to say.

"Yes—I came back to this room," he at length continued, "having done, as I thought, the deed of vengeance, and accomplished the traditionary vow which from generation to generation had descended unto me. I sat down here—on this very spot where I am now seated—and I gazed upon that chest. Apostrophizing its ghastly tenant, I said, 'Roger, thou art avenged!'—and then it struck me that I again heard the awful sound as of bones rattling within. Starting up from my seat, my first impulse was to fly in horror from the place: but regaining my courage, I said, 'No, no, there is naught for me to dread! For many long, long years have I made my couch upon the coffin wherein those bones lie hidden, and they have never been a source of fear to me until now. Nor shall they at present!'—To convince myself therefore that the sounds which I had heard could only be an illusion of the brain, I opened the chest—took out all the things it contained above the false bottom—and then with trembling hand raised that also. But, oh! how can I express the mortal terror which seized upon me, when, as I bent over the chest with the lamp in my hand, I saw that the skeleton had shifted its position, and that instead of lying flat upon its back (as it was when last I beheld it) it had turned completely round on its right side!"

"Old man, you are dreaming—you are endeavouring to frighten me!" said the King's Secretary: but his countenance was again ghastly pale, and he was actually shivering from head to foot.

"It is true—solemnly true," returned Dunhaven. "Wherefore should I deceive you?—are these things fit subjects to jest upon? No, no, Master St. Louis: I dare not, even if I wished, convert this awful topic into one of bantering or jocularity."

The young man answered not a word, but gazed with a sort of speechless stupefaction upon Dunhaven, while the solemnity of look which the latter wore, full well corroborated his assurance that he was not jesting.

"Then do the very dead manifest an interest," observed St. Louis at length, "in the vows which the living have sworn to avenge their wrongs!"

"It is even so," answered Dunhaven. "He who proves faithless to such a duty will himself become the object of vengeance—but a vengeance emanating from the tomb and wreaked upon him by the dead!"

"Yes, yes—I feel that it is so," murmured St. Louis, evidently much troubled. "But what think you, old man, of one who instead of wreaking his revenge upon an hereditary enemy, accepts boons from the hands of that enemy—aye, and even serves him?"

"I think," replied Dunhaven, already suspecting the meaning that lurked in the young man's words, "that the day must come sooner or later when all bounties thus received will turn into the most fearful curses. Gerald St. Louis! speak out and tell me frankly—have you proved treacherous and faithless to the memory of your ancestress Arline? have you received bounties at the hands of Lionel Danvers?"

"I have, I have," answered the young man, fearfully excited. "There was a time—aye, and until very lately too—when I would have given the best years of my life for the opportunity of avenging Arline's wrongs: but in a moment of weakness, when rendered desperate by my position— penniless, rushing headlong on in the mad career of crime, and compelled to herd with such as Benjamin Welford,—at that moment was it, I say, that I yielded to the offers of Lionel Danvers; and it was through *him* that I obtained my post at Court. But there I am a tool—a very tool—the tool of Danvers too! I comprehend not the intrigue—I cannot fathom the machinations in which he plays the part of principal, and I that of an instrument or puppet: but this I know, that it is serious, it is dark—most serious, most dark!"

"Then if all this be the case," exclaimed Dunhaven, his countenance expressing mingled joy and suspense, "doubtless the means of vengeance are in your hands? Yes, yes—I see by your looks that it is so. Then, by the wrongs of Arline, whose history I have read in your manuscripts, I adjure you, Gerald St. Louis, to prove faithful to the legacy of hatred and of vengeance which has come down to you. Behold! I have endeavoured to strike the blow, and have failed. It is your turn now. You cannot flinch— you dare not refuse. Have not I—an old man, well stricken in years, and bearing the load of infirmities upon my back—have not I, I ask, done my duty and proved faithful to the name I bear? Oh! I have disgraced it in a thousand other ways—disgraced it by crime, by usury, by meannesses, pettinesses, and rascalities of all sorts—but in the one sacred sentiment of hereditary vengeance I have proved worthy of it! Shall you, then, a young man with health, and vigour, and strength to sustain you,—shall you, I ask, hesitate to deal the blow which I, the old man, feared not to strike? St. Louis, be not a recreant to that cherished vengeance which should be regarded as a worship, a devotion, and a faith! Do you fear to lose the place which Danvers himself procured you? are you afraid of relapsing once more into poverty? If so, I will set your mind at ease on that account. Behold! I am rich—yes, I am rich—no matter how the money has been made—you yourself are not too nice nor delicate upon those points to refuse it. Swear then that you will devote yourself to vengeance—and from this moment I constitute you mine heir."

The young man grew greatly excited while Dunhaven was addressing him in this long and fervid speech. Glancing down upon his own person, he beheld himself tricked out in a courtier's garb, and he felt the sickening sensation that for the post whereof it was an emblem he was indebted to a man whom instead of regarding as a friend, he ought to look upon as a mortal enemy. Then he fixed his eyes upon Dunhaven; and instead of marking the sordid garments and ignoble as well as repulsive features of that individual, he beheld only an old man whose fervour and enthusiasm seemed to make his form dilate and his spirit soar high above the squalor of a penurious life and the physical traits of a miserly greed, and setting him a glorious example which he dared not hesitate to follow!

"Dunhaven," exclaimed St. Louis when the old man had finished his speech, "you have aroused within me a feeling which, though it has slumbered for three months and upwards, has not been extinguished altogether. And now that feeling again flames up in my soul; and I yield to your arguments—I receive inspiration from your lips—I accept your generous proposals! Master Dunhaven," added the King's Secretary after a moment's pause, "I swear to devote myself to vengeance; and from this day do I look upon myself as your heir!"

Thereupon these two individuals—that young man in the splendid apparel of a Court, and that old man in the sordid rags of miserly penuriousness—shook hands together, and their solemn compact was thus ratified.

"But now," continued St. Louis, resuming his seat upon one of the rude stools and speaking in a slow thoughtful manner, "let us understand each other well relative to the vengeance that is to be wreaked. Hath it not occurred to you that these Danvers are a race different from other men and seeming to bear a charmed life? How was it Lord Ranulph, when carrying away your ancestress, was enabled with a slim rapier to ward off the deathblow from himself and deal the stroke of doom to the powerful and warlike Roger? How was it that the mighty Sir Poniers, so terrible in battle and so famed in border-strife, should have become paralysed and powerless at the very moment when, his daughter being borne away before his eyes, he should have stricken the youthful Ranulph down? Peradventure, if we were acquainted with all the minute details of other histories and legends which rumour vaguely declares to be associated with the several Lords of Danvers, we might be led to mark additional proofs of this unaccountable power which they possess of defying the arm of death. At all events, coming down to the most recent period—within the last two or three years indeed—we ourselves have had signal evidence of that almost preterhuman power. For by what miracle was it that Lord Lionel escaped from the death which would have overtaken any other mortal man when you flung him down yon trap-door on the night of storm? And I also have a tale of equal wonder to impart to your ear: for on that occasion when Welford and myself encountered Danvers under the circumstances that you partially know of, his life remained proof against four pistol-shots fired at him point blank in a manner which seemed to defy escape!"

St. Louis then proceeded to sketch the details of that meeting with Lord Danvers in the lane near Greenwich, which had resulted in the offer of situations both to himself and Welford. He also explained several important matters wherein he had been made the tool of Lord Danvers since his nomination to the office of Royal Secretary. Dunhaven listened with the profoundest attention and interest; and when St. Louis had ceased speaking, they both reflected deeply for several minutes.

"It must have been as you said," at length observed old Dunhaven: "Lord Danvers bears a charmed life! It were vain, then, to renew any past attempts of violence against him. Had there been but *one* instance of his escape from death—namely, that of the trap-door—we might account for it by natural means,—either that he swam strongly despite the eddying of the waters, or that the current itself in its maddening violence threw him upon the land. But when we consider his subsequent escape from the double attack made upon him by yourself and Welford, it is scarcely possible to account for this by natural means also. Let our vengeance therefore be directed to the frustration of his schemes, the counterfoiling of his intrigues, and the combining of circumstances in such a manner as shall unmask him to the whole nation and cover him with infamy, disgrace, and shame. Perhaps, too, when proved a traitor to his King, he may not escape the royal vengeance so easily as he has eluded our's: peradventure the Tower may have a dungeon strong enough to hold him, and the headsman an axe sharp enough to do the work which my trap-door and your pistols failed to accomplish!"

In this manner did old Dunhaven and Gerald St. Louis continue talking for some time longer, until they had come not merely to a thorough understanding with each other, but likewise to a full settlement of those proceedings that were to be adopted in order to hurl the thunderbolt of ruin at the head of Lionel Danvers.

It was late in the afternoon when Gerald St. Louis took leave of old Dunhaven, and mounting his horse, rode forth from Deadman's Place on his way back to the Royal Palace at Greenwich.

CHAPTER XXXIV.

THE MYSTERIOUS VISITOR.

It was about a week after the incidents just related, that Gerald St. Louis was pacing to and fro, one evening in his own chamber, at the Royal House at Greenwich, revolving the many grave and important subjects which were uppermost in his mind. It was the hour of sunset, and the last beams of the departing orb were flickering through the lattice of the young man's apartment, so that they played fitfully upon his countenance as each turn in his agitated walk led him to approach the window. The vacillating uncertain light gave to the workings of St. Louis' features—pale with thought and anxiety as they were—a somewhat ghastly aspect; and of all the young gallants who envied the Royal Secretary his post at Court, few would have consented to change conditions with him, if once the secrets of his heart were read.

"Yes—I am pledged to vengeance," thought St. Louis to himself; "and since that day when I visited Dunhaven and heard his tale, I myself have experienced all the intenseness of a heartfelt longing to wreak that vengeance upon the head of Lionel Danvers. How many times within the past week have I read and re-read—aye, and brooded over—the manuscripts which contain the narrative of Arline's wrongs! Yes! my blood boils again at the mere thought thereof, as it was wont to do ere I sold myself as the vile instrument and grovelling tool of a scion of the hated house of Danvers! But how wreak this vengeance? how fulfil my pledge to old Dunhaven? how prove myself worthy to inherit the immense wealth which in the latter portion of our interview he admitted himself to possess? how, in short, prosecute all those plans which he and I settled as we thought so admirably? Fool that I was! I had forgotten that document which I signed, and which at any moment may be produced to brand me as a forger. Yes: that bill—that fatal bill, which Sir Edward Poynings made me put my hand to—not with my own name—but to fabricate that of Danvers—Oh! is not this felon-made bill an insuperable barrier in my path? Malediction upon the diabolic cunning of those who thus involved me in their treacherous web!—curses upon the foul conspirators who thus succeeded in binding me hand and foot! I dare not move farther in all this, nor venture to betray a single syllable of what I know. It is true that I might ruin others by a full disclosure: but would not the blow rebound upon myself? Ah, and more!" ejaculated the young man, recoiling with a sort of horror from the new idea which at this moment suddenly struck him: "they might deny the truth of all and everything which I could proclaim—and Sir Edward Poynings, while branding me as a forger, would triumphantly say to the King, 'Is it not evident that he who could fabricate this bill for money, would likewise do all the rest for his own private and special purposes?'—Such would be the question put; and the King would heed not anything that I might say. O wretched young man!" continued St. Louis, apostrophising himself: "what wilt thou do? how wilt thou act? Thy very life is in the hands of those whose instrument thou hast become! A word—a single word from Sir Edward Poynings' lips, and away with thee to the gaol— away with thee to the tribunal—away with thee to the scaffold!"

Sorely troubled—and indeed cruelly racked with these harrowing thoughts, Gerald St. Louis continued to pace to and fro in his apartment, while the sun went down and the gloom of evening gradually deepened around him. Unmindful however of the gathering obscurity, he continued to pace to and fro, like a restless tiger chafing in its cage; and though he no longer mused aloud, yet were his thoughts as active as at first in revolving all the circumstances of his position. Suddenly he was startled from his painful reverie by the opening of his chamber-door; and in the twilight glimmering which now prevailed in the room, he had little difficulty in recognising the person of the King.

"Is this you, St. Louis? and are you alone?" asked the monarch, as he entered the apartment with an evident stealthiness of manner, and closing the door cautiously behind him.

"My liege, it is I, your Grace's devoted servant," answered the Secretary, sinking upon one knee in the presence of the monarch, whose somewhat portly person was but ill-defined in the gathering gloom.

"Rise, rise, young man," said the King: "I have business for you to perform—and no time to tarry. But is it your humour thus to be in the dark? or were you preparing for rest when I entered? Yet methought that I heard you pacing to and fro as I opened the door——"

"My liege, I was giving way to certain reflections," answered St. Louis, so confused that he scarcely knew what he said.

"Reflections—eh?" echoed the King, with a good-humoured laugh. "But we will not waste words, Master Philosopher——"

"Shall I light a lamp, sire?" asked the young Secretary.

"No—it is better for the room thus to be enveloped in darkness," rejoined the King. "And now listen. Throw your most capacious mantle over your garments, so as to escape particular attention; and hie you forth from the private door of the palace. You will pass the sentry by means of the watchword, which is *Plantagenet*. Then proceed straightway to the stairs at the landing-place in front of the terrace; and if the boat that is expected be already there, good and well: if not, wait you until it arrives. A certain individual will give you the watchword of *Plantagenet*, which shall be a sufficient guarantee for your further proceeding. And this further proceeding is that you forthwith conduct the individual alluded to, into the palace by the private door, and escort him at once to this room—observe! *this* room—where I shall in the meantime wait. Be expeditious—and what is more important still, be prudent: for the mission I am now entrusting to you must pass without exciting observation. Now go."

"But is it not your Grace's pleasure to have a light?" asked St. Louis.

"Again I tell you," replied the King, "that it suits me better to remain here in the dark. The conference I am about to have with the individual whom you are to escort hither is of importance—as you may well suppose by the secrecy of these proceedings. Therefore the deeper the veil that darkness throws over them, the better. And now once more I bid thee depart."

St. Louis said not another word; but enveloping himself in a large Spanish mantle, and putting on a cap with a dark feather which overshadowed his countenance, he quitted the room. Threading the passage on which it opened, he descended the staircase and issued forth from the private door. He was now in that division of the enclosure on which the Royal apartments looked, and which was therefore strictly guarded by sentinels placed at short distances. Giving the watchword *Plantagenet*, St. Louis passed on without interruption, and soon reached the terrace on the bank of the Thames: but on gaining the stairs, he could perceive no boat. The night was very dark: but still there was that dim halo or glimmering on the water which makes objects upon its surface discernible; and in a very few minutes the Royal Secretary beheld a barge shooting in towards the landing-place. There were six rowers, who plied the oars so noiselessly that it seemed as if they were muffled: for not the slightest sound of a ripple, much less a splash, was heard. In the stern of the barge there was a canopy, with draperies closing all round in the form of a tent; and St. Louis at once felt assured that the individual whom the King expected was one of no mean distinction.

The barge ran alongside the stairs, on the lowest step of which St. Louis waited to receive the personage who was now arriving under such circumstances of secrecy. Not a syllable was spoken by the rowers as they threw up their oars perpendicularly between their feet. An individual then came forth from beneath the tent-like canopy; and assisted by St. Louis' arm, he at once stepped ashore, giving utterance to the word *Plantagenet* at the same time.

By the very manner in which he laid his hand on St. Louis' arm—by the tone in which he gave the watchword—and by the way in which he continued to lean on the young Secretary, it was easy for the latter to conjecture that this personage was of no mean consequence. With becoming respect therefore did he conduct him up the landing-steps; and so far as the deep obscurity would allow him to form any idea of the stranger's personal appearance, he seemed to be a man of middle age, with a handsome countenance, a somewhat portly figure, and of elevated stature. He wore the cap of an ecclesiastic; but his form was so completely enveloped in a large dark cloak that St. Louis was unable to judge whether the raiment thus completely concealed, was also of a clerical description.

In silence the Secretary and the visitor walked side by side towards the private door of the palace, passing the sentries without interruption, as the former hurriedly whispered the watchword in their ear. On entering the building, the light that was burning at the foot of the staircase showed St. Louis that the estimate he had already formed as to the personal appearance of this mysterious visitor, was a correct one: but he was now enabled to note the additional observation, that the countenance of the individual was pale—marked with wrinkles, evidently premature and indicative of profound study rather than of age—and wearing an expression the austerity of which was not altogether unmixed with worldly-mindedness, cunning, and sensuality.

On his side, the individual of whom we are speaking, fixed his sharp piercing eyes upon St. Louis, as if to read his character at a glance,—saying at the same time, "I presume, young man, you hold a confidential post about the King's person?"

"I have the honour to be his Grace's Private Secretary," answered St. Louis, in a tone of the deepest deference: for there was something so commanding and at the same time so benevolently condescending in the demeanour and voice of him who spoke, as to confirm St. Louis' previous impression and proclaim his companion a personage of exalted rank. Indeed St. Louis was already convinced that he must be some high dignitary of the Church.

They now ascended the staircase; and St. Louis conducted the visitor to the chamber where King Henry was waiting.

"Is that you, my lord?" asked the monarch, speaking from the darkness of the room the instant the door was opened.

"It is I—your Grace's devoted and duteous servant," was the response, delivered with a bland and courtier-like tone rather than with the solemn gravity of a high churchman.

"St. Louis, wait you in the passage," said the King, "and see that no one intrudes hither. Devise what excuse you may if you be seen loitering about in the corridor: but be careful that no one enters this room. Come, my lord, give me your hand and I will conduct you to a seat."

These last words were addressed to the high personage whom St. Louis had just introduced into the palace; and immediately afterwards the door was shut.

The young Secretary had remained, as the reader will observe, in the corridor, which was but very feebly lighted by a lamp at one end, and was pretty nearly enveloped in darkness at the spot where he was now standing. But still it was light enough for any one passing that way to notice him; and if thus noticed, what excuse could he make for being seen lounging about at that hour, when, according to the custom of the time, the dependants of the Royal Household were supposed to retire to rest:—for it was now past ten o'clock. The King had left it to his invention to devise some excuse, if observed there; but this he felt would not prove so easy, should the emergency arise—while on the other hand it would be as much as his head was worth to proclaim the truth to any questioner and reveal the royal proceedings. It was therefore clear that St. Louis must *not* remain in that passage. Besides, he was inspired by an immense curiosity to ascertain what could be the meaning of this visit, paid under circumstances of such mystery and precaution—and who the visitor himself was. Suddenly he remembered that the adjacent room was at the moment unoccupied, and that there was a very thin door of communication between the two. Without another instant's hesitation St. Louis passed into that empty chamber, leaving the door which communicated with the passage wide open, so as to be ready to afford him instantaneous egress whenever the conference between the King and the visitor should break up and his services should be needed to conduct the other back to the boat. Then, planting himself at the partition door-way, St. Louis held his breath while listening to the conversation that had already commenced in the adjacent room, and every word of which he could distinctly hear.

CHAPTER XXXV.

THE CONFERENCE IN THE DARK.

"And so, my Lord Archbishop," the King was saying at the instant when St. Louis thus commenced his eavesdropping, "you agree with me that the circumstances under which your lordship has been brought hither, are sufficiently consistent with caution and prudence? But assuredly, if any of these circumstances—such for instance as receiving you here in a dark

room—should appear disrespectful to your lordship, you have but yourself to thank for it."

"Gracious King," replied Wolsey, Archbishop of York,—for such indeed was the eminent personage now in such strange conference with
Henry,—"no circumstances under which your Highness might deign to
receive me could be deemed disparaging to my personal dignity or my ecclesiastic rank. But, as your Grace has said, it was I myself who craved that
this audience should be of the strictest privacy, so that neither curiosity
might be awakened nor espial risked."

"And moreover, in the private despatch which your lordship sent me
yesterday, beseeching this audience," observed the King, "you enjoined me
to envelope it with as much mystery as possible—lest, as you observed,
the very walls should have eyes and ears for what was to take place. At
first I was puzzled how to meet your wishes and arrange an interview
under such peculiar circumstances: for, as your lordship is doubtless well
aware, when a King surrounds himself with courtiers it is but so many
spies whom he plants upon his actions—and the more courtiers the more
spies. However, after some deliberation with myself, I resolved to make a
confidant of my youthful Secretary: it was he therefore who conducted
your lordship hither—and this is his chamber. I would not have the lamp
burning, because the light seen through the lattice at this hour might
chance to attract the very notice your lordship is so anxious to avoid. Have
I done wisely? and have all these arrangements been carried out well?"

"Most dread Sovereign," answered Wolsey, "your Grace does everything both wisely and well."

"Humph!" said the King, with a tone proving that he could not help
thinking the courtier-like churchman had his own private reasons for dealing in flattery. "But now, without farther waste of words, your lordship
will be pleased to explain what pressing and urgent matter it is that you
have to treat upon?"

"Pardon me," returned Wolsey, "if I open what may be termed the
business-portion of our conference, by hinting that if your Grace will at
once fix your thoughts upon the most serious, most important, and most
solemn act which you have lately performed, it will spare me much unnecessary and even painful preface, by immediately affording your Grace
a clue to the purport of my visit."

"Eh, my lord! is it to deal in enigmas," exclaimed the King, somewhat
angrily, "that you have come all the way from your palace at Westminster
this night, and under such clouded and mysterious circumstances?"

"Forgive me, sire, if I came not to the point at once," said Wolsey, in
a humble and deferential tone: "but although heaven knows the welfare

of your Highness is uppermost in my heart, and would at all times em-
bolden me to speak frankly and candidly, the business which hath brought
me hither is somewhat difficult to approach. Again therefore do I beseech
your Highness to throw out a few words—even one word—to show that
you have already obtained a clue to my meaning, so that I may be encouraged to proceed."

"Well, well, then," ejaculated the King, still somewhat impatiently,
"if it be necessary to prove that I divine your meaning, and have perhaps
an inkling of your motives,—in order to encourage you to proceed,—you
shall find me pretty frank and candid. But mark, my Lord Archbishop of
York! if your object be such as I conjecture, and if you have given all this
trouble and created all this anxiety and suspense on my part for the bare
purpose of reaching my private ear in an underhand fashion, you will find
that I am not likely to remain well pleased at the proceeding. However, I
suspend farther comment thereon until I hear your explanations. As for
my suspicion or conjecture relative to the purport of your visit, you shall
at once learn what I think. At present," continued Henry, in a sarcastic
tone. "Lord Warham, Archbishop of Canterbury, is the High Chancellor
and Prime Minister of the Kingdom;[6] and there is a certain Lord Wolsey,
Archbishop of York, who longs to rise to that post. Now, my lord," asked
the King, with a still more biting irony, "have I conjectured the truth?"

"No, your Highness—no!" was Wolsey's firm and even somewhat indignant answer. "Had my purpose been one of underhand political intrigue
and base selfish manœuvring, I should indeed expect to draw down upon
my head your Grace's direst indignation. Besides, by virtue of my rank I
possess the privilege of approaching your Grace at proper times, and under ordinary circumstances could solicit a private audience on Court-days
in the wonted manner. But this is no ordinary circumstance; and hence the
mystery, the secrecy, and the precautions with which I deemed it prudent
that my present interview with your Grace should be accompanied."

"Then speak out frankly at once," exclaimed the King, impatiently.

"I will," rejoined Wolsey: "and therefore, without further preface, I
will mention to your Highness the name of Father Paul, Superior of the
Monastery of Twelve."

"I have heard of that establishment," answered the King, "and believe
it to be one of good repute. But who the Superior may be, is a matter with
which I am unacquainted: nor do I trouble myself thereon."

"Reflect—consider, great King," urged Wolsey, "whether the name of
Father Paul be indeed altogether unfamiliar to your ears?"

"Totally unfamiliar," rejoined Henry. "But what of this ecclesiastic of
whom you speak?"

"A fortnight back," answered Wolsey in a solemn voice, "Father Paul the Superior of the Monastery of Twelve was found dead at the foot of the altar in the church belonging to that establishment."

"And what have I to do with a dead monk?" asked Henry, in a tone that seemed half careless and half impatient.

"Permit me to continue," said Wolsey. "Indeed, I must crave your Highness's patience to listen to a short narrative. It will not occupy many minutes, and it is of importance."

"Then in heaven's name proceed!" ejaculated the King.

"I will, sire. On the evening of the 13th of this month—namely, the month of August," continued Wolsey, with solemn sententiousness, "Father Paul issued instructions to his eleven brethren to repair to their cells, and not to stir thence until the peep of dawn should announce the time for matin-prayer. Accustomed to obedience, the eleven monks shut themselves up in their respective cells, without seeking to learn the motive for which the order had been given. Soon after ten o'clock, it appears, some of them heard the sounds of horses approaching the monastery: but they gave no rein to undue curiosity. A little later on that night, a tremendous storm broke forth——Your Highness may perhaps recollect," added Wolsey, with an evident meaning in his accents, "that such was the case?"

"I recollect the storm well," answered the King. "It was a fortnight back, as you have said; and the thunder shook this palace to its very foundation. But go on, my lord."

"The eleven monks who had been consigned to their cells," continued Wolsey, "prayed with a devotion well becoming their own sacred character and the awful solemnity of the hour. Some of them heard the sounds of horses' hoofs again, but at this time in rapid retreat from the Monastery. Not until the first glimmer of the dawn began to peep into the cloisters and through the loopholes of the cells, did the eleven monks come forth from their stone tenements; and then they repaired in procession to the chapel to offer up their matin praise to heaven. On entering the sacred place they beheld lights flickering upon the altar-piece: the tapers had been evidently burning all night, and were now sunken down into their sockets. As the holy men advanced they perceived their venerable Superior, Father Paul, kneeling upon the steps of the altar, but with his head bowed down in such a manner that his brow rested upon the cold marble. They thought he was praying devoutly and in silence. They drew nearer still: but gradually a cold tremor crept over them like a presentiment, as they observed how still and motionless he remained. They advanced to the steps of the altar—but he arose not to give them his blessing; he made no sign of life. They raised him—he was stone dead. The corpse was cold—the limbs were rigid—it was but too evident that the breath had left his body many hours."

Here Wolsey paused—most probably to ascertain what effect his narrative would produce upon the King: but the room being dark, he could not of course see the monarch's countenance; and his Highness did not immediately speak.

"There is something in the tale solemn and awful enough, no doubt," at length observed the monarch: "but it was not merely to tell me this history, tragic though it be, that your lordship has this night come all the way from Westminster? There must be more behind: so I pray thee, proceed."

"I will, sire," returned Wolsey. "When the corpse was borne from the church into the Monastery, it was placed upon the humble pallet where the living anchorite had been wont to sleep; and the good monk who was deputed by his brethren to perform the last offices for the dead, discovered a slip of parchment amidst the folds of the deceased's garments. Mark, my liege! a slip of parchment! Am I to proceed?—or have I said enough?"

"By heaven, my lord!" ejaculated the King angrily: but immediately checking himself, he said, "Go on—go on: I will hear you out. 'Twere perhaps better—although—But go on!"

"I will do so, then—since such is your Grace's command," observed Wolsey, with a sort of subdued wonder in his accents; as if the King's conduct amazed him much—more indeed than by his voice he dared show. "On perusing the contents of that parchment-slip," he continued, "the worthy monk who had discovered it, was stricken with the profoundest astonishment; and he at once understood why he and his brethren had been consigned the night before to their cells. But he also saw the necessity of keeping the secret which accident had thus revealed to him: it was his late Superior's secret—and it had fallen into his hands like a heritage from the dead! he therefore said nothing of the circumstance unto his brethren, but kept the parchment-slip safe about his own person. The very next night the monk dreamt that he beheld the spirit of Father Paul standing by the side of his pallet, and gazing down upon him with a look of mingled mournfulness and reproach. For several successive nights was this dream repeated—until at length the monk resolved to consult the new Superior, who had just been elected from amongst his brethren. He did so: and the Superior at once advised him to place the parchment certificate in the hands of one of the high dignitaries of the church. The monk, acting upon his counsel, lost no time in proceeding to Lord Warham's residence at Greenwich: but his lordship was absent at Canterbury. Thereupon the worthy monk bent his steps to Westminster—sought an interview with me—narrated all these particulars—and placed the parchment in my hands. I enjoined him to maintain the strictest secrecy,—sending a similar message through him to his Superior. This occurred yesterday morning; and after due deliberation with myself, I resolved to seek an early audience of your Highness—but an audience clothed in the deepest mystery, veiled in the profoundest secrecy, and accompanied with all possible precautions."

Wolsey stopped, evidently awaiting some observation or comment from the lips of the King: but Henry spake not for nearly a minute;—and then he said, in a tone which seemed filled with blended astonishment and impatience, "Well, my lord, why tarry you thus? Proceed with your tale: for as yet I am at a loss to conceive how it hath anything to do with me."

"Great King," resumed Wolsey, with the deepest solemnity, "this transaction is assuredly not one that may be trifled with. The parchment slip which I received from the monk, and which I have now about my person, speaks of a Papal Bull issued at a very recent date, and granting certain licences and dispensations. Now, most potent Sovereign, be not offended with your faithful servant—but pardon my boldness, I conjure you—when I remind your Highness that I, though a most unworthy servant of the Sovereign Pontiff at Rome, do exercise the functions of his special Legate at this moment in your Grace's Dominions; and every document emanating from Rome, stamped with the keys of St. Peter, and having the three leaden seals appended, must of necessity pass through my hands, and be duly recorded in the archives whereof I am the custodian. Shall I continue, sire?—do you wish me to proceed?"

"Instead of asking my *permission*," quickly responded the King, "you receive my *command* to do so. And now delay not: for I am growing weary of this long discourse, my lord."

"God keep your Highness!" said Wolsey with a deep solemnity of tone: "and again I must take leave to observe, even at the risk of offending my beloved monarch, that this is no matter to trifle with. Ah! will your Grace compel me to speak out plainly, and to declare that the Papal Bull mentioned in the slip of parchment which I received from the monk, never emanated from Rome—never passed through my hands—but though most cunningly devised and skilfully confectioned, is but a fabrication and a forgery!"

"By heaven! this grows too tedious for even the patience of a saint!" ejaculated King Henry. "Here! what, ho! St. Louis, come quick!" he shouted forth at the top of his powerful voice.

The young Secretary bounded away from the partition-door at which he was listening; and the next moment entered his own chamber, where the King and Wolsey had been conversing.

"Light the lamp, Master Secretary!" cried the King, still speaking in a loud and angry tone. "Were the eyes of all my Court fixed upon the lattice of this room, and able to penetrate, we would have a light! Be quick, I say—be quick!"

"Has this young man been listening to our discourse, my liege," asked Wolsey, "that he responded so quickly to your Highness's summons?"

"No—he would not dare!" answered the King. "But I raised my voice aloud—and being in the passage, he was quick to fly to the summons. Haste, St. Louis—the lamp, the lamp! I see it is the only thing to throw light upon his lordship's story!"

"But, great Sovereign," urged Wolsey, "will you admit this young man to our confidence?"

"Silence, my lord!—not another word!" interrupted the King petulantly: and he was heard to stamp his foot violently upon the floor.

The next moment the lamp flamed up;—the strong spirituous oil catching the match which St. Louis applied to the wick; and the three persons who were in the apartment—namely, the King, Wolsey, and the Private Secretary—were in a moment revealed to each other's eyes.

"Now, my lord—the parchment—the parchment!" said the King. "Come—give it quickly—fumble not thus beneath your garments—quick, I say——there!—at last!"

The King snatched the slip of parchment from Wolsey's hands, and hastily ran his eye over its contents. An extraordinary expression rapidly spread itself upon his countenance; and turning aside for an instant, he seemed to deliberate what course he should pursue.

"Up to the very last moment," muttered Wolsey to himself, "did the infatuated monarch hug the belief that the document might not reveal the whole extent of his imprudence: and now——"

"St. Louis!" cried the King, suddenly turning towards the young Secretary, "go you down to the stables—prepare two horses—have them in readiness at the private gate—and in ten minutes I will join you there. You will accompany me to the place whither I am going."

St. Louis hastened away to execute his royal master's orders; and the King remained alone with the Lord Archbishop of York. What more passed between the monarch and Wolsey—who was already intriguing to raise himself to power—we need not pause to describe. Suffice it to say, that after a few more words of brief and hurried discourse, Wolsey returned to his barge,—while the King hastened to join St. Louis, whom he found ready with the two horses at the private gate of the palace-grounds.

CHAPTER XXXVI.

A MEETING.

ON the same evening of which we have just been writing in the previous chapter,—but a couple of hours earlier than when the King first went to St. Louis' apartment in the Royal House,—Musidora was walking alone in the garden of Grantham Villa. The sun was then bright, though descending towards its western home: the air was filled with the warmth of the glowing autumnal season—the borders and parterres, amidst which the gravel walks meandered, were beautiful in all the myriad varieties of floral hues—and the ripe fruits clustered upon the laden boughs of the trees.

Musidora was clad in a dark dress that set off the alabaster fairness of her complexion to its fullest advantage, and developed the gracefully voluptuous contours of her splendid form. The masses of her hair, shaming the most lustrous hue of the raven's wing, fell in luxuriant ringlets over the ivory shoulders and on the proud bosom which the low-cut corsage of her dress half revealed;—and even below the slender waist did the rich tresses descend, floating heavily around her, like a veil which the warm sluggish breeze can but languidly agitate. Her countenance was more than usually serious. That smile, which in its cold brilliancy was wont to linger upon and soften the lower portion of her countenance, was not there now: the features of chiselled marble were well-nigh as rigid as the marble itself, though not altogether expressionless, but profoundly solemn. Neither proudly radiant nor coldly proud at this hour, Musidora appeared as if there were a deep and painful pre-occupation of all her thoughts, and as if she were seriously and deliberately endeavouring, not merely to analyse feelings of which she was conscious, but also to read the meaning of others which dimly and vaguely yet oppressively haunted her.

Her step was slow, and seemed measured to the mournful tenor of her thoughts: her large dark eyes, though not absolutely cast down, had their looks inclined;—her arms, white and dazzling as modelled alabaster, and bare to the shoulders, were curved in such a manner that the wrists crossed as if listlessly thrown the one over the other, at the peak of the stomacher: while the gentle inclination of the head gave a most graceful arching to the neck; so that there was something elegantly statuesque, mingled with a soft abandonment, about her entire form.

The long skirt of her dark dress swept with a slight rustling sound over the gravel pathway; but being shorter in front, the flowing drapery concealed not the admirably shaped feet and ankles, as the lady slowly pursued her way towards a shrubbery at that extremity of the garden which was farthest from the villa.

Seldom was it that Musidora gave audible utterance to her thoughts: rare were the occasions on which her habitual caution, and the strong control which she was wont to exercise over herself, were so far forgotten as to lead her to run the risk of being overheard by any curious listener who might happen to be near. But now, in that same serious mood which had thus as it were beguiled her with its mournful influence to abandon somewhat of the glacial dignity of her demeanour to a slightly drooping gait, was she also led to allow her thoughts to flow in audible musings from her lips, and she the while unconscious of the proceeding.

"I might have seen—I might have know that this marriage would not merely fail to secure my happiness, but that it would even stamp my misery. Happiness!—no, no; *that* is what I never could have hoped for! The green returns not to the withered leaf, nor the delicate bloom to the blighted flower: still less its early poetry to the heart. I have sacrificed myself—I feel that I have done so. But wherefore did I accept this destiny? Was it through ambition? Yes—a lofty, towering ambition! And yet God knows it was not ambition at all! No—it was for my beloved father's sake as well. Yes—and more than this likewise—that I might have the power of dispensing benefits to the poor, the wretched, and the down-trampled members of the human race. If then ambition be an evil, my motives in accepting the dignity of Queen of England were not all evil: for besides ambition, there were some softer and gentler if not nobler sentiments. But am I Queen of England? Ah! now I have asked myself a question that seems to touch the chord which, hitherto unknown, has been vibrating with a mysterious pain in my heart. Yes—and at this moment, while giving substance and shape to the doubt itself, and calling up into palpable existence that misgiving which has hitherto lurked in the darkest depths of my soul, I feel a dull sickening sense of terror come over me. That feeling, which for some days past has haunted me like a weird presentiment of evil, now assumes the shape of a real phantom in my path. Then, *am* I Queen of England?"

Asking herself this question in a louder tone than that in which she had previously been speaking, Musidora stopped short; and while a more than ghastly pallor sat upon her features, a strange feverish lustre shone in the depths of her superb dark eyes, and the next moment an expression of mingling anguish and bewilderment swept over her countenance.

"Yet why do I put that question to myself?" she suddenly resumed, still speaking audibly, and at the same time continuing her slow and seemingly measured walk through the shrubbery. "Were not all the ceremonies complete? was not the Papal Bull read? were not the witnesses present? was not the priest's blessing given? was not my hand united to the King's? and is not the certificate here—yes, here in my bosom?"

Thus speaking, she again stopped short; and drawing forth the slip of parchment from its resting-place in her corsage, she opened it and slowly read its contents: then folding it up again, she returned it to her bosom.

"Yes—all the proceedings were regular and legitimate. Then wherefore this strange and bewildering uncertainty? why this gloom that creeps in upon my spirit? why this presentiment of evil that takes possession of my soul? Only fourteen short days have passed since that night—may I not even say that *dreadful* night?—on which the bridal ceremony took place; and from all the King has told me, is it not plain enough that it were dangerous for him to proclaim immediately this secret marriage? Wherefore, then, should I be already impatient for the public recognition of that rank which is assuredly mine. Is it that my soul still trembles and my brain still reels beneath the influence of those omens which seemed to mark the evening of our bridal? or is it that the memories of *the past* have been vividly re-awakened within me? No, no: those memories needed not arousing: they never slumbered!"

And as Musidora gave utterance to these last words with a strange, a wild, and yet a deeply concentrated emphasis,—again did an expression of anguish sweep over her countenance; and stopping short, she covered her face—that ghastly pallid face—with her delicate white hands. Thus she stood for upwards of a minute, still and motionless as a statue. No tears trickled between her fingers—no sobs broke from her lips—no sighs convulsed her bosom: all that passed, was passing *inwardly*—and deep indeed, mysterious too as deep, was the lady's unutterable woe. At length she slowly withdrew her hands from her countenance, and resumed her walk as well as her audible musings.

"No, no—such memories as those never slumbered!" she said, thus again giving utterance to the thought that was uppermost in her mind. "Besides—that day, six weeks previous to the bridal-evening, when old Landini whispered certain words in mine ears——Ah! *they* indeed would have caused all *the past* to flame up into a vivid glare before me, even if the dark shades of forgetfulness had ever for a single moment begun to envelope it! And during that interval of six weeks, what strange fancies tortured me—what wild and frightful visions haunted me! No wonder that my moods were versatile as those of the most capricious girl who knows not her own mind from one instant to another!—no wonder that my conduct towards the King was marked by as many variations as the tenor of my inward thoughts! Oh! there were moments when the idea fastened upon my soul that a hideous deception was being practised towards me; and being tortured by the fiery agonies of that suspicion, did I often find myself gazing upon the King to acquire the certainty that it was really he, and not some demon taking his place. At other times the fancy would seize upon me that he himself must be made the sport of malicious fiends who were filling his mind with the delusion of love, only to dispel it again when it should reach the point at which retreat was impossible, but aversion and regret most certain! And, O heavens! how arduously did I struggle against those torturing dreams—how fiercely did I battle against those frightful misgivings!—and in my zeal to conquer them, to what strange moods of unnatural mirth and buoyant spirits did I seem to abandon myself! My conduct must have been most singular;—and yet the King appeared to notice it not. But why?" she suddenly exclaimed, "do I thus give way to these painful thoughts? why do I now recall every fitful fancy that tortured me during those six weeks? Musidora, Musidora!" she said, apostrophizing herself in a reproachful tone, "all this is unworthy of you! You, who for three long years and upwards entombed the past as it were so deeply in your heart's sepulchre, and covered that grave of perished feelings, *not* with the flowers of artificial smiles, but with the snows of a cold and frozen mien!—you, who until the last few weeks had exercised such sovereign sway over every sentiment of the soul and emotion of the mind, that not even a blush could rise to your cheeks against your will nor an unpremeditated glance flash forth from your eyes!—you, who had thus succeeded in converting yourself into a statue, and rendering your very countenance as inscrutable as the mystery itself which lay buried in your heart!—you, Musidora," she continued, still reproachfully addressing herself, "are now becoming weak, nervous, and apprehensive as the silliest girl,—torturing every passing shadow into a phantom of fear, and brooding upon every transient image until it assumes the shape of a palpable spectre. Musidora, Musidora! you must take courage—you must be firm—you must become yourself again!"

Inspired as it were all in a moment with the very courage which she sought thus to summon to her aid, and animated with the fortitude which was natural to her soul, Musidora suddenly raised her head—stepped out with a firmer pace—and assumed a look of mingled hauteur and defiance, as if she were prepared to combat even destiny itself. Back to her countenance came that smile of ice-like brilliancy which she was wont to wear: her eyes flashed strange and living fires; she put back the cloud of raven hair which had somewhat obtruded over the alabaster expanse of her brow; and her fine bust seemed to swell into nobler contours as if queenly thoughts were springing up within. Proudly now she walked—proudly too she looked; but combining elegance and grace in every movement and in every gesture, and with that cold glacier-like brilliancy shining over all, she seemed the Queen of Winter transported from the frozen regions of the north to the warm sunshine of that garden-scene!

At the very instant she had thus resumed this icy calmness of demeanour, which, if not exactly natural to her, at least had been her habitual bearing for nearly four years,—she heard the sounds of footsteps advancing from behind. Deliberately turning round, she suddenly started—and something like a suppressed shriek seemed to escape her lips, as she found herself face to face with an individual who thus appeared no stranger to her.

This was Lionel Danvers!

The nobleman was apparelled, according to his wont, in dark raiment, but of the costliest materials and most elegant fashion; and nothing could be better adapted to set off his tall, slender, and faultlessly symmetrical figure than the costume of that age. The cap, with its gracefully drooping feather, seemed to sit proudly upon the masses of his long curling raven-black hair, and above his forehead of noble height. His splendid dark eyes, glorious as Musidora's own, flashed forth fires as bright though far more sinister; and upon his classically cut lips, shaded by the thinly but darkly pencilled moustache, sat that half-scornful, half-disdainful smile which seemed to have been a characteristic of all the scions of the Danvers race, but more especially of Lord Lionel.

The excitement which seized upon Musidora at this meeting, evidently so unexpected and so unlooked for, disappeared as quickly as it came;—and all in an instant resuming her dignity of mien and her glacier-like look of haughty beauty, she said in a cold passionless voice, as if her very words were ice, "What would you with me?"

"Will not the fair Musidora honour me with a brief interview?" asked Danvers: then, without waiting for her assent, he placed himself by her side on her right hand, and with an easy but graceful gesture, went on to observe, "Do not let me interrupt your walk; but suffer me to become the partner of your ramble in this delicious garden for a few minutes. Behold! the sun is sinking towards the western horizon: in half-an-hour or so he will disappear from our view. Grant me, then, the interval which will thus elapse ere the twilight commences?"

"But for what purpose this meeting?" asked Musidora: and though her words and looks were still calm—nay, more than calm—cold even unto freezing point—yet was it evident to the eye of Lord Danvers that it cost her an almost superhuman effort to sustain such an unnatural composure.

"Did you think, Musidora," he asked, fixing his eyes with a strange searching look upon her, "that we were never to meet again? did you believe that when we parted last—I need not allude to the how or the where——"

"No, no!" suddenly ejaculated Musidora, her eyes flashing a wild fire, and a look of anguish sweeping over her countenance, as if Lord Danvers' words had suddenly conjured up a crucifying remembrance: but again, the next instant, did she conquer her emotions and resume the cold hauteur of her looks.

"You see, Musidora," observed the nobleman, with a slightly perceptible irony in his words, and an expansion of the mocking smile upon his lips, "that I have but to breathe a few syllables to your ear in order to startle you from this icy inanimation of your's, and send the torrent of a living fire pouring through every vein."

"My lord," responded Musidora, her deep eyes glowing with a strange unnatural lustre, and her lips blanching as she spoke, "your words may conjure up memories that are torturing to a degree: but is not my conscience pure? Whatever fearful mystery there may be in those past circumstances to which you have alluded—yet if crime be connected therewith—if awful horror lurk in its scarcely fathomable profundities—surely it is *you*, my lord, who should tremble more than I?"

"Think you, Musidora," said Lionel Danvers, now suddenly becoming strangely excited himself, and glaring down upon her as if with those fierce and fiery looks of his he could pierce into the depths of her soul and fathom its most secret thoughts,—"think you, Musidora, I ask, that you have ever, even in the wildest flight of your imagination or in the loftiest soaring of your conjecture, penetrated the tremendous mystery to which we are both alluding?"

"May God have mercy upon you, Lionel Danvers!" suddenly answered Musidora, in a singularly earnest and impressive tone: then as if all her unnaturally assumed courage and calmness abruptly broke down in a moment, she literally wrung her hands, crying, "Oh! it is impossible that I can continue to regard you without emotion, knowing what I *do* know and thinking what I *do* think!"

"But that emotion, Musidora?" exclaimed Danvers: and in his dark eyes shone still more brightly and more glowingly that strange lustre which shot forth fires terrible to encounter.

"That emotion?" repeated Musidora, her blanched lips quivering and her whole form trembling likewise, as if she were now actually shivering with a real and not an assumed glacial coldness: "do you ask me to explain what that emotion is? I will then. It is a pity—a commiseration boundless,

Oh! boundless as the illimitable immensity of that ill which, heaven knows how or why, you have wrought unto yourself!"

"Ah!" ejaculated Danvers, an awful expression of mingled rage, and hate, and diabolic malignity suddenly distorting his sublimely beautiful countenance: "have you then so far penetrated my wild and wondrous secret as to make me the object of such grovelling, despicable sentiments as those? Perish all pity!—beneath the heel of contempt do I crush all commiseration! Such as my destiny is, do I follow it: such as my fate is, do I pursue it——"

"But your doom—your final doom, unhappy man?" exclaimed Musidora, her whole appearance so full of convulsing horror and wild affright, that she seemed not the same being she was when clothed in her ice-like dignity a few minutes back.

"My doom, Musidora!" returned Danvers, his voice suddenly sinking to a tone awfully low, and yet filled with the accents of fierce despair: "speak not to me thus! dare not to breathe that word in my ear! Besides," he added, in a wild voice of passionate vehemence, "you are wrong—you err deplorably—your conjecture has misled you—you have followed the promptings of a fevered fancy——"

"Would to heaven that I could think so, Lionel!" responded Musidora quickly: then appearing suddenly to recollect that she was speaking in a tone and likewise in terms all too familiar for her position as a married woman, especially a bride in the first days of the honeymoon, she went on to say with a graver look and colder voice, "Lord Danvers, do not mistake my meaning. Attribute not the words I have uttered, to any revival of the sentiment of other times. No—*that* has perished for ever! But when I expressed myself so vehemently—perhaps *too* warmly in behalf of your welfare—it was as a fellow-creature that I regarded you; and to any other human being whom I fancied or feared to be similarly situated, should I have spoken in precisely the same terms. But enough of this, if it offend you. And now perhaps, my lord," she added with a still more dignified manner and even in a tone of command, "perhaps you will be kind enough to inform me for what purpose you have sought me here this evening?"

"Let the course of conversation carry us naturally on to the issue of explanation," observed Lord Danvers, who had now recovered not merely his wonted equanimity, but likewise his haughty ease of manner, his scornful smile, and his slightly mocking tone. "From what you have ere now said, I cannot flatter myself that you are particularly well pleased to behold me?"

"My lord, we never ought to have met again—and you know it!" was Musidora's calm but resolute reply.

"Ah! the disdainful beauty means to dictate to me!" said Lord Dan-vers, his accents becoming bitterly mocking.

"My lord, are you coward enough to insult me?" demanded Musi-dora, stopping suddenly short, and bending upon him all the fire of her magnificent eyes.

"Really," responded Lionel, with a sardonic laugh, "this is not the lan-guage which you, of all women, should hold to me."

"My lord," answered Musidora, still speaking with dignity but firm-ness, although a hectic flush, like that of suppressed indignation, suddenly appeared upon her cheeks, which were wont to be of such marble purity; "you have no right to revert to the past. It is not only ungenerous, it is even mean and dastardly—Besides," exclaimed Musidora, suddenly raising her head proudly, "if we look each other in the face, *who* ought to blush and be ashamed for the past? *whose* eyes ought to quail before those of the other?"

"All the solemn vows, the oaths, the protestations," returned Lionel Danvers, with bitter accents and diabolically mocking looks,—"where are they? what became of them? List! there is a breeze passing gently amidst these verdant evergreens, those shrubs, and those trees—but it is not more fleeting nor more idle than the vows, the pledges, and the protestations to which I allude. Again—those sunbeams which are now flickering above the western horizon, are not so transient nor so evanescent, as that same catalogue of promises and protestations!"

"Lord Danvers," interrupted Musidora, "is it possible that you can dare address this language to me? Just heaven!" she cried, stamping one of her delicate feet fiercely upon the ground, "with whom lay the deception? with whom the foul treachery? O God!" she continued, now clasping her hands wildly together, as the whole train of torturing memories swept back like a flight of fiery arrows through her mind: "from what appalling fate was I not rescued? I shudder—Oh! I shudder at the bare idea—it is fearful to contemplate!"

"Ah! you escaped me *then*, it is true!" cried Danvers, with accents so savagely bitter that Musidora quailed and shrank back.

"Yes," she murmured in a low and half bewildered tone—for her thoughts seemed falling into confusion beneath the influence of conster-nation and dismay: "I escaped you then—and heaven grant that I may escape you for ever!"

"You escaped me!" echoed Danvers, his lip curling with fiendish scorn and diabolic mockery. "Yes, in one sense you have escaped me but——"

And suddenly checking himself, he surveyed the affrighted Musidora with a look of such ineffable sardonism and malignant triumph, that she felt the maddening sensations of wildest terror springing up like living flames within her.

"Tell me what you mean?" she said, with short quick gaspings. "Your words are vague—but your looks—O God! your looks are full of direst omen!—Lionel—my lord—Danvers—for heaven's sake I conjure you, regard me not thus! Whatever your power may be—and I fear it is great—I dare not think *how* great, nor to what extent of mischief it may be exercised—but I beseech you, my lord, to spare me!"

Frenzy had collected in her wild dark eyes as she thus spoke; and the hectic on her cheeks had gathered into two crimson spots, which seemed to burn upon that countenance where the marble's paleness was wont to dwell: and so vivid indeed were these spots that they appeared as if all the heart's blood had been suddenly concentrated there.

"Musidora," said Lord Danvers, in a deep penetrating voice, "calm yourself, if you can—and listen to me. You have said that you believe my power to be great: but whatever it be, I am compelled by its influence at this moment to reassure you so far as to declare that I have no wish to deal with your life——"

"My life?" echoed Musidora. "But my happiness—all that remains to me of what the world calls happiness—all that *you* have left—can you deal with *that?*"

"Aye, by the Power to which we have both alluded, can I!" exclaimed Lord Danvers, in a swelling voice of malignant triumph. "Your happiness, Musidora,—see! I hold it in my hand, and can crush it thus in my grasp!"

As Lord Danvers spoke he plucked a pear from the overhanging branch of a tree, and crushing it so that the juice spurted out upon his garments from its ripe pulpiness, he tossed it away; and where it fell upon the gravel-walk it seemed as if a wheel or a heavy boot had passed over it. Then calmly wiping his hand upon a beautiful worked kerchief, he said in a quiet tone, but full of an implacable wickedness, "Now, Musidora, what think you of my power over your happiness, since at any moment I can crush it even as I have crushed that fruit?"

No words can describe the appalled and dreary look of mingled consternation and despair which Musidora fixed upon Lionel Danvers as he crushed the fruit and addressed her in those terrible terms. Gone was all her wondrous power of self-composure!—gone that mask of ice with which she had been wont to cover her countenance!—gone that glacial serenity beneath which she had for years concealed the harrowing memories of the past! Unhappy Musidora! she was now experiencing an ordeal of the most frightful and excruciating description: it seemed as if fingers of red-hot iron were tearing in her brain and grasping at her vitals: it was an awful moment, full of horror, anguish, blackness, burning!

"Proud soul of ice!" exclaimed Lord Danvers, "have I moved you now? But listen—and hear what I have to say. Doubtless when we parted nearly four years back—you well remember when and how—you thought that it was for ever: you imagined that ne'er again should we meet upon earth. But, O insensate fool that you were, to hug the hope that when the love of a Danvers was rejected, it would not turn to deadliest hate!"

"Love, love!" shrieked forth the agonizing Musidora: "desecrate not thus the name of love! That love was mine, not your's. It was I who cherished your image as the beacon of life's hope—the guiding star of my destiny. But you—you, false, treacherous man!" she continued, her countenance now flushing with sudden rage; "it was you who would have made me a victim—it was you who sought to sacrifice me to that same tremendous mystery which had previously engulfed Clara Manners!"

"Yes," observed Lionel, with a strange mocking smile, and a bitter irony of tone, "I know full well that you are acquainted with that history. I watched your features when the old man related it word for word, some three or four months back in yon villa——"

"You!" exclaimed Musidora in utter amazement; and all the flush of recent indignation faded into more than the wonted paleness of her countenance: "you! What, were you present—or were you near—upon that occasion?"

"Yes—I was present on that occasion," returned Danvers, gazing upon her as if Lucifer himself were looking out of his eyes, so diabolic was their expression. "I heard all—I beheld all. Remember you, that in your sympathy for the poor old ruined merchant," he continued with withering sarcasm, "you handed him a cup of wine ere he commenced his history? and when he had brought it to a conclusion, you expressed your sorrow and your commiseration. Ah! but when he implored you to intercede against *that cruel pitiless Danvers*—those were his very words—your countenance became ghastly. I saw it all, I tell you: yes, I beheld it all: and it was not difficult to read what was passing in your mind—for in proportion to the sympathy which you bestowed upon old Manners, was the sentiment of loathing and execration with which you thought of me!"

Again in utter dismay and with an appalled look did Musidora gaze upon Lionel as he thus spoke: then, as he ceased, she said, while a cold shivering passed visibly over her form, "You tell me that you saw everything that night? Dreadful man—but as incomprehensible as you are dreadful—was it at the casement or behind the tapestry that you were listening? or am I to believe that you have the facility of rendering yourself unseen—invisible?"

A smile of ineffable malice and triumph, but wicked beyond the power of language to describe, wreathed the haughty lips of the nobleman as Musidora thus addressed him: but without answering her question, he said in taunting accents, "Perhaps the history of Clara Manners is not the only one into which your curiosity has led you to penetrate? and it may be that you intend to follow up your researches with regard to each and all of those names which you beheld——"

"Enough, enough! you are driving me mad!" shrieked forth the wretched Musidora, pressing both her hands to her throbbing brows.

"The history of Clara Manners," pursued the implacable Danvers, as if he revelled in the tortures which he was thus inflicting, "is known to you: that of Bianca Landini is also known to you: and perhaps in process of time you will glean the histories of Margaret Dunhaven—Dolorosa Cortez—and Arline de St. Louis?"

"O heavens! is not your's a fearful race?" exclaimed Musidora: "and, Oh! what a fearful destiny that makes you tread in the path of your ancestors——like them, seeking victims!"

"Ancestors!" echoed Lionel: and again did that terrible smile of wickedness and malice mingled with haughty scorn, expand upon his countenance. "But time is passing—the sun is sinking to its western home—and its expiring rays are now flickering over yon trees. Our present interview shall not exceed the limit which I prescribed at its commencement."

"Our present interview?" repeated Musidora, recoiling with fresh terror from the observation: "are we then to meet again?"

"Yes—and shortly too——Very, very shortly," rejoined Danvers. "But listen, I say, while I give utterance to a few more words of explanation. Musidora, we once loved each other: but this love on your part has turned to abhorrence, hatred, and loathing—while with me it has changed to the craving for an implacable vengeance. Nearly four years have elapsed since we parted—I need not say where nor how: but when we did thus part, it was with the determination on my side to make you sooner or later feel that power from which at the time you so miraculously escaped. During the three years and nine months which have elapsed since that memorable night when we parted, I have watched you—I have kept my eye upon you—and you the while unconscious that you were thus observed! I beheld you seeking to conceal all the memories of the past beneath that air of glacial sereneness and freezing dignity which almost became a second nature, so well did you wear your mask of ice! But I laughed within myself as I thought that the time must come when I should be enabled to thaw all this coldness on your part and make your marble frame feel as if liquid fire were gushing in your veins——yes, and melt that proud soul which had learnt to pride itself upon its power and strength, and break too that spirit which to the world seemed characterized with an adamantine firmness! Now, Musidora, you understand me well—you know me better than ever you knew me before; and the deep terror which sits upon your soul makes you feel—aye, and deeply feel, that your happiness is but too surely in my grasp, to be treated at any moment as that bruised and crushed fruit which lies *there!*"

As these last words fell from the lips of Lionel Danvers, the expiring sunbeams disappeared behind the trees. Musidora, filled with consternation and horror, passed her hand over her eyes as if to dissipate any illusion that might be upon her brain; for she could scarcely believe that all that was now passing could be aught more than a frightful vision: but when she looked again at the spot where Danvers had an instant before stood in her presence, she beheld him not—he was gone, having disappeared like a phantom that vanishes into the thin air.

CHAPTER XXXVII.

THE KING.

For upwards of a minute did Musidora remain standing where she was, in a sort of dream-like amazement, blended with dismay. Her eyes were dilated and vacant—her features were rigid—her form was still and motionless as marble. The colour had even left her lips; and there was no vital hue upon her countenance. She seemed like a statue personifying consternation and despair.

Was it all a dream—a terrible illusion through which she had been passing? Clutching greedily at the thought, she exclaimed, "Yes, yes—it must be!"

But at that instant her eyes fell upon the crushed fruit which lay upon the gravel-walk; and then she clasped her hands together in a new paroxysm of wildest anguish. The hot tears gushed over her alabaster cheeks— —scalding, burning tears that might have left searing marks even upon the marble whose paleness those cheeks resembled. It is a terrible thing to contemplate the rending anguish thus endured by one of such grand and marvellous beauty, and who, judging from what she herself had said during her discourse with Danvers, deserved not so wretched a fate!

All of a sudden a thought struck her. The sun had set—it was the hour when the King, her husband, would arrive at the villa—and she must return in-doors to receive him! Oh, not for worlds must she suffer him to notice the terrible traces of that poignant anguish which she had been enduring, and was enduring still! If he were to mark the evidences of her grief, what explanation could she give? What could she possibly say to account for the desolate dreariness of her looks! Again did the lady exert a wondrous—nay, almost preternatural effort to resume her wonted air: and more than ever did she experience the necessity of veiling the tortures of her harrowed heart beneath that mask of ice which she had been wont to put on. In proportion to the utter need of the emergency, so did her power of concealment appear to come back to her aid;—and once more with the glacial dignity of bearing—once more too with the cold refinement and icy elegance of mien, did she re-enter the villa.

She ascended to her chamber, to make some little alteration in her toilet, and likewise to rest herself for a few minutes, the more effectually to regain the full measure of outward composure that was requisite for her meeting with the King. Annetta was in the room; and a perfumed lamp was lighted upon the toilet-table. Then, except for the increased pallor of Musidora's cheeks as the flame of the strongly-burning lamp cast its glare upon her,—and except too for the partial drooping of her richly-fringed eyelids,—Musidora's countenance revealed not a trace of the crucifying agonies through the ordeal of which she had just passed. The faithful Annetta merely observed that her beloved mistress spoke in a somewhat lower and more bewildered tone, and that there was the slightest amount of abstraction in her air—but perhaps even a kinder softness towards the abigail herself.

The reader has seen that during the last hour some of the strongest of all human feelings had not merely been excited within the bosom of Musidora, but had struck as it were upon her heart like so many successive blows. Considering therefore how quickly these sudden shocks had followed one upon another, and all within so comparatively brief a space of time when viewed in reference to their violence and their fierceness, it must seem astonishing that Musidora had not completely succumbed beneath their tremendous influence. But certain it is that she now gathered a preternatural strength from the very necessity of concealing all that had taken place; and this circumstance affords the most striking illustration we can adduce of the wondrous power with which Musidora's mind was naturally endowed.

But let it not be thought that she had been enabled to banish from her soul any of the impressions which her interview with Lord Danvers had left upon it. No: there they were, stamped as it were with a red-hot iron—seared as indelibly upon that soul as the murderer's brand was upon the brow of Cain! And yet there was this tremendous difference—that Musidora suffered innocently, with these frightful traces of imperishable agony upon her heart; while the first murderer had suffered righteously, with the open stigma upon his forehead.

Of all the incidents of her interview with Danvers, none was more deeply impressed, amidst those searing marks upon her soul, than the frightful illustration of the crushed fruit. Nor less did she remember with the most vivid keenness, how he had declared that they were to meet again shortly—*very shortly*: and that assurance, given by one who was but too capable of accomplishing all that he menaced, filled her with the direst dismay. But this, as well as every other feeling which she experienced or emotion that had been excited, was now veiled beneath the habitual serenity which she again put on.

Thus armed with that most unnatural fortitude, she suffered Annetta to arrange her hair, and then to deck her person with the resplendent gems that were the King's gift, and which he so much loved to see her wear.

"Your Majesty does indeed look like the Queen of England!" were the words which the faithful Annetta ventured to breathe softly in the ears of her mistress when her toilet was concluded.

This was the first time that the abigail had ever addressed Musidora by her royal titles: for that the secret of the marriage might be the more effectually kept, in compliance with the King's wish, Musidora had desired that she might be spoken to in the same terms as before her union,—lest the very walls might have ears to catch up those swelling titles and proclaim the mystery to the world. She therefore started as Annetta thus spoke in venial disobedience of the standing order; and it appeared to Musidora as if she had just been addressed by a strange name. Then, at the same instant, a thought struck her! Was not the secret of her marriage most probably known to Danvers? had he not discovered it? in short, was it not certain to be very far from a mystery to *him?* That he possessed the faculty of rendering himself invisible, and thereby penetrating whithersoever he chose, Musidora was fully convinced: and as he himself had declared that he had kept watch upon her actions, was it likely that the circumstance of her marriage—one of the most important incidents of her life—should have remained unknown to him? This thought filled her with a new presentiment of approaching evil. The knowledge of such a secret might furnish to his unscrupulous hands a weapon that his vindictive feelings would love to wield. And might he not use it to prejudice the King against her? might he not suffer the monarch to believe that it was she herself who had betrayed a secret which his Highness had for the present so many reasons to wish inviolably kept?

All these reflections, sweeping hurriedly through Musidora's brain, aggravated if possible the dismay already harbouring in her soul; and Annetta could not help noticing an expression of anguish flit across the countenance of her mistress. But it disappeared again as rapidly as it had sprung into existence; and the faithful dependant ventured upon no comment.

"If Lionel Danvers in his fearful wickedness," thought Musidora to herself, "should attempt anything to alienate from me the regard of the King, or alter my position from what it ought to be, and from what it must be made when once this marriage is proclaimed to the world,—I will deal frankly with my husband and tell him everything. Perhaps it was my duty to have done so at the very outset: perhaps it would have been better for us both! At all events, if the dreaded emergency should arise and the necessity should present itself, I will not hesitate any more, but will deal candidly with my royal husband at once! Lionel Danvers has been compelled to admit that he dares not practise upon my life: let me see if I cannot shield my happiness—or at least, as much of happiness as *he* has left me—from the influence of his terrible power!"

Consoled, or rather strengthened, by these reflections which she hurriedly made to herself, Musidora descended to the saloon where she was wont to receive her royal husband. Since the marriage, the Earl and Countess of Grantham were in the habit of leaving them alone together on these occasions, except when the evening repast was served up. The King had just arrived when Musidora entered that apartment; and with all his wonted affection of manner he hastened forward to strain her in his embrace.

"How fares it with my sweet spouse this evening?" he asked, as he conducted her to a seat upon an ottoman: and placing himself by her side, he passed one arm round her waist, and with the other played with the long rich tresses of her shining hair. "Tell me, sweetest, are you pleased to see me? do you think of me when I am away?"

"In all respects your Grace will ever find me a dutiful wife," answered Musidora.

"Eh! but this is parrying with my question," exclaimed the King, with a good-humoured smile. "Come, tell me, charmer, do you think of me during the day, when I am absent from you?"

"Can you ask me such a question?" rejoined Musidora, in a tone of gentle reproach. "Think you, my royal husband, that I am unmindful of him who has lavished all bounties upon my family, and who has bestowed such especial favour upon myself?"

"Then tell me, Musidora, are you happy? are you altogether happy?" inquired the King: and he gazed upon her with a penetrating earnestness.

"Would it not savour of ingratitude were I to answer otherwise than in the affirmative?"

"But I require you to answer me truly," he insisted, though mildly and gently.

"There is no condition of life, my liege lord and husband," returned Musidora, "without its care in a greater or lesser degree. But tell me in your turn," she asked, bending upon him her sweetest smile, "whether you yourself are happy?"

"Yes—you know not how happy in having won you!" answered the King. "You are aware that from the very first moment I saw you I loved you devotedly and fondly; and had it depended upon me, our hands would have been united some weeks before they were."

"And then you would have thought all the less of me," rejoined Musidora. "But permit me to ask a question——"

"Ten thousand if you will, my sweet queen," was the response. "Proceed."

"How is it that your Grace contrives so well to escape the observation of all that host of domestics, courtiers, and dependants who throng at the palace? It is a circumstance that has often bewildered me; and seeing the many grave reasons which your Highness has advanced for keeping our marriage secret yet a few months, I am constantly trembling lest by some accident it should be discovered."

"Do not make yourself uneasy on that score," replied the King. "I know full well how to elude the observation of my dependants. Besides, dearest Musidora, love sharpens the wit and gives a wondrous keenness to the ingenuity. Think you that your own hand-maiden Annetta, and the old housekeeper Dame Bertha, are as guarded and as prudent as we could wish them to be in keeping this secret?"

"I am convinced of it," returned Musidora.

"And now, what of your father in the Isle of Wight?" proceeded the King: "how fares the worthy old gentleman?"

"I showed you, my liege husband, the letter which I received from my father in reply to the one I wrote acquainting him with my marriage: but I have received no communication since. Indeed, there has been no time for farther correspondence between us."

"Truly not!" remarked the King: "our marriage is as yet but a fort-night old. Your sire, sweet Musidora, seems well pleased with that Dr. Bertram whom I sent to be his companion?"

"Yes—my father has always written, since the first day Dr. Bertram became his guest, in a cheerful strain of gratitude concerning him."

"And that cousin of your's, Master Percy Rivers—or as I ought rather to call him, Governor Rivers?"

"I have not heard from him since he was here at the villa," replied

Musidora: "but in the letters which I have received from my father, I learn that he is most assiduous in his duties, and by various administrative measures which he has adopted, has given great satisfaction to the people of the Isle of Wight. But of course your Highness knows all these things much better than I."

"To be sure," rejoined the King. "And now tell me, Musidora, do you not look forward with some degree of impatience to that day when the public recognition of our marriage is to take place, and when you will be saluted with acclamation as Queen of England?"

"It would be a miserable affectation on my part," returned the lady, "and one which would serve to render me contemptible in your Grace's eyes, were I to deny that I do anticipate with much joy and hope the hour when it shall suit your sovereign pleasure to acknowledge me as your wife. But do not think, my royal husband, that it is altogether from mere ambition that I entertain this feeling: it is that I long to have the opportunity of doing good—an opportunity for which the station whereunto you will elevate me, must prove most favourable."

At this moment the Earl and Countess of Grantham made their appearance to pay their respects to the King; and shortly afterwards it was announced that supper was served up. To the banqueting-room did the party accordingly repair; and when the repast was over, the King and Musidora went back to the saloon where they had previously been discoursing, and where they were wont to pass an hour together in conversation ere retiring to rest.

"What topic were we talking upon when your relatives interrupted us just now?" asked the King, as soon as he and Musidora were again by themselves. "Ah! I remember—we were speaking of the time when your public recognition as Queen of England will take place. Musidora, that will be a proud day for you! Apparelled in your most splendid raiment—glittering with jewels—but the light of your own magnificent beauty shining above all—you will be at once the envy and the admiration of the highest-born ladies in the land. Will not that be a glorious day for you, Musidora?"

"It will be a happy day, and a proud one," she answered. "But wherefore, my royal husband, do you dwell upon this topic to-night—so much more than usual?"

"Is it not a topic which we ought to speak upon?" asked the King: and it struck Musidora at the moment that there was something peculiar in his smile.

"Are you able as yet to calculate the day when publicity shall be given to our marriage?" she asked, with a slight glitter of uneasiness in her eyes.

"No—not yet," he answered: and she fancied that the cause of her temporary apprehension must have been a mere passing illusion, for the King's look had instantaneously resumed its wonted appearance. "Why did you gaze upon me in so singular a manner for a moment? Surely my Musidora does not entertain any suspicion of my honour—my good faith—my love?"

"No, no—heaven forefend!" she cried, with a sudden outburst of passionate vehemence.

"I thought you could not—I flattered myself that it was impossible," he whispered, drawing her towards him and covering her countenance with kisses.

At this moment the quick trampling of steeds, as if horsemen were furiously galloping towards the villa, reached the ears of Musidora and her husband. In a few moments the sounds ceased, and then the bell at the gate was heard to ring violently.

"What can this mean? what can this be?" muttered the King in a low and hasty, but still audible tone: then rising from his seat, he stood calm, cool, and resolute, as if the consciousness of sovereign rank enabled him to triumph over every feeling of apprehension.

But Musidora, seized with a sudden and terrible presentiment of evil, clung to his arm, and gazed up into his countenance as if to watch what was passing there and gather from his looks the means of tranquilising and reassuring herself.

In another moment the Earl of Grantham, rushing into the room, exclaimed, "Did your Highness hear that ring? Two persons on horseback—I could just distinguish their figures from the hall-window through the darkness——"

"Go yourself, my lord," interrupted the King, "and give them admittance. Bid your servants retire to their own apartments, so that if anything disagreeable be about to happen, there may be no unnecessary witnesses of the scene."

The Earl rushed out of the room into the hall, closing the door behind him;—and Musidora, still clinging to her husband, while a sickening sense of terror crept in upon her soul, murmuringly asked, "Do you really apprehend anything unpleasant? What can be done? what would you have me do?"

"Nothing, nothing—but remain here with me," was the response, given almost sternly.

Musidora gazed more intently still up into her husband's countenance; and its expression augmented her terrors. It was fierce, haughty, and implacable—seeming to portend the inward conviction that some crisis was at hand.

Meanwhile the Earl of Grantham, having hastily dismissed the porter from the hall, unfastened the front door; and the two horsemen, who had just alighted from their steeds outside, immediately entered the villa.

Hark! what was that ejaculation of mingled consternation and dismay which at this instant reached Musidora's ears? It was a cry that burst from the lips of Lord Grantham. The very next moment a voice—*another* voice—addressed a few quick but peremptory words to the Earl. But that *other* voice—heaven! why did it sound like the knell of doom upon Musidora's ear? A sensation of sickly horror seized upon her;—she looked up to her husband and beheld so strange an expression upon his countenance, that instead of cheering her, it enhanced her dismay. She tried to speak, and could not—but rushed towards the door and then stopped suddenly short without opening it, as that voice which had thus filled her with consternation was speaking again. With one hand she held back the luxuriant tresses of her raven hair—her lips, colourless as her countenance, were parted—pale and statue-like she stood—and listened. That voice was speaking still: but she could not gather the words it said.

Again she turned towards her husband: but at that same instant the door was flung violently open; and the two horsemen who had just arrived, rushed into the room. Yes—they entered thus abruptly: and a wild terror shot into Musidora's eyes; for she at once perceived——eternal heaven! could it be possible?—that the foremost individual was the exact resemblance of her husband.

To that husband she flung her frantic looks but in this one wild glance of agony was revealed to her the terrible astounding fact, that he whom she knew as her husband had in a moment changed to the form of Lord Lionel Danvers!

A thunderbolt falling upon her head, would have been mercy at that moment: she placed her hands before her eyes—shrieked aloud—and, as a mocking laugh rang in her ears, dropped senseless upon the floor.

CHAPTER XXXVIII.

LIONEL DANVERS.

It would be very difficult to convey an adequate idea of the singularity, together with the awfulness and the terror, of the scene so rapidly sketched at the end of the previous chapter: but though so hastily hit off, no words were quick enough to keep pace with the celerity of the actions themselves. The sudden bursting in of the *real* King and his Secretary—the instantaneous transformation of the *false* King back to the real shape of

Lionel Danvers—the wild cry bursting from Musidora's lips as the whole ghastly truth flashed like searing lightning to her comprehension—then her falling down in a death-like trance,—all these circumstances constituted a scene to which no powers of language can do justice. But now survey the group! Lionel Danvers, drawn up to the full height of his slim and graceful figure, and his handsome countenance bearing the Lucifer-like reflex of that diabolically vindictive feeling which also found expression in his mocking laugh,—the King, who on bursting into the room had caught sight of the exact image of himself, and then the next moment, quick as the eye can wink, beheld Lord Lionel Danvers upon the same spot,—the Earl of Grantham and St. Louis, who had likewise witnessed the astounding transformation and were paralysed with horror—and last of all, Musidora lying stretched senseless upon the floor, pale as marble, but with the bright gems shining upon her raven hair, her bosom, and her arms, as if in mockery of the corpse-like form which they now embellished,—such was the picture the full effect of which our readers must exert all the powers of their imagination to conceive!

"Let this lady be attended to!" said the King, recovering his presence of mind before the Earl of Grantham or St. Louis had even begun to surmount their first sensation of horror at what they had seen: "minister unto this lady, I say: for it is clear that some astounding treachery has been practised towards her. But perhaps she is dead?"

"I will place her upon this ottoman," said Danvers; and raising Musidora in his arms, he bore her to a sofa; but while so doing, he rapidly took from her bosom the marriage-certificate which she kept treasured there.

"My lord, do you hear me speak?" exclaimed the King, addressing himself in a fierce and angry voice to the Earl of Grantham. "That lady may be dead, I say: or at least she will die unless timely succour be afforded her. Lead the way to some other room where we may converse: and send her handmaids without delay to minister unto her."

The Earl of Grantham, recalled by the King's words from the torpor of consternation,—but still feeling like one under the influence of a confused somnambulistic dream,—opened the door, and was leading the way to another apartment, when he encountered his wife and Annetta in the hall,—Musidora's piercing scream having brought them thither. Being utterly unconscious of what had occurred, they of course regarded the King as Musidora's husband, and fancied whatever extraordinary had taken place must be connected with the presence of Danvers and St. Louis.

"Go quick to Musidora," said the Earl, in a confused manner and bewildered look. "When she recovers—if she ever do—keep her quiet: let her not move—or rather convey her up at once to her own chamber—and let her have speech with none but yourselves. Whatever may happen—whatever danger may seem impending—send not for a doctor: no stranger must have access to her! The ears of yourselves alone must receive the first words to which she will give utterance. I will explain all presently."

Both the Countess and Annetta saw that something dreadful had indeed occurred: and they noticed that the countenance of the King was filled with a sort of gloomy indignation. But Lady Grantham dared not pause to ask her husband for any farther explanation now: for he waved her peremptorily away, urging her and Annetta to hasten to the succour of Musidora. Ere the Countess and the abigail, however, passed on to the room where the unfortunate young lady lay senseless upon the sofa, they caught a glimpse of the countenance of Danvers—that countenance of such dark and fearful beauty!—and without knowing who he was, they felt stricken with the deepest terror, as if instinctively aware that they were in the presence of some being of no common order. Then they hurried on into the saloon where their services were required; while the Earl of Grantham continued to lead the way to another apartment, followed by the King, Lionel Danvers, and St. Louis.

On entering this room, which was lighted by a chandelier suspended to the ceiling, the Earl of Grantham said in a faint trembling voice, "Where will it please your Highness to be seated?"

"Here," answered the King, placing himself in a large arm-chair near the central table.

The Earl of Grantham took his stand upon the monarch's right, while St. Louis placed himself behind the chair. But Lord Danvers, without even doffing his plumed cap, or in any way testifying the slightest obeisance towards King Henry VIII, leant his elbow upon a protecting image sculptured on the upright part of the huge overhanging chimney-piece; and with the other hand upon his hip, he lounged there with a sort of graceful ease and elegant indolence, as if all that had taken place or that still might occur was a matter of the most perfect indifference to him.

"Lord Danvers," said the monarch, in a tone full well evincing the latent terror that was mingled with the other feelings which the recent scene had conjured up, "you must be conscious of some wondrous power thus to bear yourself in the presence of your Sovereign. But tell me, Lord Danvers—was it really true—or did my eyes deceive me——"

And the King stopped short; as if, with a sudden return of convulsing terror, he was altogether unable to give utterance to the question he was about to put.

"It is not in my habit to be discourteous to those whom the world has invested with a rank above my own," said Danvers, slowly and leisurely taking off his cap, but replacing upon his hip the hand in which he held it, so that the plume branched out from behind his curved arm; and altogether there was an unspeakable air of elegance and grace investing that man of wild and wondrous destiny.

"I claim not courtesy from you, Lord Danvers," said the King, still in a moody voice, as if well-nigh afraid to speak, yet compelled to do so, at any peril, in vindication of his sovereign rank: "nor do I ask for homage at your hands; for it is clear enough that King though I be, you are in one sense invested with a power enabling you to defy mine—perhaps even——But no, I will not think that you are capable of working me an injury."

"Monarch," answered Danvers, "I never seek to work wanton harm upon any one. I deal only with those who in the first place are necessary to my purposes, or who in the second place by their own deeds have provoked my vengeance. I know what question you were about to put to me ere now; and I will answer it. Yes," he continued, slowly raising himself up from his leaning posture and assuming an attitude full of dignity, hauteur, and conscious power, "I took your shape, O King, for the purpose of melting the proudest soul of ice that ever sought to defy the influence of human passions and human feelings—to bend the pride of the haughtiest female beauty that ever enshrined itself in a temple hewn from a glacier— to melt the coldest virtue that ever took refuge amidst the snow-drifts of an Alpine height! This I have done—my triumph is achieved—and I regret not that the catastrophe has come so soon. Of course I well knew that the deceit could not last forever: nor did it suit my purpose that it should so. Within a few days should I myself have proclaimed the tremendous truth to the ears of Musidora, and overwhelmed her by the sudden assumption of my own shape while she fancied that it was the King whom she was clasping in her arms. But it appears that by some accident you, O Monarch, have been led hither this night. Perchance that youth who stands behind your chair——"

"No—I learnt nothing from his lips," interrupted the King; "and if he had the power to betray you, he has not exercised it."

"It is well then for his sake," rejoined Danvers: and still in the same calm tone of self-possession as before, he went on to say, "As I was observing, some accident, for the nature of which I care not, brought your Highness hither this night, thus precipitating somewhat the catastrophe which sooner or later was to ensue. It is now for you, O King, to decide what amount of publicity you choose to give to the affair: but for my part I am indifferent—and having no farther need to tarry here, bid ye all farewell."

"No, by heaven!" ejaculated the monarch, now suddenly inspired with all the courage of his race, and feeling the hot blood of the Plantagenets boil up in his veins; "the matter cannot end thus! I were a very coward to let you escape the law which you affect to trample upon. The foulest forgeries have been committed—the most damnable treacheries practised! At all risks I make thee my prisoner!"

Starting from his chair as he spoke, King Henry drew his sword from its sheath: brightly it flashed in the glare of the overhanging lamps—and the next instant it was pointed at Danvers' heart, the very tip penetrating his doublet,—while the monarch's left hand clutched him forcibly by the arm.

"Be quiet, foolish King—I bear a charmed life!" said Danvers: and without any apparent effort, he shook the monarch off.

"Ah! this to *me*, your King?" ejaculated the now infuriate Henry. "Draw and defend thyself! I would not like to murder thee in cold blood!"—and he placed himself in an attitude of attack.

Lord Danvers drew his rapier from its sheath—not hastily, as one does who feels that his life is in danger—but with a cool and leisurely delibera-tion, as if there were not the slightest necessity for exertion on his part. The King, fearfully exasperated, and in his boiling rage losing sight of all the circumstances which should have convinced him of Danvers' super-human power, aimed a tremendous blow at the nobleman: but the rapier catching the massive sword, seemed to twist and twine its thin blade like a coiling snake all in an instant round the heavier weapon, and thus literally tore it from the King's grasp.

"Now I give you your life," said Danvers, his lip curling with scornful triumph: "for we were not upon equal terms."

"Traitors! villains! dastards!" thundered the King, turning furiously towards the Earl of Grantham and St. Louis: "will ye stand idly by and see your monarch thus treated—thus insulted? On your allegiance, I com-mand you to aid me in arresting this man,—whose punishment is required alike by the laws of humanity and of heaven!"

But the Earl of Grantham shrank back with a horror which he could neither conceal nor subdue; while on the other hand St. Louis, drawing his sword, sprang towards Danvers, exclaiming, "I obey my King; but it is my life that I am giving him!"

"No, no—foolish boy," said Danvers, not even condescending to use his rapier now, but pushing back St. Louis' weapon with his hand: "I do not want your life. I seek not lives when they are worthless to me. No, no—I do not!" he exclaimed, his voice suddenly thrilling with the excite-ment of some horrifying emotion which flamed up within him; and at the same instant an expression of unutterable anguish passed over his counte-nance.

St. Louis' sword dropped as if the hand which had just held it were stricken with sudden palsy; and then Danvers, returning his own rapier to its sheath, and slowly replacing his plumed cap upon his head, moved towards the door.

"O terrible man!" said the King, all his maddened rage having subsided again beneath the influence of an overwhelming horror: "you are not as other men are!—you are either infinitely above or below them!—you must be in league with the Evil One!"

Lionel Danvers turned at this moment, just as he reached the door; and no words can describe the look—the awful look—which he bent upon the King;—a look which while it lit up his countenance into a perfect blaze of superhuman beauty, at the same time expressed that undefinable mingling of triumph, anguish, and horror which the great masters have given to the features of Lucifer when, even in the hour of his fall, still hurling defiance against the Majesty of Heaven. Danvers passed slowly out of the room; and for several minutes after he had thus disappeared, not a word was spoken—not a soul moved—but the King, the Earl of Grantham, and Gerald St. Louis stood statue-like, transfixed with horror by that awful look which had been bent upon them.

At length the King, suddenly breaking as it were from the attitude in which he was spellbound, said, "It is a relief thus to be rid of the presence of that dreadful man. My lord of Grantham, order your menials to bring wine hither."

The Earl issued from the room with trembling steps; and as he traversed the hall, he flung frightened glances around, lest the dreaded form of Danvers should emerge from some dark nook or from behind some marble column, armed with terrors of a more crushing nature than any he had yet displayed. But his apprehensions were not realized; and having ordered a domestic to carry a silver tray with wine and other refreshments into the room which he had just left, he hastily sped up-stairs to Musidora's chamber. On knocking at that door the Countess came forth, terror and dismay depicted upon her countenance. Few and hurried were the words that passed between the Earl and his wife in the passage outside Musidora's apartment. It appeared that the unhappy young lady had recovered once from her deep trance, and had given utterance to lamentations and cries which, though generally vague and incongruous, still were just intelligible enough to afford the bewildered and affrighted Countess and Annetta an idea of what had passed: but then she had relapsed off into a swoon again. The Earl, in a low deep voice full of terror and dismay, confirmed the dreadful suspicion which Musidora's incoherent words had already excited in her ladyship's mind; and as the last faint hope that what

Musidora had said might be mere delirious raving, was destroyed in the bosom of the Countess, she clung to the bannisters for support.

"Heaven only knows how it will all end!" said the Earl, trembling from head to foot, as if shaking with the palsy. "Oh, what a night of horror! But whatever may be the issue, there is one thing that must be religiously observed—and that is *secrecy!* At all events let none but yourself, Annetta, and of necessity Dame Bertha, know of these things. If Musidora should survive, it will be for ye three to take turns in watching her. But heaven only knows," repeated the unhappy nobleman, seeming as if almost crushed by the incidents of the evening, "how it will possibly end! It is for the King to decide in some sense; and I now return to him."

The Earl accordingly hurried away, and the Countess re-entered Musidora's chamber. Retracing his steps to the apartment where he had left the King and St. Louis, he found the former drinking deep draughts of wine, and the latter also refreshing himself with a goblet which the monarch had bade him take. But beyond the few words conveying this invitation to partake of the wine, the King had not spoken a syllable to St. Louis during the ten minutes that the old nobleman was absent.

"How fares it," asked the monarch in a deep gloomy voice, "with the unhappy Musidora now?"

"She is still in a grievous plight, my liege," answered the Earl of Grantham; "and I fear me it will be the death of her—especially if the shame that will redound upon her from this mock marriage be published to the world."

"Tell me, my Lord of Grantham," said the King, "everything that has occurred from first to last,—when this imposture commenced—how it has been sustained——In short, prove to me that ye have indeed been all the victims and the dupes of the most detestable of cheats, and none of ye accessory to it,—and ye may rest assured that I will consult your feelings in the course that I may hereafter pursue with regard to it."

The Earl of Grantham accordingly sat down and gave the King a circumstantial account of all those incidents with which the reader has been made acquainted,—how Danvers, in the guise of the royal person, first introduced himself to Musidora, and how he became a regular visitor of an evening—how on one occasion Musidora wrote a letter to the King, requesting a favour on behalf of Percy Rivers—how this letter was duly forwarded to the palace at Greenwich—and how it was productive of the double appointment of Musidora's cousin and father respectively to the Governorship and Rangership of the Isle of Wight,—how the marriage had been celebrated in the chapel of the Monastery of Twelve—and how Danvers, exercising the privileges of a husband, had since passed each night with his bride at Grantham Villa.

King Henry did not listen to this narrative without frequent demonstrations of anger and excitement. Had it been under ordinary circumstances, his rage would have known no bounds: the inflammable materials of his temperament would have blazed up into the fiercest conflagration: but now, although Danvers was no longer present, yet did a certain lingering terror overhang the monarch's mind, like the influence of a hideous nightmare even after the dream itself has passed away. Still, as we above hinted, the King did occasionally interrupt the Earl of Grantham's recital with sudden starts of impatience and half-subdued ejaculations of rage— especially at those points which described how the false King—or rather Lionel Danvers personifying the King—had bestowed the appointments upon Sir Lewis Sinclair and Percy Rivers.

"Your lordship tells me," said the monarch, when the narrative was brought to a conclusion, "that Father Paul, the Superior of the Monastery, gave a certificate of marriage, and that Musidora has it? Go and fetch it to me."

The Earl accordingly left the room a second time; and the moment the door closed behind him, St. Louis threw himself at the King's feet, saying, "My liege, pardon me—pardon me—for the treacheries and duplicities in which I have been a sharer! There are many things in the narrative of the Earl of Grantham which are still involved in mystery, but on which I can throw some light."

"Rise, young man," said the King, rather in a compassionating tone of voice than otherwise. "I saw from a certain observation which Lord Danvers made, that you were to some extent in his confidence: but I mean to hear you first ere I condemn. I have this night seen sufficient of the wondrous power of that dreadful man to feel assured that over whomsoever he chooses to enthral, he must necessarily exercise a fearful influence. Rise then, I say; and when we return to the palace presently, you shall tell me everything. Then, if I see that you also have been made a victim and a dupe, and have become entangled in the meshes of this diabolical enchantment, I will not deal harshly to you. Besides," muttered the King to himself, "I shall take very good care to do nothing that will draw down upon me the vengeance of this all-powerful Danvers: and there are other considerations too that must make me deal with becoming prudence and policy in these things."

While the King was thus musing to himself, St. Louis rose from his knees, considerably cheered by the manner in which his royal master had spoken: and almost immediately after this little scene, the Earl of Grantham returned to the apartment.

"My liege," he said, with trembling voice and the direst apprehension in his looks, "I cannot find the marriage-certificate given by Father Paul."

"Not find it!" ejaculated the King, angrily.

"Such is the truth, sire, as I have a soul to be saved!" answered the Earl of Grantham. "Annetta, Musidora's handmaiden, declares that her mistress was wont to carry that marriage certificate in her bosom; and the girl declares positively that when Musidora performed her toilet this evening ere descending to the supper-room, she as usual deposited the certificate in the body of her dress: but when the Countess and Annetta ere now disapparelled Musidora on bearing her up to her room, that certificate was nowhere to be found."

"May it please your Highness," St. Louis ventured to suggest, "was there not something strangely zealous and suspiciously over-strained in the conduct of Lord Danvers when he lifted to the sofa the poor lady whom his own treachery had plunged into that death-like trance? It was not probable that after seeking so terrible a vengeance upon her, he could have been moved by her swooning state."

"You are right, St. Louis!" ejaculated the King: "it must be so! Danvers behaved thus to Musidora in order to have the opportunity of pilfering back the marriage-certificate—the only barrier which perhaps might, under eventual circumstances, stand between her and fullest shame!"

"Your Grace's Secretary has doubtless furnished the clue to the mysterious disappearance of the marriage-certificate," observed the Earl of Grantham. "And now, may I venture to beseech your Highness to relieve me from the acutest suspense——"

"In what respect?" demanded the King abruptly.

"In this, my liege," rejoined the Earl,—"that the Countess and myself are as yet utterly uncertain regarding the issue to which the terrible occurrences of this night may lead."

"I acquit you and your Countess of being in the slightest degree accessary to the base perfidy of Danvers," answered the King; "and it by no means suits my purpose that publicity should be given to the affair. Were it known that any man in my dominions possesses the power of assuming any shape he chooses—and chiefest of all, mine—heaven alone knows to what extent it might impair my royal authority. Therefore, mark you well, my Lord of Grantham! let all these transactions be consigned as much as possible to oblivion: at all events let them be preserved as inviolable secrets. For the sake of that poor unhappy lady who has been the victim of so much treachery, do I confirm her father and her cousin in their appointments, respectively as Ranger and Governor of the Isle of Wight. You told me, I think, that this Percy Rivers knew not of the mock-marriage?—did you not say so ere now in your narrative?"

"I did, my liege," answered the Earl of Grantham.

"Then mind he never does hear of it. But Sir Lewis Sinclair and that physician who is with him,—doubtless a creature whom Danvers sent to amuse the old man,—have been duly informed of the marriage, or rather of the hideous treachery which dared sport with the solemn nuptial rite?"

"It is even so, great King," rejoined the Earl. "Sir Lewis and Dr. Bertram are acquainted with the so-called marriage."

"Then see that they are disabused by some means of that belief," continued Henry. "But all this I leave to Musidora herself to regulate in the manner that shall suit her best, when she recovers from the shock sustained from this night's occurrences. Tell me, how fares she now, as you have again so recently visited her chamber?"

"Her senses have come back again—she is no longer in a swoon," replied the Earl, "but an awful stupor is upon her. She seems thoroughly crushed and broken by the tremendous blow she has this night received."

"Then, at all events, the assurances I have given your lordship," said the King, "relative to the appointments of her father and her cousin, will be to some little extent a source of solace. If she hesitate to allow her relatives to retain situations so fraudulently bestowed, I will issue fresh letters-patent conferring the appointments,—or lather conferring them all over again. But upon this subject you can communicate with me in a few days, when the unhappy young lady shall be in a better frame of mind to converse with your lordship upon the subject."

"Most sincerely do I thank your Grace for all the bounteous words that have issued from your royal lips: and these thanks are tendered," continued the Earl of Grantham, "not merely on my behalf, but likewise on that of the Countess and the hapless Musidora."

"See you, my lord, that the most religious secrecy be observed; and I shall not regret having spoken thus kindly to you. And now, St. Louis, we will take our departure."

The obsequious Earl of Grantham flew to open the doors for the royal egress; and the King went forth, accompanied by his Secretary. Remounting their horses, they galloped back to the Royal House, and entered that palatial dwelling unperceived by any one save the sentinel at the gate.

"Take you the horses to the stables," said the King to St. Louis; "and see that you disturb not the grooms. Use all possible despatch; and then rejoin me in your own chamber, to which I shall proceed."

CHAPTER XXXIX.

FARTHER EXPLANATIONS.

THE reader might fancy, from the latter portion of the preceding chapter, that King Henry possessed a generous and compassionating disposition, and that in so readily confirming the appointments bestowed by forgery and fraud upon Sir Lewis Sinclair and Percy Rivers, he sought to indemnify Musidora for the villany of which she had been the victim. But his Highness was totally incapable of such benevolent sympathy; and for anything that he would have cared, Musidora and all her relations might have been plunged into shame, poverty, and ruin, as the result of the transaction, ere he would have stretched out a hand to help or uttered a word to console them. The real truth is that the King acted, throughout his seeming benevolences, under the influences of terror: and this terror was two-fold.

In the first place, the King reasoned with himself that if the two appointments were suddenly cancelled, inquiries and investigations would ensue as to the cause,—if not on Sir Lewis Sinclair's part, at least on that of Percy Rivers; and the result would inevitably be the making public of the whole transactions. In this case the world would not for an instant believe that a necromancer had assumed the likeness of the King, but would very naturally jump to the conclusion that the King himself had seduced a young lady of virtue by means of a fraudulent marriage, to aid which even the very signature of the Pope had been forged; and if such a belief as this were to get abroad, it would heap an odium upon Henry's name which he shuddered to think of. In the second place, the King reasoned that if publicity were given to the whole affair, and even if the public *did* believe in the preternatural power of Danvers, the discontented nobles of the land (and there were many at the time) might get hold of Danvers, inducing him to assume the royal likeness and declare that he was the real Henry Plantagenet—an imposture which his superhuman resources, backed by the enormous wealth he was known to possess, would be pretty sure to render successful. These were the considerations which prompted the King to do his best to hush up all that had occurred; and therefore had he not only spoken in terms of sympathy with respect to Musidora, but had also confirmed the appointments of her father and cousin. For the same reason had he borne himself in a conciliatory manner towards the Earl of Grantham, and had also held out hopes of forgiveness to Gerald St. Louis for whatsoever faults he might have committed.

But there was another person to whom it would be necessary to enter into the fullest and completest explanations: and this was Wolsey, Archbishop of York. The reader will remember that after the King had perused the parchment-slip which Wolsey showed him, they had some little private discourse together while St. Louis went to get the horses in readiness. During this brief and hurried colloquy the King had emphatically sworn to Wolsey that he was altogether innocent of whatsoever treachery had been practised towards Musidora Sinclair, and that therefore somebody must not only have forged the Papal Bull, but also have personated himself. Wolsey was thus so far initiated into the secret that it would be impossible to avoid telling him the rest; and therefore the King suddenly found himself, for all the reasons above specified, under the necessity of purchasing the secrecy of the ambitious Wolsey at any price. The reader is thus in possession of the key to that sudden rise which the haughty prelate was now on the point of experiencing in the favour of the monarch.

Having given these necessary explanations, and shown how Henry was swayed by a two-fold terror in hushing up the transactions which had been so strangely brought to his knowledge, we resume the thread of our narrative. Ascending to his Private Secretary's chamber in the palace at Greenwich, he waited with some degree of impatience till St. Louis made his appearance. A quarter of an hour thus elapsed: for the young man had to unsaddle the steeds and stable them ere he could ascend to the room where the King was tarrying. At length he hurried thither; and lighting the lamp—(the King having remained the while in the dark)—he awaited with fear and trembling to be questioned by his royal master: for notwithstanding the forbearing manner in which his Highness had ere now spoken to him at Grantham Villa, St. Louis was afraid, because he well knew not only that the treacheries he was about to recite were of a very black character, but also that the King's mood was apt to change as frequently as a weathercock.

Placing himself at the table, the King said, "Sit down, young man, and speak out with candour and frankness. Upon the sincerity of your words and the fulness of your avowals, will depend the manner in which I purpose to deal with you. Let me be assured that you tell me the whole truth without reserve or suppression; and I promise you an unconditional pardon. But if I detect you in the least duplicity or deception, I shall not fail to visit you with condign punishment."

"I will speak frankly and candidly, sire," replied St. Louis, much cheered by the words just addressed to him. "Does your Highness recollect that when you came to my chamber this evening, your Grace found me walking to and fro in the dark; and I declared that I was giving way to my reflections? Ah, my liege! I was pondering upon the best means of making your Highness acquainted with all that was going on in respect to these frauds and forgeries. But of the object for which they were intended I was altogether ignorant: nor until to-night was I ever aware of the tremendous fact that Lionel Danvers possessed the power of assuming the shape of another. As I was however saying, my liege, I had resolved to throw myself at your royal feet and confess the treacheries of which I was a vile instrument and tool."

"And wherefore, then, did you not do so at once?" asked the King. "The moment I entered the room, why did you not obey the impulse of those resolutions which you state to have been uppermost in your mind? why did you not throw yourself at my feet and confess everything?"

"Ah! sire," responded St. Louis, "there was one consideration—one fearful consideration—which made me hesitate; and this was because not only my honour, but also my very life is in the hands of those who originally placed me about your royal person!"

"Those?" echoed the "King. "To whom do you allude?—are there many in this plot?"

"I mean, sire," answered St. Louis, "that Sir Edward Poynings is the creature of Lord Danvers as well as I am—but with this difference, that it is I who am made the vile instrument and tool of the villanies which they suggest. It is I also who have had the dangerous part to perform, and have been urged on step by step in this nefarious career by the terror of exposing myself to infamy and disgrace—perhaps death upon the scaffold, if I dared refuse to do the bidding of my masters!"

"Ah! Sir Edward Poynings is a traitor, then?" observed the King, with an increasing gloominess of look: for he thought to himself that there was now *another* person whom, instead of punishing, he would have to conciliate. "But think you," he demanded, after a brief pause, "that Sir Edward Poynings is altogether in Lord Danvers' secrets?—think you that he is aware of the course this dreadful man was pursuing towards Musidora?"

"No, sire—I am convinced that he was not," replied St. Louis. "He, as well as I, have been kept as much in the dark as possible respecting the real object for which the various frauds and forgeries were intended;—and by many an expression which has fallen from the lips of Sir Edward Poynings, am I certain that he knew but little more than myself. As for the fact that Lionel Danvers was assuming your royal likeness, and thus practising his diabolical treacheries towards Musidora, I can positively assure your Grace that Sir Edward knew naught thereof."

"Well, well—so much the better," observed the King. "But I think that without any farther parley, you had better enter at once upon a continuous narrative of such matters as you may have to reveal; and I will listen with all due attention."

"Most potent Sovereign," answered St. Louis, "I shall commence at once: but with the earnest hope not only that I may receive your royal pardon for the share I have taken in the things whereof I am about to speak, but likewise that your Grace will command Sir Edward Poynings to surrender up to me, or burn before my eyes, a certain document which he holds, and which places me so completely in the power of himself and Lord Danvers."

"Be frank and candid, St. Louis," rejoined the King, "and you will have nothing to fear. Not only will I use forbearance towards you, but will see that you are emancipated from the terrorism of the document which so deeply menaces you."

"I must commence by informing your Grace," began St. Louis, "that some four years and a-half ago, a worthy uncle of mine departed this life, bequeathing to me a handsome fortune. But on his death-bed he placed in my hands a certain casket, which I will presently show your Highness, and which contains the portrait of a great-aunt of mine, together with certain manuscripts describing how Arline—for so the ancestress alluded to was called—became the victim of Lord Humphrey Danvers, father of the present nobleman. The history of my ancestress was well known to me previous to that death-bed scene when my uncle placed the casket in my hand: but he bade me receive that casket, and treasure it as a sad memorial of Arline's wrongs—those wrongs which he solemnly enjoined me to avenge either upon Lord Humphrey, if he were still alive, or upon his descendants. I swore to obey the old man's command; and upon that condition did he leave me the heir to his property. Immediately after the funeral I made inquiries respecting the Danvers family, and ascertained that Lord Humphrey had been dead a few years, and was succeeded by Lord Lionel, who was then abroad. Instead of proceeding to the Continent in search of him—which, having youth, vigour, and courage on my side, I ought to have done—I gave way to dissipation and debauchery. Into these vile courses, however, I did not fall of my own accord: but happening at the time of my uncle's death to form the acquaintance of a certain Benjamin Welford,—by profession a medical doctor, but in principle the most finished of scoundrels,—saving your Highness's presence—I was initiated by him into those ways which I now blush to look back upon. Following his example with an infatuation which can only be accounted for by my youth and inexperience, I led for four years a life of profligacy and extravagance: so that at the end of the period my fortune was gone. Welford then suggested the most desperate of pursuits in order to replenish our purses;

and without entering farther into detail, I may proceed to state that one night, when we had sallied forth to put our concocted projects into execution, we encountered Lord Lionel Danvers in the lane which runs behind the grounds of Grantham Villa. Comparing the date of that night with the particulars which the Earl of Grantham ere now gave your Highness, it is plain enough that when I and Welford thus met Danvers, it must have been at the very commencement of the intrigue which, in the shape and form of your Highness, he has been carrying on in respect to Musidora Sinclair. On that night he escaped in the most marvellous manner from the attack which Welford and myself made upon him; four pistols, fired point blank, had no effect: and our swords were equally unavailing. Ah, it was no wonder!" added St. Louis: "for that wicked nobleman must have made some compact with the Evil One, and bears a charmed life."

"It is dreadful to think of," observed the King. "But proceed."

"Lord Lionel Danvers," continued Gerald St. Louis, "appeared anxious to return good for evil; and under the pretence of offering atonement to me for the foul wrong which his father had done towards my ancestress Arline, he proposed to befriend me. What could I do? In desperate circumstances—a reckless adventurer—without money, without credit, and almost without a home,—I yielded to his insidious offers, and accepted his bounty. But this was not all. He likewise undertook to provide for my companion Welford, whom he arranged to see on the following morning."

"And that Welford," observed the King, "is no doubt the Dr. Bertram who, as Lord Grantham ere now told us, was despatched to keep old Sir Lewis Sinclair company in the Isle of Wight."

"Beyond all doubt, my liege," replied St. Louis. "With respect to myself, it was in consequence of the instructions which I received from Lord Danvers, that I made application to Sir Edward Poynings for the post of Private Secretary in your Grace's household. Without entering into details respecting the conversation that took place on the occasion between Sir Edward Poynings and myself, suffice it to say I was given to understand that I could only be inducted into the wished-for office on condition that I placed myself altogether in Sir Edward's power. Not only with regard to my honour and my reputation, but also my very life, was I thus to be at the mercy of the Comptroller of your Grace's household."

"By my crown and sceptre, this is beyond all endurance!" exclaimed Henry, his cheeks flushing with indignation, and his blood boiling with all the ire of the Plantagenets. "Sir Edward is a traitor——But go on, go on, young man," he added, suddenly checking himself, as the necessity of pursuing a conciliatory course recurred to his mind.

"The desperate condition of my fortunes, to which I have before alluded," continued Gerald St. Louis, "constrained me to fall entirely into the views of Sir Edward Poynings, who played his part so skilfully, that I was led at the moment to fancy it was in *his* power I was to place myself, and *not* in that of the prime mover of all who kept in the background. To be brief, Sir Edward Poynings suggested to me that I should place in his hands a forged bill, which would thus furnish him with the means of exercising a constant terrorism over me. I did so—and at his suggestion forged the name of Danvers. This bill, for one hundred pounds sterling, purporting to be payable at the banking-house of Master Landini in Lombard Street, is now in the hands of Sir Edward Poynings; and it is against the power—the awful power which the felonious document gives him over me, that I beseech your Highness's shielding protection."

"You shall have it—you shall have it," responded the King. "I have already promised you as much: and ere you retire to rest this night, that document shall have ceased to trouble you. Proceed."

"No sooner had Sir Edward Poynings possessed himself of the paper and presented me to your Highness, when he took the earliest opportunity to let me know that Lord Danvers had merely procured me the situation through his (Sir Edward's) influence at Court, in order that I might become the slave, the instrument, and the tool of that nobleman's private interest. It being a part of my duty to receive and open all despatches or letters addressed to your Grace in a private manner, I was instructed by Sir Edward Poynings to suppress, or rather to keep back, any letter or document which might at any moment come from Grantham Villa, or that any one might seek to deliver under circumstances of evident privacy and secrecy. Accordingly, when one day a messenger arrived with a letter which he earnestly requested might be at once placed in your Grace's hands, I took it to Sir Edward Poynings, who applauded my fidelity in obeying his instructions, and bade me return to his apartments in about an hour. I did so—and found Lord Danvers with him. I was then told to sit down, and carefully draw up two documents in the style and phraseology that Lord Danvers would himself dictate. This I also did; but when I began to discover the nature of those documents, I hesitated to proceed. Then was I threatened with exposure, arrest, trial, and condemnation on account of the forged bill. I was therefore compelled to proceed. Both those documents were letters-patent, drawn up in your Highness's name,—the one conferring the appointment of the Governorship of the Isle of Wight upon Master Percy Rivers, and the other bestowing the Rangership of the woodlands in the same island upon Sir Lewis Sinclair. When the task was completed, Lord Danvers addressed me, saying, 'You have doubtless several documents in preparation which you will have to submit in the course of the day to the King, in order to receive the royal signature; and you will therefore contrive to thrust these papers in amongst the rest, so that they may be likewise signed by the royal hand.'"

"By heaven!" ejaculated the King, starting from his seat and laying his fingers upon his sword. "But no," he added, again suddenly checking himself: "I must be calm:"—then sitting down once more, he said in a moody tone, "Proceed."

"Your Grace," resumed the Private Secretary, who had been for the moment terribly frightened by his royal master's manner, "need scarcely be reminded that when I was wont to submit divers letters and papers for your sovereign signature, your Highness never read them, but was contented with such hurried description as I gave your Grace of each successive one in the order in which they occurred. It was therefore by no means difficult for me to obtain your royal signature to the two letters-patent which, under Danvers' dictation, I had drawn up. And those signatures *were* given. Then I affixed your royal seal to those as well as to all the others; and when the work was completed, I took the documents to Sir Edward Poynings, who no doubt immediately afterwards conveyed them to Lord Danvers. Your Highness will give me credit for truthfulness when I declare that I trembled with the direst apprehension at the crime of which I had thus been made an instrument; and I could not help questioning Sir Edward relative to the ulterior motives of it. He answered me very frankly, that he himself was under such obligations to Lord Danvers that he dared not refuse to do anything his lordship might command: but that he also was ignorant of the object which these documents were intended to serve, unless it were to further an amorous intrigue of Lord Danvers with Musidora Sinclair, who was at Grantham Villa."

"Have you anything more to tell me, St. Louis?" asked the King.

"Yes, my liege," rejoined the Private Secretary: "one thing more respecting these nefarious courses into which I have been led. Some three weeks ago I was sent for to Sir Edward Poynings' room; and there I again found Lord Danvers. He said to me, 'In the Royal Closet where you transact business with his Grace, all his family archives are kept in a cupboard of which he alone possesses the key. That cupboard must doubtless contain, amongst other documents, several Papal Bulls, duly signed by the reigning Pontiff, stamped with the Keys of St. Peter, and with the three leaden seals appended. The very next time that his Highness has occasion to refer to any documents contained in that cupboard, you, St. Louis, must contrive to possess yourself of one of these Papal Bulls. Herein see that you fail not.'—Vainly did I represent both to Lord Danvers and Sir

Edward Poynings the immense peril of detection that I should incur: the forged bill was again flung in my teeth, and I was ordered to obey. That very same evening the opportunity served: your Grace wished to consult certain papers contained in the cupboard; and while your Highness was seated at the table in the Royal Closet, you ordered me to search for the deeds you required. I took that opportunity to fulfil the dangerous and treacherous commission enjoined me by Lord Danvers. And now your Highness knows all."

"Ah! I understand the meaning of this latter piece of villany," said the King in a musing tone. "Doubtless, by some chemical process, the writing originally in that document was obliterated, and the traitorous Danvers was enabled to fill it in with whatsoever suited his purpose, the signature of the Sovereign Pontiff having been left at the bottom. Now, St. Louis," continued the monarch, bending his eyes upon the Secretary, "I will not fly from my royal word. I promised to be merciful unto you if you dealt frankly with me; and although this frankness on your part has revealed high crimes and misdemeanours, treacheries and treasons, wherein you have played no mean part,—yet inasmuch as you acted under coercion and in obedience to an unnatural influence, I pardon you."

"O King, it is more than I deserve!" exclaimed St. Louis, falling upon his knees at the monarch's feet, and bursting into tears. "I know that I have done wrong—much grievous and fearful wrong; but from the very depths of my soul am I contrite and penitent!"

"Enough, enough!" exclaimed the King: "I believe you. Rise and fol-low me. Take the lamp in your hand—and come speedily."

St. Louis did as he was ordered; and the King, passing out of the room, hastened along the passage, which he threaded until he reached the door of Sir Edward Poynings' suite of apartments. These he entered, followed by St. Louis, bearing the lamp. Traversing the outer room, which was the Comptroller's office, they entered an adjoining one, which served as a parlour; and proceeding onward, they entered a third, which was Sir Edward Poynings' private chamber.

The Comptroller of the Royal Household was in bed and fast asleep when his privacy was thus broken in upon: but as the light of the lamp which St. Louis carried, flashed upon the sleeper's countenance, he opened his eyes and started up in mingled astonishment and dismay on beholding the King close at the head of the couch. Then, as his glance turned upon St. Louis, he felt that everything had been betrayed; and the cold perspira-tion broke out visibly upon his forehead.

"You have nothing to fear, Sir Edward," immediately observed the King; "provided you obey me promptly in the commands I am about to issue. Rise first of all, and dress yourself."

St. Louis placed the lamp upon the table; and while Sir Edward Poynings, leaping from the couch, huddled on his garments, the King walked to the further end of the chamber, while the Secretary retreated into the obscurest nook. In a few minutes Sir Edward Poynings was dressed, though with considerable negligence, inasmuch as his hands trembled so that he could scarcely adjust his raiment.

"Now," said the King, speaking in a calm but firm and collected tone, "I must begin by informing you, Sir Edward Poynings, that everything is known relative to the conduct of Lord Danvers. But in justice to St. Louis I have to state that it was through no treacherous betrayal of your proceedings on his part, that they have thus become revealed to my knowledge. An accident, totally unconnected with him, gave me the first clue, which, being followed up speedily, led me on to the unravelment of this complicated web of treachery. Then, seeing that the leading features were discovered, St. Louis confessed the remainder."

"Spare me, O King!—spare me, I beseech your Highness!" exclaimed Sir Edward Poynings, falling at the monarch's feet: and he began to pour forth the most piteous lamentations.

"Rise, sirrah," said the King, "and explain to me how you fell into the power of this Lord Danvers. Be candid as St. Louis has been; and I will deal mercifully with you."

"My liege, I will speak the truth," answered Sir Edward Poynings, rising up from his suppliant posture. "Some few years ago accident made me acquainted with Lord Danvers. It was at the time he visited England after his father's death, and when he came to prove his own rights and titles to the peerage which he inherited. During his short stay in London on that occasion, a friendship grew up between us; and as I was in embarrassed circumstances at the time, he advanced me a considerable sum of money. Suddenly he disappeared from the metropolis; and I saw him no more until between three and four months back. He then called upon me at this palace; and in the course of conversation I expressed my regret at being unable for the present to return the money he had lent me some years ago. He pressed me for the reasons; and I was led to admit the truth—which was that although holding so good and excellent a situation in the Royal Household, I had nevertheless fallen into arrears, and was deficient in the moneys entrusted to me by your Highness for the management of your establishment. Thereupon Danvers probed me to the very bottom of my heart, and discovered—alas! that I should be compelled to confess the ignominious truth—that the gaming-table had occasioned these defalcations which I was fearful that every day would bring to light. Danvers at once proffered me all that a seeming friendship could suggest, and volunteered to place large sums of money at my command, not only to supply the deficiencies in my accounts, but also to purchase an estate which I had for some time longed to possess. I yielded; and he got me into his power,—the condition of his seeming generosity being that I should induct a nominee of his own into the post of Private Secretary, at that time vacant. That nominee was St. Louis. Your Highness can now full well understand how a stern necessity has rendered me the slave and tool of Lionel Danvers."

"As a reward for your frankness," answered the King, "I forgive you. Indeed the humiliation of having to reveal this tale to my ears, and in the presence of Gerald St. Louis, is almost a sufficient chastisement for a personage of your rank, family, and station. But I pardon you, Sir Edward, only on condition—that you immediately give up to this young man a certain forged document which you hold——that is to say, if you do indeed still hold it."

"Yes—it is in my possession," answered Sir Edward. "Lord Danvers bade me keep it to serve as a source of terrorism in respect to St. Louis."

Thus speaking, the Comptroller of the Household took up the lamp, and begged the King to accompany him into the room which served as his office. Thither also did St. Louis follow; and Sir Edward Poynings produced the forged bill from the iron safe, where he kept the cash book and accounts connected with his high post at Court.

"Take and burn it," said the King, addressing himself to St. Louis.

The young man lost not a moment in obeying the command thus given; and as he lighted the felonious document by the flame of the lamp, it seemed as if an immense weight were gradually passing away from his soul. Throwing it into the grate, he watched it burning; and when it was consumed, the animation of unspeakable joy shone upon his countenance as he tendered his gratitude to the King.

"Now, Sir Edward Poynings," resumed the monarch, once more addressing himself to the individual, who still stood pale and trembling before him,—"you must be well convinced that after all which has taken place, it will be impossible for you to continue in the post of Comptroller of my Household. But inasmuch as I wish to deal kindly towards you, and furnish you with every opportunity of atoning for your past errors, I have resolved upon placing you in another office as high as that which you have hitherto enjoyed,—or it may be a more elevated rank still. I mean the Lord-Lieutenancy of Ireland. Now, Sir Edward Poynings, summon your grooms—take horse at once—and depart! Some excuse shall be found for the urgency and precipitation of your withdrawal from the palace. Moreover, messengers shall be despatched after you to-morrow, bearing the necessary documents for your appointment."

Sir Edward Poynings again fell upon his knees at the King's feet, to thank him for this (as he believed) most generous demonstration of mercy and forbearance; but the monarch bade him rise, with renewed injunctions for prompt departure.

"And, Ah! while I bethink me," said the King, "immediately on your arrival in Ireland, you may proclaim to my loving subjects in that kingdom, that Lord Warham Archbishop of Canterbury is no longer High Chancellor and Prime Minister of these realms, but that the great seal has been transferred from his hands to those of Lord Wolsey Primate of York."

Sir Edward Poynings bowed in humble intimation that he would not fail to promulgate the intelligence on his arrival in Ireland: and the King quitted the ex-Comptroller's apartment, followed by St. Louis.

"Now, young man," said the monarch, when they were once more alone together in the Private Secretary's chamber, "you spoke to me of a certain casket containing a portrait and written papers. My curiosity is excited in all that seems to relate to the family of Danvers; and I will thank you to fulfil your promise by showing me that casket."

St. Louis hastened to a cupboard behind the flowing tapestry of his chamber, and drew forth his cherished casket of sandal-wood inlaid with gold—that casket which through all his spendthrift follies and consequent embarrassments he had managed to keep. The King opened it, and beheld the portrait of a lovely female set in the lid. It represented a sweet creature of about eighteen, with magnificent auburn hair and deep blue eyes. Beneath it was the following inscription:—*"Arline de St. Louis, Victim of Lord Humphrey Danvers, in the year 1463."*

The King gazed for several minutes upon the portrait which thus riveted his attention with its exquisite fascinations; and his curiosity being still more deeply excited, he at length said, "I presume there will be no indiscretion in demanding leave to peruse this manuscript which the casket contains?"

St. Louis bowed assent; and the King went on to say, "After all that has occurred this evening, I feel but little inclination to sleep; and will therefore while away an hour or two in the perusal of these documents. To-morrow I will return you your casket, and will then decide in what manner I mean to act towards yourself. But rest assured that, as in the case of Sir Edward Poynings, if I make up my mind to banish you from any farther service about my person, I will provide you with an equally honourable and lucrative situation elsewhere."

Having thus spoken, the King repaired to his own chamber, where the lamps were burning; and seating himself at a table, he commenced the perusal of the manuscripts, the contents of which will now be laid before the reader.

CHAPTER XL.

THE HISTORY OF ARLINE DE ST. LOUIS.

"The present narrative opens in the year 1463. At that time an old and gloomy-looking tower, on the verge of one of the vast forests of Normandy, was inhabited by a brother and sister of the name of St. Louis. They were the remaining scions of a family that had been once powerful and rich: and their decaying tower was the only relict of the immense possessions that in former times had belonged to their ancestors. Scarcely an acre of land pertained to it; and this was a flower-garden where the sister, whose name was Arline, was wont to while away the hours in the genial season, when her brother was occupied in the chase. We will speak more particularly of him first. His Christian name was Philip: he was about twenty-eight years of age, of tall athletic form, and remarkably handsome countenance. His disposition was generous and good: his humanity and his charity, to the extent of his means, had never been vainly put to the test; while his affection towards his beauteous sister had become proverbial throughout the district. He was devoted to the sports of the forest—was of tried bravery—and excelled in all manly exercises. Indeed, he was the most dauntless well as the most indefatigable huntsman ever known in that part of the country; and while pursuing the ardours of the chase in company with other inhabitants of the district, he would often laugh at their fatigues when evening came; and instead of riding home to his tower, he would pass the night in the forest, so that he might mount again at the first glimpse of dawn and renew the exciting sport.

"It was frequently whispered amongst the dwellers in those parts that it was not altogether through mere love of the chase that Philip de St. Louis prosecuted it thus devotedly; but that the narrowness of his pecuniary circumstances rendered the produce of his hunting exploits very desirable additions to the household requirements at the tower. Indeed, Philip himself hesitated not to say that his fortunes were so broken that if it were not for the bounty of a wealthy friend of his deceased father's—living at Rouen, the capital of Normandy—he should find himself altogether without pecuniary means. It was understood that this kind friend, who had known the family in better days, was wont to allow the brother and sister a half-yearly stipend; and accordingly, at Midsummer and at Christmas, did Philip visit Rouen to receive the income so generously bestowed. The distance from the tower to the old capital city of Normandy was not above two days' journey; and thus, as the brother's absence was never very long, and he journeyed quick on his good steed in order to save the expenses of travelling as much as possible, his sister Arline was wont to remain at the tower on the occasions when her brother was thus away.

"It is true that some people wondered how a high-spirited, brave, and chivalrous young man like Philip de St. Louis could condescend to live as it were upon the bread of charity, instead of going forth into the world and carving out his fortunes with his sword. But he himself, doubtless with a delicate prescience of the comments that public opinion might make upon his dependent position, frequently met the objection by volunteering an explanation to the few friends with whom he was intimate. He was accustomed to say that if it were not for his beloved sister Arline he would go forth into the wide world and seek by his own endeavours to place himself in an independent position: but were he to do so, what would become of her? He dared not abandon her, young and beautiful as she was, to the loneliness of that gloomy old tower upon the verge of a forest, and in a very thinly populated neighbourhood. Besides which, the difference that existed between their ages—she being nearly ten years younger than he—made her look up to him as a child clings to its parent, rather than as a sister looks up to a brother.

"Such indeed was the affectionate and confiding disposition of the beauteous Arline; and it would have broken her gentle heart to be separated from that brother whom she loved so fondly. She knew full well the sacrifice of pride and every lofty feeling which her brother must be making in order to accept this dependent position for her sake, rather than hie away to the distant scenes of warfare in which fame was to be won and gold earned: but if ever she ventured to address him upon the subject, he invariably avoided the topic and compelled her to speak of something else. For this delicate regard which he paid to her feelings she loved him all the more fondly; and never was huntsman welcomed with more winning smiles and cheerful looks than was Philip de St. Louis, on those occasions when after a day or two's absence at the chase, he returned to his tower laden with the spoils of the forest. Then that old grey tower no longer seemed gloomy in his eyes: it was lighted up with the radiant smiles and sunny looks of the lovely Arline. Beauteous indeed she was too! Her hair was of the richest auburn—of that precious hue which the sunbeams love to sport with, and which seems to imprison their rays to increase the glory of its own effulgence. Her eyes were of the deepest blue, a heavenly lustre shining in their depths, and reflecting the innocent purity of her soul. Her complexion was beautifully fair, with a rich carnation glow upon the cheeks; and her lips of the brightest vermilion, revealed teeth of pearly whiteness. She was not above the middle height, but exquisitely modelled, and with just that sufficient fullness of contour which was neither too voluptuous on the one hand nor detrimental to the sculptural elegance of symmetry on the other. Her disposition, without being absolutely buoyant, was naturally happy: yet at times the idea of the sacrifices which her brother was making for her sake would throw a tinge of sadness over her features—especially when he was absent. But, generally speaking, when he was at home at the tower with her, she was all gaiety and smiles.

"At the period, however, when we thus introduce Philip de St. Louis and his beauteous sister to those who may peruse this narrative, the tinge of sadness was beginning to appear more frequently upon the countenance of Arline, and likewise to remain longer when it did overshadow her. This was caused by a deepening anxiety on her brother's account—not altogether, *now*, because he was sacrificing the best years of his life to her, but also on account of his personal safety. For certain rumours which had been vaguely current for some years past relative to the existence of banditti in the forest, had latterly become more rife as well as more positive, and had assumed a graver aspect. At first, when these rumours originally commenced, it was merely an occasional traveller who was plundered in the forest; and these cases were at very long intervals, so that either the stories were disbelieved altogether, or else it was imagined that the robber, whoever he was (for there never appeared to be more than one thus spoken of) did not habitually haunt the forest, but merely paid it an occasional visit from a distance. Latterly, however, the reports of this kind of outrage had become more frequent and more defined, the instances occurring at shorter intervals: but still there was no evidence to warrant the belief that the forest was infested by an extensive gang, as in every case it was a solitary traveller plundered by a single robber. At last the statements of the plundered seemed to furnish more circumstantial details relative to the daring bandit whose existence in the forest it was no longer possible to doubt or disbelieve. He was represented as a most terrible-looking object, clad entirely from head to foot in the hairy skins of wolves, with a mask of the same material over his countenance, and his eyes glaring fiercely and brightly through the openings made for the convenience of vision. He was said also to be mounted on a colossal steed, of immense power and extraordinary swiftness: but in no instance was it stated that he ever used more violence than was necessary to accomplish his purpose, and that he prevailed rather by the terror which his appearance excited than by anything like a savage assault. As for taking life or shedding blood, no such allegation was ever made: but on the contrary, it was asserted that he was in reality a dastard and a coward, not daring to remain and fight when resistance was offered; but that if the terrific nature of his appearance did not at once produce the desired effect, he would wheel his horse round and disappear like lightning amidst the depths of the forest.

"At the time when this narrative opens, the rumours thus hastily sketched had assumed an alarming aspect: for there were very few who believed in the alleged cowardice of the bandit. On the contrary, it was supposed that in the two or three instances which were reported of this wheeling round of the colossal steed and precipitate flight, the circumstance might be accounted for by the bravado of the travellers who related the tale rather than the cowardice of the robber who was the subject of it. Certain it is, that the rumours had lately filled the entire district with terror—not so much because the presence of a single bandit was in itself calculated to frighten men who generally went out in large parties to hunt; but because superstition lending its aid to enhance the wild interest of the whole circumstances, it was confidently whispered that the supposed brigand was some fearful demon, or else a wehr-wolf. The belief in wehr-wolves had always been popular in the French forests,—the idea of a wehr-wolf being that of a man compelled periodically by some infernal destiny to assume the form of one of those much dreaded animals.

"Arline de St. Louis, though gifted with a strong intellect, was by no means free from the superstitions prevailing in those forest-regions; and the alarming aspect which the above-mentioned rumours had of late assumed, were but too well calculated to render the affectionate girl uneasy on her brother's account. But he only laughed at her fears,—declaring that if the bandit were really a human being, he was but a solitary enemy and therefore not to be dreaded: but that if he were a wehr-wolf, he would have no power against one who had done no harm and wore a cross-handled sword. Nevertheless, Arline was not pacified by these representations; therefore each time that she saw her brother go forth to hunt in the forest, she charged him not to separate from his companions; and when he did so,—remaining in the wild depths of the wood after they had returned to their homes,—she invariably chided him as soon as he came back. Meanwhile the cases of robbery in the forest grew more frequent; and instances were now constantly reported of solitary travellers being despoiled of the gold they might have about them. Several parties of the huntsmen in the district were formed to scour the forest and catch the plunderer, if possible; and on all these occasions no one was more zealous in the undertaking nor more arduous in the search than Philip de St. Louis. But all was of no avail; and the robber, were he a man or wolf, baffled all the endeavours thus instituted for his capture.

"Such was the state of things in the vicinage of the great forest of

Normandy at the time when this narrative opens; and now we have to record an incident which was destined to exercise a material influence upon the life of Arline St. Louis. One day, in the middle of January, 1463, when Philip was hunting in the forest, a cavalier, mounted upon a horse as splendid in appearance as its caparisons were rich, rode up to the gate of the tower to make some inquiry. He was attended by a suite of six pages, also mounted upon beauteous steeds covered with gorgeous trappings. The cavalier himself was of striking appearance,—tall, slender, and admirably formed,—his figure uniting elegance with dignity, gracefulness with lithe and supple vigour. His hair, dark as night, but glossy as the raven's plumage, was worn long; and parted above a high and open forehead, it clustered in rich natural curls around the well-shaded head. His complexion was dusky, but clear and healthy: his eyes were large, dark, and luminous; and his look, though haughty and not untinged with a natural disdain, was nevertheless full of chivalrous generosity. His moustachio, black and glossy as his luxuriant hair, set off the short upper lip, and made the ivory teeth shine all the more brilliantly with the contrast. He had no whiskers nor beard; and thus the term *beauty* might be all the more appropriately used in reference to the singularly interesting appearance of this individual: indeed a more perfect masculine beauty was perhaps never seen. His age seemed to be about two-and thirty; and his aspect, his apparel, and his suite, all bespoke him to be a personage of rank and consequence.

"The inquiry which this elegant individual paused at the old tower to make, was respecting the road to the castle of the Count de Montauban, which ancient feudal fortalice was situated at a distance of about fifteen miles from the tower. It was a splendid day, the sun shining brightly; yet the ground was hard as marble, and the frost gleamed in its transparent net-work upon the skeleton boughs of the trees. Arline was taking exercise in her garden at the time when the cavalcade rode up to the tower: and immediately supposing that the chief horseman was some acquaintance of her brother's she hastened forward to give such greeting as might be suitable. But when she beheld a handsome cavalier who was utterly unknown to her, she shrank slightly back with a natural maiden modesty; and the carnation deepened upon her cheeks. Supremely beautiful did she appear at that moment; and the cavalier was evidently at once struck by her appearance. The groom and the old housekeeper,—who were the only domestics that the circumstances of Philip de St. Louis allowed him to keep,—had come forth from the tower on hearing the sounds of so many horses' feet; and, as they on a subsequent occasion declared, they noticed the sudden look of mingled ardour, interest, and adoration which the handsome cavalier bent upon the lovely Arline as she thus stood bashfully in his presence.

" 'Lady,' he said, doffing his plumed cap, and addressing her in a soft voice and with courtly manner, 'pardon me that I have given you the trouble to come forth from the grounds where you were walking. My object in approaching your habitation, was to learn the most direct path to Montauban Castle.'—Although the cavalier spoke the French language with perfect fluency, yet was it evident from a slight accentuation as also from his general bearing and appearance, that he was not a native of France but seemed to be an Englishman. Arline de St. Louis, replying in the silver tones of her fluid voice, gave him the necessary directions which he sought; and the cavalier, with a graceful salutation, thanked her for her courtesy. He then moved away at the head of his retinue, but slowly as if reluctantly; and when at a little distance, he turned to look back, Arline was still standing where he had left her, gazing in a kind of abstraction— or was it with an irresistible fascination—after him? He again raised his plumed cap in graceful salute; and she, turning somewhat abruptly away, appeared vexed with herself that she had thus seemed to be bestowing any particular interest upon him. She hastened up to her own chamber, while the groom and the old housekeeper exchanged significant looks, as much as to imply that the handsome English stranger would make a suitable bridegroom for their lovely young mistress.

"The Count de Montauban, who has just been mentioned, was a powerful feudal chief, possessing immense domains in that part of Normandy. But for some years he had resided on another estate which he possessed in a more southern province; and it was only from time to time, at long intervals, that he visited Montauban Castle. Even on these occasions he remained but a few days, for the purpose of inspecting his steward's accounts and attending to such affairs as his vassals might have to submit to his consideration. Then, so soon as these duties were performed, he would speed away again to his southern estate, where, as rumour alleged, he was wont to pass his time with the gayest company and in voluptuous pleasures. He was a man of about forty-five years of age, of dissipated appearance, though not altogether ill-looking; but with a constitution enfeebled and impaired by the course of life that he led. Thus, a countenance that had once been handsome, was rendered prematurely old in appearance by the effects of debauchery; and a frame, originally athletic and well-knit, was slightly bowed by the enervating influence of dissipation. Such was the Count de Montauban. He was unmarried, and possessed no heir to his vast estates: but it appeared that, at the very time of which this narrative is now treating, he had quitted his southern domain so that he might shake off his boon companions, and had come to settle down at Montauban Castle,—there to pursue a more steady life and recover if possible a portion of his lost health and strength. He had returned thither a week or ten days previous to that morning on which the cavalier and his retinue stopped to make inquiries at St. Louis' tower; and it was therefore surmised by the groom and the housekeeper that the gallant Englishman was proceeding to Montauban Castle to become the guest of the Count.

"When Philip de St. Louis returned home from the chase in the evening, Arline mentioned the incident of the forenoon; but the moment the name of the Count de Montauban passed her lips, she could not help observing that her brother's countenance grew suddenly troubled. She looked surprised, and was evidently on the point of inquiring the reason; when Philip immediately recovering his wonted gaiety, began to describe the success he had experienced in the forest—so that Arline no doubt speedily forgot the little incident which had for a moment astonished and even alarmed her. About a week afterwards, as she and her brother were rambling together in the vicinage of their tower, they observed a horseman approaching; and as he drew near, the damsel at once recognized the English cavalier. He was alone—not even attended by a single page; and as he advanced towards the brother and sister, he doffed his plumed cap in graceful salutation to the young damsel. He then proceeded to observe that having ridden forth alone to inspect some Roman ruins which existed in that neighbourhood, he had lost his way, and was uncertain how to proceed until he saw the tower which he remembered to have passed when journeying to Montauban Castle. Philip de St. Louis invited him to enter the tower and partake of such hospitality as it was able to afford; and the Englishman at once accepted his courteous offer. Leaping from his horse, as if he thought it ungallant to continue riding while the lady was walking, he led the noble animal by the bridle, and then began to converse in a strain of such courtly ease, but at the same time in so affable and unpretending a manner, that he speedily ingratiated himself into Philip's favour:—*that* of Arline he no doubt already possessed! He informed them that his name was Humphrey Danvers—that he was an English nobleman—but that he owned a castle and estate in Normandy, which had been purchased more than seventy years back by his ancestor Lord Walter. The name of Danvers was already known by repute to Philip and Arline, as they were aware that there was a fortalice and a domain belonging to an English family of that title on the southern confines of Normandy, and therefore at a considerable distance from their own tower. It farther appeared, from what Lord Humphrey Danvers then said, that being acquainted with the Count de Montauban, he had received an invitation to pass a few months with that nobleman; and he concluded his remarks by gallantly observing that he felt doubly indebted to the hospitable friendship of the count, inasmuch as the invitation had been the means of procuring for him the pleasure of forming the acquaintance of Arline de St. Louis. The maiden blushed and looked confused at the compliment; of which her brother however took no particular notice, as it was perfectly consistent with the bearing of courtly gallants towards lovely maidens in those times.

"On reaching the tower, the groom came forth to receive Lord Danvers' horse; and as Philip and Arline conducted their guest into their gloomy-looking and shabbily furnished sitting-apartment, they both made apologies for the rudeness of the hospitality which they were enabled to offer. But Danvers, in the most affable manner possible, at once placed them at their ease on this account,—declaring that the pleasure of forming their acquaintance rose above every other consideration in his thoughts and that since they had once tempted him into their abode they must expect that he should regard it as a permission to return and pay his respects to them on a future occasion. A substantial meal, consisting of venison, dressed in several ways, and a fine boar's head in the centre of the table, was served up. Wine and cider was also placed upon the board; and Danvers did justice to the fare, finding every thing excellent. In a word, by his affability—his generous readiness to gloss over everything that was rude, humble, or deficient in the domestic economy of the tower—the brilliancy of his conversation—the interesting anecdotes of adventure and travel which he related—and by his whole bearing, he completely won Philip's heart; while the lovely Arline listened in silent rapture to the discourse that flowed in the melody of a fine masculine voice from the lips of the guest. The time passed away with astonishing celerity; and it was late in the afternoon ere Lord Danvers thought of taking his departure. Then, as he rose to bid farewell to his kind entertainers, he requested Arline's permission to call again on an early day. The question was somewhat pointedly put to her instead of her brother: but with a blush upon her cheeks, she glanced towards Philip, as much as to imply that it was he who must answer for her. The response which he gave was not merely courteous—it was friendly: and a glow of delight overspread the olive complexion of the handsome Danvers as he declared that he should not fail to take advantage of the permission thus hospitably accorded.

"As he was about to mount his horse, Philip de St. Louis said, 'My lord, it wants but an hour to sunset, and darkness may overtake you before your good steed's hoofs shall clatter over the drawbridge of Montauban Castle. If your lordship thinks fit, I will gladly guide you to within such a distance of the Count's fortalice that you will readily achieve the rest of

the way unaided.'—But Danvers, thanking him for his courtesy, declared
that he had no apprehension as to missing his path any more. 'On the
contrary,' he added, 'I am now so well acquainted with it, that it will not
be long ere I retrace it for the purpose of visiting you again.'—'My lord,"
said Philip, in a low and somewhat deep voice, as if he were inwardly troubled, 'I have a parting request to proffer to your ear. Most welcome will
your lordship ever be at this humble abode of mine; but I beseech your
lordship on no account to breathe a syllable to the Count de Montauban
which may excite his interest or raise his curiosity relative to any inmate
of my habitation. The Count is a friend of your lordship's; and therefore,
through delicacy, I say no more.'—'I understand you fully,' replied Danvers; 'and also for the same reasons which are at this moment uppermost
in your mind, should I studiously refrain from mentioning to Montauban that this tower is graced by the presence of an angel in female shape.
Do not think, however, that because, as society is now constituted, I am
to some extent compelled to maintain intercourse with such nobles as
the Count de Montauban, that I myself sympathise with their licentious-
ness or even join in their debaucheries. No,' added Humphrey Danvers,
drawing himself up with a proud dignity and a lofty bearing, 'I loathe and
abominate their vices and depravities.'—'I have already seen too much of
your lordship, though our acquaintance is but of a few hours' duration,'
rejoined Philip, 'not to be convinced of the truth of this averment on your
part.'—They then separated, Lord Humphrey Danvers galloping away in
the direction of Montauban Castle; and Philip de St. Louis re-entering his
tower to converse with Arline upon the brilliant qualifications and varied
merits of their new acquaintance.

"Four months passed away—it was now the middle of the smiling
May season—and along the outskirt of the thick forest, once again clothed
in richest verdure, Lord Humphrey Danvers and the beauteous Arline
were walking together. His arm lightly encircled her slender waist; and
with downcast eyes and blushing cheeks she listened to the soft music
of love's delicious language which he was breathing in her ears. From a
window in the tower Philip beheld them, and was rejoiced. During the
past four months Danvers had been a frequent visitor at the gloomy old
habitation,—gloomy not however for him, but irradiated by the halo of
beauty, innocence, and purity that invested the lovely Arline. During that
interval, Philip had observed, with increasing satisfaction, and hope, and
joy, the attentions which Humphrey Danvers paid towards his sister; and
now as he beheld them roving together in a manner which indicated that
the nobleman had at length avowed his love, and was making honourable
proposals to Arline,—for to none other was it possible she could listen,—

Philip experienced feelings of indescribable exultation. And all that Philip supposed and depicted to himself, was indeed taking place. Humphrey Danvers was telling the tale of love to the ear of Arline, in strains which sank down soft and low, like a heavenly harmony, in the depths of her soul. He offered her his hand—he declared it would be the proudest day of his life when he could bear her as his bride to his castle and present her to his friends as the sharer of his brilliant rank and his immense fortune. And what said the gentle Arline? She spoke not: but her down-cast looks and the blushes which suffused her cheeks, were a reply more eloquent than words could have been; and when she withdrew not her waist from the arm wherewith her lover encircled her, he could not doubt for a moment but that his suit was accepted. When they returned into the tower together, Lord Danvers frankly explained to Philip de St. Louis all that had just taken place between himself and Arline, and demanded the brother's assent to his suit. This was cordially given; and unspeakable happiness prevailed that day at the tower. In the course of conversation with Philip, when Arline had temporarily retired to her chamber, Lord Danvers said, 'To-morrow I shall take leave of the Count de Montauban, and return to my own domain in order to make preparations for the approaching bridal, which I venture to hope will be allowed to take place two months hence. But in the meantime, as I wish to be separated as little from my beloved Arline as possible, it will afford me pleasure if you will bring her to pass a month at the castle, so that she may have the opportunity of superintending such arrangements and preliminaries as under circumstances are now required.'—Philip cheerfully accepted this invitation; and it was settled that in ten or twelve days Lord Danvers should send a fitting escort to conduct his intended bride and her brother to his castle. He then took a temporary leave of Philip and Arline, and mounting his horse, rode away.

"When Philip de St. Louis mentioned to his sister Arline the arrangement thus made with Danvers, a shade fell upon the damsel's countenance; and as she instinctively glanced down at her apparel, her brother comprehended what she meant: for her raiment, although plainly neat and simply elegant, was yet altogether unfitted for one about to become the bride of an opulent nobleman. Moreover, as there were likely to be guests and visitors at the castle, it seemed almost indispensably necessary that both she and her brother should appear in suitable garments. Philip bade her be of good cheer, as he would at once set off for Rouen, and represent to his kind friend there the position in which they were placed. He accordingly mounted his horse, and commenced his journey at once. While he was absent, a little incident occurred, which for the moment somewhat perplexed and astonished the gentle Arline. This was nothing else than the discovery which she made of a tolerably large sum of money, in coins of all species, concealed in the depths of an old cupboard in her brother's apartment. That he must be aware of the existence of the little treasure, was beyond all doubt; inasmuch as it was buried beneath a heap of his own clothing. Wherefore, then, had he not taken some of that money to make purchases in the nearest town, instead of going all the way to Rouen to ask for succour at the hands of a friend who, as it seemed, had already done so much for him? But then, Arline thought to herself, this money in the cupboard might be a sacred deposit entrusted to him by some friend, and which he would not violate. This was the only solution of the mystery; and therewith the damsel satisfied herself. Indeed, the discovery of the treasure soon slipped out of her mind: for she was in love—and the image of Danvers engrossed all her thoughts. In five or six days her brother came back, attended by a young page whom he had taken into his service, and who was mounted upon a handsome steed. They led two other steeds, also newly purchased, and which were laden with bales and packages; so that the delighted Arline at once perceived her brother's mission to Rouen had not been in vain. The packages contained elegant apparel both for Philip and herself,—that portion of the wardrobe which was destined for her own use, comprising many costly stuffs, and also such jewellery as would best befit her style of beauty. Overjoyed at her brother's safe return, she poured forth her gratitude for the splendid presents he had brought her; and diligently did she ply her needle so as to adjust the various articles to their uses and purposes.

"At the end of ten days, and in pursuance of the arrangement already made, a brilliant escort of pages, grooms, and gentlemen-at-arms, consisting altogether of twenty persons, arrived at the tower; and the brother and sister were duly conducted to the castle belonging to Lord Danvers on the southern confines of Normandy. The edifice was spacious; and the state-apartments were sumptuously furnished. On every side were the evidences, not merely of the colossal wealth, but also of the refined taste of the noble proprietor of this habitation, which united feudal strength with palatial magnificence. Several guests—great barons and titled dames, who dwelt in the same neighbourhood—had been invited to meet Lord Danvers' intended bride and her brother; and preparations were being made, with all the despatch that ample means could ensure, for festivities, entertainments, pageants, and dramatic exhibitions, on the most varied and extensive scale. Thus the time passed happily enough,—Arline receiving the most assiduous and delicate attentions from Lord Danvers. Amongst the various persons of a professional character who had been engaged to contribute to the more refined amusement of the guests assembled at the castle, was an eminent painter; and at the request of Philip he undertook to delineate in a miniature-form the charming countenance of Arline. For Philip said to him, 'When my sister becomes the wife of Lord Danvers, it is my intention to travel into distant lands; and I would fain take with me the portrait of her whom I love so tenderly.'—The miniature was accordingly executed, to the admiration of all who saw it and who had an opportunity of comparing it with the beautiful original.

"During the month which was thus passed by the brother and sister amidst the festivities at the castle, Lord Danvers was, as we have above stated, unremitting in his attentions to Arline; and all the time that could be spared from the entertainments and pageantries was passed by the fond couple in rambling through the spacious grounds attached to the fortalice. The more Arline saw of her lover, the more deeply did she become devoted to him; and though there were times when his eyes seemed to flash with strange fires and his lips to wreath into a singularly scornful smile,—yet these circumstances failed to make any serious impression upon the mind of the innocent and unsuspecting girl. Occasionally Philip de St. Louis himself noticed that wild flashing of the eyes and that haughty scornfulness of look: but he conceived these mental indications to be merely the expression of a conscious superiority on the part of a man of large experience, rare intelligence, and boundless wealth. In short, the month passed most pleasantly for all who were gathered at the castle; and at the expiration of that time Arline took a temporary leave of her lover, and returned with Philip to the tower,—there to pass with him the three weeks which were now to elapse ere Danvers would come with a princely escort and fetch her away as his bride.

"No doubt the old tower seemed particularly gloomy in the eyes of the brother and sister after the splendours of the castle: but its sombre aspect and mean interior produced no disagreeable influence upon their minds,—for Arline felt assured that her's was to be a brilliant and a happy destiny—while, on his side, Philip was rejoiced that his beloved sister should have won the affections and was to be the cherished bride of such a man as Danvers.

"A fortnight elapsed, during which interval Philip had not once gone forth to hunt in the forest: for he resolved to devote all his time to his sister, until the wedding-day should become the signal for their separation. One evening—soon after sunset—it being now the beginning of July, in that year 1463, of which this narrative treats—Philip and Arline had just returned from a ramble in the vicinage of their abode, and were sitting down to their repast, when the quick trampling of many steeds suddenly reached their ears. Those sounds ceased at the gate of the tower; and a violent knocking immediately followed. The young page hastened to answer the summons; and half-a-dozen individuals, having leapt from their horses, at once crowded into the vestibule, bearing amongst them one who seemed to be either seriously ill or else dangerously hurt. Philip and Arline came forth from their sitting-room to see who the arrivals were; but scarcely had they thus made their appearance in the vestibule, when an ejaculation of mingled anger and surprise burst from the lips of the chief of the party that had just entered. For a moment Philip de St. Louis seemed stricken with dismay: he became ghastly pale, and staggered backward. Arline gazed upon him in wonderment and terror: for she was at a loss to conjecture the cause of this strange emotion on his part.—'My Lord Count of Montauban,' said Philip, suddenly recovering himself and advancing towards the nobleman, 'I humbly beseech a few moments' private conversation with your lordship.'—The Count seemed to hesitate for an instant: then making up his mind how to act, he said in a cold haughty tone, 'Be it so: I will accede to your request. But first you will give orders that my dependant here, who has been thrown from his horse and is severely injured, receives all requisite attentions.'—'Arline,' said Philip, turning to his sister, who with continued misgiving observed that he was still ghastly pale, 'see you to his lordship's servant.'—He then took a lamp and conducted the Count de Montauban into an apartment, the door of which was immediately closed behind them.

CHAPTER XLI.

CONCLUSION OF THE HISTORY OF ARLINE DE ST. LOUIS.

"Arline de St. Louis was much troubled with her brother's looks: for she could not possibly conceive wherefore he should thus have been stricken with consternation and dismay on meeting the Count de Montauban. She however with the ministering spirit of woman's angel character, lost no time in paying attention to the injured servant, who was at once conveyed to a bed-chamber, and the old housekeeper was appointed to nurse him. Arline then directed the groom and the young page to serve up refreshments to the rest of the Count's dependants; while she herself hastened to make such additions to the supper-table as the state of the larder and cellar permitted, in anticipation that the Count himself would most probably partake of the meal. Half-an-hour thus elapsed; and the excitement of all these preparations somewhat abstracted Arline's thoughts from the disagreeable topic which nevertheless still remained in her mind. But scarcely had she sat down and again begun to reflect deeply and seriously upon her brother's conduct, when he and the Count made their appearance. It has already been said that his lordship was a man of about forty-five years of age, with looks marred and a countenance impaired by the effects of dissipation; and though he possessed the manners of a courtier, yet he could also assume when he chose the rakish air of an insolent gallantry. It was something of this sort of appearance that he wore as he advanced towards Arline, and taking her hand, began to pour forth a tirade of empty compliments such as would at no time have been palatable to the pure and innocent maiden, but were still less agreeable now that she was the affianced bride of another.

"She could not conceal her displeasure, nor did she attempt to do so, as the Count de Montauban gave vent to this string of fulsome gallantries; and snatching away her hand, she turned her eyes upon her brother as if to beseech that he would relieve her from importunities which she could not tolerate. But to her surprise and grief she observed that Philip's countenance was clouded with a sombre mournfulness, his looks being wrapped in a gloom such as she had never seen them wear before.—'His lordship,' he said in a voice which was deep and hollow, despite his endeavour to use its natural tones, 'will honour us with partaking of a morsel of food and drinking a cup of wine.'—'His lordship is welcome,' said Arline, in a somewhat cold voice, for she observed the Count's gaze fixed with a sort of libertine boldness upon her countenance: 'but I must leave you, Philip, to entertain our noble guest, as it is incumbent upon me to assure myself that the injured horseman is properly cared for.'—'Leave my lacquey to those whom you have doubtless placed around him,' said the Count; 'and do you, fair lady, remain here to grace the board the hospitality of which I shall accept upon no other condition.'—'Your lordship will excuse me,' said Arline firmly; 'but we are not so rich in menials as your lordship's castle doubtless is, and therefore I have household duties to attend to.'—'Nay, by heaven! this pretext will not serve thee, beauteous Arline,' exclaimed the Count: 'whoever heard of the lady-mistress of a dwelling thus abandoning the table at the moment when it best becomes her to preside at its head, while I, as a most obedient gallant, am prepared to seat myself at your right hand?'—Thus speaking, the Count placed himself before Arline in such a manner as to bar her way to the door; and then the young girl, with blood mantling on her cheeks and the fire flashing for the first time in her beauteous eyes, exclaimed, 'My lord, this conduct is most unknightly on your part!'—'Sweet lady, you must positively and truly remain here to favour me with your presence,' persisted Montauban, again endeavouring to take her hand.

"Arline, drawing away that fair hand with greater indignation than before, threw her looks upon her brother in the natural expectation that he would at once interfere to save her from this continued rudeness; but she became as it were aghast on perceiving how truly woe-begone and distressed he looked. Instantaneously forgetting the Count's presence altogether, she flew to her brother, and threw her arms round his neck, crying in a tone of mingled endearment and entreaty, 'What is it that has thus altered you so suddenly, my beloved Philip?'—'Nothing, nothing, Arline,' he whispered in strange hoarse tones, while his looks also showed that horrible feelings were agitating within his breast: 'I can explain nothing now; I will tell you everything to-morrow: but do for my sake sit down at table and endeavour to be as civil to his lordship as you possibly can.'—These last words were uttered in the lowest whisper; but as they fell upon Arline's ear, she started back in dismay, her looks inquiring with all the eloquence of her astonished and frightened feelings, what mysterious power it was that the Count had so suddenly obtained over her brother? Philip however gave no answer to that appealing look, but led her to the seat at the head of the table,—she mechanically suffering him to do so; for she was too bewildered and distressed to offer any farther remonstrance. The Count de Montauban placed himself at her right hand, while her brother took his seat in a moody manner at a distance. The nobleman then resumed that complimentary style of conversation which, though not transgressing the actual bounds of delicacy, was yet of too fulsome a character to excite any other feeling than annoyance or disgust in the bosom of the gentle Arline. Reared in that forest, she had seen too little of aristocratic life to take with simperings and coquettish smiles, as high-born ladies were wont to do, the flatteries and soft nothings—those sugar-plums of conversation—which constituted the staple topics of courtly life: and feeling herself in a manner abandoned by her own brother to the company of the Count, she could only testify her disagreeable sensations by the alternating distress or anger of her looks. De Montauban seemed little to reck these demonstrations on her part, but continued to throw off flattery after flattery, and compliment after compliment from his tongue, as if his speech derived fresh glibness from the deep draughts of wine which during his pauses he imbibed. Not once did he address a syllable to Arline's brother, nor even turn his looks in the direction where he was seated; but appeared to behave as if he were disdainfully unmindful of the presence of such an individual in the room at all. On his part, Philip remained wrapped up in a gloomy silence, neither eating a morsel of food nor touching a drop of wine; but with his elbows resting on the table and his two hands supporting his head, he kept his eyes bent down as if not to be compelled to notice his sister's distress at her unpleasant position.

" 'And so, fair lady,' said the Count presently, when his string of compliments appeared at length to be exhausted, 'I understand that you have pledged yourself to become the bride of my friend Lord Danvers? It was really most ungenerous of him not to invite me to be a partaker of the festivities at his castle: but he doubtless had his reasons. The intelligence that such festivities had taken place and that he was engaged to be wedded to a fair damsel of this district, never reached me until a day or two ago; and then, on hearing those things, I paid but little heed to them. Thanks however to the accident which my lacquey has sustained, and which, whether he die or recover, I must henceforth regard as a most fortunate occurrence in respect to myself, I have this night had an opportunity of judging of Danvers' good taste. By my lordly title! I had not an idea that so charming a flower was blooming in such a hiding-place on the verge of the forest. Beautiful Arline, I drink another cup of wine in honour to thee!'—This speech, commingling as much brutality as flippancy, disgusted the young damsel more than anything else the Count de Montauban had yet uttered: her cheeks grew rapidly red and pale by turns—there was even a moment when her distress was so great it seemed as if she were about to burst into tears; but conquering this weaker emotion, she assumed all the indignant pride of maiden dignity, and rising from her seat, said, 'My lord, you will excuse me if I decline to remain any longer in the presence of one who makes a servant's serious injuries, perhaps his death, a subject for self-congratulation.'—'No, haughty beauty,' exclaimed the Count, also rising from his seat and again barring her progress towards the door, 'you shall not escape me thus. There! now you look ten thousand times more lovely in your indignation. I adore a woman of spirit: but it is doubly adorable when manifested by a girl of your youthful age.'—'Unhand me, my lord!' cried Arline, her countenance now suffused with the deepest crimson: for Montauban had once more seized, and with some rudeness too, upon her delicate taper fingers.—'No,' he returned, violently retaining that fair hand in his grasp, 'you shall resume your seat!'—'My lord, is it possible that you, a nobleman and a courtier, are guilty of this unheard-of insolence?' and with a sort of struggle she succeeded in snatching away her hand.—'But you shall stay all the same,' he cried passionately. 'I have not half done talking to you yet.'—'Philip!' cried Arline, in a voice of reproach, 'is it possible that you can sit tranquilly by and behold your sister subjected to this cowardly treatment?'—'Your brother, beauteous Arline,' said De Montauban, in a tone of such triumphant confidence that it almost sounded as if accentuated with a mocking laugh, 'will bid you resume your seat.'—'No, no, he will not; he cannot!' cried Arline, cruelly distressed at this scene. 'Philip, Philip, why do you not speak?—'Because I am well-nigh driven mad!' he exclaimed, suddenly starting up and striking the table furiously with his clenched fist. But the Count de Montauban threw upon him a look which, though only momentary, and instantaneously withdrawn, had the effect of cowing him completely, as a rebellious child is suddenly over-awed by the glance of a stern father.—'Philip, Philip,' almost shrieked forth Arline, 'I beseech you to tell me what means this horrible mystery?'—'My lord,' said the brother, not daring to look at his sister, but addressing the Count with the tone and manner of the most grovelling humiliation. 'I do beseech your lordship in mercy's sake to let Arline seek her own chamber now; and to-morrow I will prepare her to give your lordship a kinder reception on the next occasion of your visit.'—The Count seemed to hesitate whether he should yield to this request or not; while Arline flung looks of mingled consternation and alarm upon her brother; for there appeared something ominous to a degree in that invitation for the nobleman to repeat his visit, and in the accompanying pledge that she should be prepared for it.—'Well,' said the Count, 'be it as you say. Beauteous lady,' he added, turning towards Arline, 'I will detain you no longer now: but to-morrow I shall have the pleasure of seeing you again. One kiss on that fair hand——'

"But these last words startled the young damsel from the stupor of dismay in which she had been transfixed; and gliding past the Count de Montauban, who no longer made any effort to detain her, she quitted the room. It is impossible to say what thoughts agitated in the bosom of the gentle Arline when she reached her own chamber. Conjecture alone can follow her thither, and imagine her a prey to all the tortures of alarm, suspense, and misgiving,—tortures that must have been of the most crucifying description! Half-an-hour after she had left the supper-room, the Count de Montauban and his dependants (the injured one excepted) mounted their horses and took their departure, the lacquey who was hurt remaining at the tower in the care of the old housekeeper. Soon after the nobleman and suite had thus ridden away, Philip de St. Louis ascended to his sister's chamber; and as he opened the door, he beheld her seated on the foot of her couch, looking the image of sorrow and despair. A lamp was burning upon the table: and its light fell upon her pale countenance, the expression of which struck the direst anguish into the heart of Philip, as with ghastly features, ashy lips, and uneven gait he advanced slowly towards her.—'Philip,' she said, suddenly starting up and nervously catching hold of one of his hands, 'tell me the meaning of all this: do not deceive me: I beseech and implore that you relieve me from suspense at once!'— 'Arline,' he replied, in a deep voice so full of woe that it was unutterable even in such accents and such words as those in which he spoke, 'you have not felt, and you are not feeling, more truly miserable than I. Let us sit down together; and pray listen to me without excitement.'—The poor girl shuddered visibly; for every species of evil presentiment rushed to her brain, as she saw that there was nothing to cheer or reassure her in her brother's words or manner. They sat down side by side; and Philip did not immediately speak.—'Oh, this suspense is torturing!" cried his sister with hysterical wildness. 'What meant all that has taken place? why were you so troubled on first meeting the Count? why did you suffer him to treat me as he did? what dreadful power does he exercise over you? why did his very look make your proud heart quail and reduce you to submission? wherefore is he coming hither again? and in what manner are you to prepare for his next visit? Speak, I conjure you! You know not what harrowed feelings are now torturing me.'

" 'Arline, said her brother, as he slowly turned and bent upon her a look so full of utter woe that all the hysterical paroxysm of her affliction was subdued in a moment, and she gazed upon him with renewed consternation; 'if you love me, if you have ever loved me, and if you be sensible of those sacrifices which I have made on your account, giving the best years of my life to an ignominious sloth instead of seeking occupation and fame in the ranks of war, you will now testify that affection by promising to obey me blindly and without asking for explanations.'—'But you promised them,' said Arline, frightened at his words. 'Oh, whatever terrible mystery there may be at the bottom of all this, I could better support a full knowledge of the tremendous truth than endure the agonizing tortures of suspense.'—'If you force me to tell you everything, Arline,' said Philip, 'you will deeply repent it. Better, my poor girl, for you to remain in ignorance of the causes of your doom, while you accept that doom, the bitterness of which, heaven knows, will be enough for you to bear!'—'And that doom?' inquired Arline, gasping for breath with the excruciating torture of suspense.—'Prepare yourself, my sweet sister,' returned her brother; 'for what I am about to say is terrible.'—'Speak, Oh! speak,' she cried, with frenzied vehemence.—'Not if you are thus excited,' he answered: 'be calm and tranquil first.'—'I am calm and tranquil now,' rejoined the young creature; and she shivered, as if with a cold chill.—'Know then,' said her brother, 'that you must renounce all hope of marrying Lord Danvers, and must prepare to receive the Count de Montauban as your future husband!'

"As Philip de St. Louis slowly and gloomily uttered these words, Arline gave vent to a suppressed shriek, and then suddenly became pale, motionless, and transfixed as a statue. There she sat in her chair, gazing upon vacancy, her hands lying listlessly in her lap, her lips apart, as if she had just received some awful shock from which she could never recover. Philip looked upon her with a fixed contemplation of profoundest sympathy: then all of a sudden he covered his face with his hands and gave vent to his own ineffable anguish in sobs and tears. For a moment, but it could not be for more than a single moment, Arline appeared to lose sight of her own colossal woe; and starting up, she threw her arms about her brother's neck, imploring him in the most endearing language to be tranquillized.—'No, no, it is impossible, Arline! it is impossible!' he exclaimed. 'How can I be happy, how can I even be calm and tranquil, when I am compelled to know and feel that in one brief hour all your happiness, which is dearer to me than life, has been destroyed? Ah! if by immolating myself and driving a dagger deep down into my own heart, I could remove the barrier which has suddenly sprang up to separate you from Danvers, and at the same time rescue you from the power of Montauban, I would do so! But my death would not wipe away disgrace from the name of St. Louis; and even were I to perish in the blood of a distracted suicide, yet still Montauban would exercise his infernal influence over *you* by threatening to reveal that dread secret which would give your brother's name to lasting infamy. Then Danvers would not wed you, Arline; and you would still remain at the mercy of the Count!'—'Oh! what wild words are these, my poor brother?' shrieked forth Arline, who had hitherto listened in awful bewilderment to Philip's speech: 'you distract me. Is it possible that I am awake, or am I dreaming? Good heavens, Philip! gaze not thus upon me: there is the darkness of despair in your looks!'—'It is no dream, my unhappy sister: it is all a most unfortunate reality. But do you still insist that I should enter into explanations?' he asked.

"Arline reflected for a few moments, during which brief interval wild and terrible imaginings flashed through her brain; and by some association the reminiscence of that hoard of money, in so many various coins, which she had found in the cupboard during her brother's absence, rose prominent amongst her thoughts. An expression of ineffable anguish gradually settled upon her countenance; and Philip saw that she more than half read the tremendous truth.—'Arline,' he said in a low voice and with downcast looks, 'your conjectures have placed you upon the right track; and therefore it were needless to attempt any farther concealment of the whole truth. Perhaps, too, it is better that you should know the worst at once, because *that* will enable you to understand the magnitude of the sacrifice which you will have to make in order to save the name of St. Louis from a branding infamy.'—Arline took her brother's hand in her own, and said, 'Proceed, dear Philip: I will not interrupt you.'—Her brother gazed upon her for a few moments; and seeing that she was indeed nerved with

the unnatural tranquillity of despair, he continued in the following manner:—

"I do not say it in self-justification, Arline, but to render myself less
odious in your eyes, that it was through my sincere affection for you I have
been led into those courses which you already more than half-suspect and
which I am about to explain fully. Had I been alone in the world, with
nothing but my good sword by my side, I might have done as other for-
tuneless youths have been wont to do—go forth where the brazen notes
of war were sounding, and seek honour and gold on the fields of battle.
But I could not leave you, my poor sister, without bread and without protection; and, as you are well aware, we had no relations left. Therefore did
I resolve to remain with you until such time as your beauty and your ami-
ability might win for you the hand of some eligible suitor. The slender
resources left by our parents were soon exhausted; and I knew not how to
obtain even the small supply of coin that was needed to support our frugal
home. Then in the hour of my deep distress and utter despair, the tempter
whispered in my ear, and I went into the forest, not in pursuit of game as
heretofore, but to perform the deed of a bandit. Oh! well may you press
my hand convulsively: and well may that expression of anguish pass over
your countenance! You cannot feel more poignantly now, than I felt after
the perpetration of my first crime! But how was I to account for the possession of the resources thus obtained? A falsehood was needed to do this;
and hence the fabrication of the tale of a friend at Rouen whose purse
supplied me with funds. But in course of time the sum was exhausted; and
I was compelled to repeat my guilt. To avoid as much as possible the
chances of discovery, I manufactured a dress of skins stripped from wolves
which I slew in the chase. But let me not dwell on these incidents which
harrow up my own soul, and make you shiver from head to foot. Observe
however one thing—that never has human blood stained the hand which
you now hold clasped in your own!—no, no—never! Were it otherwise,
not for another instant should it remain in contact with the hand of my
pure and spotless sister! And now for the occurrence which will account
for the power that the Count de Montauban has obtained over me. It was
about eighteen months ago that I was one night roaming in the forest,
waiting for an opportunity to replenish my exhausted purse by the same
vile means as heretofore, when I heard the sounds of a horse's hoofs approaching. The moon was shining brightly; and through the openings in
the forest its silver flood poured down with powerful splendour. Disguised
in my garb of skins, and mounted upon my strong steed, I remained concealed in a thicket until I beheld the traveller close at hand. He seemed to
be alone, for I heard not the sounds of other steeds, and I therefore hesi-

tated not to spring forth and demand his gold. Quick as thought he drew his sword from its sheath; and ere I had time to grasp it in my skin-gloved hand so as to wrench it from him, he dealt me a blow, which striking me at the side of the head, cut the ligatures that fastened the mask to the remainder of the head-gear. The mask therefore fell off, and in the bright moon-beams was my countenance revealed to the traveller, whom at the same instant I recognised to be the Count de Montauban. 'Who are you, wretched man?' he demanded: and the question sent a thrill of delight through my entire form. Without answering him, I dashed the spurs into the flanks of my steed and galloped away into the depths of the forest. But wherefore had I experienced the relief of so sudden a joy at the question which the Count put? Because it proved that though I knew him by sight, yet he had not a similar acquaintance with me; and therefore I hoped that my crime might yet remain concealed, especially as the Count came so very seldom to his castle in this neighbourhood, and then only for two or three days at a time. The incident which I have just related took place, as I ere now said, eighteen months ago, on one of those occasions when the Count was paying a flying visit to his castle. He was doubtless riding a little way ahead of his suite at the time; and had I not thus taken precipitately to flight, his dependants would have come up and I should have been overpowered. Throughout the three or four successive days I was a prey to a constant terror lest the Count should repair with his followers to search the forest, and by accident be led to visit our abode. However, my fears in this respect were not realized; and after a brief stay at his castle, his lordship departed for his southern estate once more. But I now began to reflect that my honour—nay, even my very life—hung by a thread, and that on some future visit to his castle in Normandy, the Count might meet me, when recognition would be almost certain and I should be handed over to an ignominious fate. I accordingly resolved to accumulate a sum of money sufficient to enable me to bear you, Arline, away to some other part of France, and thus place me beyond the reach of exposure and peril. Animated with this intent, I multiplied my depredations in the forest, and began to amass the money that I required. Still my ill-gotten gains were scanty in amount: for I invariably made it a rule to waylay only single horsemen, so that there might be the less chance of resistance being offered me and therefore the less probability of my shedding the blood of another or being myself overpowered. I had not accumulated near a sufficiency for my purpose, when a few months ago the intelligence suddenly reached me that the Count de Montauban had come to settle altogether at his castle. This intelligence at first struck me with dismay; and I resolved to hurry you off to some distant part as speedily as possible. But then accident threw Lord Danvers in our way, and I immediately saw that he was struck by your beauty. He became your admirer; and I could not find it in my heart to remove you from your native place, where there was every chance of your forming so brilliant an alliance. Besides, I soon observed that the love which he evidently conceived for you was reciprocated; and I thought to myself that by remaining as much as possible at home, and especially avoiding the vicinage of Montauban Castle, I might succeed for at least a few weeks or months in keeping out of the Count's way. When Lord Danvers, having offered you his hand, invited us to his castle, I repaired to Rouen to make the purchases that were required, because it was necessary to sustain in your mind the belief that I derived the funds for the purpose from the bounty of the supposed friend living there: otherwise I should have bought what was needful at a nearer town. But let me hasten and bring my narrative to a conclusion. With joy and satisfaction—with hope and confidence—had I seen the time slipping away, and no encounter between myself and the Lord of Montauban taking place. It was my intention, immediately after your marriage with Danvers, to hie away to more distant scenes where I might carve out for myself a more honourable career than that which I have been pursuing. But heaven has willed that it should be otherwise; and this evening has all my hopes and all my plans been suddenly annihilated by the accident which brought the Count de Montauban hither. You saw that he recognised me instantaneously; and it only remains for me to tell what took place between us in the apartment where at my request he granted me a private interview. I flung myself upon my knees at his feet, beseeching and imploring that he would have mercy upon me and not expose my infamy to my sister and the world. The cold-blooded monster! Though his eyes had lingered but for so short a space upon you ere he followed me away from the hall, yet did he see enough of you to become all in a moment enamoured of your charms: and moreover he suddenly grew jealous of Lord Danvers who had never mentioned to him the existence of such a being as yourself in this district. He was also piqued at having been excluded from the festivities at Lord Danvers' castle; and being no doubt naturally revengeful and malignant, he at a glance saw an opportunity for mortifying and punishing your affianced Humphrey. Accordingly, he made me rise from my knees, and said there was one condition—and one only—on which he would consent to spare my name from dishonour and my life from the executioner. This condition was that you, my sweet Arline, should transfer your troth from Danvers and pledge yourself to become the bride of Montauban! Vainly did I fling myself at his feet again, and beseech a revocation of that dreadful sentence: vainly did I assure him that he was dealing a death-blow not

merely at the happiness but at the very life of my sister! He was inexora-
ble: and neither my prayers nor tears availed in the slightest degree. Arline, I have no more to say. You now comprehend the full measure of your
brother's guilt, and also of his unhappiness: and you understand the nature of the sacrifice that circumstances require from you. As I ere now
said, if by my suicide or by my precipitate flight from the country your
happiness would be ensured, I should rejoice to immolate myself for the
purpose of securing that end. But the calamity would not be thereby
averted. For were I to plunge a dagger into my own heart, Montauban
would still insist that you should espouse him, under the threat of proclaiming to the world that you are the sister of a vile bandit, and thus leading Danvers to spurn an alliance with you. Then what would become of
you, my poor unhappy Arline? Better that you should accept, under existing circumstances, the destiny which is forced upon you; and as the Countess of Montauban you will at least possess a proud name, a high station,
and the enjoyment of wealth. Then your unhappy brother can fulfil his
original intention of hastening to the wars, where perhaps a speedy death
may hush his own poignant memories for ever, and to some extent atone
for the criminality of the past!'

   "Such was the history which Philip de St. Louis narrated to his sister,—a sad, sad history, intermingled with many bitter self-upbraidings on
his part, and listened to with many bitter outbursts of anguish and floods
of weeping on her's. For the greater portion of the wretched night did
the brother and sister remain in discourse together; and the result was
that Arline consented to sacrifice herself to the Count de Montauban. He
came next day, attended by a numerous suite, bearing presents for Arline;
and when, with a pale countenance and trembling form, she murmured
the syllable 'Yes' to the question which he breathed in her ear, his manner
no longer continued flippantly supercilious or insolently libertine, but he
at once treated her with the respect due to the lady who had just promised to become Countess of Montauban. But how was the intelligence
of Arline's broken plight to be conveyed to Lord Danvers? Montauban
himself undertook to make him acquainted with this piece of successful
rivalry on his part. Arline was too completely miserable, and Philip too
much in the power of the Count, to offer any objection to such a course;
and accordingly the nobleman despatched a messenger with a letter to
Lord Danvers, acquainting him that Arline had transferred her affections
to himself and had agreed to become Countess of Montauban. Now, it
must be here mentioned that the castle of Lord Humphrey Danvers was
two days' journey distant from the district where St. Louis' Tower and
Montauban Castle were situated; and therefore, even supposing that Lord

Danvers should hurry off immediately on receipt of the letter, to insist upon the fulfilment of Arline's pledge to himself, it was calculated that four clear days must elapse ere he could possibly be at the tower. But the Count de Montauban resolved that in the meantime his own marriage with Arline should be celebrated; and he fixed it to take place on the third day thence. He himself dictated all the arrangements, to which neither the brother nor sister had the heart nor the power to offer a single word of objection. His lordship's plan was, that on the morning of the third day he and his suite should arrive from Montauban Castle to fetch away Arline and bear her to her future home, where the marriage would be immediately celebrated with as much pomp and magnificence as the shortness of the notice would permit. Having settled all these things and partaken of some refreshments, the Count and his suite took their departure from the tower.

"Arline retired to her chamber and passed the remainder of the day there. On the following day her brother went to her, threw himself upon his knees, and besought her to forgive him for all the unhappiness of which his crimes were the fatal cause. She said in reply, 'I cannot reproach you, Philip; for all that you did was for my sake:'—and though she forgave him as he asked her, it was with a smile so sickly and a look so laden with despair that the unhappy man felt as if all the woes of the universe were upon his head. That day passed; and the next was if possible fraught with more gloomy prospects still: for the brother and sister now said to each other, 'To-morrow!' as they exchanged the darkest and most sombre looks. They walked together in the evening, feeling it was for the last time, because it was Philip's intention to take his departure to the distant scenes of warfare immediately after the bridal of the ensuing day. The sun went down, and in the twilight the unhappy man and his sorrowing sister still continued their walk in the garden: nor did they re-enter the tower until it was dusk. Just as they were about to separate for the night, a loud knocking was heard at the gate; and for a moment a presentiment that it was Humphrey Danvers struck athwart the brain alike of the brother and sister. But no! another moment's reflection made them feel that this was scarcely possible: for only two days and a half had elapsed since the messenger had set out with a despatch for Lord Danvers' castle, and consequently there was not time for Danvers himself to make his appearance at the tower. Nevertheless, when the door was opened by the youthful page, it was none other than Lord Humphrey Danvers who entered the hall of the tower!

"Philip and Arline were in the hall at the moment when the English nobleman made his appearance; and a faint shriek escaped the lips of the young damsel, while her brother fell back in shame and confusion. Never perhaps had Humphrey Danvers appeared more sublimely handsome than on the present occasion. His tall slender form, instead of having the easy gait of an elegant indolence, was drawn up with the proudest dignity—a grave solemnity sat upon his features—the classic lips were slightly compressed with an air of decision and firmness—but his eyes were shining more brightly if possible than ever. With a rapid but imperious motion of his hand he bade the youthful page leave the great folding-doors open; and advancing towards Arline, he took her hand, saying in a voice that was mournfully solemn, 'Lady, after all that has passed between us, you will not refuse me one boon, which is that you favour me with an interview of five minutes. I do not ask for more: but we must be alone. The night is beautiful, and with your permission we will walk in that garden of your's where I first beheld you, and of which you seemed to be the choicest and sweetest flower. Lady, I do not mean to reproach you: but it will somewhat mitigate the bitterness of my disappointment and the poignancy of my woe, if we may exchange farewells ere we part for ever. Philip,' added the nobleman, turning towards the brother, 'you will not interpose your authority to prevent Arline from granting this last request on my part?'— 'No, my lord,' replied Philip in a gloomy voice, 'I dare not say nay to that demand on your part.'

"The trembling Arline, from whose cheeks all colour had fled some days past, but who was now paler if possible than before, had suffered her hand to remain locked in the clasp of him who possessed her heart's best and purest affections; but she said not a word, though some syllables seemed to be wavering upon her lips—yet only as the zephyr may slightly agitate the opening leaves of the rose; and mechanically she walked forth with Lord Humphrey Danvers into the garden. The night was serene and beautiful, with that soft twilight which in the summer season keeps back the wing of darkness from altogether expanding its sable shadows over the earth; and as the tall slender form of Danvers and the graceful figure of Arline issued forth from the tower, Philip de St. Louis dismissed the page with a wave of his hand, and sat himself down in a window-recess to wait for the return of his sister. From that point he could observe Arline and Danvers in the garden: but it was with no premeditated intention to watch them that he had posted himself there. The state of his mind had reduced him to the condition of an automaton, obeying mere mechanical impulses; and in a sort of semi-unconsciousness was it that he took his seat in the window-recess. But still his eyes remained fixed upon the forms of the lovers—for such indeed they were still, though Arline had pledged herself to become Montauban's bride. At first they walked hand in hand with very slow steps along the central avenue of the garden; and so far as Philip de St. Louis could distinguish them through the twilight, Danvers was inclining his head towards Arline, who appeared to be bending her own looks downward. Was he, then, dealing in remonstrance despite his assurance to the contrary? or was he pleading with eloquence his own suit of love? Ah, now his arm encircles Arline's waist—and a feeling of uneasiness begins to creep into the soul of Philip de St. Louis, arousing him as it were from his automaton state of listlessness. What if Arline were to yield to the blandishments of her own devoted lover's language? what if she were to recant her promise to Montauban and at any risk give back her troth to Danvers? Now she seems to be sinking to the ground, as if beneath the influence of ineffable emotions: but his arm sustains her. Now he suddenly quits his hold upon her—steps back—and addresses her with passionate gesticulations. She clasps her hands, as if in bewilderment how to act. Then she suddenly flings herself into the arms of Danvers—he strains her to his breast—long and fervent is their embrace. Philip de St. Louis starts up: he knows not what to do, or what to think. Can he or dares he interfere? No: for, after all, what could he say? Might it not be the farewell embrace which they are now taking? and who could blame Arline for thus remaining a few moments pressed to the bosom of him whom she loved so fondly although now pledged to become Montauban's bride? Yes—doubtless it is their farewell embrace: for now they return hand in hand up the avenue. But, Ah! wherefore do they suddenly diverge into a path leading towards a little shrubbery at the side of the garden?—and now, too, why do they abruptly quicken their pace? why does Danvers once more encircle her elastic shape with his arm? why does it seem as if he were hurrying her half-fainting along?

"At this moment the sounds of horses champing their bits and pawing the ground with their impatient hoofs, are borne to Philip's ear. A wild misgiving shoots like a barbed arrow through his brain, and he rushes forth into the open air. But it is only in time to see Lord Humphrey Danvers spring upon the back of a sable steed, with Arline in his arms,—thus lifting her as if she were a thing of no weight. And then away, away, thunders that coal-black steed, with its rider and his fair burden; and another steed, likewise of the deepest sable, gallops by the side of its companion. In an agonizing voice Philip shouts forth, 'Arline! Arline!'—but his voice is answered only by the echoes of the forest; and the next moment Danvers, with Arline and his horses, disappears from the brother's view.

"Philip de St. Louis was transfixed to the spot in amazement. Had anyone, two or three minutes previously, told him that Arline was capable of thus abandoning her brother as a sacrifice to the Count of Montauban's wrath, he would not have believed it. But what was he now to do? His first thought, on regaining his presence of mind, was to hurry to the stable, saddle a horse, and speed in pursuit of Danvers and his sister. But suddenly a revulsion took place in all his ideas, and in a moment he beheld the whole transaction in a new light, so that he became filled with an enthusiastic joy.—'Doubtless Arline has explained to Danvers the entire circumstances which compelled her to pledge her hand to Montauban? and Danvers, through his devoted love for her, cares not for her brother's shame? It is to make her his bride, therefore, that he has borne her away; and there is no chance of his spurning an alliance with her. Arline will be happy; and therefore it is for me to rejoice!'—Such were his reflections: and indeed, now that Philip de St. Louis was enabled to look calmly upon all that had just occurred, he did rejoice at it and wondered that he should have been filled with misgiving even for a single moment.

"But now it was necessary to shield himself against the vengeance of the Count de Montauban. There was no time to lose: for on the following day his lordship was to come with his suite to fetch Arline away,—that Arline whom he would not find at the tower! Without delay Philip de St. Louis commenced his preparations for departure. Ascending to his chamber, he secured about his person the hoard of coins which he had concealed in his cupboard; and he did not forget to take Arline's miniature with him. He then made known his intention to his old groom and housekeeper, telling them that he was about to quit Normandy for a long time, if not for ever, but bidding them regard the tower and the garden as their own for the remainder of their days. Having taken leave of the old people, he went to the stable, followed by his page; and there he ordered three of the four steeds which he possessed, to be immediately saddled. The page gazed upon his master in surprise, wondering wherefore three horses were to be thus gotten in readiness for two riders: but Philip bade him use despatch, and in a few minutes the preparations were complete. Philip and his page then mounted their horses, leading the other one with them; and in this manner they took their departure.

"Into the depths of the forest did they ride; and in about two hours they reached an open space, where a small hut was situated. At the sounds of the trampling steeds a young woman, of about seven-and-twenty, and of great beauty though dressed in a humble peasant's garb, came forth from the cottage. She was evidently bounding forward with the joyousness of a first impulse to welcome St. Louis: but on seeing that he was accompanied by another person, she stopped suddenly short. Leaping from his steed, Philip de St. Louis embraced the young woman, and gave her a few hurried explanations as well as instructions in a whispered voice. She at once re-entered the hut, and in a few minutes came forth again, leading a little boy, about ten years of age, by one hand, and carrying a younger child in her arms. Philip assisted her to mount on the led horse, she still retaining her younger son in her embrace. The elder boy Philip took up before him on his own steed; and the whole party then galloped away.

"A few words will explain the incident which has just been recorded. When a mere youth of seventeen, Philip de St. Louis had become enamoured of a woodman's daughter of the humblest birth, and had persuaded her to marry him privately. The nuptial blessing was accordingly pronounced by the venerable pastor of a neighbouring village; and the young bride had continued to dwell with her parents at that cottage in the depths of the forest. Two children were the fruit of this union. A few years after the marriage the young wife's parents died within a short period of each other: and she continued to inhabit that cottage alone with her children. Thus the frequent absences of Philip de St. Louis from the tower arose not altogether from his bandit-exploits, as these until lately had been few and far between: but it was to devote as much time as he could well afford to his peasant-wife and his children that he had thus so often remained away from home. But why had Philip never acknowledged this marriage to his sister Arline? Surely she would have allowed no prejudice of gentle birth to induce her to scorn the companionship of her brother's wife? No; but it was because Philip de St. Louis had all along hoped that his sister, who from her childhood had been of a ravishing beauty, would form some alliance that should shed the lustre of rank and wealth upon her name; but if he were to introduce to the tower that peasant-wife of his own, he would sink in the esteem of the neighbouring chiefs, and the family would fall into contempt. Philip thought that it was already sufficient to be poor, without increasing the prejudice of society by acknowledging a marriage that would be deemed a degradation. Besides, he himself felt that he had committed a folly by contracting such an alliance; and therefore a sentiment of pride had invariably restrained him if ever in a moment of tender confidence he had seriously thought of confessing his secret to Arline.

"With his wife, his two children, and his page, did Philip de St. Louis journey on, allowing no more leisure for repose than was absolutely necessary until they were beyond the confines of Normandy. In due course they reached Calais, and thence they embarked for England, Philip feeling that he should not be safe from the vengeance of so powerful a noble as the Count de Montauban if he were to remain in France. Settling in London, he lost no time in embarking his little capital in trade; and his first speculations proved eminently successful. At the expiration of a short time he despatched his page to France, with instructions to hasten into Normandy and convey letters to Arline, who he had not the slightest doubt was the happy wife of Lord Humphrey Danvers. After some considerable absence the page returned to London with the most astounding information. He had proceeded to Lord Danvers' castle in Normandy, and to his surprise had learnt that the marriage with Arline de St. Louis had never taken place at all—that she had never been seen at the castle since the time she was there on a visit in company with her brother—and that Lord Humphrey was still unmarried. The page had then visited the tower, where he saw the old groom and housekeeper; but they had heard nothing of Arline since the night she was borne away by Lord Danvers. As for the Count de Montauban, he had died through illness brought on by rage and disappointment at finding that his passion was thwarted by the disappearance of Arline, and that her brother had likewise eluded his vengeance.

"Philip knew not what to think on receiving this intelligence; and he resolved to undertake a journey to his native district in Normandy, for the purpose of instituting still more searching inquiries relative to his lost sister. This plan he carried into execution,—disguising himself however, when nearing the forest, lest the Count de Montauban should previous to his death have spread the tale of who the real bandit for so many years had been. Having called at his tower and received from the old couple the same account which they had previously reported to the page, he continued his way to the castle of Lord Humphrey Danvers; and learning that the nobleman was staying there at the time, he besought an interview with him. Giving a feigned name and being thoroughly disguised, he was not recognised by the menials of the castle. The interview was accorded, and Humphrey Danvers at once knew who his visitor was. Philip demanded of him what had become of his sister: but without giving any satisfactory answer, the English nobleman ordered Philip to quit his presence immediately. St. Louis remonstrated and threatened. A diabolical smile of malignity then appeared upon Lord Humphrey's countenance, as he exclaimed, 'Vile bandit of the forest, depart hence at once; or ere sunset shalt thou hang to a gibbet on the top of the highest tower of this castle!'—Overwhelmed with shame and quailing with terror, the unhappy Philip de St. Louis was compelled to hurry away without obtaining the slightest satisfaction relative to the lost Arline. That she had become a victim to the base seducer, he felt certain: but he dared not tarry in those parts to make farther inquiries concerning her. Well nigh heart-broken, he went back to the tower to inform the old couple where he resided in England, so that if they ever did behold Arline again they might be enabled to acquaint her where she might see or hear of her brother. Philip then retraced his way with all possible despatch to Calais, whence he embarked for the British shores.

"Years passed—and no tidings reached him of his lost sister. His sons grew up; and when his wife died, they became a solace and a comfort to him. His worldly affairs prospered, and he amassed considerable wealth. Several times, at the interval of a few years, did he despatch his faithful dependant to France to inquire for Arline: but all that related to her since the memorable night when she fled with Danvers, was a perfect blank. In short, Philip never heard of her again. As years grew upon him he caused this history to be faithfully chronicled on parchment; and he had a box of sandal-wood made to contain manuscript records, as well as the miniature of his lost sister. But wherefore did he thus preserve the memorials of his own past guilt in the form of those written parchments? It was in obedience to an impulse which he could not control: it was the irresistible sway of destiny governing his actions independently of his own will. For a sentiment of implacable hatred had gradually been growing in his heart against Humphrey Danvers, and he felt within him a deep craving for revenge against him or his posterity. That sentiment of hatred, and this craving for revenge he resolved to perpetuate in the hearts of his children; so that if ever opportunity should serve, they might hesitate not to wreak the effects of this fearful wrath upon the head of Humphrey Danvers or those who might inherit the detested noble's name."

CHAPTER XLII.

THE KING'S ARRANGEMENTS.

SUCH was the legend of Arline de St. Louis, which King Henry read ere retiring to rest. When he sought his couch he could not immediately sleep, his thoughts being full of all that had happened on this eventful night, and his mind being not altogether free from terror in respect to any future manifestation which Lionel Danvers might make of his superhuman power. The royal bed-chamber was spacious and lofty; and though four silver lamps were burning in as many different parts of the room, yet there were recesses, nooks, and corners involved in the deepest shade; and the King more than once found himself lifting his head from the pillow, and plunging his looks into those obscure parts with the cold creeping apprehension that some terrible form would come forth. But at length sleep fell upon his eyelids: yet even then a host of terrors pursued him in his dreams: and when he awoke in the morning, he felt feverish and unrefreshed.

His toilet being completed, and the early repast hastily disposed of, the King sent to command the immediate attendance of Gerald St. Louis. The young man, who had expected to be thus early summoned to his

royal master's presence, lost no time in proceeding thither; and on entering the apartment where his Highness was walking to and fro in a mood
of mingled thoughtfulness and agitation, the Secretary made a low obeisance and remained standing with a profoundly respectful demeanour
near the door. The King ordered those who were in attendance to leave
the apartment; and bidding Gerald approach him, he took a seat at a table
on which the casket was standing.

"Young man," said the King, "I have not forgotten my promise to you
of last night. In compelling Sir Edward Poynings to surrender you up that
document which you had been led to fabricate, I gave you a proof of my
royal leaning in your favour. The assurance of my forgiveness for whatsoever share you had in past complots and treacheries, I now repeat. This
casket I return to you. The wild and wondrous legend which it contains,
I read last night with mingled interest and alarm: for it seems to me that
every time my ear is to catch the name of Danvers or my eye is to fall upon
that name in writing, 'tis to be in connexion with things calculated to excite the strongest feelings of human nature. But there are one or two questions which that narrative suggests, and which I would fain put to you.
Have no tidings ever been received by your family of the lost Arline?"

"Never, sire," responded St. Louis. "Her fate seems to be beyond the
reach of even the wildest conjecture."

"Was it supposed that Lord Humphrey Danvers dealt foully with
her?—in short," asked the King, "was it imagined that he had murdered
her?"

"That she disappeared, my liege, never to be heard of more, is too
certain," rejoined St. Louis: "but what interest could a great and powerful
noble like Lord Humphrey Danvers have had in making away with her?"

"True!" said the King: "it is a mystery of the most incomprehensible
character:"—then after a pause he asked, "In what degree of relationship
do you stand to the Philip de St. Louis who figures in that narrative?"—and
the King pointed to the casket.

"Your Grace will have observed," replied the Royal Secretary, "that
Philip had two sons. The elder succeeded him in his business and remained
unmarried: the younger married a worthy citizen's daughter, and I was
the fruit of this alliance. My parents died when I was young; and I was
adopted by my uncle—my ancestor Philip's elder son. Having amassed
a handsome fortune, he retired from business, and purchased a beautiful
little villa-cottage in Islington fields. There, in the summer time, the old
man in the last years of his life was wont to sit beneath the rose-covered
portico, enjoying the warmth of the sunshine: and there too, as it would
appear, Lord Lionel Danvers—the present bearer of that proud title—he

whom we beheld last night—saw my venerable uncle on some occasion or another. At least so Lord Lionel stated to me on that night when I first encountered him in the lane at the back of Grantham Villa."

"And did your uncle likewise see him?" asked the King.

"It does not appear so, my liege: for my venerable relative never mentioned such a circumstance to me. From his father Philip had he received the legacy of hereditary vengeance, which on his death he in his turn bequeathed to me, enjoining me as the condition on which his whole fortune was left at my disposal that I would seek some means of avenging the wrongs of Arline."

"From all that I have seen of Lionel Danvers' power," observed the monarch abruptly, "I would advise you, Master St. Louis, to scatter all thoughts of vengeance to the winds: for Danvers appears to me a being whom it is better to propitiate than provoke. However, this business regards yourself; and it is for you to decide upon the importance to be attached to the advice I now give you."

"I thank your Highness most sincerely," answered St. Louis, "for this undeserved proof of interest on my behalf—likewise for the assurance of forgiveness which your Grace vouchsafed me last night, and which has been repeated this morning. In whatsoever manner your Highness purposes to dispose of me, I shall ever prove myself the devoted servant of my King."

"You speak well and wisely, young man," answered the Sovereign. "Nevertheless, after all that has occurred, it does not suit me to retain you longer about my person. You must prepare to take your departure forthwith from the palace. I am about to send an embassy to my august ally and cousin his Majesty of France; and the post of First Secretary to the Ambassador whom I may appoint, is the one that I destine you to fill. But I must warn you to beware how you talk lightly or openly of aught relating to these adventures in which Lord Lionel Danvers has played so conspicuous a part. Indeed, it will be treason and punishable as such for you to breathe even to your bosom-friend if you have one, or to your wife, if you marry one, the tremendous secret that there is in my dominions a man who possesses the power of assuming my shape. Be wise and wary on this head, and I will not lose sight of you; your interests shall be my care, and promotion will follow. You may now retire."

St. Louis knelt down and kissed the royal hand which was extended towards him. He then rose—took up his casket—and went forth from the King's presence. In less than an hour his preparations for departure were made; and leaving the palace, he repaired to London, where he took a temporary lodging until such time as the embassy for France should be in readiness to start.

As we have hinted in a previous chapter, the King found himself compelled to make Wolsey a complete confidant in all which had occurred. That prelate was accordingly summoned from London to an immediate audience of his royal master; and after an hour's secret conference, the ambitious churchman received the object of his ambition and his intrigues—namely, the post of High Chancellor and Prime Minister of the realm. The very next day, as accident willed it, a messenger arrived from Rome, bearing Wolsey's nomination to the rank of Cardinal; and thus did he almost at the same moment rise to the highest grades in the temporal and spiritual hierarchies.

After his conference with Wolsey the King sent to command the attendance of the Earl of Grantham at Greenwich House. This nobleman lost no time in repairing to the palace, his thoughts fluctuating between hope and fear. On reaching the royal abode, he was at once shown into the presence of the King, who received the Earl alone in his Private Closet.

"How fares it with Musidora?" was the monarch's first question.

"She has altogether regained her self-possession," answered the Earl. "The violence of her grief has subsided, and she has relapsed into that cold and almost unfathomable state of mind which was wont to characterize her ere the mock-marriage. When assured that it was your Highness's expressed wish and command that the whole terrible transaction should be maintained a profound secret, she declared her thankfulness for so much gracious consideration on her Sovereign's part; and she likewise observed that it afforded a considerable relief to her lacerated spirit."

"And what says she relative to the appointments of her father and cousin?" inquired the King.

"I made known to her the message with which your Highness condescended to entrust me respecting those appointments," was the Earl of Grantham's response. "That her cousin Percy Rivers should retain the Governorship of the Isle of Wight, and her father the Rangership of the woodlands in the same island, Musidora is naturally anxious; and she has charged me to express her most humble devotion to your Highness for having guaranteed those offices to her relatives. She however ventures most deferentially to suggest that it would be more satisfactory were your Highness to confirm them by fresh letters-patent,—or rather by *genuine* letters-patent,—at the same time without exciting a suspicion in the minds of her father and cousin that the former documents were mere felonious fabrications."

"This shall be done," said the King. "I presume therefore that it is Musidora's intention to veil her calamity altogether from her father and her cousin?"

"From her cousin altogether—and from her father as much as possible," answered Lord Grantham. "Such is her wish—such is her hope. She likewise purposes to remain for a short time longer beneath my roof—not merely for the sake of the requisite leisure to regain the natural balance of her mind after the cruel shock it has sustained, but also to acquire the certainty as to whether her unfortunate connexion with Lionel Danvers be likely to promise issue. It is this eventuality which the unhappy girl seems to hold in appalling horror; and when she spoke of it to my wife this morning—as I understand from the Countess—it was with a sudden paroxysm of such anguish and despair as was piteous to contemplate. It lasted however but for a few minutes; and Musidora has since been cold and ice-like in her demeanour as it is in her nature or at least her habit to seem."

"Think you not, my lord," asked the King, "that Musidora was previously acquainted with Danvers ere the terrible incidents of last night? Else what meant his words that he had a vengeance to wreak upon her—to melt her stubborn virtue—and thaw her icy soul—or something to that effect?"

"The Countess of Grantham, my liege," replied the Earl, "has ventured to put some questions to Musidora upon that point: but the unfortunate girl insists upon remaining silent as to the past. She has even declared that the only condition upon which she will remain at Grantham Villa, is that the name of Danvers shall never again be mentioned in her hearing."

"And you will do well to fulfil her wishes in this respect," said the King. "Now observe, my Lord of Grantham! all that you know in respect to these dreadful transactions is to be the same as if you knew it *not*. I mean that you are to preserve an inviolable secrecy; and on that condition will I again receive you at Court, and in due time give you back the pensions of which you have been deprived. In a few weeks the Queen, who is now at Windsor, will join me here at Greenwich House, and your Countess may then present herself to her Grace."

The Earl, overjoyed at what he now heard, fell at the King's feet and poured forth his gratitude: but the monarch, penetrating easily enough through the egotism and selfishness of the old courtier, bade him rise and hasten back to Grantham Villa to convey to Musidora the assurance that her wishes should be promptly attended to in reference to the new letters-patent.

"But by the way," exclaimed the King, as the Earl was about to take his departure, "there is one thing more concerning which I have to speak to your lordship. That physician Dr. Bertram, as he calls himself, is none other than a worthless profligate character, named Benjamin Welford. I have gleaned all particulars concerning him from my late secretary St. Louis. Now this Welford was sent to the Isle of Wight by Danvers; and being in old Sir Lewis Sinclair's confidence, he has doubtless been told that Musidora is privately married to the King."

"Perhaps, my liege, this Bertram—or Welford," suggested the Earl, "is aware that Lord Danvers took your Highness's form?"

"No—I do not think so," observed Henry. "From all I have learnt since I was at your house last night, it seems to me that Danvers was but little communicative to the tools and instruments whom he employed. However, it is my desire that this Benjamin Welford should be propitiated, and not dealt harshly by, and that he be strictly enjoined to keep secret whatever he knows, or suspects, or has been led to believe. In what way is this to be managed? But first give me, my lord, some definite idea of how Musidora intends to act towards her father? The old knight must be disabused of his belief that his daughter is Queen of England through a secret marriage with myself."

"My liege, all this is arranged," answered the Earl of Grantham. "Musidora has decided that I shall proceed to the Isle of Wight to see her father, and that without entering into any more particulars than are absolutely necessary, I shall do my best to disabuse him of the fond belief which he hugs, and at the same time tranquillize his feelings so far as I may be able——in short, to do the best I can in such difficult circumstances, but religiously to keep in the back-ground the full horrors of the cheat of which she has been made the dupe."

"The plan is a good one," observed the King. "When does your lordship depart for the Isle of Wight."

"Now that I have had the honour of this audience of your Highness to-day," said the Earl, "I shall set off to-morrow morning. As a matter of course I shall see Bertram, or Welford, or whatsoever the man's name may be, at Sinclair House in the Isle of Wight; and if your Grace will entrust the management of the whole affair to me——"

"I not only do so," interrupted the King, "but I place the utmost confidence in your discretion. From what I have learnt, this Benjamin Welford is a man addicted to deep potations: but I have not heard that he is indiscreet in his cups. However, you will see him and judge for yourself. If his present position with the old knight suits him, you may leave him there, and can give him this purse of gold as a guarantee that he will from time to time be thought of if he holds his peace in respect to past matters. And perhaps it would be as well," added the King, who had just thrown a heavy purse upon the table, "to drop a hint at the same time that any breach of secrecy on the points in question will be regarded as treason and punished as such. Now, my Lord of Grantham, you understand my wishes. See that you execute them faithfully!"

"Your Highness may rely upon me," answered the old courtier: and having taken up the purse he made his obeisance and went forth from the presence of the King.

"Now," said Henry to himself, when he was once more alone, "I think that I have settled these divers matters in the most prudent manner possible. I have sealed the lips of all who can speak upon the subject, and have thus quenched the flame which might have burst forth into a perfect blaze of alarming scandal. Poynings is on his way to Ireland—St. Louis will in a day or two be off to France—the Earl and Countess of Grantham will be too well pleased at regaining their lost station at Court not to keep the secret—Wolsey has attained the height of his ambition—Sir Lewis Sinclair and the physician will be duly silenced by the cunning and artful Grantham—and as for Musidora, she, heaven knows! is but too deeply interested in cherishing the secret for her own sake. As for Danvers himself, it does not appear that he either gossips or vaunts relative to his proceedings; and therefore, all things considered, I may look upon this most disagreeable transaction as settled in every detail."

Ere we close this chapter we must mention two occurrences in order to render the present portion of our narrative complete. The first was that the very same evening fresh letters-patent were prepared, confirming the appointments of Sir Lewis Sinclair and Master Percy Rivers in their respective appointments,—the plea for these new documents being based on the change in the Ministry which had that day taken place: and as Wolsey's counter-signature was procured for these parchments, both the old knight and Percy Rivers could be easily led to look upon them as the requisite formulas for confirming them in their offices under a new Minister. These letters-patent were duly forwarded to the Earl of Grantham, that he might become the bearer of them on his journey to the Isle of Wight.

The other incident to which we have above alluded, can be explained in a few words. At ten o'clock on the same night, Musidora issued forth from the front entrance of Grantham Villa, and with slow steps advanced to the very margin of the Thames. It was high water—and the soft glimmering light of the autumn evening was playing like a dimly shining halo upon the river's bosom. Musidora held in her hand a small packet tied round with a piece of riband; and on reaching the edge of the water, she flung it in with a firm hand. Then, with the same slow walk as before, she retraced her way into the villa: but not the slightest change of expression on her marble features afforded an indication to whatsoever feeling she might have experienced at the deed she had just done. The packet she had thrown into the river was the casket containing the brilliant set of diamonds she had received as a present from Lord Danvers at the time she believed him to be the King!

CHAPTER XLIII.

THE PURSE.—SOPHISTRY AND WINE.

It was about noon, when a vessel from the Hampshire coast touched at that part of the Isle of Wight which was nearest to Sinclair House. A plank was run out to enable the passengers to land without wetting their feet. These consisted of three persons, the foremost of whom was an elderly man, apparelled in a rich travelling-suit; and the other two were evidently his pages or lacqueys—for each of them carried a small valise filled with the necessaries of the toilet. Taking the nearest pathway towards Sinclair House, and which one of the mariners indicated, the elderly personage and his two attendants began ascending the acclivity; and in due time they reached the entrance of the grounds in the midst of which the building was situated. A tall ungainly figure, dressed in black, was walking in the garden; and on seeing strangers approach, he at once accosted them with a somewhat sour and forbidding look: for it by no means suited Dr. Bertram's purposes that any one should arrive at the mansion who stood a chance of being able to interfere with the control and ascendancy he had gained over Sir Lewis Sinclair.

"Is the knightly owner of this dwelling at home? and if so, can I have immediate speech of him?" asked the elderly personage.

"As for Sir Lewis Sinclair being at home, he is in one sense and not in another," was the physician's rude reply.

"And these contradictory senses, what may they mean?" asked the elderly visitor.

"They mean that Sir Lewis is at home in body—that is to say he is indoors: but he is not at home to visitors—which, also being interpreted, means to say that he cannot be disturbed."

"If I mistake not," said the elderly personage, smiling, "you are that learned and accomplished personage, Dr. Bertram?"

"The same—physician, licentiate, surgeon, apothecary, leech, and divers other qualifications."

"You bear titles sufficient for at least a dozen persons," said the elderly individual, still smiling, but with a good-humour that was to some degree forced.

"And pray what the deuce may your titles be?" demanded Bertram, impudently.

"Earl of Grantham, Viscount Mowbray, Baron Thornfield, Knight-Banneret, and Knight," was the reply.

An immediate change came over Dr. Bertram. At the mention of the first title he took off his cap—at the second he bowed—at the third he made a lower obeisance still—at the fourth he stepped back a pace or two as if aghast at his own former impudence—and at the fifth he fairly sank down upon one knee, exclaiming, "Most potent lord, I pray your noble lordship to excuse your unworthy servant's coarse behaviour."

"Rise," said the Earl of Grantham, laughing; "you and I shall be better friends presently. Of course your distinguished merits are no secret to me; and I shall know how to treat them with due honour."

"You see, my lord," said Dr. Bertram,—for as he was known at Sinclair House by this name, we had better continue to call him by it in order to prevent confusion,—"you see, my lord," he said, rising from his knees, but still standing cap in hand, "my most worthy and excellent friend Sir Lewis Sinclair, whose health is specially entrusted to my charge, is at this moment suffering with a grievous malady——"

"A grievous malady?" echoed the Earl. "What! is the poor knight ill? Is there any danger?"

"No danger but what a comfortable nap will remove," answered the physician.

"But this grievous malady—what is it?" asked the Earl.

"In plain terms," rejoined Dr. Bertram, "Sir Lewis has a vinous affection——"

"A what?" cried the Earl, considerably mystified. "Those are not plain terms. Tell me what you mean."

"I mean, my lord, saving your lordship's presence," answered Dr. Bertram, "that Sir Lewis took a cup of wine too much at breakfast this morning, and I have therefore recommended the worshipful knight to lie down for an hour or two."

"Then this grievous malady is nothing but——"

"A little touch of intoxication," rejoined Bertram; "which is grievous enough while it lasts—especially for a moral and sober man like me to contemplate."

"Well, well," said the Earl, "I am not altogether sorry that I have an opportunity of speaking a few words alone with you before I see my worthy relation, the good Sir Lewis:"—then looking round towards his lacqueys, he bade them enter the house, but not to have the knight disturbed by any announcement of the present arrivals. "Now, most erudite and

accomplished Dr. Bertram," continued the Earl, when the servants were
beyond ear-shot, "let us take a turn or two in this garden——"

"Will not your lordship first take a turn or two at a cold sirloin and a
flask of Canary?" inquired the physician, who had now become as excruciatingly polite as he was doggedly insolent at first.

"Not for the present," rejoined the Earl; "we will have a little conversation first. Perhaps, Dr. Bertram, you are somewhat surprised to behold
me a visitor to the Isle of Wight? But you need be under no apprehension
on your own account. I am well aware you have represented to Sir Lewis
Sinclair that it is the King himself who has sent you hither, whereas in
reality it was none other than a certain Lord Danvers——of whom, be it
understood, I do not mean to speak the slightest harm," added the Earl
hastily, as he flung a rapid and somewhat apprehensive look around: for
since the memorable night of tremendous incidents at his Villa he had
never been able even to think of, much less to breathe, the name of Danvers without a certain sensation of tremor.

"Well, my lord, I must candidly confess," said Dr. Bertram, "that your
lordship has hit the exact nail on the head. But no matter who sent me, I
am not the less a devoted friend to Sir Lewis Sinclair. Besides, my object
in coming hither was innocent enough—just to bear the old gentleman
company, relieve him from monotonous feelings during the absence of his
daughter, and convince him that the King was taking a very great interest
in him. Indeed although it was Lord Danvers who did really send me, yet
was not he expressly empowered by his Highness the King to do so?"

"Observe, Dr. Bertram, that I have not demanded these explanations
of you," said the Earl; "and therefore, should you again see Lord Danvers
soon, pray do not whisper aught in his ear to prejudice him against me:
for I entertain a most particular aversion at even the idea of being placed
at variance with that nobleman. But now to the point. You believe, Dr.
Bertram, that Musidora, the worthy knight's daughter, has married King
Henry?"

"I have not a doubt of it, my lord!" exclaimed the physician. "I have
seen her own letter to her father, announcing the circumstance of the
marriage, and stating that your lordship was one of the witnesses."

"Then, without entering into any particulars," said the Earl, "I wish
you to understand at once that nothing of the kind has taken place."

"How, my lord?" ejaculated Bertram, becoming utterly aghast. "Then
what in heaven's name *has* taken place?"

"Why, that somebody has sent you this purse of gold," immediately
replied Lord Grantham, "as a proof of good-will; and a like donation will
be repeated annually on certain conditions."

"Ah! this is a sort of reasoning that pleases me," exclaimed Bertram, as he clutched the purse. "It is heavy—and therefore the argument is all the weightier. Now, my lord, what am I to think? and what am I to believe?—because such powerful logic as this will make me think and believe whatsoever your lordship chooses—the more so as it seems my faith is to be refreshed in a like manner every year."

"Dr. Bertram, you are a wise man—a man of the world—and a philosopher," said the Earl; "and you are prepared to see, to hear, and to think in proportion to the weight of the arguments placed before you. Now, therefore, what I wish you to think is that through some extraordinary mishap an erroneous account has been sent to Sir Lewis Sinclair, and that no such marriage as that of his daughter with the King has taken place. Then what I want you to believe is that the young lady's honour has in no way suffered through this mistake, the circumstances of which I cannot however explain to you."

"I think and believe everything your lordship chooses," cried the physician: then as he tossed up the purse and caught it in his hand again, he said, "Another such argument as this would make me believe that the sun is as black as ink and that this is the middle of the night."

"Dr. Bertram," remarked the Earl, if not sternly at least gravely, "we must have no jesting—for I pray you to observe that it is treason, and punishable as such, to deal lightly with these matters. As for making them the subject of gossip or scandal, do you know what the result will be?"

"No—not exactly," answered the physician, now looking terribly frightened. "What?"

"Hanging, drawing, and quartering."

"Then never shall it be said that honest Ben Welford has been hung, drawn, and quartered!" cried the physician. "Henceforth I am silent—dumb—wordless—speechless, upon the point."

"I do not mean to threaten in an unhandsome manner," said the Earl, now resuming his conciliatory tone; "because I would rather trust to your prudence and discretion. At the same time I thought it best just to hint at the consequences of any breach of that secrecy which ought to be inviolable."

"Forewarned is forearmed," said Bertram. "But when I just now styled myself Benjamin Welford, I do not mean to say that it is not my real name—at the same time I do not wish your lordship to understand that it is——"

"I shall know you only as Dr. Bertram in the presence of Sir Lewis Sinclair and the other inmates of the house," interrupted the Earl. "And when I think of it, I may add that the object of my visit is by no means to interfere with your position in respect to the knight; so that if it suits you to remain here as his companion and professional adviser, it will be through no fault of mine if you abandon your post."

"Every sentence your lordship utters places me under greater obligations," rejoined Bertram, confounding himself in obsequious salaams.

"Your influence with Sir Lewis is doubtless great?" remarked the Earl interrogatively. "I hope it is so—I wish it to be so," he added, seeing that the physician hesitated what reply to give.

"Well, my lord, it *is* great then," was the answer.

"And you will use it in the way which I shall suggest?" continued the Earl.

"Your lordship has but to speak, and I obey."

"Good. Then it suits me, Dr. Bertram, that Sir Lewis Sinclair shall be led to understand precisely the same relative to his daughter as I have already hinted to you: namely, that she is not married to the King, nor will she be—but at the same time so far from anything dishonourable having taken place between herself and his Highness, I swear that it is not so!"

"All this Sir Lewis Sinclair shall be led to believe," answered Bertram, "and whatsoever else your lordship chooses. But is the Rangership safe?" he abruptly inquired.

"Perfectly. Cardinal Wolsey is now Prime Minister, and I am the bearer of fresh letters-patent with the signature of his Eminence attached, and confirming the appointments of Sir Lewis Sinclair and Master Percy Rivers."

"Then what more can the old knight want?" exclaimed Bertram, as the Earl displayed the documents to his view. "He is already as happy as the day is long, and will doubtless continue so."

"And Percy Rivers?" said Lord Grantham: "has anything ever been whispered to him relative to this supposed marriage?"

"Not a sentence," responded Bertram. "I have taken good care of that. A part of my instructions from Lord Danvers was to see that whatsoever Sir Lewis Sinclair might hear in respect to his daughter, was never to be told to Rivers. Indeed I have done my best to keep this upstart Governor as much as possible away from the house; and I have succeeded too," added the physician, with a coarse chuckle.

"Then as Rivers has heard nothing, there is no trouble to be taken on his account," remarked the Earl. "This is just as I thought and expected. But one word more, Dr. Bertram, ere we enter the house. Mistress Musidora purposes to remain at Grantham Villa for a short time longer—I cannot exactly say how long—it all depends upon circumstances: but during her stay there, you must keep her father's mind perfectly tranquil on her account. Do you understand me?"

"I do, my lord. And your lordship may rest assured that my best shall be done to obey all your instructions. Your lordship is certain that I am to receive a similar purse every year?"

"I will guarantee it—in writing if you choose."

"Your lordship's word is better than a bond. And now, what says your lordship to a slice of the sirloin and a stoup of the wine whereof I have before spoken?"

"We will enter the house," said the Earl, "and see if Sir Lewis Sinclair be now awake, and also in a fit condition for discourse—as the sooner I accomplish the object of my journey the better."

"I will warrant that the excellent knight shall wake up with a wonderful freshness alike of head and of appetite," responded Bertram. "Let us go and see."

The nobleman and Dr. Bertram accordingly entered Sinclair House. Sir Lewis was at the moment waking up; and on being told that his relative the Earl of Grantham had arrived, he hastened to make some improvements in his toilet and efface the signs of the morning's dissipation. He then repaired to the room to which Bertram had already conducted the Earl, and where by the physician's order the domestics had promptly covered the board with the dainties of the larder and the choicest produce of the cellar. The Earl feigned the most enthusiastic delight at meeting his relative; while the welcome which Sir Lewis gave the nobleman was equally cordial, and far more sincere. The worthy knight instantaneously began to overwhelm Lord Grantham with questions relative to Musidora: but the nobleman cut him short by explaining that it was on purpose to clear up certain misunderstandings respecting her actual position that he had come to the Isle of Wight.

To enter into detail with regard to the long discourse that now took place, would be to extend this part of our narrative far beyond the requisite limits, and to weary the patience of the reader. Suffice it to say that the Earl proceeded to break as delicately as he could the fact that Musidora was not married to the King, nor was to marry him. At first Sir Lewis was astounded: but Dr. Bertram was close at hand to tender him a brimming goblet and to help to tranquillize him. Then the Earl proceeded to assure the old man that the honour of his daughter was untainted, and that the King had never looked upon her otherwise than with respect. Another goblet of wine and the artful exercise of Bertram's influence were wonderfully efficient in backing up the Earl of Grantham's sophistry. Still the knight demanded farther explanations: for of course he was at a loss to understand how Musidora could have written to announce her marriage when no such marriage had taken place at all. But instead of attempting anything like a direct answer to Sir Lewis's queries, the Earl of Grantham displayed before his eyes the new letter-patent confirming him in his post; and at the same time Dr. Bertram was in readiness with a third goblet and some more specious observations of his own. To be brief, the old knight was brought into precisely the train of thinking and believing that suited Lord Grantham's purposes: his mind seemed as plastic as could well be desired beneath the tutorings of the two artful men who plied him alike with sophistry and wine; and the result was that the Earl achieved his mission in the most successful manner possible.

On the following day Lord Grantham proceeded to Carisbrook Castle, where he presented the new letter-patent to Percy Rivers; and having passed an hour with the young Governor, he returned to Sinclair House. There he remained until the next morning, when he took his departure, leaving Sir Lewis entirely happy in the possession of his Rangership and in the society of Dr. Bertram.

CHAPTER XLIV.

DANVERS AND THE POWERS OF DARKNESS.

IT was midnight. The winds swept sullenly over the sea, which was tossing and heaving in its mighty bed, and like a many-headed angry monster, erecting crests of foam upon its rolling billows. Dark clouds were passing rapidly over the face of heaven, not with one continuous mass of sable drapery, but in tattered shreds and fragments: so that the full round moon shone at intervals between the openings as if seen through the chasms and fissures of a moving panorama of celestial crags and rocks.

It was a wild and fearful night—the wind moaning with a deep sound, or speaking in a hollow voice, as it swept around the cliffs on the south-western coast of the Isle of Wight. Between those beetling rocks, too, known as the Needles, did the wind pour with a gushing noise, mingling in that spot its loud accents with the heavy plash of the waves as they broke against those natural pillars which shot upward from the sea. High upon the summit of the escarped cliff stood the vast pile of buildings—ramparts, turrets, and towers—which seemed solid as the rock over which they frowned, and to exist there in defiance of the lapse of ages—belonging not to time but to eternity! No light shone from within that gloomy edifice; and so dark were the windows with accumulated dust and dirt, that they reflected not even the moonlight which poured from the openings in the broken masses of the clouds. Yet as the wind swept around that castle—along the ramparts—amidst the battlements, the turrets, and the towers—it seemed to evoke strange echoes and to waken sounds more ominous and gloomy than were heard elsewhere.

And so perhaps might have thought Lord Danvers himself, as he stood upon the very edge of the cliff at a short distance from the castle-wall, and with folded arms looked down upon the wide expanse of sea which stretched before him. It appeared as if that mighty volume of water were agitating, and heaving, and tossing in uneasiness at the presence of some unearthly being: it seemed too as if from the dark horizon the waves came rolling forth like living things, to dash themselves against the foot of the high towering cliff on which Lord Danvers stood.

Yes: with folded arms and fixed gaze did he stand motionless there,— the long sable plume of his cap stretching forth like a fluttering pine-bough, and his short Spanish cloak spreading behind him as if sable wings projected from his shoulders. His tall slender form, so inimitable in its Apollo-like symmetry,—and with all its modelled perfection and sweeping length of limb set off by the tight-fitting garb which he wore, and which was of a foreign fashion,—was drawn up to its full height, in an attitude which seemed as if he were boldly confronting an approaching storm to bid it defiance. One foot was a little advanced before the other, thus increasing that air of resolute boldness and calm courage which invested him at the moment. A kindred expression was upon his countenance,— that countenance of such wondrous beauty, but which at times bore the fearful stamp of the fallen angel!

"Sixteen more years in which to accomplish my work!" he said aloud, as if in apostrophe to the sea on which he was gazing, or to the wind that sounded so ominously to his ear: "sixteen more years of that power which may perhaps terminate with life itself! Aye—and not merely with life, but also with the annihilation of even hope! Yet wherefore should I despair? Have not five names already been inscribed upon the tablets in yon tower?"—and he glanced towards the loftiest building of the pile constituting his castle: "may I not therefore reckon upon filling up the sixth within a period of sixteen years? Ah, Musidora! thou didst escape me: but I have been fearfully avenged!"—and then a look of blighting scorn and satanic triumph appeared for a moment upon his Lucifer-like features.

He ceased to speak for a brief space, and slowly moving away from the spot where he had been hitherto standing, for some time walked slowly along the edge of the cliff. Yes—upon the very verge was it that he thus proceeded, as if reckless of life or conscious of a power that enabled him to scorn all thought of danger: for assuredly it was a path of peril which no human being under other circumstances would have ventured to pursue, on the margin of the giddy height whence the least false step might precipitate him down into the waves beneath, or a sudden change in the wind hurl him right over. But Danvers walked on slowly there, not heeding where he trod, but as calmly and unconcernedly as if in the midst of a beaten road with no danger on either side. Ah! for a moment the edge of the crag gave way beneath his feet—he had trodden upon a ledge of overhanging soil, and his weight had at once broken it away. That circumstance would have been followed by an instantaneous fall and a speedy death to any other being on the face of the earth: but it was not so with Danvers! For a moment he stood as it were upon the air—and then without an effort, without even so much as that spasmodic start and clutching at something—anything—which is the instinctive impulse in such a case, he stood on the firm cliff again, and continued his way as if nothing had happened. Truly that man bore a charmed life!

Again he paused—looked towards the sea—folded his arms—and spoke aloud, once more giving audible expression to the ideas that were uppermost in his mind.

"Sixteen more years! and if I succeed not in obtaining one other victim—Ah! but I shall succeed—I must—I will!" he exclaimed wildly: and for an instant an awful expression of mingled terror and anguish swept over his countenance, as if a barbed arrow-head had suddenly penetrated his heart. "Yes, fiend! I will baffle thee yet: the means are within my power, and I will use them. But, Oh, what a life is mine! Ever in search of a new victim—and with all the Past frowning upon me like a tremendous vision of evil, and the Future still wrapped in utter uncertainty! But why is it that I have sought this place to-night?—what strange influence is it that hath driven my wandering footsteps hither now? Is it because I have resolved to restore to freedom a wretched old man whose captivity is needful to my purposes no longer? or is it because from time to time I have before sought this spot where first I met the tempter—where I have since encountered him—and where perhaps my destiny wills that I shall meet him again to-night?"

Lord Danvers ceased; and with folded arms he stood, still gazing into that distant darkness where the sullen sea and the gloom of the horizon met, but with no definable boundary between them. Suddenly, in the midst of that far-off gloom, an object like a black cloud seemed to come forth from the prevailing obscurity: and then as it swept rapidly over the sea, there was a terrific sound which might have been deemed that of a furious gust of storm-wind to the inhabitants of the island, but which sounded like the rushing of mighty wings to the ear of Danvers. His countenance grew for an instant ghastly pale in the moonlight—his lips were firmly compressed—his high and ample brow became corrugated—and something like a shudder passed through his form as he stepped back a pace or two. The phenomenon that thus strangely moved him, might be described as if that black cloud had rushed with wild flight over the sea towards the cliff, and in a moment had settled there, but instantaneously condensing into the shape and form of a human being.

"Ah, thou art come!" said Danvers, immediately recovering all his wonted calmness and self-possession, as the being, whatever it were, thus appeared before him on the summit of that cliff.

And this being—can language describe it? A human shape it wore, as we have just said—the shape of a man invested with a beauty whereof that of Danvers himself might be regarded as the reflex, yet which was still more unmistakably marked with all the attributes of a fallen angel. Of the same height as Danvers—habited in a similar style—with the distended plume and the outstretched cloak—possessing too the same cast of features, the same duskiness of complexion, and the same slender elegance of figure—that being would have looked the exact counterpart of Lionel himself, were it not that his eyes shone with a fiercer and more terrible light, his lips wreathed with a more sardonic smile than even in his darkest moments Danvers had ever worn, and in his whole appearance there was a loftier air of conscious power than the hero of our tale had ever assumed.

"Again we meet, Lionel Danvers!" said that being—and surely he belonged not to this world? "Again we meet!" he repeated; "and thine expectation is fulfilled: for thou didst come hither this night knowing that it was thy master's influence which urged your footsteps to this spot."

"Master?" said Danvers scornfully: "not yet, not yet! 'Tis I who am still the master."

"Oh! be it as thou wilt, miserable mortal!" exclaimed that unearthly being, his deep voice accentuated with mocking tones of irony; "we will not dispute upon that point. And yet, gifted as thou art with a power that should raise thee above the meanness and the pettiness of that human race to which thou dost belong, thou shouldst display a loftier spirit than to cavil for a mere word, as any despot of a day or grovelling worm of an earthly tyrant is wont to do if his authority be for an instant questioned."

"Dost thou never seek me out save to provoke me with thy sardonic taunts, O fiend?" demanded Danvers, folding his arms once more across his breast, and now as calmly and resolutely confronting the Evil One as when anticipating his approach from that ocean or that horizon whereon he was a few minutes previously gazing so fixedly. "Wherefore hast thou sought me this night? It was not I who summoned thee; and yet as thou thyself hast said, I knew by some intuitive warning that we were to meet here ere yon dark clouds should disperse before the presence of the sun and yield to the glory of another day."

"Why do I seek you now?—why have I ever sought you?" asked Lucifer in a voice more sonorous and deep-toned than that of Danvers, and though not without its harmony, yet as different from the other as that of Lablache from Rubini. "Is it not to remind you of our compact—to tell you of the lapse of time—to bid you mark that years are flowing on and that the great day approaches?"

"Think you, O demon," demanded Lionel Danvers, "that I require thine hateful presence to tell me that which is indelibly seared upon my mind?—think you not that the poisoned arrow rankles too deeply within my soul not to make its own presence felt?—think you that if you have placed the intoxicating chalice of power in my hand, I do not feel its poison also smarting upon my lip?—think you that the words which you spoke when first we made our compact, have not ever since rung as a knell in my ear?—think you that the terrific secret of my destiny is not interwoven with the very fibres of life itself?—think you, in a word, O fiend, that dark as my thoughts too often are, and excruciatingly keen my memories, the former need thy presence to make them darker still, or the latter thy biting words to sharpen them to a more anguished poignancy?"

"And yet with all those thoughts and with all those memories," responded Satan, "thou darest to hope?"

"Hope?" echoed Lionel Danvers, looking and speaking as if his first impulse were to deny that which was both meant and received as an accusation: but the next instant resuming a look of the haughtiest defiance, he said, "Yes, fiend! I dare hope—and where is the human creature whose lot is so desperate that hope does not remain? Here—look—behold!"—and tearing open his doublet, Danvers produced a gold chain which he wore, and on which were five rings of the same metal, but enamelled in black, and each with a name upon it. "These are my constant companions: in these exists my hope. It requires but another to complete the number— and then I bid thee defiance!"

"Is it in vain and ridiculous vaunt that thou thus displayest the tokens which come from me?" demanded the Evil One, a withering expression of scorn appearing upon his countenance, more terrible than ever swept over the features of Lionel Danvers himself; and at the same time the fiend's dark eyes shot forth lightnings which played vivid and lambent about his brow.

"I show thee these tokens," replied Danvers, "in the same manner and for the same purpose that thou dost from time to time come to recall our compact to my memory. If thou on thy part thinkest it needful thus to remind me of those things which it were impossible I could forget, equally needful must it have been for me to convince thee, O Satan, that there are conditions and casualties, and hopes still existing in my favour."

"Be it so!" rejoined the demon, with a subdued laugh of malignant mockery: and there was something horrible even to Danvers in that malice-mirth. "It would seem, then, that power, and wealth, and long life, and all the means of enjoyment which have been placed within thy reach, have not effaced from thy memory the conditions of our compact—no, nor even deadened that memory as to the horrors of the Future which I sketched out for thee in times past. But wherefore, O Danvers, abandon thyself by night and by day to this hope which renders thee restless and deprives thee of the opportunity of plunging deep into those pleasures which would make the remainder of thy time flow on amidst all blandishments and blisses?"

"What language is this which thou darest to hold to me?" demanded Lionel, with a look of proudest defiance. "Is it that thou art so well assured of my eventual success in escaping thy power, that thou seekest to turn me aside from the indulgence of that hope which thou foreknowest will be crowned with triumph?"

"Mortal, I have told thee on former occasions," replied the Evil One, "that it is not mine to read the Future. *He* alone whose name I dare not mention, can penetrate the abyss of eternity which lies beyond the present moment."

"And yet thou canst doubtless carry thy looks backward throughout the illimitable vista of the Past?"—and as Danvers spoke he fixed his eyes with curiosity and interest upon the tempter's countenance.

"Yes," answered the Evil One: "I can send my looks retrospectively throughout ages and ages; and they see no beginning—settle themselves at last upon no origin—stop at no point beyond which it is impossible to look farther?"

"Oh! eternity is awful to think of!" said Danvers, shuddering in spite of himself.

"Yes—awful," rejoined the fiend, malignantly, "when it is to become an eternity of woe!"

"Give me some idea of this eternity whereof we are speaking," said Danvers with a gesture of impatience.

"An idea of eternity?" exclaimed the Evil One, with a laugh of insulting mockery. "What, to you—a denizen of earth—a mortal—whose ideas are limited to your own perishable existence? It were impossible! How can a finite being be made to comprehend the meaning of infinity? As well ask me, thou whose ideas are limited to a space, to give thee an idea of that space which is illimitable. The intellect which knows things only by measurement, can understand naught of things which are immeasurable: the mind which even in its loftiest soarings and wildest flights of conjecture, must stop short at certain bounds, cannot be made to conceive the nature of that which is boundless. Yet pause awhile, and think! Take for example a million of years—divide them into days—the days into hours—the hours into minutes—and the minutes into seconds; then suppose that all those millions and millions of seconds are themselves not merely years, but centuries; and even then you will not have marked out so large a space of time from the great ocean of eternity as a single drop of water would be in comparison with that immense sea, stretching before you!"

Lionel Danvers spoke not: the darkest cloud had gathered upon his brow—his lips were compressed—there was a deadly pallor appearing through the olive of his complexion—and it was evident that his powerful mind was profoundly troubled.

"If man possessed an imagination," resumed Lucifer, "capable of embracing all the wonders concerning which he dares conjecture, he would know no peace, but would live in constant horror and amaze, as if surrounded by myriads of hideous haunting-phantoms. I know that when a few years ago thou wast at Rome, thou didst visit the philosopher Copernicus, while pursuing his astronomical studies there; and I know also that when he imparted to thee the extent of his discoveries, thou didst smile inwardly at the thought that he had but obtained a glimpse of those mighty truths which were radiant with illumination to thee, and that he should be wasting an entire lifetime in the search of that knowledge which from my lips thou hadst obtained in a few brief minutes long years before! But even thou, with all thy knowledge, Danvers—to what extent can thine imagination reach? Thou knowest that infinite space is dotted with millions and millions of worlds, all circling in their orbits and moving round their respective centres of attraction. Thou knowest also that this planetary system to which your Earth belongs, though grand in its own immensity, is nothing in comparison with the myriads and myriads of other planetary systems, which stretch away, and away, throughout infinite space, so that there is no end to these assemblages of moving worlds. But has it ever struck you what an awful thing it is to contemplate how this Earth, for instance, goes ever rushing as if madly on—flying with a velocity which would make the mortal brain all dizzy and whirling to contemplate it— and surrounded by an atmosphere cradling the thunder and rife with the elements of the lightning? Suppose I were to take you in my arms and fly with you for a million of miles away from this earth, then suddenly stop and bid you look down and see the world which you had just left,—what would you behold? A ball shooting onward with tremendous speed, carrying dark clouds with it in its atmosphere, and those clouds parting and breaking and pouring forth the vivid lightning. Would it not make your hair stand on end, and your brain whirl, and your sight grow dim, and your heart shrink appalled within you, to think that upon that globe, thus pursuing its wondrous and rapid way without visible support, are millions and millions of human beings whom a whirlwind more furious than usual might sweep away like grains of dust? And is it not strange that these myriads of sentient, living, moving creatures are all ignorant or careless of the circumstances attending their whirling route through the impalpable expanse and amidst the stars?"

"Wherefore dost thou talk to me in this strain, O Satan?" asked Lionel Danvers, suddenly starting as it were from a sensation of ineffable awe which had crept over him, and which had held him silent for some minutes after the fiend had ceased from speaking.

"It may be to excite thy wonder—it may be to excite thy terror," was the response. "But no matter. Assuredly," added the demon, a malignant smile once more appearing upon his countenance, "it was not *only* to bestow upon thee a lecture on such topics, that I sought thee, Danvers, this night. It was to tell thee, as I ere now said, that time is passing, and give thee due warning that thirty-two years hence thou wilt be mine—unless indeed that hope which thy heart dares cherish should be fulfilled. Thou can'st not reproach me that I thus appear in thy presence from time to time, to give thee such warnings as these. On the contrary, thou should'st confess that I am just and generous after my own fashion——"

"Yes!" interrupted Danvers, with scornful tone and bitter laugh: "just and generous as the executioner is, who ere the day comes on which he hopes to pounce upon his victim, visits him from time to time in his dungeon-cell and warns him of his approaching doom!—just and generous as those tyrants with crowns upon their heads, who shut up their victims in cages, having fixed a distant day on which they are to be put to death, and who in the interval go now and then to gloat over their sufferings! Is it thus, O Satan, that thy mercy is shown to me?"

"Wherefore liken thyself unto the victims destined for the gibbet or the fire?" demanded Satan, "since thou hast thy heart full of hope—aye, and a hope too which ere now was proclaimed so confidently and asserted so proudly from thy lips! Lionel Danvers, there is a hope which mortals woo back to them when the very threshold of despair itself is passed,—a hope that is thus wooed in despair's despite, and because despair is too intolerable to endure! But the hope which is begotten of despair—what is it? Shall I liken it to the will-o'-the-wisp produced by the very quagmire in which the wretched traveller is floundering?—shall I compare it to the straw at which the drowning man clutches, and which floats in light mockery upon the very waters that are swallowing him up?"

"Enough, enough!" exclaimed Danvers, stamping his foot with mingled rage and impatience. "I will hear thee no more, Satan! Begone—I command thee to begone!"

"Farewell, then, for the present, thou who *only for the present* may'st command me!"—and as he thus spoke in a mocking voice, the Evil One rapidly dilated as it were from his human form into the impalpable and shapeless expansion of a cloud of ominous blackness, and again with the noise as of the rush of mighty winds, swept away over the ocean until lost in the deepening gloom of the horizon.

Lionel Danvers was once more alone upon the summit of the cliff; and for several minutes he stood in the spot where Lucifer had left him, gazing vacantly in the direction which the vanishing black cloud had taken in its retreat. Heaven alone can tell what thoughts swept through the brain of that fearful man: but dark and ominous was the expression of his features—aye, as dark and as ominous as the cloud-like form in which Lucifer had just parted from him. But suddenly turning away from the spot on the edge of the cliff, he walked with a rapid step towards the entrance of his castle close by.

CHAPTER XLV.

DANVERS' CASTLE.

THE huge and heavy gates of the entrance-tower fell back of their own accord as Lionel Danvers imperiously waved his hand; and when he entered, they closed behind him with a similar spontaneousness. He passed through a spacious vestibule, lighted only by the feeble glimmerings of the moonbeams which penetrated through the loopholes; and he entered the court-yard of the castle. All was deserted, but not silent: for the wind raised mournful echoes round the buildings, and seemed to speak in ominous voices to the lord of the castle as he thus revisited the home of his ancestors.

The doors of another entrance-way opened to his presence; and now he passed into a spacious hall, where the moonbeams shone through a range of lofty windows. This hall, of heavy gothic architecture, and with its lofty roof sustained by many pillars, was hung with suits of armour, implements of war, and trophies of the chase; and above them the tattered and dusty banners of battle waved lazily, like pendant masses of cobwebs as the night-wind swept through the place.

Many long, long years had passed since that hall had resounded to the shouts of revellers, or had blazed with lights upon the banqueting-board. The armour was rusting on the walls—the flags were mouldering—the marble pavement, with its diamond-like arrangement of black and white slabs, was covered with dust—and its range of high narrow-arched windows were all defenceless against wind, or rain, or sleet, or tempest, as well as they were open to pure moonbeams or gorgeous sunlight.

Through this hall did Lionel Danvers slowly bend his steps; but ever and anon he paused and gazed up at the armour and the banners—then down upon the marble pavement; for the warlike accoutrements and the flags of battle doubtless reminded him of his heroic ancestors whose remains reposed in the vaults dug deep below the castle-foundations. But whatever his thoughts were, he gave not audible expression to them,— though once or twice a look of regret, amounting almost to the anguish of remorse, appeared upon his countenance, as if a secret voice were whispering in his soul, "Better would it have been for thee, Lionel Danvers, had'st thou imitated the pursuits of thine ancestors whose memories are now conjured up in thy brain!"

Passing through the hall, he reached an immense staircase of solid oak, the balustrades of which were of enormous size and massively sculptured. At the foot thereof stood two suits of armour upon pedestals; and as the vizors were closed and the attitudes were perfectly life-like, they seemed like real sentinels stationed there to guard the spot. Ascending the stairs, which were but dimly lighted by the moonbeams as they glimmered through a high window of stained glass, Danvers at length reached a landing where a door instantaneously opened before him; and now he entered a gallery the walls of which were covered with pictures. The light fell upon them through a row of narrow windows; but Danvers scarcely paused to throw a glance on any one of the portraits of his ancestors. Indeed, so blackened were they all with dust, and so great had been the ravages of time with many, that there were few whose subjects were discernible; and even these were fast yielding to neglect and decay.

From that gallery Danvers passed into a suite of spacious rooms, where the moonbeams entered, as in other parts of the castle, through rows of gothic windows. In former times, when the castle was inhabited, these apartments must have been of the most splendid description; for they were embellished with elaborate sculpture-work in the windows and doorways, and the furniture though blackened with dust and rotting with damp and decay, still bore sufficient evidences of its pristine richness and elegance. But in these apartments the dust had collected even more thickly upon the floor than elsewhere—probably because there was less draught to disperse it; and scarcely had Danvers entered when his eyes fell on the traces of footprints that were plainly visible from door to door. He started at the sight; and a singular expression swept over his features as his looks rested upon some prints which were smaller than others, and which seemed to indicate the delicate tread of a woman as well as the bolder and more deeply indented one of a man.

It must not be inferred that Lionel Danvers was at all astonished by observing those footprints there: he knew full well whose they were, both the male and the female ones! But he was startled as a person is who suddenly beholds something of which he is not thinking at the moment, and which vividly recalls strong and painful memories.

"It is not quite four years since *she* accompanied me hither," he said in a musing tone, as he stopped short and looked down upon the footprints, which not only led onward but also in the contrary direction—that is to say, back again towards the door by which he had just entered. "She escaped me—but I have been avenged! Ah, and this vengeance so dire, so terrible, was better far than immolating her at once to my wrath. Yes: for thereby two passions have been sated—the passion which her beauty kindled, and the passion that craved for revenge. And she too was the only woman who ever retraced her way from yon tower after accompanying me thither!"

Lionel Danvers, having thus mused, proceeded through the suite of apartments, until another door opening of its own accord, admitted him into a room which has been minutely described in the Prologue to this tale. The door closed behind him—the secret spring whereby it was held fast making a sharp clicking noise.

The room presented precisely the same appearance as when, six years previously, Lionel Danvers had led Clara Manners thither. There were the six black panels, each duly numbered, and on five of which appeared in characters of fire the names of as many females who had been consigned to some dark and unknown fate:—

1. Bianca Landini	1390.
2. Margaret Dunhaven	1407.
3. Arline de St. Louis	1463.
4. Dolorosa Cortez	1500.
5. Clara Manners	1510.

Yes—there were those five names: but would the sixth panel ever be filled up? This was the question which Danvers asked himself, as pausing in the middle of the room, he folded his arms and gazed steadfastly upon the six black squares marked with the bold red outlines, and with the fiery names upon five of them.

"Aye, even Lucifer himself," mused Danvers audibly, had there been any one near to listen, "could not succeed in banishing hope from my breast—no, not with all his sophistry!"

Then Lionel sat down near the great oaken table; and leaning his face upon his hands, he gave way to a long train of reflections. But his thoughts we cannot fathom. Perhaps he was pondering regretfully upon the past—perhaps he was thinking of those whose names were traced in characters of fire upon the five black panels—perhaps he was devising plans for the future? We cannot say.

For a long time did he remain wrapped up in that profound reverie; and when he raised his head again, there were traces of care and anguish upon the dark and fearful beauty of his countenance. Slowly he rose from his seat, opened a drawer in the table, and drew forth a phial containing a white fluid. This phial he uncorked, and was about to apply it to his lips, when he suddenly stopped short as an idea struck him; and returning the cork to the phial, he again reflected profoundly for some minutes.

"What age shall I assume?" he at length asked himself aloud, thus giving verbal utterance to the question he was evidently pondering in his mind. "With my present appearance I am far too young to have a grown up son—and I have never spoken to those who know me of a younger brother. And yet it were not wise to pursue my search for another victim—*the last*—as Lionel Danvers. The tale of Clara Manners is already known to several; and all that has ever taken place between Musidora and myself, even to the incidents of the last few days, may be bruited abroad, and the name of Lionel Danvers will perhaps become associated with the reputation of an infamous seducer. Would it be wise, then, to continue as I am—to wear this present shape—and with the name of *Lionel* also, continue my search for that being whose name must fill up the sixth square? No: it were scarcely prudent—it were scarcely wise. Yet if I take another and a younger form, how am I to represent myself? Not as the son nor as the brother of Lord Lionel. No! But wherefore not the cousin? Aye—the idea is happy. The requisite papers to establish the identity are speedily fabricated—and that is sufficient. Besides, as a beautiful youth—what age shall I say?—of eighteen? Well, then—as a beautiful youth of eighteen I may stand a better chance of speedily captivating the heart of some young confiding girl, than by retaining my present appearance. Yes—be it so!"

With these last words Lionel Danvers again uncorked the phial; and placing it to his lips, he imbibed a few drops of the fluid which it contained. Instantaneous was the change accomplished in his looks;—and on the spot where a man seeming to be about thirty years of age had just stood, there now appeared a youth of about eighteen!

And of what exceeding beauty was this youth! Tall as ere the transformation had taken place, but the least thing more slender, the elegant and graceful figure was characterized by all the willowy elasticity and litheness properly belonging to that age when boyhood has shot up into a somewhat precocious manhood. There too was the same classic beauty of the features, but a trifle more delicate in their chiselling—without, too, any of that sardonic haughtiness which had marked the countenance of the man when figuring in the world as Lionel Danvers—but yet wearing an expression of high-bred dignity, mingled with an air of youthful ingenuousness. Instead of the dark moustache, there was but a thick down upon the upper lip; and that lip, as well as its companion, was red and fresh as the lips of a woman. The eyes, still dark as night, retained all the glory of their lustre, with naught of a sinister expression; and the hair, still long and glossy in its even blackness, was of a more silken fineness, if possible, than before. The apparel was precisely the same; but in all other respects it was now a brilliant and beautiful youth of eighteen who stood in the place of the wondrously handsome man of about thirty.

Approaching one of the oaken panels which surrounded the walls up to the high window-ledges, the transformed being—or rather, should we not say the renovated one?—drew back one of those panels and surveyed himself in a large mirror which was thus disclosed. Well satisfied did he seem by the change he had accomplished in his personal appearance: the carnation flush of exultant emotion mantled upon the pure and delicate olive of his complexion—his eyes shot forth diamond-like jets of fire—his beautiful lips wreathed with a triumphant smile—and he exclaimed, with the sweetest melody which belongs to the voice of youth when between boyhood and manhood, "Dared the fiend tell me that I should abandon hope? No, no! With such a shape as this, it is not only *one* female heart that I may conquer if I will!"

Having thus spoken, Danvers drew back the oaken panel over the mirror, and approached the door, which instantly flew open to give him egress. He passed on through the suite of rooms where the costly furniture was mouldering; and his feet left fresh prints upon the dust that lay thick upon the floor: but these prints were a trifle smaller and more delicate than those which his steps had made when he passed inward. He went on, threading the long picture-gallery, and reached the oaken staircase. This he descended, once more gaining the immense hall, where the high-arched roof, the many tall columns, and the range of gothic windows, with the moonlight pouring in, produced so solemn and awe-inspiring a cathedral-effect.

But he did not immediately issue forth from his castle. Proceeding
into one of the obscure nooks of the immense hall, he drew forth a bunch
of keys and a lamp: this he lighted, and then approached a little low door
in another recess. But it was not needful for him to use any of the keys on
that bunch unless he chose to do so: for with the slightest wave of his hand
the door flew open at his presence, and he descended a flight of stone
steps which seemed to go winding on and on—down, down—deep below the foundations of the castle. At length he reached an immense long
passage, hollowed out of the cliff on which the fortalice stood, and into
which the air was admitted by an opening at the end—this aperture being
in the face of the escarped rock overlooking the sea. Selecting a particular
key on the bunch, and which he instantly knew by a touch of the fingers
rather than by the aid of the lamp-light, he approached one of the many
doors which appeared in the side of the long passage; and opening that
particular door, he said, in the gentlest tones of a voice which was filled
with the flute-like melody and fresh harmony of youth. "Prisoner, where
art thou? 'Tis a friend who seeks thee!"

"Ah! who calls?" exclaimed a voice from the farthest extremity of the
dungeon, into which the beams of the lamp could not entirely penetrate.
"Those are not the accents of my base persecutor."

"Come forth, poor old man—come forth!" said Danvers. "I am here
to deliver thee."

"Oh! is this a dream? Yes—it is too delightful to be true——"

"No—it is a reality. Come forth!"

Then from the interior of the dungeon, did Manners, the ruined merchant, issue; and by the light of the lamp which Danvers carried in his
hand, the two individuals were enabled to observe each other. Of course
Danvers knew the old merchant well: but the latter was unfeignedly surprised on beholding this beautiful, and indeed exquisitely lovely youth appearing there as his deliverer.

"It is a Danvers—yet not the same," said the old man. "There is the
likeness—but in the person of a youth——What does it mean?" he demanded, a cloud of doubt and distrust settling upon his countenance.

"It means simply," was the response, given in a mournful tone, as if
the speaker had the death of a kinsman uppermost in his mind, "that Lord
Lionel Danvers is no more, and that I, his cousin and his heir, obedient to
his dying instructions, am here to deliver you. Hasten however away from
this place; and whatever questions you may choose to put to me, I will
answer in a spot where it will be more pleasant to converse."

Thus speaking, Danvers led the way towards the ascent of steps, taking however the keys with him; for he did not choose to display his super-

natural power by allowing doors to open of their own accord, now that observing eyes could mark the circumstance.

He ascended the flight slowly, with every appearance of the most delicate consideration for the old man, whose feebleness could not have kept pace with his lithe agility. He even tendered a hand to help the ruined merchant up; and in this way did they ascend to the great hall. There Danvers locked the door with the keys; and placing the lamp in a niche, said to the merchant, "Worthy Master Manners, I am well pleased at having been commissioned thus to release you from the most undeserved captivity."

"And is Lord Lionel really no more?" asked the old man anxiously.

"Three days ago he expired, in consequence of injuries sustained by a fall from his horse," was the response.

"His horse!" echoed Manners, to whose memory rushed all the circumstances of his frightful journey in a few hours from London to that castle in the Isle of Wight. "Was it one of those colossal black steeds——"

"My deceased cousin told me everything," interrupted Danvers with a significant look: "but it were useless for us, poor old man, to remain here and discourse upon the details of those mystic occurrences which are uppermost in your mind."

"But my daughter, my lord—my daughter, good youth?" exclaimed old Manners. "Tell me—what of her? Did your deceased kinsman, the fearful Lord Lionel, mention aught of my poor Clara?"

"Alas! yes, Master Manners," replied the young nobleman: "your daughter has been dead some years. More I cannot tell you."

"Now then I know the worst!" said the old man; and staggering back against the wall, he covered his face with his hands and sobbed aloud. "Alas! alas! wherefore have I survived her?—wherefore have I lived to hear this? O Clara, hast thou indeed perished without receiving either my forgiveness or my blessing? Oh! my beloved daughter—my poor lost child— that I could but have embraced thee once ere thou wast taken from me! My lord,—for from your words I glean that you bear the proud title of Danvers—have pity upon a poor old man and leave him not in a state of suspense. Tell me—under what circumstances did my daughter die?"

"She died happy—happy in the love of Lionel Danvers," was the response.

"But her remains—where do they repose? Tell me where she lies, that I may drag my weary limbs to her grave and weep over her last resting-place?"

"Ah! that I know not," responded the young nobleman. "It was in one of my deceased's cousin's Continental castles that she died: but where I cannot say. On this point the late Lord Lionel did not speak. Death came upon him with such rapid strides that he had barely leisure to give me his last instructions; and of these the very first was to enjoin me to lose no time in coming hither to release you from captivity."

"Know you, young man," asked the old merchant, wiping away the tears from his eyes, and gazing fixedly upon the youthful countenance before him, all the exquisite beauty of which was visible as the glare of the lamp fell upon it,—"know you that your deceased relative was a man of dark and fearful character—possessed of powers which no good Christian could righteously possess, and which were not exercised to any worthy purpose?"

"I know—indeed I learnt from the dying words of Lord Lionel, that he had devoted some degree of study to those black arts which cannot be alluded to without a shudder."

"And you should pray to heaven that no such terrible heritage may descend to you," rejoiced old Manners, with something like malignant bitterness in his tone.

"In consequence of the injuries you have sustained at the hands of my predecessor," said Danvers, somewhat haughtily, "I forgive you a remark which under other circumstances would be an impertinence, and which even now is fraught with ingratitude towards one who is thy deliverer and not thy persecutor."

The old merchant endeavoured to force himself to make some apology for the words he had uttered: but there was a feeling within him which hushed the syllables that rose to the very tip of his tongue—for he could not think of all his wrongs without experiencing a bitter hatred for every one bearing the name of Danvers.

"Ah! you do not choose to answer me," said the youthful noble, who appeared instantaneously to comprehend wherefore the bereaved father's lips remained sealed. "But it is no matter. I have fulfilled the commission entrusted to me, and have given you your deliverance. More generous in my endeavour to make atonement for what you have suffered, than you are grateful for the zealous promptitude with which I have hastened to set you free, I proffer you my purse. 'Tis well filled with gold: there are likewise a few diamonds and other precious stones in it, which may afford you the means of living in competency and ease for the remainder of your existence."

"No, my lord," said old Manners, resolutely and gravely—indeed almost sternly: "you, as the heir of the deceased Lord Lionel, doubtless owe to him everything which you possess; and not for worlds would I receive even so much as the smallest coin which has emanated from the treasury of my persecutor. For three months and a half have I been a pris-

oner in that deep dungeon below! Every morning, when awakening from
the sleep into which the exhaustion of anguish and sorrow plunged me,
I found a loaf of bread and a pitcher of water placed just inside the door
of that cell. But never once did I hear that door open—never once could I
ascertain by whose hand the food and the water were placed there. Who,
then, was my gaoler? Answer me that question, my lord! Has there not
been fearful magic in all this? Vainly did I more than once endeavour to
keep awake throughout the whole night, in the hope that if Lord Lionel
himself came, I might endeavour to move him by my prayers and entreaties, or by my remonstrances and reproaches, to set me free—or at least to
give me some positive intelligence relative to my poor deluded daughter.
But ever at a certain hour towards the dawn of morning, did sleep fall
upon my eyes; and when I awoke again and groped through the darkness
towards the neighbourhood of the door, I still found the daily supply of
provision there. My lord, I tell you that you belong to a fearful race; and
even apart from the wrongs I have received at the hands of your predecessor, there are sensations of terror and misgiving in my soul which forbid
me to receive the slightest succour at your hands."

"Then let us say no more," rejoined Danvers, impatiently: "and respecting the question you have put to me, I know not how to answer it.
Now let us part and pursue our separate ways in the world."

"God grant, young man, that yours may be for purposes of good!"—
and as the old merchant uttered these words in an ominous tone, as if
swayed by dark doubts and misgivings in the depths of his soul, he turned
away, and moving slowly through the hall, approached the great folding
doors.

Lord Danvers gave him egress by means of the keys which he carried
in his hand; and when they reached the threshold of the outer gate the
ruined merchant said in a grave tone, "Farewell, my lord. I can scarcely—
—no, I cannot even force myself to give utterance to a single syllable of
gratitude for the freedom to which you have restored me!"

Lord Danvers merely said "Farewell," and stood at the outer gate of
his castle watching the retreating form of the old man as he took the pathway leading into the interior of the island.

CHAPTER XLVI.

SCENES IN LOMBARD STREET.

WE must now again transport the reader to Master Landini's establishment in Lombard Street. It was a week after the incidents recorded in the preceding chapters, and therefore now the end of August.

At about three o'clock in the afternoon, as Mark was closeted with his uncle in the private office behind the counting-house, one of the clerks threw open the door exclaiming, "Lord Reginald Danvers!"

Both the uncle and nephew started at this announcement, being struck with the idea that there was some error in the Christian name; and ere they could well recover from the astonishment into which they were thrown, the visitor himself, passing into the office, appeared in their presence. Old Landini doffed the black velvet cap which he habitually wore, and made a low obeisance; while Mark testified his respect and also endeavoured to conceal his confusion by bowing profoundly.

But still an expression of surprise and curiosity lingered upon the countenances of the old banker and his nephew, when, raising their looks again, they took a more attentive survey of that tall elegant youth about eighteen years of age, and not merely of the most perfect beauty, but likewise of a beauty in the peculiar style which seemed hereditary among the race of Danvers. Still however they tried to conceal their astonishment as much as possible, lest they should appear rude in staring too intently upon their noble visitor.

"I have the pleasure of making acquaintance with Master Landini, I presume?" said Lord Reginald, extending his hand with the most affable condescension towards the old man.

"I am your lordship's obedient servant," was the response, accompanied by a low salutation. "This, my lord, is my nephew Mark—my assistant in the business—my heir—and I might almost say, my adopted son."

"I have heard you both most admirably spoken of by my cousin the deceased Lord Lionel," said Danvers, who, having shaken the old banker by the hand, now bestowed the same mark of friendship upon the nephew.

"Ah!" exclaimed the elder Landini, putting on a most mournful expression of countenance: "is my excellent patron Lord Lionel indeed no more?"

"He is no more," rejoined Lord Reginald: "he exists no longer. Some ten days back, when on a visit to a friend in Hampshire, he experienced a

fall from his horse, and received such severe injuries that they proved fatal
in a few hours."

"And your lordship was with your noble kinsman at the time?" said
the elder Landini interrogatively.

"I was staying at the same friend's house, but was not riding out with
my cousin on the occasion of his accident. Conceive my horror and dismay when he was brought to the dwelling, in a dying state, by some peas-
ants who had picked him up!"

"It is most lamentable, my lord!" said old Landini. "But pardon me—
it is somewhat strange that his lordship never mentioned in my hearing
the existence of a cousin——"

"Until very lately—indeed till within the last month," interrupted
Reginald, with all the ingenuousness and frankness of youth, "we were
much estranged from each other: but it is a happy reflection for me that,
since heaven willed that my cousin's fate should be so near at hand, circumstances brought us together at last and made us friends. And now,
perhaps, I should inform you, Master Landini, that I am the only son of a
younger brother of Lord Humphrey Danvers, who, as you are aware, was
the father of Lord Lionel."

"I never heard, my lord, until now," responded Landini, speaking
with the profoundest respect, and by no means doubtingly, "that Lord
Humphrey had any brother at all."

"Yet you see that it was so," observed Reginald, with a look and tone
of the most affable frankness. "Here are all the papers requisite to prove
my claims and substantiate my identity. I have this day been to his Eminence Cardinal Wolsey, and have submitted these documents to his perusal. The peerage will therefore be mine on the attainment of my majority:
it is indeed mine already—except the power to take my seat, were I so
disposed, amongst the Barons of the realm. In respect to the castles and
estates, those are all hereditary, and therefore mine by right; and with reference to whatsoever sums of money may be in your hands, to those also
can I substantiate my claim—for in his last moments Lord Lionel signed a
document enjoining you to hold the same for my account and benefit, and
subject to my disposal."

Thus speaking, Reginald Danvers drew forth a packet of papers from
the folds of his doublet, and tossed them upon the table. He then threw
himself carelessly upon a seat, and with a motion of the hand indicated
that Landini was to peruse them. The old man accordingly sat down at his
desk and looked over the documents, all of which he found to be perfectly
exact and accurate in their nature and details.

"My lord," he said at length, turning towards the youthful noble—for youthful we must call him, inasmuch as so he seemed;—"as a matter of course your lordship's word would have been sufficient for me; but in the ordinary way of business it was necessary to cast an eye over these papers which your lordship has done me the honour to submit to me. While deeply deploring the untimely death of my excellent patron and friend Lord Lionel, I may nevertheless without affectation congratulate your lordship on having succeeded to the proud title and immense wealth of your deceased kinsman."

As he thus spoke, the elder Landini assumed a demeanour so profoundly respectful, and his accents seemed so full of sincerity, that it was scarcely possible to imagine he cherished in his heart so implacable a vengeance against the bearers of the name of Danvers.

"I thank you, Master Landini, for your felicitations," replied Reginald; "and I hasten to inform you that my deceased cousin Lionel, in his last moments, spoke of you in the highest terms. It is therefore my wish that you should continue as the banker and agent for my English as well as my Continental revenues. Indeed, I seek to introduce no change into the arrangements as they have hitherto stood between yourself and my kinsman Lionel."

"My lord, I thank you for this mark of confidence and kindness on your part," said old Landini. "But I must inform your lordship that in pursuance of instructions given by your late cousin, I have begun to invest the surplus capital amassed in my hands, in such enterprises where it may be usefully and safely employed, productive of good interest, and——"

"In all these respects I leave myself entirely at your disposal," interrupted Lord Reginald. "It is my intention to return to the Continent forthwith——"

"Like your ancestors, then, my lord," remarked the old banker, "you entertain no particular affection for England?"

"I prefer the Continent," answered Reginald carelessly, "where I have passed the greater portion of my life."

"Your lordship must have been in constant communion with English persons," said the banker, "to be enabled to speak our language so fluently."

"From the time that I was eight until twelve I was educated in England," rejoined the young noble; "and I have always had English domestics in attendance upon me, and several English friends constantly staying with me in France."

"Does your lordship purpose to make a long stay abroad?" inquired the old man.

"According to my present ideas I shall visit England only from time to time, in order to confer with you respecting such business-matters as you may have to submit to me."

"That will be necessary, my lord, considering the various ways in which your capital is to be laid out. But may I venture to suggest that your lordship will continue the same plan which your deceased kinsman commenced some months back—I mean the concentration of all your surplus revenues in my hands: for, looking at the troubled state of the Continent, and the probability of wars between France and Germany——"

"Again I assure you, Master Landini," interrupted Reginald, "that I shall in no way deviate from the course pursued by Lord Lionel."

At this moment Mark, who had quitted the private office at the time his uncle was in the midst of perusing the papers, came back, followed by a domestic bearing a massive silver salver covered with choice wines, fruits, and other light refreshments, of which Lord Reginald was most respectfully invited to partake.

"I will cheerfully drink a cup of wine to our better acquaintance," was the young noble's response: and having done so, he rose to take his departure.

"Shall we have the pleasure of seeing your lordship again ere you leave England?" asked the banker. "There are certain documents which your lordship should sign, empowering me to make use of your lordship's moneys in the same manner as I have hitherto done in respect to your predecessors."

"Let what papers you deem necessary be got in readiness at once," exclaimed Reginald; "and to-morrow at noon I will call to affix my signature unto them. Meantime I bid you farewell."

The youthful noble thereupon took his departure, attended to the outer door of the establishment by the obsequious old man and his nephew. They stood regarding him as he passed slowly along the street; and they could not help noticing to each other the exceeding elegance of his figure, the grace of his movements, and the effect which his appearance produced upon all who passed him by. Indeed, it was impossible to observe that youth of such exquisite beauty without turning round to regard him more attentively.

"Now, my dear nephew," said the old banker, when he and Mark were once more alone together in the private office, "the day of our vengeance is nearer at hand than even an hour ago we could possibly have hoped or expected. The premature death of Lord Lionel is a fortunate event for us: inasmuch as he was shrewd and keen, and it would have required a most wondrous amount of caution as well as artifice and duplicity, to have carried out our aims towards *him* with the fullest success. But with this youth it will be different! A stripling in years, he has but little experience of the world, and none in those financial affairs which will now beyond all doubt become the means of consummating our vengeance."

"Is it not strange," said Mark, "that we never before heard of this kinsman of Lord Lionel?"

"The circumstance itself is not strange, nephew," exclaimed the old man: "but it is the character of all these Danvers which is strange! Sometimes an unaccountable reserve, and a most mysterious suppression of even the most trivial little incidents which are wont to be revealed in ordinary conversation—sometimes an equally singular appearance of bestowing a confidence that is unasked—such are the characteristics of every scion of the Danvers family."

The uncle and nephew pursued the theme of their discourse in this manner for some little time longer, until the hour came for the jewel-workers and the clerks to withdraw and the establishment to close for the evening.

Shortly after dusk a summons at the front door was heard; and the female servant who answered it, announced to the Landinis that an old man who refused to give his name, but who said that he had come upon important business, requested an interview. The uncle and nephew were seated at the time in an upper apartment, and had just finished the evening meal: they accordingly directed the servant to introduce the visitor to their presence. The command was promptly obeyed; and an old man, shabbily attired and with a sinister countenance, was ushered into the room. At once did the two Landinis recognise him as a person whom they had seen before, but of whom they had a very dim recollection—at all events not sufficient to make them receive him with any degree of welcome.

"What is your business?" inquired the uncle, somewhat sharply. "Your face is not altogether unfamiliar to me——"

"I have taken the liberty of calling from time to time at your establishment," was the response given by the old and ill-looking visitor, "to ask a certain question, to which however I have on no occasion received a satisfactory answer."

"I recollect!" exclaimed Mark. "Your inquiries have been relative to Lord Danvers?—and if my memory serves me aright, you never gave your name nor even stated for what business you sought our noble patron. Under such circumstances, how could you expect that either my uncle or myself, or any of the persons in our employment would answer your queries? Therefore, if it be with the same object that you are now come hither, the information you will obtain is not likely to be of a more satisfactory character than on former occasions."

"I come not upon my old errand," replied the visitor. "Indeed," he added, with a cunning smile, "I have recently heard something of Lord Danvers——Perhaps more than he himself has chosen to communicate to *you*."

"Ah!" ejaculated the elder Landini. "And is it with a view of imparting to us your knowledge on this head that you have come hither now?"

"Have I not positively declared that my business has no reference to Lord Danvers nor his affairs?" returned the man gruffly.

"Then what *has* brought you hither?" demanded the old banker in a sharp tone.

"If you grant me your patience for a few minutes, I will explain myself," responded the visitor, as he took a chair though unbidden. "Pardon me if I make thus free to sit down in your presence: but perhaps my very freedom is not an altogether unnecessary rebuke for your want of courtesy in keeping an old man like me standing thus."

"One would think," exclaimed the banker in an angry voice, "that you were our very best patron by the airs which you give yourself. However, I am listening, and await such explanations as you may have to afford. In short, what would you with me?"

"You bear the repute, Master Landini," rejoined the shabbily-dressed and ill-mannered visitor, "of being the most eminent dealer in precious stones in all London; and as circumstances have thrown in my way some diamonds which strike me as being of wondrous brilliancy, I thought it best to come at once to you and see if you were disposed to purchase them."

"It is a rare thing, though," said the elder Landini, satirically, "for circumstances to throw such things in a poor man's way; and therefore I would rather have nothing to do with the matter."

"You fancy that they were stolen, then?" said the visitor, with a sort of grim smile.

"I think it not unlikely," rejoined the old banker drily; "and therefore the sooner you depart from my house the better."

"But you are mistaken, Master Landini," said the visitor, not offering to move from his chair. "I was of course prepared for your suspicions, and likewise to answer any questions that might be put to me."

"Then what account can you give of the diamonds which you allege to have fallen into your possession?" demanded the banker. "Speak quickly, and also with frankness—if you can."

"I must begin by informing you, Master Landini," proceeded the stranger, "that I live in a house situated on the bank of the river, and a portion of which actually overhangs the water, being supported on piles.

Now, I noticed this morning that there was a crack in the wall of one of the rooms in the overhanging part of the building; and it struck me that the piles might possibly be giving way. Therefore, when the tide was out, I descended the bank to examine the woodwork which supports that part of my house of which I am speaking. The water had ebbed so low that the ground from which the piles shoot up was left bare; and while groping about to examine the state of those huge wooden posts, I observed something like a small box or casket. I picked it up, and found it to be indeed a casket tied round with a bit of ribbon. On opening my prize to see what it contained, I was astonished to find it filled with precious stones, all beautifully set in jewellery for a lady's ornaments. Perhaps you may blame me," added the visitor, with a cunning leer, "for not taking the casket to the Lord Mayor or the City Marshal, so that proclamation may be made inviting the owner to come forward: but methinks that it were more discreet and prudent to avail my own especial self of this signal bounty of fortune."

"Let me see the diamonds," said the elder Landini. "But first, before I have anything to do with them, tell me where you live and what your name is, as a guarantee of good faith in respect to the story you have just related."

"Yes—if you agree to purchase the diamonds," answered the visitor: "otherwise it will be useless for me to enter into further details."

"Well, well—then be it as you will," said the elder Landini, not choosing to let the opportunity of driving a good bargain slip through his fingers. "Where are these diamonds?"

The shabbily-attired old man thrust his hand into the bosom of his sordid and greasy jerkin, and drew forth a parcel enveloped in a dirty rag. This rag he deliberately took off, observing the while, "I have carefully washed away the mud and slime from the casket, both inside and out; and though the velvet lining is all soiled and damaged, and indeed still damp, yet the jewellery itself is uninjured and the gems are perfect."

At this moment he had completely taken off the rag, and the casket was thus revealed to the eyes of both the uncle and nephew.

"Ah!" ejaculated Mark, completely thrown off his guard as he at once recognised the casket: "the diamonds which Lionel Danvers——"

"Danvers! Danvers!" echoed the visitor, starting up from his seat, the sudden mention of the name at that moment producing a magical effect upon him: "what has this casket to do with Danvers? wherefore did the first glimpse of it instantaneously recall him to your mind?"

A glance from the elder Landini, rapidly thrown across the table, had already reproved Mark for his indiscretion in letting drop that name; and the nephew bit his lip with vexation at his fault.

"Let me see the diamonds," said the elder Landini, extending his hand to receive the casket: then, as he opened the lid and threw his eyes upon them, a certain expression which flitted across his countenance at the instant, confirmed his nephew's suspicions that these were the very diamonds which Lionel Danvers had some months back purchased at their establishment, and which had subsequently been repaired for Mistress Musidora Sinclair when she visited Lombard Street in company with Lord and Lady Grantham.

"Ye both know that casket? ye recognise these diamonds?" exclaimed the shabbily-dressed old man who had brought them; and he glanced rapidly from the uncle to the nephew, and back again to the uncle as he spoke. "But what connexion have they with Lord Danvers? Again I ask how they reminded you of him? Speak! You must tell me! Everything that relates to Danvers is of consequence to me."

"First let us ask," said the elder Landini, "what is the meaning of all this excitement on your part, and how it is that you are so deeply interested in the affairs of Lord Danvers?"

"Perhaps I have shown too much excitement," said the visitor, now evidently angry with himself at having been hurried away by his feelings: "and perhaps too on account of that very excitement, you will now refuse to answer the questions I have put?"

"Methinks there is in all this some reason and motive for mutual confidences," observed the elder Landini, speaking with the slow deliberation of a man who weighs every word as he utters it. "Come—deal frankly with us, and say wherefore you are so interested in the movements and proceedings of Lord Danvers?"

"Would'st thou know wherefore I have sought Lord Lionel Danvers—wherefore I have inquired about him from time to time?" said the visitor, a cloud gathering and deepening over his features. "But, no!" he suddenly ejaculated: "not to you, the agent—the banker—the friend of Lord Lionel Danvers, must any explanation be given! Let us change the discourse. In a word, tell me—will you purchase my diamonds or not?"

"You speak of Lord Lionel Danvers," answered the elder Landini, not heeding the old man's last questions; "perhaps you are unaware, then, that Lord Lionel is no more, and that Lord Reginald is the present bearer of the title?"

"What! Lionel Danvers dead?" exclaimed the visitor. "When did this take place? It is barely three weeks since I saw a young man who told me much about him, but whom I have not seen since; though he promised great things, and——"

Here he checked himself, for he was musing audibly rather than purposely addressing his observations to the uncle and nephew.

"The intelligence I have just given you is correct," said the elder Landini. "Lord Lionel is no more: he died ten days ago—and his kinsman Reginald, a mere youth of eighteen, has succeeded him."

"How and where did Lionel Danvers die?" demanded the old visitor.

"He was killed by a fall from his horse, when staying with a friend in Hampshire. But now," added the old banker, "I have answered you divers questions; and it is your turn to answer mine. Perhaps however you have no longer any interest in the family of Danvers, now that he whom you have been wont to inquire for is no more?"

"Yes—I am as interested in the movements and proceedings of this youthful Lord Reginald, as ever I was in those of Lord Lionel."

At this answer the two Landinis surveyed him who gave it with an earnest and fixed attention: and then they exchanged a rapid glance with each other, expressive of astonishment and also of a suspicion which had sprung up in their minds.

"Perhaps," said the elder Landini, addressing himself to the visitor, "you think I am too friendly disposed towards every one bearing the name of Danvers to be entrusted with your secrets. But what if I have already to some extent penetrated those secrets?—what if it has struck me that you or your family have in some way been injured by a scion of the house of Danvers, and that you are either seeking for redress or an opportunity of vengeance?—and what if I were solemnly and sacredly to declare that, should you give me your confidence, I will not betray it?"

There was something in the look and also in the tone of the elder Landini, as he thus spoke, which made the visitor observe, "Perhaps *you* then, after all, are not so friendly with the Danvers' family as the world believes?"

"I see that we are drawing nearer and nearer towards each other," remarked the old banker, "and touching upon the threshold of confidence. Stay—I will give you some encouragement to proceed! Has the whisper never reached you that an ancestress of mine suffered some grievous wrong at the hands of a scion of the house of Danvers?"

"Ah! is it possible?" ejaculated the old visitor, with a strange expression of countenance. "No—such a rumour never did reach mine ears! And yet, if what you say be true—or rather if what you have hinted at did really happen—there is indeed something in our respective circumstances which may lead to mutual confidence."

"It is for you to give a proof of your desire for such interchange of confidential revealings," observed the old banker: and he looked his visitor full in the face with an expression which was as much as to imply that the hint he had thrown but relative to an ancestress of his own was indeed the truth.

"Did you ever hear of a tale of Cumberland, in which the name of Dunhaven figured?" asked the visitor.

"Yes—some whispering rumour of that wild legend was wafted to my ears when I was a mere youth," responded the old banker: "but never could I glean the particulars thereof—no, nor even assure myself that it was otherwise than a mere fiction."

"It was a truth—a solemn truth," exclaimed the visitor: "and my name is Dunhaven."

"Then it is vengeance you seek against the family of Danvers?" asked old Landini, literally trembling from head to foot with the violence of his feelings.

"Yes—vengeance!—the deepest, darkest, most implacable vengeance!" rejoined Dunhaven, his eyes flashing back the same malignant look that had shot from those of the elder banker.

"Then, so far from your having aught to dread at my hands, you have every succour to look for. We are friends!"—and Alessandro Landini grasped the hand of the old dweller in Deadman's Place. "Now let us give you a word of explanation," he continued. "So long as Lord Lionel was alive, vainly might you have called time after time at this establishment to seek information concerning him: for he was a man whose keenness I dreaded, and in respect to whom I knew that the utmost precaution, care, and prudence were necessary. But now that the name of Danvers is borne by a stripling—a mere boy of inexperience, and indeed of unsophisticated frankness—a child in the ways of the world, suspecting nothing, but full of confidence—it is different; and I no longer feel the same dread to step beyond the narrow circle of that reserve which I and my nephew had drawn around all our actions in respect to Lionel Danvers."

At this moment the door opened and the female servant entered to announce that Master Manners, the once eminent merchant, requested an immediate interview with Master Landini.

"Ah, this is strange!" muttered the elder banker to himself. "Usher him hither at once," he said to the domestic: then turning towards Dunhaven as soon as he had retired, he observed, "He who is now coming has likewise suffered an irreparable wrong from a scion of that same family whence the woes of your ancestress and mine alike emanated!"

Scarcely were these words spoken, when old Manners entered the room. On perceiving a stranger in company with the banker and his nephew, he stopped short and seemed fearful of intruding: but the elder Landini, hastening forward to great him, exclaimed, "You have come at a singular crisis, Master Manners, and your presence is very far from amiss. But say—have you found your daughter Clara? have you learnt her fate? Know you what has become of her?"

"I know that Lord Lionel Danvers was a vile seducer and a base cowardly villain," responded the ruined merchant, with energetic tones and gesticulations; "and were it not that the snows of age have fallen thickly upon my head, and my limbs are frail and feeble, and my strength wellnigh worn out, I would avenge the wrongs of my lost Clara even upon the kinsman of her seducer—yes, even, I say, upon the youth who now bears the name of Danvers!"

"Ah! then you have learnt that Lord Lionel is no more?" said the banker, inquiringly.

"A week only has elapsed," answered Manners, "since I was delivered by the youthful Reginald from a fearful captivity, to which Lord Lionel had consigned me. It was at his castle in the Isle of Wight whither I was borne by magic means, and where I was fed by the invisible hand of enchantment."

"What mean you?" asked the old banker, who, as well as Dunhaven and Mark, surveyed the ruined merchant with mingled astonishment and curiosity.

"How can I tell my tale to you, Master Landini, if you be the friend of this accursed race of Danvers?"—and old Manners gesticulated vehemently as he spoke. "Still, after all, 'tis but right to do so; and yet——"

"Wherefore have you sought me this night?" asked the banker, as the ruined merchant stopped short abruptly.

"I scarcely know—I cannot altogether account for the feeling which prompted me to bend my steps hither. When liberated from captivity seven days back, I had fortunately gold in my pocket,—gold which was given to me by a royal hand some months ago. I therefore possessed the means not only of sustaining life, but likewise of procuring a steed to save my weary limbs from a sore travel. To be brief, from the Isle of Wight did I take my way to a mansion near Greenwich where I had experienced hospitality and kindness before. I obtained an interview of the fair and excellent lady whose name must ever be mingled with my prayers; and she gave me her sweetest sympathy, as she listened to the recital of the fresh wrongs I had experienced. I told her all that had occurred to me since last I beheld her beauteous face: I told her also that Lord Lionel was no more, and that his kinsman Lord Reginald had succeeded him. Ah! she was moved—aye, even much moved—by everything that I said: she pitied me deeply! She gave me gold too; and, therefore, Master Landini, it is not as a beggar that I have sought you now. But on leaving that lady of whom I have spoken, and on bending my steps to London, methought that as you are so intimately connected with the family of Danvers, it were not amiss to afford you a farther proof of what an accursed race it is. You know, Master Landini, the details connected with the loves of Lionel and Clara—you know also my poor girl's sudden flight and disappearance—you have likewise shown me some sympathy, and have even given me gold at times; and therefore, it was, perhaps, with these circumstances in my mind that I was impelled to visit you once more—to communicate all that has befallen me—all the fresh injuries I have endured from the hated Lionel, since I saw you last!"

"My worthy friend," said the old banker, taking the hand of the ruined merchant, "I felt assured it was something more than a bare coincidence which brought you hither now. This is an evening of mighty importance to all who are at present assembled here: and it must be an evening of fullest and completest revelations. Let us sit down and explain to each other those things which are desirable to be known, and concerning which there need be no farther reserve nor secrecy on the part of any one of us towards the others. For, believe me, the hour of vengeance is not far distant!"

Both Manners and Dunhaven, as well as Mark, gazed with a sort of grim exultation upon the old banker, as he thus spoke; and then they all sat down at the table—the ruined merchant, the dweller at Deadman's Place, the wealthy goldsmith of Lombard Street, and the acknowledged heir to his wealth! Yes, these four sat down together to engage in earnest and solemn discourse—to enter into mutual explanations relative to the wrongs which they cherished—and to deliberate upon schemes of vengeance.

CHAPTER XLVII.

REGINALD DANVERS.

IT was not till midnight that the conference broke up: and at that hour old Manners and Dunhaven took their leave of the Landinis and issued forth into Lombard Street. They continued their way together towards London Bridge, conversing as they went along.

It was a beautiful clear night, and the blended lustre of moon and stars flooded the air with argentine splendour. The Thames shone like quicksilver, as the two old men paused upon the bridge to contemplate the scene. But how different that scene then, from the spectacle which the mighty metropolis affords at the present day to the eye of the observer similarly placed, at a like hour, and when the heavens are bright and cloudless! In those days there was no miraculously crowded assemblage of buildings, covering either bank far as the eye could reach, and from the midst of which a thousand towers and pinnacles, and spires shoot upward in all the varieties of architecture: but at that time of which we are writing, the metropolis, in comparison with its extent and grandeur of these days, was a mere collection of a few middle-sized houses and a most disproportionate number of huts and hovels. And yet it was great and grand to the people of those times and to the dwellers within its precincts!

Old Manners and Dunhaven, we say, had halted upon the bridge in a part where there was an open space between the houses standing upon it; and they gazed for a few minutes in silence upon the river, which, eddying beneath the narrow arches, speedily grew calm again and pursued its way in a tranquil but majestic volume. Soon however were the thoughts of the two old men diverted from the serene loveliness of the night: but still wooed by it to remain there for a short space longer, they began to discourse again—and their conversation at once took up the topic which they had previously been debating. They thus reviewed all that had taken place at Landini's house: they commented upon everything that had been said in respect to the Danvers family;—and they gloated anew over the scheme which old Landini had explained to them as the one he had already initiated some months back, and which he now intended more actively than ever to carry out, in order to involve the fortunes of the house of Danvers in unredeemable ruin.

It was natural that the two old men should linger thus to converse with each other, though at so late an hour. For all their ideas, all their thoughts, all their hopes indeed, were concentrated in one focus: they were animated only by one passion. Having wrongs to avenge, every worldly concern was now put aside to make room for the immensity of this craving for vengeance which filled their souls. It was natural therefore, we repeat, that they should thus pause and review in all its details the deliberations which had just taken place in Lombard Street.

For nearly half-an-hour did they remain talking upon the bridge, ere they thought of moving onward. Their path lay in the same direction for a little while yet; inasmuch as old Manners had stabled his horse and therefore meant to take up his quarters at a tavern in Southwark. They accordingly walked on together, until they reached the foot of the bridge, where they stopped to exchange farewells: for this was the point where old Dunhaven had to turn off to gain the Sanctuary of Deadman's Place.

But still they had a few parting words to say relative to the already well-conned topic that was uppermost in their thoughts: and so they lingered for a minute or two.

"Hush!" said Dunhaven suddenly: "here is some one approaching over the bridge!"

Old Manners accordingly stopped short in the middle of the somewhat vehement remarks he was making at the instant, and gazed in the direction of the bridge. Thence a courtly-looking gallant was saunteringly approaching. Even while he was yet at a distance, Manners and Dunhaven could see in the powerful moonlight that he was elegantly dressed: for a tall sable plume waved gracefully above his cap, and the diamond clasp in which it was fixed reflected the moonbeams in jets of fire. The gems upon the hilt of his rapier also gleamed brightly, as did the other ornaments that decorated his person. As he drew nearer still, they could observe that he was tall, slender, and exquisitely formed; and when still nearer, they perceived that he was quite a young man.

"Just heaven!" suddenly whispered old Manners, "'tis Reginald Danvers!"

"Ah! say you so?" muttered Dunhaven with a quick start: then in a low hissing whisper, he added, "Perhaps the hour of vengeance has already come? Who can tell?—it may be for us to wreak it, and not for the Landinis?"

"The trap-door of which you spoke ere now?" hurriedly suggested Manners.

"Aye—it were well to try if Reginald bears a charmed life as his kinsman did:"—and old Dunhaven's eyes twinkled with basilisk-like malignity.

"Let us trust to circumstances," quickly rejoined Manners, "and in the meantime seem to be discoursing unconcernedly."

This little colloquy took place with exceeding rapidity: indeed it was an exchange of words so rapid that half their meaning was conveyed as well by the looks of the speakers as by the sentences so jerkingly and whisperingly spoken. They now affected to be bidding each other farewell, and did not seem to take any notice of Reginald Danvers' approach.

"Good citizens," said the young nobleman, as he drew near, "can you tell me where I may obtain a respectable lodgement for this night—or rather the remainder of it——What? Master Manners!" he ejaculated, with all the appearance of exceeding amazement: "is it indeed you whom I thus meet again and at such an hour?"

"Yes, my lord—it is I, your humble and dutiful servant," answered the old merchant, with a low bow and assuming a most respectful demeanour. "Urgent business has kept me and my friend here out thus late; and we were at the moment bidding each other farewell——"

"And I also am abroad late, as you perceive," said the youthful noble, laughing. "To confess the truth, I have spent the evening with some gay gallants; and when I refused to sit any longer over the wine-flask, I could not induce one of them, either for courtesy or for friendship, to conduct me to the hostelry where I am lodging. It was an oversight not to order my grooms to come and fetch me at a given hour: but I little foresaw that my friends would leave me thus to find my way about this maze of London as best I might."

"And your wandering steps, my lord, brought you to the bridge?" said Manners interrogatively.

"It was even so," answered Reginald, with every appearance of youthful ingenuousness and candour: then, as he took off his plumed cap and pushed aside the raven locks that had intruded somewhat over the high and noble forehead above which they were parted, he said with an accent of pettishness, "How foolish of me to yield thus to the dissipation of London! But it shall be for the last time. My head aches, and I would that there were some hostelry or tavern near where I might retire to rest."

"Your lordship is therefore inexperienced and strange in London?" said Dunhaven, now addressing the young nobleman for the first time.

"Yes—and hence this uncertain wandering of mine," answered Reginald, as he carelessly tossed his cap again upon his head. "I know not what led me to cross the bridge, unless it were that the fresh breeze of the river fanned my heated cheeks and gave them a refreshing coolness."

As he was thus speaking, Dunhaven and Manners exchanged glances fraught with significancy, but so rapid that it appeared scarcely possible for Danvers to notice them. But there was a world of meaning in those glances: they seemed to say, "Here is this artless, ingenuous, and inexperienced youth in our hands—accident has thrown him into our power—the present bearer of the hated name of Danvers is at our mercy! Let us strike the blow at once!"

"What could be done for his lordship?" asked old Manners, as if compassionating the awkward predicament in which the youth was placed.

"It were vain to expect that any hostelry will open its door to a stranger at this time of night," said Dunhaven, in response to the ruined merchant's question.

"My lord," said Manners, addressing Reginald in a serious tone, "although I have little reason to feel sympathy for any one of your race or name, yet am I friendly disposed towards you now. I will even admit that when we parted a week back in the Isle of Wight, my conduct was churlish and ungrateful towards your lordship——"

"Say not another word upon the point, Master Manners!" interrupted Reginald, taking the old man's hand and pressing it with every appearance of the most frank-hearted cordiality. "But," he exclaimed, as if suddenly recollecting something, "your friend here is not acquainted with all those circumstances?"

"Assuredly not, my lord," old Manners hastened to reply: and thus he who only a few months back would have scorned to utter a falsehood, and who had passed through a long life in truthfulness and in sincerity, now unhesitatingly and unblushingly proffered a lie in response to Reginald's question—so completely were all his better feelings absorbed in the hope of wreaking that vengeance which he believed to be at hand.

"My lord," said Dunhaven, again breaking silence, "my house is close by—in this immediate neighbourhood indeed—and though somewhat dark and gloomily situate, is nevertheless such as an honest man need not blush to acknowledge as his own. It appears that your lordship is well acquainted with Master Manners: and he will at once testify to the truth of my assertion."

"Of a surety," rejoined the old merchant, "the house is of the highest respectability."

"Do you mean, worthy citizen," asked Reginald, addressing himself to Dunhaven, "that you are kind enough to offer me a lodging for the night?"

"I do—if your lordship will accept it."

"Aye—that will I right cheerfully!" exclaimed Danvers. "And now lead on: for I am almost dropping with fatigue."

Old Dunhaven passed on in front, Manners and Reginald following close behind. The ruined merchant, fancying that he was playing his part with wonderful astuteness and cunning, kept Reginald in conversation, so that he might not observe too closely the sombre aspect and repulsive features of Deadman's Place and thus take the alarm as the little party turned into the sanctuary. And the youthful noble seemed completely to fall into the snare, as he walked with a kind of graceful indolence by the side of old Manners, and chatted with an artless gaiety, through the midst of which there ran a certain languor, thus appearing to bear out his assertion that he was very much wearied. In a few minutes they reached the house overhanging the river, and passing down the stable-yard were at once admitted by old Dunhaven, who had the door-key about his person. Having escorted his two guests—for Manners, be it observed, had never in his life been there before—into the sordid-looking and mean little apartment, Dunhaven lighted a lamp, and bustled about to produce a flask of wine, so as to divert Reginald's attention as much as possible from the repulsive aspect of the place.

But the youthful noble, leaning against the wall, yawned and rubbed his eyelids as if overcome by sleepiness, and therefore too tired and drowsy to pay particular attention to his host's quarters.

"One goblet of wine, my lord," said Dunhaven, as he presented a brimming cup to the young nobleman.

"Well, just one draught, that I may pledge thee in gratitude for the rites of hospitality which thou art affording me: and then I pray thee that I may be conducted to some place where I can stretch my limbs, no matter whether upon mattrass or straw."

Having thus spoken, Reginald drank a portion of the wine which Dunhaven proffered; and the latter taking up the lamp, said, "Now, my lord, I will conduct you to a chamber which in itself is comfortable enough, and must not be forejudged by its approaches: for I warn your lordship that you will have to pass through an entrance-way but little inviting."

"What matters it, so long as the accommodations to which your entrance-way leads, be good?" asked Reginald, in a still more languid voice and with a more sleepy look than before. "Proceed, I pray thee, good citizen."

Dunhaven accordingly went first, Reginald Danvers following close behind him.

"I will bring this flask and the goblet," exclaimed old Manners, "in case his lordship should be athirst during the night:"—and with this pretext for accompanying the others, he brought up the rear.

They traversed the narrow passage, and entered the room with which it communicated. As before described, it had no window, was totally denuded of furniture, and its walls were green and mildewed with the damp. Old Manners halted upon the threshold: for from what Dunhaven had said at the Landinis' house, he was already aware of the existence of the trapdoor and the mode of its operation. He accordingly remained in the doorway to be safe from danger, and also to gloat his eyes with the spectacle of vengeance which he believed about to be consummated. Nor had he, any more than Dunhaven, the slightest sentiment of pity for that beautiful youth—no, nor the faintest remorse for the crime which was now meditated!

Immediately on entering the room, Dunhaven advanced in such a way that as Reginald followed him, the latter was just in the middle of the treacherous trap-door, when Dunhaven exclaimed, "Halt there a moment, my lord!"

Instinctively as it appeared, Reginald did stop short—as a stranger under such circumstances might be supposed to do at the bidding of a host who was conducting him. Then, quick as lightning, Dunhaven wheeled round—a couple of steps brought him close up to the wall—and swift as the eye can wink, he pressed the iron knob let into the masonry.

The hidden mechanism failed not to do its work—the effect was instantaneous—and the trap-door, tilting vertically half upward and half downward on its axle, suddenly made a frightful chasm in the floor. But

what words can depict the consternation and amazement that all in a moment seized upon Manners and Dunhaven, when instead of being precipitated into the gulf below, the youth with a light spring gained the solid
part of the flooring at the very instant that he felt the trap-door falling
beneath his feet!

It was done so quickly that the eye could not follow the movement:
it was done too with scarcely an effort—certainly with no struggle, much
less with any desperate exertion. All in a moment his feigned sleepiness
and languor had been cast off: all in a moment, too, his looks changed
from the ingenuousness and confidence of an unsuspecting youth, into
the fierce indignation mingled with haughty scorn of a true Danvers.

Bitter too, and mocking, was the laugh which broke from his lips, as
he bent his brilliant eyes first upon Dunhaven, then upon Manners—so
that his looks seemed to wither them up with a blighting, blasting, scorching effect. There was the power of annihilation in those looks!

"Wretched old dotards—vile grovelling fools!" he exclaimed, in a
voice that was rather sardonically taunting than fiercely irate: "thought
ye thus to accomplish your black treachery? But it is time that I should rid
myself of my enemies. I sought to let ye live—I was willing to spare ye—I
wanted not the lives of such drivelling imbeciles as ye. But ye would not let
me be merciful! Ye thought the farce ye were playing was good: but mine
was better still—for while ye aimed but at outwitting *one*, I was outwitting *two!* Miserable dotards, all your conversation on the bridge was heard
by me. Accident willed that I should be passing that way at the moment
when ye loitered to review the schemes propounded at Landini's. Yes—I
heard it all, and chuckled inwardly to think how ye would be baffled. But
enough of words! It is deeds now that are required—and all enemies must
disappear from my path!"

So terrible grew the looks of Reginald Danvers as he gave utterance
to the last syllables of his speech—such fires flashed from his eyes—such
lightnings played around his brows—such satanic malice wreathed his red
lips—and such a Lucifer-like vengeance seemed to inspire his whole dilating form—that the two wretched old men simultaneously fell upon their
knees, while the lamp dropped from Dunhaven's hand and was instantaneously extinguished.

The awful work that was then done, took not long to do: but it was
horrible—most horrible—in that profound and pitchy darkness! No cry
betrayed the anguish, terror, and despair of the two old men, as they felt
themselves in the power of the fiend-like Danvers: a spell was upon their
lips during the few brief moments which followed the extinction of the
lamp ere they themselves were plunged into a darkness deeper still—the

darkness of death! For there was first one heavy plunge in the deep water—another immediately followed: then the trap-door fell into its place
again—and all was over!

A few moments afterwards, Reginald Danvers passed out of the house
with a scornful smile of malignant triumph upon his countenance, which
thus beamed with a wild and fearful beauty, as emerging from Deadman's
Place he again passed into the pure effulgence of the moonlight.

CHAPTER XLVIII.

THE RETURN.

A YEAR had elapsed since the occurrences last mentioned; and it was now
the close of the month of August, 1517. One evening, within about an
hour of sunset, old Sir Lewis Sinclair, supported between Dr. Bertram
and Percy Rivers, descended the sloping path leading from the eminence
on which his mansion stood down to the shore immediately facing the
Hampshire coast. The worthy knight was feeble in limbs, broken in health
and getting childish in intellect. His temper had become nervous and ir-
ritable, the results of habitual intemperance: but of Dr. Bertram he ever
stood in awe, and allowed that individual to domineer over him without
daring to exhibit the slightest will of his own.

Oftentimes, during the past year, had Percy Rivers endeavoured to
rescue his uncle from the evil companionship of the physician: but all the
measures he had taken to that effect, had failed. The doctor felt himself
in too comfortable a position at Sinclair House to abandon his quarters;
and thus so far as he was concerned, neither threats nor offers of bribery
on the part of Rivers could induce him to depart elsewhere. As for the
old knight himself, if ever Percy managed to obtain a few minutes' private interview with him and endeavoured to persuade him to get rid of
Dr. Bertram, Sir Lewis would fly into a rage with his nephew—bid him
mind his own business—or else accuse him of entertaining interested motives by desiring to cause a breach between himself and the doctor. Several
times had Percy written to Musidora, urgently representing the necessity
of her return home to take care of her father: but the young lady's replies
were always of a character to postpone indefinitely the period of her visit
to Grantham Villa. She however evinced by the tenor of her letters that
she felt deeply on behalf of her parent; and though still remaining absent
from home, she was earnest in her exhortations that Percy would visit
Sinclair House as frequently as he could and see that the old knight was
well treated and tenderly cared for.

Thus the year had passed; and now at length the long absent daughter was expected home again. She had written alike to her father and to Percy Rivers, appointing the time when she should once more set foot in the Isle of Wight; and it was to meet her on her landing that Sir Lewis was at present being conducted to the shore by the doctor and his nephew, as above described.

We have already said that it was within an hour of sunset on an autumn evening, that the knight was thus escorted by Percy Rivers and his boon companion to the beach. The day had been sultry: but the evening was fresh and beautiful. A gentle breeze swept over the sea, slightly ruffling its surface, and filling the sail of the ferry-boat which was already in sight. Sir Lewis and his two companions sat down upon the beach, watching the little vessel that was approaching; and in the conversation that took place Percy Rivers could not help observing that Dr. Bertram now treated him with a respect and friendliness as fawning and sycophantic as his demeanour was wont to be rude, rough, and repulsive. The truth was that the return of Musidora had filled the doctor with serious misgivings as to the stability of his own position at Sinclair House; and he therefore deemed it politic and prudent to conciliate Percy Rivers as much as possible, in the hope that the young Governor would not make to Musidora any communications hostile to his interests. Percy full well understood the motives which actuated Dr. Bertram in this change of tone and manner towards him: but instead of being softened thereby, he only experienced a deeper loathing and contempt for the individual who could thus enact the bully at one time and the parasite at another. He accordingly treated the physician with the most chilling reserve; and the consequence was that the nearer the vessel approached, the more uneasy did Bertram grow in his mind.

At length the ferry-boat touched the strand; and Musidora from the deck waved her handkerchief to those who were expecting her. The planks, to facilitate her landing, were put out; and in a few minutes she was clasped in her father's arms. Long and fervent was the embrace in which the young lady retained her sire: she wept too, as she lavished upon him the tenderest caresses;—and by the endearing words she uttered, as well as by her entire manner towards her father, was it evident that she strove to make up in her present kindness for that prolonged absence from her home which she felt was too unjustifiable not to need every atonement she could offer. On his side, the old man cried with childish delight at welcoming his daughter again to the little islet of her birth; and though his nature was exceedingly selfish, as we have hinted at the commencement of our tale, yet his increasing infirmities, his enfeebled intellect, and his long separation from his only child, all combined to make him feel that her presence was necessary to soothe and minister unto the wants of his old age.

When the first ebullitions of feeling attendant upon this meeting on the part of the father and daughter were over, Musidora gave her hand to Percy Rivers with a more affectionate cordiality than for years past she had ever demonstrated towards him; and with a look full of grateful meaning she thanked him for all his kind endeavours to promote her sire's happiness during her absence. She then turned towards Dr. Bertram; and to the surprise of Percy Rivers, as well as to the mingled joy and triumph of the physician, addressed him in terms of affable friendliness. But then Musidora knew that the doctor was too well acquainted with certain secrets regarding her, to render it safe or prudent to convert him into an enemy.

Musidora was attended by the faithful Annetta, and also by one of Lord Grantham's pages. The grooms in charge of the horses which had borne the travelling party from Greenwich to Portsmouth, had not of course crossed in the ferry-boat,—their services being no longer required when once the sea-coast of Hampshire was reached. With regard to Musidora, slight was the change that had taken place in her appearance during the past year. Her countenance, always of marble paleness, might possibly be still a trifle paler—that is to say, of a less animated fairness than heretofore; and instead of that gleam of a half-vanishing smile upon her lips, there was a settled expression of melancholy. But it would have required a very close observer indeed to mark these trivial changes: yet that close observer was there present, in the person of her cousin Rivers.

But if Sir Lewis Sinclair perceived not the slightest alteration in his daughter's appearance, she on the other hand was shocked and afflicted at the change which she observed in him. As the party ascended from the beach towards Sinclair House,—the old man being now supported by Musidora's arm,—Percy Rivers noticed that the gaze of the young lady was frequently fixed upon her sire's countenance, and that a certain slight quivering of the lips, a half-suppressed sigh, and other little symptoms of uneasiness, showed how much she felt at marking that great and signal change. Moreover, these symptoms of feeling on her side, though outwardly so slight, were in reality great and important when it is considered how passionless her demeanour was wont to be, and how little of what was passing in the depths of her soul could ever be read on her inscrutable countenance.

Then, too, as Percy Rivers, when unperceived by his fair cousin, gazed upon her as she supported her father's tottering steps up the pathway to the house—and as he contemplated those magnificent features and that superb figure, all the beauty and youthful freshness of which were still so brilliant and striking,—he could not help wondering within himself wherefore she had remained so long absent from home, and what extraordinary attractions Grantham Villa could have presented for one who by intellect and nature was so elevated above the frivolities, the vanities, and the hollow enjoyments of aristocratic life!

The sun was setting in the western horizon, descending to its couch amidst curtains of orange and purple, and crimson, and gold,—flinging its parting light in rich effulgence upon the thick woodlands, and spreading a ruddy glow over the gently rippling sea,—when Musidora again entered the home of her birth. The servants of the household were all thronging in the hall to proffer a respectful welcome to their young mistress: but they were far more numerous than when she had left Sinclair House sixteen long months back—and there were many stranger-faces amongst them; for in consequence of his restoration to the Rangership and increased revenues, Sir Lewis had placed his establishment on its former footing of splendour. To the old servants of the mansion Musidora spoke with the most cordial fondness; to the new ones she returned affable acknowledgments for the greetings with which they welcomed her. The former were overjoyed at the return of their well-beloved young lady: the latter were much pleased with the demeanour of their mistress.

On conducting her father into the parlour where the evening meal was already spread, Musidora threw herself upon a sofa; and all the iciness of her nature dissolving for a moment beneath the influence of ineffable emotions, she exclaimed with a sudden paroxysm of fervour, "Thank heaven, I am once more at home!"

"Yes, dear 'Dora," cried her father, whimperingly, "and you shall not leave me again. There have been times when I have missed you very much—much more than I expected I should when you left me. But you have come back, my dear girl—and——and——Give me a cup of wine, Bertram!"

"Wait, dear father, till you have partaken of some solid food first," said Musidora: and with a quick but commanding gesture she motioned the too willing Bertram to desist from pouring out the wine from the flask which he had suddenly snatched up the instant the words fell from the old knight's lips. "Dr. Bertram, I am afraid, has been too indulgent and too kind to you," continued Musidora: "but now that I am come back, I shall alter all that. Indeed, my dear father, you must henceforth listen to me. I am going to be your nurse, and shall take you entirely under my charge. You do not look well; and I must see if I cannot have you restored to your wonted health."

Musidora perceived that the countenance of Percy Rivers brightened up at this display of firmness on her part. On the other hand, Dr. Bertram's looks had suddenly grown dark and gloomy at that imperious gesture on the part of Musidora: but they somewhat cleared up again as she went on to speak in a kind of propitiatory tone of his indulgence to her father. As for the old knight himself, he gave vent to a few pettish remonstrances against being deprived of the liquor which he craved: but finding that even his friend Bertram yielded to Musidora's authority, he himself could not do otherwise than submit.

They then all sat down to supper; and during the meal Musidora took good care that her father should not fall into any excess with regard to wine. She allowed him a sufficiency to cheer his spirits and put him in good humour, but resolutely refused to suffer his goblet to be refilled when once the limit of moderation was reached. Yet she pursued this course with so much affectionate tenderness, saying so many kind things, and exercising her influence rather through the medium of gentle entreaty than the positive assumption of authority, that the old knight yielded to her wishes with a better grace than Percy Rivers himself had anticipated. The result of this supper was that the first step was taken by Musidora towards reclaiming her father from the sottish habits into which he had fallen during her long absence from home: while Dr. Bertram was made to understand that his authority was no longer dominant at Sinclair House.

When Percy Rivers took his leave that evening, he said in a whisper to Musidora, "You have begun well, fair cousin. Pray continue in the same manner, and my uncle's health may yet be restored. But methinks that so long as a certain person is beneath this roof, there will ever be the danger of a relapse."

"Fear nothing on that head," replied Musidora, with firmness in her accents, though speaking also in a whisper. "It would not be politic to do anything that should give too rude a shock to my father's feelings; and therefore I shall not immediately separate him from his friend: but in less than a fortnight, depend upon my assurance, Percy, that this Dr. Bertram will no longer be an inmate of Sinclair House."

And the promise which Musidora thus made her cousin was fulfilled. During the first two weeks which followed her return home, she gradually weaned her father as much as possible from the pleasures of the table. In the same affectionate manner which she had adopted on the first evening of her arrival, did she succeed in regulating the quantity of his potations; and as the worthy knight was of a temper by no means easy to drive contrary to his inclinations, but on the other hand facile to lead in silken strings, Musidora's management progressed most favourably. Thus, even within the lapse of a couple of weeks, a marked improvement took place in her sire's health, spirits, and intellect. By rendering the companionship of Dr. Bertram less necessary to him, and as it were taking the physician's place in keeping the old man's mind continuously amused, Musidora enabled him to dispense more and more with that individual's presence. She made him rise early in the morning and ride forth with her alone: she also took him out to walk with her in the orchard and the forest: she assisted him in the little business details of his office as Ranger of the Woodlands; and in the evening she sat with him in the garden, conversing with a gaiety most unusual on her part, and which indeed was assumed for the purpose of cheering the enfeebled mind of her parent and enabling him to dispense with artificial stimulants. In a word, the whole tenor of her conduct was a devotedness evidently based on the resolution to atone as much as possible for sixteen months' neglect of her father, and to repair to the extent of her power the moral and physical injuries he had sustained during her absence.

Yet while pursuing this course, she treated Dr. Bertram with no coldness, much less with open hostility—so that while he day by day beheld his authority in the household slipping out of his grasp, he had no defined and positive ground for complaint. Though Musidora regulated her father's application to the wine-flask according to her own sense of propriety in that respect, she attempted not the slightest interference with the doctor's predilection for the same exhilarating beverage; and even while gradually alienating the physician from the worthy knight's society, she permitted him to use the house just as if it were his own. Thus, by judicious management, by consummate prudence, and by a true womanly tact, Musidora performed her duty to her father without any unfriendly treatment in respect to Dr. Bertram.

But when a fortnight had passed, the young lady one morning sought an opportunity of entering into certain explanations with the physician. Accordingly, while her father was engaged inspecting his stables and issuing orders to his huntsmen and grooms, Musidora desired Dr. Bertram to accompany her into the garden; and leading him to a shady avenue where they could not be observed from the house, she said in her wonted quiet manner, and with the even flow of her harmonious voice, "The time is come when I must speak to you, Dr. Bertram, upon a subject of some little importance."

"Fair lady," replied the physician, who was walking beside her, cap in hand, "I am your most obedient servant, and ready to obey you to the extent of my power."

"I know and appreciate the friendly feeling you entertain towards my father," replied Musidora: and if Dr. Bertram had been a very keen observer, he would have noticed a slight contemptuous wreathing of the young lady's lips as she gave utterance to these words; for her heart at the time loathed the little piece of duplicity which policy and prudence compelled her to enact. "I am also aware," she continued, "that the Earl of Grantham, when he visited Sinclair House a year ago, had a long and serious conversation with you, during which certain topics of importance were discussed and the strictest secrecy concerning them was enjoined,— the penalty being nothing short of that due to high treason, and the reward being the promise of an annual pension. Now, Dr. Bertram, how stands your feeling upon those points at the present time?"

"In the same way that I assured his lordship of my readiness to obey his wishes in all respects," replied the physician, "am I now equally prepared to submit to your commands."

"You speak well and wisely, Dr. Bertram," rejoined Musidora; "and in a style best calculated to advance your own interests. I presume that so long as you are well provided with the means of ministering to all your wants, it is indifferent to you where your abode is fixed?"—and as she thus spoke, she bent upon him the full power of her magnificent dark eyes, as if the eloquence of her looks should even more forcibly than her words suggest the answer that was awaited from his lips.

"Fair lady," he replied, at once comprehending the intimation he was about to receive, "if my presence at Sinclair House be in any way distasteful, I am not the man to persist in remaining there—especially," he added with promptitude, "as there is so much kind promise in your words seeming to assure me that my future interests are to be cared for according to the understanding settled between me and the Earl of Grantham."

"It is my object to preserve that understanding," said Musidora: then producing a heavy purse from beneath the folds of her garments, she handed it to the physician, observing, "Behold your pension for one year—at the expiration of which time, if you present yourself at Grantham Villa near Greenwich, you will receive a similar sum from the hands of the Earl. Thenceforth at the close of each successive year—reckoning from August to August—may you call at the villa with the certitude of receiving a like amount so long as the Earl and Countess of Grantham, or either of them, remain alive. When they die—as in the common course of nature may be expected ere your time or mine may come—it will rest with me to make some other arrangement for the payment of your pension. But understand me well, Master Welford—for you see I know your name—should aught relative to the past ever escape your lips, not merely will your annual pension cease, but you will draw down upon your head the vengeance of one who has power to punish."

"The warning is unnecessary," rejoined the physician, "though all words are sweet that come from your lips. But rest assured that I prefer the double enjoyment of receiving the annual pension and keeping my head upon my shoulders to the dismal alternative of losing the former and having the latter paraded most ignobly on the summit of Temple Bar."

"And now one word more," said Musidora. "I do not wish my father to know that it is in consequence of any interference on my part that you leave Sinclair House. You will therefore when bidding him farewell this day, suffer him to believe that you are acting in accordance with your own spontaneous will, and that urgent business necessitates your speedy departure hence."

"I comprehend you, fair lady," replied the physician: "and herein shall you also be obeyed faithfully and truly, as in every other respect. It will not be difficult for a man of ready wit, such as I flatter myself to be, to invent feasible causes for my abrupt leave-taking—such, for example, as the sudden death of a relative in some distant part, and the consequent inheritance of a large estate."

"Make what excuse you will, Dr. Bertram," rejoined Musidora: "only let it be done today."

"Within the hour, fair lady," exclaimed the physician. "I observed that the ferry-boat from Hampshire touched the shore ere now; and I can easily pretend that it bore a messenger for me!"

"Good!" said Musidora: and with a slight bow, she intimated that there was no farther need of his remaining in her presence.

According to the arrangement just settled, Dr. Bertram communicated, within the hour, to Sir Lewis Sinclair, the sudden necessity for his departure. The knight was grieved: for though having been lately led by his daughter's ministrations to dispense with much of Bertram's companionship, he still liked the man too much not to sorrow at separating from him. But he was tranquillized by the assurance that so soon as the learned physician had settled his affairs, he would come back to make a long sojourn at Sinclair House.

That afternoon Musidora and her father sat down to dinner without the doctor; and when Percy Rivers galloped across from Carisbrook in the evening, he was infinitely delighted to learn that the physician was no longer an inmate of his uncle's mansion. From this day forth the improvement in the worthy knight's health, spirits, and intellect went on increasing most satisfactorily, and at the expiration of five or six months his mind was restored to its wonted tone, while his frame had recovered as much vigour as at his age it could be expected to develop.

CHAPTER XLIX.

A YEAR had passed since Musidora's return; and it was once more the month of August. One delicious evening, too, of that autumnal season was it that the young lady was walking with her cousin and her father in the orchard attached to the mansion. The knight had been expatiating at great length upon the complete renovation of his health, and congratulating himself upon having adopted habits of temperance with respect to the wine-flask: he had likewise been reciting the many improvements which during the past twelve months he had introduced into the management of the forest-lands in the Isle of Wight;—and altogether he was in the best possible spirits, laughing and talking with the most rational cheerfulness and gaiety.

"Well, my dear 'Dora," he observed at the end of his long speech, "I must freely confess that much of all this whereof I am vaunting, is to be attributed to you. Indeed, since you returned home to me, I have felt happier than perhaps I ever did before in all my life. But still there is one subject which at times gives me a little uneasiness—and this is that you are not settled in the world as you ought to be."

"My dear father," said Musidora, with the least perceptible accent of excitement, "this is a topic which you and I can best discuss alone."

"I am not so sure of that," exclaimed Sir Lewis, with a sly glance towards Percy Rivers, who, somewhat suspecting the old knight's drift, became confused in his looks. "It is my opinion that this is the very time and opportunity to discourse upon the matter. Here you are, three-and-twenty years of age, and not married yet——"

"My dear father," interrupted Musidora, in a peremptory tone, "it is my desire that we should talk on something else."

"Nay, my dear child," persisted Sir Lewis, taking her arm as if to prevent her escaping from him, "you surely will humour your old father by allowing him to give utterance to his thoughts, and in his own way? There was a time, 'Dora—and it was not very long ago either—when I did not care so much about you as I have done lately: but ever since your return home, I have felt that you are dearer to me than I was wont to suspect. You must not be angry with me, therefore, if your welfare is uppermost in my mind."

"You have told me, my dear father," said Musidora, apparently emotionless and passionless as she habitually was, "that you love me better than you used to do. It is because I have become more necessary to you; and therefore I beg that you will suggest nothing which would have the effect of separating me from you."

"No, no—I would not do that!" cried Sir Lewis: "depend upon it, I would not do that! But now that we are all three walking pleasantly together, and talking in a confidential manner——though, by the bye, you, nephew, are not giving utterance to a word——nevertheless, as you are one of the family, and as what I am about to propose regards yourself——"

"My dear uncle," interrupted Percy, bewildered and confused at the turn the discourse was taking, "you really ought to listen to my cousin's entreaty and talk upon some other topic. For example, you were proposing just now to have a new road cut through the forest——"

"Never mind the forest-roads for the present, nephew," interrupted Sir Lewis, pertinaciously adhering to the subject which had risen uppermost in his mind. "Musidora's welfare is of much greater consequence to me than a stupid road through a forest; and when I reflect that in the ordinary course of nature I cannot have many years to live, it is natural enough I should wish to see her comfortably settled. Upon this subject I have been thinking for some time past; and I consider it to be a burning shame that a young lady of her good looks—for it is no flattery to tell her that she is a very fine handsome young woman——"

"Really, my dear father, I must beg and beseech that you will at once abandon this topic!"—and Musidora spoke with a firmness that was alike imperious and peremptory.

"Then, daughter, I shall do no such thing," exclaimed Sir Lewis, half angrily and half jocularly. "It is your duty to listen when your father confidently believes he is speaking for your good. Percy, do not lag behind. Here, give me your arm. There! that's right! It is in this manner, between you both, that I wish to pass the remainder of my existence. And now perhaps, 'Dora and Percy, you understand what I mean?"

Neither Musidora nor Rivers made any observation. Perhaps it was, with regard to the former, that she knew not what to say; and she accordingly walked on by her father's side, supporting his arm, with her looks bent downward, but with no betrayal of any inward feeling upon her countenance. In respect to Percy Rivers it was not altogether confusion now that sent the blood mantling up to his cheeks: he possibly entertained a revival of that hope which he had long thought dead within him.

"When I bethink me," resumed Sir Lewis, "it was the general opinion that you two, when boy and girl together, were destined for each other; and I can't imagine how it was that everybody's expectation was disappointed. Now in respect to you, Percy, having hitherto remained unmarried, the inference is that you have never met anybody whom you have considered worthy of becoming your partner for life. It is time that you *did* marry: and whom could you better wed than your cousin whom you have known from her infancy?"

"Enough, father!" suddenly exclaimed Musidora, with a strange expression of countenance and an unearthly flashing forth of fires from her unfathomable eyes. "It is indelicate for you to talk in this manner!"

"Nay, daughter," cried the knight, "I pray thee to curb this pretty indignation of thine. It makes thee look handsomer, no doubt: but thou hast not need of such sudden display of emotion to enhance thy beauty. My mind is set upon the point; and let me tell thee," added Sir Lewis, his voice and look suddenly becoming full of endearment, "that it would be the happiest moment of my life to behold thee the bride of Percy Rivers. Then might I take up my residence with ye both at Carisbrook; and the remainder of my existence would pass on without a care. Now, Percy, you shall answer me first. Will you make your old uncle happy? do you love him enough for this? But since I have broken the ice, I had better leave you together to settle the matter between you."

And having given utterance to these last words with uncommon haste, Sir Lewis Sinclair abruptly turned away and hurried off towards the mansion at a very quick pace. Indeed the movement was altogether so sudden on his part, that Musidora and Percy were left thus alone together ere they even had an instant's leisure to anticipate the old man's intention.

A profound silence existed on both sides; and their position was most awkward and embarrassing. But Musidora was the first to make up her mind to any settled course; and in a low deep voice, which for her was indicative of extraordinary emotion, she said, "Percy, had not my father gone to such a length, and had he contented himself with mere hints or allusions, I should not have appeared to notice the subject when we were alone together. But as his observations have been so pointed and his desire has been so definitely expressed, it is impossible for you and me to avoid all mention of the topic."

"And is it a painful one for you to speak of, Musidora?" asked Percy in tremulous accents.

"Yes—painful," she responded, still in that same low deep voice as before, "because I am unable to obey my father's wishes, even if you yourself——"

"Oh! do not raise the slightest doubt as to the state of my feelings towards you!" cried Rivers, with the enthusiasm of a love that would never die though hope itself should perish. "Those feelings are ever the same! And there was a moment, Musidora, while your father was ere now speaking, when the thought thrilled through me that it was possible you yourself might now——But no!" he suddenly ejaculated, with a voice of despair, as he marked the iciness of manner which his cousin had all in a moment put on again after it had appeared to be thawing somewhat. "Pardon me, then, Musidora, if I did venture thus to hope!——pardon me also if I have alluded to that love of mine which now is devoid of hope once more. Not for worlds should I have touched upon the forbidden topic, had not my uncle thus forced it upon us! But hear me declare, Musidora, that if I remain unmarried it is for your sake—if I have never even thought of marrying another, it is still for your sake—and if I invoke Heaven to witness my solemn vow that I never, never will marry any other——"

"Hold, Percy! swear not thus rashly!" exclaimed Musidora, with a sudden paroxysm of excitement; and again did a wild unearthly lustre shine in her deep dark eyes as she turned them full upon her cousin. "Record no vow of that kind for my sake—because——because I shall never marry."

And as Musidora spoke these last words, her voice grew suddenly cold, as if it were borne upon breath chill as the breeze which sweeps over the glaciers of the north.

"Oh! there is something dreadful to hear you speak thus, and in such a tone!" cried Percy, gazing upon her with mingled affliction and surprise. "Wherefore should you never marry? Heaven knows it is not on my account that I ask this question? for if you loved another, and it ensured your happiness to espouse him, I should be the first to persuade you to the alliance. No, no, Musidora," he added, with passionate vehemence, "love has not made me altogether selfish: but the hopelessness of that love has taught me to sympathize with others whose hearts cherish an affection. Wherefore should you declare that you will never marry—you so young, so bright, so beautiful? Oh, it is unnatural to hear you talk thus! Is your heart an icy chaos over which the spirit of love can never move with power to quicken its best and holiest feelings? Believe me, it is terrible—Oh, 'tis terrible indeed, to hear one so young and loveable as you declare that you cannot love!"

"I did not say so—no, I did not say so!" exclaimed Musidora, thrown off her guard by the impassioned accents and vehement words of her cousin; and her whole frame trembled visibly with a cold shudder.

"But you said you would never marry—and is not that the same thing?" he immediately demanded. "Oh! why did you speak thus? Heavens! is it possible, Musidora, that anything has ever happened to you to render that idea a settled resolve in your heart?"

"Percy," said Musidora, having regained all her wonted presence of mind, and speaking with her habitual iciness of look and passionless continuity of tone, "this conversation must not be prolonged. Yet for my own sake I must declare that if aught that I have said has excited in your mind a suspicion—even the faintest—injurious to the purity of my character or the innocence of my soul, then banish that suspicion from your mind as most dishonouring to your cousin!"

"Musidora," said Percy, alike humiliated and afflicted by his fair relative's words, "I believe you—heaven knows that I believe you! But yet it is strange to hear you proclaim so firmly and so resolutely that you will never marry. However, we will not continue this painful topic. At the same time, your father will presently demand of me what has passed between us. How am I to answer him?"

"My father will put a similar question to me," rejoined Musidora: "and I shall tell him that in his zeal for my welfare, he was led into an indiscretion bordering upon indelicacy. I shall tell him also that I will not marry where I cannot give my heart, and that much as I esteem Percy Rivers as a relation—much as I value him as a friend—much as he is endeared to me in one sense, as the companion of my girlhood—yet that I do not love him in that other sense which can alone justify a right-minded female to think of marriage. That is what I shall tell my father; and I believe that my words will have sufficient weight to prevent him from ever placing you and me in so embarrassing and unpleasant a position again. What you will say, Percy, I must leave to your own sense of respect for yourself, and kindness towards me. And now that we bid farewell to the topic, let us be affectionate cousins and faithful friends as we were before."

Thus speaking, Musidora, with the most affable frankness, proffered her hand, which Rivers took with a kindred air of honest candour. Then, in order to relieve his cousin from the painfulness of saying more to her father than was absolutely necessary upon the topic just discussed, he himself at once sought an interview with the worthy knight, and made to him such representations as to convince him that he had taken a rash and unwise step in endeavouring to persuade his daughter and nephew into an alliance which under circumstances was unfitting and unsuitable.

CHAPTER L.

THE DEATH-BED.

TIME sped onward,—that never ceasing tide which bears everything upon its surface: a year and a-half glided away, and it was the month of January,

1520. The snow lay thick upon the fields and the woodlands of the Isle of Wight—the sky was of a leaden hue—and the atmosphere was filled with a nipping cold.

Why treads every foot so gently within the walls of Sinclair House? wherefore is there a gloomy foreboding upon the countenance of every inmate? It is because Sir Lewis Sinclair lies stretched upon a bed of sickness, whence there is no hope that he will ever rise again. For six weeks has death been slowly but steadily advancing; and now the grim destroyer seems to be near at hand.

From the first moment of her father's illness Musidora was unremitting in her assiduities and attentions. Scarcely allowing herself even a few brief hours each night to snatch the repose that was necessary to sustain her strength throughout the ordeal, she was almost constantly by the side of her father's couch; and nothing could exceed the affectionate gentleness with which she ministered to the old man. Percy Rivers, too, never allowed a day to pass without riding over from Carisbrook to spend some hours in the sick-chamber, and as much as possible relieve Musidora in the task of soothing the mind of the departing knight.

Thus the cousins were thrown together more than ever they had been since their youthful playmate-days. The effect was that all the cherished love of Percy Rivers for Musidora acquired a tenderness of an ineffable character; while on the other hand, the lady herself experienced a deeper and sincerer friendship for her generous-hearted relative. When a young man and a young woman are thus forced to pass hours together in each other's society, and under such peculiar circumstances, an intimacy of no ordinary character must inevitably arise: and intimate though the cousins were before, yet now this intimacy was drawn as closely as that which subsists between a brother and a sister. The task of watching by the couch of an invalid develops many new traits in the character of individuals; and it was impossible for a generous disposition, as that of Musidora naturally was, to remain untouched by the truly filial attentions which Percy Rivers demonstrated towards her father. Nevertheless, she did not love her cousin in the true meaning of the term: but she learnt to love him in the light already alluded to—namely, as a sister loves a brother. She experienced a sense of deep obligation to him for the zeal which he thus manifested in his endeavours to soothe the last days of the old man's life: she felt that in Percy she possessed a true and sincere friend; and knowing how fondly, how deeply he loved her, she more than ever compassionated that hopeless affection which he had so long and so faithfully cherished.

On the other hand, Percy Rivers discovered in Musidora's character many admirable traits for which he could scarcely have given her credit.

From the circumstance of her too protracted absence from home at the time she was staying at Grantham Villa,—an absence, too, which was thus prolonged despite the many letters he had written to urge her return,—he had naturally fancied that her regard for her father was not so great as that which under any circumstances a daughter should exhibit; and when, after she did come back, he had observed the attentions she bestowed upon the old man, he had looked upon her conduct as arising rather from remorse on account of previous neglect, than from a sincere filial devotion. But now, under the trying and peculiar circumstances of the sick-room, he speedily beheld enough to convince him that he was mistaken as to his previous estimate of Musidora's sentiments towards her sire. He saw, indeed, that she was most tenderly attached to her parent—that she cherished him with a love the most genuine and profound—and that however resolutely she might hitherto have cloaked the natural emotions of her heart beneath a garb of ice, this same heart could melt into softness and send forth the warmest tears to flow from her eyes and scald her cheeks at the thought of losing him. In a word, all the manifold proofs of filial affection and sterling devotion which her nature now put forth, might be likened unto those beautiful Alpine flowers which lie long unsuspected and unknown beneath a thick surface of snow, but which become revealed in all their unaffected simplicity and ineffable purity when the snow melts away from above them.

The illness of the old knight had originated in a very severe cold, and was followed by what may be termed a rapid breaking up of his constitution: but he retained his consciousness until the very last. Often and often, during the six weeks that he was thus gradually sinking into the embrace of death, would he lie, propped up by the pillows of his couch, gazing in silence upon his daughter and his nephew, while his looks showed what was passing in his mind. But since that memorable day when he had committed himself so awkwardly in respect to them both, as described in the previous chapter, he had never once alluded to the same topic: indeed he appeared to have banished it from his memory until illness thus prostrated him upon that couch whence he felt that he was never to rise again. *Then* did that topic come back to his thoughts, gradually assuming a strength which increased in proportion as his own physical powers were wasting away: so that it soon became as easy to read what was passing in his mind as to observe the pebbles at the bottom of a crystal stream. Still the old man appeared unwilling to give utterance to his wishes, though with his looks were they expressed as eloquently as eyes that were glazing beneath the touch of death could express anything at all!

Now, as Musidora failed not to observe the tenor of her father's

thoughts on those occasions, she could scarcely do otherwise than prepare herself for the arrival of that moment when he would be certain to
overcome his reluctance and give verbal utterance to his wishes. We may
therefore suppose that Musidora experienced all the battlings of a deep
and painful inward struggle as to the course she ought to pursue when the
supreme moment should come. She did not love Percy in any other sense
than as a friend and a sister: she had loved once—and never could love
again! The power of love was dead within her: *that* sentiment at least was
frozen in her heart, never to be thawed by human influence—nor in this
world! Yet if it were her father's dying wish that she should marry him,
ought she to refuse? ought she again to say that she could not comply with
that injunction because she dared not bestow her hand where she could
not give her heart? No: she dared not nerve herself to answer in the negative upon such grounds: for had she not consented to marry him whom
she had believed at the time to be the King, though she loved him not? To
refuse to become the wife of Percy, therefore, on such a plea, was a duplicity, a deceit, a falsehood, which she dared not practise by the side of the
bed of death.

The hour so long foreseen, and so much dreaded, came at last. It was
one evening, when Sir Lewis awoke from a short and troubled sleep, that
he fixed his eyes more earnestly than ever, and with a deeper significancy
also, upon his daughter and his nephew, as they sat together by the side
of his bed. The medical attendant was in the room at the time; and from
certain symptoms familiar enough to the experienced professional eye,
he knew that the moment of dissolution on the part of his patient was
not very far distant. In terms of befitting delicacy he hinted to the old
knight that if he had any parting instructions to give to those that were
nearest and dearest to him, it were better not to delay doing so. The medical attendant then gently quitted the room; and Musidora, with the tears
streaming down her cheeks, threw herself upon her father's breast and
poured forth the abundance of her sorrow.

"Don't weep, dear 'Dora—don't weep," said the dying parent, in a
feeble and tremulous voice. "You have been a good daughter to me—and
have nothing to reproach yourself for. I am not sure that I have altogether
done my duty towards you: perhaps I have been selfish—thinking too
much of myself and of my own interests——"

"Dearest father, do not speak to me thus!" cried Musidora, with passionate accents of grief: and there was nothing ice-like—naught of glacier
coldness—in her looks, her voice, or her conduct now!

"Well, well," said the old man, "we will not speak of the past more
than is necessary. But for the present, and for the future, there is some-

thing in my mind—something I should like to say—but which I know not
how to speak——Percy, my nephew, you will be kind and good to my
poor girl when I am gone?——she will be all alone in the world——"

"Oh, my dear uncle!" exclaimed Rivers, pressing to his lips the hand
of his dying relative, "I will be unto her as a brother——"

"As a brother," faintly repeated Sir Lewis, with a subdued gasp—for
the tide of life was ebbing away and all his powers were sinking. "Yes—
but——Oh, 'Dora! there is one last wish—Percy, I have but a single thing to
desire——"

"My dear father," said Musidora, "hesitate not to give utterance to
all that is in your mind. I shall be unhappy for the rest of my days—Oh!
more unhappy than——But speak, dear father! say what you will! Give
me your commands—impart your wishes——and all, everything, shall be
obeyed!"

"God bless thee, my child! Now I shall die happy! Percy," added the
old knight, as he turned his glazing eyes to his nephew, "will you also
promise to attend to my last words?"

"Yes, dear uncle—faithfully—most faithfully!" was the fervid answer.

The light of satisfaction—we might even say of joy—flamed up for an
instant in the eyes of the dying man: but the same emotion which caused
it, likewise choked his powers of utterance. Instinctively aware that his last
moments were at hand, Musidora and Percy sank down upon their knees
by the side of the bed. Sir Lewis Sinclair made another effort to speak,
but could only give utterance to a few inarticulate and broken syllables:
he however placed the hand of Musidora in that of Percy Rivers—and the
next instant was no more!

* * * * *

A week had passed—the funeral was over—and Musidora Sinclair sat
alone in her own chamber, in that spacious mansion of which she was now
the mistress. But how cold—how dreary—how desolate it seemed!—for
mighty is the change which death works in human abodes, when it bears
away a loved and cherished being to those habitations in another world to
which the eye cannot penetrate and which are beyond the stars!

Musidora reflected upon her position. It was her sire's last wish, expressed in a manner too solemn and too full of meaning either to doubt
or disregard, that she should become the wife of Percy Rivers. But never,
never could she inform her cousin that she had been made the victim of a
vile and detestable necromancer! No: there was an awe—a horror—even
a despair, sitting too heavily upon her soul, to allow it to find vent for

that tremendous secret. Yet, on the other hand, how could she possibly accompany him to the altar, allowing him to be deceived as to her real condition? That her marriage with the false King—or rather with Lionel Danvers—had all along been utterly null and void, she well knew, based as it was on fraud and deceit. But in addition to that knowledge she had heard from old Manners, three years and a-half back, that Lionel himself was dead and had been succeeded by his cousin Lord Reginald. Thus, in no way did the mock-marriage act as a legal barrier against her contracting a new and legitimate alliance. But were there not moral grounds upon which she should refrain? And yet how was she to disregard her sire's dying wish—that wish too, which she had so fervently and so solemnly promised to obey?

What was she to do? how was she to act? Never, never in all her life, had the unhappy lady been so cruelly bewildered! True, it was still early after her parent's death to devote attention to the subject: but in the first place it forced itself upon her thoughts; and secondly she was in duty bound to let her cousin know upon what footing they were thenceforth to meet—whether as mere friends and relatives, or whether as having been solemnly affianced and betrothed by the bedside of death?

We have already said that not for a single instant could Musidora entertain a thought of unbosoming herself frankly and unreservedly to Percy Rivers respecting the past incidents of her life. Even if she herself were inclined to do so, she felt that she would not have the power; for there was that intuitive feeling within her which made her deeply sensible that an irresistible spell would choke her utterance and seal her lips if she endeavoured to enter upon a narrative of the past. And yet, on the other hand, she shrank from the idea of practising so gross a deceit and so profound a duplicity towards a generous-hearted, confiding, and noble-minded young man, as to allow him to conduct her, with the belief that she was a virgin-bride, to the altar—she who had been made, though innocently so, the victim of a remorseless magician!

Such was the tremendous conflict that raged in Musidora's mind, as she meditated upon the course which she ought to pursue. The next day she again shut herself up in her room, and reflected long and painfully upon the subject: but still without coming to any decision. Nevertheless, she gradually felt the strength of her moral objections diminishing beneath the weight of an imperious necessity; and on the third day, when she once more meditated on the topic, sophistry—that bane of every honourable feeling—still farther weakened her delicate sense of propriety. For this same sophistry whispered in her ear, that it was not she who had given encouragement to Percy Rivers—that she on the contrary had suffered him to know she did not love him, and had even told him at one time positively and frankly that she would never marry; but that still he had gone on hoping—or if not hoping, at least loving as fondly as ever—and that it was through no fault of her's her father had been led to express the dying wish that had thus plunged her into so much perplexity and embarrassment. The conclusion, therefore, to which she came was that if Percy Rivers, who had himself so fervidly promised to obey his uncle's last wishes, chose to act upon that pledge and receive her as his wife, he must take her as she was, with all the mysterious past hanging around her—and that if *he* sought no explanation, she was not bound to offer any.

Musidora was far too intelligent, much too strong-minded, and also endowed with feelings naturally too frank and generous, not to be well aware that this reasoning was mere sophistry, and that the conclusion to which it brought her was illogical and devoid of all rectitude of principle. But she felt herself the creature of circumstances—the victim of an imperious necessity. She believed that she was swayed by destiny itself, and that it were vain and useless to attempt to battle against fate. With such a tone of mind—or rather, having been brought to such conclusions—Musidora acted in the way which in nearly all similar cases is the course that frail human nature adopts. For the best of human nature is too often but frailty after all, when the development of an immense amount of moral courage is needed to accomplish a painful duty.

Not to dwell, however, at any greater length upon this portion of our narrative, we may observe that at the expiration of a few days Musidora suffered Percy Rivers to understand that it rested with himself to decide upon what terms they were thenceforth to meet.

"You have before told me," he replied, "that you can never love me save as a friend: but on the other hand, so illimitable is my love for you, that it fills me with the presentiment that my affection will beget a kindred sentiment in your heart. If therefore you do not absolutely recoil from the idea of becoming my wife it will be with joy, and gratitude, and hope, that I shall regard myself as your affianced husband."

For an instant—but only for a single instant—a strange and almost ghastly expression appeared upon Musidora's countenance: yet it flitted away again so suddenly that Percy Rivers instantaneously fancied he was mistaken in believing that he had even caught a vanishing glimpse of any such look upon her fine features at all. At the same moment, too, she placed her hand in his own; and with a smile that was coldly sweet, she said, "Percy, I will be unto you a dutiful and devoted wife."

Twelve months afterwards the marriage of Percy Rivers and Musidora Sinclair was celebrated at Carisbrook Castle, which thenceforth became the home of our heroine.

CHAPTER LI.

THE LANDINIS' PLOT.

It was about the time of Musidora's marriage to Percy Rivers—namely, in the month of January, 1521—that the following scene took place at the establishment of Master Landini in Lombard Street, London.

It was evening—and old Alessandro was closeted with his nephew Mark in the private office behind the counting house. The outer shutters were closed—business-hours were over—the front door was made fast—and the clerks of the establishment as well as the jewel-workers upstairs had left some time. A cheerful fire blazed in the grate of the private office—a lamp burnt upon the table—and the light, playing upon the countenances of the uncle and nephew, showed that they were grave and serious, as if subjects of immense moment were under discussion. The lapse of a few years since last we spoke of the Landinis had produced a marked effect upon the old man,—his form being more bowed, his limbs more enfeebled, and his countenance indented with deeper wrinkles. But he retained all the vigour of his intellect—aye, and likewise that insatiate thirst for vengeance which in one sense appeared to exhilarate its powers, rendering it keen and astute for purposes of mischief. With regard to the nephew, being in the prime of life, the lapse of a few years had worked but little change in him—unless it were to trace that line across the forehead which usually belongs to the countenance of the avaricious, greedy, and grasping individual whose life is passed in the pursuit of gain.

Upon the table at which the uncle and nephew were seated, lay the immense volume containing the history of Bianca Landini; and it was open at the concluding page of that ill-fated lady's narrative. There were also vast numbers of papers and deeds, tied round with string, and endorsed with the name of Danvers—thereby showing that they related to the affairs of that family.

"It is good, nephew," said the elder Alessandro, "to refresh our memories in respect to every point connected with the history of our ancestress—even though our minds were already impressed with each and all of these details. But especially was it needful that we should read that narrative again this evening, to sharpen as it were the keenness of our appetites for vengeance, now that the moment is so near at hand when this vengeance is to be consummated! As the repetition of the same war-song, though so familiar to the ear, is useful to inspire not only the stalwart warrior rushing on into the ranks of battle, but even the mettled courser that proudly bears him in his career of glory—so does the recapitulation of Bianca's wrongs kindle into a more vivid glow those cravings for vengeance which are hereditary with us. Now, Mark, turn to the volume once more; and read slowly and deliberately that passage in the instructions which the dying Nino Landini gave to his son Ludovico, relative to the nature of the vengeance which he recommended as the more terrible because the more lasting in its effects."

Mark, in obedience to his uncle's orders drew the mighty volume towards him, and read in a low, deep, measured tone the following words:— "But to wreak this vengeance effectually, it must not be by means of your weapon nor of the hired assassin's dagger. There is a vengeance more terrible than that of taking away life. If you take the life of an enemy, you place him beyond the reach of farther pain at once; and this is scarcely a vengeance to be contemplated with satisfaction. But if you get your enemy into your power—involve him in a web of difficulties that shall be inextricable—insidiously draw in the meshes tighter and tighter around him, so that utter ruin at last stares him in the face,—*this* is true vengeance; because he remains alive for you to tell him that you *are* avenged, and he lives on in wretchedness and misery to feel day after day and hour after hour the effects of your vengeance!"

"It is well!" observed old Alessandro, when his nephew had concluded this quotation from the history of Bianca Landini. "Never have I lost sight of the recommendations contained in that passage; and it was in pursuance of the advice thus given that I began by so artfully leading Lord Lionel Danvers to invest his fortune in my hands and entrust me with its whole and sole management. Fortunate was it for the success of our plans, that at Lord Lionel's death the youthful Reginald enabled us to continue in the same course. You have seen, Mark, how I have taken advantage of his inexperience to enmesh him in our toils: you have beheld how I suggested a variety of ways in which he could dispose of his immense capital in a manner which he has been led to regard as most lucrative. With what blind confidence has he continued to pour into our bank the surplus of his Continental revenues, which together with the produce of his English estates have all been laid out according to my advice. Four years and a half have elapsed since Lord Reginald Danvers entered into possession of the family titles and estates; and during that period the work of ruin has been slowly but not the less surely progressing. And you have seen too, Mark, that on each of the occasions when Lord Reginald has paid one of his abrupt, brief, and volatile visits to London, I have obtained at his hands written acknowledgments, all in due form, not merely approving of the mode wherein his treasures have been laid out, but likewise positively and definitely enjoining each particular proceeding. And what is the result?" exclaimed old Landini, with a fiendish smile of satisfaction. "It is this—that I have so contrived as to dissipate the entire fortune of Reginald Danvers, and strip him of every coin that he possesses! Nay, more—I have brought him immensely into my own debt, so that the very title-deeds of his estates both in England and on the Continent—all of which I have induced him to entrust to my keeping—will be held as security for the payment of the immense amounts in which I have contrived to make him my debtor!"

"And think you not, my dear uncle," asked the nephew, trembling with mingled satisfaction and fear—satisfaction at the hope of a terrible and speedy vengeance, and fear lest by any means the old man should over-reach himself,—"think you not, my dear uncle, that Reginald Danvers may appeal to the law-courts, alleging fraud and robbery, or malversation, against us?"

"No—it is impossible!" responded Alessandro in a firm and decisive tone. "I have played the game too cautiously and too well. Wherever I heard of a mercantile house that was running into speculations which the world at large believed to be full of promise, but which my own shrewdness and experience told me must result in inevitable failure—there have I laid out the riches of Lord Reginald Danvers. When argosies were trading to such Mediterranean ports where they stood the best chance of being captured by pirates—in those vessels did I send rich freights of merchandize in the name of Danvers. But all this you know full well: and it is needless for me to recapitulate the measures which have been taken to dissipate the enormous wealth which his confiding folly placed in our hands. Mark," added the old man, with another malignant smile, but lowering his voice to a whisper as if the very walls had ears,—"I have adopted such a course that while Reginald Danvers is ruined beyond redemption, no human being can impute dishonesty to me!"

"But will you not be accused, dear uncle, of ignorance, carelessness, imprudence, and want of sufficient forethought?—will you not," continued the nephew, "be charged with having pursued the most reckless game? Indeed, if the tribunals were appealed to, would it be held rational or reasonable that such enormous wealth could be dissipated in comparatively so short a time? Consider, my dear uncle—it is barely five years since you first began thus to lay out the money of the Danvers family——"

"And if those papers," interrupted the elder Landini, pointing to the documents on the table, "be produced before any judge in England, it must be admitted that everything was fair, honest, and straightforward. But let me anticipate every objection which might possibly be offered.

Supposing it were said that while I have been thus dissipating the fortune of Lord Danvers, I have not impaired my own—that while he is ruined, I am a richer man than ever. Then, what would be my response? That I ran no risk myself and incurred no hazard of my own, because I was a mere agent of Lord Reginald's speculations. If it be asked wherefore, when I saw venture after venture fail, I did not counsel him to pause,—my reply would be that it was impossible to check the headlong career of an obstinate, vain, and self-sufficient young man, who was intent upon gambling with his resources, and who grew the more venturesome in proportion as his fortunes became the more desperate."

"I am satisfied with all that you say," replied Mark. "Indeed, it is impossible to dispute the justice of your reasoning, or to doubt the admirable precautions you have taken."

"And now, nephew," resumed the old man, "will it not be a glorious sight for us to behold Reginald Danvers stand pale, ghastly, and trembling in our presence—perhaps a suppliant for means to live—and at all events entreating that we will not press too hardly upon him for the payment of those sums in which he is made our debtor? Oh! if those two men who disappeared so strangely some few years back were with us at this moment—how would they rejoice at the prospect of approaching vengeance!"

"Uncle, was there not indeed something strange in that disappearance to which you have just alluded?" said Mark, shuddering visibly. "You remember, they sat with us until a late hour, discussing this very scheme of vengeance which we have been carrying out, and which now touches upon the threshold of success: they were to return again in a few days to review the plans laid down;—but we never saw them more! Think you, I ask, that of their own accord they kept away?"

"Nephew, you seem to tremble as you speak?" said old Landini, gazing fixedly upon Mark. "What is this that you feel?—is there any misgiving in your mind?"

"To speak soothly, dear uncle," was the reply—and Mark flung a hasty, shuddering glance around,—"I *do* feel as if the weight of an evil presentiment were upon my mind. I know not how it is—but the nearer we advance to what we hope will be the consummation of our revenge, the more do I tremble lest by any accident it should all redound upon ourselves. Does not this tale,"—and he pointed to the volume containing the legend of Bianca Landini,—"seem to prove that Lord Walter, the seducer of my ancestress, was endowed with strange powers? And remember you not the wild tale which old Manners told us, of how he was borne along upon the coal-black steed at a preternatural pace—how he was fed by the hand of enchantment in his dungeon—and how Lord Reginald himself confessed to the old man how his predecessor Lionel had dealt in the black arts?"

"I have forgotten nothing that Master Manners told us the night he was here," responded the elder Landini; "and no one knows better than I that the race of Danvers is a dread and a fearful one. But there is not the slightest reason to believe that Lord Reginald inherits any of those wild and mysterious powers which may have been possessed by his ancestors. On the contrary, does not every circumstance tend to prove that he is an ingenuous, frank, confiding young man—very different in disposition and character to his predecessors, though inheriting all their wondrous beauty? Nephew, it is with regret I have heard you confess to these misgivings and sentiments of evil, which argue weakness on your side. What!" exclaimed the elder Landini, his wrinkled cheeks flushing, and his eyes flashing forth fire,—"do you stand in awe of this inexperienced and harmless young man who has suffered himself to fall so easily into our meshes? do you fear, I say, this Reginald, when I, an old man, feel my heart throbbing with de-light—aye, with ecstasy too, at the thought of approaching vengeance? Why, the bare idea that after the lapse of long, long years it should be reserved for us to wreak this vengeance which has so long remained unac-complished,—the bare idea, I say, sends a thrill of ineffable joy through my veins, makes my blood tingle, and even fills me with the most fervid fires of youth!"

"Pardon me, uncle," exclaimed Mark, "if for a moment I seemed wanting in that amount of courage which ought to inspire me at such a crisis. Whatever be the result, you shall not have to complain of any pusillanimity on my part. When do you think it probable that Reginald Danvers will visit London again?"

"From the letter which I sent him to his castle in Normandy some weeks back, it is reasonable to expect that he will be here without much farther delay. In that letter," continued the old banker, "I impressed upon him the necessity of coming at once to England to look into the state of his affairs, so that he might ascertain precisely how his finances stood. Therefore, under these circumstances, he may arrive at any moment."

"Hark!" suddenly ejaculated the nephew: "was not that a loud rap-ping at the street-door?"—and he started up. "Yes—it continues, and grows more imperious——"

"Let the domestics, as in duty bound," said the old banker calmly, "respond to the summons."

The nephew accordingly resumed his seat; and for about a minute, silence prevailed in the private office. At the expiration of that brief interval, a domestic of the household threw open the door—announcing Lord Reginald Danvers!

This nobleman now wore the appearance of a man bordering upon three-and-twenty. He had suffered his moustache to grow; and those two delicately curving lines of glossy blackness enhanced the red richness of his classically cut lips and the enamel of the pearls shining between them. He wore no whiskers nor beard; and the exceeding beauty of his countenance was therefore only relieved from feminine softness by the hair upon the upper lip. As he doffed his cap, his locks of raven darkness and brightness were seen to be parted above his noble brow—thus admirably setting off, without concealing, the statue-like shape of the head. He was richly dressed in dark raiment, and wore a short Spanish cloak hanging over his left shoulder—so that in personal appearance he retained much of the aspect which he wore when passing through the world as Lionel.

The banker and his nephew had more than suspected who it was that gave so imperious a summons at the door of their establishment; and during that minute's silence which had preceded Reginald's entrance they had composed their looks in order to give him such a reception as they might deem suitable ere the moment came for flinging off the mask and proclaiming that the ruin they had worked him was the immediate result of revenge. They therefore received him with the wonted air and language of respectful obsequiousness; while he on his side bore himself with the high-bred demeanour of frank and gracious affability.

Taking a seat near the fire, and tossing his cap upon the table, Reginald said, "I duly received your despatch, worthy Master Landini and should have been with you a week or two ago, had not pressing matters detained me in Normandy. But at length I am here: and now let me request you to tell me the precise object for sending so urgent a summons. Are there any fresh disasters relative to the moneys you have laid out on my account?"

"Your lordship must prepare," replied old Landini, "for a very sad history of the several transactions in which your lordship's funds have been embarked."

"Indeed!" ejaculated Reginald Danvers, as if beginning to be frightened. "Is it as you say?"

"It is, my lord," responded Landini. "I have no good tidings to give your lordship at all. In not a single instance has any success resulted from the ventures in which your lordship's treasures have been embarked."

"Then it is indeed time to stop short," observed Danvers, his words and looks appearing to express an increased anxiety.

"It is too late, my lord!" rejoined the old banker.

"Too late!" cried Danvers. "What mean you?"

"I mean, my lord, that your whole fortune is dissipated."

"And you tell me this to my face? Do you mean that I am ruined?"

"I mean that you are ruined, my lord!"—and as old Landini spoke, there was the commencement of a malignant expression upon his countenance, like the first glimmering of an incendiary fire against the dark clouds of the horizon.

"Then doubtless we are fellow-sufferers in misfortune?" observed Danvers, not appearing to notice that slight change in Landini's looks.

"I do not understand, your lordship," was the reply, accompanied by a growing sneer.

"Not understand me?" ejaculated Danvers angrily; "and yet I spoke plainly enough. What I meant was, that if I am ruined, you must be ruined also."

"How so, my lord?" demanded the banker, now assuming an independent look and tone—the first time he had ever dared thus to deport himself in the presence of any one bearing the name of Danvers.

"How so?" echoed Reginald, still more angrily. "You would not have me understand that it is with my money only you have been speculating thus insanely?"

"What the state of my affairs may be, has nothing to do with your lordship," replied the old banker. "To those who have a right to put the question shall an explanation be given. It is enough for you to know, Reginald Danvers, that you are a beggar upon the face of the earth!"

"Yes—a beggar upon the face of the earth!" exclaimed Mark, thus repeating his uncle's words.

As the old man announced and the nephew echoed that intelligence which was to overwhelm Danvers with confusion, they both started up from their seats; and this was the instant for flinging off the mask. Then what hideous malignity gleamed forth from the reptile eyes of the elder Landini! and what savage hatred suddenly glared in the looks of his nephew! Terrible indeed was the aspect of those two men, thus influenced as they were by feelings of such remorseless implacability—of such gloating, savage, inhuman revenge!

"What means this insolence—this astounding impertinence of manner on your parts?" demanded Reginald Danvers, affecting to be bewildered and amazed—indeed somewhat frightened—by the fierce and malignant aspect so abruptly assumed by the old man and his nephew.

"You ask what all this means, Reginald Danvers?" said the elder Landini, with the most savage fierceness: "it means that you are ruined, and that I have purposely consummated this ruin for you! It means that the wrongs of my ancestress are now avenged upon the descendant of him who inflicted them! It means that the voice of Bianca Landini, crying up from her unknown grave for this dark and implacable revenge, will have to cry no more, but may sink into silence, and her spirit into rest! It means that the cravings for the day of retribution which has been dissimulated in our family towards your's for a hundred and thirty years, need be dissimulated no longer! It means that the vindictive aspirations which have been cherished for more than a century and a quarter, are now appeased and gratified! Yes: the aim is accomplished—the work is done. I have lived to see the hour of vengeance—and I care not how soon I may pass hence and be no more. Embrace me, Mark—my nephew—my adopted son—embrace me!—for this is a moment of supreme triumph and ineffable happiness for us!"

Then the old man and Mark threw themselves into each other's arms, and embraced with all the enthusiastic self-gratulation that might have been supposed to accompany the consciousness of some good and virtuous deed, instead of the gratification of one of the darkest passions of human nature.

During that long and vehemently delivered speech which the elder Landini, with a gloating malignity, had addressed to Reginald Danvers, this nobleman had remained so calm and passionless that it was impossible to read in his features what was passing in his mind: but the old banker and his nephew imagined that Reginald was in reality confounded and stricken with the stupor of despair, at the intelligence of his ruin, as well as by the announcement of the motives which had prompted them to work it. When however the old man and Mark threw themselves into each other's arms, and their looks were thus withdrawn for a few moments from the face of Danvers, then did a proud expression of scornful defiance sweep over that darkly beautiful countenance—so that the handsome features, with the unearthly glory of the eyes, did indeed resemble at that moment the aspect of Lucifer in his fall!

"You tell me that I am ruined," said Danvers, speaking in a calm and even cold voice of indifference, while his countenance immediately regained its youthful expression of ingenious frankness; "and you tell me also that you yourselves, from motives of vengeance, have purposely accomplished that ruin? Of this horrible vindictiveness which you have cherished and sought to wreak against me, we will speak anon. First of all, ye will, as in duty bound, prove to me that I am ruined. Show me the accounts—give me a satisfactory explanation of the way in which you have disposed of the immense treasures placed in your hands—convince me that you have a right to retain the title-deeds of my estates—and also that you have had my authority for playing so venturous a game with my fortune."

"All this can be speedily done," answered the elder Landini, whose countenance now wore a settled look of the darkest hatred, mingled with the sinister light of fiendish malignity. "First of all," he continued, spreading open a long roll of parchment in which numerous financial entries were made, "here is an account showing the disbursement of two millions of pounds sterling*—that being the precise sum for which I have to be answerable unto you."

"Good and well!" observed Danvers, hastily glancing over the paper. "I have not the slightest fault to find with that statement. On the contrary, it is a satisfactory proof that you have received altogether on my behalf the sum of two millions sterling."

"And you will perceive," rejoined Landini, pointing to an item at the foot of the account, "that you are indebted to me in the sum of three hundred and sixty thousand pounds, for which I retain the title-deeds of your several estates both in this country and on the Continent."

The old man spoke with a sort of harsh and rude insolence—not seeming any longer to regard the lordly title and patrician rank of the nobleman, but to treat him as a man of ruined fortunes, an outcast, and a beggar.

"Now then, there is but one thing more which I require to be shown," said Danvers, still cool and even careless—which manner on his part did not in any way alarm the old banker or his nephew: for they fancied it was merely an air which from motives of pride he assumed in order to conceal the actual condition of his mind. "Where is my authority empowering you to lay out my revenues according to your own discretion and pleasure?"

"Ah!" ejaculated Landini, with a horribly malignant expression of countenance: "you would fain find some loophole by which you may escape from this vortex of utter ruin? But I have you fast—I have you fast—and within these four walls, where you have no witness in your favour, I hesitate not to declare that I have so well combined my plans as to leave you powerless and defenceless. Behold!" he added, opening the great book which contained the chronicles of his family: "Here is the record of Bianca's wrongs—and this night, ere I retire to rest, shall I append these few words, '*Bianca, thou art avenged!*'"

"That is a subject," rejoined Danvers coldly, "which we shall discuss presently. First of all show me the papers I have demanded to see."

"Here," answered Landini, taking up a bundle of documents and untying the string which held them together, "are all the acknowledgments

---

* An enormous sum in that age—many times greater, considering the relative value of money, than what we may estimate two millions to be at the present day.

and authorizations which on different occasions you have signed, empowering me to act on your account, and even specifying each particular venture and transaction."

"Show me my signature to one of those documents," said Danvers: and there was a slight wreathing of a scornful smile upon his lips, which the old man did not notice, but which met the eyes of Mark and suddenly conjured up in his mind that presentiment of evil which he had experienced ere the arrival of Reginald Danvers.

"Your signature?" exclaimed the old man contemptuously: "it is attached to every one of these documents. Here, for instance, is the first that comes to hand."

He took up the paper and spread it open: but a sudden change came over his countenance as he glanced at the foot of the deed.

"Here, Mark! my sight seems to fail me," he said, with nervous haste. "Look——"

"Good God, uncle!" ejaculated the nephew, staggering back as if struck with the blow of a hammer, while his features became blank with dismay: "the signature is not there!"

"Not here, not here?" exclaimed old Landini, now trembling from head to foot. "Then perhaps it is a mere copy which by accident has got amongst the other deeds. Here—let us look at the next."

Mark rushed eagerly forward to clear up the torturing suspense which had seized upon him; and something resembling a wild cry of mingled horror and anguish burst from his lips as the first glance at this second deed showed him in an instant that there was no signature attached to it.

"Look at another," said Danvers, who having risen from his chair, was now leaning in a posture of graceful indolence against the mantelpiece, while his countenance wore an expression of mingled defiance, scorn, and contempt.

"O uncle, uncle!" gasped the nephew, a prey to the most excruciating feelings—the wildest and most harrowing emotions: "what does this mean?"

"Silence, nephew!" interrupted the old man: "there must be signatures to some of these deeds—and even one would be a sufficient authority to prove all we want."

"Look through them all!" were the ominous words which fell from the lips of Danvers, and smote the ears of the two Landinis as if with the voice of doom.

Ghastly pale—quivering in every nerve and fibre—scarcely able to turn over the documents in their trembling hands, the wretched old man and his miserable nephew examined them one after the other with feverish impatience: and piteous indeed became their looks as each successive paper proved to be devoid of signature. The last dropped from their grasp as they both had eagerly clutched it together; for this was blank as to signature likewise!

"Not one, not one!" muttered old Landini, as he sank upon a seat, gasping for breath, pale and hideous as a corpse.

"No—not one!" echoed Mark: and staggering back against the wall, he flung his frightened and dismayed looks in utter hopelessness upon Reginald Danvers.

"Well," said this nobleman, "how stands the matter now? Where is the authority to prove that I ever gave you leave or license to play with my revenues? Master Landini," he added, his voice and look suddenly becoming stern and implacable, "I demand the immediate payment of two millions of pounds sterling!"

"My lord," gasped the old man—and he could say no more, but sat gazing in utter vacancy upon Reginald.

"Two millions sterling!" repeated the nobleman, still more stern and implacable. "I demand it all at once! Let it be in gold—in precious stones—in bills of exchange—no matter in what shape or form—but I require it all now. Come, Master Landini, you are so business-like and punctual, give me up my treasures!"

"No, no—you shall not ruin me thus!" literally screamed forth the miserable old man, "Two millions! I am not worth half the sum—barely a quarter! It would sweep away everything I possess—reduce me and my nephew to beggary, destitution, and want——No, no—some hideous trick has been played!——Reginald Danvers, those signatures have not disappeared by natural means! You are a detestable magician!"—and the wretched Landini, who had started up from his seat in wild excitement, fell back again quivering, and gasping, and trembling, as if battling desperately against death itself.

"Oh, my lord!" said Mark, falling upon his knees at the feet of Reginald Danvers and speaking with accents of the most piteous entreaty: "have mercy upon my uncle—have mercy upon me!"

"Rise, wretched man, and hear me!" exclaimed Reginald, literally spurning the nephew who grovelled at his feet.

Obedient to that commanding tone, Mark rose, and stood the picture of consternation and dismay in the presence of the young nobleman.

"Yes—listen both of ye, I say," he continued drawing himself up to the full of his superb height, so that all the slender gracefulness and lithe elegance of his Apollo-like form appeared to the fullest advantage—while the dark beauty of his features wore that strange and weird-like mystery of expression which indicated the consciousness of some preterhuman power. "Listen to me! Nearly five years have elapsed since one afternoon Lionel Danvers called at this establishment on business-matters. He remained some little time, conversing with you, old man, alone in this very room; and then he took his departure. But recollecting that he needed a set of diamonds from your collection, he came back to procure them. You, Mark, had in the meantime joined your uncle in this office, at the door of which Lionel Danvers paused for a minute ere he entered,—thus pausing because some words which you, Mark, were speaking in a loud tone and with vehement accents at the time, met his ears. Those words spoke of the *implacable vengeance which you both cherished against the accursed house of Danvers!* Such was the expression. Lord Lionel paused to hear no more: he had heard enough to convince him that ye both meant to work him the foulest wrong. Not in your presence however did he suffer his looks to betray the fact that he had overheard you, He received the diamonds, and went away. I now pass on to another incident with which it is requisite ye should be made acquainted. One night—some months after the circumstance just alluded to, and at the very time when I, Reginald Danvers, had assumed the lordly title which then became mine—I was passing late through the streets of London, when I beheld two old men issue forth from your dwelling. These were Manners and Dunhaven. I knew them both—and following them at a distance, kept them in sight till they reached the bridge. There they paused to converse. I drew close, but unperceived by them—and listened. Then did I obtain a complete insight into the project which you, miserable old man, had devised to work my ruin. Well, upon Dunhaven and Manners I wreaked a vengeance which they full well deserved!"

Here the elder Landini groaned in horror; and Mark, who had hitherto remained standing while Danvers was speaking, fell back into a seat, pale and trembling, and looking as if he were about to give up the ghost.

"Yes," continued Reginald Danvers, "I punished them as they deserved—no matter how. I did not travel out of my way to seek their wretched lives; rather would I have let them live—for already there is enough upon my mind to answer for!"—and as he murmured these last words, in a low whisper to which his voice suddenly sank, a terrible expression of anguish passed over his countenance—the too evident reflex of feelings that were harrowing him within. "But of all that, no matter!" he abruptly exclaimed. "I punished those men as they deserved—for they compelled me to trample them in my path. And now, with regard to yourselves. You perceive that for some years—aye, even from the very first moment when you devised the scheme which you hoped was to engulf me in ruin—I have been acquainted with it. But why did I suffer you thus to go on dissipating my treasures? Because the amount you have thus deliberately squandered, and which you so idly thought was the whole substance of my worldly possessions, is but a drop of water to the sea in comparison with the wealth which I can command. Poor insensate creatures!" said Danvers, turning his eyes from the nephew to the uncle, and back again to the nephew, with a look of the most contemptuous scorn: "ye thought to beggar me by the dissipation of two millions—me who can command twenty or two hundred millions, if I think fit! But I suffered you to go on, because if you chose thus to labour for the accomplishment of my ruin, it was but natural that I should leave the blow to rebound upon yourselves. And it will do so! Master Landini, I take this account which shows the amounts you have received on my behalf: I take back my title-deeds also—not that I value them even to the extent of the poor wretched pieces of parchment themselves; for were my present possessions to pass away from me, I could command gold enough to purchase not mere estates, but kingdoms! I however take these documents, so as to leave ye without the means of raising the funds requisite to liquidate my claims; and to-morrow morning, the moment your bank opens, the new agent whom I shall appoint will present himself on my behalf to claim two millions at your counter."

"My lord, in mercy spare me!" exclaimed the old man, dropping upon his knees, and extending his clasped hands wildly to the young noble.

"Oh! in mercy spare us!" cried Mark, also sinking upon his knees, and bursting into tears.

But Danvers, who meanwhile had gathered up the documents to which he had alluded, flung upon the two wretched men a look of the most withering scorn and blighting contempt; and turning with graceful ease upon his heel, quitted the room.

An hour afterwards, Lombard Street and its neighbourhood were alarmed by the sudden bursting forth of a terrific fire on the premises of the eminent goldsmith and banker; and with such fury did the flames rage, that it seemed as if they were fed by some oily or bituminous substance. The whole building speedily gave way and fell in with a terrific crash, burying the inmates of the house beneath the burning ruins. Not a soul within those premises at the time was saved—nor a single article of furniture, nor any of the valuables constituting the goldsmith's store, were rescued from the conflagration. The servants, the old banker, and his nephew, all perished; and the origin of the fire was, as a matter of course, attributed to accident by every one who heard of it, save Reginald Danvers. But he full well comprehended its cause: the Landinis had preferred self-immolation to ruin and dishonour!

CHAPTER LII.

THE DREAM.

TEN years passed away from the date of the incidents just related; and it was now the beginning of the year 1531. Many events of importance had in the interval taken place in the great, busy, bustling world. There had been wars, in which Henry of England and Francis of France were engaged—there had been treaties of peace, by which fresh lustre was added to the diadem of the English monarch—Wolsey had fallen from the eminence of power, and had died breathing the memorable wish "that he had only served heaven as faithfully as he had served his king"—Cranmer had succeeded him—Henry had openly professed the Protestant faith—and Parliament had repudiated the spiritual jurisdiction of the Pope in the affairs of this country.

The life of Gerald St. Louis had been for many years past a happy and a prosperous one. The King, having his own private reasons, as the reader is aware, for keeping St. Louis in his favour, had never omitted any opportunity of befriending him. In the first instance he was sent as a dependant of the English Ambassador to France: next he was entrusted with a diplomatic mission to some German Court; and on his return to England, he received the honour of knighthood for his services. Then he was despatched as Envoy-Plenipotentiary to the court of the Emperor Charles V; and so well did he advance the interests of England, that when he came back he was rewarded with a peerage. Thus some years passed away; and now, in February 1531, we behold Lord St. Louis embarking on board an English ship, attended by a numerous suite, and charged with a diplomatic mission to the Sultan of the Ottoman Empire. At this time Lord St. Louis was about forty years of age. In consequence of the busy active life he had led in King Henry's service, he had found no opportunity—even had he experienced the desire—of forming a matrimonial connexion; and thus we still find him unmarried. Indeed, with such heart and soul had he pursued the diplomatic career which was accompanied with increasing wealth and honours to himself, that all his thoughts and ideas were absorbed therein. Seldom was it that even the name of Danvers recurred to his memory; and when it did, he experienced no revival of any vindictive feeling in respect to that nobleman. Once or twice, however, he had felt some little curiosity to ascertain what had become of old Dunhaven, and if he were dead, who had inherited his wealth; but even upon this point he had at length ceased to think, so engrossing became the duties and the attractions of the prosperous career he was pursuing in the school of diplomacy.

We will not weary our readers with any description of Lord St. Louis' voyage from England to Constantinople upon that mission in which we find him engaged. Suffice it to say that, having narrowly escaped being captured by the Barbary corsairs in the Mediterranean, the ship which bore the Ambassador and his suite anchored at length in safety in the waters of the Bosphorus. Lord St. Louis and his numerous dependants landed upon the Turkish shores, and took up their abode in the mansion provided for their reception in the suburb of Pera, one of the quarters of Constantinople. If we have not entered into any minute particulars with regard to St. Louis' voyage, neither shall we stop the continuous flow of our narrative to dwell upon the particulars of his diplomatic mission, but leave it to our readers' imagination to fancy the splendours with which he was received by the Grand Vizier and the Sultan, and how the Envoy of so powerful a monarch as the King of England became an object of curiosity to the Turkish capital.

We must however pause for a few moments to observe that during the diplomatic career of Lord St. Louis, he had not failed to become acquainted with the principal European languages. In the French tongue from his boyhood he had been proficient; and now he was equally the master of Spanish, German, and Italian. It was this quickness on his part in acquiring the Continental tongues, that had enabled King Henry to push him on with such rapidity in his diplomatic career; and it will presently be seen why we have thus halted for a moment to notice his skill in one of the languages above enumerated.

St. Louis had been about six weeks in Constantinople and had made some satisfactory progress in the purposes of his mission, when he was informed by the Grand Vizier that all further negotiations must stand over for three or four months, as his Imperial Highness the Sultan was about to make a tour through his Asiatic provinces. St. Louis had now the prospect of an interval of idleness and inactivity, so far as his diplomatic business was concerned; and he was deliberating with himself upon the most eligible manner of passing the time, when an incident occurred that seemed to furnish suggestions upon that point.

One night, as Lord St. Louis lay buried in a profound sleep, in the splendid bed-chamber of his Turkish mansion, he dreamt that the apartment became slowly filled with a preternatural lustre, upon which he gazed with mingled rapture and awe. Then, in the midst of the unearthly halo a female shape gradually became apparent; and to his increased surprise and veneration it took the form of his ancestress, the lovely Arline, according to the portrait which was preserved in the casket of sandal-wood. But the figure was clothed in dark mourning garments; and the countenance was pale and full of a deep melancholy. For some minutes she appeared to fix her blue eyes with an expression of tender and mournful reproach upon the sleeping St. Louis: then slowly raising her right hand, she held up her forefinger with a warning impressiveness,—at the same time breathing these words in a soft, plaintive, but still earnest tone—"Is the name of Arline obliterated from thy memory? is the legacy of vengeance forgotten? wilt thou do naught to give repose to the troubled spirit of thine ancestress? Rise, I enjoin thee—rise! betake thyself to the Holy Land, and ascend to the highest eminence of the mountains of Lebanon!"

Having thus spoken—or rather appeared to speak—the form rapidly began to fade away; the light which enveloped her diminished—and Lord St. Louis awoke. The moon was shining brightly in at the lattices of his chamber: but he beheld not the slightest trace of anything he had seen in his vision. He endeavoured to compose himself to sleep again, but could not: the figure of Arline, dressed in mourning garments, seemed to hover around him, while her voice continued to ring in his ears. He rose—dressed himself—and descended to the garden, where he walked about till morning dawned above the Asiatic hills. Then he re-entered the mansion, and for the remainder of the day endeavoured by a variety of pursuits to chase from his mind the impression made upon it by his vision.

On retiring to rest, when night came again, he fell asleep sooner than he had anticipated: but once more did he behold that preternatural light rising in the room, until it filled the entire chamber with its effulgence; and then in the midst appeared the form of Arline, dressed in sable garments as before, and which seemed to flow about her feet as if she were standing upon a dark cloud. The aspect of her features was more pensive, more melancholy, and likewise more reproachful than it had appeared on the preceding night; and she also gazed longer upon the sleeping St. Louis. It was moreover with an air of deeper significancy and more impressive warning that she raised her hand and uplifted finger, while she said in a voice full of remonstrance, "Is it possible that thou can'st thus remain faithless to the solemn pledge which thou didst give thine uncle on his death-bed? Arise, I repeat—and betake thee to the mountains of Lebanon!"

Then the preternatural light gradually faded away—the form of Arline becoming more and more shadowy, until it ceased to be visible—and St. Louis awoke with a sudden start. Again was the moon shining in at the lattices, its serene argentine lustre occupying the space where the supernatural light had ere now shone. St. Louis felt sorely troubled. He sat up in his couch, reflecting seriously and solemnly upon this vision which had appeared to him a second time. He could sleep no longer; therefore rising, put on his apparel, and descending to the garden, wooed the refreshing breeze that blew from the waters of the Golden Horn upon his feverish brows. Throughout the remainder of that day he vainly endeavoured to divert his thoughts from the vision; it haunted him more completely than at first—and when night came again and he retired to rest, he resolved that if the same appearance revisited him for the third time, he would not fail to obey the mandate given by the spirit of the unfortunate Arline.

And the vision did come back,—under the same circumstances as before, except that the countenance of Arline appeared so profoundly mournful that St. Louis fancied he wept as he gazed upon it, so deeply were his feelings touched. Long and earnest was the gaze which she fixed upon him; and in the most impressive manner did she raise her hand, saying in a voice that was even menacing as well as full of remonstrance, "This is the last time I am permitted to appear before thee for such a purpose. Disobey my injunctions, and nothing more shall prosper thee in this life: but obey, and it shall be well with thee. Arise therefore—depart for the Holy Land—and ascend to the summit of the highest mountain of Lebanon!"

The figure ceased to speak—the supernatural lustre gradually faded away—and the form itself grew proportionably more dim and indistinct, until it seemed to melt into thin air. Then St. Louis awoke; and he felt the tears upon his cheeks, and found also that his pillow was moist, so that he knew he had really been weeping in his slumber. He did not now rise from his couch, nor experience any trouble in his mind. His feelings were those of a solemn awe and holy veneration, but tranquil and serene. He resolved to obey the mandate he had received. Yet for what earthly purpose could he thus be sent on a pilgrimage to the Holy Land? what was he to see or whom was he to meet on the summit of Mount Lebanon? Vainly did he ask himself these questions: all conjecture was defied by the mystery enveloping the circumstances of the vision, the mandate, and the pilgrimage. Sleep came upon his eyes again—and he slumbered on calmly and tranquilly till the usual hour for rising in the morning.

So soon as he was apparelled and had partaken of some refreshment, he commanded immediate preparations to be made for a voyage to the coast of Palestine. The British ship which had brought him to the Ottoman shores, had remained at his disposal, and was therefore soon in readiness. Having signified to the Grand Vizier that he purposed to make a tour in the Levant, in order to see the Greek Isles and visit the Holy Land,

Lord St. Louis embarked one morning in the beauteous month of May, on board the ship, which set sail and was soon clear of the Dardanelles. The wind was favourable; and in a few days the vessel neared the coast of Palestine. Without affording any intimation of the mysterious object of this voyage, Lord St. Louis desired the captain to put into the port that was most convenient so as to enable him to visit the mountains of Lebanon. The captain, who was well acquainted with the shores of Asia Minor, accordingly guided the vessel into a bay, at the bottom of which was a miserable little fishing village; but the heights of Lebanon formed the sublime background of the landscape. In the immediate neighbourhood of that wretched village, were immense heaps of shapeless ruins, above which troops of eagles were constantly soaring and hovering. Those ruins were all that remained of the once mighty and populous city of Tyre—in ancient times the most important sea-port of the Levant, and the place which furnished the stately cedars for the building of Solomon's temple. But now Desolation seemed to have made those ruins its chosen home! The sun could give no cheerfulness to these remnants of a once proud and opulent city, nor find reflection in any bright hues upon those dreary shores. At night the moon appeared to rise mournfully upon the scene, and fling her melancholy rays upon the cliffs whitened by the moaning sea, and upon those blackened heaps of ruin beyond which rose the vast and sterile hills of the chain of Lebanon.

It was upon this desolate and cheerless shore that Lord St. Louis landed early one morning; but he nevertheless experienced strange feelings of mingled rapture and awe as he thus planted his foot on the land of miracles. Leaving the dependants who had accompanied him from the ship, he ascended the mountains alone. Well armed with weapons of defence, and furnished with provisions in a wallet, St. Louis pursued his path amidst the sterile hills, where he met no human being, but which he knew had been trodden by prophets in the olden time. For two or three hours did he thus advance, until he reached an immense slope covered with trees. Here he sat down to rest, and also to partake of some refreshment: for a scorching sun was above his head, and he experienced much weariness in consequence of the uneven and sometimes difficult nature of the path which he had been pursuing.

But not long did he tarry in that spot: for he was anxious to get to the end of his journey as speedily as possible, and ascertain the mystic purpose for which he had been sent thither. Rising from his seat amidst the long soft grass which grew in luxuriance on that slope, he threaded his way amongst those trees—the cedars of Lebanon! Two hours did he thus continue climbing the ascent; and the limit of the grove of cedars was reached. But still the mountains stretched onward and upward, more dark, more gloomy, more sterile, than any portion of the chain he had yet seen. Sometimes an immense eagle with its wide outstretched wings came swooping so near that he drew his sword in expectation of an attack from the fierce bird: sometimes his foot startled the dark mountain-snake, which glided away with meandering coils and hissing noise—and sometimes the cry of the jackal from some cavern amidst the hills, sent a thrill of terror through the form of the Englishman. But, save when interrupted by the rush of the eagle's wings, the hissings of the snake, or the mournful voice of the jackal, stupendous was the silence which enveloped that region—a silence which in one sense seemed like the Egyptian darkness of patriarchal times, inasmuch as it could be *felt!*

Sometimes startled by the alarms above-mentioned—but for the most part with a deep and solemn awe sitting on his soul, as that silence itself sat like a spell upon the desolate mountains—Lord St. Louis pursued his way. It was about three o'clock in the afternoon that he reached a point whence he could embrace the whole of the highest portion of the range, and could therefore distinguish which summit of the many eminences was the highest of all. Thither did he bend his steps, the path every minute becoming more rugged and difficult. Once he was stricken down by an eagle that dashed against him; though as if satisfied with this proof of its strength, the king of birds attempted no farther mischief, but shooting high up into the air with tremendous velocity, was out of sight. Another time a large snake suddenly coiled itself round his leg; and had he not with amazing presence of mind instantaneously clutched it by the neck and held its head so far away that it could not bite him, its envenomed teeth might have sent the dark poison of its jaws into his blood and he never would have left the mountains of Lebanon to tell the tale of his adventures there. Having strangled the snake, he pursued his way sword in hand, so as to be prepared for the onslaught of any fresh enemies. But he experienced no farther dangers worth recording; and after another interval of rest, began the ascent of that sterile summit which is the highest of the range, and which specially bearing the name of Lebanon, bestows it upon all the other mountains of the rocky border of Palestine.

It was five o'clock in the evening when St. Louis found himself upon the barren top of that immense mountain. The Holy Land lay at his feet, stretching out before him far unto the southern horizon. He could see the ship too which had borne him to Palestine, floating like a speck in the port of Tyre; and upon the blue waters of the Mediterranean the sun was pouring the flood of its effulgence.

But as St. Louis stood alone on the summit of Mount Lebanon,—shivering with the bitter chill of the atmosphere which prevailed at that height, although it was the warm and glowing month of May,—he said to himself, "For what object have I been sent hither? Surely not for the mere purpose of contemplating this panorama, where the wild scenery that forms the theatre on which I am placed is scarcely relieved by those shining waters on the one hand, and those green plains which stretch far as the eye can reach towards the south."

"My son, what dost thou here?" said a deep and solemn voice, speaking in the Spanish language.

Lord St. Louis started, and turning round, beheld a venerable old man issuing from what appeared to be a cave or grotto, the entrance to which was in a projecting mass of rock a few feet below the summit of the mountain. This old man could not have seen less than eighty winters. His hair was thin and white as silver; his beard, also of glistening whiteness, reached down to the rude leathern girdle which confined the coarse black gown that clothed him. To that girdle was suspended a rosary and crucifix: he held a long staff in his hand to support his tottering limbs; and altogether he had the air of some venerable pilgrim who having quitted his native European clime to seek the Holy Land, had fixed his abode amidst the time-honoured heights of Lebanon.

He had spoken in the Spanish language, we say; and now the reader will comprehend wherefore at the opening of this chapter we intimated the necessity of pausing to observe that Gerald St. Louis was well versed in the principal Continental tongues.

"Venerable anchorite—for such I presume you to be," answered the English nobleman, taking off his plumed cap through respect for that awe-inspiring figure, "are you astonished to behold a fellow-Christian amidst these barren regions? or have you in any way been led to expect such a visit? In a word, holy father, have you aught to say unto me—any instructions to give—any secrets to communicate—any particular course to point out?—for I am full of suspense to learn the object of my mysterious mission hither."

"Who art thou? and what is thy name?" inquired the old man: "for though thou speakest my own native tongue with fluency, yet do I perceive by thy accents that thou thyself art not a Spaniard."

"No, venerable man," rejoined St. Louis; "I am of French origin, but may term myself an Englishman, not only through having been born on the shores of Albion, but likewise because it is the country of my adoption, and I am in the service of its King. My name is St. Louis—I am a peer of England, and the ambassador of Henry VIII to the Ottoman Court. It is in consequence of a vision, thrice repeated, that I have now sought the summit of Mount Lebanon."

"Tell me thy vision," said the old man, gazing earnestly with his mild dark eyes upon St. Louis.

"To tell thee my vision, holy father, were to deal merely in words which thou could'st scarcely understand, unless prefaced by other explanations. Know, then, that an ancestress of mine, Arline by name, suffered cruel wrong at the hands of a nobleman who bore the title of Danvers——"

"Danvers!" suddenly ejaculated the old man, an extraordinary change coming over him; for all in a moment an expression of hatred and fierce malignity sprang up on his countenance: but as speedily regaining the natural calmness of his demeanour, he turned his eyes upward, saying in a voice of the deepest fervour, "Forgive me, O Lord! that for a moment the dark thought should have intruded itself upon my soul. My son," he continued, again addressing himself to St. Louis and speaking with true patriarchal benevolence, "I can understand wherefore thou hast been sent hither. Thou hast mentioned a name—the name of Danvers—which affords a clue to that mystery which I may solve for thee. Follow me."

St. Louis was thereupon conducted by the old man into the grotto whence the latter had ere now emerged, and which was a spacious cave, not hollowed by human hands, but evidently existing naturally in the mountain. Rude and rough were the accommodations of the place, such as well became the abode of an anchorite: but the old man set dried fruits and cakes of bread, together with an earthen vessel of water, before St. Louis, and bade him welcome to the frugal fare. The nobleman ate a morsel and drank of the water, so as not to appear to disdain the hospitality of the old anchorite, though, he had more succulent viands, together with a flask of wine, in his wallet. But these he dared not produce in that abode of humility and self-denial.

"Now," said the venerable hermit, "you must give me your patience while I tell you a tale which it is requisite for you to hear. My name is Antonio Cortez; and it is of a loved and lamented daughter of mine—the wronged and hapless Dolorosa—of whom I am about to speak."

The old anchorite then related the particulars which will be found in the ensuing chapter.

CHAPTER LIII.

THE HISTORY OF DOLOROSA CORTEZ.

"I AM descended from a Jewish family, which had long been settled at Toledo, one of the most ancient and celebrated cities of Spain. My ancestors were devoted to commercial pursuits; and though frequently subjected to the most bitter persecutions, of which heavy fines were not the least, they succeeded in amassing considerable wealth. My father became a convert to Christianity; and abandoning commerce, he settled down in a comfortable mansion in the hope of living undisturbed upon the wealth which he possessed, part of which had descended to him from his progenitors, and part of which he had acquired by his own industry. I was his only son, and was reared in the doctrines of the Christian faith. At the death of my parents I inherited their wealth and this being great, I was not compelled to pursue any avocation or profession. I married a young lady of good family, and who was likewise a convert from the Jewish persuasion. Two children were the issue of this union—a son named Juan, and a daughter called Dolorosa. My wife died when these children were still very young; and being devotedly attached to the memory of my deceased partner, I resolved to remain single as a tribute of respect towards her whom I had loved so fondly. All my care and attention were now bestowed upon Juan and Dolorosa; and my heart swelled with a father's pride as I saw them grow up everything I could wish—beautiful, virtuous, and intelligent.

"The incidents I am about to relate happened thirty-one years ago—consequently in the middle of the year 1500. At that time Juan was twenty and Dolorosa eighteen. Both of them were tall and admirably formed: both were likewise eminently handsome, with dark hair, fine black eyes, and the rich hues of health glowing through the transparent olive of their complexions. In respect to Dolorosa, a more lovely being it were impossible to conceive. She had just sufficient of the Jewish profile to indicate that she was descended from a family in whose veins flowed Hebrew blood; but in her manners, the graces of her person, and the elegant attractions of her sex, she combined all the most captivating and fascinating qualities of the Castilian maidens. Although we lived in comparative retirement, yet in consequence of her own exceeding beauty and of my wealth, she had many suitors; but none of them appeared to make any impression upon her heart, and she was too intelligent to be dazzled by the mere artificial attractions of rank. For amongst the aspirants to her hand there were several individuals of authority and position in the city: but the most arduous in pressing his claims was the Count of Segovia—a nobleman belonging to a very ancient family, but of dilapidated fortunes. He was a young man of about twenty-five years of age, and had at one time been somewhat notorious for the dissipated nature of his pursuits. Latterly, however—that is to say, within two or three years of the particular time of which I am speaking—a marked change had come over his conduct: he had grown suddenly steady, and from having been totally indifferent to his religious duties, became a frequent attendant at mass in the splendid cathedral of Toledo. With his alteration of conduct there also appeared to be an amendment in his pecuniary condition. He extended his establishment by increasing the number of his domestics and by the purchase of several beautiful horses: in short, he not only lived in better style, but also honourably paid his debts. There was some little degree of mystery attached to the sources whence his finances emanated: but as he was connected with some of the best families in Spain, it was supposed that his opulent relations had replenished his treasury on condition that he should amend his course of life. Being, as it appeared, a thoroughly reformed character, and even more steady and better conducted than any other young nobleman of the same age and position in the whole province, his former irregularities would not have induced me to reject him as a suitor for Dolorosa's love: on the contrary, the circumstances of his previous wildness and subsequent reformation were such as to afford ample promise that he would make a good, devoted, and steady husband. He therefore received my countenance to a certain extent—that is to say, I gave him to understand that if he succeeded in winning Dolorosa's love I should throw no obstacle in the way of their union.

"But Dolorosa herself—as it soon appeared, when I spoke seriously to her upon the subject—entertained a feeling that well-nigh bordered upon aversion, in respect to the Count of Segovia. Yet, as I learned from her lips, she herself could not account for this feeling. Perhaps it might have been that there was a boldness which she did not like in the manner in which he proffered his suit: perhaps, notwithstanding his handsome person, she beheld something sinister and suspicious in his looks;—or perhaps she mistrusted the sincerity of his reformation and considered the improvement in his fortunes to be involved in too much unpleasant mystery, despite the rumours concerning his opulent relations. Or it may be that all these causes combined to render the pretensions of the Count of Segovia unpalatable and repugnant to her feelings.

"I must here interrupt the course of my narrative for a few minutes to state that while the horrors of the Inquisition were raging at the period throughout the principal part of Spain, Toledo had hitherto been mercifully dealt with in that respect. But within the three or four years previous to the time of which I am speaking, a new Inquisitor-General had been appointed to the district; and taking up his abode at the Alcazar palace, he speedily gave proofs that he was not disposed to adopt the lenient course practised by his predecessors. In short, a reign of terror commenced in Toledo; and under the new Inquisitor-General Don Guzman Valdez a terrible spy-system was organised—so that it even became unsafe to trust one's own familiar friends, lest the slightest word inadvertently uttered should be reported to the authorities of the Holy Office. At the time of which I am specially speaking—namely, in the year 1500—this reign of terror had already progressed to a fearful extent: the dungeons of the Alcazar were filled with prisoners—hundreds of victims daily and nightly were subjected to the torture in those deep subterraneans where the massive walls beat back the cries of anguish and the yells of pain; and there had already been one *auto da fé* at which several unhappy beings, male and female, were burnt. Consternation prevailed throughout Toledo: thousands of families had to deplore the loss of some loved members, torn away from their bosom under circumstances of the darkest treachery and most terrible mystery, the offences with which they were charged being scarcely known and only possible to be guessed at; while those who had thus to deplore their loss dared not complain, much less attempt to interfere, in case they should share the same fate.

"Such was the condition of Toledo at the time of which I am speaking; and at this period was it that the Count of Segovia became more pressing in his attentions than ever towards my daughter. Vainly had she given him to understand, with as much plainness and firmness as became the delicacy of her sex and her own naturally gentle disposition, that she could not accept his suit: he persevered in his pretensions, which at length became so disagreeable to Dolorosa that her brother Juan took it upon himself to remonstrate with the Count. This led to an altercation between them, and which coming to my knowledge, filled me with apprehension lest a duel should follow. I accordingly interfered; and taking the Count into my private apartment, addressed him in terms of friendly remonstrance and rebuke. 'Wherefore,' said I, 'should you continue thus to persecute my daughter? You cannot complain that I have acted unfairly or unhandsomely towards you. No, my lord; I gave you free permission to make Dolorosa an offer of your hand; and had she replied favourably, I should have yielded my assent. But she does not love you; and she will not wed where she cannot bestow her heart. If your lordship be content to visit at my house as a friend, you will be well received as heretofore; but it ill becomes a nobleman and a gentleman thus to persist in asserting claims which are not recognised, and on the contrary positively discountenanced.'—Never shall I forget the fiendish look which Segovia suddenly fixed upon me. All the bad passions that can possibly disgrace the heart of man, were concentrated in that look; and it seemed as if the most malignant of fiends were gazing out of his eyes.—'Ah!' he said, in a low deep voice which was strangely altered at the time, 'my pretensions are spurned? my suit is treated with contempt? But I will ask you three times, Don Antonio

Cortez, whether you will think better of this and compel your daughter
to receive me as her accepted suitor? Once then, do you promise?'—'No,
my lord,' I answered, firmly: 'I cannot consent to seal the unhappiness
of Dolorosa.'—'Your refusal will effectually do that which you pretend
to be anxious to avoid,' he answered: then after a brief pause, he said, 'A
second time do I demand Dolorosa's hand.'—'Your lordship,' I responded,
'must fancy that I am gifted with an extraordinary degree of patience thus
to tolerate a behaviour which has already become a most unwarrantable
insolence.'—'You little know whom you are provoking,' exclaimed the
Count de Segovia with a look that troubled me. 'For the third time I ask
you whether Dolorosa shall become my bride?'—'And for the third time,
my lord, I am constrained to answer thee in the negative.'—He said nothing more, but flinging upon me another of those strange menacing looks,
rushed from my presence and quitted the house.

   "Though very far from apprehending the dreadful consequences that
were to ensue, or the fearful channel in which the Count's revenge would
flow, yet I experienced a deep uneasiness at the interview which had thus
taken place. There was something in the nobleman's looks that appeared
to reveal the direst capacity for mischief: a mask had fallen from his face,
exhibiting him in his true colours; and I saw that notwithstanding his pretended reformation and his assumed piety he was in reality possessed of
an evil disposition and a vindictive nature. I however feared that whatever
revenge he might contemplate would be directed against my son Juan,
who had first offended him; or else that he would endeavour to carry off
Dolorosa by force: and therefore I resolved to keep a vigilant watch over
the safety of my beloved children. To this same effect I also instructed
the servants of the household. But the blow came in a manner I had little foreseen, and with a speed which proved how quickly his measures of
vengeance were taken. For in the middle of the night following the interview I have just described, the house was invaded by the Familiars of the
Inquisition, who bore off both my son and daughter to the dungeons of
the Alcazar palace. Vainly did I fall upon my knees and implore mercy for
my children: the Familiars only shook their heads gloomily—while one,
perhaps more friendly inclined than the rest, gave me a warning whisper
that I might thank my guardian saints my own name was not included
in the warrant of arrest. But heedless of the intimation thus conveyed,
I implored for permission to accompany my children,—declaring that I
would gladly share their dungeon and any fate that might be in store for
them, rather than be separated from those whom I loved so tenderly. The
Familiars would not listen to me, but took Juan and Dolorosa away: and
it was only in compliance with the earnest entreaties of those affection-

ate children that I did not persist in following them to the gates of their prison.

"The mystery with regard to the Count of Segovia was now horribly cleared up. From the date of his pretended reformation he had become a spy and coadjutor of the Holy Office; and well paid was he for his detestable services. Hence the improvement in his fortunes. As the whole power of the Inquisition was vested in the hands of the Dominican friars, and as they were rigid sticklers for the observance of all the outward ceremonies of religion, the assumed piety of the treacherous nobleman was likewise accounted for. In the first effusion of my anguish I went amongst my friends and acquaintances, to make known the villanous conduct of the Count: but none would listen to me. Some turned away in horror, lest by even giving ear to my tale they should bring down upon their own heads the vengeance of the Holy Office: others conjured and entreated me not to draw them into conversation upon such a dangerous topic. Some few threw upon me looks of sympathy, and then shudderingly hastened from my presence. I proceeded to the palace and besought an audience of the Grand-Inquisitor, Don Guzman Valdez; but I was cruelly repulsed from his gates. I flew to the Archbishop of Toledo—a kind and excellent man; threw myself at his feet and besought his interference: but he only shook his head compassionately, giving me to understand that the dread tribunal exercised a power above his own. I consulted the father-confessor who attended my house: but this worthy monk had no counsel to give, and could merely exhort me to the exercise of patience and resignation. Patience and resignation for me, who had seen all the sources of happiness in this world suddenly torn away by the rudest and most treacherous hands! For several days I went wandering about like a madman, and at length fell upon a bed of sickness, where for a month I lost all consciousness of my calamity in the delirium of fever.

"At the expiration of that time when I regained the faculties of reason, I received an intimation, secretly delivered by one of the Familiars, that if I chose to visit my son and daughter in their dungeons, I had permission to that effect; and moreover that if the result of my interview with Dolorosa should be to persuade her to accept the hand of the Count of Segovia, she and her brother would be set at liberty. Gladly, Oh! how gladly, did I avail myself of this leave to behold my children. Not that for an instant I expected Dolorosa would change her resolve in respect to the Count—nor that I intended to use my authority with her for such an end. But, though scarcely able to drag myself from my sick bed, I lost no time in repairing to the gaol department of the Alcazar palace. It was a lovely evening in the middle of the month of May, when, supported by two of

my domestics, I reached the gates of that fearful prison. But there I had
to dispense with the assistance of my menials, and drag myself on as best
I could, down the steep flights of stone stairs and through the gloomy
passages and corridors, until the Familiar who conducted me stopped at
a huge massive door which he opened. I passed over the threshold and
found myself in the cell containing my daughter. The Familiar placed a
lamp upon the stone pavement just inside the door; and closing that door,
left me alone with my child.

"Dolorosa flew into my arms. I strained her to my breast; and we
mingled our tears together. Presently—by the light of the lamp, dimly
though it burnt—we gazed upon each other. She knew that I had been
very ill—that I had suffered much; and she wept abundantly. I did not tell
her how ill I had been; for I was necessarily averse to increase her afflictions. She was not so much altered as I had tremblingly expected to find
her. Not having yet appeared before the tribunal, upon whatsoever charge
might be laid against her, she had not been subjected to any extraordinary
severity of treatment: the cell in which I found her was clean, and might
even be termed comfortably furnished—that is to say, it was provided with
necessaries, though these were of the rudest and humblest description.
She had moreover been supplied with good and sufficient food, though of
the plainest kind; and she had been given to understand that her brother,
who occupied an adjoining cell, was similarly treated. Thus, to some little extent, the rigours of incarceration had been mitigated; and knowing
herself innocent of any offence against the Holy Office, she had buoyed
herself up with the hope of acquittal when the day of trial should come.
Nor was this all that occurred to sustain her fortitude: but there was something of a still more cheering character which had taken place. This I must
explain in her own words:—

" 'The dungeon, my dear father,' she said, 'is dimly lighted in the day-
time by means of that window which you behold there with the huge iron
bars. On the first day of my imprisonment—and as nearly as I can guess,
about noon, as the light was then most powerful—the door opened, and
giving admittance to a person, instantaneously closed again. This person
was not a Spaniard, although his complexion had somewhat of the duskiness of the Spanish race. He was a tall, handsome, and elegantly dressed
man, apparently about thirty years of age—or it may be, a year or two
more; with raven black hair descending to his shoulders, a moustachio
upon his haughtily curving lip, but no beard. He was apparelled in the
Spanish fashion, with a sable plume in his cap, and a short Castilian cloak
hanging with graceful elegance upon his left shoulder. There was something mysterious but likewise compassionate in his look; and I may here

at once observe that his manners were those of a most polished courtier. I naturally took him for some official of the Inquisition; but advancing towards me, he in a few words gave me to understand that so far from having any connexion with the dread tribunal, he loathed and detested it with the utmost abomination. He then proceeded to state that his name was Humphrey Danvers, and that he was an English nobleman, possessing estates in various parts of the Continent, one of which was in Spain. I was astonished to hear him talk thus: for I not only wondered how he had obtained access to my presence, but also why he had come at all. Then, with a delicacy of language and of manner that I cannot describe—but a delicacy that was mingled with an air of the most frank and chivalrous sincerity,—he proceeded to state that having for some few weeks past been visiting a friend at Toledo, he had seen me on several occasions, had taken an interest in me, and was profoundly shocked on hearing that I had been arrested. He added that he had come to ascertain whether I knew the nature of the charges against me, so that he might take measures for my efficient defence. I thanked him with the warmest gratitude for his kindness; but replied that not until the day of appearing before the tribunal should I learn the nature of the accusations, although I had little doubt that my accuser was the Count of Segovia. I asked him how he had obtained access to my dungeon: to which question he responded that a golden key would open any lock, and that my gaolers were not above the influence of bribery. He remained with me for nearly an hour,—his language, his bearing, and his manner being all fraught with the utmost delicacy towards me, but at the same time with a most fervid interest on my behalf. When he took his departure, he solicited permission to return again shortly. Could I refuse this demand on the part of so disinterested a friend? I accordingly gave my consent. At the expiration of a week he came back, at about the same hour of the day; and he told me that you, my dear father, had not been molested by the officers of the Inquisition. This was a great source of consolation; and I cordially thanked Lord Danvers for such welcome intelligence. He likewise assured me that in a short time he should be enabled to learn the particular charges on which myself and Juan had been arrested; and having again tarried about an hour, conversing with me, he went away. Again at the expiration of a week did he return, repeating his assurance that you, my father, continued at liberty; but adding that he had not as yet obtained information on the other point. He remained with me about an hour, as before, and then took his departure. A fourth time, at the expiration of a week, did he visit me again and give me consolatory assurances respecting yourself as regarded your freedom: but he added that you had been ill, a circumstance which he had withheld before through

fear of afflicting me. I wept, Oh! how bitterly I wept, at such sad intelligence: but he assured me the crisis was passed, and that you were out
of danger. Having remained the usual time discoursing with me, he went
away, promising that at his next visit he would bring me tidings relative to
the nature of the accusations against Juan and myself. Dearest father, the
fifth visit of Lord Danvers was paid yesterday; when he informed me that
the Count of Segovia has accused my dear brother Juan and me of being
secretly attached to the Jewish faith, although openly professing Christianity, and that we have spoken in disrespectful terms of the Holy Office.
Lord Danvers, having given me this information, inquired what could be
done to serve me and Juan in our defence? What could I tell him? Nothing, but that the accusation was false—for that I and my brother are both
firmly and sincerely devoted to the Christian faith which we profess. I then
implored Lord Danvers to see you, my dear father; so that you might become aware that heaven had raised us up so kind a friend. He assured me
that if he had not already presented himself to you, it was in consequence
of your illness; but that he would do so within a very few days. And now,
my dear father, I have but a few more words to say relative to these visits
which I have received from Lord Danvers; and as your own dutiful daughter, who has never in thought nor word deceived you, I must confess that
on each occasion he has contemplated me with a deeper interest and with
a more tender sympathy; but his language has been only that of the most
delicate and generous friendship.'

"Such was the extraordinary statement which Dolorosa revealed to
me; but I read in her blushing countenance something more than she herself had explained. Yet it was with no studied reserve that she had failed
to mention the tender impression that Lord Danvers had made upon her
own heart: she at the time, poor girl, comprehended not her own feelings
in that respect. I asked her under what circumstances the English nobleman obtained access to her, and whether the Familiar whom he bribed let
him in and out of the dungeon? She answered that on each of the five occasions of his visit he seemed to be in possession of the key that unlocked
the door, as he let himself in and out. I then began to tremble lest after
all, this mysterious visitor should be a mere spy of the Inquisition, intent
upon taking advantage of her confidence and gleaning from her lips those
natural complainings against the tyranny of the Holy Office that might
supply the deficiency of more substantial evidence to procure her condemnation. But while I was thus giving utterance to my fears, the door of
the dungeon opened, and the gaoler came to announce that it was time
for me to take my departure. Dolorosa clung to me with all the tenacity of
mingled anguish and devoted love: but the rude Familiar separated us, and

I was hurried away. From my daughter's cell I passed to that of Juan, with whom I was only allowed to remain a few minutes, but just long enough to make him acquainted with the singular tale which Dolorosa had told me, and put him upon his guard so that he might speak cautiously in case he should receive a similar visit. I returned to my lonely habitation, and passed a sleepless night, thinking of all Dolorosa had said, and offering up the most fervid prayers to heaven on behalf of my poor children. On the following day, as I was seated in an apartment pondering upon my misfortunes, a servant entered and announced Lord Danvers. I experienced a thrill of joy as my visitor entered the room; for I at once felt assured that he was really a friend and no spy after all. I accordingly received him with befitting courtesy, and gave him a cordial welcome. We conversed long and earnestly upon the circumstances of the position in which Dolorosa and Juan were placed; and he not only manifested the liveliest sympathy on their behalf, but likewise gave me to understand that he was deeply enamoured of my daughter. While we were yet speaking, a domestic entered to inform me that the Count of Segovia demanded an interview. My first impulse was to give an indignant refusal to see the traitor: but Lord Danvers, as if struck by a sudden idea, bade me order that he might be introduced. I accordingly did so; and the false nobleman entered the room. He stopped short, near the threshold, on observing that I had some one with me: but I immediately said, 'This is Lord Danvers, an English nobleman and a man of honour. It is my desire that he should remain a witness of whatever may take place between us.'—'In that case,' said the Count of Segovia, 'I am to presume that you have given Lord Danvers such a version of the story as suits your own purposes? But I refuse to hold any communication with you in the presence of a witness.'—'Such is invariably the conduct of all foul traitors,' said Lord Danvers, in a coldly sarcastic voice, as he bent a look of mingled scorn and indignation upon the Count.—'Ah! this to me?' cried the latter, placing his hand upon his sword and half drawing it from its sheath.—'Yes; and more too,' rejoined Danvers with the same tone and manner as before. 'I tell thee, my lord of Segovia, that thou art the basest of villains as well as the vilest of dastards!'—'Such words as those,' said the Count, pale and trembling with rage, 'convey an insult which can only be wiped away with blood.'—'Be it so!' answered Lord Danvers, with the most contemptuous indifference. 'Name the hour and the place where I may have an opportunity of ridding the earth of a cowardly traitor who wages war on defenceless damsels!'—'At once, and in the garden of my mansion,' exclaimed the Count, scarcely able to restrain his fury.—'Proceed thither,' rejoined Lord Danvers, 'and I will follow shortly, with a friend to serve as my second.'—'I shall await you, my lord,' exclaimed the Count of Segovia: 'and then, having chastised you for your insolence, I shall return to hold my conference with Don Antonio Cortez.'

"With these words he turned upon his heel and quitted the room. The scene I have just described commenced so abruptly, progressed so rapidly, and ended with such a kindred speed, that I had not time to throw in a single word while the arrangement for a death-duel was taking place. A sort of consternation was upon me; but the moment the Count of Segovia had taken his departure, I turned towards Danvers, saying, 'Heavens, my lord! what have you done? Through your kind interest on my behalf and that of my children, you have rushed headlong upon a danger which may prove fatal. My lord, the Count of Segovia is the best swordsman in Toledo.'—'And he may wear the best Toledo blade by his side,' responded Danvers, with a smile of contemptuous indifference; 'but I shall not fear to cross it with my French rapier.'—'At least, my lord,' said I, 'let me furnish you with a weightier weapon: yours is but slight indeed.'—'Strong enough to punish that foul traitor,' replied Danvers, now in an easy tone of confidence, but without any more perceptible emotion. 'If I slay him,' he added, 'your children will be free; for he is the only accuser who is to appear against them. Remain tranquilly here, Don Cortez, until my return.'—I snatched his hand and pressed it to my lips; for I already beheld in him, as I thought, the saviour of my dearly beloved children. He left me; and for an hour I was prey to the most acute suspense—a suspense so poignant that I wonder my heart-strings did not crack with the excruciation I thus endured. At the expiration of that interval the door was thrown open and Lord Danvers re-entered the room.—'Your enemy is no more,' he said: 'that villain, I have killed him!'

"I sank down upon a seat, overwhelmed with ineffable emotions: then starting up, I sprang towards the English nobleman, threw myself at his feet, and almost worshipped him as a friend whom heaven had raised up in the moment of bitterest need to vindicate outraged innocence and punish foulest perfidy. On the following morning Juan and Dolorosa were placed before the Grand-Inquisitor in the tribunal at the Alcazar palace; and three times was their accuser summoned to make his appearance. But no witness stood up against them: they were accordingly liberated, and ere noon were restored to their home and to their father's arms. Lord Danvers was present when they thus re-entered the dwelling from which they had been torn away so cruelly, and to which they were now restored as it seemed, so happily. I beheld the rich blood mantle upon Dolorosa's cheeks as she expressed her warmest gratitude to the nobleman for having so chivalrously constituted himself her champion and her brother's; and methought that it would be a day of rejoicing on which my daughter should become Lord Danvers' bride. For to gaze upon them, they seemed admirably suited for each other; and there appeared to be a remarkable fitness in the union of that fine elegant noble of an almost wondrous beauty, and that tall, graceful, charming girl, of a loveliness surpassing that of any other maiden in Castile. As for my son Juan, he was delighted with the new friend whose acquaintance he made now for the first time: and indeed, the conduct of Danvers in having risked his life for the purpose of punishing a traitor was full well calculated to win the esteem and admiration of a frank, confiding, and high-spirited youth as Juan was.

"Lord Danvers now became a constant visitor at our house, where he was received as the affianced suitor of Dolorosa. I learnt from an eminent goldsmith in Toledo, with whom I was well acquainted, that Lord Danvers was the richest nobleman in Europe, as he not only possessed three or four estates in England, but likewise immense territorial properties in Spain, France, Germany, and elsewhere. Thus, in every point of view did the alliance appear to be the most eligible that Dolorosa could possibly form. And she loved Humphrey Danvers with the sincerest and most heartfelt devotion: it was a love based not only upon admiration, but also upon gratitude—a love too which seemed to be fully reciprocated. I was supremely happy: for the more I saw of Danvers, the more was I possessed in his favour. His mind appeared to be of the most wondrous contexture—stored with all possible accomplishments, and with funds of knowledge which were rare indeed on the part of even the most erudite sages, much more so on that of a nobleman who did not appear to have yet reached the prime of life.

"The day was fixed for the bridal: it was to take place exactly three months after the release of Dolorosa and Juan from the prison of the Alcazar palace. Lord Danvers had suggested that it should be celebrated with as little ostentation as possible; and to this I willingly yielded my assent. A few select friends only were invited: but I had given orders for a banquet of the most elegant description. Never did a man rise from his couch with a happier heart than I on the morning which I fondly believed was destined to give me a son-in-law every way worthy of my esteem and my daughter's love. Scarcely was I dressed, when Juan came to my apartment, apparelled in his gayest costume, and with radiant looks, to offer me his filial congratulations upon the blissful event which we both deemed about to take place. We embraced each other, and then descended to the apartment where the banquet was to be held. But our happiness was of brief duration, and was destined to be destroyed by a blow as violent as it was sudden. A domestic came hurrying into the room with consternation upon his countenance: he had just heard from Dolorosa's maid that her young mistress had disappeared! I could not believe the statement—it seemed utterly preposterous: but the next moment the maid herself came to confirm the dreadful tidings. Yes, Dolorosa was gone: her bed had not been slept in all night—and she had departed in the same apparel she had worn on the previous evening. It was therefore evident that she had been absent some hours: but what could it mean? Juan rushed frantically to the house where Lord Danvers had been living during his residence in Toledo. There my son learnt that his lordship had abruptly taken his departure on the preceding evening, between ten and eleven o'clock—and that his attendants had risen very early on that same morning of which I am speaking, and had likewise quitted the city of Toledo. It farther appeared that on the previous evening Lord Danvers had ordered his two most splendid horses to be saddled, but that dispensing with all attendance, he had mounted one and led away the other. These were all the particulars that could be gleaned: and not the slightest clue existed as to the route which the fugitives had taken.

"When Juan returned to me with this intelligence, I was nearly distracted. Too clear—too evident—was it that Dolorosa had been beguiled away by the treacherous Danvers, at whose perfidy I was as much enraged as I was shocked and astounded by Dolorosa's frailty. Juan was perfectly infuriate. Falling upon his knees and drawing his sword from his sheath, he kissed the blade, calling heaven to witness his vow that he would never rest until he had either compelled the treacherous Danvers to make reparation to the dishonoured Dolorosa, or else had wreaked upon him a fearful vengeance. Catching the infection of the same spirit which animated my son, I promised to accompany him in pursuit of the fugitives. Mounting our horses, and accompanied by six well armed retainers, we commenced our journey, bending our way in the first instance to Lord Danvers' estate in the neighbourhood of Madrid. But on reaching his castle on that domain, we learnt that he was not there. Cruelly disappointed, but by no means dispirited, we now resolved to proceed into France; and accordingly journeyed with all possible rapidity to Danvers' estate in Normandy. But the treacherous seducer was not there. Thence we continued our way to the coast and embarked for England, where we visited the several domains belonging to Lord Danvers in Essex, in Cumberland, and in the Isle of Wight. Still we could hear naught of him. At the two first-mentioned castles he had not been seen for some years past; and that in the Isle of Wight was untenanted and shut up. After a long absence we returned to Toledo, where nothing had been heard of Dolorosa during the time we were away.

"I was now seized with a serious illness; and for some time my life was despaired of. Juan attended me affectionately day and night: but where was my daughter, who should have been with me to smooth my pillow and minister unto me in my sickness? Alas! no tidings of her came; and as soon as the physician pronounced me beyond the reach of danger, Juan, in accordance with his vow, set off again in search of Danvers. A year passed away, during which I suffered the tortures of suspense relative to my son, dreading lest it were heaven's doom that I should thus be deprived of both my children. Another year passed—and still no tidings of my absent Juan! Then, reduced to despair, I breathed a solemn vow to heaven, that if he were restored to me, even though it were but for an hour, I would retire from the world, make a pilgrimage to the Holy Land, and devote the remainder of my life to prayer and religious observances. Within a week after I had made this vow, Juan returned. But heavens! how changed was he—and in what a condition did he come back to his afflicted parent! Pale—emaciated—worn out with fatigues, privations, and sufferings, my well-beloved son returned to die in my arms! He had wandered over Europe in search of Danvers. Often had he heard of him; but never could he succeed in meeting or overtaking him. Terrible were the dangers he had encountered and the adversities he had experienced: at last, plundered by banditti, despoiled of all resources, his dependants slain or dispersed, he had been compelled to drag himself, a mendicant and a beggar, through Germany, France, and a considerable part of his own native Spain, until he thus reached the paternal threshold once more. But, as I have already said, he only came back to die: and that noble-hearted, chivalrous, and handsome youth—my pride and my hope—my beloved Juan, expired in my arms, with his last words invoking heaven's vengeance upon the head of Danvers, and imploring me never to rest until I had punished the seducer of my daughter—the author of our calamities and sorrows!

"Yes: and I felt, too, an ardent and almost irresistible longing to follow the dictates of my fiercer passions and obey the dying injunctions of my son: but on the other hand, there was the solemn vow which I had registered—that if Juan came back I would thenceforth devote myself to the service of heaven. He *had* come back: and though it were but to die in my arms, yet it would have been a wretched quibble and an unpardonable sophistry on my part, to assume that because he was thus abruptly snatched from me again and for ever, I was absolved from my vow. I therefore decided upon keeping it; and bestowing all my riches upon the church, I retained but a sufficiency of gold to bear my expenses to Palestine. Twenty-seven years have elapsed since, alone, and with my heart full of sorrow, I ascended the mountains of Lebanon, to choose me a grotto for my future home;—and for twenty-seven years has this cave been my abiding-place."

CHAPTER LIV.

THE GROTTO ON MOUNT LEBANON.

THE venerable anchorite ceased speaking; and Lord St. Louis, who had listened with the deepest interest to the tale, continued to gaze upon Antonio Cortez with mingled respect and curiosity. At length he said, "Holy hermit, you have recited a narrative which has enchained my attention: but there was one point at which you might have observed that I suddenly started in astonishment, and even gave vent to an ejaculation which I could not repress."

"I noticed the circumstance, my son," responded the old anchorite: "it was when I stated that Lord Humphrey Danvers appeared to be a man of about thirty years of age, or perhaps a year or two more."

"And it was this same Humphrey Danvers," said Lord St. Louis, "who inflicted upon my great-aunt Arline a similar wrong to that which he perpetrated in respect to your daughter Dolorosa. But it was in the year 1463, that Lord Humphrey Danvers bore away Arline: and then, as the written records declare, he was thirty-two years of age. How, therefore, could he still be but of the same age and of a like appearance in the year 1500, which is the date of your history?"

"Little does it matter what Christian name that man of dread and mystic destiny may bear," was the solemn response given by the old anchorite: "for whatever iniquities have been perpetrated for the past hundred and fifty years by the bearer of the name of Danvers, are all accumulated upon the head of one and the same individual!"

"What mean you, holy father?" exclaimed Lord St. Louis, gazing with the wildest astonishment upon Don Antonio Cortez.

"I mean," was the old man's answer, still given with the gravest and deepest solemnity, "that a hundred and forty-nine years have elapsed since Lord Walter Danvers formed a compact with the Evil One—and that this same Danvers still lives at the present day!"

"Just heaven! is this possible?" said St. Louis. "And yet it may be so: for I myself have seen wondrous proofs of that man's preternatural power. I beheld him change—it was some fifteen years ago—from a shape which he had assumed, back to his natural form——"

"My son, you know not the extent of that mysterious being's power," interrupted Antonio Cortez, shaking his head solemnly. "It is a subject fearful to think upon; because all his attributes, of whatever kind they are, have been purchased at a tremendous price."

"And that price?" asked St. Louis, shuddering from head to foot: for he anticipated the answer.

"His immortal soul!" rejoined the anchorite: and then there was a long silence in the grotto, during which the nobleman and the venerable hermit sat gazing upon each other with mingled awe and subdued consternation.

"Venerable father," at length observed St. Louis, "you have told me things which have filled me with dismay: but you have not yet informed me for what purpose I have been sent hither. Yet, if I remember aright, you said ere now, when we first met upon the summit of this holy hill, that you were enabled to afford me a clue to the mystery. The sun is setting in the Mediterranean wave—and unless it be your will that I should pass the night amongst these mountains, it is urgent that I should take my departure soon."

"My son, thou wilt tarry with me till the morning: for I have yet many things to say unto thee," replied the Spaniard: "and as thou hast already experienced the danger of wandering amidst these hills when the orb of day pours its effulgence upon them, thou mayst estimate the perils which would be attendant upon retracing thy steps at night."

Having thus spoken, the venerable hermit rose from his seat; and striking a light, he set fire to a quantity of dry wood collected at the extremity of the grotto. Then, as the faggots blazed and crackled, he threw thereon several large logs; and a genial heat was speedily shed through the cave,—the smoke escaping by an aperture above, which served the purpose of a chimney.

"For twenty-seven years, as I have already informed you," he said, as he resumed his seat, "have I made this grotto my home,—dwelling thus a solitary hermit upon the height of Lebanon! During this long space of time, my existence has been devoted to heaven; and I have endeavoured to the utmost of my power to banish from my mind the recollections of the past and the affairs of the great busy, bustling world, so that naught should interfere with my devotions. But at times I have felt arising within me a dark hatred for that man whose treachery wrecked all my earthly hopes of happiness. Aye—and I have longed, too, to rush back into that great world which I have deserted, and fulfilling the dying injunctions of my son, pursue Lord Danvers with an unrelenting vindictiveness. But on those occasions, when the thought of revenge has thus stolen into my mind, have I recollected the sublime maxim which enjoins us to leave vengeance unto the Lord: and thus has my sense of duty toward heaven triumphed over the remnants of earthly passions which smoulder in my heart. And to a rigid perseverance in the life of seclusion which I have adopted, has my soul been encouraged by visions from above. In those visions much that relates to the author of my sorrows has been revealed to me; and it is doubtless for the purpose of hearing from my lips the revelation of these deep and mysterious secrets, that you have been sent hither. Listen, then, Gerald St. Louis, to what I am about to say."

The countenance of the venerable anchorite assumed, if possible, a deeper solemnity than it had previously worn, as he thus spoke; and as the lambent light of the fire played upon his features, St. Louis thought that never had he beheld a figure so venerable and so entitled to the profoundest respect as the hermit of Mount Lebanon.

"A hundred and forty-nine years have elapsed," continued the anchorite, "since Lord Walter Danvers—then only twenty-five years of age—made his compact with the Evil One. This compact, as I have already informed you, involved the peril of his immortal soul. For a period of one hundred and fifty years was the lease of life, and power, and riches, extended, in one year more that lease will expire; and *then*, unless certain conditions be fulfilled, the unhappy Danvers must surrender up his soul to Satan!"

"One year more?" murmured St. Louis, a cold shudder quivering throughout his frame. "Oh! how dark, how dreary, how desolate his thoughts must be!"

"Perhaps less so than you may imagine," rejoined the hermit: "for if the conditions of his compact be fulfilled by him, he emancipates himself from the power of the Evil One."

"And those conditions?" asked St. Louis with mingled curiosity and awe.

"That he should furnish six victims," replied the old man, "who, for the love of him, pledge themselves to surrender up even their immortal souls at his bidding!"

"Heavens! unhappy Arline!" ejaculated St. Louis, a light suddenly breaking in upon his mind. "Was it thus that thou wast beguiled, O Arline?"

"Alas! and my unhappy daughter likewise!" rejoined the old man, clasping his hands and bending his head down in deep despondency. "But let us hope," he observed, somewhat suddenly looking up again, and with the sacred light of a sublime confidence beaming upon his countenance, "that your mission hither to me was to prepare the way for breaking the spell which has already given five victims to the infernal compact that Danvers made with the Enemy of Mankind."

"Five victims?" echoed St. Louis interrogatively.

"Yes—five," rejoined the anchorite. "I have seen them in my visions; and amongst them was my hapless daughter Dolorosa. So recently as last night did I behold them flitting in shadowy shapes before me, as I lay stretched upon my bed of dry leaves; and thus it is certain that Lord Danvers has not as yet found a *sixth* victim! He therefore has but one year left in order to find that sixth and last victim who in the infatuation of a virgin love will consent to be his both body and soul!"

"One year to find his sixth and last victim?" said Gerald St. Louis, as he repeated in a musing tone the old man's words.

"Yes—it is so," responded the anchorite. "But I have yet more to reveal. In my visions I have beheld the interior of a chamber containing six black panels bordered with red lines, and originally planned for the inscription of the names of six victims. I know not where upon the face of the earth that chamber is situated: for my dreams have been limited as to circumstances, and shadowy as well as indistinct in respect to many things connected with these awful mysteries. But upon five of those panels have I read as many names, traced in letters of fire and fearfully distinct. There are times when my memory becomes confused, and I recollect not all that I have seen in my visions: but at this moment everything which has thus been so mysteriously revealed to me, is wonderfully distinct in the cells of my brain. Yes—now I behold those panels; and I can read the names which burn upon five thereof. Bianca Landini—Margaret Dunhaven—Arline de St. Louis—Dolorosa Cortez—and Clara Manners!"

"Arline, Arline!" muttered the nobleman between his teeth; "thou shalt be avenged! thou shalt be avenged!"

"Say rather, my son," rejoined the old man, in a tone of mingled rebuke and encouragement, "that the soul of your ancestress shall be rescued and saved, and not that her spirit shall be avenged. Have I not already made thee understand that vengeance belongeth unto heaven, and not to man? It was one of the circumstances of Lord Danvers' wild and mysterious destiny that whenever he succeeded in finding a victim, he should leave the germs of a dark and almost implacable vengeance behind. Thus, so far as the revealings of my nights' dreams have lifted the veil of my comprehension, have I been made to know that each family which experienced the sad destiny of furnishing a victim to Lord Danvers, has likewise cherished hopes and projects for revenge. Such would also have been the dominant thoughts and aspirations of *my* soul, had not I devoted myself to the service of heaven, and abandoning the world, sought the holy seclusion of this grotto on the heights of Lebanon. Therefore is it that heaven in the working out of its own inscrutable will, hath made such revelations unto me as will perhaps lead to the emancipation of the souls of the five departed maidens from the power of the Evil One, and frustrate the designs of Lord Danvers in his search for a sixth and last virgin-victim!"

"And perhaps also," added St. Louis, deeply touched by the old man's piety, "it is because for many years past I also have renounced all thoughts of vengeance, that I am now destined to become an instrument of good to accomplish the high purposes of heaven?"

"Let us hope so, my son," answered the old anchorite, crossing himself devoutly: "and I already feel a presentiment arising within me that our anticipations will not be disappointed. Let us now lie down to rest; and it may be in the morning that I shall have farther revelations to make and positive instructions to give, so that your mission to Mount Lebanon will not have been accomplished in vain."

The old anchorite and the great English nobleman then stretched themselves side by side upon the bed of leaves; and in a few minutes a deep slumber fell upon them both. The visions of Gerald St. Louis were cheering and full of hope. He fancied that he beheld that same preternatural lustre which he had seen in his magnificent chamber at Constantinople, now diffusing itself throughout the grotto, and supplying with its holier and more translucent radiance the light of the fire which had died away;—and in the midst of that shining halo he perceived the figure of Arline gradually appear. The shape was still apparelled in sable garments; but its countenance was no longer pensive and mournful. It shone with the radiance of hope; and her features were beaming with smiles of approval and thankfulness, as she fixed her blue eyes upon Gerald St. Louis. Then she appeared to raise her hand—not in a warning manner, but as if invocative of a blessing: and she said in a soft musical voice, "Again am I permitted to appear unto thee! Thou hast done well to obey my injunctions; and all things shall henceforth prosper thee in life if thou dost pursue thy mission faithfully until the end. See that thou obeyest to the very letter the words the venerable anchorite will breathe to thee in the morning!"

Having thus spoken—or rather having thus appeared to speak—the figure of Arline gradually grew dim and indistinct, the lustre also fading away; and utter darkness once more prevailed in that grotto. St. Louis dreamt no more, but slept on tranquilly and serenely until the morning—when he awoke, as the orient heavens were glowing with the effulgence of a new-born day.

Rising from his bed of leaves, St. Louis found that he was alone in the grotto; and having performed his ablutions—the conveniences for which, rude though they were, he found at hand—he issued forth from the cave. Antonio Cortez was now descried kneeling on the summit of the hill, and offering up his prayers to heaven. St. Louis, silently advancing to the spot, knelt down by his side, and joined in the old man's devotions. Presently they rose; and the anchorite said, "Let us first break our fast, and I will then impart to you the inspirations of my sleep's visions."

They sat down at the entrance of the grotto, and partook of the frugal fare which the anchorite produced.

"For this," he said, "as well as for every morsel of food that I have put into my mouth for twenty-seven years past—yea, also for the garments which clothe me—am I indebted to the piety of a few Christians who dwell amongst the hills farther along the chain of Lebanon."

Antonio Cortez gave St. Louis a few more particulars relative to his mode of life: but these would prove but little interesting to the reader. We will therefore suppose the frugal meal ended and a thanksgiving pronounced by the venerable hermit. Then addressing himself to Lord St. Louis, he spoke as follows:—"The presentiment which had arisen in my mind ere we retired to rest, and which was to the effect that the visions of my slumber would follow up the chain of previous revelations and divine promptings, has been fulfilled. Angel-voices have whispered the most cheering language to my ears, and have indicated yourself as the instrument whom heaven has chosen to accomplish its high purposes. But of the future I can read little: and what I have to say is limited to a few instructions, which nevertheless I feel assured are destined to serve as the means for accomplishing all desired aims. Return you without delay to Constantinople: in a few months' time your negotiations there will be accomplished successfully; and this shall be a sign unto you that you may likewise hope for success in the holy and mysterious mission with which you are entrusted by a power superior to all earthly kings. In due course you will retrace your way to England. And now mark well what I am about to say. On the last night of the month of May of the next year—namely, the year 1532—and soon after ten o'clock on that same night, do you present yourself at the gate of Carisbrook Castle in the Isle of Wight, and accost the first person whom you shall see coming forth thence. In that person's ear thou wilt whisper these words: '_This night a victim must be saved from the power of Lord Danvers!_' Then that person—I know not whom it will be, nor whether male or female—will aid thee to the accomplishment of the rest. But one word more. Thou wilt require a talisman to save thyself and thy companion from the vengeance of Lord Danvers: and this holy relic shall suffice."

Thus speaking, the old man drew forth a small ebony crucifix from beneath the folds of his garment; and having devoutly kissed it, he gave it into the hand of St. Louis.

They then parted,—the venerable hermit bestowing a fervid benediction upon the English nobleman, who forthwith began to retrace his way down the slopes of Lebanon to the fishing-village where he had left his dependants. They were rejoiced to behold their master return; for they were apprehensive that some evil had befallen him amidst the mountains. Without farther delay, St. Louis and his menials embarked on board the ship, which set sail on its voyage back to Constantinople.

CHAPTER LV.

MARIAN

THE town of Chelmsford was already a thriving and by no means unimportant place in the age of which we are writing. It is to the environs of this town that we are about to direct the attention of the reader.

A neat little cottage, standing in the midst of a flower-garden upon the bank of the Chelmer, was occupied by an aged gentlewoman and a beautiful young maiden. The former was the widow of an officer who had fallen when fighting the battles of his country many years previous to the date of which we are speaking. There were no pensions in those times for widows in such cases: but as Captain Musgrave had been a distinguished and highly respected townsman of Chelmsford, the wealthy inhabitants of the place had taken care that his widow should be placed above want. She had no children nor any relations to care for her: but she had adopted the young maiden to whom we ere now alluded.

The circumstances of this adoption were so singular as to require special mention here. It was in the summer of the year 1517, that a man and woman bearing the name of Bradley, and having an infant female child with them, came to settle in the town of Chelmsford. The man was about thirty years of age—the woman two or three years younger. They hired a respectable house, and appeared to be possessed of ample means, although the sources of their income were not known, the man pursuing no trade, profession, or calling of any kind. They did not appear to be of the rank of gentlefolk; and indeed it somehow or another got whispered about that they had held menial offices previous to their marriage—or in plainer terms, had been servants in some wealthy family. However, be this as it may, they conducted themselves with the utmost propriety; and if they lived in a manner which appeared to be somewhat above their real condition in life, they at all events paid their way honourably. The house which they occupied was at no great distance from Dame Musgrave's cottage—a little way out of town, and on the bank of the river. The man

Bradley's chief amusement consisted in angling in the stream; and for this purpose he purchased a little boat which he kept moored at the bottom of his garden. Sometimes his wife, with the child in her arms, would accompany him in his fishing excursions; and he seemed fond of rowing his boat up and down the river when his wife thus became his companion. It was about a year after the Bradleys had settled at Chelmsford that the tragedy took place which gave the child over to the care of Dame Musgrave: for one day the boat upset in a wide and deep part of the river, and Bradley and his wife were drowned. The child, buoyed up by its garments, floated upon the water: and some persons who witnessed the accident, hastened to tender such assistance as they could. Bradley and his wife had sunk to rise no more: but the child was rescued from a watery grave.

Dame Musgrave's cottage being nearest to the scene of the catastrophe, the child was taken thither; and the worthy woman, kindly receiving the little girl, lavished upon her the most affectionate attentions. The Bradleys had no friends in the town who knew anything about them beyond what has been already stated: it could not therefore be ascertained whether they had relations anywhere in England to whom their death ought to be reported, and to whose charge their orphan child might be consigned. But a considerable sum of money, all in gold and silver coin, was found secreted in their house—whether honestly come by in the origin, could not of course be known. The authorities of Chelmsford, upon being applied to, thought it advisable that the money should be appropriated to the maintenance of the child in the care of any respectable person who would take charge of her; and this Dame Musgrave at once volunteered to do.

These were the circumstances under which Marian became the adopted daughter (or grand-daughter as she was subsequently called) of worthy Mistress Musgrave. The child's surname of *Bradley* was dropped, and that of her protectress was bestowed upon her in accordance with the custom of the times in such cases of adoption. Marian Musgrave, as she grew up, gave promise of becoming one of the loveliest creatures that ever graced this earth with her presence; and at the time when we now introduce her to our readers—namely, in the month of May, 1532—she was at that sweet and interesting age of fifteen when the light step, the beaming eye, the gay sunny smile, and the merry laugh of girlhood are only just beginning to be subdued into the bashful sedateness which precedes the dawn of womanhood. And Marian's charms were somewhat precocious—she looked two years older than she really was, and in height had attained her full growth. Eminently beautiful was she! Her hair was of raven darkness, but lustrous also as the wing of the bird to which we have just likened it. Her eyes, of deepest black, were sparkling with intelligence, innocence,

and gaiety. Her complexion was naturally pale: but there was the hue of
health upon her cheeks—and that hue could mantle into the softest or
richest blush, according to the emotions that stirred in her soul. Above
the medium stature of her sex, and upright as a dart, her figure was of the
most exquisite symmetry, and seemed invested with a gracefulness that
only needed courtly apparel to enhance it into a brilliant elegance. Her
disposition was artless and lively; but nevertheless her soul was susceptible
of feelings the deepest and most sensitive. Whatever impression was made
upon her, was at once indelibly stamped. Indeed, her's was a disposition of
precisely that plastic and tender nature which a poet would describe as the
one calculated to imbibe the holy essence of love almost at first sight, and
to receive it into her being never more to be separated therefrom.

Such was Marian Musgrave at the age of fifteen; and from what we
have already stated concerning her, it can scarcely be necessary to inform
the reader that she was devotedly attached to her benefactress. Dame
Musgrave was now well stricken in years; and she loved the lively but gentle and innocent Marian as tenderly as if the damsel were really closely al-
lied to her, instead of there being a total absence of all kinship whatsoever.
Of an evening the worthy woman and her sweet charge might be seen
walking along the bank of the river, enjoying the refreshing breeze; or else
inspecting the flowers which it was Marian's delight to rear and tend not
only because she herself was fond of them, but because their luxuriant
beauties were pleasing to the eye of her whom she revered and loved so
well. The catastrophe which had deprived Marian of her early protectors
had been with the most delicate consideration carefully concealed from
her, so that no cloud should be permitted to overshadow the mind of that
charming and ingenuous creature. She had likewise been led to believe
that she was a relation of Dame Musgrave's—another precaution adopted
by the good woman to prevent her young charge from feeling a too complete dependence upon her. Thus was it that up to the time of which we
are writing Marian's existence had flowed on without a care, like a crystal
stream pursuing its way between its banks of flowers, without a ripple to
disturb the glassy uniformity of its surface.

One evening—we must here be particular in dates, and observe that
it was the opening of the month of May, 1532—Marian Musgrave was
rambling forth alone on the bank of the river, her aged protectress having gone up into the town to minister to the wants of some poor female
acquaintance who was lying upon the bed of death. Dame Musgrave had
not thought it right to make Marian her companion on a visit to so mournful and distressing a scene; and thus it was that the charming damsel was
roving forth alone. But she did not purpose to proceed any great distance

from the cottage, because she expected the good dame to return at the expiration of an hour, when they were to have their usual ramble in the little garden together. As Marian walked along she thought to herself that she would only venture as far as a group of trees which were about a mile from the dwelling, and that then she would retrace her way. These trees stood upon a gentle slope, gradually shelving down to the bank of the river, and covered with wild flowers. On nearing this spot Marian observed an elegantly-dressed individual reclining indolently upon the verdant declivity, beneath the shade of an overhanging bough. The nature of the path and the windings of the river had thus brought her within a few yards of the stranger ere she perceived him; and then she was about to turn away and begin retracing her steps homeward, when he suddenly sprang to his feet, and doffing his plumed cap, made her so courteous a salutation that she was of necessity compelled to return it. Then he advanced towards her, putting some question relative to the direction in which certain paths, branching away from that point, led off; so that she found herself constrained to pause and give him the information which he sought.

While thus conversing with the stranger, Marian could not help noticing the beauty of his person, the elegance of his manners, and the sweetness of his voice. Moreover, he was quite a youth—apparently not more than two or three years above her own age; and thus there was less real awkwardness or embarrassment on her part in conversing with him, than if he had been farther advanced in manhood.

But his personal beauty—it was indeed of a rare perfection! The reader cannot fail to remember the description which we gave of Reginald Danvers at the time when he assumed that boyishness of appearance after imbibing the liquid from the phial at his castle in the Isle of Wight. That very same description will exactly suit the elegant stripling who thus introduced himself to the notice of Marian Musgrave. His long dark hair, curling as beautifully as that of a woman, and parted above a brow of noble height—the classic regularity of his delicately chiselled features—the brightness of his splendid eyes—the pure vermilion of his lips—the pearly whiteness of his teeth—and the soft carnation appearing through the clear olive of his complexion,—all were precisely the same as those characteristics which distinguished the exquisite beauty of Reginald Danvers. There was likewise an ingenuous frankness and a captivating affability in his manner, as well as a softness in his speech, with the gloss of the most polished courtesy and well-bred refinement thrown over all, that it was no wonder if the susceptible heart of Marian Musgrave at once experienced a feeling of interest in her new acquaintance.

He had asked her those questions concerning the pathways, and he had received the information which he appeared to seek. But still he found some additional queries to put—some more intelligence to obtain; and Marian, even without the secret and scarcely comprehensible promptings of her own heart, would have been compelled for mere courtesy's sake to linger a few minutes thus to converse with the elegant stranger. Insensibly, too, did she find herself listening to some tale which he had already begun to tell concerning himself. He stated that the family to which he belonged, and which was of the highest rank and greatest wealth, had given displeasure to the King and been much persecuted. He went on to say that he himself at that moment, though so young, was an object of the same rancorous proscription; and that his head would be forfeited if he were entrapped by the royal emissaries.

It required nothing more than such a tale as this to enlist the tenderest sympathies of Marian's generous heart; and as she fixed her fine dark eyes with a compassionating look upon the stranger, she could not help thinking how shocking it would be if so handsome and graceful a young man were to undergo a violent death. He saw what was passing in her mind—he read all her emotions in her eloquent eyes; and taking her hand, he said, in that soft musical voice which in its very tones is laden with the language of love, "Fair damsel, I perceive that you sympathize with me—and I thank you—Oh! I thank you, from the bottom of my heart! But there is a boon which, were I bold enough, I should beseech at your hands—a boon that will give you little trouble to grant, and which may perhaps be the means of saving my life."

What could Marian do? what could she say? Guileless herself, she was unsuspicious of guile in others: never having harboured a deceitful thought in all her life, it occurred not to her for a single moment that there was a possibility of being deceived. She therefore at once declared, with a blush upon her cheek and a tear glistening in her eye, that she would cheerfully do all that lay in her power to assist one who seemed to be so cruelly persecuted, and over whose head such imminent peril was hanging.

"All that I require, sweet maiden," he responded, "is to be informed whether any of the King's officers are at present lurking about in the town of Chelmsford. If at this same hour to-morrow evening you would not deem it indiscreet to come hither and bring me information on that head, you would be conferring a lasting obligation upon me."

"My grandmother"—(for so was Marian accustomed to call Dame Musgrave)—"is in the town at this moment, and I will presently seek from her the information you require. To-morrow evening therefore—or earlier if you wish—I will return hither in company with my relative."

"Ah! fair maiden," cried the youth, a cloud suddenly settling upon his countenance; "if you breathe to a single soul, even your nearest and dearest relation, that I am concealed in this neighbourhood, I should not consider myself safe. Without the intention to do me harm, the most fatal result might be produced by a mere word inadvertently uttered."

"Then I will take the task upon myself," at once replied the generous-hearted Marian, not understanding in her girlish artlessness that it was nothing more nor less than an appointment she was thus making with the youthful stranger.

"Thanks—a thousand thanks!" he exclaimed, his beauteous features suddenly lighting up with joy. "For heaven's sake do not disappoint me!"

Without giving her time to reply, the elegant stranger doffed his plumed cap once more in graceful salutation; and then plunging amidst the trees, disappeared from her view. Marian retraced her way to the cottage, her mind filled with the image of that captivating youth whose alleged misfortunes had already enlisted her warmest sympathies.

CHAPTER LVI.

THE LOVERS.

It was not till the gentle Marian reached the threshold of the cottage that it struck her how she had given a pledge to the beautiful youth from whom she had just parted, that would compel her to keep all the particulars of their meeting, and indeed the meeting itself, rigidly secret from Dame Musgrave. The young girl stopped short; and a painful sensation smote her heart, even with the violence of a pang. She stood irresolute how to act. On the one hand was a deep and affectionate sense of the duty which she owed to her kind guardian: on the other hand was the promise she had given the youth to observe a strict silence in respect to all that concerned him. Ingenuous, sincere, and open-hearted as Marian was, she naturally looked upon everything that savoured of dissimulation as a crime; and she felt sorely distressed at the embarrassment in which she was placed.

For nearly a minute did she remain at the door ere she lifted the latch: and then she entered the dwelling without having been able to make up her mind to any particular course. The little parlour was empty: Dame Musgrave had not yet returned. Greatly relieved at thus finding she had leisure for reflection, Marian sat down and continued her communings. She felt towards that youth as never she had yet felt in respect to any human being: his image had made a sudden and deep impression upon her heart. Chaste and ingenuous though she were—guileless even to an angelic simplicity—she could not help experiencing a secret desire to behold that youth again; and when she caught herself sighing, she wondered in her innocence wherefore what she believed to be so trivial a circumstance as the mere encounter of a stranger, should have produced such an effect upon her. Still, as she went on thinking, she could not satisfactorily settle the point whether she should tell her grandmother (as she called Dame Musgrave) everything, or whether she should maintain a rigid silence. But then, as she reflected—and shuddered, too, as she thus reflected—upon the words which the youth had spoken, to the effect that the least inadvertent syllable let drop would send him to the scaffold, she was naturally led to the conclusion that it would be more prudent to say nothing upon the point. Yet, even as Marian made up her mind, she felt some slight compunction and some little misgiving at the course on which she resolved: then again, as the dread of in any way compromising the safety of that beautiful and elegant youth recurred to her heart, she was confirmed in the decision to which she had come.

Therefore, when Dame Musgrave re-appeared, Marian held her peace as to the adventure on the river's bank. She and her worthy protectress took their usual little walk in the garden; and though the young maiden was more pensive than ever she had been before, yet her kind guardian did not perceive it, she being herself somewhat pre-occupied with the solemn thoughts excited by the visit which she had just paid to a dying friend.

It was a long time before Marian could compose herself to sleep that night: the image of the beautiful youth was never absent from her mind. The charming girl was in love—but she knew it not. It was love at first sight,—that love which poets have depicted, but which serious-minded people have seldom put faith in. Nevertheless, whether affording an instance of the rule or the exception, matters not to our story: for certain it is that Marian Musgrave had been smitten by the tenderest sentiment in respect to the elegant stranger. When sleep fell upon her eyes, his image was re-produced in her dreams: the soft melody of his voice seemed to be wafted to her ears—his fine dark eyes appeared to be gazing upon her with all the witching tenderness of love—and her heart beat with raptures as new as they were ecstatic. Her first thought in the morning, when she awoke—or rather the continuous chain of her thoughts, still kept the image of the youthful stranger present in her mind; and she experienced an inward rejoicing at the prospect of meeting him again, although she felt the colour mounting to her cheeks as she became aware that she was harbouring such a thought.

Immediately after the morning meal Dame Musgrave bade her put a few little things into her basket, and take them, together with a nosegay of flowers, to her invalid friend in the town. Marian lost no time in obeying these directions, as it afforded her an opportunity to make the inquiries enjoined her by the youthful stranger. On entering the town, she soon acquitted herself of her errand in respect to the invalid; and then, in a guarded manner, she questioned two or three of the shop-keepers at whose houses Dame Musgrave was accustomed to deal, upon the point whether any of the King's officers had been observed in the place? Such queries, although by no means pointedly put, nevertheless excited some degree of astonishment on the part of those to whom they were addressed; and Marian blushed when she found herself the object of the wondering gaze of the trades people. Nevertheless, she did not satisfy their curiosity; but inwardly rejoicing at the answer she received, betook herself homeward. In the evening Dame Musgrave again went forth to visit her invalid friend; and again was Marian left to ramble by herself. With a beating heart and a blushing cheek did the young damsel repair to the place of appointment; and the moment she reached the vicinage of the group of trees, she beheld the elegant unknown issuing forth from amidst the depth of their shade. Joy beamed upon his countenance; and for a moment the eyes of the gentle Marian sent forth a kindred reflection. But she was suddenly overwhelmed with confusion as the youth seized her hand and passionately pressed it to his lips. Of a vivid crimson became Marian's cheeks, and her heart throbbed more violently than before. Feelings hitherto unknown took possession of her: she had not the courage nor the power to withdraw her hand—so that it lingered in the clasp of the youth after it had left his lips.

"Sweet maiden," he said, in the most touching tones of his melodious voice, "all the effusion of my heart's deepest gratitude is your due for this kindness on your part. And now, what intelligence have you for me?"

"From the inquiries which I made," she answered in a tremulous voice, "I have no reason to fear that your presence in this neighbourhood is suspected by your enemies."

"Heaven be thanked!" cried the youth fervidly: "I shall therefore be enabled to remain. Oh! after having formed your acquaintance, sweet girl, it would have been sad indeed for me to depart hence!"

Again did Marian blush: but she withdrew her hand, and made a movement as if about to take her departure and retrace her way homeward.

"Surely you will not leave me yet?" he said, in a voice of such mild and mournful reproach that the young girl felt at the instant as if she were actually treating him with unkindness. "Ah! if you only knew how I have counted the hours—aye, even the minutes—since we separated last evening, until I beheld you approaching along the bank of the river ere now, you would indeed comprehend that it is not a mere passing sentiment of gratitude which I feel for the kindness you have rendered me, but that in you I behold the personification of everything bright and beautiful that has ever visited me in my dreams. Ah! sweet girl, turn not away—plunge me not into despair: for you are dearer to me than life itself!"

Marian trembled all over, but not with painful sensations: a flood of happiest feelings seemed to be gushing forth from the fountains of her heart and rapidly diffusing itself through her entire being. The veil had dropped from her eyes—she understood wherefore she had contemplated with such ineffable emotions the image of the youthful stranger ever since she parted from him on the previous evening—and she now knew that she loved! At that moment all thought beyond the bliss of the present scene was lost—she remembered not her venerable protectress—she reflected not whether she were guilty of imprudence in lingering with the beautiful youth, who had again taken her hand and again pressed it to his lips: the blissful consciousness of a first virginal love was in her soul—and though she was yet even ignorant of her lover's name, and their acquaintance dated back for a few hours, she nevertheless felt as if she had known him for years!

He continued to address her in that soft and melting language of love which appeared to flow with the natural eloquence of his own heart's feelings, and which sank deeply down into the heart of Marian. She listened in silent rapture, as one who suddenly finding herself transported to a strange land, may drink in the ravishing music of sweet birds unknown to the clime to which she herself belongs. Existence had in a few brief minutes appeared to assume altogether a new and brighter aspect; as if she had gone to sleep amidst the ordinary scenes that were familiar to her, and wakened again in the bowers and roseate atmosphere of a hitherto unknown paradise. She raised her blushing countenance timidly and bashfully towards him who addressed her in a strain that filled her with such new and delightful sensations; and as she beheld mingled joy, and tenderness, and hope beaming in the eyes of her youthful companion, it seemed as if that brilliant and adoring gaze which he bent upon her was flinging a shower of light and love upon her heart. In the rapt trance of her feelings it appeared to her as if the dawn of another day, with the radiance of the sunniest clime, were bursting around her; and her soul, naturally so sensitive, thrilled with emotions of indescribable bliss.

Think you then, reader, that it was difficult for her youthful lover to exact from her a promise that she would return to the same spot and at the same hour on the following day? or that he experienced any trouble in persuading her of the necessity (whether real or assumed, matters not now) of keeping their acquaintance, their love, and their appointments a profound secret? Marian, unsuspicious as she was sensitive, and confiding as she was guileless, promised everything that the youth demanded:—and they separated.

But it was not altogether an easy task for the maiden to conceal the state of her mind from Dame Musgrave. Utterly unpractised in the art of dissimulation, the damsel could not prevent herself from blushing when she returned to the cottage and found that the worthy woman had got back before her. The dame, noticing this confusion on the girl's part, at once questioned her as to the cause. Then, in that moment, did Marian feel an almost resistless inclination to throw herself into Dame Musgrave's arms and confess everything: but the next instant all that the youth had said to her, warning her of the consequences of revealing their love, rushed to her mind, and she declared that nothing unusual had occurred to her. The dame believed Marian, because she had never known her descend to the slightest subterfuge or deceit: the young girl had taken her first lesson in dissimulation—and it was not without a pang that she did so!

For several days following, did Dame Musgrave regularly go into the town to visit her sick friend; and the young damsel as regularly repaired to the trysting-place to meet her lover. In the course of those tender conversations which they had together, and which daily developed new charms to fascinate the soul of the gentle and confiding Marian, he told her that he was Lord Danvers, the owner of the vast domain and castellated mansion which were in the neighbourhood of Chelmsford; and while breathing the language of love into the ears of the maiden, he artfully depicted, but in glowing colours, the delights, the splendours, and the dazzling circumstances attendant upon that rank to which she would be raised when she became his bride. He told her that the persecutions to which he had been subjected at the hands of the King, were now at an end, and that he was no longer in fear of his enemies: but still he made her understand that there were certain circumstances which for the present compelled him to keep their love a secret—at least until after their marriage. Marian was neither vain nor ambitious: but yet she could not be indifferent to the brilliant prospects of rank and wealth that were thus spread out for her contemplation; and when Lord Danvers, with every appearance of the most tender sympathy, represented how she would be enabled to transport her grandmother from a cottage and place her in the splendid saloon of a castle, Marian thanked him with tears of joy for his considerate kindness on behalf of her relative. Believing herself, as we have already stated, to be the grand-daughter of the worthy dame, she had all along spoken of her to Danvers in that light; and therefore the young nobleman himself was led to entertain the same belief. For that preternatural power which he possessed through his compact with the Evil One, was limited in many respects, and afforded him no extraordinary facility of plunging into the mysteries that enveloped the affairs of strangers.

Thus day after day passed; and the love of Marian for the youthful Conrad Danvers—that being the Christian name which he now bore— grew into an all-engrossing worship. It was an enthusiasm of the most rapt and holy kind. If an angel had appeared to her from heaven, she could not have placed a more sublime confidence in the purity, the sincerity, and the virtue of the holy visitor, than she reposed in her lover. Besides, she had never heard of damsels being deceived, and knew naught of the wiles of treacherous and designing men: there was consequently naught in her mind to impair or for a moment check that chaste reliance which she experienced in Conrad Danvers. Fair and beautiful did the future seem to stretch before her;—the bow of hope was ever shining in the heaven which love had thus created for her; and the paradise through which in imagination she was proceeding, was gemmed with flowers far brighter, more fascinating, and more fragrant than those real ones which bloomed in her now somewhat neglected garden.

We must likewise observe that the behaviour of Conrad Danvers towards Marian was of a nature to sustain that sublime confidence and holy trust which she placed in him: for even when most passionately pleading the suit of love, his language and his manner were invariably characterized by a delicacy that was best calculated to secure the heart of a damsel so chaste, so pure, and so innocent as she.

Meanwhile Dame Musgrave had more than once observed that Marian's demeanour was somewhat changed—that there were times when she would sit wrapped up in a deep reverie—and yet that there was ever the beaming smile of a softly subdued happiness upon her angelic features. The dame likewise noticed that the garden was neglected, and that when the damsel went forth to tend her flowers she would stand gazing upon them in a mood of soft and dreamy abstraction. Now and then Dame Musgrave would question Marian upon the subject: but as the young girl invariably recovered her wonted gaiety and sprightliness of demeanour in an instant, and appeared so full of radiant happiness as she pushed back her raven hair and lifted her beaming countenance, the worthy woman failed to suspect anything serious. Indeed she herself had latterly become so assiduous in her attentions to her dying friend, that she did not observe to the full extent those numerous evidences which, under other circumstances, must have betrayed the young girl's secret;—and that same devotedness with which the kind-hearted woman ministered unto her invalid acquaintance in the town, afforded Marian so many opportunities of meeting her lover without exciting the suspicion of her old guardian. Thus did nearly a month pass, and the close of the genial spring-time of May was about to be succeeded by the summer warmth of June.

CHAPTER LVII.

THE LAST APPOINTMENT.

It was the evening of the thirty-first of May. The sun was descending to his western home—a gentle breeze had begun to agitate the heavy sultry air—and the birds were pouring forth their blithe carols from amidst the trees and the hedge-rows, as Conrad Danvers and Marian Musgrave walked slowly along the verdant bank of the Chelmer.

Had they been observed by a stranger utterly unconscious of the fearful destiny attaching itself to the young nobleman, they would have been admired with a tender and almost a saint-like enthusiasm: for each was so faultless in face and in form, and both were so characterized by an air of youthful ingenuousness, that there seemed a remarkable fitness in the circumstance that two such beings should cherish so deep a passion for each other. Marian was listening with downcast looks to the tender words that Conrad was breathing in her ears; and the language of love was far sweeter to the young maiden than the delicious harmony of the warblers on every bough.

With one arm lightly engirdling the slender waist of the fair damsel, Conrad bent gracefully towards her in a manner which, though so completely unstudied, displayed the slim elegance and willowy elasticity of his tall stripling figure; and as the sunbeams shone horizontally from the west upon his beardless countenance, his features seemed lighted up with the radiance of a glorious beauty, as well as with the reflection of the heart's inward happiness. Yet, was he happy? Ever and anon for a moment—and only for a single moment—did a withering expression of mingled anguish and horror sweep over that countenance: but as the maiden's eyes were bent down in the bashfulness of her virgin love, she perceived not those occasional and transient indications of a soul that was inwardly ill at ease.

"To-morrow, my angel," said Conrad Danvers, in tones more melting than ever lover had yet spoken in to his enraptured fair one,—"to-morrow shall behold you the bride of him who worships and adores the very ground upon which you tread. Oh, dearest Marian! what happiness

awaits us! Restored to the favour of my King—about to possess the greatest treasure existing upon the face of the earth—what more can I need?
what more can I desire?"

It is scarcely necessary to pause here for a moment to acquaint the
reader that the alleged persecutions of Conrad Danvers were utterly false,
and had merely served as a pretext in the first instance to enlist the sympathies of Marian Musgrave in his behalf. For, on the one hand, King Henry
experienced too profound a dread of the terrible name of Danvers even to
dream of working him a mischief; and on the other hand, Danvers himself
could as easily have triumphed over every such attempt, as a giant could
crush a miserable worm beneath his heel.

"Yes—to-morrow, sweetest Marian," continued the treacherous Danvers, speaking as if honey only were upon his lips, untainted by the gall
which was distilling from his heart,—"shalt thou be the bearer of my
name—the sharer of my fortune—the partner of my rank! And then too,
my well beloved, when the priest has united our hands in sacred bonds,
we will repair with a brilliant cavalcade of attendant knights and ministering ladies, to that cottage which has hitherto been your home; and then
shall I experience the ineffable bliss of conducting thee by the hand, arrayed as thou wilt be in thy rich bridal garments—and thus shall I present
thee to thy venerable relative, bidding her embrace thee as the chosen and
cherished wife of Lord Danvers. And then the good dame shall quit her
humble abode and depart with us; and in our mansion shall she dwell, a
witness of our happiness, until the end of her days."

"Dear Conrad," murmured Marian, in the low soft voice of the heart's
most deeply-stirred emotions, "what prospects of bliss do you present to
my gaze?"—and she looked up with love beaming in her fine dark eyes,
and the radiance of ineffable joy sitting upon her countenance as if it were
a heavenly halo.

"And art thou not worthy, dearest Marian," cried Danvers, straining
her to his breast, "of all that I can do for thee? Hast thou not given me thy
first and purest affections? In one short month hast thou not learnt to love
me as if by a year's unwearied devotion I had studied to win that love of
thine? Ought I not to be grateful to thee for thus consenting to render me
the happiest of mortals?"

"O Conrad, you speak of gratitude," said Marian, once again raising
her looks with a most earnest and trustful devotion: "but it is I who should
experience gratitude towards you! I, the humble and obscure girl—never
dreaming of love at all, and scarcely knowing of its existence,—I who
never entertained the thought of what might occur to me beyond the day
itself, and who never sent a single aspiration beyond the limits of the poor

cottage in which I dwell,—for me, I say, to be loved by you, and to be told that to-morrow I shall become thy bride,—O Conrad, how can I ever testify towards thee all the gratitude I experience? Would to heaven that in return for so much love, and goodness, and generosity on your part, there were some way in which I could afford thee a proof of my fondness in return!"

"Ah! now I am reminded," said Danvers, "that there is a certain ceremony which we must pass through—a ceremony in assenting to which my sweet Marian will be enabled to afford me the proof of love which she so much longs to give."

"Oh, name it! name it!" cried Marian, in a voice ringing melodiously with the exultation that gushed up as it were from the fountains of her soul. "Tell me what I may do to prove my trusting and confiding love in you, my worshipped Conrad!"

"Listen, sweetest," rejoined Danvers, pressing her still more closely to him as his arm encircled her waist. "There was a certain eccentric and whimsical ancestor of mine, who some centuries ago decreed that every descendant of his, when about to enter the marriage state, should receive in a particular room of the family mansion the solemn pledge and plight of love from the lips of her whom he proposed to lead unto the altar. And now that I bethink me, this singular injunction on his part becomes all the more important, not only as an hereditary duty, but likewise in a legal point of view; for it is on fulfilment of the condition thus laid down that the tenure of my titles and estates is made to depend. Do you understand me, sweetest Marian?"

"Yes, dear Conrad," she answered: "But was it not a strange wild whim on the part of your ancestor?"

"Yes—a strange wild whim," he responded, looking anxiously, or rather earnestly for a moment into the depths of her gazelle-like eyes, as if to assure himself that no expression of doubt or mistrust was lurking there: then, as he perceived that naught but the most endearing confidence and the tenderest devotion were to be read in the lustrous depths of those black orbs, he said, "But there are many noble families in England who hold all their titles and estates upon a tenure fraught with conditions still more preposterous and absurd."

"But it is enough for us to know, dear Conrad," replied Marian, "that such was the will of your ancestor—and it must be accomplished."

"You assent then, my own adored one?" he asked: and his arm, rising from her waist to her neck, drew her gently towards him, so that his cheek rested against the clustering tresses of her raven hair.

"Yes—can you doubt it?" exclaimed the artless, unsuspecting girl; and in the effusion of her innocent love and impassioned gratitude she kissed him unasked.

"To-night then, dearest Marian," resumed Conrad Danvers, "must you steal forth from your cottage-home to meet me here. I will have steeds waiting in readiness: your absence will not last beyond a couple of hours—and long ere the dawn of morning shall peep through the lattice of your grand-dame's chamber, will you have returned. It is a mere ceremony—but one which you yourself have with so much good sense observed must be fulfilled. This, dear Marian, is the proof of love I ask."

"And is that all?" exclaimed the fond confiding girl, in the heartfelt fondness of her devotion, as she gazed tenderly up into Conrad's countenance. "It is a mere duty which we have to perform; and yet you regard it as a proof of my attachment."

"Nevertheless, beauteous Marian," he rejoined, "I do receive it in such a sense, because it is a testimony of thy trust and confidence in me."

"How can I doubt thee? what is there to doubt?" exclaimed the innocent girl, gazing upon him in the simplicity of her surprise. "I love you—and you love me—and we are everything to each other. Have you yourself not said so? am I not repeating your own words?"

"Yes, yes, my angel—my adored one!" he cried, and abruptly straining her to his breast—as if to prevent her from catching a glimpse of the expression of mingled anguish and horror which he felt at the moment to be springing up from his soul and passing over his countenance.

The lovers now separated, with the understanding that so soon as night should have spread her veil upon the earth, and the eyes of Dame Musgrave should be sealed in slumber, the young damsel was to come stealthily forth and meet Conrad at the usual trysting-place. Then utterly unsuspicious of evil—mistrusting naught—but, on the contrary, as full of a sublime confidence as such a loving heart as her's could possibly be—Marian tripped lightly back to the cottage, pausing and turning now and then to wave her kerchief to her lover who stood lingering on the spot where she had left him.

On re-entering that humble home which Marian believed she was soon to exchange for a castellated mansion, she found Dame Musgrave waiting for her. Then ensued some serious conversation—or rather some revealings made by the good woman to the young girl,—but with which we need not trouble the reader at present. Suffice it to say that when the dame retired to her own room and Marian found herself free to keep the appointment with her lover, all that her kind-hearted guardian had told her, slipped completely out of her memory. How could it be otherwise? Were not all her thoughts engrossed by the image of Conrad Danvers?

The appointment was therefore duly kept; and by the soft glimmering moonlight did the lovely Marian steal forth from the cottage and hurry along the bank of the river, her heart throbbing with a fond impatience to meet her lover. It was a beauteous night—and the stars shone with diamond brightness, like gems upon the purple robe of an imperial bride. Danvers was waiting for Marian at the trysting-place. He had with him two splendid steeds whose coal-black coats were glossy as his own raven hair, or that of the sweet girl who was now clasped in his arms. Magnificent steeds were they—of colossal height, but of Arab fineness of limb; and as they impatiently pawed the ground and tossed their beautiful heads, their sable manes were gracefully agitated and their rich caparisons clanked and rattled.

But Marian, who had never ridden on horseback in her life, expressed her fears to her lover that she should not be able to retain her seat upon the back of one of those spirited steeds—much less manage it. He laughed, but tenderly and affectionately; and assured her that the noble animal which was to be her own, would feel that its future mistress was seated on its back. So, with a fond and girlish gaiety, the intended victim of the treacherous Danvers mounted the steed by her lover's assistance. He sprang upon the back of his own—and away they sped.

Marian found that the horse, though proceeding at a tremendous rate, bore her in a manner so gentle that this first equestrian experiment of her's was replete with a thrilling and exciting pleasure. But in a short time she became aware that they were literally flying along the road; trees, hedges, and houses—in short, all objects, gliding fast as if they also were galloping, but in a contrary direction. A dizziness came over the damsel— her head swam round—and she cried out in a voice of alarm for Conrad to rein in both her horse and his own. But pouring forth re-assuring words in her ears, he held her with one hand on her steed; and then her head drooped towards his shoulder, where she became if not altogether insensible, at least enwrapped in a sort of dreamy repose—as if she were being whirled with thrilling celerity, yet with ecstatic sensations, through the phantasmagorian details of a vision.

In this manner they rode on side by side, the two horses almost touching each other. Away, away they sped, as if borne on the wings of a whirlwind! Never did mortal steeds fly so fast: the careering eagle in his swiftest course would have been outstripped in a moment and left far behind. Scarcely an hour had passed, when Marian suddenly woke up; but with complete consciousness of where she was, with whom she was, and what was taking place. Then the delicious musical tones of her lover's voice floated upon her ears; and she was happy—Oh! happy as a bird just loose from its cage and essaying its wings in a long and rapid flight after a tedious captivity.

Ah! now it appears that they reach a river's brink: and yet it can be but a rivulet—for scarcely do the horses' feet touch the shining water when it is passed—and on they speed upon what seemed an instant before the opposite bank. Nevertheless it was the sea itself that had been thus passed,—the sea which lies between the Hampshire coast and the Isle of Wight! Yet such was the velocity with which the demon-horses had flitted across the watery strait, that their hoofs were scarcely wet and there was not so much as a spray thrown up to damp the garments of either Marian or her lover. Another minute—and they halted at the gate of Danvers Castle in the Isle of Wight.

"Is it here?" asked Marian, glancing up at the long range of turrets, battlements, and towers; and she at once saw that it was not the castellated mansion near Chelmsford, which she had occasionally seen.

"It is my ancestral castle," responded Danvers; "at no great distance from the one which is familiar to your eyes:" thus alluding to that castellated mansion near Chelmsford of which we have just spoken.

We should here observe that the entrance-gate looked towards the interior of the island; and having a protecting wall on each side, it was impossible to obtain a view of the sea from that point—so that Marian could behold nothing but the castle before her and the groves and woods of the island behind. Still altogether unsuspecting—indeed as dreamless of treachery as the infant child when pillowed on its mother's breast—Marian was assisted by her lover to dismount from the steed that had brought her thither; and straining her to his breast, he poured forth words of the deepest and most melting tenderness. When she looked round again, the entrance-gates stood open—although she had not observed that her lover had touched them; but naturally presuming that he must have given some summons which she had failed to observe, and that the doors were unclosed from within, she leant upon his arm as he conducted her into the building.

He led her on through the court-yard, into that vast Gothic hall which has been before described, and where the decaying banners of battle, as well as the suits of armour and weapons of the chase, were suspended to the walls: and Marian failed to observe that there was no one in attendance to have opened the door, so completely engrossed was she by the fond and affectionate language which Danvers was still pouring in her ears and the delicate caresses he lavished upon her. Then, in the artless simplicity of girlhood, she began to admire that mighty hall with its range of high narrow-arched windows, its two rows of pillars sustaining the vaulted roof, and the warlike embellishments of mouldering flags and rustling panoplies that decked the walls. She felt not afraid: she was too virtuous and too good to fear—too guileless and too confiding to suspect—and too fondly devoted to her lover even to have a doubt of his sincerity flash to her mind.

Through the hall they passed, and soon reached the spot where the two suits of complete armour stood like giant-sentinels to guard the broad and vast ascent dimly lighted from the painted glass window. Marian had started for a moment on beholding those figures looming through the obscurity: but a word from Conrad Danvers instantaneously re-assured her—and Oh! it was so sweet to be frightened for no more than a moment, that the loving girl might cling all the more tenderly and tenaciously to her worshipped companion!

Up the staircase they went; and passing through an interval of darkness, they entered the long gallery crowded with pictures. Nor here did Marian tremble, but still with girlish simplicity gazed in silent wonder upon the scene, and then looked up with trustful devotion to the countenance of her lover.

From the gallery they passed into that suite of spacious rooms where the furniture was all blackened and the footprints were on the floor: and here for an instant did that strange wild look again flit over the countenance of the treacherous one as he thought within himself, "It shall not be with Marian as it was with Musidora. The female steps that now leave their marks in the dust shall never be retraced!"

But the young creature, so sweet in her confiding artlessness, beheld not that wicked look which for a moment marred the god-like beauty of her stripling lover's countenance; and in a few moments they entered a narrow passage where utter darkness prevailed. Then the click of a secret spring was heard—a low narrow door flew open—and Marian was conducted by Danvers into the room where the fiery names were traced upon the wall. Thus:—

1. Bianca Landini	1390.
2. Margaret Dunhaven	1407.
3. Arline de St. Louis	1463.
4. Dolorosa Cortez	1500.
5. Clara Manners	1510.

CHAPTER LVIII.

THE TALISMAN.

PERCY RIVERS and Musidora had now been married upwards of eleven years. No children had blessed their union; but Sir Percy (for he had received the honour of knighthood) was happy in the possession of his first and only love. To say that Musidora was happy also, would be an exaggeration. Attached to her existence there was a past too full of trouble, and pain, and anguish to allow her memory so far to lose sight of it as to leave scope for the complete tranquillity of her mind. But that she found in Percy a sincere friend and affectionate husband, and therefore a great solace and comfort, we can safely aver. She had gradually discarded somewhat of that iciness of mien which in the beginning she had only tutored herself to assume as a veil beneath which she might the more effectually conceal the inward emotions of her wounded spirit, and likewise as a mask to protect her against the betrayal of any feeling suddenly stirred by the passing remarks that might in any way conjure up distressing reminiscences. Yes—she had studied to lay aside, after her marriage, that glacial demeanour to some extent: for she felt that having accepted the destiny of a wife, she had no right to seem cold and reserved, distant and passionless, towards one who loved her so fondly and so well. Eleven years had passed, we say; and Lady Rivers was now in her thirty-seventh year. The lapse of time had enhanced rather than diminished the splendour of her beauty, developing her form into all the richness of the most glorious contours, without in any way marring its noble symmetry. Her hair retained all its raven darkness and superb luxuriance; her eyes had lost no spark of their fire; nor her lips the brightness of their vermilion tint; while that half-vanishing smile which ere her mock-marriage with the treacherous Lionel Danvers had been wont to linger upon her countenance, but which had disappeared altogether on her return home from Grantham Villa, had gradually came back again with all its pristine serenity, yet devoid of its glacial coldness.

Nevertheless, there were times when Musidora experienced intervals of real unhappiness—almost of anguish: yet carefully did she conceal these seasons of despondency and pain from her ever-loving and affectionate husband. The faithful Annetta, who still remained in her service, was the only living being who ever beheld the silent and secret grief of her beloved mistress; and on these occasions she said nothing, attempting no consolation—because she knew that the dark hour would pass all the more quickly if Musidora's mind were not forced to dwell upon it by means of discourse relative to the sad topic of the past.

Lord and Lady Grantham had been dead some years: Dr. Bertram, *alias* Benjamin Welford, was likewise dead: Dame Bertha, the Earl of Grantham's housekeeper, had equally gone to her last home; and thus all who were acquainted with Musidora's terrific secret in respect to Danvers (save the King, St. Louis, and Annetta) were no longer denizens of this world. Yes—Danvers himself was: but Musidora knew not that the Danvers now living was *the same* who had practised his foul treachery against her. Thus in most respects did she consider her secret to be safe; and therefore it was not through fear of its betrayal that she experienced those intervals of despondency and anguish to which we have ere now alluded.

Let us however resume the thread of our narrative. It was about ten o'clock at night; and Musidora was seated alone in the handsomely-furnished saloon at Carisbrook Castle. Some urgent business, connected with the affairs of the island, had compelled Sir Percy to repair that morning to Portsmouth; and he was not expected to return till the following day. Musidora experienced a strange restlessness for which she could not account. There was in her mind a feeling amounting to a presentiment that something was about to take place; but whether for good or for evil, she knew not. Vainly did she endeavour to shake off this growing uneasiness: it gained upon her;—and it seemed to her she must do something to escape from its influence. She rose—walked to the window—and drawing back the curtain, gazed forth into the beautiful starlit night. But still she could not divert her thoughts from this presentiment that was growing up within her. Then she determined to look it as it were in the face, and by analysing her feelings endeavour to ascertain the cause of this trouble. But she could no more give shape and substance to her imaginings than if it were a vaguely outlined shadow seen at a distance through the gathering gloom of the evening.

She felt the want of fresh air; for her brows began to throb and her cheeks to feel feverish. Descending therefore from the apartment, she threw a light scarf over her shoulders, and passed out of the castle to take a short ramble in the grounds attached thereto. The sentries at the gate respectfully saluted their Governor's wife; and she graciously acknowledged their courtesy. Proceeding onward, she reached the outskirt of the fortifications, and was about to turn into a beautiful garden the cultivation of which she herself superintended, when she was suddenly accosted by a personage whose appearance, so far as she could judge in the starlight, was dignified and noble, and whose travelling-suit was of the richest materials. He immediately doffed his plumed cap, and said in a low but earnest and impressive tone, "This night a victim is to be saved from the power of Lord Danvers!"

Musidora started as if suddenly stung by a serpent, and gave vent to a cry resembling a half-suppressed shriek: then instantaneously recovering her self-possession, she said with exceeding rapidity of utterance, "What mean you? Explain yourself! For heaven's sake, speak!"

"It is for you, lady, to read the enigma—not I," was the answer. "If I mistake not, I am addressing Lady Rivers: for I have this night learnt, since I arrived at the island, that the daughter of the late Sir Lewis Sinclair now bears that name."

"Yes. But who are you? whence come you? who sent you?" demanded Musidora, with passionate vehemence.

"I am Lord St. Louis."

"Ah! the Secretary of the King at that time——"

"The same," rejoined the nobleman; "and I immediately recognised your ladyship. A holy man in Palestine has sent me hither; and I bear a talisman which will protect us from evil."

As he thus spoke, Lord St. Louis produced a little ebony crucifix from the breast of his doublet.

"But the holy man—who was he?" demanded Musidora, still rapidly and nervously.

"The father of Dolorosa Cortez."

"Ah! one of the victims of the terrible Danvers!"—and a ghastly pallor overspread Musidora's countenance—a pallor more deathlike far than the natural paleness of those splendidly chiselled features.

"Lady, what is to be done?" inquired St. Louis, himself labouring under a strong excitement. "The sixth and last victim——"

"Must be saved!" responded Musidora, with firm emphasis though rapid utterance.

"But where—how?" asked St. Louis.

"Has your lordship a steed at hand?"

"Yes—yonder—tied to that tree."

"Then there is not a moment to be lost. Lead on!"

St. Louis instantaneously turned round and sped in the direction where he had left his horse, Musidora following close behind.

"You are without attendants?" she inquired, flinging her quick glance around.

"Yes: I am alone, lady," was the nobleman's response. "Methought the mission was too sacred to bear the presence of witnesses."

"And you thought well, my lord," rejoined Musidora. "Now mount—and you must take me with you. Assist me to seat myself behind you—this is no time nor occasion for false delicacy."

"No," added St. Louis solemnly: "for it is not *one* soul that must be saved to-night, but the *five* other victims who have already been consigned to a dark mysterious fate."

St. Louis mounted the steed: Musidora seated herself behind him; and with her hand upon his shoulder she retained her place with facility, for she was an accomplished horsewoman. Then guided by her, St. Louis urged on his steed in the direction of Danvers Castle. The distance was not great; and despite its double burden, the animal careered onward at a gallant pace. In less than an hour they were within sight of the vast range of buildings constituting the Castle.

"Let us halt here," said Musidora when within fifty yards of the gate: then having lightly descended from the horse she murmured, "Heaven grant me a sufficient amount of fortitude to witness all that is too well calculated to conjure up the most terrible memories!"

But she had not spoken so low as to prevent Lord St. Louis from catching at least the meaning of her words, if not the precise words themselves; and with a generosity as chivalrous as it was delicate, and as high-minded as it was courteous, he said, "Lady, take you the talisman: it will be better in your keeping."

Thus speaking, he placed the ebony cross in her hand: and Musidora instantaneously felt herself inspired by a courage which, strong-minded though she naturally was, far surpassed any amount of fortitude she could by other means have summoned to her aid. Then having rapidly expressed her thanks to Lord St. Louis, she said, "You must follow me: for alas! I am but too well acquainted with the interior of this dread fortalice."

With these words she proceeded towards the gate, her step being firm, her looks decisive, her heart strong; and even by her very walk, as St. Louis kept close behind, could he perceive that his fair guide was armed with no ordinary degree of self-possession.

The gates of the castle were closed: but as Musidora touched them with the crucifix, while in the act of merely trying them with her hand, they instantaneously flew wide open. She turned round and threw a significant glance upon St. Louis, as much as to say, "Behold the first proof of the virtue with which this talisman is endowed!"

The nobleman comprehended the meaning of that glance, and crossed himself in a reverential manner, as he thus recognized the heavenly intervention which had given wisdom to the words of the old anchorite of Mount Lebanon.

With a firm pace did Musidora pass onward, and in a few moments enter that antique gothic hall which was not strange to her, but whither St. Louis penetrated now for the first time. In the dim cathedral-light did they observe the mouldering banners slightly waving with the draught which poured through from the open doors; and then they drooped heavily again. Onward proceeded Musidora, passing the colossal figures on the pedestals at the foot of the staircase; and then without hesitation did she ascend those stairs, Lord St. Louis keeping in her track. The picture-gallery was reached: but not an instant did they tarry to contemplate the portraits in their blackened frames; and thence they passed on into the suite of apartments where the furniture was mouldering and the footprints were visible in the dust. Still without pausing, on they went,—Musidora sustained by the sublime courage derived from the holy talisman, and Lord St. Louis preserving his own self-possession not merely from the remembrance of the prophetic assurances which the old man of Mount Lebanon had given him, but likewise from the example of fortitude thus set him by Musidora.

From the suite of apartments the lady and the noble passed into a narrow corridor where utter darkness prevailed; and on reaching the end, Musidora suddenly stopped short—for the sounds of voices at that instant met her ears. Catching St. Louis by the wrist to intimate that they would pause for an instant, and likewise that it was necessary to remain perfectly still, she listened attentively. St. Louis also listened with suspended breath. A male and a female were speaking within the room, on the outside of the door of which they had thus halted; and though the door was massive and well set in its frame, yet it was doubtless through the talismanic power of the crucifix that they were thus enabled to hear what was passing within that room as plainly and clearly as if they themselves were present there.

"And thus, sweetest girl," said Lord Conrad Danvers, "thou art happy in being the object of my love? and thou hast experienced no alarm in being brought hither this night for the purpose of pledging thyself unto me?"

"Alarm, dearest Conrad?" exclaimed the damsel in the silver melody of her delicious voice: "wherefore should I be alarmed? I am happy everywhere with you; and being happy, I cannot be alarmed. You say that we shall soon return to Chelmsford, and that I shall be enabled to re-enter the cottage before Dame Musgrave can possibly miss me?"

"Yes—assuredly, my charming one," replied Danvers: and he caressed her with every appearance of the most fervid affection. "But wherefore did you speak of your grandmother in such a manner?"

"Ah!" exclaimed Marian, as if suddenly struck by a reminiscence: "in the hurry of our journey hither I forgot to mention to you, dear Conrad, something that occurred this evening. Dame Musgrave is no relation to me: she is not my grandmother—and my name is not even Musgrave. You know that when I left you at sunset, after our appointment to meet again for the purpose of coming hither, I hastened back to the cottage. The worthy dame had already returned from her sick friend's house, and was waiting for me. I know not in what mood she was that she began speaking of my earliest years; but she bade me sit down and listen to her. Then she said that she thought I was now old enough to be made acquainted with the real truth of my position in respect to herself; that she had intended to sustain unto the end the belief which I cherished that I was her grand-daughter; but that on mature reflection, she considered it more prudent to undeceive me on that head. You may judge, dearest Conrad, of my surprise at being thus seriously and solemnly addressed: and I *did* prepare to listen with attention. Then she went on to tell me that my father and mother bore a name very different from that of Musgrave—that they were drowned—alas! poor parents!—in the river Chelmer when I was yet quite an infant; and that they left a considerable sum of money in gold pieces concealed in their dwelling. This money was at the time placed in the hands of Dame Musgrave as a reward for taking care of me; but according to what the worthy dame told me this evening, she has all along kept the money intact, reserving it as a little dowry for me. The kindness of friends—for Dame Musgrave is highly respected in Chelmsford—has enabled her to maintain herself and me without infringing upon that little treasure; and thus you see, dear Conrad," added Marian in her artless simplicity, "I do not come to you altogether a portionless bride."

"Sweet girl," answered Danvers, again lavishing upon her the warmest caresses—at least so they appeared to the intended and unsuspecting victim,—"had you the wealth of the Indies, you would not be more acceptable to me than when I thought you a poor dowerless maiden!"

"Oh! everything you say, my noble-hearted Conrad," replied the damsel, "is full of generosity! But was it not strange that on the very evening before the day of our nuptials, Dame Musgrave should thus be impelled to make me acquainted with those secrets? Ah! I remember now, she said that in case she should die suddenly it were better that I should know the true secret of my birth, and also the source whence came the treasure that would be found concealed in a spot which she explained to me."

"Yes—the coincidence was singular enough," observed Danvers. "But you have forgotten to tell me, my angel, what your proper name really is?"

"Marian Bradley," was the young girl's immediate response.

A wild shriek now thrilled from the lips of Musidora as this name suddenly met her ears; and St. Louis started in amazement and terror, not knowing the cause of her sudden excitement. But this was speedily explained. For well-nigh frantic, Lady Rivers touched the door with the crucifix—it instantaneously flew open—and bursting into the room where Marian was clinging fondly to Danvers, she caught that young maiden in her arms, exclaiming wildly, "Marian, my child! my child!"

CHAPTER LIX.

THE CHAMBER OF MYSTERIES.

STRANGE wild words were those which thus sounded on Marian's ear;— scarcely less strange and wild too, did they seem to Lord St. Louis. But instead of producing the same thrilling and startling effect upon Danvers, they struck him with a mingled consternation and dismay. Vivid as a flash of lightning that suddenly reveals every object in a cavern a moment before enveloped in pitchy darkness, did the whole truth blaze upon his mind—but not to disappear again and replunge his memory into the gloom of night, as the cavern is restored to darkness when the play of heaven's fire has vanished!

The young girl,—in whose soul Musidora's revelation had touched a chord which suddenly vibrated with the instinctive feeling of nature,—felt at once that she was indeed being pressed in the arms of a mother: but in the whirl and confusion of her ideas she had neither ability nor time to reflect how this fond close tie could possibly exist between them. With frantic vehemence did Musidora continue to strain the young girl to her bosom: then she held her back for a few moments while she gazed upon Marian's countenance; and beholding some traces of her own features and lineaments there, but with a softer and sweeter beauty, she again pressed her in her arms—again covered her cheeks with caresses!

For upwards of a minute did this strange and affecting scene last; while Danvers, pale and haggard, petrified with astonishment and dismay, stood gazing upon the mother and daughter. Then did *he* also observe that there was some resemblance between them—the same fine eyes, the same dark glory of the hair, the same facial outline;—and he marvelled that this likeness had not struck him before. Yet really there was no cause for wonderment, inasmuch as the resemblance was far from strong; and when that mother and daughter were far apart, a person acquainted with them both would not be reminded of the one while gazing upon the other.

St. Louis, being well acquainted with the particulars of Musidora's mock marriage with Danvers, guessed the whole truth as soon as he observed the effect which the lady's words had produced upon that terrible man; and profoundly shocked he was at the idea that Danvers should have been led by circumstances thus to attempt the offering up of his own daughter as a victim to the Enemy of Mankind.

But one word of explanation is here necessary. For during the rapid ride from Carisbrook to Danvers Castle, Lord St. Louis had given Musidora a few hurriedly outlined particulars of all he had learnt from the old man of Mount Lebanon relative to the mysterious existence of Lord Danvers; and thus Musidora was aware that he who she now beheld, was the same whom she had known as Lionel, and that though wearing a shape of youthful beauty, he was a man of a great and wondrous age! For upwards of a minute, as we have already said, did Musidora continue lavishing all a mother's fondest endearments upon that young creature whom she had not only all in an instant discovered to be her daughter, but whom she had thus so providentially rescued from the terrible power of Danvers. A thousand conflicting ideas swept like a flight of birds through Musidora's brain: a thousand different feelings agitated her heart all at the same moment. Her soul seemed to be tossing on a buoyant but troubled sea, where billows of pain rolled under surges of joy. Her conscience smote her for having ever abandoned her child at all; and her heart thrilled with rapture at having thus arrived in time to rescue her. The Past came sweeping before her with bitter memories; while the Present had its emotions of relief. Yet even with this Present, there were sensations of horror derived from the consciousness that Danvers—the father of her child—was devoted to the Enemy of Mankind. But it were impossible to find space for the complete analysis of all that Musidora remembered, thought, felt, sorrowed over, or rejoiced at, during the swift brief interval which elapsed ere Danvers, recovering somewhat of his presence of mind, accosted the injured mother of his daughter.

"Musidora," he said, in a low deep voice which seemed laden with despair, "it were better that Marian should remain here no longer."

Lady Rivers at once comprehended what Danvers meant. There was deep contrition in his words—remorse in his looks; and she felt that for once in his life he had spoken with sincerity. Indeed, what he meant, and what she understood him to mean, was to the effect that it were better for Musidora's sake that the veil should be lifted no farther from the secret of her birth.

"I will take her away with me," at once said Musidora, still clasping Marian fondly round the waist with one arm.

"Tell me—Oh! tell me," exclaimed the young girl, "what is the meaning of all this?"—and she gazed up with a kind of anguished entreaty into Musidora's countenance; for she felt that there was something wrong in respect to him whom she had loved so tenderly—but what the wrong was, appeared to be enveloped in the deepest mystery to her.

"Do not ask me now, my sweet child," responded Musidora: "but come away with me—come away!"

"No—*you* will not depart thus?" said Danvers, as he fixed a look of mournful appeal upon Musidora's countenance. "Ah! think not——"

She knew what he was about to say—but she checked him with a gesture; for she would not have her daughter hear him promise that he meditated no injury to her—that girl's mother! besides, Musidora suddenly felt herself inwardly prompted to remain with Lord Danvers; while the possession of the talisman was felt to be a sufficient safeguard against evil, should any be attempted. Her mind was therefore promptly resolved how to act; and turning to St. Louis, she said, "My lord, you will conduct my daughter Marian away from this chamber. I will rejoin you presently in the great hall below:"—and she spoke quickly with nervousness and excitement.

The young girl threw an affrighted glance from her mother towards St. Louis, and then upon Danvers: but she was shocked, now that her eyes settled upon the latter, at observing how strangely altered he had within the last few moments become. It is true that he was still in appearance the same youthful being she had known and loved: but upon that countenance of eighteen the care of ages might be traced. There was a blank despair in his looks: it seemed as if the touch of a reed would strike him down.

"Marian, I beseech you to go with Lord St. Louis," whispered Musidora, in a still more hurried voice than before, but with endearing manner. "He is a friend—he will take care of you—he is a great nobleman—a man of honour: and besides, I shall join you again in a few minutes. Depart, my child—depart!"

St. Louis hastened forward to take the hand of the young damsel whom Musidora had now disengaged from her maternal clasp; and the door having remained open, Marian was led away, though somewhat reluctantly, by St. Louis. As her foot touched the threshold she cast a rapid glance over her shoulder towards Danvers: but he made no sign—he said not a word—yet he gazed on her as she was departing from his view in a manner that she could never afterwards forget. It was no longer the fervid look of love which he thus bent upon her retreating form: but it was a look of profound and ineffable sorrow—of remorse—of entreaty—almost of utter despair,—as if he would have asked her forgiveness for something which she could not comprehend, but that yet he dared not!

A dizziness suddenly came over the poor girl: some instinctive feeling made her aware that she was parting from Danvers for ever;—and yet, blended with that feeling, there was a vague and unknown sentiment, likewise whispering in her soul, which made her equally aware that it would be wrong to think of him thenceforth as she had been wont to do. Her brain appeared to turn—her footsteps faltered—and Lord St. Louis, perceiving that she was about to faint, took her into his arms and hurried away from the vicinage of that chamber. The door closed behind them of its own accord; and Musidora now remained alone with Lord Danvers.

"Fear nothing," said the latter, in a voice so low, so broken with utter misery, that it filled Musidora's heart with compassion notwithstanding all she had suffered at his hands: "I would not attempt to harm you, even if I had the power. But that power I possess no longer in the presence of the holy symbol which you carry in your hand. Besides," he continued, in tones of a deepening despondency, "a great and sudden change has been wrought within me during the last few minutes. I no longer cherish vindictive sentiments towards you, Musidora: and I have asked you to remain that you may witness the last moments of my troubled existence!"

"The last moments?" echoed Lady Rivers, a cold shudder passing through her entire frame, as if an ice-snake had crept from the crown of her head to her very feet. "What mean you, unhappy man? Is it indeed so near the time——"

But she stopped short: she could not give utterance to the horrible question which had risen up to her lips;—and she stood gazing on Danvers with the profoundest commiseration.

"Yes—this is my last hour; and at midnight it will be my last moment!" he said, perceiving that she hesitated. "Now, alas! there arises within me— too late—a cry of despair and woe,—a cry which comes up from the uttermost depths of my soul, and which, though you cannot hear it, is full of the awful wail of lamentation and bitterness for me! Mine are now feelings so infinitely beyond all human experience that you can comprehend them not. You have had your sufferings, Musidora—you have known what anguish is—you have writhed upon your couch in fearfullest agony—and, alas! it is I who have been the cause. Oh I would that I could recall it all: but it is impossible! It belongs unto the Past: and the Past is absorbed in its own irrevocable self. The Future is mine—and, ah! what a Future!" he added, the withering look of unutterable despair passing slowly over his countenance. "But I spoke of your sufferings, Musidora: I reminded you of all the afflictions which you have known, and which were entailed upon your head by the love which you bore for me. Yet wherefore have I alluded to all this? It is to make you understand that the direst anguish which you have ever known, is bliss—elysian happiness—joy ineffable—aye, ecstasy beatific, in comparison with the tremendous horror which sits at this moment upon my appalled soul. And not horror only—but an agony in my heart so poignant, so excruciating, that even at this instant, deliberately as I am speaking to you, I could scream forth—I could tear out my hair by the roots—I could rush away madly, madly—for my soul is scourged by the lashes of invisible fiends!"

He ceased for a few moments, and shook shudderingly from head to foot, as if grasped by the hand of some unseen power. It was a horrible whirlwind of the mind's tempest that was evidently passing through him. Musidora felt as if she herself must fall down and faint: but as she grasped the talisman all the more tenaciously, her strength of mind returned—her courage revived—and she again bent her looks full of compassion upon that man, the father of her child!

"Musidora," he continued, after a brief pause, "mine has been a wild and fearful life—I will not say *how* wild, *how* fearful! That you have this night learnt much concerning me, I am aware. There is a voice whispering in my soul which tells me whence came the inspirations that brought about the circumstance of your presence here this night, in company with St. Louis. Ah! Antonio Cortez, though thou hast buried thyself in a grotto on Mount Lebanon, and though devoting thyself to heaven, thou didst renounce the thought of vengeance in respect to me—yet art thou avenged! Yes—even from the Holy Land hath thy vengeance overtaken me: but it is the vengeance of that heaven which thou, Antonio Cortez, dost serve—a holy, a sacred, and a righteous vengeance, which I acknowledge, and to which I bow!"

Thus speaking, the unhappy man slowly inclined his head forward until it drooped to his breast: and thus he stood for upwards of a minute, evidently absorbed in the profound despair of his ineffable thoughts. During that interval an idea full of hope flashed to Musidora's mind. Would not the talisman which she held, have the power to emancipate the unhappy Danvers from the thrall of the Evil One? With a sudden start of joy at the prospect of being enabled thus to save the soul of that erring man, she lifted the crucifix, exclaiming, "Lord Danvers, herein behold your salvation!"

He raised his looks slowly—shook his head with an awful despondency—and observed, "No, Musidora! my crimes have been too great—my guilt has proved too enormous! Midnight is approaching—and then my doom will be sealed. You will behold strange sights; but I need not say that there is no cause for *you* to fear, inasmuch as the consciousness of possessing that holy emblem will sustain your courage and allow you to experience no other feeling than joy at the emancipation of the souls of those five beings whose names are inscribed on yon tablets!"—and he pointed towards the black squares on which the names were inscribed in letters of fire. "Yes," he added slowly, "there may be another feeling besides joy, which you will entertain. Perhaps you may feel some sentiment of pity for him who at the same time will be borne away to a doom the appalling horrors of which are even now forcing themselves in anticipation upon his mind!"

"Oh! yes—I will pity you, I will pity you! I do already pity you—deeply, deeply!" exclaimed Musidora: "and I will pray for you——Ah! shake not your head thus despondingly—I will pray for you! Morning and night will I kneel and pray that a higher power than that to which you have devoted yourself, may have mercy upon you! And there is *another* who shall kneel and pray by my side for the welfare of her father's soul; and yet her innocent mind shall not be shocked by having the veil of mystery torn away from before it—nor shall she know that he for whom she will thus pray was her sire, the author of her being!"

"Say then, Musidora, you forgive me for the past?" exclaimed Danvers: "for even amidst the tremendous horrors which now sit upon my soul, it will be some consolation to hear that I am forgiven by you whom I have outraged so cruelly!"

"Yes—I forgive you—from the very bottom of my soul do I forgive you!" answered Musidora. "Not once during this last interview have I experienced a revengeful feeling against you. No, Danvers—your punishment is now too great at the hand of heaven, for me, a mortal pigmy of earth, to superadd the mere atom-weight of any wretched hate or vengefulness on my part. Besides, I pity you—yes, I pity you—and I forgive you! Would to heaven that I could save you also!"

"Musidora, I thank you for those generous words which you have spoken," answered Danvers: but he offered not to accost her—made not the slightest movement even to touch her hand. "I have persecuted you bitterly: but my heart at the time was filled with a demon-hatred. It was the rage of disappointment in having lost you as a victim—and likewise the mad desire to possess you! Thus was it that I hated and loved you at the same time—and I resolved that at the same time also would I wreak my vengeance and gratify my passion. Therefore did I watch for the opportunity of achieving this twofold aim. And at length the occasion presented itself. Your father, the late Sir Lewis, was one day walking with yourself and him who is now your husband, in the orchard attached to Sinclair House. I was concealed in the forest. Presently you and Percy Rivers entered the house; and your sire remained alone in the orchard. He drew forth a letter and read it: it filled him with joy—and in the excitement of his feelings, he dropped it. I possessed myself of that letter, which proved to be one of invitation for you to visit the Earl and Countess of Grantham. The wily courtier and his equally astute lady had conceived the project of throwing you in the King's way that your beauty might attract him and lead to your elevation to the queenly rank. Need I say another word to explain how this letter suddenly prompted me with the idea of gratifying the two passions which I entertained towards you?—need I add——"

"Enough, Danvers—enough!" interrupted Musidora, with feverish haste. "Recall not that terrible past to my mind!"

"Ah! you would have me think then only of the present?" he said, his voice and look becoming deeply, Oh! so deeply despondent again—"this present which is so brief and fleeting for me, and which is but the threshold of a long and terrible future—a future stretching away like an illimitable ocean that is bounded by no shore and stops at no horizon! Well then, Musidora, if I am thus to fix my ideas upon the present, how is it possible that I can avoid a retrospection over the past, and recall those dread circumstances which have brought me to this sad present and is about to plunge me into so tremendous a future? Listen! It was in the year 1357 that my eyes first opened to the light of this world. Oh! accursed be that year of my birth! would that I had never been born! would that the date of my existence could be blotted from the annals of time, and my own existence erased from the history of the human species! But these repinings are vain; and what I have to say must be briefly said—for midnight is approaching! Know then that at the age of twenty five, and in the year 1382, I made my fearful compact with the Enemy of Mankind. No matter how it was done. I will not harrow up your soul by the details of the tremendous night on which the fell agreement was concluded. Suffice it to say that on my side the conditions stipulated for, were long life—riches wherewith to bless it—and unfailing youth to enable me to enjoy them. Add to these the faculty of assuming whatsoever shape I chose, and that of transporting myself from place to place, no matter how great the interval, with a wondrous rapidity—and you may then estimate the extent of the temptations thrown in my way by Satan, and to which I succumbed. Rest assured that I even asked for more: but more it was not in the Evil One's power to grant. For the period of one hundred and fifty years was the compact made, with the condition that if during that interval I could find six young virgins, who, never having loved before, would bestow their love on me—and who in the purity, the chastity, and the holiness of that love, would devote themselves in soul as well as in body unto me——"

"Oh! dwell not thus upon the details of your terrific history!" exclaimed Musidora, with a cold shudder from head to foot.

"And yet you must listen," said Danvers, with a sudden access of vehemence: "for there is some feeling within me that compels me thus to speak. Five victims have been offered up—five young, beauteous, and confiding maidens, who in the stainlessness of their virgin purity have been snatched away from the earth which they have adorned and plunged into the gulf of death! Yes—and the arm of Death, too, thrusting its fleshless hand forth from beneath those panels, hath on each occasion given me a token in acknowledgment of the offering up of a victim. Behold them!"

With these words Danvers tore open his doublet, and produced a gold chain on which were five rings of the same metal and enamelled in black.

"Take them, take them," he said with passionate vehemence; "and when the fatal moment comes let the crucifix which you hold in your hand be placed in contact with those five rings. The spell which binds the victims whom they symbolize, in a profound and dreamless trance, will be broken—their souls will be emancipated from the dull deep lethargy in which they are now held—and they will ascend to the mansions of the blessed;—those mansions which I may never hope to enter!"

Musidora took the chain on which the rings were suspended; and in so doing her hand came in contact for a moment with that of Danvers. She started, even with a sensation of pain as well as of horror: for the hand which she thus touched was as hot as if it were burning with a fierce internal fire.

"Oh! did I not tell you ere now," exclaimed Danvers, "that I already experienced tortures so maddening that you yourself could not possibly comprehend them? Nearer and nearer approaches the dreadful moment; and I have but a few more words to say. Think not, Musidora, that when I sought to make *her*—your daughter—*our* child——Oh! what fire is there in my brain—what agony in my heart!——think not, I say, that when I sought to make *her* a victim, I knew who she was. No—vile as I have been, I was not so vile as that: desperate as my condition was and is, I would not have redeemed it at such a sacrifice—the sacrifice of my own child! I knew her not. Believe me when I give you this assurance. From the moment that you and I parted on that tremendous night when the presence of the monarch whose shape I had assumed so suddenly compelled me to take back my own, I ceased to watch your movements—ceased almost to remember that there was such a being as yourself in the world. I knew not therefore that you had become a mother. No, no—I would not have been so base as to offer up my own child to Satan! For every good feeling has not been altogether dead within me during the strange wild life I have led for a hundred and fifty years since the date of my dreadful compact. I have known what love is! Each of my victims did I love—and my heart was torn as if with vulture-talons and goaded as if with scorpion-stings, when I was wont to gaze upon those fond, loving, and too-confiding creatures, and felt in my desperation that there was an imperious necessity compelling me to make them my victims. Oh! I have felt that in spite of myself—in spite even of the iron bands with which I have girt and strengthened my soul—that there were moments when an expression of ineffable anguish would sweep over my countenance; and as years flitted away and I drew nearer and nearer unto the last, more frequent in their recurrence and more anguished in their expression would grow those looks which in that transient appearance on my features reflected the dire anguish of my heart. And now, Musidora, I have no more to say. Midnight is at hand— and I feel a sensation coming over me that warns me of the approach of the fatal moment when Satan will come to claim his own. Oh! the last fatal instant is near—it is now present—its dire influence is upon me! Musidora, Musidora, be not surprised at the change which is already beginning to take place in my form!"

While the unhappy man was thus speaking in a voice of mingled anguish and mournfulness, horror and despair, he was rapidly losing the exquisite beauty of his youthful appearance; and with an extraordinary simultaneousness did his shape and all his features receive the impress of advancing decrepitude and old age. His figure, losing its willowy elasticity, became bent—his limbs lost their straightness—wrinkles gathered upon his countenance—his hair turned grey, and then white—his eyes grew dull and glassy—his mouth fell in—and in less than a minute, that being late so bright and beautiful, tottered towards a seat and fell upon it a withered, silver-haired, powerless old man!

Awfully shocked by this appalling change, Musidora herself staggered back with a sensation of faintness: but as she grasped the little crucifix all the more firmly, her presence of mind returned, and she felt herself armed with the necessary courage for the terrific crisis which she now knew to be at hand.

Hitherto the chamber where all these incidents occurred had been lighted not merely by the beams of the stars which shone through the windows of the four walls of the tower, but also more brightly still by the preternatural lustre shed by the names inscribed by characters of fire upon the panels. But now almost immediately after Lord Danvers had sunk down upon the chair, a miserable old man—a strange and awful gloom began deepening in the apartment. Danvers himself and all other objects gradually disappeared from Musidora's eyes; and the fiery names simultaneously subsiding, the darkness increased, until in a minute or two it filled the room with the in-tensest blackness. Musidora held the crucifix firmly in her hand, and pressed it to her lips; so that she was inspired with a marvellous courage, as well as by the deep inward consciousness that no harm could happen to her.

And now from the midst of the more than Egyptian darkness which filled the chamber—a darkness which could be *felt*—piteous moans, and subdued lamentations began to arise, sent forth upon the voice of extreme old age; and therefore Musidora knew that they came from the lips of the unhappy Lord Danvers. Her first impulse was to raise her voice, and entreat him to pray: but a spell was on her lips, sealing them in silence—and therefore she sank down upon her knees, and from the depth of her own soul sent up mute but fervid intercessions on behalf of that wretched man who now hovered upon the threshold of doom.

Suddenly there was a sound as of huge and mighty wings sweeping through the heavy black atmosphere which filled the chamber; and then the voice which had previously been sending forth such piteous lamentations, swelled into tones of the wildest agony—so that yells and cries, shrieks and screams of the most terrific character, struck upon Musidora's ears, and pierced like barbed arrows of fire through her brain. But all in a moment these appalling sounds ceased—not gradually, but with a strange and fearful abruptness, accompanied by the repetition of the mighty gush of those huge invisible wings through the air. And then all was still!

Musidora, instantaneously recollecting the directions she had received relative to the five rings, placed them in contact with the crucifix; and at the very moment this was done, the glimmering of a light appeared in the midst of the chamber. Misty and indistinct was it at first: but gradually it expanded and grew stronger, brightening more and more until it spread throughout the room—chasing away every vestige of the black darkness that had previously prevailed. It was a halo of the most transcendent effulgence; and yet, though enveloping Musidora in its glow, it hurt her not to gaze upon it. All over the floor in the middle of the room, clouds of blue and fleecy white were spread; and from the midst thereof five shapes gradually ascended,—the shapes of females of transcending beauty, clad in robes of azure and gold, which floated around them, and with smiles of soft ecstasy and angelic bliss upon their countenances. Bending their looks, which were full of gratitude and beatific joy, upon Musidora, they slowly ascended,—borne upward by those clouds of white and blue on which they seemed to float; and in this manner they appeared to pass through the roof of the tower—the halo of lustre gradually subsiding, so that at the instant when they ceased to be visible there was no other light in the chamber than that soft faint glimmering which the stars shed through the windows.

Then Musidora knew that if on the one hand Satan had possessed

himself of his Own, on the other the souls of the five maidens whom
Danvers had sought to make his victims, had been released from the spell
which had hitherto retained them in dull dark lethargy—that they were
emancipated—and that they had ascended to the mansions of the Eternal!

But Musidora likewise became aware that the gold chain with the
five rings had departed from her hand—in what manner she knew not,
and at what moment she had not perceived. They were gone—they had
vanished: and in her hand she held the crucifix alone!

All this while still remaining on her knees, she offered up fresh prayers
to heaven,—prayers of thankfulness for the salvation of the souls of Bianca Landini, Margaret Dunhaven, Arline de St. Louis, Dolorosa Cortez,
and Clara Manners,—and prayers of intercession on behalf of the soul of
Lord Danvers!

Then Musidora, rising from her knees, issued forth from that chamber; and passing rapidly through the suite of apartments with the mouldering furniture—next threading the picture gallery—she reached the staircase, which she descended. At the foot thereof she beheld the two colossal
suits of armour fallen from their pedestals and stretched upon the pavement of the gothic hall—as if the duty of those sentinel-panoplies was
over, and there were no more mysteries in Danvers Castle to guard and
defend against the approach of intrusive steps.

In the middle of the mighty gothic hall Lady Rivers perceived her
daughter clinging in affright to the arm of Lord St. Louis, who, though
himself under the influence of awe-stricken feelings, was saying all he
could to cheer and reassure the young maiden. It appeared that the sudden fall of the two suits of armour, accompanied by a terrific crash, had so
dismayed poor Marian that she had not recovered from the effects of the
fright at the time Musidora thus rejoined her and St. Louis: but the presence of that being whom she now regarded as her mother infused hope
and confidence into her gentle breast.

"Let us speed hence," said Musidora, as through the cathedral light
of that gothic hall she flung upon St. Louis a rapid but significant look
to make him aware that all was over in the chamber of mysteries. "Now,
dearest girl," she added, straining her daughter to her bosom, "you will
accompany me to Carisbrook Castle, which is my home—and God grant
that it may likewise prove your's!"

These last words Lady Rivers murmured to herself, so that they
were inaudible to Marian. But why did Musidora entertain a doubt as to
whether Carisbrook Castle might be regarded as the future home of her
daughter? Because, after everything that had occurred, and under existing

circumstances, it would be necessary to make a full and complete confession of the entire past to her husband; and though she had the sublimest faith in his love, his generosity, and his compassionate disposition, yet she could not be altogether sure of the course which he might decide upon adopting towards herself and her child.

Issuing forth from the castle, Lord St. Louis assisted Musidora and Marian to mount his horse, which he led by the bridle. But where were the demon steeds belonging to Lord Danvers? how was it that St. Louis and Musidora, when arriving at the Castle, had seen them not at the gate? It was because they had vanished the moment that holy crucifix which St. Louis had given to Musidora, was near enough to the castellated edifice to shed its talismanic spell upon those unearthly steeds which belonged to the Power of Darkness: and thus had they disappeared even before either St. Louis or Musidora had reached the spot where Danvers had left them.

Few words were spoken by Lord St. Louis, Lady Rivers, and Marian on the way to Carisbrook Castle, which they were nearly two hours in reaching, as the steed that bore the ladies could only proceed at a gentle pace, and the distance was upwards of ten miles. But at length the governor's residence was gained, and Lord St. Louis was courteously invited by Musidora to take up his quarters there.

Ere sleep fell upon the eyes of either the mother or daughter during the rest of that eventful night, they remained long in conversation together: for Musidora was anxious to learn from Marian's lips all the particulars of her past life. But in respect to the young damsel, Musidora avoided giving any precise explanations relative to her birth: for this was a proceeding which for several reasons she desired to postpone until she had first communicated everything to her husband. Marian longed to ask what had become of Conrad Danvers: but she dared not. Though far from suspecting aught that had occurred in respect to the past life or the fearful doom of that unhappy man, the young maiden nevertheless could not help feeling that there was some dark mystery in connexion with all that had just taken place at Danvers Castle, but into which she ventured not to inquire. Musidora, seeing what was passing in her mind, gave her to understand that she must never hope to see Lord Danvers again, and that there were imperative reasons wherefore his name should never be breathed except in her prayers!

But ere the conversation between the mother and daughter terminated that night, the former gave the young damsel the welcome assurance that no unnecessary delay should occur in despatching a messenger to Chelmsford, to set at rest any apprehensions which Dame Musgrave might naturally entertain relative to Marian's absence from home.

CHAPTER LX.

CONCLUSION.

IT was not till six o'clock in the evening of the day which followed the memorable night whose incidents have just been related, that Sir Percy Rivers returned home from Portsmouth. Musidora, who had been anxiously watching his arrival, went forth to meet him the instant that from the casement she beheld him approach and before he entered the castle or had any opportunity of seeing Marian, she besought him to walk in the garden with her as she had matters of the most serious consequence for his ear.

Sir Percy at once complied with this request: and retreating to the most shady bower which the garden afforded, the husband and wife seated themselves beneath the umbrageous foliage.

Musidora then, without circumlocution or many prefatory words, began the history of the past, which we will give in a purely narrative form rather than in her own words, so that we may supply any little deficiencies or fill up any slight gaps which would otherwise occur in her own personally related history.

It appeared that when Musidora was in her seventeenth year, and was wont to ramble alone in the forest near Sinclair House, or on the shores of Brading Haven, she one day encountered an elegant young cavalier who saluted her gracefully. Managing to get into conversation with Musidora, the cavalier succeeded even at the first interview in making such an impression upon her that when they separated his image remained uppermost in her mind for the remainder of the day. On the following morning she met him again: another and a longer conversation took place—and deeper still was the impression made upon Musidora by the extraordinary beauty, the elegant figure, the fascinating discourse, and the courtly manners of the cavalier. Thus, for several successive days did they meet—entirely by accident, as it would seem,—and yet it was not really so. For of course the cavalier had his object in following up his acquaintance with Musidora; while she was secretly, if not altogether unconsciously, impelled by the germinating power of love thus to repair day after day to the very spot in the forest where she was accustomed to meet the cavalier. In a word, she became profoundly enamoured of him before she even knew his name: for be it remembered that Musidora was at that time a mere artless, ingenuous, and confiding girl, without any of that knowledge of the world which subsequent experiences had so sadly but impressively given her.

At length she learnt that the unknown object of this devoted love of her's was Lord Lionel Danvers, the owner of the uninhabited castle which stood on the south-western point of the Isle of Wight; and when he declared his affection, she in her unsuspecting simplicity at once invited him home to Sinclair House that he might form the acquaintance of her father. But Lord Lionel had a tale ready as a pretext for keeping their love secret. There could be no doubt that he feared lest her cousin Percy Rivers might prove a successful rival. At all events, whatever his motives were, he did invent some specious excuse, but which it is needless to record in detail. Musidora, in whose noble heart love and confidence were closely blended, put the most implicit faith in her lover's representations;—and thus some weeks went on, each day being marked by a fresh interview, and each interview by the deepening of the pure and chaste affection which the knight's daughter had formed for her lover.

Then came another pretext on his part; and this was to induce her to accompany him to Danvers Castle. The tale that he told for this purpose was the same which, as Conrad Danvers, we have seen him insidiously whispering in the ear of the gentle Marian—the same too which in the Prologue we saw him repeat to Clara Manners—the same, in short, with which on former occasions and at different times he had deluded other confiding damsels whose names are well known to the reader. Musidora listened and believed: the story seemed so simple—the ceremony one merely to be accomplished in fulfilment of the stipulation of some whimsical ancestor of her noble lover! She therefore readily promised to steal forth from the house and meet him at the usual place of appointment. Her pledge was kept—the ride to Danvers Castle was short, consisting only of some sixteen or seventeen miles from Sinclair House; and she was conducted by her lover into the deserted fortalice.

But now, from this point the history of Musidora Sinclair in its relation with Danvers differs from that of all the other maidens whom he had succeeded in deluding to his castle. For from the very first moment that she entered the gothic hall a misgiving sprang up in her mind,—a misgiving which continued to increase the farther she advanced in that lonely and awe-inspiring place. Vainly did Danvers breathe the tenderest and most reassuring words in her ear: the misgiving was enhanced into suspicion;—and a presentiment of evil, stronger even than her love, fastened itself upon her soul. Still she went on, and at length reached the chamber of mysteries. There, on beholding those fiery names upon the wall, she was seized with a wild affright; and turning suddenly round to her lover, she caught upon his countenance a look so strange, so wild, so wicked that all her suspicions were confirmed, and she felt assured she had been brought thither for no good purpose. Danvers threw himself at her feet, pouring forth the most impassioned protestations of love, and sincerity and honourable intents: so that Musidora, wrestling against her terrors, suffered herself to be cheered, encouraged, reassured, and almost deluded. Believing her to be entirely at his mercy, Danvers led on the discourse, which was accompanied by the tenderest caresses, unto that point when obtaining from her the fondest avowals of love, he ardently besought her to pledge herself unto him body and soul. Then, all in an instant, did her suspicions come back with renewed force: a sense of terrible danger seized upon her—she felt as one who, suddenly awakening from a walking dream, finds herself upon the brink of a precipice—and without precisely comprehending the nature of the peril which threatened her, she exclaimed, "No, Lionel—no! I will not pledge myself thus fearfully."

It would be impossible to describe the look of rage and disappointment which all in a moment seized as it were upon Danvers' countenance, distorting every feature and giving to it a fiend-like expression. At the same instant a wild mocking laugh, coming from unseen lips, rang through the apartment—a veil fell from Musidora's eyes—and a secret voice whispered in her soul that she had escaped from becoming the victim of a treacherous deceiver!

Wild and precipitate was the flight of Musidora from the chamber of mysteries and without once looking behind her, she gained the outer gate of the castle. There was she overtaken by Lionel Danvers. Too much a prey to terror to be able to lavish reproaches upon him, she listened almost in total silence to what he said. His words were few but they were impressive; and the tones in which they were uttered, were terrible. He bade her beware how she ever betrayed the secret of what she had seen within the walls of his castle; and having compelled her by threats of instantaneous death to swear that so long as he lived she would retain the secret, he seized her in his arms, sprang upon one of his demon-horses, and bore her rapidly back to the place where they had met. There they parted!

When Musidora descended to the breakfast-table in the morning, her countenance was marble-pale—her look was as cold as ice—her very nature seemed to have been frozen. And no wonder: for was not her heart the depository of a tremendous secret? The reader has already been informed how from that time forth she preserved the glacier-aspect with which horror had at first invested her, and how she adopted it as a mask to conceal her inward feelings, and also to guard against the betrayal of that fearful secret in a moment of surprise. The colour had fled from her cheeks to return no more: the shock she had received was powerful enough thus to produce this physical change with regard to the bloom that was wont to rest upon her countenance like the vermeil on the damask of the peach.

Leaping over a period of upwards of three years and a half, let us now follow Musidora to Grantham Villa at Greenwich. From the first moment that the supposed King made her the offer of his hand, she resolved to accept it. She felt that the power of love was dead within her—that she could therefore never marry from motives of affection—and the void thus left in her heart afforded room for the entrance of a feeling of ambition. But her ambition was not selfish: for if she experienced a glow of pride, and satisfaction, and triumph at the prospect of placing a queenly crown upon her brow, she likewise longed for the possession of power in order to do good. Besides, she was an affectionate daughter; and it was naturally agreeable to her filial feelings to become instrumental in restoring her father to wealth, prosperity and happiness. She knew not that Lord Grantham had written such a letter to her sire as that which had led to her visit to the villa. Had she for a moment suspected that it was through a coldly calculated and selfishly contrived pre-arrangement between her noble kinsman and her father that she had been invited to Grantham Villa in the hope of attracting the King's notice, she would at once have spurned the idea of reaching a sovereign rank in such a manner. Of the contents of that letter she had all along remained in ignorance, until Lord Danvers explained it on the memorable night when she saw him for the last time.

The history which she heard from the lips of old Manners had justified her suspicion that she had narrowly escaped being made the victim of Lord Danvers; and if farther confirmation thereof were required, it was furnished a few weeks afterwards when accident threw in her way the Memoirs of Bianca Landini at the old banker's house in Lombard Street. The reader will recollect that the Landinis were both much alarmed on that occasion, when they learnt that Musidora had not only been dipping into the volume, but had actually read the very history which least of all would they have had thus meet her eyes. But here some explanation is necessary. In the diamonds which Musidora, accompanied by her noble relatives, had brought to be repaired, the Landinis had recognised those which they had sold to Lionel Danvers. They therefore inferred that Danvers had presented them to Musidora—consequently that she must be well acquainted with him; and they naturally feared that she might mention to him the circumstance of having read the history of Bianca Landini, whom they believed to be the victim of an ancestor—little suspecting that Walter and Lionel were one and the same person! Therefore was it that the elder Landini had on some pretext requested Musidora to accompany him into the recess opening from the saloon of his house. When thus alone together, old Landini had said to Musidora, "You have read a history in which the name of Danvers occurs. Should you ever meet the present bearer of that name, may I implore that you will not betray the circumstance that such a history, bequeathing an hereditary vengeance to myself and nephew, is in existence?" Musidora promised; and no wonder was it that when she issued forth from that recess, her countenance had even more of the marble's whiteness than usual: for the mere mention of the name of Danvers had profoundly stirred all the keenest emotions of her heart.

We need not recapitulate how, after having prescribed a becoming interval of courtship so as to satisfy her feminine feelings of strictest delicacy and propriety, Musidora gave her hand to the mock King: nor need we remind the reader of all the painful circumstances which occurred when the astounding truth was so soon after revealed to her that it was Lionel Danvers whom she had thus received to her arms. But what language can depict the feeling of horror and despair which seized upon the poor lady's mind when in due course she found that she was in a way to become a mother? The idea of bringing into the world a being that would have for its father a man whose fearful doom she more than half suspected, was ten thousand times more horrifying than the sense of that disgrace which would attach to herself if her condition became known to her relatives and friends. And with regard to this disgrace, she could not avert it by displaying her certificate of marriage: for Danvers, with a fiendish malignity of purpose, had taken it from her when she lay in a swoon at his feet. His object in thus acting was no doubt to deprive her of the only valid testimony to show that she had been deceived by a mock-marriage, and thus rob her alike of the consolation and the power of displaying to the world, in case of need, that she had been beguiled and that she was innocent!

The Earl and Countess of Grantham were of course interested in many ways in hushing up the secret of Musidora's condition; and thus, by the aid of Dame Bertha and the faithful Annetta, she became a mother unknown to the other domestics of the household. At that time a tenant upon an estate which Lord Grantham possessed in another part of Kent, some distance from Greenwich, arrived on business at the villa. His name was Bradley; and he had recently married. To this man and his wife was the child confided, the name of Marian having been given to it. A considerable sum of money was placed in Bradley's hand; and he was ordered to betake himself, with his wife and the child, to some part of England where he was altogether unknown,—there to settle down, with the understanding that from time to time Lord Grantham would furnish him with farther funds. But the reader has already seen how Bradley and his wife were prematurely cut off by an accidental death, and how Marian fell into the hands of Dame Musgrave. As so short a time had elapsed since the receipt of the first sum of money, and as it was not near exhausted, Bradley did not in the interval apply for a replenishment of his resources; and thus the Earl remained in ignorance of where the man had settled.

The reader now knows why it was that Musidora's stay at Grantham Villa was so prolonged ere she came back to Sinclair House. After that return home years elapsed—and in her occasional communications with Lord Grantham she learnt from him that he had never heard any more of the Bradleys. Death in due course summoned the Earl and his lady to their last account; and thus all means of ever again hearing anything more of the Bradleys and her child appeared to be totally cut off. But there were of-ten moments when Musidora, with a mother's natural longings, yearned for some tidings of her offspring; and hence that secret grief which often seized upon her, and to which Annetta knew that no consolation could be administered! It was however willed by Providence that the child should be ultimately restored to its parent: and this end was brought about in the manner already described.

Such was the history which Musidora, with frankness and candour, related to her husband as they sat together in the shady arbour to which they had retired for the purpose. And now did Sir Percy Rivers exhibit all the noble generosity of his heart. Flinging his arms round Musidora's neck, and straining her to his breast he said, "My beloved wife, I adopt your Marian as my own! Let the world believe it is our child, lost in its infancy, and recovered in a miraculous manner. By these means also will you be saved from blushing when Marian shall again ask you concern-ing her father! And now, dearest Musidora, from this time forth let not a word—no, not a single word, ever be breathed relative to the past. I attach no blame to you. In the belief that you were the legitimate wedded wife of England's King, you received a traitor in your arms. The treachery was most foul: but you were innocent. And if, when you bestowed your hand on me, you kept this tremendous secret treasured up in your own bosom, it was natural—most natural! Again therefore, do I say, Musidora, let a veil be thrown over the past; and never by word, or look, or deed, will you experience reproach from one who loves you so fondly and so well!"

Musidora wept in her husband's arms; and never had she bestowed upon him such warm, such affectionate caresses as those which she now lavished, and felt a joy and delight in thus lavishing!

Marian was thus owned as the daughter of Sir Percy Rivers; and Lord St. Louis was sincerely rejoiced when he learnt from Musidora's lips the noble conduct of her generous-hearted husband. His lordship remained some days at Carisbrook Castle; and when he took his leave it was with the satisfaction of knowing that he left a happy family living in love and contentment there.

On repairing to London, Lord St. Louis visited Deadman's Place, where he learnt that many long years had elapsed since old Dunhaven had disappeared in a sudden and mysterious manner: but the nobleman felt convinced in his own mind that the cause thereof had been in some way connected with Lord Danvers. The hoarded wealth of old Dunhaven had been pillaged and self-appropriated by the lodgers in the house: but singularly enough the huge trunk though emptied of its valuable contents, had not been removed, and the false bottom covering the skeleton had remained without discovery. The room itself had never been tenanted since old Dunhaven's disappearance; and it was in a sad dilapidated condition when St. Louis penetrated into it. He caused the trunk containing the skeleton to be privately interred in consecrated ground; and thus, after all, the vow of old Sir Poniers Dunhaven, recorded so many long years back, was ultimately fulfilled—the bones of his nephew having remained above ground until after vengeance was wreaked upon Danvers! But that vengeance had been awarded by no mortal power—though the venerable hermit of Mount Lebanon was made the instrument of ensuring its accomplishment through the rescue of the last intended victim of the terrible Danvers.

THE END

NOTES

1   Henry VII reigned from 1485, when he murdered King Richard III, until 1509. His second son Henry succeeded him, and reigned until 1547.

2   One of the main streets running off from the Bank of England, in the City of London. Italian bankers were welcomed to England in the Middle Ages, but encouraged to live in one particular area of London, which now bears their name.

3   Reynolds was living above a grocer's shop in Kings Square, just off Goswell Street, when writing *Wagner the Wehr-wolf*.

4   A sanctuary, or liberty, was traditionally granted to a servant of the Crown, and gave him immunity in his own place—one such was the county of Durham. Later, the privilege remained, and the places became the haunt of thieves, who returned there with impunity. Fielding's *Amelia* is set in a liberty.

5   By dynasty, Henry VIII was not a Plantagenet, of course, but a Tudor. His mother, Elizabeth of York, was a Plantagenet.

6   An anachronism. Warham, as Chancellor, certainly performed some of the roles of a modern Prime Minister, but the phrase was not used until Robert Walpole, in the 1720s.

AFTERWORD

WHAT is Reynolds's place in English literature?

Many people would smile at such a question, with its bold implication that he *has* a place. To the best of my knowledge only one of his works is still in print (in 2007), and before it appeared there had been only one, highly abridged, reprint of *The Mysteries of London* in over 120 years. A few essays, mainly on the man's politics, have surfaced in the last twenty years or so, from a small and distinct knot of scholars. In the enormous activity of putting books out online, Reynolds is notably absent, with not a single complete e-text to his name. Lee Jameson's excellent Victorian London website is currently bringing out the *Mysteries* in its unabridged fullness, but it is as yet incomplete. Apart from that, there are only endless reprints of the grave-robbing episode from the *Mysteries*. If we accept George Orwell's test of the survival of a book as the indicator of its author's quality, then we would have to say that Reynolds's place in literature is tenuous and tangential, if indeed he has one at all.

In his own day, he was more popular than Dickens; in 1868 *The Bookseller* declared he was the best-selling author in Britain, and we can accept the truth of this the more as it was said with a sneer. Writing in 1852, Thackeray quotes a bookseller he met at Brighton station, who told him *The Mysteries of London* "was by many, many times the most popular of all periodical tales then published, because, says he, 'it lashed the aristocracy!'" Reynolds did not keep this reputation long. We have already seen Dickens's opinion of him—which may even be honest—and this is the one that stuck. In November 1914, Horace Breakley wrote to *Notes & Queries*:

> A writer of historical novels, like his famous contemporary Harrison Ainsworth, he rivalled that author in popularity, but was incomparably a much inferior artist. Of all his works 'Faust' alone has any claim to distinction, and 'Pickwick Abroad,' in spite of the demerits of plagiarism, is not without humour. [...] 'The Mysteries of the Court of London,' which I have called despicable, is still, I believe, in a publisher's list, but many of the indelicate passages in the original edition appear to have been expurgated. Gilbert's illustrations, like the novel itself, are full of absurd anachronisms; and though intended as a scathing attack upon the manners and morals of the English nobility at the close of the eighteenth century, the book loses all its sting through exaggeration. It has some interest, however, for the historical student who is acquainted with the *dramatis personæ*, and who can trace the source of many of its canards. Otherwise, as a work of art, it is beneath contempt.

He is not in Dickens's league, when Dickens is at his best—though Dickens is not always at his best, and many people would prefer *Wagner the Wehr-wolf* or *The Mysteries of London* to *The Old Curiosity Shop* or *The Chimes*, any day of any year. On the other hand, Reynolds is far above the best of the Penny Dreadful writers, such as Thomas Prest and J.M. Rymer (much of whose work is, anyway, only dubiously their own). Perhaps the best comparison with him in his own age is with William Harrison Ainsworth (1805-1872). Here, too, we must distinguish Ainsworth at his Gothic best (*Guy Fawkes*, *Old Saint Paul's*, *Rookwood*) from the weakened, timid writer of *Jane Shore* and *Beatrice Tildesley*. At Reynolds's best, as in *The Necromancer*, he approaches and matches the best of Ainsworth; he is far better than "the Lancastrian Novelist" in his later years.

There was a thriving School of Ainsworth, to which Reynolds owes a great deal. The typical plot device (adapted from Scott) of these writers is to take a crucial moment in history, and explore it through fictitious characters who find themselves caught up on the edge of real events. Thus Stephen Blundel and his apprentice, Leonard Holt, struggle to keep their family together in the face of the Plague, the Fire of London, and the evils emanating from Old Saint Paul's Cathedral. Real people such as the Earl of Rochester and Charles II intervene and interfere, and the result is a slice of "real" history, seen through the eyes of ordinary people.

Albert Smith, later editor of *Punch*, followed Ainsworth with his *Marchioness of Brinvilliers*, an Ainsworthian reworking of a piece by Dumas, exposing (they would have said, "revealing") the horrors of the court of Louis XIV. George Bonaparte Rodwell wrote a rather more diffuse account of the early years of Charles II, *Old London Bridge*, which ended with the Fire. Both are still extremely readable, though we might agree that they are not up to Reynolds's standard. Neither man seems to have an agenda beyond telling a good story.

A far more notable and complex disciple of the Lancastrian Novelist was Emma Robinson, a Catholic from Hammersmith, West London. Ainsworth in his early years had a distinctive political bias to his writing: he speaks from the point of view of the One Nation Tory, thus bridging the years between Scott, a romantic Tory of the old school, and Peel and Disraeli, often far more socially liberal than the official Liberals of their day. Ainsworth is conservative, paternalistic, and believes in honour and duty, and that *noblesse oblige*. His novels such as *Windsor Castle* and *The Star Chamber* show what happens when these values are forgotten. He hates cruelty, as only he can who understands its attractions from within himself. Robinson has a similar project, but has none of his cruelty, which makes her values the purer, if it takes the bite from her writing. She presents a revisionist Catholic view of history, analogous to Ainsworth's Tory view. Where he is knowing, she (as Ann Humpherys says) is naïve, but her fundamental decency often makes her more attractive than her Master. The villain of her *Westminster; or, The Days of the Reformation* is (naturally) Henry VIII, and it is likely, from reading both books, that Reynolds was influenced by Robinson in his writing of the Murdering Monarch. What he does not do is present a vision of History from his own point of view, the Republican, Socialist, Chartist position. As we shall see, he had reasons for not doing so.

If we put Reynolds at the level of Emma Robinson, that is no bad thing for either of them. But the truth is that GWMR was vastly inconsistent in his quality. Much of his work is below his best, but at his best he is better than most of his rivals. Perhaps we should put him in Chesterton's famous category, as a writer of "good bad books." Since G.K. included Conan Doyle in their number, that is no bad thing, either.

★ ★ ★

In 1843, Ainsworth serialised a short and rather strange novel, *Auriol; or, The Elixir of Life*. It started to appear in *Ainsworth's Magazine*, under the title of *Revelations of Old London*, but then Ainsworth sold the magazine, and took *Auriol* with him to his new post on the *New Monthly Magazine*. Many people were (and are) under the impression that Auriol ended in *Ainsworth's*. They were (and are) surprised to read the true ending, which seems even more inconclusive than the one in *Ainsworth's*.

Auriol concerns the adventures of one Auriol Darcy. On New Year's Eve 1599 he tries to rescue his father's head, which has been set on a pike on London Bridge; he is arrested, and rescued in his turn by Dr. Lamb, an ancient alchemist. Lamb has almost perfected the Elixir of Life, which must be taken *tonight*, at the turn of two centuries; but at the critical moment Auriol seizes the brew and drinks it himself, letting Lamb die. He thus becomes immortal. The story lurches forward to 1830, when a young woman, Ebba Thorneycroft, and her lover are preparing to marry. We enter a world of low dives in Rookeries, and characters such as the Dog-Fancier, the Tinker, and the Sandman. It is a world just like that of *The Mysteries of London*, but without the politics, and less of the grime. Ebba's lover is Auriol Darcy; but he is being pursued by a man in a long black cloak, with whom he has a dreadful appointment—what it is, we are not told. Through several subplots we are led to the first denouement, in The Chamber of Mystery. Ebba is seized and abducted, and taken to a mysteries house. There she is visited by the spirits of dead women:

"Who, and what are ye?" she cried, wild with terror.

"The victims of Auriol!" replied the figure on the right. "As we are, such will you be ere long."

"What crime have you committed?" demanded Ebba.

"We have loved him," replied the second figure.

"Is that a crime?" cried Ebba. "If so, I am equally culpable with you."

"You will share our doom," replied the third figure.

"Heaven have mercy upon me!" exclaimed the agonized girl, dropping upon her knees.

At this moment a terrible voice from behind the curtain exclaimed:

"Sign, or Auriol is lost for ever."

"I cannot yield my soul, even to save him," cried Ebba distractedly.

"Witness his chastisement, then," cried the voice.

And as the words were uttered, a side door was opened on the opposite side, and Auriol was dragged forth from it by two masked personages, who looked like familiars of the Inquisition.

"Do not yield to the demands of this fiend, Ebba!" cried Auriol, gazing at her distractedly.

"Will you save him before he is cast, living, into the tomb?" cried the voice.

And at the words, a heavy slab or marble rose slowly from the floor near where Ebba sat, and disclosed a dark pit beneath.

Ebba gazed into the abyss with indescribable terror.

"There he will be immured, unless you sign," cried the voice; "and, as he is immortal, he will endure an eternity of torture."

"I cannot save him so, but I may precede him," cried Ebba. And throwing her hands aloft, she flung herself into the pit. [Ainsworth 1843: 127]

Though Auriol Darcy is a very different character from Lionel Danvers, the resemblance between *Auriol* and *The Necromancer* is immediately clear, in both style and content. In both, a man will attain eternal life if he can provide the Devil with the souls of virgins, who give themselves for love. By cheating the Fiend, Ebba has also left Auriol with a teaser: how to find another such before the expiry of his contract with Cyprian de Rougemont, alias Satan. In the end he does not, and he is taken: but his doom is stranger by far than what we expected, after Ebba's death. He is chained in a dungeon, for all eternity; but a spell, a glamour, convinces him that he is back in the London of 1599, in Dr. Lamb's laboratory:

Auriol looked at him earnestly, but could not catch another glance, so intently was the old man occupied. At length he ventured to break the silence.

"I should feel perfectly convinced, if I might look forth from that window," he said.

"Convinced of what?" rejoined the old man, somewhat sharply.

"That I am what I seem," replied Auriol.

"Look forth, then," said the old man. "But do not disturb me by idle talk. There is the rosy colour in the projection for which I have been so long waiting."

Auriol then walked to the window and gazed through the tinted panes. It was very dark, and objects could only be imperfectly distinguished. Still he fancied he could detect the gleam of the river beneath him, and what seemed a long line of houses on the bridge. He also fancied he discerned other buildings, with the high roofs, the gables, and the other architectural peculiarities of the structures of Elizabeth's time. He persuaded himself, also, that he could distinguish through the gloom the venerable Gothic pile of Saint Paul's Cathedral on the other side of the water, and, as if to satisfy him that he was right, a deep solemn bell tolled forth the hour of two. After a while he returned from the window, and said to his supposed grandsire, "I am satisfied. I have lived centuries in a few nights."

Here the book truly ends. In our days of uncertain novels, and *opere aperte*, it is as satisfying as any other, and more so: there is a lot of arguing and exegesis provided for in such an ending. Reynolds takes a far safer, less existential path: Lionel Danvers doesn't have the dual nature of Auriol Darcy, and gets his comeuppance as he deserves. But that Reynolds based the plot of *The Necromancer* on *Auriol* is undeniable.

Most readers will have spotted, too, the close resemblance between the project of both men, Danvers and Darcy, and Captain Vanderdecken, alias the Flying Dutchman. He was a staple figure of the Penny Dreadful, having first appeared on stage in 1827. A version of the story, Frederick Marryat's *The Phantom Ship*, was published in *The New Monthly Magazine* in 1838-1839: since this was the direct rival to Reynolds's former fiefdom, the *Monthly Magazine*, it is hard to see how he could not have read it. It was published as a three-volume affair in 1839 by Colburn, Emma Robinson's publisher, and an up-market version, *The Flying Dutchman: A Legend of the High Seas*, by William Johnson Neale, came out the same year. Although the theme is similar—Vanderdecken must sail the Seven Seas until Doomsday, unless he can find a woman who will die for love for him—the treatment is quite different; all the same, the many versions of the Flying Dutchman legend schooled the public into accepting *Auriol* and *The Necromancer*.

A better-known antecedent of *The Necromancer* is Eugène Sue's *Le Juif Errant*. Serialised from 1844 it was extremely popular in France, and Reynolds undoubtedly knew it. The legend is too well-known to need repeating, and it had received several treatments in the years before Reynolds wrote. We must not forget Maturin's *Melmoth*. Having made a pact with the Devil for eternal life, Melmoth now seeks to be rid of it, but before he can do so he must find someone wretched enough to take his place. He seeks them out and torments them further, but none of them will give up their soul for him. Both these novels approach the subject of *The Necromancer*, and their episodic, portmanteau structure feeds directly into Reynolds; but it is *Auriol* alone that provides the true model for the plot.

This episodic structure is partly a function of the penny-part system, in which *The Necromancer* appeared. The lurches between competing strands of the novel assist the attention of the reader over the six months—or six years—the serial will run. Many of his contemporaries were less than able to keep track of these changes themselves: even in great and influential stories such as *The String of Pearls*, the author introduces plots that will fail abortively, or even be forgotten completely. Reynolds's control of his material is admirable. The six interpolated stories, of Danvers's victims, all feed into the main linking-tale of Musidora Sinclair, and the villain Danvers's dreadful secret is not revealed until the right moment, again in contrast to *The String of Pearls*. The reader may like to test my opinion against her or his own, but of all the works I have mentioned as antecedents of *The Necromancer*, none of them displays the same narrative skill, or authorial confidence.

One rich source for Reynolds's novels is his own life, and his own past works. All writers write from their experience—it is impossible to conceive how they could not do so—even if only their experience of writing. One benefit of expanding his biography is to see how frequently, and how richly, he draws on his own life for character and incident. A couple of examples:

—In *The Mysteries of London*, Richard Markham bids farewell to his brother Eugene. Richard has been through Sandhurst. Many critics have drawn attention to the resemblance between the two brothers and Sade's two siblings, Justine and Juliette; and doubtless they are right. We now see that the incident has a direct parallel in GWMR's biography, when, after Sandhurst, he left his younger brother behind and went off to seek his fortune and his freedom.

—Again in the *Mysteries*, the Resurrection Man, Anthony Tidkins, is from Walmer in Kent. In order to raise money, to marry his childhood sweetheart Katie Price, he and his father plunder the burial-ground belonging to Deal Hospital, where there were many sick sailors. Reynolds's grandfather, Purser Dowers, was Commandant of Deal Hospital. Then they are commissioned to snatch a certain body:

> ... my father came in and asked me if I felt myself well enough to accompany him on a little expedition that evening. I replied in the affirmative. He then told me that a certain surgeon for whom we did business, and who resided in Deal, required a particular subject which had been buried that morning in Walmer Churchyard. I did not ask my father any more questions; but that night I accompanied him to the burial-ground between eleven and twelve o'clock. The surgeon had shown my father the grave in the afternoon; and we had a cart waiting in a lane close by. The church is in a secluded part, surrounded by trees, and at some little distance from any habitations. There was no danger of being meddled with:—moreover, we had often operated in the same ground before. [*Mysteries*: 194]

In real life, the surgeon in Deal was Reynolds's godfather, Duncan McArthur; and as a naval surgeon, and close friend of Purser Dowers, he was connected with Deal Hospital. This is slander by association (or would have been, had McArthur still been alive), but it is also probably true. Trefor Thomas points out the realistic detail in the Resurrection Man's methods, as depicted by Reynolds, in Shoreditch churchyard: especially interesting is the idea that you dig down, not directly onto the body, but at an angle from behind the foot of the coffin, then pull the body up the slope. We can well believe that McArthur used body-snatchers—very few surgeons didn't. And Reynolds would have known Shoreditch church well, living barely half-a-mile away in Suffolk Place.

There are other, smaller cross-overs between life and art. Otto Pianalla meets the virtuous Italian peasant Mazzini; Ida tells Faust she is pregnant, in a conversation that must have had flaming resonances for GWMR. When we know a little more about Reynolds, we will doubtless know far more about his works.

* * *

Mention of *Faust* brings us to another source: Reynolds's own works. On the whole, he did not produce many supernatural works, and it often seems that, even in these, he is not really interested in the supernatural *per se*. There are incidents of the uncanny in certain of his novels, but it is not thematic, and neither does it push the plot forward. But three of his finest serials have an occult theme and motivation: *Faust, Wagner, the Wehr-wolf,* and *The Necromancer.* The first ran in the *London Journal* from 4 October 1845 to 18 July 1846, and was published in America as *Faust and the Demon.* Wilhelm [*sic*] Faust, a penniless student, loves Theresa, daughter and only heir of the powerful Lord of Rosenthal—who, to complicate matters, has been betrothed to the Arch-duke Leopold of Austria. As a result, Faust is thrown into prison in Wittenberg and, as the story begins, he is about to be broken on the wheel in the public square, having been convicted on a trumped-up charge. He finds a spell scratched on the wall, and by it summons a demon. At first reluctant to sell his soul, he is persuaded by the trickery of the demon, who shows him Theresa mooning over a picture that is (says the demon) that of Faust's rival. Enraged and desperate, Faust signs the pact. A point of interest: he will have twenty-four years of dominion, ending on 30 July 1517. The year apart, this is the eve of Reynolds's wedding.

This is not the Faust of legend, of the *Faust-Bücher,* nor even of Marlowe. The story as it unfolds is original, and firmly within the Gothic-Dreadful genre. Faust takes a lover, Ida Pianalla, who ends up poisoned by her new rival, Lucreza Borgia. Her brother Otto, an upstanding hero, sorts out various trickery on the part of his sister's husband, the false Baron Czernin. After many more such adventures, Faust is finally dragged into the crater of Vesuvius, on 31 July 1517.

We have the same theme of selling one's soul to the devil, but without the escape clause of providing enough substitutes to buy back the contract. Despite Breakley's admiration of it, *Faust* is a rambling novel, though highly readable, that loses much by failing to learn from Goethe and Marlowe. And though we have Lucreza Borgia, she is not yet the icy, enigmatic goddess Reynolds so loved to portray. That figure comes in the sequel: *Wagner, the Wehr-wolf.*

Wagner began on 6 November 1846, in *Reynolds's Miscellany,* and ran till 24 July 1847. In the prologue, set in January 1516, an ancient man living alone with his granddaughter is bewailing his fate, since young Agnes seems to have been lost in the storm. A stranger arrives: although unnamed, he is Wilhelm Faust. He persuades the old man to serve him for the last year of his life, until 31 July 1517. In return, the man's youth is returned to him: and so is Agnes. But, once a month for ever afterwards, he will become a wehr-wolf.

The nature of Fernand Wagner after Faust's departure is odd. The mechanics of his lycanthropy owe nothing to tradition: it is part of a curse, but one he takes on himself in order to regain his youthful vigour. There is no sin in his actions as a wolf, because he is not himself at the time, and he is not damned, even through his association with Faust. There are some excellent wehr-wolf scenes (I use the spelling Reynolds used) but the real point of the novel is the lovely Nisida, daughter of the Count of Riverola.

Nisida is described at long and lingering length, as a staggering but glacial Italian beauty. As a child, she was struck deaf-and-dumb by something terrible she saw: but, of course, being mute, nobody knows what this terror was. In fact, as we learn, Nisida is not mute at all: she has chosen to be silent until she can solve the mystery of her family. In the meantime she falls in love with Wagner, the only man who moves her in this way, and together they escape the clutches of the Inquisition, to end up on a deserted island in the Mediterranean. There is a lengthy subplot, involving the Ottoman Empire Reynolds admired so much, and in the end the secret is revealed: Nisida's family is descended from the public hangman! She and Fernand expiate their crimes in repentance, quickly followed by death.

The wehr-wolf theme takes up surprisingly little of the book. In general it is very like Reynolds's other works—a unifying theme, with a great deal of digression and diversification of plot. But *Wagner* improves on *Faust* in at least one respect: we have a mystery, the solution of which is not revealed until the end of the story, and which is carried by the female lead. In *The Necromancer* this goes a step farther, with each apparent subplot shown, at last, as an integral part of the main Musidora theme. The first two books were not rehearsals for the third, but we can trace Reynolds's learning of the art of the mystery novel through the three.

* * *

There is no question that Henry VIII was the worst king to reign in England. He is reputed to have executed more than 80,000 people in his reign, for political reasons alone; he had the octogenarian Katherine Plantagenet, daughter of the oinophobe Duke of Clarence, beheaded, simply because she had a better claim to the throne than he did. His pursuit of wealth destroyed the social fabric of medieval England, and having created thousands of beggars, he responded to the crisis by making begging a criminal offence. He died, bloated and syphilitic, in 1547: his body is said to have exploded as it was carried by boat from Windsor to London. Such a tyrant, with so many cruelties to his name, is surely a godsend to a Gothic novelist, and even more to a Red Republican: but Reynolds goes curiously easy on the monstrous man.

If you followed my suggestion, and read the book before this introduction, you will know that Henry VIII is not a main character in *The Necromancer*; his semblance is used by Lionel Danvers to seduce and ensnare Musidora Sinclair. Nonetheless, for the larger part of the book we are under the impression that it really is the King of England we are reading about, and, on the whole, although he is portrayed as a crafty and heartless seducer, his statecraft in general is hardly mentioned. There is condemnation enough of tyranny, and a lengthy portrayal of cruel torture and state-sponsored murder: but it is all fictitious, and set in Genoa, in the Bianca Landini section of the book. It is a fairly straightforward Gothic trope, in the familiar setting of medieval Italy, and, strangely for Reynolds, he does not point out links with the situation in his own day. The closest he gets to vintage Reynolds is in a brief passage:

> Musidora has her ambition I am convinced of it!" exclaimed the Countess of Grantham. "The very style in which she discusses what she is pleased to term your Highness's *faults*, has once or twice caused her to let slip a word or two——"
>
> "Well, and that word or two?" asked the King. "And about the faults too? Tell me what are my faults in her estimation, that I may know how to amend them."
>
> "Musidora thinks, from all she has heard, that your Highness attends too much to pleasure and too little to the interests of your people—that there is a vast amount of misery and poverty into which your Highness never condescends to look; and she has once or twice observed that if she had the power, she would accomplish such and such reforms and effect such and such beneficial changes."
>
> "Ah! then her's is the ambition to do good?" and a look very much resembling scornful disgust appeared upon the monarch's countenance. "However," he immediately added, "if such be her desire, we will see if it cannot be gratified."

Compared to the howls of outrage we find in the *Mysteries*, that is hardly Reynolds at all.

Of course this is not to say that none of Reynolds's preoccupations are to be found: that would not be possible. He is still deeply admiring of the Ottoman Empire, and Musidora is still the typical, glacial-but-simmering sex-goddess that GWMR worships. But by 1851 things were different: the Great Chartist Foment was "all over bar the shouting," except that few people were still shouting; the Great Exhibition had come and gone; a new mood was in Britain, which was coming to seem far more like the Victorian Age as we picture it today. The Second Golden Age of the Gothic was coming to an end, and people were starting to prefer their ghosts as domestic beings, or not at all. Publishers such as Edward Lloyd, who had pirated Dickens with the best of them, were now starting to think about respectability, and with his growing family so was Reynolds. His output turned more towards social novels: simultaneously with *The Necromancer*, *Reynolds's Miscellany* was bringing out *Mary Price; or, The Adventures of a Serving Girl*. Although he was still to write episodes of *The Mysteries of the Court of London* for another four years, *The Necromancer* therefore might represent a more mature style, concentrating more on story-telling, and less on shocking and proselytising. The structure of the novel bears this out. We have a portmanteau of four tales, with a unifying tale about how the families of Danvers's victims try to exact their revenge. On top of this we have the apparently separate story of Musidora Sinclair and her intrigue with Henry VIII. Only towards the end do we see that this outlying section is in fact central to the whole work: Musidora is Danvers's next victim, and his greatest challenge, and will end up his Nemesis. Such a well-worked out structure is in sharp contrast to the sprawling, picaresque line of the *Mysteries*, in its various series.

One of the most important factors in this change is that from 1850 Reynolds had an outlet for his political writings, that he himself controlled completely. In short, he had *Reynolds's Newspaper*. From the very outset, as editor of the *New Monthly*, he had used sensational fiction to get people in, so that they would read his opinions as well; but for the most part this very fiction was the only place he could lay out his stall, so to speak. This led to the out-of-place, unwieldy political diatribes that interrupt and unbalance the *Mysteries*. Though many people read them, many more must have bleeped past them, waiting for Reynolds to climb off his hobby horse and get on with the gory story. Now he could separate the two. What we have, therefore, in *The Necromancer*, is the mature Reynolds, free to be a pure story-teller: still willing to engage with thought and issues, but far better able simply to relax and give the public what it wanted. *The Necromancer* is my favourite book of Reynolds's, and I am not sure the two things are not connected.